THE DROWNED REALM SERIES BOOK II

THE GHOSTS OF ASHUR

KHALID UDDIN

Can't Put it Down
BOOKS
An Imprint of Open Door Publications

The Ghosts of Ashur
Book Two of
The Drowned Realm Series

By Khalid Uddin

ISBN: 978-1-7365979-3-4
Copyright © 2022 by Khalid Uddin

The following is a work of fiction. Names, characters, businesses, places, events and incidents are either the products of the author's imagination or used in a fictitious manner. Any resemblance to actual persons, living or dead, or actual events is purely coincidental.

No part of this book may be used or reproduced in any manner whatsoever without the written permission of the author except in the case of brief quotations embodied in critical articles and reviews.

All rights reserved.
Printed in the United States

Cover Design by Eric Labacz, labaczdesign.com
Map Design by Kaira Marquez

Published by
Can't Put It Down Books
An Imprint of
Open Door Publications
2113 Stackhouse Dr.
Yardley, PA 19067
www.OpenDoorPublications.com

For Ahmed/Kirby/Chach (who are all actually the same person)
It's rather common for a little brother to grow up emulating his big brother's haircuts, taste in music, sports, sayings, and mannerisms in general, all of which I'm guilty.
I think it's rare, however, for the little brother to grow up and realize that his big brother is his biggest fan, and is always there, promoting his little brother's endeavors as an author.
I can't thank you enough for all of the time and energy you've put into helping me become me, and for all of the unconditional support that you've given. This book is for you, and hopefully it makes up for all of the rass over the years.

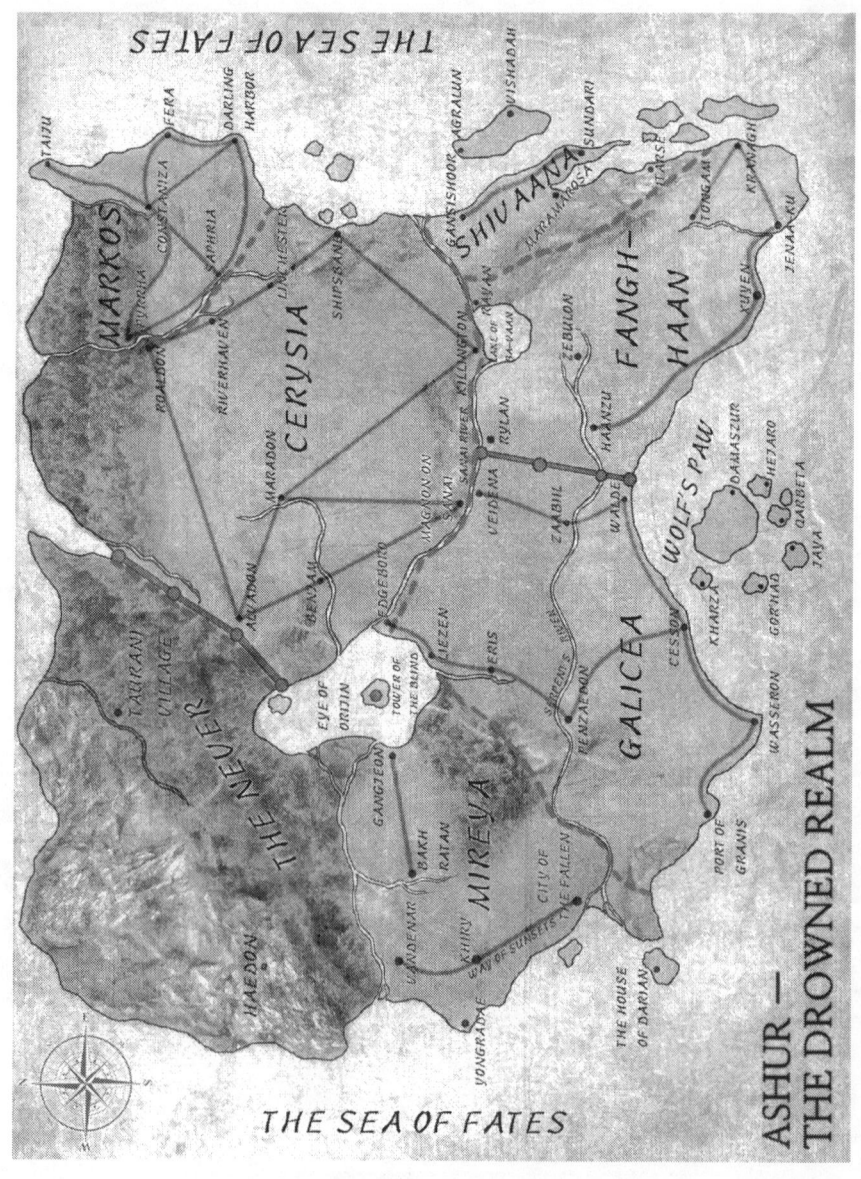

CHAPTER 1
A DANGEROUS KISS

From **The Book of Orijin**, **Verse Three Hundred Forty-Nine**
O Chosen Ones, Not a single one of you is irredeemable.
We have seen your hearts and souls.
We know your capabilities far better than anything made of flesh can ever know.

LIGHT SNOWFLAKES SKIPPED and danced in the fickle wind. Regular travelers in the City of the Fallen prepared themselves well with cloaks, hoods, and coats. Despite it being a mild winter day, the ocean's proximity offered a robust breeze that turned a tolerable chill into an uncomfortably cold morning. It also, however, provided the ideal cover for anyone looking to go unnoticed.

Farrah adjusted her hood once more and slightly turned her head to each side. The City of the Fallen was notorious for being friendly and welcoming to Descendants. Unfortunately for her, Farrah could not say the same for herself. Most people in the city would have no idea of her identity, but if any Descendants had managed to flee the House of Darian and find shelter here, there was a small chance they might recognize her.

Jahmash was currently leaving her mind at peace, but the directive was clear: find any Descendants who might be lingering in the city and kill them. Farrah would be allowed one week in the city and then would have to ride north through the Never and board a ship back to Jahmash. He wanted her to return for a voyage to the nations beyond Ashur. Farrah had somehow managed to convince Jahmash to give her a small reprieve. After the weeks-long journey to and the destruction of the House of Darian, Farrah had hoped for some rest and some time on land. To her surprise, Jahmash had softened and compromised by allowing her to come to the City of the Fallen, where almost no one would bother her, and hunt down any remaining Descendants. Farrah was shocked when Jahmash allowed her a week to stay.

She had gone to Jahmash without much prodding from Maqdhuum. The man had found her at a time when her anger and desire for revenge had been at its apex. However, Farrah now wondered how well she could carry out Jahmash's order. Ever since killing the Descendant on the boat, she'd had doubts about whether her anger was properly directed. The stupid girl they'd held captive didn't really help with her confusion, either. *Adria. Bitch.* In truth, the only reason Farrah disliked the girl was because she'd made a point that Farrah had difficulty arguing. Chances were that some Descendants were nothing like Prince Garrison. Gunnar and Adria had done nothing to her. Farrah steeled her resolve. *No. If they were in the same fortress as Prince Garrison, then they are sympathizers to him and his cause. No Descendant in their right mind would take him in unless they forgave his crimes. Even if he is the Prince of Ashur.*

Whenever she doubted her decisions, Farrah reminded herself of what Garrison had done to Melina, her little sister, and their friends in Rayan. She coughed to stifle a sob and scurried into an alleyway. She pressed her forehead against the cold brick side of a building and let the chill numb her emotions. The memory of Melina's beheading always brought the worst out of her, but she needed to steel her resolve. She kept it all down, but allowed some of the anger to surface. Farrah was equally as furious with herself as with Garrison. A part of her wished she had died there with her sister, instead of leaving her broken and lifeless body surrounded by cowards and enemies. *I'll kill every last Descendant. And then I can die. And before I see her, I'll kill the damn Orijin, too. Curse him for these manifestations.*

As Farrah was finishing the thought, a sympathizing voice inquired from her right, "Schatza, no need to be out here in ze freezing cold! Vhy not come inside and fix your troubles viz some hot soup? Or a nice big mug of our honey ale?" Farrah looked up at the man, a portly, middle-aged Galicean in short sleeves and an apron. Upon seeing her face, the man gasped and looked at his feet, but spoke again. "I am so sorry, sveet girl. I am truly so sorry. I didn't realize you're a Descendant. Obviously ve have all heard of ze attack. Zhere are only a few of you zhat I have seen since ze attack last veek. Sad, sad news. But please come inside, schatza. Ze fact zhat you are a Descendant makes it even more important. Zhere are ozhers inside. Maybe zhey did not know you survived."

Farrah perked up and pushed the anger aside. "There are other Descendants inside?"

The man set down his sack of trash against the wall. "Yes. Zhere are two inside. Badalao is a regular at Zhe Colored Road. Sindha I have only met a few days ago. Zhey have been here since escaping zhe attack. I cannot believe it is all true."

"What is true?"

"Jahmash. Zhat he is back. I don't zhink many people believed it vould happen in zhis lifetime. It is getting cold. Ve should go inside. I vill have zhe kitchen fix you some breakfast and I vill tell Lao zhat you are here. Vhat is your name, schatza?"

Farrah hesitated. "No. Please do not tell them that I am here. I have not yet been to the House of Darian. I was on my way there when…my companions and I heard the news. I do not want to bother them yet. Let the two of them have their peace for now. I cannot begin to understand what they are feeling. Perhaps I will come inside, though. Is there a crowd inside?"

"Oh yes, nearly full to zhe brim. I vill likely be in trouble for being gone so long, come to zhink of it. You should come in soon as vell. I will not tell zhem you are out here, but you should go in and find a table. Some food and varmth vould do you vell, dear."

Farrah nodded. "I will be in shortly after you. Thank you. May I have the pleasure of your name, sir?"

"Name's Uli, my dear. And yours?"

Farrah hesitated. "Melina."

"I vill see you inside, Melina. Pretty name for a pretty schatza."

"Schatza?"

"Little treasure. I knew vhen I saw you out here zhat you vher a treasure." Uli smiled at her and walked away. Farrah rolled her eyes. The man was clearly not flirting with her, but his mannerisms were excessive. Farrah waited long enough that she would hopefully not have to encounter him as soon as she walked in. She shifted her pack at her shoulders and walked slowly. Maqdhuum had taken her around the city, after rescuing her from the sinking galley, and ensured she'd had enough clothing and personal effects. She had wanted to like him even before his generosity, but something about Maqdhuum seemed off. She shrugged off the notion and walked into the inn. Chances were likely slim that she would cross paths with Maqdhuum again, anyway. He was always in a rush to be somewhere else.

The common room of The Colored Road was all hustle and bustle. Barmaids danced through crowds or sat on laps. Men and women crowded around tables and most of the conversations were too loud. *Let me just find them and kill them so I may leave.* Farrah pulled her hood up and close to her face as she walked through the aisles. *Uli said there were two. Male and female. Shouldn't be difficult to – there.* Two Descendants sat at a large table with a group of others. They sat in plain view, not attempting to hide, except that several men had crowded around the male as he spoke. The others hung on his every word. Farrah found a small unoccupied table in the corner, several feet away.

She could see the male through bodies and limbs. *He is too charismatic to leave his seat. Someone else will bring him a drink. Even buy it. Badalao, Uli said. Old Markosi name, just like that hairstyle, but he wears it well. Likely from one of the old families, which means his funeral will be lavish. It's a shame I have to kill him; he's too handsome to die alone in some dingy inn.* Farrah barely noticed the female Descendant rise and walk away. Her eyes followed as the Shivaani girl walked to the edge of the room and up a staircase. Farrah glanced back at

Badalao. He still told his story with great intensity in his face as the crowd around him sat and stood, frozen in anticipation. Farrah could only guess that the boy told was telling them of the House of Darian's destruction. She flinched suddenly as Badalao looked directly into her eyes.

Dammit. It will be fine; stay calm. Badalao glanced over again a few moments later and smiled. *Sea of Fates, why does he keep looking? I should have kept my hood up!* She looked about the room and signaled to a barmaid, hoping Badalao would get the hint that she was not interested. The wrinkly, squat, woman neared, "By yourself, are ye? Can I get ye a drink, sweetie?"

"Wine, please. Red, dry if you have." Farrah put on her most innocent smile before the woman nodded and turned to walk away. *Why do Mireyans talk like idiots? That accent is the worst!* She hadn't seen much of Ashur. Her father was a stubborn Markosi and her mother a Galicean, which meant that she and her sister had been raised in Markos until both of her parents fell ill of Crimson Pox when Farrah had barely reached eight years. Her mother had contracted it first and eventually passed it to Farrah's father, as he refused to leave her bedside. Melina was only two when their father died, less than a month after their mother.

Farrah twitched out of her reminiscence, realizing that Badalao no longer sat at his table. *Shit. Where is he?* She knew she wouldn't find him from her table; the room was too full. She would have to walk around again, but then would also risk him finding her first. Farrah stood, though she wasn't tall enough to see over most people in the room. She focused on her left first, scanning tables and what she could see between bodies, arms, and legs. *Nothing. This is impossible.* She strained to see through people, looking over and under bodies.

"If I did not know better, I'd assume you were looking for me."

The voice startled her, and after turning to her right to see Badalao sitting at her table, Farrah felt her face redden. "Excuse me? No, I don't even know who you are. I was looking for a barmaid. They take forever in this place."

"Strange. I would have sworn that you just spoke to one." He smiled at her while gently tapping his fingers on the table.

Farrah rolled her eyes, more in embarrassment than annoyance. Badalao was too clever for her to get away with simple lies. "How long have *you* been watching *me*? Next, you'll be trying to read my mind. Maybe then you would know that I wanted to ask her for something else."

Badalao chuckled, "Oh no, I don't read minds without consent. It would be rude otherwise." He continued smiling then pointed to the black line down his left eye.

So that's his manifestation. "Just like that? What am I thinking then?"

"Well it isn't *that* simple. I would need physical contact to initiate the bond. After that, I can come and go just about whenever I'd like. Now what about you? I've shared mine…how about yours?"

Farrah smirked. "Well, I suppose you'll just have to read my mind to find that out." She liked him more than she cared to. He carried a certain charisma about him that made her want to sit there and talk to him for hours on end. *Who am I kidding, I want to talk to him AND flirt with him. For hours on end.* She felt her mind slightly tighten. *Do not fear, my master. I know my mission. I simply want to have some fun with my target first.*

By the time Farrah had finished her thought, Badalao had leaned across the table and pulled her lips to his. Countless thoughts and feelings eclectically barraged her so strongly that she didn't even think to seize her manifestation. Badalao gently held her face just under her ear so that his fingers simultaneously passed through her hair. For the first time in as long as she could remember, the tension drained from Farrah's shoulders. Badalao paused for just a moment and then resumed kissing her gently. In that short moment, Farrah felt the grip on her mind dissolve and it was shortly replaced with a cozy warmth, as if Jahmash no longer cared to control her. Badalao suddenly pulled back and stared at her.

Farrah looked back at him wide-eyed and bewildered. She asked him sharply and suspiciously. "Why did you do that? Who do you think you are?"

"I…did not even know that…"

"You don't just grab a strange girl and kiss her! That is exactly how people get hurt! You know nothing about me!" *Shut up you kolos, you'll give too much away!* She took a deep breath but continued before he could get in a word. "And what did you do to my head? Did you bond your mind with mine? Did I tell you that you could do that? You have no idea who I am; what if I killed you for doing that? I could have stabbed you before you had a chance to even read one thought of mine!" Farrah felt relieved that the room was as crowded and noisy as it was.

Badalao put a hand up, signaling her to stop. "It was simply a kiss. You seemed to be enjoying it for those few moments, which felt like millennia, but still too short a time if you ask me. Why are you so offended now? So I bonded you – that does not automatically mean that I will intrude upon your mind whenever I want. You *just* said that I would have to read your mind to discover your manifestation. To me, that is an invitation to bond you. And besides, not for a single second did I try to read your thoughts!"

"So then why do it in the first place?" She shut up as the barmaid returned with her wine, then resumed as the woman walked away. "Is that what you do? Go around touching people so you can go into their minds whenever you like? If you *ever* invade my head, by the Sea of Fates, I swear I will kill you!"

Badalao shrugged his shoulders, "I just thought there was something here. Between us. You kissed me back and I thought that if our minds were connected, I could show you that you don't need to…spy on me from the corner of a crowded room. And besides, you obviously let someone else have the pleasure. When I attempted to connect with you, I felt a strong presence in your head, like a sheath around your mind. But then I applied pressure to it, unsure if you were resisting. I assumed that if you were still kissing me, then you were likely not fighting me in your head. Whoever was in your head before me is gone now. Completely. So I apologize for that."

Farrah grew nervous. "You got rid of him?" Badalao nodded. Her mind filled with panic at the notion that Jahmash was no longer connected to her. *Will he hunt me down and kill me now? No, stop thinking. Stop. Thinking. Jahmash has to know it wasn't your fault. He would know.* Relief slowly smothered out the panic. Impulsively, Farrah smiled and leaned over the table, then kissed Badalao passionately. She knocked over her glass of wine in the process, but made no move to get it or to clean the mess. She'd never actually initiated kissing a boy without using her manifestation. The feeling was almost as freeing as knowing that Jahmash was not preying on her every thought. Without Jahmash in her head, she couldn't even be sure whether the notion of murder was still hers or just a memory borrowed from someone else.

Badalao pulled back. "Who was it? Former lover? Overprotective brother? Father?"

Farrah's face reddened as she stared at him. She clenched her teeth and fist, somewhat angry that they were no longer kissing so that she could just kill him for mentioning her father. *Calm down; he obviously doesn't know about father or anything about you.* "Long story. Maybe I'll tell you another time, if we're still talking in the distant future."

"You're a Descendant. I'm a Descendant. Way I see it, we should stay together." Badalao paused and smirked. "For protection, of course. Sindha and I are lucky that we both ended up here after the destruction of the House. Who knows whether any of the other survivors are stranded alone in some city that hates us."

"How *did* you end up here? It has been less than a week, and you've apparently been here for a few days."

Badalao's eye cocked. "How did you know that? I'm supposed to be the mind reader." He studied Farrah for a moment, but she merely shrugged. "One of our Mavens, Savaiyon, can create doorways in the air that will take you anywhere. You could travel from here to Markos in a single step. Once everything started to look bleak for us, he was running around like a madman, creating doorways and helping the last of us to escape."

"How fortunate for all of you," she said coolly. She placed her hand over his, which was resting on the table. "How many are left? And what do we do now if there's no House of Darian to go to?"

"There's no way to be sure. I have not bonded every Descendant so I cannot keep track of everyone. I know the whereabouts of about ten, but they are all scattered throughout Ashur. Most in less fortunate situations than myself and Sindha. And you. I think first we will all have to regroup in a common location. However, I do not have a bond with Maven Savaiyon. If he is even still alive, there is no telling where he could be. So, without Savaiyon, it will take a long time before we can all be reunited. Those whom I have bonded know to go to the Tower of the Blind. It is our best chance of survival at this point."

"Interesting. When are you leaving for the Tower? Just you and Sindha are going?"

"We will wait another day or two. Just in case we find any other Descendants. We've been here for days and only met you today. There could still be others hoping to reach the House who have no idea what happened."

"Am I going with you?" She smiled out of the corner of her mouth, still unsure of whether she wanted to kiss him or kill him.

Badalao raised his eyebrows, "I don't know. Are you?"

He really isn't in my head. So honorable. I would have been intruding on his thoughts within a moment of creating that bond. "We shall see. I have not decided yet. I have heard that the Way of Sunsets can be unkind to Descendants. There is talk in the city that King Edmund is sending more soldiers to watch the road. How do you plan to avoid them?"

"We will have to avoid all roads. Perhaps ride along the Serpent and then use Mireya's southern forest as cover to reach the Eye of Orijin. It will not be easy, no matter which course we choose. But Sindha is exceptional with her manifestation and my combat skills are formidable. If you come, we welcome any help that you might provide, manifestation or otherwise." Badalao stared at her intensely for a moment.

"What? What is it?"

"You never told me your name. We've kissed twice, and despite your anger and distrust, *you* have asked *me* for a great deal of information and have not had the courtesy of telling me your name or asking for mine. Unless you already know it. Regardless, I am Badalao

Majime. You?"

Farrah's eyes widened. "Majime. The hair was telling enough that you were from an old family. But Majime is about as high as it gets in Markos. I was only seven or eight years when I left Markos, but even I know how well-connected you and your family are. I mean, how does a Majime even get into a situation to develop a manifestation? Surely your life could never have been in danger." Farrah caught herself. It was rude to ask a Descendant how he or she acquired their manifestation. Offending Badalao wouldn't help her mission. "I apologize. That was rude." Badalao casually dismissed it. "But, you're sure it has to be a difficult journey to the Tower of the Blind? Oh." She took a deep breath. "I am Farrah. I do not really use my father's surname any longer. Just call me Farrah. Please."

"Fine. Farrah it is. The name is beautiful enough by itself anyway." Badalao turned his hand over so that their palms were touching. "So will you come with us?"

Farrah looked down and then back at Badalao. "I am unsure. I made it this far by hiding. Even still, I am all that is left of my family. The thought of leaving this city for the dangers of the world and risking my life all over again…it…it would make my sister's death in vain. Perhaps I should stay in the City of the Fallen and find work. It would at least be a peaceful life." She played coy, hoping to see how insistent Badalao might be willing to get in order for her to join him.

"There will be no peace in our lifetime. Jahmash has awoken and we must kill him. The only way to do that is for us Descendants to gather and determine a strategy to defeat him. We are better than most of the people in Ashur. We were chosen by the Orijin for something more." He shook his head. "Dammit, we are trying to save these very people from extinction and they still hate us. But that is our path. You are not some old crone whose days are numbered. You are young, beautiful, and have a lifetime ahead of you. If we must, we will reach the Tower of the Blind in secret, so that no one will even know when we are sneaking right past them. And if they have an issue with it, then we kill them before they kill us. Our lives are too important now to be wasted trying to live like common folk."

I need to change the dynamic of this conversation soon. He's getting too convincing and any argument I pose will likely expose me. She sighed, "Are you and Sindha sharing a room?"

"No, no. It is not like that between us. Why?"

"I don't feel comfortable having this conversation down here, and I have not requested a room yet. Might we go up to yours and continue talking?" Badalao eyed her suspiciously. "You can tie me down if you don't trust me. I just want to be able to talk about all this and process it without having to worry about eavesdroppers." *Calm down, you idiot. You cannot sound too eager.*

Badalao glanced back at the table where he'd been sitting before, then back at Farrah and smiled. "Fine. Let's go up." He signaled to the same barmaid who'd brought her wine and shouted for her to bring some up. Farrah looked around the room as they stood and walked to the stairs. Badalao must have understood her concern, but did nothing to comfort her. "Don't worry, if anyone is looking at us, they'll simply assume we're going upstairs to sleep together."

"Oh, is that all?"

"Most do not need much of a reason to assume two people are being intimate. Look at you – you needed clarification about whether I was sleeping with Sindha, simply because you saw us together."

Farrah rolled her eyes, "Whatever. You seem too comfortable with this. Why do I get the feeling that you've walked quite a few girls up to your room in this place?"

"It was you who said that we should go upstairs and that I could tie you down. Just because I'm willing to go along with it doesn't make me a bad person. It's not like you're the first girl who's asked me to tie her down."

"Now you're scaring me. Perhaps I should go." Farrah wasn't serious, but she was curious how he would take that.

"Oh please, you know you like me. Give me a few more minutes and you might even love me." He turned his head to her and grinned.

Give me a few more minutes and maybe I'm going to kill you. "We'll just have to see then, won't we?"

"YOU ARE AN AMAZING KISSER," Badalao said after a deep breath. Their lips had barely separated in the last several minutes.

Farrah blushed. "I've had some practice." *However, most of my 'practice' tends to stop men from breathing shortly after. What am I going to do with you?* Her desire to kill Badalao had reduced exponentially now that Jahmash could no longer simply drop in on her mind whenever he felt like it. Even more embarrassingly, she allowed him to tie up her wrists to the bedposts. Something about Badalao made him easy to trust and made Farrah eager for his attention. His demeanor made her feel like it was an honor to be in his presence, and at the same time, like she was the only thing that mattered to him. She was almost annoyed that she did not dislike him.

"With beauty like yours, it must be so difficult for men to restrain themselves."

She was likely blushing again, or still, but Farrah managed a cool smile. "Well, *you* could hardly restrain yourself." Badalao leaned down towards her and kissed her again. At first softly, and progressively more passionately. Thoughts and emotions fluttered back and forth through Farrah's mind, but she took the time to only entertain two. She knew for sure that she had no intention of using her manifestation on him. And that was because of the other thought she acknowledged. *At any moment, he could be in my head. Of course I would know, but he hasn't attempted to even once since pushing out Jahmash.* It was the first time a man had initiated a kiss with her and she was not apprehensive about ulterior motives. It was also the first time she willingly kissed a man without intending to kill him. *Stop thinking, kolos. Just enjoy it.* "Do you really want me to come with you? Or is that just because you want to be able to keep kissing me?" She whispered to him.

Badalao slightly backed his face away. "Of course I want to keep kissing you. But I'd like you to be with me. You are one of us. You are safest with the other Descendants. Now, more than ever, we have to look out for each other. We no longer have the House of Darian as a safe haven. It will be much easier for us to be attacked. Especially if we are found divided."

"So you are saying that you *need* me to come with you."

"It would deeply affect my well-being if you did not." Badalao grinned slyly and gently kissed her neck. A thought poked at her, but Farrah instantly forgot what she intended to ask him next. Guilt nudged at the back of her mind, but she pushed it back. She could not remember the last time she'd been able to let her guard down and enjoy the moment. She thought she'd enjoyed some of the killing, but she could no longer tell if those emotions belonged to her or Jahmash. In truth, she did not remember a single happy day since before her parents had gotten sick. *I deserve this. I deserve at least a night of happiness.*

"You can untie me now. I want to be able to use *my* hands, too." Immediately after Badalao loosened the knots, she pulled him back to her and kissed him again. She ran her hands softly under his shirt and allowed him to do the same to her. Her first instinct had been to flinch, but Badalao's touch was warm and gentle, making her welcome more. Farrah had never actually slept with a man. Many had tried against her will and paid the consequences with their lives. It was how she'd developed her manifestation in the first place, when she had only Melina as company, shortly after their parents died. Farrah shook the thought from her head as subtly as she could, but Badalao pulled back to look at her anyway. "I'm fine, I just got lost in a thought." He smiled and continued kissing her neck and shoulders. She took a deep breath and smiled, then pulled his shirt off.

BADALAO SNORED NEXT TO HER as she stared at the shadows on the ceiling. She'd finally had knowledge of a man, a few times over the past few hours, at that, and it had been rapturous, though somewhat painful at first. Eventually, they'd tired themselves out and could no longer keep their eyes open. Farrah couldn't be sure what the hour was, but it was still the middle of the night. She still felt sore from everything they'd done. She also could not decide whether Badalao's snoring had awoken her or if her conscience was to blame. She knew that something had bothered her before in what Badalao had said, but the moment had gotten swept away in her infatuation. *Something he said. Being on the run? Not safe? No...attacked! He said that we would only be attacked by the King's soldiers. That was it!* "Prince Garrison."

Badalao grunted, "Hmm?"

Shit. If I reveal that I know that they were harboring the Prince, will that give me away? Will that ruin things? Is he not just as guilty for sharing the same roof as that bottom feeder? Is it common knowledge that Garrison is there? Sea of Fates, what do I do? "Nothing. Go back to sleep," she unwittingly whispered aloud. Luckily for Farrah, Badalao rolled over and faced the other way. She gingerly sat up in the bed and found her clothes on the floor. She slowly got dressed, despite how much her body ached. She'd also been lucky that she'd left her pack intact. She grabbed it and left the room. She wasn't sure how she felt about everything, but it would be better to process the situation and the information somewhere else, where she wouldn't have to worry about talking to other people.

BADALAO WOKE UP TO SOMEONE nudging his shoulder. He opened his eyes, startled to see that it was Sindha and not Farrah. "Wait, how long have you been standing there?"

"Long enough to see you in all your glory, for better and worse."

He glanced down at his body only to remember that he was completely naked, and pulled the sheet up for cover. "Sorry."

Sindha rolled her eyes, "Nothing I haven't seen before, right? I'm assuming you were not alone last night, then?"

"I definitely was not. Farrah came up here with me. She was here for quite a while; she definitely fell asleep here. Where could she have gone?"

Sindha's grin was a little too wide. "You look quite put off. Are you alright?"

"It's just...usually I am the one who leaves in the middle of the night after a good romp. This has never happened to me before. Now I know what it feels like. Not that great. But why would she leave? Everything had been going so well."

"I feel *so* horrible for you, my dear. Come, let us get breakfast downstairs. I am starving and it is still early, so there should not be much of a crowd."

Badalao got up slowly, his body achy from all of the fun he'd had with Farrah during the night. *At least I thought it was fun. What could have happened that would make her leave? Should I open the bond with her? No, she does not know me well enough yet for that to be smart. Dammit.* He put his clothes on in front of Sindha. If she was comfortable with it, then so was he. They'd spent one night together shortly after he'd first arrived at the House, but then she lost interest in continuing when she saw him flirting with another girl a few days later. "I'm ready. After you."

As they walked down the stairs to the main common room and dining hall, a crowd was gathered close to the entrance. People were looking down at the ground and murmuring, talking, or shouting. Badalao stepped in front of Sindha and maneuvered his way to the front. On the ground lay Uli, one of the cooks. His face bore a blue hue and his eyes were open wide. "What happened?" He shouted to a woman next to him.

The woman answered Badalao, but remained staring at Uli's lifeless body. "No one knows. He was found like this not that long ago. No heartbeat. No breath. No one can see any wounds. No blood has left his body, either. It is the strangest thing."

CHAPTER 2
MARK OF THE JINN

From **The Book of Orijin, Verse Four Hundred Thirty-one**
It is impossible to live a meaningful life without love.
Let love exist in everything you do. In every decision you make.
But be wise to not let love cloud your sense of right and wrong.

BALTASZAR GINGERLY STOOD BACK up. He was almost certain that something in his face was broken. He could only see clearly out of his right eye, but even still, there was no doubt that several Jinn towered around him, ready to continue their onslaught. *This doesn't make any sense. I have been with you for several days, and now you choose to attack me?* There was no sense in speaking aloud, they only communicated with him mentally.

I have made clear why this is necessary. While you are intended to lead us, you will not be deemed worthy until you defeat me.

The whole concept of individuality had been lost on the Jinn. They spoke as one, thought as one, and shared one collective mind—all capable of individual thought, yet always connected. They regularly interchanged words like *I*, *me*, *we*, and *us*, as if each one meant the same thing. *So essentially, I have to defeat all of you. Except you can manipulate heat and fire, just as I can, and you are impervious to fire, so my manifestation is useless against you.*

You think too much, and yet, you do not think enough. Another Jinn struck Baltaszar from behind, knocking him face-first into the hard ground. His eyes were tearing from what was sure to be a broken nose. Before he could muster the strength to push himself off the ground, one of the Jinn pulled him up to his feet. He opened himself to his manifestation and summoned a flame to each hand. He had no idea how the flames would help him, but it was the only thing he could think to do. Baltaszar swiveled his neck as his attackers drew closer. He threw his flames at two of them, only to see the fires disappear against their skin. He summoned a ring of fire around him, thanking Lincan for making him impervious to his own fire. The Jinn drew closer, stepping right through the circle of flames.

On two feet they stood more than twice his size. On four, they were slightly less intimidating, but still the size of horses. Curved tusks grew from behind each side of their jaws and extended past their mouths. Their thick pale skin was off-putting, especially with the earthy colors always shifting. Jinn generally could only be seen if they wanted to be. Baltaszar wished, at this moment, that he couldn't see them. It would have been less terrifying to be attacked by invisible creatures than to be surrounded by the grotesqueness of the Jinn, knowing they wanted to hurt him, and perhaps kill him.

Another Jinn advanced to him and punched at his chest. Baltaszar attempted to shield himself with his right arm, but the blow shattered the bones in his forearm, which then slammed into his ribs, likely cracking some in the process. Baltaszar doubled over and fell to his knees. He sucked at the air and grasped his broken arm. He labored to breathe and bent forward to put his forehead to the ground. If the Jinn planned to kill him he could not do much to stop them. A warm foot pushed him flatly to the ground, and Baltaszar screamed at the pressure on his nose, arm, and ribs.

The Jinn rolled him over to lay face up. He could feel the blood still running from his nose, now all over his face. Four of them surrounded him and each held down an arm or leg with seemingly minimal effort. A fifth crouched over him, its large head directly over his.

"I don't understand. I've been here for several days and everything was fine." The blood trickled into his mouth as he spoke. "Why were you so nice to me then if you only planned to kill me?" Baltaszar decided that talking made it easier to distract himself from the pain, rather than just using his mind to communicate.

We are not going to kill you. We treat you as you deserve. You deserve kindness. You deserve punishment. You are young and naïve. You are also impulsive, stubborn, and not in control of your emotions. These are things you must master before you return.

"So then why…" He paused to wince at a sharp pain from his broken ribs, "Why all this? What is the purpose of attacking me?"

As we said, you are impulsive, stubborn, and cannot control your emotions. You set your own village on fire with no remorse. You were also willing to end your own life, all because you were faced with a difficult situation that you were not emotionally equipped to handle.

"You were there?"

We are everywhere you are. We know everything you do. Even when you tell us to leave. Most of your flaws are justifiable. Most of your mistakes can be corrected. But the intent to sacrifice the lives of innocents because of your anger…that is not an action that can go unpunished.

"Then…?"

Before Baltaszar could finish his question, the Jinn put its enormous hand over Baltaszar's mouth and, with its other hand, placed a finger to its own mouth, indicating for him to stop talking. With the same finger, the Jinn placed its claw on Baltaszar's right cheek and sliced a line from his cheek to his forehead, intersecting his right eye. Baltaszar screamed immediately, unable to writhe or move, left only to fully embrace the burn of the gaping open wound against the winter air. The creatures themselves were created by the Orijin from smokeless fire. They could make themselves hot to the touch if they desired. Baltaszar was sure that was what had happened while the Jinn sliced the right side of his face open.

You bear the Mark of the Descendant so the world always knows that you are capable of more, and that you are pure of heart, chosen by Orijin itself. You now bear another mark, so that you will always remember the evil you are capable of. This one will not be beautiful like the one on your left eye. It will truly be a scar. It will burn and itch and bother you for some time, the way the guilt of your actions should.

Baltaszar composed himself enough to respond, "I understand and I accept your…" but once again, the Jinn struck him before he could finish his thought. The same claw that pierced his face briefly hovered over his chest. With the other hand, it sliced a cut into its fingertip and then quickly struck through Baltaszar's shirt and into his chest. This time, Baltaszar barely managed a scream, instead croaking and gurgling as the Jinn's bleeding finger pierced his heart. Baltaszar convulsed wildly, despite the four other Jinn holding him down.

The fifth Jinn removed its finger from Baltaszar's chest, but still stared him in the eyes. The tusks originating from the back of its jaw brushed the side of Baltaszar's face. It placed a hand on Baltaszar's chest, applying pressure to where it had gouged him. Baltaszar felt great warmth in his chest for several moments until the Jinn lifted its hand away.

I have healed the opening in your chest. You will go now. You will find that we have equipped you with what you need to better yourself. You may not see it today, but you will come to understand in time. With that, the five Jinn simultaneously arose to their feet and disappeared as they walked away from him.

Baltaszar lay on the ground for what felt like several hours, though he knew it had been less than one. He sat up and looked around at the lightly snow-covered ground and the darkness of the forest. Once again, he was somehow alone in the forest with barely an inkling about which direction to proceed. He knew better than to try asking the Jinn for help at this point. Baltaszar took his time in standing up, unsure of whether his broken nose, burning eye, or broken ribs would make him fall down again. To his surprise, Baltaszar managed to stay standing, although it was more of a hunched over type of stance. He didn't dare turn in a different direction; the pain from his ribs had subsided and he dared not tempt it to return. He would simply just walk straight ahead until it brought him somewhere, hopefully somewhere hospitable that would be willing to help him heal. Thankfully, the Jinn hadn't hurt his legs, so the only pain from walking was from the motion.

Surprisingly, Baltaszar was able to walk on for quite a while. He was too tired to think about all of the events that had just happened, so he continued forward, appreciating that the only break in the silence of the winter night was the crunch of his boots on the snow. He'd had no warm clothes, but he supposed that would never matter for him. Four fireballs floated around him as he walked, maintaining his warmth. Ironically enough, before the Jinn had attacked him, he'd shared a meal with them. They'd killed two Ranza cats and allowed him a portion of the leg. Of course, he had to cook his while they ate theirs raw, but it had been a substantial meal and would sustain him until the next day.

He decided he would settle down for the night once he found the right setting. The trees were too dense here, and he would have to wait until they cleared a little. He would have to surround himself with fire to keep safe while he slept, and the last thing he needed was his fire causing a tree to fall on him in his sleep. Baltaszar paused for a moment to take a breath. He was proud of himself. Despite everything he'd just faced, he was upright and on the move. He hoped that if Bo'az was okay, he was able to do the same thing. He also hoped that Anahi would be happy to see him again, because sooner or later, he would find his way back to her. "I'm going to get back to her. I'm still standing."

"I'M STILL STANDIN'. Ya don't have ta worry about me." Anahi insisted. She wasn't sure if she was more annoyed about Fae pushing the topic or about Baltaszar having never returned.

"So then ya wouldn't mind if another boy showed some interest, then?"

Anahi continued folding sheets. It was easier to mask her frustration if she was focused on a task. "I haven't got time fer boys, Fae. Boys make promises an' then don't come back. Sure, it's only been a couple o' weeks, but he told me he'd be back in a couple days. My life was fine before Baltaszar. But he taught me not ta get caught up with *boys*. Now if a *man* wanted ta sweep me off my feet, that's a different story."

Fae chuckled as she ironed a sheet. "Ha! Are there any men in Vandenar sweepin' women off o' our feet? All I know is, if we had as many elephants as we have boys, *or men*, talkin' 'bout ya, all o' Vandenar'd be fat."

"Fae, I've known ya fer years now. Why are ya all of a sudden concerned about my love life?"

Fae looked downward, still smiling. "Look Anahi, I don't get looks an' glances like ye do. Sure, someone here an' there might say I'm cute. But they all gawk at ya. Maids like us don't get the best selection ta begin with, so I…"

"So ya figure if I'm spoken fer, then ye'll get the pick o' the parade?"

"That's the story." Fae attempted a sheepish smile.

Anahi furrowed her brow and stopped folding. She crossed her arms and stared directly at Fae. "Listen ta me, girl. Any man who only wants ya fer yer looks is a waste o' yer time. Any man who thinks he's too good fer ya because yer a maid is a waste o' yer time. Yer a wonderful girl, sweet as can be. An' ye'd make an even better wife. An don't fool yerself, ya *are* beautiful. Any *man* who doesn't see that is blinder than Munn Keeramm. Ya think I was smitten with Baltaszar because o' his looks? Mind ya, he was a bit handsome, but it was our connection. We just had a spark that I'd never felt before. I knew it the firs' time he spoke ta me. He could be uglier than yer uncle with all the scars, no offense, an' I'd still feel the same fer him. When he starts talkin' an' he smiles at me, an' he's excited about what he's tellin' me, he makes me feel like no one else in the world matters ta him. An' the one time we did kiss, fer a moment I swear I didn' even know where I was." Anahi blinked a few times, realizing that Fae was staring at her intently. "What's yer problem?"

"Ya just admitted that yer still a fool fer Baltaszar! Ya talked about him like he's still courtin' ya!" Fae eyed Anahi for a moment and then softened her intensity, "I mean, thanks fer all the nice things ya said 'bout me, that was real sweet. But ya definitely still wish Baltaszar was around."

"What do ya want me ta say, Fae? That I still fancy the boy? O' course I do. It was special, an' candid, an' profound, an' except fer the girl he was runnin' off ta break things off with, it was almost perfect. But where does that get me now, Fae? He's not here, is he? He may never come back, so am I supposed ta wait around fer just a possibility? He's a Descendant fer Orijin's sake. Even if he wanted ta come back, who knows if he's already off huntin' fer Jahmash or captured or hurt or maybe even dead."

"Anahi, how could ya say that?"

"Don't start talkin' down ta me. I know just what kind o' world we live in. If it could happen ta my brother, it could happen ta Baltaszar. Put enough soldiers in front o' him an' any Descendant will run out o' luck. I told him ta be careful the first time he left here, but trouble has a way o' findin' them, doesn't it. If the rumors are true, the House o' Darian was just destroyed by Jahmash's soldiers. If that's true, then a whole lot o' Descendants are dead. Some who we've probably met." She saw that Fae had stopped what she was doing. The petite girl's demeanor had become somewhat limp. "I'm sorry, Fae. I know that's not what ya want ta hear, but we're livin' in some difficult times. There's so much that we shouldn't take fer granted. An' that's why I can't hold my breath fer Baltaszar. It's possible that I could even love him one day, I may even love him already, but who knows how long we've got ta live our lives. I want ta make the most o' mine while I can."

"Wow. That was a defensive rant if I ever heard one. I was just pointin' out that ya admitted yer feelins fer Baltaszar." She smirked at Anahi, whose face remained stoic. "Obviously I'm jokin'. An' I understand that this might not be the best time fer that. But we're two maids at an inn. We don't get the luxury o' adventure an' glamor. An I'm sorry; I know yer likely worried about him an' the other Descendants. So if ya don't want ta wait fer him, by all means, go ahead an' find a good ol' Vandenari man. My advice, though, is ta pay a visit ta Munn Keeramm before ya decide. Maybe he can tell ya if fate has already decided."

Anahi started folding sheets again, this time more aggressively. "Well then if it's already decided, why even see him? If I'm meant ta be with Baltaszar, then he'll return before I can even find someone else. Right?"

"Aren't ya even a little curious about the future? About whether there are any clues for who ya might end up with?"

"No. What if I find out somethin' worse? What if I go ta Munn an' he tells me I'm goin' ta die next week? Then not only do I have ta hear bad news, but I have ta live the next week knowin' I'm goin' ta die. Those prophecies are never wrong."

Fae set the iron down into a bucket of water, which caused a hiss and plumes of steam. She grabbed Anahi by the hand and tugged. For such a slight stature, Anahi was surprised at the girl's strength. "Come on, we're goin' ta go there together. An' you can tell Master Keeramm that if yer goin' ta die next week, that he shouldn't tell ya. Fair?"

Anahi sighed and grabbed a thick cloak on the way out. "All this over a boy? Two intelligent girls like us should be spendin' our energy on more worthwhile things." She allowed herself to be pulled along anyway. Although she knew the Blind Man well, she had never asked Munn Keeramm for a prophecy; in fact, most people in Vandenar tended to leave him alone for the same reasons as she. Despite her curiosity, Anahi preferred to be ignorant of everything rather than risk knowing about something bad. But she supposed as far as Baltaszar was concerned, if there was some piece of information that could help her know what to do, she should consider it.

"If boys aren't worthwhile, why do intelligent women keep getting' married an' havin' babies with 'em? If anythin', this is how intelligent women handle things like this." Fae kept the grasp on her arm the whole way to the man's house. Anahi had been to Keeramm's home quite often. Cyrus had insisted that the inn provide Keeramm with food and tea regularly. As the head maid of The Happy Elephant, Anahi took it upon herself to personally bring everything to the Blind Man. In all that time, she never once asked for a prophecy, nor did he ever ask her to sit for one. She never knew whether that was a bad omen, but Ahani assumed it was just the man's way of being respectful. They'd sat and talked about other things from time to time, but there was never a need to talk about prophecy. She appreciated that about their interactions. Sometimes she thought that he appreciated being able to talk to someone without having to worry about visions and prophecies. Sure he'd had Farco to keep him company, but as nice a boy as Farco was, there was only so much intelligent conversation an old man could have with a boy who'd only seen twelve summers. Fae chirped again, "Here, I'm comin' in with ya ta make sure you at least ask him fer somethin'."

"Fae, are ya sure this isn't all some ruse? I'm beginnin' ta think that maybe yer in love with me an' that's why yer so insistent about this."

Fae glanced at her plainly, "Ha, I don't think ya could handle me, dear. I'm too much woman fer ya. Men are simple-minded, easy ta push around. Yer too difficult an' strong-willed fer me, even if I did manage ta get ya here. Now stop stallin' an' let's go."

"Fine." She followed Fae up Keeramm's steps where the shaggy haired boy tended to sit. "G'day, Far!" She gently touched his head as Farco smiled and stood to show her and Fae in.

"Hi Anahi. Hi Fae. Come in, he's just relaxin'. No delivery today?"

Fae answered before Anahi could. "Not today, Far. We're on official business this time. Our friend Anahi needs a prophecy. We're curious about her future."

Anahi spoke up, "No, Fae's curious about my future an' she convinced me ta come here. So here we are. About ta bother Master Keeramm fer a bunch o' nonsense."

Farco looked somewhat confused and uncomfortable to be caught in the middle of her banter with Fae. "Right." He waved for them to sit at Keeramm's main table, which was littered with open books and scrolls. "Just…just wait right here an' I'll bring him in. Tea?"

Fae spoke up again, "Oh yes please. Fer both o' us. Thanks!" Farco nodded and scuttled out of the room.

Anahi eyed Fae sideways. "Ya can stop speakin' up fer me now. I think I can manage from here."

"Ya sure? I don't mind tellin' him exactly what yer lookin fer."

"I'll be fine. Just sit there an' drink yer tea an' look pretty."

Fae smirked at that. "Whatever ya say, dear."

A few moments later, Farco returned with Keeramm at his arm and guided the man to his chair at the table. "Master Keeramm, yer company is Anahi an' Fae. Believe it or not, they request a prophecy. I shall bring the volume ya need an' then I will make some tea. What kind fer today?"

Keeramm smiled and rubbed the top of his head. "Thank ya, dear boy. I would prefer the black this time, if our guests don't mind."

Anahi looked at Farco, "No that would be just fine. Black tea warms the bones when it's cold outside."

Farco nodded, "Very well, I will return shortly."

Keeramm used his fingers to scan through pages. "Unusual that either of you girls would come lookin' fer a prophecy. But not unwelcome. May I ask the reason? Unless ya prefer not ta share. No judgment here. Just an old man pryin'."

Anahi could feel Fae's gaze upon her and rolled her eyes. "Yer goin' ta think we're silly little girls, Master Keeramm. But Fae here has convinced me ta come see ya regardin' the future o' my love life. Ya see, I've fancied Baltaszar—ye've met him—since the first time he showed up here, an' I'm unsure o' whether ta hold onta hope that he'll come back here ta see me again, like he promised. My head says ta move on an' live my life, an' my heart still believes that he'll fulfill his promise, however late, an' come back here ta see me. Fae suggested that perhaps ya might have somethin' in yer books that might help me make a decision."

Keeramm closed his eyes and continued to run his fingers at the edges of the pages. Anahi assumed he was searching for her name. "Like I said, dear friend, I don't judge. Even in my brief time at the Tower, people would come ta us fer all kinds o' reasons. Everyone has their reasons fer wantin' ta know what comes ahead. Just because I am blessed ta have some o' that information, it is not my place ta say that any reason is good or bad or anythin' else. Ya have concerns about yer future. Good. We live in troublin' times, ya should be able to make the most o' it." He continued scanning his book.

Anahi turned to Fae and whispered. "See. That's just what I said. Times are troublin'. I should make the most o' it instead o' this."

Fae raised an eyebrow at her and whispered back. "Stop it. He was makin' a different point by sayin' that. It's not the same thing."

"Oh shush." Anahi pursed her lips together.

"Aha!" Keeramm whooped just as Farco returned with their tea. "I found it. Farco, why did ya not just open ta the page fer me? All that searchin' when ya could have made things easier."

"I apologize, Master Keeramm. I didn't know if it was definitely in there. I was waitin' fer ya ta tell me if ya needed a different book. Looks like we got lucky on the first one. There's only one fer Anahi anyway."

Keeramm shook his head. "Lucky my foot, boy. Ya just got lazy. Thanks fer the tea, ya can go back outside now." Farco set their cups in front of each of them and then returned outside. "He's startin' ta get too old fer this. Got other interests an' I can't blame him. I think he spends more time outside now than in here, even in the cold. Somethin' out there's more interesting than me. He's a sweet boy, though. Never rude, never disrespectful or disobedient. Sooner or later, I'm goin' ta have ta find another helper. I get the feelin' I'll have ta ask the Tower ta send someone though. Don't know anyone else in Vandenar who can read Augur writin'." Keeramm sipped his tea and then paused for a moment. "My apologies, Anahi, where were we?"

"No, it's fine, Master Keeramm. Far is a great boy. Perhaps he'll decide against Anonymi trainin' an' he'll stay with ya. Or perhaps he'll come back here once he's finished."

"Ah yes, perhaps an' perhaps. I suppose we shall see. Or you shall see an' I shall not. Ha! I apologize, I could not help myself." Anahi giggled. She was used to Keeramm's humor – always making fun of himself and making light of his blindness. It was one of the reasons she enjoyed being in his company, because he didn't allow her to feel uncomfortable around him. "Let us find out what we have here."

"Yes, if we must." Anahi felt a tinge of nervousness. She knew it would be something bad. She already regretted coming here and somewhat resented Fae for convincing her to come. She resented herself even more for giving in. Whatever it was, she would have to live with it for the rest of her life and she would constantly dwell on when the prophecy would actually come true, until it actually happened.

"Now, I can't be sure who yer talkin' ta, because it seems that I saw this prophecy through the eyes o' whoever ya were addressin'. Seems ya were talkin' ta a larger man – tall an' husky, a soldier." His fingers slowly passed over the dots and dashes on the page. "Yer wearin' grey, I believe that's what they call that color?"

"Yes, that would mean I'm workin' at the 'Elephant' then. Go on."

"Yer voice is somewhat raised, but yer not yellin'. Whoever I am, yer tellin' me an' another man—me an' him we're standin'—yer tellin' me that yer betrothed ta a Descendant who can wield fire. An' he's powerful enough ta kill me if I lay a hand on ya. I can't be sure what would spark this, maybe one o' us propositioned ya? Sorry Anahi, it's a short vision, an' I'm not sure what ya can do with it, but it's all I can give ya. Ya look young, but then again, what, by Orijin do I know about who looks young an' old. I couldn't even tell ya if this is goin' ta happen ta ya tomorrow or in five years. I do hope it's some help, though."

Anahi looked at Fae and then back at Keeramm. "That's not

comfortin' at all. Sounds like a man is goin' ta want ta assault me." She didn't want to make Keeramm feel bad, so she changed her tone. "It's somethin' at least. Can I help ya put that back before we go?"

"Oh no, no, o' course not. Farco'll take care o' it when he comes back. Thank ya fer the visit. I always enjoy yer company; an' yers as well, Fae. Come back any time ya want, fer whatever reason!"

She arose with Fae, who gulped down the rest of her tea. "Course we will, Master Keeramm. Thank ya fer all o' yer help. We'll see ya soon!" She led Fae out the front door. As they walked down the porch stairs, Anahi noticed Farco talking to a girl up ahead at fruit stand. The girl bore the Mark of a Descendant. Fae was about to speak to the girl, but Anahi stopped her. "Hold on, let me just say bye ta Far." She walked up to Farco's side and tapped him on the shoulder, which was almost at the height of hers. "So this is what's got ya so busy these days."

Farco looked at her obliviously, "I don't understand."

"I'm just teasin' ya. But he knows. He doesn't *know*, but he knows somethin'."

"I still don't really understand. Who knows what?"

Anahi chuckled, "Who's yer friend here? Introduce us."

Farco quickly reddened. "Oh. This is Avenira. Avenira, this is um…this is Anahi an' Fae. They're from the 'Elephant' an' Anahi visits Master Keeramm often." Avenira smiled genuinely and waved at Anahi and Fae. She was of a height with Farco, which meant she was nearly as tall as Anahi. She was a beautiful girl, with wild brownish-orange eyes. Anahi at first wondered why she'd never seen Avenira before, but then realized she barely did much outside of the inn, save visit Master Keeramm. *An' I'm so caught up with livin' my life ta the fullest.*

"It's a pleasure, Avenira. He's one o' a kind, ya better be good ta him."

Avenira responded with a smile, "So am I, so likewise ta him."

Anahi liked her already. "Enjoy yerselves. An' be nice ta Master Keeramm, Far. He's goin' ta be a bit lost when ya leave him." Anahi waved at them and signaled for Fae to follow her as she walked away.

Farco raised a hand to stop her. "Wait. I couldn't help but hear ya were talkin' about Baltaszar in there. Right?"

Anahi's eyes shifted around, "What's yer point?"

"Don't ask me how I know, because I won't tell ya. But when Baltaszar came that night with all o' his Descendant friends an' then they all left fer The Never, there was a fire, a huge fire, well inta the forest. Seems kinda fair ta assume that if Baltaszar went inta The Never, an' Baltaszar can control fire, that maybe it had somethin' ta do with him. I don't know if that helps ya at all, but when I heard ya talkin' 'bout Baltaszar an' not comin' back an' all, it reminded me o' that night that he came here with the other Descendants."

Anahi didn't even know where to begin. "How did...sorry." She took a deep breath and then pulled Farco in for a hug, wrapping both of her arms around him. "Thank ya, Far. Thank ya. Ya don't know how much that news means ta me. Now really, go back ta Master Keeramm an' help him back ta his relaxin'. He's waitin' fer ya. An' let him meet Avenira. He deserves as much. So does she." She released him and looked him straight in the eyes, intently.

"I will, I will." To Anahi's surprise, Farco took Avenira by the hand and led her toward Keeramm's porch. She smiled and wiped away a tear. Despite the winter chill, she felt warmth inside. *Maybe he will come back ta me, after all. Maybe somethin' did happen that didn't allow him ta come back here.*

LIGHT OF ORIJIN, couldn't they just slice my hand instead of my face? Maybe the back of my head or my leg or anything else? Baltaszar threw the handful of berries in frustration. Chewing even soft foods had proved torturous. He'd had to resort to crushing any fruits he found in order to just swallow without chewing. It had been several days since he'd left the Jinn and eating brought great anxiety. Moving the right side of his face irritated the cut, which had barely started scabbing. He'd stopped speaking, which had been made easier by the lack of company. Even when he didn't move his face, it burned and throbbed.

I wonder what anyone else would have done in my situation. Of course no one else would have set everything on fire, because they can't control it. And what the hell do the Jinn know about what I've been through? They don't understand courtship and betrayal. They don't have a twin brother who's pretended to be them just to impregnate the woman they love. For the love of Orijin, they are all twin brothers of each other! And they all share the same damn mind, so they would never have to worry about that. What was I supposed to do, just tell her it's fine, and then walk away knowing that Bo'az is the father of her child? That's stupid. I get it, we're supposed to master our emotions to have full control of our manifestations, but some things don't allow us to be in the best emotional state.

He let go of his thoughts and walked on, focusing only on his surroundings. After several minutes of walking through the same setting, Baltaszar grew bored of appreciating the forest. He thought back to one of his conversations with the Jinn. He wondered if anyone in Ashur knew about them. *Maybe people have seen them. Maybe that's why people are so afraid to come into The Never. I wonder if that's it.*

According to them, they were created by the Orijin centuries ago and had lived in the forest ever since. They were created from smokeless fire, so they could regulate their body temperatures. Baltaszar learned the lesson the hard way that the Jinn could even make themselves hot enough to burn to the touch. That remarkable feature was compounded by the fact that they could turn invisible, which is what they chose most of the time. They didn't care to be seen by people, and invisibility made it easier for them to hunt. Even when they were "visible," their skin could blend into the environment. The hues of their skin shifted when they allowed it, which Baltaszar found uneasy to look at. All in all, they were serious weapons and Baltaszar deeply regretted angering them. They were so much more than predators in a forest. If they wanted to, they could leave The Never and wipe out most, if not all, people throughout Ashur. Baltaszar felt incredibly lucky that they were on his side.

That was another troubling point in itself. *Because of our connection, I'm supposed to be their leader? Just because of the fire? They said they were created as a safeguard if humans couldn't defeat Jahmash. So what, I have to lead them against Jahmash if everything else fails? I don't understand any of this. And then they welcome me in and take care of me for days, but all of a sudden they decide I'm not worthy of their kindness? How is that any better than what I did in Haedon? Never mind, who am I kidding, I deserved that pummeling and probably more. I'd hate to see what they do to people they actually want to kill. Those ranzas that they killed never stood a chance. But why even wait to see if we fail? Why not just kill Jahmash and let it all be over with? Is the Orijin toying with us or testing us or something?*

What would I have to even do to prove I'm worthy of leading them? What if I never figure it out? Do the Jinn just stay in The Never forever and do nothing? Does Jahmash win? What kind of stupid rule is this? And who decided it? Did Orijin tell them to wait for me, Baltaszar Kontez, to be born and show up and that I would lead them someday? That seems so asinine. And what if I don't even want to lead them? Why am I even caught up in all of this 'Red Harbinger' nonsense to begin with? I just wanted to find a place to be safe after my father died and even they kicked me out. Whatever; all of them at the House of Darian can rot in Opprobrium. Fools. I'm not going back there. If my friends want to find me, they'll find me. If not, I find my own path. I'll heal up, then go to Vandenar and Anahi, and forget about everything and everyone else. I'll eat elephant for the rest of my life. I'll even make it a point to find Bo'az before Anahi and I settle down and start a family. By then, I'm sure I'll no longer be angry at him and I can prove that damn prophecy wrong. I've learned my lesson; even if this gaping wound in my face does ever heal, and even if it disappears, I'm done doing stupid things and letting emotions get the best in me. There is no chance in the

Three Rings that I would or could actually hurt Bo. I like Keeramm, but he's wrong. Maybe he thought it was me in that vision, but it was actually Bo'az. Maybe...wait, that would mean Bo will...kill...me? Baltaszar shook his head at the thought. He had been so consumed in his thoughts that he only now realized that the forest was clearing and a giant wall towered in the distance.

He scanned the expansive structure, noticing that soldiers littered the top of it. At this point, most of them had turned their attention toward him. Baltaszar did his best to straighten up, then raised his left arm and showed his palm, hoping they would understand he meant no harm. He waited for some type of signal from them, or at for at least someone to speak. He looked around at the top of the wall again as something struck his right shoulder and knocked him backwards to the ground. His head slammed hard against the cold hard dirt and as he tried to blink away the dizziness, Baltaszar realized he'd taken an arrow through his shoulder and it was pinning him to the ground. The notion horrified him, but before he could panic, his eyes closed and everything went dark.

Baltaszar awoke with a shock and had no opportunity to get his bearings. His arms were bound in front of him, and his ankles were tied together by a thick rope, which was being pulled by a horse. *At least it's not running.* The last thing he remembered was being struck by an arrow and falling down. He was being dragged face up at the moment, and judging by the distance of the wall, he hadn't blacked out for very long. It took a few more minutes to reach the wall. He was grateful that he hadn't turned over while being dragged. Everything burned and ached, and it would have increased the pain tenfold if he'd been dragged on his arm and face.

He couldn't ignore the pain enough to be able to channel his manifestation. Whatever the people wanted to do to him, they would. As the horse reached the gate, soldiers walked over to him and lifted him up. They put a dark sack over his head and one of them must have lifted him over their shoulder. The pressure on his arm and the bouncing of his shoulder didn't do anything to ease his pain, but it was better than being dragged.

Baltaszar was carried for several minutes before being dropped carelessly to the ground. The impact did nothing to help his already aching head, and only made the gash in his face burn even more. The soldiers untied his ankles only to bind each one separately in chains. Once again, he was dragged along the ground. He was then lifted to his feet and pushed backwards against a cold, hard wall. Someone punched him in the stomach, making him double over. In the process, they unbound his wrists and secured each one in chains. His arms were pulled upwards until they both extended straight out from the side of his body.

Baltaszar had no strength to keep his head up, and as it drooped forward, the sack fell off and he vomited immediately after. His eyes watered, but he looked upwards without moving his head. Even that hurt. His vision was still blurred, so somewhere between four and eight soldiers stood around him, talking to each other. After the group laughed heartily, most likely at his expense, they turned and left. The only comfort that Baltaszar felt was that he was too exhausted for any of the pain to keep him awake. His right arm had thankfully gone numb. He could barely even stop the drool from flowing down his bottom lip. His eyelids proved too heavy to be stopped and he quickly drifted off to sleep.

He awoke again to the sounds of chains clanking around him. Baltaszar realized quite quickly that turning his head would not be possible. His neck ached almost as bad as his head, so he allowed himself to just slump under the weight of the chains. *My wrists and ankles are going to be raw in no time. Just add them to the list of what's wrong with me, I guess.* He did his best to mutter a word. "Hello?" *Well, that still burns like crazy.*

"Greetings, Descendant. I was unsure of whether you died in your sleep. You were out for so long that it seemed likely you had not survived. I would show some happiness for you, however you likely would have been better off dying in your sleep."

Dammit. I'm going to have to talk if I want this to go anywhere. Baltaszar clenched his teeth and did his best to speak clearly. "Why? Who are you?"

"I have been here for nearly a year. There is no indication that I shall leave this place. Sure, from time to time they take me down from the wall to help with my blood flow and ensure that I still function. My name is Virgil. You likely cannot see me in your state, but I barely have any flesh covering my bones. Before the dungeon, I was one of King Edmund's Royal Guard, one of his personal protectors. Now look at me; I am useless. Even if I could leave this place, what would I do? No one in Cerysia would take me in after my treason."

"Why are you here?"

There was a pause before the man answered. "Prince Garrison entered the throne room one morning requesting that the king allow him leave from his princely duties so that he could study at the House of Darian. King Edmund would not have it. He asked the Royal Guard to fight the prince right there. Some of us actually followed the order, despite the fact that Garrison had been a better leader to us than the king ever had. Of all the guards who fought Prince Garrison, I am the only one who might still be able to be a knight again. Regardless, I suppose I will waste my life in here. Broderick cannot lift his arms all the way up. I believe he fled Cerysia shortly after. The same is the case for Connor, who cannot use his right hand. I am unsure of whether he had it cut off or not. Brandon made the mistake of questioning the king in a crowded throne room. He was beheaded on the spot. Tell me, which of the four of us would you choose to be? I would switch places with any of them. You cannot see my face, but it bears a scar from my left eyebrow diagonally down to my right jaw. I have not had the luxury of seeing my nose, but it is surely misshapen from having my face shoved into the floor."

Baltaszar took it all in. The conversation was worth the burn in his face. It had been so long since he'd had a conversation with another person that he was willing to deal with the pain of continuing to talk. "Sounds like you blame the king and not the prince. I actually met Prince Garrison once at the House of Darian. He seemed like a rather humble person. That being said, he injured three of you and was responsible for another's death. Why do you only blame the king?"

Virgil responded, "You have not had much exposure to King Edmund, I suppose. The man ordered us to kill his own son, with not a speck of shame. Simply because Prince Garrison, who as you know is a Descendant, asked to learn more about his manifestation so that he could use it for the benefit of Cerysia. The fault does not lie with Prince Garrison for harming us. The fault is with us for attacking in the first place. One of the first things we are taught as knights and soldiers is that loyalty is everything. We abandoned our loyalty to our general when we should have done right by him and refused the king's order."

"You are too hard on yourself, Virgil," a foreign voice said. Baltaszar had been listening so intently to Virgil that he hadn't realized anyone else had entered the room. It didn't really matter, considering he couldn't lift his head. The voice continued, "As you said, what man orders his son killed? What king asks his personal knights to murder the prince? The fault is solely King Edmund's. Entertain no other thought than that." Baltaszar heard the voice draw near along with accompanying footsteps. To his surprise, he saw two pairs of black boots and legs in front of him. Both squatted down in front of him. While the dizziness had mostly gone away, Baltaszar's vision still remained blurry. The two faces before him bore smiles. One belonged to a young golden-skinned man likely near his age. Long blonde locks flowed from his head. Next to him was another golden-skinned man, similar in age. Baltaszar felt a notion of familiarity in looking at him. "I thought I heard you mention that you met Prince Garrison at the House of Darian? Wait, do not answer that yet. Wendell, help Virgil down, I will help this one." Baltaszar heard more clanking of chains and realized he was being let down from the wall.

"Thank you." Baltaszar sat back against the wall and immediately clutched his right arm to his torso.

"It is nothing. You have injuries. We will tend to them shortly." He passed Baltaszar a metal pitcher of water that the other man had handed him. "Drink. Then tell me who you are as well as about Garrison."

Baltaszar gulped down the water so fast, it spilled down his chin and chest. "My name is Baltaszar Kontez. Garrison was a prisoner at the House. I only had one encounter with him, which was my first day of dungeon duties. He had mentioned something about a prophecy he'd heard from a Blind Man. It peaked my interest, because I'd actually experienced the vision he'd been told. We also realized in the process that it meant Jahmash's return had already been set in motion. Shortly after that I was kicked out of the House for some unfortunate decisions I made. Not sure what's become of him. He might still be in the dungeon."

The familiar face stared at him wide-eyed. "Wow. I thought our lives here were laced with hyperbole. I suppose no outsider truly knows what happens inside the House of Darian, so we can only make assumptions. There is a great deal that needs to be shared with you." He sat down against the wall next to Baltaszar. "I am Donovan Brighton. Garrison is my older brother. Wendell here is our best friend, also the new commander of our army. First, your removal from the House of Darian, how long ago was that? Is that also why you were traveling through The Never?"

"Interesting that I'd meet both of you in dungeons. Maybe you and your brother are bad luck for me. I was dropped into The Never about a week ago." Donovan eyed him curiously. "One of the Descendants there, Maven Savaiyon, can create doorways out of thin air. At the order of Zin Marlowe, I was to be dropped into The Never from high enough not to kill me."

Donovan nodded, "I see. Then you would have no way of knowing until now. I regret to inform you, Baltaszar, that the House of Darian has been destroyed. It is also rumored that Zin Marlowe has been killed."

"What? When? How?" Baltaszar didn't have energy to match his reaction. "Are they all dead? Who did it?"

"Our sources say it was roughly a week ago, so perhaps the same day or the day after you were banished. They say the army was massive, brought by hundreds of ships west of Ashur. We have heard that survivors are minimal. Most of them have been spotted in Mireya in cities friendly to Descendants. While you despair over your friends, I do the same for my brother. If, as you say, he was in the dungeon, I cannot hold out much hope that he survived. I know that if we were attacked here our last priority would be to open the dungeons to let out the prisoners."

Baltaszar clutched his ribs and slumped a little more. "I know what you're going through. I have a twin brother, Bo'az. I haven't seen him since we both left home and I have no idea if he's still alive. I also have no way of finding out anything about him. What he's doing. Where he is. The ironic thing is, I have to assume that he's alive because a Blind Man gave me a prophecy about me and my brother. Only thing is, the prophecy is that I'll kill him. Even without the prophecy, I would always hold out faith that my brother is alive, unless I know for sure otherwise. You should do the same."

Donovan shook his head, "Damn. I'm sorry for your situation. You have not asked, but you must have wondered why Wendell and I came into your cell and let you and Virgil down. No?"

"Hey, if someone wants to come in and let me out of being chained to a wall, why would I question it?" The more he talked, the more manageable the burn in his face became. He did find it curious that Donovan and Wendell would come in, unchain them, and then just sit down to talk. "But I would gladly listen to your explanation."

Donovan laughed quietly. "You are only in here by accident. You see, after Garrison left Alvadon—that is where you are, if you have not come to that conclusion—he was followed by my father's soldiers. They were under orders to find him and kill him. The man sent just about every soldier he had. Wendell and I took a handful of soldiers we knew would be loyal to us, and tried to keep pace with wherever Garrison went. We finally caught up to him in a forest just south of the Eye of Orijin. We managed to save Garrison and his two Taurani companions, but we parted ways there. Wendell and I left to come back here while our soldiers traveled with Garrison to protect him. That was the last I saw of him. Wendell and I were tasked with ensuring that the Royal Vermillion Army is loyal to us and to Garrison, rather than to my father. However, not everyone is so keen to leave my father's employment. I cannot necessarily blame them; some of these men have families and children to support. Most of the men who still support my father have stationed themselves at the wall, as it minimizes their interaction with everyone else. You just happened to be unlucky enough to be traveling this way, which is why you were attacked."

Baltaszar snickered. "I could have gone in any direction, but I chose to go straight because it was too painful to turn. I've got a broken nose, this gash down my face, a broken arm, broken ribs, there might still be a hole in my chest, but I'm not sure because it doesn't hurt anymore, and now a hole through my shoulder. Imagine that. I travel in the one direction that lands me shot by an arrow and placed in a dungeon."

"Actually, many directions might have gotten you littered with arrows. You might be lucky that you ended up here. Wendell and I shall bring you to a new cell, a private one in which we can control who sees you. We can have someone see to your injuries and keep you nourished.

Once you are well enough, we can arrange for you to escape Alvadon unnoticed by anyone who might be interested in killing you."

"You expect me to say no to any of that? Virgil should come, too. He doesn't deserve to be in here. What do you need from me in return?"

"Virgil must stay here for the time being. He is here under direct orders from my father. Moving him now would draw unwanted attention. But do not worry; we will take care of Virgil as well. If the timing is right, perhaps we may let him escape with you." Donovan stood and walked over to Baltaszar, then helped him to his feet. "Wendell." He nodded to Virgil. "Sorry, my friend."

Wendell bound Virgil in the chains once more and secured the thin, scarred man to the wall. Virgil responded once back in place, "There is nothing for you to apologize for, Prince. You come here when you can and give me relief from the wall. Thank you."

Donovan nodded to Virgil and then led Baltaszar towards the cell door. Wendell followed them out. Baltaszar realized that Wendell hadn't spoken a word the entire time. "Does he talk? Wendell?"

Donovan laughed and looked back at the blonde-haired man. "Oh, he talks."

Wendell spoke for the first time. "Yes, I talk. Donovan simply likes to dominate the conversation. He also enjoys bossing me around. He is making up for nearly two decades of being Garrison's younger brother and having to always be second."

They walked on through several corridors and down two flights of stairs. "You are truly hiding me, I see."

Donovan nodded, "It is the only way to keep you safe. You asked what I want in return. And you also advised me to have faith that Garrison is alive. If, by the small chance that my brother is alive, I want you to find him and tell him that he has his army waiting for him in Alvadon. Tell him to return home when he is ready. I will give you a lengthier message to relay once you are ready to leave. For now, your primary concern is to heal. Here, on the right. This is where you will stay. For better or worse, there is nobody else in this corridor."

"That's fine. I could use some time to myself without worrying about getting more injuries."

"Good. Then you will also not mind staying as quiet as possible. Loud sounds have a habit of echoing throughout these halls."

Tasz?

Baltaszar flinched. The voice in his head was familiar, and it certainly not the voice of the Jinn. "Oh, yes, I will stay as quiet as possible. Thank you for your help. I'll be fine for now. I could use some rest."

Wendell spoke this time. "We will send a nurse down to you

shortly. If they are not accompanied by either of us, do not be alarmed. We are burdened with several responsibilities as requested by the king."

"I understand, thank you." Donovan and Wendell walked away. Baltaszar found some hay in the corner and lay down, using the hay pile as a pillow. *Lao, is that you? Where are you? Are you safe? I just found out that the House was destroyed!*

Yes it's Lao. I'm fine. Some of us managed to fight back and survive. I'm traveling to the Tower of the Blind with Sindha. Where are you? I attempted to connect with you a few times in the past couple of days.

I was in The Never. It's a long story. But I'm in Alvadon now; in a dungeon actually. But I am receiving some help from some friendly people. Once my serious injuries have healed, I will be out of here.

Serious injuries? Do you have non-serious injuries as well?

Baltaszar sighed. *Broken nose, gash down my face, broken arm, broken ribs, stabbed in the chest, arrow hole in the shoulder. But I can deal with it, especially now. What about all of our friends? Were there many casualties?*

Tasz, it would take way too long to go over all that with you like this. As far as I know, our group of friends is safe. Everyone is split up, but surviving. Listen, Tasz, we are about to set out again. When you are better, head for the Tower. We will all meet up there to discuss what to do next. I will try to connect with you as frequently as I can, to keep you updated. Come to the Tower as soon as you can.

I will. Thanks for finding me. I was wondering what happened to all of you. I'll see you soon. Baltaszar tried to think about what must have happened at the House of Darian, but his eyes shut before anything materialized and he drifted off to sleep.

CHAPTER 3
AN OLD FRIEND

*From **The Book of Orijin**,* **Verse Four Hundred Seventy-two**
An enemy can only remain an enemy if there exists no common ground. Once a common purpose or objective has been identified, it is the duty of both sides to come together and cast aside their differences.

ADRIA STARED OUT OF THE THIRD story window, wrapped tightly in a thick blanket. They'd been in Shipsbane roughly a week, and she'd had plenty of nourishment in that time. Despite that, she still had some ways to go in order to not look like a walking corpse any longer. She could barely remember how long she'd been captive on Drahkunov's ship, but the food deprivation had been long enough to make her already thin frame look skeletal. *And somehow, he still managed to fool me with the occasional fancy meal, like he was doing me a favor. It's amazing how starving me turned me into such an idiot.*

Nights had been cold. The town sat right on Ashur's eastern shores of The Sea of Fates. Maqdhuum had lit the fireplace just before leaving her and Garrison in the room. Adria wondered how the man had been able to afford a room as resplendent as this. These types of rooms were generally reserved for important guests. Each of them had their own bed and the room took up half of the third floor. She'd made the decision to refrain from asking, though. Adria had enough questions for Maqdhuum. Asking about his coin was lower on her list of priorities. She was stuck in a strange town with Garrison, who'd, until recently, had had no qualms of hunting and killing Descendants like her. And then there was Maqdhuum, the Harbinger Abram in a mortal body, who also had a hand in killing some of her friends as well as the entire Taurani population. She would have to pick her battles.

Beneath it all, she remembered that Jahmash had still had access to her mind. Since being rescued from Drahkunov's ship, she had yet to feel the Red Harbinger's presence in her head, but Adria wondered whether he could poke around in her head without her knowing. Or perhaps he could simply be present in her mind and listen in on everything. She hoped that, perhaps, the Harbinger was simply too busy to remember to pay her mind a visit. She thought about telling Maqdhuum or Garrison, but she barely trusted either, and knew that neither could do anything to help her anyway.

Adria turned from the window and glanced at Garrison, who'd

curled up in his bed. As malnourished as she was, Garrison was completely emaciated. She'd seen him once a little over two years ago, after he had started delivering Descendants to the House of Darian instead of killing them. She remembered him as well built and muscular. The man she saw now was a shadow of his former self. It must have been an incredible shot to his pride to accept what he'd become. Adria had difficulty feeling pity for him, though. The teachings of Orijin always stressed balance in the world, or "tauzun," the notion that sooner or later, people would get what they deserved. She had little difficulty convincing herself that this was exactly what was happening to Garrison.

Regardless of how she felt, Garrison's kindness to her had been perpetual, to the point where she couldn't be sure if she was actually annoyed by it. If she hadn't known about his earlier exploits, Adria would have believed that Garrison was one of the nicest and most humble people she'd ever met.

He spoke up, startling her. "I can feel it, simply by your intent gaze."

Adria shook out of her reverie. "Excuse me?"

"You turned around and looked at me, and then you got lost in thought for several moments. I can guess the nature of what you are thinking. Look Adria, you can say to me whatever is on your mind. Chances are, I have most likely thought it about myself already."

Adria took a moment to compose herself, then sat at the foot of her bed and faced him. "I think you are a hypocrite, a murderer, and lower than a firestag beetle. I think it is disgusting that you came to our home asking for asylum and protection. I think it is even worse that Marlowe allowed you to stay, even as a prisoner. And I think it is a shame that no Descendants even attempted to try and kill you in your cell."

Garrison sat up in his bed, still engulfed in blankets. "Like I said, I do not disagree with you. It is unfair to ask your understanding, but there are some things that you should know about me. First, my father raised me to hate Descendants. That meant also hating myself. Do you have any idea what it is like to want to do everything to make your father proud as a young child, while also realizing that he hates your very existence? I thought what I was doing would gain acceptance."

"You hunted and killed dozens upon dozens of Descendants, and you knew it was wrong. And now you justify it by saying that it was all so that your father would love you? Is that really your defense, Garrison?" She clenched her fist.

"I will not pretend that I was better than that for most of my life. My father *never* valued life. It was how I was brought up. It is how the wealthy and the regal are bred. We have everything given to us and we assume that we may stroll through our existences taking as we please."

Adria was about to counter, but Garrison raised a hand to stop her, "No, let me finish. It took one moment for me to comprehend your intellect and wit, so my words are not meant to talk down to you. But unless you have ever had a taste of a royal upbringing, you will never relate to how I have been raised. How many lords have you ever met? How many kings, queens, or princes? How much time have you spent in the daily lives of any of them?"

Adria would let him make his point. She knew she could get the best of him by the end. "None."

"Then you have no idea how confining it can be. We are expected to be a certain way and act a certain way by our families, friends, and associates. Even if we do not like it, we must maintain the facade. As bad as that is, what is worse is that most people in that position will live their whole lives doing what is expected of them, because it is worth the life of entitlement and excess. You have no idea how difficult it is to give that up. Not only did I break away from it, I convinced my brother and best friend to do so as well, and they are not even Descendants. Yes, I killed Descendants, and for a time I thought what I was doing was right. But I stopped because I had the courage to educate myself about the truth of this world. Believe it or not, I also killed my own soldiers who wished to continue hunting Descendants."

Adria could not help herself. "Perhaps you just enjoy killing, then."

Garrison looked down. "For a time, I am sure I did. When I was killing Descendants, just as when as I was killing soldiers, I was always killing my own people. But things need to change. My father is not worthy to rule Ashur. I left Alvadon because I want to be able to overthrow him one day." He took a deep breath, looked at the window and then back at her. "I never told anyone this, but I could never decide whether it would be better if he died before I return to Alvadon, or if I kill him myself. The thing I fear most now is, if confronted with the opportunity, whether I could actually go through with killing him."

Adria glanced at him and then away. "Are you looking for sympathy?"

"You are so passionate about Descendants and so sure that I am irredeemable, but then why would the Orijin choose me as a Descendant if I was only meant for destruction and evil? By the mere fact that I bear the Mark, does that not mean that I am worthy of fighting for His cause?"

Adria took in the question for a few moments. Garrison was right about bearing the Mark. The Orijin would not bless him with a manifestation if he was unworthy. But then a thought dawned on her, "You had better hope that what's written in the Book of Orijin is correct. Because you are now the second *Descendant* I have met that has no trouble killing other Descendants."

Garrison shot her a puzzled look. "What?"

Adria nodded deliberately, "You heard me. When I was captive on Drahkunov's ship, there was another. I don't remember her name, but she was a beautiful blonde girl, likely our age. She kissed Gunnar and he died instantly. She bore the Mark and she killed one of our own, one of *her* own, just like you used to do. And you want to know the interesting thing about it? She told me to my face that it was your fault. She told me that you were allowed into the House and swore that she would murder more Descendants for Jahmash because you—you, Garrison—beheaded her sister. Farrah. Her name was Farrah."

Garrison's eyes widened more than she thought could be possible. "She's..."

Before Garrison could get his thought out, Maqdhuum appeared in the room, right in front of the fireplace. "The people in this town are so terrible at pretending to be clueless." Maqdhuum paused to look at Adria and then Garrison. "Oh. Did I interrupt something? Didn't peg you two for...ah, never mind." He smirked at Adria. "You are definitely angry. Did he say something stupid?"

Adria huffed air through her nostrils. "No, he actually said some rather enlightening and intelligent things. But unfortunately for him, he's still a murderer. Even if he feels bad about it now."

Maqdhuum looked over to Garrison, who still sat up rigidly and wide-eyed. "Don't worry about it, boy. I've killed plenty of people in my life. Some good, some bad. People will always have something to say about it."

Adria leaned forward, "How can you be so cavalier about such a thing? I understand that killing might sometimes be necessary. But not in his case. And who even knows what your motives have ever been. At least now your days are numbered. Imagine what the world would come to if they knew what their beloved Harbinger, Abram, had become. You're pathetic."

Maqdhuum chuckled. "So why don't you go around and tell everyone that it's me, then? You could just expose me for what I really am."

"Right, I'll just walk around the cities of Ashur telling everyone that Abram has returned in a different man's body, and now goes by the name 'Maqdhuum,' because he wants to finally help rid the world of Jahmash." She glared at Maqdhuum, "Even saying it to you sounds stupid and unbelievable. Nobody else in the world would believe it either."

"They'll end up finding out one way or another."

"When the time is right, I'll expose you for what you are. Stop with the pointless arguing. What were you saying when you interrupted us? Did you have something important to share?" Adria saw him flexing his burnt hand, and felt some comfort in his discomfort.

He stared at her blankly then sat next to her at the foot of the bed. "Look, I'm not as big an ass as you take me for. We have been here for a week and I have done nothing but let you be comfortable and get your strength back while I scour this city."

"Scour this city for what? You still haven't told us. I appreciate that you've kept us warm, dry, and fed, but we never asked for you to bring us with you."

Maqdhuum held up a finger. "This is where you need to know your place. I saved your life from that sinking ship." He nodded at Garrison, who'd finally let his guard down, "I saved his life from the dungeon your people put him in. You think he'd be better off with Savaiyon? Garrison, what say you? Were you treated better with me or them?"

"It is too early to tell. Some of the Descendants there were nice to me. I have yet to determine your need for me. You could simply be setting me up for a sacrifice."

Maqdhuum shrugged and flipped his stringy hair from his face, "True. It wouldn't be the first time. Anyway, since I brought the two of you with me, I have asked nothing of you except that you get yourselves better. I made it perfectly clear that I have no intention of harming either of you. I have not even asked for gratitude, although it would be nice." Adria continued glaring at him. "I know, I know. You hate me for killing Descendants at your House of Darian, and for leading the army against the Taurani. If anything, wiping out the Taurani was a favor to Ashur. They were never going to get out of their own way and now the other powers that be are on alert that they must be ready when Jahmash comes."

"You did us a favor? What powers that be? The Taurani were great warriors! You killed Descendants! In what way were you helping?"

"The Taurani were a society of fools. They lied to themselves about possessing manifestations, when they could have easily been one of the strongest armies in any nation of this entire world, Ashur and beyond."

Adria paused for a moment. "Wait, the Taurani were Descendants like us?"

Garrison spoke up. "He is right, Adria. A few of them helped me to reach the House of Darian. We were being chased at the Serpent," he paused to look Adria in the eyes, "by my own people, and our company was being decimated. The one Taurani who had made it that far, Marika, froze the river so I could cross. She told me not to tell anyone, but it seems pointless to maintain that secret any longer. Right after helping me, she was killed." Garrison stopped for a moment to ponder something. "But now that I think about it, she made it seem like there might be more Taurani. She had mentioned something about traveling east with her two companions to perhaps help save her people." Garrison cautiously looked at Adria and then Maqdhuum, "Is that what you are doing now? Trying to find the rest so you can kill them?"

Adria shook her head, "This is too much. They had manifestations, and now there might actually be more?"

Maqdhuum placed a hand on her shoulder, causing her to shift away from him. "Just hold on for a moment. Yes Adria, they had manifestations. No, Garrison, I'm not hunting down stragglers. But what intelligent society considers itself a great warrior society, yet prevents itself from using its greatest weapon? Those tattoos that they all bear? Those covered their Marks. Imagine how different things could have been if they had just embraced that about themselves. Not that all of them had manifestations, but many of them. It is of little consequence now, though. But Garrison, what you said about the east is precisely why we are here. There was one Taurani who left the society because he disagreed with their ways. He discovered his manifestation and did not wish to hide it. His name was Asarei Taurean. I know he oversees a fortress somewhere near Shipsbane, but it eludes even me. I have been out and around in this city every day since we arrived, trying to find out where it is, but no one will tell me. They all pretend they've no idea what I'm talking about, but I know they are hiding its location. I'm running out of people to ask. I can only approach so many people before they start talking about me."

Adria slowly looked up from staring at her hands. "Are you saying that there is another safe haven for Descendants? Why would you of all people be looking for that?" She stood up, "So you can kill more of us?"

"No fool. I told you I am done killing your kind. I understand your worth now. For a time, I thought of you all as some petty experiment by the Orijin. I understand your purpose now. That's why I brought the two of you in the first place. I am making my own army to fight Jahmash. If Asarei is still the way he used to be, then there is a good chance he has Descendants following him. Wherever he is."

Garrison responded, "You mean like his own House of Darian."

Maqdhuum nodded, "You could put it that way, I suppose. But that's just a guess. He is more militant than your headmaster, Zin Marlowe. More aggressive and physical. So who knows what his people would be like, if he actually has...people."

Adria still disagreed with Maqdhuum. "So what exactly is your plan? Eventually find him and then just try to join forces? Why could you not do that at the House of Darian? Why did you not come in peace, searching for us? You seem to be quite knowledgeable of Ashurian people. Did it somehow slip your mind that perhaps we were your best chance for help in stopping Jahmash? Or did you kill us because we're like how you *used* to be?"

Maqdhuum scoffed. "It's because I knew well enough about Marlowe to understand that most of you would be a waste of time. Marlowe never had you trained for Jahmash. By bloody Opprobrium, Marlowe never even trained you to survive Ashur. How many Descendants did you kill over the years, Garrison? Scores? Adria, why do you think none of them were already at the House of Darian? Ashur had no faith in that place, at least not while Marlowe has his grip on it. Honestly, girl, what have you learned in your time there? How to *hear* better? Jahmash would destroy you easily. As strong-willed and minded as you think you are, Jahmash would toss you aside like the core of an apple. I have seen him do it to stronger people."

Adria got lost in thought for a moment. She wondered why Jahmash hadn't mentally done that to her already. For a split second, she considered even asking Maqdhuum about what to do about Jahmash still being in her head, but she was too angry with the man to want his help.

Maqdhuum continued, "You might like to think you're special, Adria, but the Descendants are not Ashur's only hope. Neither are the Taurani. This fight that is coming is not just about numbers or manpower. You cannot just walk up to Jahmash and punch him in the face. It is a battle of minds and wills. And he has now had thousands of years to get even better at that battle. There are three steps we need to take if we want to stop him. First, find Asarei and any remaining Descendants who are willing to partake in this fight. Basically, any Descendants who are willing to die to stop Jahmash. You *could* be a formidable force, but your minds need to match your manifestations. You will need Savaiyon as well; he has the composition to lead you in this fight. Good thing I let him live. That reminds me of the next step. You need to meet with the Anonymi and the Kraisos. Jahmash's army is getting bigger and bigger. Between the three of you, perhaps with the Royal Vermillion as well, you might be able to defend Ashur when the armies come."

Adria didn't bother to wait for him to go through his steps. "That's way too much information to casually throw out. The Kraisos are just a legend. Something Markosi parents just tell their children to make them afraid of wandering off or leaving 'miterokaa and patosan.' I grew up in Markos, where everyone says that Kraiso thieves will steal you away if you leave your parents' side. Never once have I seen a Kraiso thief. You actually believe in those things?"

"Why do you think you never saw them? The blend into day just as easily as night. They move faster than most people and are masters of distraction. You never saw them because you never knew they were there." Adria shot him a disbelieving glance. "Unfortunately for you, exceptional hearing doesn't necessarily mean you are always listening. But take it from someone who has a knack for appearing unexpectedly."

"Well then why haven't you spoken to them already?"

Maqdhuum sighed. "You know, you don't have to be immortal to know that speaking your mind to everyone, *all* of the time, is not the most tactful way of communicating. Follow Garrison's example; he's just sitting there, shutting up and listening."

He finally stood up from the bed and walked a few feet away, so he could look at her and Garrison at the same time. "With the Kraisos, I never had a reason to communicate with them. It wasn't until recently that I knew exactly what Jahmash had planned and how heavy his influence was becoming. He has select people in many nations: Rhagavi, Aladar, Isamar, Kol, and Nachtoveel, to name the ones I know for sure, who are his eyes and voice. He can control these people and manipulate them. He is using them as his voice to continue to recruit more. The Koli in particular are fully behind him. They are a large nation built on weak leadership; all it took was the flimsy promise of a new place to settle and leadership by Jahmash, and they were ready to fight. If those five nations are all fully behind Jahmash, the only advantage you will have will be that you can attack from your own shores as they sail in. Even then, how many coastal cities in Ashur even have the means to attack? Your king," he turned to Garrison, "*your* father, would have to place his soldiers strategically. But that would also require knowing where the attack would come from and when. Now do you understand why I plan to leave Ashur from time to time to see what I can find out?"

Just as he finished his sentence, the door to their room opened and two maids walked in with dinner trays. The one in front spoke up, "Sorry for the intrusion, we were unsure of whether you said to come in." They set the trays on a table at the side of the room, a few feet away from Garrison. The same maid glanced back and forth between Garrison and the trays a few times. "I apologize for staring. It is simply that you remind me of Prince Garrison, except skinnier. You have the same eyes as he. My aunt is a maid at King Edmund's castle; I visited there several times when I was younger. Are you a relative of his?"

Garrison's eyes flitted back and forth between her, the other maid, Maqdhuum, and Adria. Finally he shook his head at her. "No, it is just a coincidence. Thank you for the compliment, though."

The maid continued to eye him. "Oh, it is my mistake. My apologies." She signaled the other maid to follow and left the room.

As soon as the door closed, Garrison insisted, "We have to leave. We cannot stay in Shipsbane. If that girl talks, even if she believed me, it is unwanted attention."

Adria countered, "It's not like you've left the room. We can continue to hide until we know where to go next."

"No, he's right," Maqdhuum corrected, "who knows who shows up at the door next, once this girl tells others that there's a man in here who looks like Prince Garrison. Especially in Cerysia. We need to leave here at once to regroup, and then we can decide what our next step is. It is clear that I will not get answers about Asarei's whereabouts here, anyway. Any destination requests?"

Adria eagerly answered, "The Taurani village. Or it's remains, I should say." She looked Maqdhuum directly in the eyes, "Or does that make you uncomfortable?"

Maqdhuum returned the stare and then rolled his eyes. Before he could say anything, Garrison spoke up. "The Stones of Gideon." Adria's focus was still on Maqdhuum, and his countenance changed drastically from annoyance to almost sad and pensive.

He looked down for a moment and then back at Garrison. "Why would you want to go *there*?"

Garrison finally stood up and walked to the middle of the room. "It is where I always used to go to think, clear my head, escape from everyone else. The castle is relatively close to it, but nobody else ever goes there. That is also why I frequented it; I never had to worry about other people bothering me. We could go there, agree on what to do next, and then leave as soon as we've come to a decision. It would also be nice to be in a familiar place that used to bring me comfort."

Adria was still fixated on Maqdhuum, who continued to be deep in thought. He responded again after a few moments. "My first reaction is to refuse outright, because of your ignorance. But I suppose that wouldn't teach you anything, Garrison. So we'll go. But only because there is something you need to learn about that place. Grab the food trays. We'll bring them and eat there. I can always bring them back after we're done, and I'm starving. Let's go."

Adria was intrigued about this decision. She'd never been to the Stones, but had always been curious about them. It wasn't a place that most people could just pick up and go to. At the same time, she could somewhat empathize with Maqdhuum for being hesitant. For him, they were not just stones.

Garrison held the trays in two hands, and Maqdhuum grasped her and Garrison by their shoulders. In a moment, after the rainbow of colors finished flashing before her eyes, Adria found herself surrounded by hundreds of life-sized stones, each vividly and intricately carved like a human being. It took her a moment to grasp the profundity of the situation that they were at one point, all actual people, not just sculptures.

MAQDHUUM FELT LIKE HIS neck was on a swivel. He had been here a long time ago, but purposely avoided coming back. Everywhere he looked, men stood ready to fight, solidified forever in their stone coffins. *This is the last time. I swear. If I didn't have to put this entitled Prince in his place, I wouldn't even be here now.* He put his head down and hand-signaled for the other two to follow him. They walked to a clearing, where the other army stood, facing them in similar positions, several yards away. Maqdhuum looked around at the rest of the scene. He found the stone statue that was once Gideon, his former friend and fellow Harbinger, and walked reluctantly toward the boy. He stood in front of Gideon, gently touched the top of the stone boy's head with his good hand, rubbed the side of his face, and then knelt down. Luckily, Adria and Garrison had been smart enough to give him some space, as they remained several feet away.

He spoke softly anyway, not wanting to chance that they would hear. He vividly remembered the day he'd come here centuries ago with Gideon, Lionel, Jahmash, and Darian. It was the last time they saw Gideon alive, and none of them knew that Gideon intended to sacrifice himself to stop this battle from happening. "I'm so sorry, boy. I'm so sorry that you had to make this sacrifice. I know this isn't you any longer, and that you are at peace in Omneitria for the rest of time, but it still isn't a fate you deserved." Tears trickled from the corners of his eyes. "I thought about looking for you when I made Raya take me to the Rings, but I want to wait until I've succeeded with my mission. They've gotten worse, mankind. They fight all of the time and most only care for themselves. They put shrines up for their heroes or follow idols blindly, without even knowing why they do anything. I wouldn't mind just killing all of them so that it can all be over with, but who knows. I'm destined for Opprobrium anyway, so it might not be so bad to make being there worthwhile. I'll have to spend eternity there with Jahmash anyway. Look, Gideon, I came here to see you once before and I didn't handle it in the best way. I'm sorry for punching you; it broke my right hand, if that gives you any satisfaction. Took forever to heal; I had to go to the nurses in Domna Orjann to get it properly set. I was mad at you for a while. I didn't want you to make this sacrifice. You were the youngest of us, and you didn't even tell us you were going to do it. Gideon, you didn't even give us a chance to say goodbye." He thought about looking behind him to see if Adria & Garrison were watching or listening, but he didn't care.

He continued, "I don't even remember how old I am, but I have been lonely since you all left. I watched you die. I watched Lionel die. I protected Darian long enough for him to escape, and then he sacrificed himself anyway. And Jahmash...well he was worthwhile before he went crazy. All of my best friends, like brothers to me, gone in a flash. I haven't had real friends since all of you were alive. It's a strange thing, being immortal. It's so hard to keep people around. I tried and then people grew old while I didn't. People died and I didn't. I can't do it anymore. I will stop Jahmash, Gideon. I'll stop him and it'll be over."

Maqdhuum looked over at Garrison and Adria, and waved them closer. "I can understand why you would find peace here, Garrison. To you, this place is nothing but statues. Statues that meant something long ago and perhaps represent an ideal to you. What an ignorant thing." Maqdhuum arose somewhat gingerly. The pain in his left hand still sharp and constant from where the lightning bolt had struck him. "I have seen most of this world several times over, and this has always been one of the few places I intentionally avoid." He looked at Garrison. "I was here when this happened. I watched him," Maqdhuum patted the stone figure's head, "he wanted to save all of these people. And look at them. Not a single damn soldier looks as if he was ready to listen to the boy. Even now, you people haven't learned your lessons. We're not worth saving—mankind. The Orijin screwed up in the first place by sending Harbingers. He should have let everyone kill each other. Leave this world to the animals. At least they respect it."

"Are you done?" Adria looked at him and rolled her eyes. "Look, I'm sorry that you lost your friend this way. And I know that once, a long, long time ago, you were probably a good person, just like Gideon was. But you're too sneaky and secretive for me to be able to stand in awe of the man who was once Abram."

"It's a shame I'm so bored of people. At one point, I likely would have courted you. Drahkunov will be a lucky man." He half grinned at her. After Adria's face turned red, his smirk turned to a full smile.

"Just decide who you are already. Are you the man who just cried for his friend or are you going to remain the prick that keeps lying to us? I still can't tell whether you want to help us or kill us. Sometimes you are more genuine and transparent than anyone I've ever met. Other times you are the exact opposite. So what, do you want to stop Jahmash and let Ashur be at peace, or do you want to kill us when you don't need us any longer?"

Maqdhuum turned from Gideon to face her, clenching his good hand. "I told you. My only care now is that Jahmash is stopped. I owe it to this boy," he nodded at Gideon, "and Darian, and Lionel, to stop him. To do that, I need help. Then, I can die and leave you all to yourselves. If I'm lucky, I'll die just after I've killed Jahmash. Chances are, I'll need you the whole way."

Adria slapped his burnt hand and he winced. "Horseshit. With a gift like yours, you could kill him at any point. I don't believe that he is just too well guarded to be prepared for you. Tell us the truth. Why can't you just appear in his chambers and stab him? I don't believe that his guards are sitting at his bedside while he sleeps."

Maqdhuum looked at her flatly. "He doesn't trust anyone. He prepares himself for threats. Sleeps in different places. He is too strong now to confront like that. Even if I did catch him off guard, he is an even better swordsman than I am."

Adria wouldn't relent. "That isn't good enough. You were in his presence as Maqdhuum and as Abram. You're telling me that you don't know his tendencies? His mannerisms? His little idiosyncrasies? Of all the people alive in however big this damn world is, *you* know him better than anyone. So what is it? What is it that you're not telling us Maqdhuum? Abram?"

Dammit. "You don't understand."

"So then tell us and we'll understand."

He was scrambling now; Adria had caught him off guard. "It's not that simp..."

"It's *extremely* simple, you coward. Tell us."

"I ca..."

Adria raised her voice. "Look, if you do not tell us, I will leave. And once I find the other Descendants, I will tell them all about you and your plan. Nobody will help you. We might not be able to kill you since you're such a coward, but you'll never see your wishes fulfilled. We'll stop Jahmash ourselves without your help."

He gritted his teeth. *I'll have to tell her sooner or later. She's relentless.* "Fine. The truth is that I'm afraid. Are you happy now? I'm afraid that I won't be able to stop him. The last time we fought, he nearly killed me and I disappeared to save myself." He closed his eyes for a moment, and reopened them. "Lionel and Darian died to stop him. And even Darian couldn't kill him. Darian who knew him better than anyone else and had a better reason than any of us to kill him. If I fail at this, then it was all pointless. Then everything that I've done in the past fifteen years is for naught. I can't risk just confronting him at a whim. It has to be planned. It has to be perfect. He defeated me before without even having to use his mind. Imagine how much more difficult it would be now. Jahmash will not be killed by one person going after him, even me. I will coordinate the attack against him. I will lead whoever wishes to fight him. But I cannot die at his hands. I wouldn't be able to face Gideon, Lionel, and Darian in the Three Rings if I died at Jahmash's hands. I failed them all once already. I cannot do that again." He noticed Adria slightly soften. "Understand something, girl. Just because he and I are the same age, does not mean that we are equal. I have spent the last two millennia trying to live a normal life. He has spent that time planning revenge. So while he has been taking steps to form armies, leave his island, and destroy a civilization, all I have been concerned with is not being lonely. And trying to find long term replacements for my friends."

"And this is the only plan we have, then?"

He shook his head in annoyance, "For the love of the Old World, girl, I am *one* person. I have designed a plan that *I* think will work. When we get together with, once again, Asarei, your Descendant friends, the Kraisos, the Anonymi, *and* the King's army, *then* I can share everything I know about Jahmash and we can collectively decide what the best plan is. Or do you have something better to offer in that overstuffed head of yours?"

She stared at him sideways. "What if they all reject you? Just because you *used* to be Abram, doesn't forgive everything you've done since. You and Garrison are two fish in a barrel. You both think that just because you're trying to do something good, the whole world needs to forgive you and forget all of the evil you committed before. But what if we meet with all of these people you're suggesting, and they refuse to work with you or they want to kill you?"

"I've considered it. If they won't help me, then we reassess the situation and make a new plan. If they are intent on killing me, I will offer to let them do so once Jahmash has been killed. The Anonymi and the Kraisos both know that Ashur comes before everything else. I guarantee you that if anyone has a problem with me, it is your Descendant friends."

Adria countered, "How many Anonymi and Kraisos have you killed?"

He nodded, "None. They're much smarter than you and your headmaster."

Garrison walked over and sat facing him. "You said you have spent all this time trying not to be lonely. What does that mean? Did you ever try to start a family? Find love?"

Maqdhuum chuckled, "In my lifetime, I've likely had more wives than Darian did. I've had children with many of them, which I guess means that I have my own set of descendants running around in the world. I've been with women, men, old, young, beautiful, ugly, fat, skinny, smart, dumb. You name it."

Garrison looked at him more intently. "You were with all kinds of people just so you would not be lonely? Men as well? Just to pass the time, essentially?"

He rolled his eyes, "You ever live for thousands of years?"

"No."

"You ever been with a man?"

"No."

"You ever sit at the side of the bed while your pregnant wife sleeps, trying to figure out how to tell her that eventually, she'll be old and broken down, as will your child, but that will never happen to you?"

Garrison looked down at the grass. "No."

"Right. Then don't judge me. Some of the men I've been with have been the most beautiful souls I've ever met. Some of the women I've been with have been monsters more savage than what you see in Sundari. Some of the animals I've kept as pets have been smarter than people I've known. You live long enough you get curious about what you haven't tried. The more of life you experience and try, the more you appreciate it. I didn't mean that I literally spent every single day of my existence trying not to be lonely. You princes are mostly cut from the same cloth, huh? Self-righteous. Condescending. Magnanimous. Sheltered more than everyone else. I'll have to help you experience the world, Garrison. Maybe find a nice man for you." Garrison coughed at that. "Who knows, you might like it. Anyway, we're wasting time. The whole reason we're here is so we can decide on where to go next. Is there a place where other Descendants might go to be safe?"

"City of the Fallen," Adria stated firmly. "Any Descendant who's stayed at the House of Darian knows that that is asylum for us. In most cities, we have an inn or two where we can hide. In the City of the Fallen, we can walk the streets without fear. It makes the most sense. Lincan would definitely head there first. I'm pretty sure that Badalao and Desmond would as well. They love the inns there."

Maqdhuum grimaced, "Orijin's mercy, I hate that place. Those statues are hideous. Tell me there is another option."

Annoyance laced Adria's tone, "You asked for a suggestion. I gave you the best possible one. The Descendants I know, if they're still alive, would head there. Not only is it safe; it is the closest point to the House of Darian. That's where they would go if they survived."

Garrison looked at Maqdhuum. "What about the Tower of the Blind?"

Adria responded to him with annoyance, "What about it?"

Garrison elaborated, "I stayed there briefly on my way to the House of Darian. They welcomed me in, and my three Taurani companions. Maqdhuum was just saying that we need to find a place where we can be safe, that is welcoming to Descendants. And he also said we need to talk to people who have Ashur's best interest in mind. That is the Tower. They potentially have information on everything we need. They may even know where to find Asarei. And how to find the Kraisos."

Maqdhuum noticed Adria attempt to speak up, but he'd had enough of her arguing. "That is exactly what we need. A neutral location with people who care about Ashur, not allegiances. That's where we're going. Trust me, I don't necessarily like the idea of going there, but it makes the most sense for us. I need to find this Baltaszar person as well. Jahmash's search party thought that he might be in the Never somewhere, but they couldn't find him. And I don't feel like searching that whole forest for him. I need to get to him before Jahmash does. Now that the House of Darian's been destroyed, if he's still alive, the Tower is probably the best resource for tracking him down."

Adria attempted again to protest, "But…"

"But nothing. Garrison is right. The Tower is neutral *and* well protected. And none of the idiots we're trying to avoid would be interested in going there. Let's go."

Garrison stared back at the food trays, "Can we eat first? We never got to enjoy our dinner and I'm starving."

Maqdhuum stated flatly, "You're always starving."

"I was locked in a dungeon cell for several months with next to nothing to eat. You would be, too. Besides, I have a lot of weight to gain if I want to get back to where I was. I do not like being this skinny."

"Fine. Eat. You too, girl. You need the nourishment just as much as he does." Garrison rose to fetch the trays and brought them over. He'd barely given Maqdhuum and Adria theirs before devouring his own food. Adria inched closer to Maqdhuum and looked at him sheepishly. Maqdhuum sighed and asked, "What?"

Adria hesitated before speaking. "This isn't the best time to ask this, but it's been on my mind for a long time and I get the feeling that if I don't ask now, I may not get the opportunity to ask for a while. I was wondering—Darian had twelve wives. How did that work? Did he love them all? Did they all love him? Did he treat them all well? I guess I can't fathom how a woman would accept being married to a man that she had to share, especially with so many other women."

Maqdhuum stopped eating for a moment and considered what she'd said. He hadn't expected her to ask about that. He also hadn't thought about Darian's wives in centuries. The memories saddened him especially, because Jahmash had had his own disciples murder almost all of Darian's wives and some of the man's children. He looked back at Adria, who waited patiently for an answer. "Well, first I suppose I should clarify that he had more than twelve wives. I don't remember the exact number, but it was well over twelve. It was twelve that were murdered by Jahmash. The thing is, Harbinger aside, Darian was larger than life. He was the type of man that everyone wanted to be around and be associated with. I don't know if he was like that because the Orijin chose him, or if it was the other way around, but you *wanted* to be around him.

You wanted to be like him and you wanted attention from him. I have met some charismatic people in my existence, but never anyone who came close to his magnetism.

"That's what attracted women to him. I think his wives were willing to have even a fraction of him in their lives. He really made you feel that important and special. So to answer all of your questions, he spent his time with all of them. I suppose if the stories have been passed down faithfully, you know that he was asked to be king. Before the flooding, our continent was called Iman Qaja." He hadn't thought about it until now, but Maqdhuum realized that he felt happy to be able to explain the old day. "For ages, we were ruled by a council of elders from each nation of the realm. After Gideon sacrificed himself, the wars and conflicts tempered. Our jobs as Harbingers were essentially fulfilled. The council wanted Darian to rule all of Iman Qaja. Obviously he declined, but it wasn't just because he didn't see himself fit for that role. He wanted to be able to spend time with his wives. All of his free time was spent doting on his wives and children. He had so much love to share.

"To be honest, I have had trouble trying to keep one wife happy, I don't know how he managed. As much as people loved him, he loved everyone back just as much. And all of his wives were good, reputable women. It's not like Darian fooled any of them into something they didn't agree to. They all knew who he was. They all knew he had other wives. They were willing to live that way. They were willing to share him. I met *all* of them. None of them came across as wanting to be with him just because he was a Harbinger. And to be perfectly clear, Darian never used that to his advantage, anyway. Myself, I may have had knowledge of a few women here and there solely because of who I was, but Darian was never interested in that type of thing. He was a good man. The best man. It was such a privilege to have known him and to have been his friend. It was definitely easier to be a good man while he was alive. I cared about what he thought of me. I didn't want to disappoint him."

Maqdhuum had become lost in his reminiscences and realized that tears streaked down his face. He didn't bother to wipe them away. It was too late to worry about showing vulnerability in front of them. Neither Adria nor Garrison said anything in response. He supposed they saw his tears and didn't want to continue on about the topic.

Adria muttered a "thanks" with a guilty looking half-smile, and then concentrated on her food. Garrison focused solely on his dinner as well. Adria looked up at him for a moment as if pondering something, then looked back down at her food.

"What?"

"Nothing. Never mind."

"I just shared a wealth of information with you that you could not find out from anyone else in this world. At least have the respect to reciprocate the transparency after all of my openness and honesty."

Adria sighed, "Fine. I was simply going to say that, all of those things that you said about Darian, every now and then I see glimpses of it in you as well. It doesn't mean that I forgive you for your wrongdoings, but I cannot fathom being alive for as long as you have, especially after bearing the burden of being a Harbinger. You were obviously chosen by the Orijin for a reason, and sometimes I see why that is."

Maqdhuum nearly blushed for the first time in what felt like centuries. "That is likely the nicest thing you'll ever say to me, so I'll take it as a compliment. I'm glad I didn't kill you."

CHAPTER 4
DELIVERANCE

*From **The Book of Orijin**,* **Verse Forty**
The only Judgment that matters is that which comes from Us.
We judge all of our creations across all worlds.
Judgment has been bestowed upon humankind as a test of character and intention.
Those who would pass judgment upon others have been blinded to their own flaws.

BO'AZ SAT WITH HIS ELBOW ON TOP of the long table, and a hand holding up his head. It wasn't that he was bored; he was exhausted. He was always exhausted. It came with the constant presence of Jahmash in his mind. Ironically enough, Jahmash was always grasping his mind to search for ways to lure Baltaszar, rather than actually controlling Bo'az or making him do anything. As a result, Bo'az was always on edge, always paranoid about his own thoughts, and always worried that Jahmash might find something he didn't like in Bo'az's memories. It didn't help that Jahmash had access to all of his private thoughts, moments, and secrets.

He realized too late that the talking had stopped, and looked directly at Jahmash, who sat at the head of the table with his fingers intertwined in front of him. Jahmash simply stared at him, as did Aric, Deacon, and Hansi. "I apologize, my lord. I am just tired and lost my focus." He looked down at the table. "It will not happen again."

"Good. See that it doesn't." Jahmash's tone had been matter of fact. The Harbinger continued, "As I was saying, Farrah is lost. Something happened to her when she encountered that Descendant, Badalao. He was in her mind at the same time as I. Somehow he managed to force my presence out and even sever my connection to her completely. This is disturbing. I did not realize that you Descendants could be this powerful." He glanced at Aric and Deacon.

Bo'az knew that neither of them would say a word in response to that. Deacon tended to look as stressed as Bo'az felt. Aric, however, always maintained a calm presence. Bo'az couldn't even be sure whether Jahmash used him the same way or perhaps left Aric alone. If Jahmash *was* controlling Aric in the same way, Bo'az marveled at how Aric could look so serene all the time. He asked a question to show he was paying attention, "My lord, what shall we do without Farrah, then? Does the mission continue?"

"It must continue. All four of you will lead an envoy to recruit other nations. There are already five nations in my army. Semaajj will not be swayed. Domna Orjann will be difficult to convince, if not impossible. And my scouts tell me that Vitheligia has already departed to lay siege to Ashur for different reasons. You will sail to Castiel, Yahaira, and Brogan. Imagine if even two of those three join our ranks? That would be seven armies under my control, *after* the Vithelegion have already launched their own attack to reduce Ashur's numbers. I do not need any of you to be violent or aggressive. You will speak to them and show them what you are capable of. I will inform you of what to say to them. Castiel may offer its support willingly, once you give Linas Nasreddine back to them. If that is not enough, Deacon, Aric, Hansi, you will show them that I have the support of some of Darian's own Descendants. You will ask each of them for half of their army. If they offer to send more when called upon, all the better. Every nation will have one year from when you arrive to prepare. I will send word to them about when to set sail for their attack and where they will set their course. In return, each nation will be able to claim a portion of Ashur as part of their empire. They may choose what they want to do with their new domain. You will stay in each nation for a week to give them time to decide. While you await a decision, enjoy yourselves. I will provide you with enough coin to ensure that you make the most of your stay. Once you return, I will reward each of you handsomely. Provided you do what I ask."

Bo'az took in Jahmash's descriptive orders. It was becoming too realistic too quickly. He hesitated before asking his question. "My lord, you had said that you want to use me as bait to lure my brother. What...what if something happens to me on this voyage? How would you be able to do that?"

Jahmash smiled widely at Bo'az. Enough to make him uncomfortable. "Oh, Bo'az. Ever the coward. You have nothing to fear. I will be paying extremely close attention to you. You are traveling with these three gentlemen here, all of whom are braver and stronger than you are. They will ensure that you return to me unharmed. There is a reason I am sending you off to gather my army, but I would be a fool to tell you everything."

The smile left Jahmash's face. "And when you return, I will send you back to Ashur for a while. There, with my guidance, we will track down your brother and confront him. He will accompany you back here, or watch you die in front of him. Once we find him, if you make any attempt to defy me, I will torture you. I'm sure if I torture you enough, it'll anger him to the point of wanting to come here to kill me anyway. Is that clear, Bo'az?"

"Perfectly clear, my lord."

"Good. While you set off on your journey, I will track down where Badalao's family lives, then send a battalion to decimate them. They will destroy the city, especially his whole family, along with a message for him to come to me. In time, I may have Badalao *and* your brother at my disposal."

"Not to question your knowledge, my lord, but are you certain that my brother is still alive?"

"It's fine, Bo'az. I understand your concern. I know for sure that Baltaszar was banished from the House of Darian before it was attacked. Therefore, unless some other threat killed him, he is alive and well, and far away from the House of Darian."

Bo'az took a deep breath. Since arriving on Jahmash's island and being separated from Slade and Linas, Bo'az had resigned himself to the fact that he had no chance of escaping or of being saved. After accepting his fate, Bo'az mostly thought of Yasaman and Baltaszar. He often wondered what Baltaszar was doing and where he was. He deeply regretted not going with his brother, but it was so difficult to give in to Baltaszar sometimes. Baltaszar was adventurous and candid and spontaneous. Baltaszar went through with things even when he was afraid. Bo'az had known ever since their fight in the Never that if he'd gone with Baltaszar, he would have just held his brother back. He would have been afraid to do something that Baltaszar was willing to do, or he would have been scared to do something that Baltaszar was excited about. It wasn't that Baltaszar would have made fun of him or judged him for any of it, but he would feel bad for holding Baltaszar back. Bo'az knew that without him, things would work out fine for Baltaszar. But with him around, Baltaszar would have to make sacrifices and difficult decisions, just because of him. Bo'az didn't want to be the reason his brother could not move forward in whatever direction he wanted.

If he *had* gone with Baltaszar, at least he wouldn't be in this position. He would rather have been a coward in his brother's company than a henchman to a prophet of the Orijin, bent on killing thousands of people.

The ironic thing about Bo'az's journey was that, while he'd never forgive himself for allowing Yas to be killed, he didn't completely regret his decision to go off on his own. When he said it to himself or thought about it, it seemed incredibly wrong. He wanted to regret the whole thing, but part of him wanted to do what Jahmash asked of him, even though deep down he knew that helping Jahmash was wrong. He knew and didn't know at the same time, that many of his current wants and desires were Jahmash's, and not his own. But a lot of Jahmash's plan was just words to him. Even the concept of Ashur was simply an idea.

Bo'az had never seen any of it. In fact, he'd spent more time on Jahmash's island than in any part of Ashur outside of Haedon. He didn't even know what Ashurian people looked like beyond Haedon. His only references were Aric and Deacon. And Aric was an insufferable bore, so half of the Ashurian people that Bo'az knew weren't worth his time.

He constantly found himself dwelling on the night he'd slept with Yasaman. It had been the first and only time he'd had knowledge of a woman, and sometimes he thought it might be the last. Thinking about that, and especially that it was with a girl he'd fancied for some time, made the memory worth reliving constantly. She'd gotten angry when he told her he loved her, but they weren't empty words to him. He thought about her every day, and sometimes his emotions got the best of him.

Jahmash continued, "You are all dismissed. Your ship will depart for Castiel in a few days. Until that time, I have relieved each of you of your duties and will refrain from entering your minds. Unless you give me any reason otherwise. I would like for you to look forward to this mission and to have clear, relaxed minds for it. Even your captivity time will be reduced over the next three days. I want each of you to get used to the feeling of freedom so that you are not awkward about it when you travel. You will be mostly free to do as you wish, but remember that you are carrying out my mission. Do you understand me?"

All four of them nodded quickly in agreement and rose from their chairs. As the other three departed the room, giving thanks to Jahmash, Bo'az hung back. "My lord…"

"Sit back down." Bo'az looked at him quizzically. "Bo'az, I do not need to read your mind to understand your concern. No, I do not plan to kill you once I no longer need you. You have been with me for about a year now. How many times have you seen me kill anyone without a reason?"

Bo'az hesitated for a second before speaking. He knew he was foolish for even attempting to gain sympathy from Jahmash, but if there was one thing Jahmash might empathize about, it would be brotherhood. "My lord, my concern was more about my own life than about my perception of you. It's just, my brother is all that I have now, and I wonder everyday whether I will get to spend an enjoyable moment with him again. Before we parted, we'd both been on edge for several weeks because of our father's sentencing. I don't even remember the last time we shared a laugh or got to share a moment in which we could both just be off our guard. I just…"

Jahmash cut him off, "The whole of Ashur either hates me or fears me, and has for millennia. Some of the reasons for that, I readily own. And I gladly hate them back for it. But what makes me hate Ashur even more is that the entirety of it believes that I murdered Darian. We were not blood brothers like you and Baltaszar, but we might as well have been. Before I was chosen to be a Harbinger, before I met Darian, I had an older brother that I idolize. I copied him in everything. I think most older brothers would have grown tired of that quite quickly, but not mine. He embraced it and became an even better role model because of it. Everything I did out of duty for the Orijin, I did also for my brother. I like to think that, if not for him, the Orijin likely would not have chosen me.

Jahmash continued, staring down at the table and rubbing his stubbly jaw, "I held Darian in that same esteem for a long time. Even after he crossed me and tried to steal my wife away from me, I don't know if I had it in me to kill him. The whole world thinks that I murdered him for trapping me here. They are all wrong. He sacrificed himself to trap me here. He collapsed in front of me on that same shore where you arrived. And as I walked over to his body, I fought with myself about whether I would kill him or not. By the time I got to him, I part of me wanted to kill him while part of me refused to go through with it. It didn't matter. He was already dead. For a long time, all I would dwell on was the good times we'd had before our relationship rotted. Despite his betrayal and deceit, I could only think of all the good times."

Bo'az wondered whether the ploy was working. Jahmash continued on about the concept of brothers, but Bo'az had no idea where the man was going with his point.

"I need you for something, Bo'az. I need Baltaszar for something. Once my plan has been carried out, if I can trust both of you not to defy me or attack me, you will both remain alive as gratitude for your loyalty. I respect brotherhood and loyalty. I am sure you and Baltaszar are very close. Brothers share an incredible bond. I am sure twin brothers share an even stronger one. Always there for each other. Always sharing that connection. That's how it should be. Brothers should always look out for each other. I considered Darian a brother and he tried to steal my wife from me. That is not brotherhood."

Bo'az looked over at Jahmash. He could hardly believe he was in the midst of a genuine conversation with the man. "Can...can I ask you something?"

Jahmash nodded, "Be my guest."

Bo'az appreciated that Jahmash hadn't already assumed what the question would be this time. "All of this. For the past...you said thousands of years. This is all because he tried to steal your wife?" Bo'az reigned himself in for a moment. "I understand that any man would be angry about that. But why would you still need revenge for that now? My brother and I are apparently descendants of Darian and we have never done anything to defy you. There are apparently thousands more throughout Ashur who could say the same thing. Why make all these people suffer for something one man did so long ago?"

Jahmash looked back at Bo'az and pressed his fingertips together. "You were never taught about the Harbingers before coming here. What of the Three Rings? Do you know of them?"

Bo'az nodded.

"Darian could have just fought me and killed me. He was a superior swordsman. Instead, he made me chase him from Ashur all the way here. You sailed here. Do you have any idea how far that is on horse? He fled all the way here so he could trap me on this island, knowing full well that I am terrified of the ocean. And he killed himself in the process. What satisfaction was I allowed? He led me here for days, chasing him, letting me think that I might eventually catch him and fight him. And when we finally came face to face, I never even got to raise my sword. Again, to this day I don't know whether I would have even swung it at Darian, but he never gave me that opportunity to get justice."

"But..." Bo'az blurted out the word before he could stop himself.

"Yes?" Jahmash raised his eyebrows at Bo'az.

Bo'az sighed, "Please don't kill me. Or make me pull out my eyes. Or tongue."

"You are asking because you want to know. Not because you are challenging me or being incompetent. I know the difference."

"You killed his wives and children before he did any of that. Why wasn't that enough?"

Jahmash stared down for a few moments before answering. "I expected him to kill me for that. I wanted him to kill me for that. When we were Harbingers, doing the Orijin's work, we killed scores of bad people. People who'd committed all kinds of horrible sins. They were brought to justice by us, the Hands of Orijin, himself. The Orijin knew this was what was needed, which was why we were chosen in the first place. Why was no one willing to kill me for what I'd done? I murdered helpless women and children out of anger, but in the name of justice and revenge. If I'd truly done something wrong, the Orijin would have stopped me then. But He didn't. He had his greatest Harbinger trap me on this island for millennia. Meanwhile, Darian's soul rests peacefully in Omneitria. So now I have the means to exact more revenge. Let Darian's restful soul and Orijin himself look down at me. Let them feel more agony and suffering for leaving me down here when they could have stopped it so long ago."

Bo'az realized his teeth had been clenched. He stroked his jaw and dared to respond. "But what if nobody stops you this time? If this all to get their attention and have the Orijin do something to stop you, what if you are victorious?"

Jahmash smiled. "I don't think I was being clear. I *want* Darian to suffer first and foremost. Especially in that damned ring of paradise. I will start with his descendants, which means I will wipe out Ashur. If that is not enough, I will destroy the whole world and all of Orijin's creation until there is nothing left living. If the Orijin would rather not stop me, I will just keep going. Bo'az, everyone in this world believes in a sense of right and wrong, even the most misguided man. If the Orijin's final stand against me is a handful of boys and girls whose powers pale in comparison to my own, then Ashur is truly in trouble."

Bo'az looked down and pursed his lips. "But..."

"But nothing. The Orijin places men and women in this world to do his bidding, and only *hopes* that it will work. These Descendants of Darian, who bear the Mark, are the Orijin's third attempt to fix his own mistakes. It is time for the Orijin to stop hiding behind fragile creatures of flesh and bone. So I will start with Ashur. I will kill every last Ashurian who opposes me until the Orijin himself faces me and stops me. Sooner or later, people will see that their faith in their god is misguided. Do you not approve of my intentions, Master Bo'az?"

Bo'az looked up, aware of the tear forming in the corner of his eye. He fought it back before speaking. "I was just putting myself in your position. From what I understand, you can choose when to die. I would just try to find a nice woman to fall in love with, marry, and have children. And then, once it's my wife's time to go, I would wait until she passes and then tell the Orijin I'm ready. All you wanted in the first place was a woman to be with and to love."

Jahmash raised a finger, "No. I wanted *my* woman. *My* wife. For the entire time I have been alive, I have had no desire to find another woman or love another woman. Come let us take a walk." He arose and gestured for Bo'az to follow him out of the room. As soon as they entered the corridor, Jahmash's personal guard surrounded them and matched pace.

"I apologize for being so forward, my lord."

"Bo'az, you have been here for over a year. In that time, you have done nothing to defy me. I have been inside your mind so many times. Enough times to know that you do what is safe. What will keep you safe. Trust me, you have done right by me and you have been loyal. If anything, I like that you are becoming confident enough to talk to me and ask me questions. But really, there is something you should see. I, myself, have not been down to that chamber in some time. It would be good to reminisce a little. Especially in light of recent events involving our friend, Maqdhuum."

Bo'az matched Jahmash's stride as they walked down a long corridor. He enjoyed the freedom; it was not too often that he got to walk freely, much less with Jahmash. "What do you mean?"

Jahmash continued looking straight ahead as they turned down another corridor. "Several years ago, this Maqdhuum fellow arrived on my shores, claiming to have a gift for me. The gift turned out to be a female Descendant, a young woman. Beautiful, feisty, with golden hair and fair skin. Young enough to be quite fertile. He'd stolen her away from her husband as a present for me to prove his loyalty to my cause. He wanted to follow me and brought her to show his good faith." They walked down a flight of stairs and then made another turn. "How does that sound as a present?"

Bo'az shrugged, "Not that great, to be honest, if she was being forced to be with you. Again, no offense, my lord."

Jahmash chuckled, "None taken. But I agree. I would never want a woman brought to me against her will. That is not exciting or fun or fulfilling. However, you know what the real prize was? Her manifestation was incredible. She could harness her mind and soul to leave her body and travel to the Three Rings. Imagine what a great gift that would be for someone like me. If I could control her mind, I could travel to Darian and the Orijin myself and confront them."

"Did you go? It doesn't seem like you did."

"That's the funny thing about it. I kept her in a cell. Fed her well and didn't bother her at all. Still, she cried a lot. Turns out she had very young children that she'd been taken from. At least, that's all I could decipher from the hysterical crying. Usually the only times she spoke were when she was crying." They arrived at a wooden door with a window cut out at eye level and vertical bars spanning the opening. "Originally, I thought that I could have her take me to the Rings and then I would be done with her. Either I would send her back or kill her, depending on how she'd acted. But when I finally came here to go through with it, I realized I didn't really want to. I have nothing to say to Darian. I don't even want to see him. I would rather leave it all in my head and perceive all this the way I want. If I had gone to the Rings and found him, chances are I would be disappointed about his outlook or perception of it all. At least this way, I can still hold onto what he did to me."

Bo'az didn't bother to utter how stubborn and petty that sounded. "My lord, I don't understand the point of all this then. Why mention this story and bring me here? We were talking about your wife before."

They still stood at the door to the cell. "After I changed my mind about going to the Rings, I thought about something else. If I could have a child with a Descendant, there might be a chance to infiltrate the Descendants in Ashur, perhaps even the House of Darian. It would take a long time for everything to unfold, but obviously I have time, if nothing else."

Bo'az's eyes shot up, "You had a child with the woman? She agreed to this?"

"Not exactly. And that is why we took this walk. I treated her quite well for a time. Tried to court her, hell, I was even romantic at times. I really thought I could force it to work. Like I said before, I've never desired another woman besides my wife. But I thought perhaps I could pretend or fake it, so that at least she might like me. At least that would be better than raping her and forcing her to carry a child."

Bo'az could not see into the cell, but he was nervous about what he might see if he looked in, considering everything Jahmash had told him. *Is this woman still in there? Is the child in there? What is he getting at?* "I'm going to assume she was not thrilled to procreate with you?"

Jahmash stared into the cell. "Never really asked her opinion. I entered her mind and persuaded her that she wanted to. As a matter of fact, I did that through the whole pregnancy to make sure she didn't have any moments of regret or bitterness or anything negative. For the whole pregnancy, she was happy to be with child and she ate well and lived a life of leisure. Even after the baby was born, she would smile and laugh and you would think she was happy to be here. But after a certain point, I was through with the facade. After the baby was old enough to not need her, I had it sent to Ashur."

Bo'az was disturbed at the thought. "Why? You had a child with this woman just to send it away?"

Jahmash kept staring into the cell. "That's the only way things would work. I didn't even name him. She might have, I'm not sure. But I ordered him sent to somewhere poor, so that he would face hardship growing up. It was the best way to ensure a manifestation. But we bonded before I sent him across the sea. I have been connected to his mind ever since."

Sadness filled Bo'az. "That seems so sad. You said you never named him. Obviously you monitored him from afar throughout his life. What is his name now?"

"Ah, Bo'az. I trust you, but not that much. My son's identity is a secret. For his safety and for my plan to remain failsafe."

"Understood. But what of the woman? What was her name? What became of her?"

Jahmash nodded towards the inside of the cell. "She's still in there. Right after I sent my son away, it didn't make sense to control her mind anymore, so I released my control of her. All of her memories must have come flooding in and I guess were too much for her. She slit her own throat that same day I released her mind. I'd been allowing her a knife with dinner every day. Never really had a reason to be concerned. To be honest, I didn't see that coming. I thought she'd just be upset again for a while. I don't like saying her name. It sounds too similar to my own wife's name. And I don't like saying my wife's name anymore, either."

Bo'az looked through the bars as Jahmash continued. On the floor by the left wall of the cell was a human skeleton covered here and there by what was once likely the woman's clothing. As soon as he realized what he was looking at, Bo'az turned from the door and vomited on the floor. Jahmash and his personal guard skittered out of the way. Bo'az took a few deep breaths with his hands on his knees, then straightened himself. "Why would you leave her there like that?"

Jahmash replied in a matter of fact tone, "She made her decision. Do you think she really expected us to bury her or honor her death? When the soul is gone, the body doesn't matter. Let it lie there as a reminder."

"A reminder of what, my lord?"

"That this physical world is meaningless. That good and evil are meaningless. That no matter what we do in this world, we will all leave it sooner or later. Even me. The Three Rings await everyone. We are all just dolls and playthings for the Orijin, a fickle god that cares nothing about justice. You want to know what really bothers me? I have killed and killed and killed. I have manipulated and destroyed. And yet, I shall end up in the same place as men and women whose sins pale in comparison. Darian drowned the world, killing innocents in the process. He tried to steal my wife from me. And yet, in the Three Rings, he is rewarded for his deeds. The more chaos I bring upon this world, the more people will realize that the Orijin cares nothing for them. The more people I kill, the more mankind will realize there is no justice. There is no balance. Their god has no plan for them. He sits back and lets them die by evils that he has allowed to happen. Sooner or later, they will give up on the Orijin and lose their faith. And when that happens, I will be satisfied. I will kill humanity until I break its faith in the Orijin. I will continue to kill until it happens, even if I have to kill every last person. Then I will allow myself to die and happily spend eternity in Opprobrium." He turned to walk away with his guard. "Now clean up this mess you made."

YASAMAN SHIFTED GINGERLY at the table. Her mother made her more uncomfortable than her giant belly, but seeing as how her mother was the only one who could help her, Yasaman had to just bear it. Not only had she gotten pregnant from the brother of the man whose heart she'd broken, but her father had been killed in the process of trying to stop her from running away with a group of strangers. The fact that her mother even allowed her to stay in the house was a miracle in itself. She remained silent through breakfast. Her mother had stopped the lecturing as of late. Yasaman assumed her mother was doing so more for the baby's health than trying to be nice.

"Will you be sitting there all day?"

Here we go. Her mother's tone was not rude, but definitely passive aggressive. "No mother. My feet are hurting more than usual today. I will arise from here in a moment so that I can be more productive."

"See that you are, " her mother stated flatly as she walked away.

Yasaman knew that it was likely a matter of days before the baby arrived. She'd told her mother that Baltaszar was the father. Perhaps luckily, her mother was too revolted by the notion of her having a baby with Baltaszar that she didn't probe into any of the hows or whys of it. Her mother still blamed her for her father's death. No one who'd been involved in chasing them out of Haedon that night had gotten a good enough look at Bo'az to be able to discern him from Baltaszar. It was an easy lie to tell everyone she was with Baltaszar. It made more sense anyway, and it helped reinforce her lie that Tasz was the father.

Yasaman put each of her feet up on other chairs. More so than having a somewhat normal body again, she couldn't wait to give birth just so the pain in her feet and back would be more tolerable. She still couldn't be sure whether her mother would actually help her with the baby. Yasaman had gotten no indication either way in terms of an answer to that. She told herself no, just to avoid being disappointed. Despite no confirmation from her mother, she'd never told Yasaman that she had to move from the house at any point, either.

It was difficult to be completely mad at her mother. She understood the amount of stress and hardship she'd placed on the woman. If she'd never tried to run away, her father would still be alive. Yasaman thought about that every day. As difficult as her father had been, she loved him dearly. Every now and then, she missed him even more because of how strained things were with her mother. Her parents had regularly bickered and argued, which allowed her some reprieve from the pestering and negativity. Yasaman felt horrible even entertaining that thought, but it managed to push its way into her mind every few days or so. Even beyond her father's death, Yasaman tried to empathize with the range of emotions her mother must have felt in the aftermath of it. First, the woman's daughter ran away in the middle of the night, with no explanation or warning, and then returned several months later with a battered and broken body, needing so much attention that she'd hired a maid to help. Her mother had been somewhat tolerable at that point, aside from telling Yasaman every now and then that she got what she deserved. It was physically and mentally impossible for Yasaman to argue with that, anyway.

And then if that wasn't enough, Yasaman told her shortly after that she was pregnant with the child of Baltaszar Kontez, whom her mother despised. The more Yasaman thought about it, the more she realized it would have been easier on her mother if she'd never returned to Haedon at all. Sometimes, she dared to think she, herself, would have been better off if she'd died when Gibreel had pushed her off the side of the mountain. She still couldn't explain how she'd survived and yet, Gibreel died.

Yasaman grimaced and gritted her teeth. Her whole abdomen tightened and cramped for a few moments, and then released. *What was that! Is the baby coming now? No, wait. Stay calm. Diya said this would happen. It's only a contraction. She said it's only when they are very close together that the baby is ready.* She forced herself to rise from the table and hobbled toward her bedroom. She hadn't gained a significant amount of weight during her pregnancy, but while her body was mostly still the same, her belly was huge. Yasaman couldn't wait for the day when her back stopped aching. She rubbed her belly. *As soon as your hands are big enough, you will be giving me back rubs every day.* She gently picked up the blanket she'd started knitting and then sat on her bed. At least she could be productive and still have some privacy. It was too cold these days for her mother to be outside, but her mother surely wouldn't occupy the same room.

She knitted for nearly an hour, feeling a couple more contractions during that time. After nearly another hour, and another few contractions, Yasaman heard a knock on the front door. The maid, Diya, stomped over and Yasaman heard the normally abrupt woman welcome the visitor in her sweetest voice. "Come in, come in, Chancellor! To what do we owe this honor?" Yasaman naturally assumed Oran Von had paid them a visit, but she could not hear the old man's response, only Diya's reaction to what he'd said, and her voice had lost its cheeriness. "Oh. She is in her bedroom, right over there. Shall I summon her to come out?"

Yasaman heard the knock of Von's cane nearing, though the heavy knock on her door was clearly from Diya. Just then, another contraction tightened in her belly. She cringed, but managed to compose herself as Von mumbled to the maid from outside the door, "If it's all right, I need to speak privately with her."

Her ears perked up at that. *What private business would he have with me?* Just as she'd completed the thought, Diya knocked again at her bedroom door. "Come in." she tried to sound innocent and welcoming.

Von opened the door and peered in with a smile, then hobbled closer to her. He shut the door behind him and Yasaman's expression must have given her away. "Oh child, do not worry. I am not here because you've done anything wrong." He sat in a soft chair next to the bed, and once again Yasaman's expression revealed too much as she glanced at the door. "Neither of them sent for me. I came here of my own accord."

Yasaman took a deep breath and let her guard down. She placed the nearly completed blanket softly down on the bed. "Then how can I help you, Chancellor?"

Von slightly raised his hand and waved it at her. "Actually, I have some questions. And depending on how those go, then I may also have some advice."

Yasaman shifted slightly. She was never comfortable anymore. And appropriately, another contraction caused her to clench her jaw. She composed herself, hoping that the Chancellor hadn't noticed. "You can ask. I'm not sure what this is about, though."

Von nodded. "Very well. Forgive me for being straight to the point. It is not my way to dawdle with my words. But, unfortunately people do what people do, and there has been much talk in Haedon about the father of your child. There are rumors that Baltaszar Kontez is the father. Is this true?" The deepness of Von's voice did nothing to put her at ease, despite that his tone was harmless.

Yasaman paused for a split second, "Yes, of course Baltaszar is the father. Who else would it be?"

Von nodded again. "I meant no offense. I was simply trying to put it together myself and perhaps I'm just too old to be trusted with numbers now, but it seemed unlikely to me that Baltaszar would be the father. The last time he was in Haedon, he didn't seem like he knew anything about that."

Yasaman frowned, "He came to me that same night and that is when he found out. I thought I had already told this to your guards. He left in a fit of anger, using some sort of magic to summon fire from the sky. You saw; we all saw what came of his anger. Why do you think that happened? He was angry that I had been suffering the whole time and he wasn't around to help me. He was even angrier that he couldn't stay here after everything that happened with his father." Her stomach clenched again, but this time it lasted a little longer than before. She stifled a groan and took a deep breath.

Von furrowed his brow, as if in thought, and then spoke after a moment. "Very well. If Baltaszar is indeed the father, then there are some things that I must share with you." He lowered his voice and pulled his chair closer to her. Von looked at the door, then again at her. "You must be careful with your child. Who knows whether Baltaszar will be around to be a present father. Regardless, Baltaszar is capable of miraculous things. Things that I must explain to you now." Yasaman was even more confused now, but Von continued before she could ask anything. Another contraction stifled her ability to speak up, anyway. "You see, Baltaszar is what the world calls a 'Descendant.' Meaning, he descends from one of five messengers, or Harbingers, of the Orijin, which is why he has that black line on his face. Beyond Haedon lies the rest of Ashur, and several other nations. We stay hidden here because almost all of Haedon's residents are originally from far away nations and do not fit in properly with Ashur's culture or society.

"Throughout Ashur, there are many of these Descendants, each with a special gift from the Orijin himself, called a manifestation. There is a threat coming to all of Ashur, and these Descendants, Baltaszar included, are our best protection against that threat. As you have seen, Baltaszar can manipulate fire. That is his manifestation. It was never his father who was responsible for the fires here, but Joakwin wanted desperately to protect his son. Joakwin came to me asking to take the fall so that Baltaszar and Bo'az could be protected, and could have enough time to escape Haedon. Because of Baltaszar's gift, he is crucial to the survival of mankind in Ashur. I wanted you to know that he will likely not return to Haedon. Even if he will be a father shortly, the world needs him for a bigger calling now. That is why, deep down, I hoped that the father was someone else, someone who might be able to be a good, present father to the child. I am sorry to put it so bluntly, but I wanted to ensure that your expectations of Baltaszar would be realistic going forward. Perhaps as you raise your child, you can explain to him or her how special their father is."

Yasaman cut in, "This threat you speak of. How serious are we talking? Are we even part of Ashur? For my whole life, I have had absolutely no interaction with anything beyond Haedon, with the exception of three strange men and a few wild animals. I have seen no person from beyond Haedon visit here. And on top of all that, I have never heard anyone in this town ever mention people or events beyond our borders. All of a sudden we are connected to something else? All of a sudden we are threatened?"

Von nodded at her. "I understand your frustration and confusion. We have never had a reason to consider the outside world. And yet, everyone in this town has come from another nation, most from Rhagavi, a nation that has much reason to dislike Ashur. Haedon is not as old as you might think. I have personally witnessed its entire growth. Most of the people here who remember their homelands would rather forget them. They are outcasts there but not truly accepted in Ashur. Nonetheless, we are only about three days from the rest of Ashurian civilization. And that means we are included in the path of this threat. Truthfully, I do not know how many people in Haedon will even take it seriously, as it does not fit in with their system of beliefs."

Yasaman needed to process the information for a moment. "Give me a moment to take this all in. You are telling me so much and I appreciate that, but you are still speaking in generalities. I have a child coming any day now. Tell me exactly what this threat is. War? Disease?" She'd had more to add, but another contraction halted her question. This one lasted even longer than the previous one.

Von quieted his tone again to almost a whisper. "Very well. But you must not mention any of this to anyone beyond this door. Haedonians are extremely sensitive about this topic." Yasaman nodded in agreement quickly. "I spoke of the Harbingers and Descendants just now. The thing is, Rhagavans do not share that belief with most of the world. They do not believe in or acknowledge any Harbingers and what little they have seen of Descendants and manifestations they assume is dark magic. Ashur, on the other hand, believes heavily in all of that; so naturally Rhagavi would have good reason to dislike most of Ashur. And now you also understand why there was no other option for Joakwin Kontez, except death."

Yasaman shifted again. "You speak about these people as if you are an outsider. Do you not believe in the same things?"

Von smiled. "Quite astute. I am Ashurian. I am originally from the nation called Galicea. So, no, I do not share the same beliefs as the rest of the people here. However, most of them took up residence in the City of the Fallen, which is likely the most tolerant and open-minded city in Ashur. Still, they had their share of difficulties, especially since that city has giant statues of four of the Harbingers at each gate on its perimeter. They lived a lie, feigning acceptance until it grew too tiresome. At the time, I was also looking for a way to leave society and just enjoy the rest of my life in relative seclusion. We migrated here in secrecy over the course of a few years. Most residents in the City of the Fallen are too busy or too self-absorbed to have even noticed that these people were different or that they were eventually gone. Haedon has existed unbothered since its inception."

"But these Harbingers were in fact real?"

Von looked at her peculiarly, then said, "Yes. In fact, one of them is still alive, which is why Ashur is in danger. His name is Jahmash, and *he* is the threat. It would take too long to explain the whole history of the Harbingers with you, and quite frankly, the only important part at this point is that Jahmash seeks to return to Ashur and decimate the population. It is quite a real and likely possibility that this happens."

Yasaman held her hand tightly against her belly. "And what kind of timeline are we looking at? I'm assuming you'd be in much more of a panic if it were a matter of days. Are we talking months? A year? A few years?"

Von took a deep breath and then rubbed his temples. "In all honesty, there is no real way of knowing. The Descendants I spoke of, their place of refuge is called 'The House of Darian.' And before you worry, I know for certain that Baltaszar was not there when this happened. The House of Darian was destroyed a little over a week ago by a massive fleet of ships, and all speculation leads to it being Jahmash's doing. It is doubtful that he was there, but it was most likely his army that attacked. But no one knows what his next move will be. It is also rumored that he sent a smaller army to wipe out the Taurani—a warrior culture that lives on the other side of the Never. But that was almost a year ago. So it could be that he is eliminating the biggest threats before waging a full on war against Ashur."

Yasaman cut in, "Perhaps it's good that we're hidden out here then. And that we're a simple society of farmers, not warriors. What threat would we pose to someone like that?"

"That is also why I asked about Baltaszar being the father of your child. You see, for most people in Ashur, it is hit or miss about whether they have descended from Darian. For anyone, there is always a chance, which means that there exists a small possibility that their offspring could eventually develop a manifestation. For Baltaszar, that question has already been answered. Baltaszar is a Descendant, and his children definitely will be, also. That means that there is a strong possibility that his children could develop manifestations of their own, if placed in certain unforced situations. Who knows what your child might be able to do? If your child proves to be a useful tool to Jahmash, he would certainly turn his attention to Haedon. And forgive me, as I do not mean to sound cold, but for anyone who would come here to kidnap a young Descendant, it would make sense to kill a frantic or desperate mother."

She thought for a moment. *At least that clears up why Tasz has that mark and Bo doesn't. But Bo or Tasz, this baby will still have the same chance of getting a manifestation. It doesn't matter if people think Tasz is the father.* Yasaman cringed once more at the long contraction. "So...then," she paused for a moment," it might be in my best interest to leave this place once it is safe for my baby to travel?"

Von's eyes perked up. "Is that something you have been considering?"

Yasaman hesitated. She realized she might be revealing too much, but at this point, Oran Von was likely the only ally she had in Haedon. "Truthfully, I don't know if I can stay with my mother. It is nearly unbearable now; she will only become more abrasive once my child is born. I don't need to be told I am a bad mother in addition to already being a bad daughter. I think it might be in my best interest that, once my child is old enough to handle the travel, we leave Haedon for good. You have made it clear that there is civilization beyond Haedon, and much of it. I think I could find a life for me and my child somewhere else."

The old man nodded his head. "In the right setting, you would be just fine. In fact, the town of Vandenar is not far beyond the Never. You would have to cross a river to get there, but there are fishing boats that would be generous enough for a young woman and her baby. In fact, I believe that is where Baltaszar went first when he left here. That is definitely where he came from when he returned to Haedon and caused all that ruckus. If they were hospitable to him, then they would surely provide you with a warm bed and a hot meal."

"That sounds nice." *If Tasz was there, then that's where I can start searching for him.* "I wouldn't end up running into him there again? You said that Tasz was not at the House of Darian."

Von grimaced, "No, he is not in Vandenar. I cannot be certain of his exact whereabouts by now, but I doubt he is anywhere even close to there. You would not have to worry about a surprise encounter."

She hid her disappointment behind a smirk. "Oh good." She surmised it would be another six months or so until she could leave, but as soon as she left Haedon, her goal would be to find Baltaszar. She wasn't sure how, but she would find a way to convince him to take her back. *I'm sure that in the next six months, I can figure out what to possibly say to him that would make him realize I made too many mistakes, but that I still love him.* What Von had told her about Baltaszar's father made her realize how cruel and horrible she'd been to have broken things off with him. And yet, she'd had the nerve to cry through it all. She felt another sharp pain in her stomach and winced noticeably. She couldn't help but let out a small groan.

"What is it, child? Is the baby coming now?" Von attempted to rise from the chair.

As Yasaman shifted and held up a hand in protest, she felt a small pop in her lower abdomen, and then something trickled down from between her legs. *Oh no.* "I...I think. I think so. I think my water just broke? Please get my mother and Diya!" She winced as Von arose and helped her to reposition herself so that her head was on her pillow. She tried to take some deep breaths to calm her nerves. Von scuttled out of the room, shouting for the two women to help. Yasaman surprised herself that she instinctually asked for her mother. *Please, let her just be a mother and not my mother. Please Orijin, let her just love me in this moment. In this situation.* Yasaman held her breath as another contraction tightened in her abdomen like a vice. It caused her to sit up and lasted so long that her mother and Diya hurried into the room before it ended.

Diya placed several blankets on the bed while Yasaman's mother eased her back so that she was laying down. Her mother held her hand and placed another hand on Yasaman's belly. "I think it's almost time.

Diya, get her legs up; I will be right back."

Diya nodded and bent Yasaman's legs so that her knees were up in the air, and then placed rolled up towels and blankets under her calves to hold them up. "This will help when it comes time to push."

"Thank you." Yasaman glanced at the door and saw Von standing at the entrance, looking the other way. "Chancellor, please come back in. I will need someone to hold my hand and talk to me while my mother and Diya focus on helping me push the baby out. Can you help distract me from the pain?"

Von turned around and walked to her with a tentative smile on his face. His cheeks were bright red as well. "Of course. I can do that, dear."

Yasaman wasn't sure if he'd caught on, but she needed someone there who she could be sure would not pass judgment. "Thank you. Diya, where did my mother go?"

Diya looked up as she was finishing with Yasaman's legs, "She has been keeping Faerie Tears in the cupboard since you told her you were with child. She went to fetch it to help with the pain."

Yasaman almost felt lucky that another contraction came at that instant. Tears welled up at the corners of both of her eyes at the thought of her mother doing such a sweet thing. Faerie Tears came from Faerie Maple trees in the Never, which were quite rare, not to mention that people rarely ventured into the Never, except in the direction of the water. *She does love me. And she is showing it.*

Her mother stormed back into the room right after and, in that moment of pain, discomfort, and insecurity, Yasaman took in her mother for a brief moment and felt appreciation for everything that the woman was. Still beautiful, though her long black hair showed strands of grey. Lines barely starting to form in her face, even after all the stress and heartbreak she'd faced in the past year. "Yas. Yasaman! Pay attention! Now is not the time for daydreaming! I've been keeping this for you; it is Faerie Tears. It will subdue the pain, but still allow you to feel sensation enough to know what your body is doing."

Yas stared at the cup. There was barely any liquid inside. "There's hardly anything in here."

"It is potent. And tasty. A dangerous combination. Many have indulged in it and lost their lives as a result. Faerie Tears, if not taken lightly, can lead to a quick and quiet death. You would simply fall asleep and not wake up. I am no expert at it, so I erred on the side of caution. What I gave you may still allow you to feel some pain. But better that than giving you too much."

Yasaman nodded and drank the golden brown liquid. It was slightly thick and definitely sweet. She understood instantly why people could easily drink too much of it. "Oh wow. I thought medicine was supposed to taste disgusting. No wonder why people die from that." She licked her lips, hoping for another taste of it. "How long does it take to start working?"

Her mother looked at her, seeming somewhat concerned. "It needs some time to get started. It should be another few minutes. You are not quite ready yet anyway." Just as her mother said that, her stomach tensed again.

Yasaman grunted. "You're right. This contraction hurts just as much as the last one. Definitely not working yet." Oran Von sat at the edge of the bed next to her head and faced away from her body. He clasped her hand gently and smiled at her. Yasaman whispered, "Thank you for being here."

Her mother pulled down her undergarments, to Yasaman's surprise. On noticing Yasaman's expression, she said, "Yas, you are not going to need those for a little while, trust me. Besides, I have to see how big the opening is and if your body is ready yet." Her mother poked and prodded her nether parts, closely inspecting between her legs. Her head popped up a few awkward moments later. "How do you feel now? Is the pain the same?"

Yasaman hesitated to answer, but another contraction began and it clearly didn't hurt like before. She felt the sensation in her abdomen, but not the pain. "No, it is better now. I can feel my stomach tightening, but it does not hurt."

Her mother smiled, "Good, then it is time to start pushing." Her mother stood up. "You are ready now for the baby to come. And your contractions are very close together. Your body is ready."

Yasaman took a deep breath. *Yes, but my mind is not. Can't you just stay in there forever, baby?* "I don't know what to do, mother. How do I even push?"

Her mother rubbed her belly softly and smiled. "Wait for the next contraction. First, put your chin to your chest. Then, you push as hard as you can, the same way as if you were relieving yourself." She stopped to chuckle, "You may even do that in the process. It is normal." Yasaman didn't find that as humorous as her mother did, especially with Oran Von standing right next to her. The last thing she wanted was to soil herself in front of likely her only friend left. She attempted a smile, which her mother must have seen through. "If you would rather Chancellor Von leave the room, I highly doubt he would be offended."

Von nodded in agreement. "Indeed, child. I could simply wait outside the room if it would make you more comfortable."

"No. Please stay and let me hold your hand. I will need to grasp something tightly when I am pushing."

Von smiled politely. "Very well. I will look away, just as I am doing now. If it is any consolation, I have been present for many births, and I have seen what your mother described nearly every time. It is a natural thing."

Yasaman blushed just as another contraction was beginning. Her mother had already noticed as well, as she started giving orders. "Here it is. Another contraction is beginning. Chin down and push as hard as you can for as long as you can."

Yasaman followed her mother's directions and tucked her chin into her chest, then pushed with all of her energy. She felt something slightly move inside of her and it gave her the strength to continue pushing. Diya had already positioned herself between Yasaman's knees, "Keep going. Nothing yet so keep pushing."

She continued to strain and clenched Von's hand so tightly that she was sure she'd break it at some point. After a few more moments she relented to catch her breath. Her mother reassured her. "Good. When the next one starts, do the exact same thing. It may take some time to push the baby all the way out, and that is normal and fine."

Yasaman caught her breath in time for the next contraction and continued to push. She gritted her teeth; sweat already dampened her forehead. She felt something moving through her birth canal as she pushed, hoping that she was making progress. Although the Faerie Tears dampened the pain, she felt the pressure of something large being pushed out. She needed to rest again after another minute. Diya provided an update on the progress, "I cannot see it just yet, but I think the next push will get the baby to crown." Yasaman felt encouraged, and continued to breathe deeply. Even pushing for only a few minutes was exhausting. *How do some women do this for hours?* She was still breathing heavily when the next contraction began. She steeled herself and pushed again, as hard as she could. Her mother and Diya offered words of encouragement, but her grunts and groans drowned them out. Yasaman thought she felt something leaving her, and she looked at Diya.

She continued to push until she couldn't strain any longer. She looked up at Diya, who was looking down confusedly and solemnly. She gasped out through heavy breaths, "Is the baby almost out? How much more pushing?" Diya and her mother both looked down and only then did Yasaman realize that Diya was already holding the baby. "Why...why is it so quiet? Mother, is it okay?"

Her mother finally looked up at her with tears streaming down her eyes. "I'm sorry Yas. He's not breathing. The cord was wrapped around his neck. I'm so sorry." Yasaman felt Von clutch her hand more tightly.

They wrapped the baby up in two of the blankets and Diya was about to leave the room with it when Yasaman stopped her. "Wait. Please let me see my son. Please let me hold him and look at him and at least say hello before I even say goodbye." As Diya passed the baby to her, Yasaman felt emotions explode within her. Sadness dominated them all, but she was still bombarded by despair, panic, anger, fear, helplessness, hopelessness, confusion, and heartbreak. Yasaman looked at its lifeless face, and with the river of tears also came terror, disappointment, inadequacy, and for a split second, relief. The sentiment had appeared and disappeared so quickly, that she didn't have a chance to physically acknowledge it or hide it, but it lingered long enough that she felt guilty. She started talking to help push it aside, "Zaid. This is my son, Zaid."

Oran Von sat on the edge of the bed, "Zaid, like the warrior boy in the children's story, who protects his family from the Ranza cats."

"Yes. Everyone underestimates him and yet, he is the only one brave enough to fight them off. Even though he will never get to be a warrior in this world, I believe he will watch me from Omneitria and protect me against future hardships." All of the emotions had somewhat subdued, but they must have affected her body because she thought she felt another contraction. "Oh, that's strange." She put one hand to her belly.

Her mother jumped up, "What is?"

"I'm having another contraction. I think it's just as strong as the ones I was just having."

Her mother reached out to her, "Let me have the...let me have Zaid. Diya, into position again."

Yasaman gently passed the baby into her mother's arms and asked concernedly, "What's wrong, mother?"

"Nothing is *wrong*, love. But there is another baby in there that wants to come out. Let us hurry. You know what to do at the next contraction." Her mother rushed out of the room with Zaid and returned a moment later, just as the next contraction was starting. "Push, Yas! Push! Let us bring this baby into the world before something bad happens to it inside of you!"

Yasaman pushed as hard as she could, fighting off the urge to take her mother's words as an insult. She grimaced and pushed until there was no force left in her body.

Diya exclaimed, "It's crowning! It's crowning!" Diya reached towards Yasaman and gingerly pulled the baby out. Within seconds, Yasaman heard it crying loudly. This time, she allowed herself to feel the relief. "You've got a baby boy, Yas! He is beautiful!" Once again, Diya swaddled Yas' baby in blankets, but this time she willingly transferred it to Yasaman.

She was crying once more, but smiling as well. "Zane. Twin boys, Zaid and Zane. And Zaid will watch over both of us like a protector. You are so handsome, Zane."

Yasaman had forgotten that Von was there. The man stood and motioned to leave the room. "Now that all is in order, if you no longer need me, I shall be off. The young mother needs some time alone with her son, anyway. Ladies, if you permit it, I shall take Zaid with me and make the proper arrangements. My guard is still outside; he can carry it back to my house."

Yasaman gulped down a ball of emotion, "Yes, Chancellor. That would be very sweet of you. Thank you. But, can we keep this as a private affair?"

"Absolutely, dear. Let us plan for two days from now, so that there is time to make all of the proper arrangements. I will return here in two days' time, early in the morning. We can perform the funeral and burial behind the house, if you like, to avoid any onlookers."

"That would be well." Yasaman responded as she looked into Zane's eyes and smiled.

"Very well then. I will send a guard tomorrow to dig a space. And I will see you in two days' time. Congratulations, Yas. I am quite proud of you." Von forced a smile as he left the room.

YASAMAN AWOKE FOR THE FOURTH or fifth time since putting Zane down for the night. She'd lost count at this point and, for the past two days, had only slept when he slept. When he was awake, she was either feeding him, holding him, or checking to see if he'd relieved himself. So far, he loved to eat, to the point where her breasts were sore from all the milk she was producing and then all the feeding. She wasn't sure if she missed Baltaszar or Bo'az, or if she was just wishing there was someone to share the burden with. Her mother and Diya had been helpful, but her mother had started to revert to her old ways of subtle insults and hidden jabs, especially because Zaid had been stillborn.

Zane wriggled and cooed in a bassinet next to her bed. He didn't cry as much as he whined and talked, but he was still always noisy if he was awake. She sat up and brought him to her chest for another feeding. She heard a knock at the front door and assumed it must be Von. Diya greeted him and invited him and his guards inside. Yasaman heard Von instructing the guards to walk around the house to the back of it where the hole had been dug yesterday. Diya asked Von to sit and then knocked on Yasaman's door. She peeked in without knocking, and quietly asked "Are you ready? Your mother is ready and Chancellor Von is here now."

"Just a moment. Zane is still eating and I then I will put him back down for a nap."

Diya nodded and then shut the door. Yasaman fed Zane for a short while longer until he fell asleep in the middle of eating. He had a habit of doing that, but she loved when it happened. She found it cute, not to mention she didn't have to put any effort into getting him to sleep. She returned him to the bassinet and then joined the others in the sitting room. When they saw her enter, they all arose and walked to the back of the house, and then to their farm behind it. Each of them was adorned in black attire from head to toe. The three women wore long, plain dresses while Von was robed in a long cloak. A hole had been dug just before the tall rows of corn began. She followed Von, Diya, and her mother toward it as one of Von's guards carried Zaid's body, now tightly wrapped in ceremonial draping. The guard knelt and placed Zaid's body gently into the ground. As the guard was about to start filling the whole back up, Yasaman spoke up. "No. Please leave it. I will do it when we are finished here." The guard looked at Von, who nodded at him, then turned and walked back around the house.

Yasaman got so caught up thinking about her firstborn son that she didn't even hear Von start speaking. She continued to entertain her thoughts and even acknowledged those feelings of relief that had caused her so much stress in the past two days. She hadn't been sure whether she could handle raising two children, but she knew she could raise Zane quite well on her own. The more she thought about Zaid, the more she felt guilty, almost at fault, for having to bury him while his brother lived. *I'm so sorry, baby. Please know that I love you so much and I will always think about you and remember your face, and I will always love you as much as your brother and he'll know all about you, too.* Tears flowed down her face once more. She couldn't explain why she felt so guilty but thought that perhaps it had to do with comments that her mother continued to make since the babies were born. She'd gotten so lost in thought that she only noticed Von had finished speaking when Diya and her mother turned to walk away. At that point, she wished she'd still been too lost in thought to hear anything.

As Yasaman's mother walked away with Diya, Yasaman overheard her mother tell the maid, "Let us go in while she covers the baby's grave. It is the least she can do for him as her mother, especially after allowing him to die." Yasaman had already stopped crying and she refused to shed more tears on her mother's behalf. She picked up the spade and started filling in the grave. Von must have sensed that she wanted him to stay, because he didn't budge from his position.

"Chancellor, you can plainly hear how she speaks of me. I cannot endure here for much longer. As soon as it is safe for Zane to travel, I plan to leave Haedon. Maybe another six months or so."

Von nodded and placed a hand on her shoulder. "Very well. I do not like to get into family affairs, but I cannot blame you for your outlook or decisions. Let me know a few days before you plan to leave. I will make arrangements for you to obtain a horse and sufficient food. We can also discuss the options you have in terms of routes of travel."

Yasaman continued to fill the hole for several moments and then dropped the shovel at her feet. She walked up to Von and hugged him tightly. "Thank you for all of your help these past few days. I don't know if I'd have kept my sanity if not for you. I am going to check on Zane, to make sure he is fine and to make sure they are not disturbing him. I will come to you when the time is right." Von hobbled back around the house once she released him. Yasaman trudged back to the house and then into her room. She shut the door gently and quietly, then searched the top left drawer of her dresser. Baltaszar had left a tiny shaving blade in her room once; she couldn't even remember why. In fact, she also couldn't remember why she'd kept it all this time. But she was happy for it now. She retrieved it from her drawer along with a small stained towel.

Zane slept quietly in his bassinet on the other side of the room, by the window. Yasaman sat at the side of her bed and rolled her sleeve up past her elbow. The good thing about winter was that she was always wearing long sleeves, even inside the house, so neither her mother nor Diya would ask any questions. Yasaman took a deep breath and then swiped the blade across the meaty part of her forearm. Because Zane was sleeping, she had no choice but to make no sound and embrace the pain of the cut. At first the open wound burned, but then she channeled her emotions enough so that they were synonymous with the physical pain. As the physical pain waned, so did the emotional stress. She wrapped the small towel around her forearm and then rolled her sleeve back down. She laid back and turned to look at Zane sleeping peacefully, then drifted off to sleep.

CHAPTER 5
THE VITHELEGION

From **The Book of Orijin,** **Verse Seventy-Nine**
The surest way to find balance in life is to live it as righteously as possible.
Live a more virtuous life than your enemies and justice will prevail.

"WHAT DO THEY SAY?" Khurt Everitas tightened his fists.

"It is nothing, father. It does not bother me. I know they are just words. Let them say whatever they want. I know I am not what they say." Khenzi continued to stare out at the sea. Khurt could never get a proper read on his son. Khenzi's thin face was always stoic, even when the boy wasn't upset. Even the pale spots of skin on his face made him look serious when he wasn't trying to be. The boy must have sensed his father's frustration. "I promise you, father, I am fine. I know I hardly fit the mold of a general's son, but I am young. I have plenty of time to live up to your standard."

Khurt punched his palm. "Very well. But the moment I think that you cannot handle it, I am going to step in. There are two of them and one of you. They are much bigger and we are out on the open sea. If those boys are even half as vicious as their father, who knows what they are capable of." Khurt was tired of his son being bullied. He didn't want to have to step in; it would not look good for Khenzi or him if he did, but Saol Suldas was an arrogant and aggressive man. He pointed out any weakness he saw, especially physical weakness. Khenzi was the perfect target for Suldas's ridicule. Saymon and Salken Suldas were not much older than Khenzi, but they were both much bigger. It would be no stretch of the imagination to assume that they would physically assault Khenzi, given the opportunity. If not for Khurt's status, he would consider knocking them overboard when no one was around. As the First General, though, he would lose everything. He stared out at the sea for a while as well and let himself calm down. If Khenzi could be levelheaded about the situation, then *he* would try to be, too. "How about some more sword practice?"

Khenzi looked at him and finally smiled, "Definitely." He rubbed the light brown stripe of hair on top of his head. Khurt had shaved Khenzi's hair on the sides, leaving it long only on the top, in the tradition of going into battle. Khenzi beamed for hours after that. *Those little pricks.* Khurt breathed deeply for a moment and punched his fist once more. *Remember, tavaz. They will get what is coming to them, one way or another. I just hope that I am there to see it.*

"Come, let's get started." Khurt led him below deck to a small open area outside their quarters. They only sparred below deck, out of sight. He didn't want to risk Saol or Saol's sons seeing them practicing with swords. It would only lead to more teasing and confrontation. It was bad enough that Khenzi was barely strong enough to hold the one handed sword with both hands. Vithelegion boys generally started with those. Khenzi was a quick learner, though. He'd already assumed his ready stance: right leg back, torso turned to the right, holding his sword upright with his hands at his hips. "Good. Let us begin."

Khenzi approached him aggressively. They'd been on the sea for nearly a week and had practiced multiple times each day. Khurt knew his son was gaining confidence, but there was anger in his eyes. He wouldn't push; despite Khenzi's aggression, he was not sparring recklessly. Khenzi spoke up as he advanced, "Why were we not allowed to tell mother and Khaira why we are truly going off to war?"

Khurt defended against Khenzi's strikes and thought of the best way to answer. "It is complicated, so be patient with my answer. And do not lean in so much when you strike. I know the sword is somewhat awkward for you, but treat it like an extension of your body, an extension of your arms. If you are off-balance when you fight, a faster enemy will kill you easily. You have a long reach, which is good. You do not need to lean in when you strike. Back to ready stance." Khenzi nodded and walked back, then assumed the ready stance. He moved forward aggressively once more, this time more calculating with his strikes and more balanced with his body. "Better. Stay focused while I answer your question. I am sure you know by now that not every leader of our armies agrees with Saol Suldas's methods. He pushed for this war more than anyone else." He caught Khenzi hesitating with an attack and struck the boy's sword out of his hands. Khenzi stroked his hair and looked at the sword in frustration. "Again. As I was saying, we all agree that the followers of Darian are blasphemers and hypocrites, and that they should be punished for following such a man. However, there are many leaders who disagree with the idea of sailing so far away to start this war when we know little of our enemy. We do not know their numbers or their terrain, or even their skill. Saol Suldas is convinced that we are superior warriors to any other nation, and that alone shall guarantee our victory."

Khenzi picked up the sword and immediately assumed the ready stance. "So then none of these soldiers told their families before they left?" Khenzi approached again, eyes narrowed with determination.

"Some soldiers told the truth, others offered a stretch of the truth." Khurt parried Khenzi's slash.

"Did you lie then? To mother and Khaira?"

Khurt looked Khenzi in the eyes as he continued the volley of attacks. "I told your mother and sister that we were simply going off to war against a new enemy. I told her that Suldas had not given me all of the details yet, and that we would learn more along the way. I did not lie to them. I simply did not tell them everything."

"Why do I get in trouble then, when I do that?" Khenzi's strikes came faster.

Greatmother, help me. "Sometimes, no, most of the time, it is not the right thing to do. Before we left I told you that you are not a child. So I will speak to you like a man. I am a general in the Vithelegion. I have a reputation to maintain. I had to decide whether it was worth it to have that argument with your mother, because it would have definitely become an argument, had I told her all of the details. You know that her role now is to defend our nation. It is better for her to have a clear head rather than be angry with me." Khenzi nodded. It was customary for the women of Vitheligia to defend the nation when the men sailed off to war. Boys and girls received different training from the time they were Khenzi's age. The boys learned a more aggressive style of fighting, heavily dependent on weapons, specifically blades, while girls practiced a more defensive combat that incorporated weapons as well as hand-to-hand fighting. Girls were also more adept at using their surroundings when fighting.

Decades ago, the first time the men left for war, the Aladari made the grave mistake of attacking. The Vithelegion women saw them coming hours before the Aladari attack. By the time the fighting was done and the Aladari decided to retreat, they'd lost hundreds of soldiers and no Vithelegion woman was seriously injured. Vitheligia did not retaliate, as there was no interest in conquest of Aladar. But since that time, no nation even hinted at an attempted strike against Vitheligia.

"Could mother beat you in a fight?"

"Yes," Khurt replied without hesitation. "Most women in Vitheligia could defeat most men in a one on one fight. Women are simply the better fighters."

"Why do we go off to war then, instead of the women?"

So smart, this boy. "It is more important to be able to defend your home. The way Vithelegion women fight, they are virtually unbeatable. We do not have to worry about losing our nation when we go off to war. The same could not be said if the women left for war and we stayed back." Khenzi paused to think once more and Khurt struck the sword from his hands. "Let us stop for now. Your head is not completely here, and that is understandable. We can come back down after we have gotten some air."

"Fine." Khenzi placed his sword on the ground next to the wall, then brought his father's there as well. Khurt watched him then turned towards the stairs to walk back onto the deck. Standing at the top was the last man he wanted to see, Saol Suldas.

Khurt punched his palm once again, this time more subtly. "How long have you been standing there, Commander?"

Saol stalked down the stairs and stopped inches in front of Khurt. Khurt himself was almost as thick as a tree trunk, but Saol was inches taller than he and even more massive. Saol sneered at him, "Enough to see that your boy is improving. In another week, he can start practicing with Saymon and Salken."

Khurt paused to choose his words wisely. "Khenzi is not to their level yet. I will teach him a while longer and then inform you when I feel he is ready for them."

Saol stroked his long goatee. Just like every Vithelegion man in the army, Saol's pale skin patches were painted black in honor of war. Somehow, they made Saol look more menacing than anyone else. Khurt wasn't afraid of the man, if anything he was afraid of what the man was capable of. "He will never fully develop as a swordsman if he only learns from you. My boys were sparring with older boys within days of picking up their swords for the first time. Now they can hold their own against any grown man in the Vithelegion. What are you afraid of, Everitas?"

Khurt ground his teeth. Saol had a habit of asking that whenever someone didn't agree with him. Khurt took it personally when it concerned Khenzi. "It is not about fear. Everyone is different. Khenzi is not ready yet. As I said, give it time and I will let you know when he is ready."

The bigger man grasped Khurt by the shoulder and squeezed firmly. Khurt knew it wasn't meant to hurt him, only to send a message. "Perhaps your family name should be *Ignavus*, then?"

Khurt swiped Saol's hand off his shoulder, "How dare you call me a coward. I am done with this conversation. What is the reason for your visit aboard my ship, Commander?"

The smile on Saol's face disappeared, leaving his mouth tight and straight. He pushed a finger into Khurt's chest. "Get your sword. I will show your son...no, I will show your whole crew the importance of taking sparring seriously. Take your sword and follow me to the upper deck." Khurt punched his palm as Saol turned and walked up the stairs. Khenzi rushed up to his side, handing him his sword.

"Sorry, father. I know this is my fault."

Khurt immediately knelt down and grabbed Khenzi's sleeveless arm. "This has nothing to do with you and everything to do with that man. He is so caught up with making sure that everyone remembers he is the commander, that he forgets that it is actual people he commands. He only cares for putting us down and exposing weaknesses wherever he can find them. He thinks you are weak because you are small. He misjudges you. He does so with many people, and I believe he is doing so with the enemies we shall face soon. Remember, *tavaz*. Life is balance, and the good always evens out the bad. One day, good will balance out the bad deeds of Saol and his sons. Let us go. And do not worry, he will not hurt me. He just wants to show a crowd that he is better than me."

He led Khenzi up to the deck, where Saol waited, already boasting to Khurt's crewmen. Saol had cleared the crew from the middle of the deck, and Khurt's men stood in a giant circle around where he and Saol were about to spar. Khurt stood at the perimeter with Khenzi, then patted the boy on the shoulder. He walked to the middle of the circle, where Saol now stood. Khurt knew that Saol would spar hard enough to make him think that Saol was trying to hurt him, but he also knew that Saol would not intentionally injure him, only embarrass him. He would almost rather be injured than embarrassed. Saol sneered at him, "Surprise me and let this last a while. For your sake." Saol patted Khurt's head for everyone to see, then turned and walked back five paces. Khurt did the same, then turned to face Saol and raised his sword.

In truth, Saol had not seen Khurt spar or practice with a sword in quite a long time. Khurt had gotten better and faster, and had practiced some new techniques of his own. Saol would be aggressive, and despite what he'd said, would try to end things quickly. Khurt would have to be faster and a step ahead. He kept his eyes locked on Saol's and entered the *steelmaiden* stance, turning his body to the left, knees bent and weight on his right leg, and holding his sword horizontally over his right shoulder. His eyes stayed focused on Saol's. The larger man seemed confused at Khurt's opening, but advanced on him nonetheless.

There would be no more talking or taunting. Saol would not allow himself to be distracted during a fight. As Khurt expected, Saol opened with an overhead strike, which Khurt deflected and spun away to regain some space between them. Though Khurt was faster, Saol was decidedly stronger. Khurt would likely have to use two hands at times to prevent Saol from overpowering him. He quickly assumed the *pillar of wind* stance, similar to *steelmaiden*, except that he held the sword straight up. He'd created several stances and attacks on his own, and had only taught the men he commanded. Once again, Saol looked curiously at him. Saol approached more cautiously this time, holding his own sword vertically in front of his body.

Khurt would only last if he let Saol get frustrated and reckless, which meant he would allow Saol to be the aggressor. This time, Saol slashed at him diagonally. Khurt once again deflected the attack, but stood his ground instead of backing up. Saol followed up with more one-handed swoops and slashes. Khurt held his own sword with two hands and parried Saol's attacks. Because he was faster than Saol, he was still able to detect Saol's strikes before they could get the best of him. Saol moved quickly and his strikes were strong and full of determination but Khurt was starting to notice more and more follow through in Saol's strikes as their volley went on. It was the only sign of frustration that Saol was likely to show, so he would have to use it. Khurt kept the volley going, defending Saol's attacks and countering for as long as he could. The unrelenting battle drew the cheers of Khurt's men and gave him a boost of confidence. Saol's strikes were getting harder and slower. Finally, after several moments, Saol telegraphed an overhand strike with his right hand. Khurt sidestepped the sword. From the moment he anticipated the move, he knew that he would counter with a two-handed strike to the base of the blade with enough force to knock it from Saol's hand. Yet, his frustration betrayed his instincts and instead he birthed the two-handed strike from beneath his shoulder and stabbed right through Saol's sword hand. Saol's sword indeed fell from his hand and Khurt withdrew his sword immediately.

Saol had been stabbed before, so the blow was not enough to debilitate him, but the gash would prevent him from using a sword for several weeks. He dropped to a knee and held his wrist, staring at the wound. Saol looked around the deck and then to Khurt. "What have you done?" He stood once more, "This was supposed to be a sparring session, not a true fight. We are on our way to battle and you stabbed my sword hand, coward."

Khurt stood before Saol and let the man have his rant. With any hope, the commander would think to get back to his ship and dress the wound. Khurt would take the insults in the hopes that that would be the worst of it. Saol would never tell his own squadron that Khurt had gotten the best of him in sparring. "I thought you were about to attempt another strike. So I struck where I thought the base of your blade *would* be. It could have been that I was too quick for the strike you intended."

Saol spit on the ground at Khurt's feet and spoke quietly. "Coward. Just come out and say that you think me to be slower than you. Either way, I do not believe you. Remember it, my sons and I will repay you...or your son...for this."

Khurt refused to take the bait, at least not visibly. He replied loud enough for most of the crew to hear, "Commander, there is a lot of blood coming from the wound. I beg you to get it dressed before it becomes too serious."

Saol glanced back at his hand and saw just how much blood was flowing from it. Khurt had given him a way to leave the ship without embarrassing himself further. Saol turned without a word and walked back to the planks that connected the two ships. He walked across to his ship without waiting for any help, and as soon as his men pulled the planks back aboard, they erupted in cheers and surrounded Khurt. Khenzi had been thrust toward him to share the praise and accolades. Khurt smiled and laughed and allowed himself to get caught up in the merriment. Saol would eventually attempt retribution, most likely on Khenzi, but that would not be this day. He could allow himself to enjoy the moment. Oftentimes he let his emotions get the best of him, and he tended to regret it in the aftermath. Yet, there was no regret in this. It was the first time he'd ever felt that Saol might have a reason to fear him. And that notion felt a little too good.

"THAT IS COMPLETE DECIMATION, and I do not see the point." Khurt punched the barrels, the makeshift table that he, Killian, and Laken pushed together for this meeting. They were two of Saol's crewmen, as Saol likely refused to be seen until his hand completely healed. That had been four days ago and, despite sailing right beside Saol's ship, Khurt and his crew had had minimal communication with Saol, aside from confirming coordinates and discussing the waves, which were growing stronger and more violent with each passing day. Khurt looked them both in the eyes, "Does Suldas really think we can eradicate the entire continent? Yes, we will get away with that for the first few cities we attack. And then word will spread and armies will come for us. They have a continent while we have one fleet. No matter how great we are in combat, we are unfamiliar with their geography, fighting styles, and the size of their armies."

Laken, an older and sinewy man, responded. "We are Vithelegion. We are better than any army that would oppose us."

Khurt shook his head, "In our brief history, we have invaded nations in the name of freedom and justice, never for conquest. We have always declared war with one nation at a time. It is said that Ashur is comprised of at least six nations. That means that if we are not careful, we could be fighting against six or more armies at one time, all of whom know their land. Our women are unparalleled fighters, but they are also successful because they know our land. I say we attack the first city we see, and take the survivors as captives. It gives us leverage against any armies that would attack us afterward."

"Khurt, we sail there to destroy their people. They follow Darian, and spit on the memory of Abram. They all deserve to die." Killian glowered at him. The man was of an age with him, but had no wife or children.

Khurt shook his head once more and glanced at Khenzi out of the corner of his eye. He wanted his son here to experience and understand the nature of these strategic meetings. It made it easier that Saol was not present. Although Laken and Killian were Saol's men, their personalities were nothing like Saol's. They could be talked to and reasoned with. "Brethren, I trust that you are speaking from your own minds, rather than simply restating what Saol would say. After our meeting is done, it is expected that all of the generals will meet within the next day or two. Our conversation is of the utmost importance. So please consider my points and take them seriously. Why must we kill all of them? What if they can be converted to see our point of view? What if we can educate them about how they are mistaken?"

Now Laken shook his head to refute the point. "No. If you were taken captive, Khurt, would you not simply agree to something like that so that your captors would be lenient with you?" A sudden strong wave rocked the boat and they all grasped the barrels for support.

Khurt looked around at Khenzi and the two men. The sudden convulsion was obviously unexpected, but he expected Laken's retort. "They would be captive and under watch. They would not simply be able to attack. And are you telling me then that both of you would be able to justify massacring children and elders in the name of Abram? Do you believe that is what the Harbinger would want? An army of his followers invading cities and murdering innocent and guilty alike all in his name?"

Laken and Killian looked at one another for a moment, neither knowing what to say. Khurt felt a tinge of smugness creep over him as he noticed the two men glance at Khenzi and then back at him. Laken finally spoke up. "But this is what Suldas wants."

"Then tell him what *I* want." Khurt stood up, knowing that his height would give him even more of an advantage in persuading the two men. "Saol Suldas quickly declared this war without proper scouting and without caring whether it was the best decision for the Vithelegion. I agree that anyone who would worship Darian must be dealt with, but that does not mean they all must die. The very name 'Vithelegion' suggests that we act as a nation, as a group. Not each man making decisions just for himself. What Saol suggests is what he wants because he is hungry for conquest. But I guarantee you that if we do only what Saol wants, most of the Vithelegion will not return to the motherland. You must talk some sense into him."

Killian stood before Laken. He picked something out of his nose and flung whatever treasure he'd found. He spoke in a hushed voice, just above a whisper. "There are rumblings, even on our own ship, that the Vithelegion would be better led by you, rather than by Suldas."

Khurt held up his hand, palm facing Killian. "Let that stay as simple rumblings. I do not want what Saol has, nor do I think I am better. The more he hears such things, the more likely he is to find a reason to do something to me. I am sure he already has something in mind for the sparring incident.

Killian rubbed his bald head and smiled as he turned to walk up the steps. "We only just found out about that when we boarded your ship. How much satisfaction did you get out of that, Khurt?"

Khurt followed them up the stairs, with Khenzi right behind him. As Killian turned back to look at him, Khurt smirked and replied, "None whatsoever. It was an unfortunate accident."

They walked along the rails of the deck gingerly and tentatively, as the sea continued its unease. His crewmen set out the planks to connect to Saol's ship once more. Laken and Killian were quite steady men and used to the sea, but they still boarded the planks on hands and knees and slowly crossed to their ship the same way. Khurt looked at the sky all around. They would be caught in this storm for at least a few days.

"ROW, MEN! ROW!" KHURT stood in the middle of the steps and shouted, holding on to a post to keep himself upright. The waves and winds were having their way with the Vithelegion. Several ships had capsized and it seemed that even the upright ships were losing men. The sea had been violent for the past day and a half, and Khurt and a few of his men thought they could see the end of the storm toward the horizon, but their eyes could also have deceived them. The waves were higher that morning, at times sending their ship almost vertical. Khurt knew they would only escape this storm by the grace of Orijin. "Row! In the name of Abram, row!" He had banished Khenzi to their private quarters, but every now and then, Khurt could see the door open just enough for Khenzi's head to poke out, then disappear just as quickly.

Khurt stayed there and directed his men for another two hours. His crew were all strong-willed and devoted to their cause, but Khurt couldn't help but be impressed by how long they rowed without any of them slowing down or asking for a break. All sixty of his rowers had maintained their position since the morning. Other crew members brought provisions for them and even went so far as to feed the rowers while they worked. Not a single man took offense; if anything, it helped to lighten the mood and bring some levity to the situation. At the moment, he'd lost nearly ten men to the sea, and that was only from the ship he was on. The rest of the First Battalion was on another ship, and he had no idea how many on that ship had been lost. This was the last thing that he or his men needed to dwell on.

Despite all the darkness from the perpetual storm clouds, it was not quite dark enough for the sun to have gone down. After another hour of battling the angry sea, the water finally started to calm. Their ship rocked less and less as the day crept into night. By the time darkness had completely set in, all that remained of the storm was a tolerable light rain.

Khurt and the faction of rowers never bothered to leave the lower deck and go up to the main deck. The rowers found a way to stretch themselves out somewhere where they sat. Khurt took the short walk to his personal cabin. The last thing he wanted was to wake Khenzi by moving around in the dark, so he simply laid down right where he was and fell asleep as soon as he closed his eyes.

He awoke the following morning to Khenzi nudging him and gently rocking him back and forth. Khurt opened his eyes to see Khenzi's face inches away from his own, and the sight startled him enough that he hit his head against the floor. "What the…? What is it?"

Khenzi stood. "They just extended the planks. Commander Suldas is boarding our ship." Khenzi pulled Khurt's hand, as if willing Khurt to stand up.

Khurt rose to his feet and realized immediately that his sweaty clothes still stuck to him. "Go find me some kahveh. As strong as you can find. Make some if you cannot find any. Go, hurry!" Khurt scrambled to the dresser to change his shirt and breeches quickly. As he changed, he realized he would have to repaint his skin, as most of the black had washed off in the storm. It was acceptable for some to wash off during a man's weekly bath, but Khurt's was almost completely gone. He only hoped that Saol was in the same state, if he was boarding this early. Khurt hopped to get his second boot on, and as soon as he left his cabin, Saol was walking down the stairs to the lower deck. *Why must always be right there?*

"Go back in. We will talk there." Saol pointed to Khurt's cabin. Khenzi came scuttling back from the other end of the lower deck with a tall mug in hand. As he saw Saol, Khenzi's hands grew shaky and he spilled some of the kahveh on Khurt when passing it. He would not dare let Saol see that it burned, though. He shook it off and wiped his hand on his pants. Saol dismissed Khenzi with a wave of his hand. "Leave us, boy. This conversation must be between men. And I would not want to embarrass your father in front of you."

Khurt nodded to his son to confirm that Khenzi should leave. *Do you mean embarrass, the way I embarrassed you in front of my whole crew? Is that why you are wearing gloves now?* As Khenzi turned toward the stairs to the main deck, Khurt held the cabin door open for Saol to walk in and then shut it behind him. Saol did not bother to sit; he simply turned around to face Khurt as soon as the door was shut. Khurt ensured he spoke first, "To what do I owe the honor, Commander?"

"This notion of mercy is going to be your undoing. Tomorrow I plan to call a meeting with the eight generals to discuss more specific plans of attack. As soon as Ashur is within sight of our ships, our entire army must be ready for conquest. Everitas, it would do you well to remember that we sail to Ashur with the intention of complete annihilation. There will be no converts, prisoners, or trophies. Any man who is found to have captives, whether for information, leverage, or pleasure shall be executed. The Vithelegion has a reputation, and I will not see it diminished in any shape or form."

"So it is safe to assume that Laken and Killian spoke to you and perhaps even partially saw my point of view?"

Saol nodded. "Yes, they reported to me as soon as they returned to my ship. It was...unfortunate that they were both swallowed by the sea during the storm."

Khurt eyed him suspiciously. "So you are so confident, especially after we have lost hundreds of men, no—hundreds of soldiers—that we shall be victorious against all of Ashur?"

Saol shook his fist, "We are the Vithelegion. I am Saol Suldas, son of Savarin Suldas. I do not lose in battle. *We* do not lose in battle."

Khurt took a deep breath. He was sure he was about to insult the man. "Saol, with all due respect, the Vithelegion has always been victorious because we fight intelligently and sensibly. We do not simply rush into war and assume we are better. I truly mean no offense, but it is the very reason why you have a hole through your hand underneath that glove. We must be smarter."

Saol leered at him, "My hand has a hole in it because I held back while you fought with full force. We are not weak, Everitas. We are the greatest army in the world. By the time Ashur will even be able to gather its armies against us, we will likely have conquered half the continent."

"If other generals agree with my point of view, will you at least consider changing your mind?"

"Why do you think I came here now? You will not speak out against me tomorrow. I am warning you now; if you question my authority or leadership, I will revoke your rank as First General and have you placed at the lowest ranking. You have already attempted to embarrass me by cheating at sparring. You wish to speak of mercy? Here is my mercy. You have defied me once. I should have demoted you already, but I am giving you one more chance. If you defy me tomorrow, there will be consequences."

"Saol, there have been multiple rumors of men and women in Ashur who have Darian's own essence manifested into their souls. It is said they can summon magic, just as he could. I am not one to daydream about fantastic stories, but I have heard this enough times that there must be a sliver of truth in it. Now suppose we are lucky enough to attack a city in which these magic wielders are not present. What happens when they do come to protect Ashur? Do you really believe that at that point, we would be better off without prisoners?"

Saol stared at him, as if dumbfounded. "That is your best argument? That you have heard stories of wizards and witches? Your boy has more sense than you do, Everitas." Saol approached him and jabbed at Khurt's shoulder with his good hand. "We shall meet tomorrow morning, an hour after sunrise, on my ship. You will hear the gongs from my deck. Be there, and remember the repercussions for your insubordination. It would be a shame for you to fall so far." With that, Saol left the room.

"Well, shit." Khurt sat on his cot and realized he had forgotten about the mug of kahveh in his hand. He took a sip, glad it was still hot. Most people in Vitheligia mixed milk and sugar into it. Khurt enjoyed it as it naturally was, black and somewhat bitter. There was a nutty flavor to the kahveh that could not be found anywhere else, and adding anything to it diminished that flavor. He drank it slowly and allowed it to clear his mind. Most times, after a conversation with Saol, he wanted to punch something or someone. Slicing Saol's hand no longer made him feel better.

He knew that Saol's plan would backfire on them sooner or later. They could get away with total annihilation if they were only attacking one or two cities. But they were sailing to fight a whole continent and they would all be killed within a week if Saol had his way. Khurt would have to be discreet in seeing how the other generals felt about the plan. Some would follow anything Saol said, but a few of them had strong enough wills to consider other strategies. He would have to plant seeds early on and then steer some of the generals in the right direction.

For the rest of the day, Khurt spent most of his time lost in thought. Even Khenzi left him alone, for the most part. The boy always knew when something was on his mind, and also knew to let him be. Khurt assumed his son was practicing with the sword. By the time nightfall came, Khurt lay in his cot, wide awake, while Khenzi snored softly in the cot next to his. Eventually he drifted off, but sleep came with the frustration of not having a very specific plan of how to get the other generals to change Saol's mind.

"SO NEARLY TWO HUNDRED MEN lost. All valuable lives, but we are still strong enough to achieve our goal. Even without them, we have over two thousand soldiers." Saol stood at the head of the table in the makeshift war room. He looked at each of the eight generals. Khurt didn't deny that the man was a strong leader, but he was too stubborn too often. He was just glad that he'd taken the time to repaint the pale patches of his skin before coming, as all of the others were freshly painted as well. He was still somewhat surprised that Saol hadn't said anything about it the day before.

Ezera, the youngest general and the lowest rank among them, spoke up. "Commander, brethren, there is something I would like to address. I bring this up only to ease my mind, in the hopes that I am not alone in my experience." What Khurt liked most about the young general was that he was outspoken and free with his opinions. "During the storm, as our ships were flailing about in the sea and men were being tossed overboard, I swore that I saw...things...in the water. Most of our men can swim strongly enough to stay adrift, even in rough seas like we faced, but most of the men who I saw in the water were taken under very quickly, and did not resurface. It made no sense to me, except that...something was taking them." Ezera looked around at the others to gauge their reactions.

Khurt had been too focused on the men still on his ship to watch the men in the water. None of his own men had reported any such thing to him though. He glanced over at Khenzi, who stood along the wall with other generals' sons. Khenzi stood at the end, next to Hector's son, Hernan. Salken and Saymon, Saol's sons, stood at another wall, behind their father.

Raffa, Second General, responded before Khurt could. "I was mostly on the lower deck with the oarsmen, but my captains expressed the same concerns. They told me they saw men scream and get sucked under in an instant. I let them tell me their stories and maintained my skepticism, but perhaps there is something to it."

Saol put a hand up to stop any other responses. "We are in the middle of the ocean with no land in sight. It should be no surprise that there are predatory creatures in the waters. Even without them, it would have been impossible to save many of those men, given how violent the water was. There is no reason to still fear whatever it was."

Ezera spoke up to defend his concern. "I agree, Commander, that it is no surprise for these creatures to be there, but we are an enormous fleet with weeks left to reach our destination. What if these things choose to follow us or actually attack us?"

Khurt cut in this time, hoping to keep Saol's patience from truncating. "Ezera, there is nothing we can do in any scenario, if sea creatures decide to attack us. All we can do is continue our course and plan our attack. If it eases your mind, we can have scouts on each ship tracking the waters for any signs of large creatures." With that, Ezera nodded.

"Thank you, Khurt," Saol glanced at him and then looked around at the others. "Now let us focus on strategy. We are several weeks away from Ashur, barring any more setbacks. Once we are close enough to its shores, we will determine which city to attack first. We will start with something small, as it will attract less attention and it will ease us into battle, as our soldiers will no doubt still be weary from being at sea for so long. After we take the first city, we will reassess, and either go full force to a bigger target, or split our army and attack on multiple fronts."

Davala, the Sixth General, cut in. Khurt found his face to be the most daunting when painted, as Davala had the most pigment-affected face, and once the black was applied, Davala simply looked terrifying. "Commander, how will we prevent them from preparing for us? Do we know how militant these nations are? What if they have sentries guarding their shores, or at the walls of their cities? We may not have the element of surprise."

Saol nodded in agreement and placed both of his gloved hands down on the high table. "We will send small scout boats out in advance to check for that. Regardless, we will hold our ships far from the shores until nightfall, then advance. We will use no fire signals or gongs for commands once we are close to the shores."

Davala agreed. "Yes. Perhaps we should all be here before that night, so we all know exactly what to do when the time comes." All of the other generals voiced their agreement to the idea. Khurt was wondering if any of them would mention or ask about Saol's intentions regarding prisoners. It would be awkward to ask about it arbitrarily.

Just as Khurt was thinking it, Saol brought it up, as if Saol could read his thoughts. "There has been a certain topic of contention that I would like to make sure everyone is clear upon. I bring this up now so that if you do not agree, you have months to come to terms with it." He looked straight at Khurt, and then around at the others. "Once our war begins, we kill every Ashurian in sight. No prisoners. I do not care if they are children, elders, men, or women. We leave no one behind to potentially retaliate. These people are all Darian worshippers. They honor a man who let his friends Abram and Lionel die while he ran away. He sacrificed thousands of people simply because he could not kill Jahmash. Ashurians are all destined to rot in Opprobrium, so we shall send them all there ourselves."

Silence overtook the room. Khurt looked around at the other generals. Raffa and Thiel nodded curtly in agreement, while Hector, Davala, and Ezera looked as if they were stifling a response. Raiza and Bragha simply looked down at the table with blank stares. *Well, this is it. Now I see how they all really feel.* "Forgive me, Commander, for questioning your authority. I understand your reasoning, but I have a question. What danger would there be in imprisoning them and allowing an opportunity to convert to our belief system?"

Saol smirked and folded his arms. "Khurt, you are a sensible man, or at least I thought so up to this point. If you were taken prisoner in war and your captors asked you to simply forget all of your beliefs and adopt theirs, would you?"

Khurt couldn't tell if he wanted to punch his palm or Saol's face more. He should have been prepared for that argument. He nodded for a moment to regroup. "I see what you mean, but I mean this more for the children. Why kill innocents when we can mold them to follow our way? Young minds are malleable and impressionable. We can teach them the right way without them even posing an argument." Some of the other generals glanced at Khurt with raised brows.

Saol stopped any chance at one of them intervening. "And did you not say the other day that some of these Ashurians have magical powers? What happens when these children grow up with *dangerous magic* and realize they are different? What will you tell them then? How will you explain their lack of parents and people who look like them?"

Khurt grew even more frustrated, "I…"

Saol cut him off, "No. That is the end of this insubordination. I warned you about your dissention and what would happen for it. Raffa, you are now my First General. The rest of you have officially been ranked up and General Everitas, you are hereby demoted to Eighth General. You dare argue about mercy when I choose to protect our people. Enough. If you and your son would rather be cowards, then we can send you back to Vitheligia and our wives and daughters can protect you."

Salken chimed in, "Cowards."

Saol grinned, "Tell me. Since you are such a coward, should we perhaps just kill you and then educate your son on the *right* way? His mind *is* young, malleable, impressionable. Generals, are all of your sons aware of how big a coward Khurt Everitas is? Khenzi might be better off with us than his own father."

Before Khurt could respond, Khenzi stepped away from the wall and shouted, "Generals, are all of you and your sons aware of why Commander Suldas is wearing gloves? He challenged my father to spar with swords, and within minutes, my father sliced a hole through the Commander's sword hand. Perhaps my father should have shown *him* mercy." Khurt stifled a smile.

Salken and Saymon immediately dashed toward Khenzi. But before Khenzi or Khurt could make a move, two generals' sons, Hernan and Darvel, stepped in front of Khenzi. Hernan, Hector's son, was a year older than Saymon, Saol's eldest. He was slightly taller than Saymon and wider in the shoulder. Darvel, Davala's son, was the oldest child in the room. He had just reached his sixteenth year before the Vithelegion sailed off, and he towered above Suldas's sons. This would not be a fight that Salken and Saymon would win. Darvel spoke up, his voice already deep like his father's. "We do not intend to fight you. We are only protecting Khenzi. It would be rather unfair for both of you, who are each much bigger than him, to physically attack him. All he did was speak the truth. Unless either of you has a truth to speak in response, I suggest you go back to where you were standing."

Saymon looked at Khenzi, rather than Darvel, "Here's a truth, Khenzi. The next time I see you without someone else to fight your battles, I will put a hole through *your* pathetic little sword hand." He and Salken turned and walked back to their father.

Saol put his hands up to quiet everyone down. "Everyone go back to your ships. Our meeting is finished. Make sure that all of your men are made aware of your promotions, and of Eighth General Everitas's demotion. We will meet again in one week." Khurt was not surprised that none of the other generals said a word. What was surprising was that Darvel patted Khenzi's shoulder, and then Khurt's, before he left the room. Saol stopped Khurt before he left, and then spoke once the other generals were gone. "Everitas, we still have months left before this war begins. It would be *unfortunate* if anything should happen to you or your son before you had a chance to die in battle. Do your best to shut up for the rest of this journey." His sons now stood at his side, and both grinned widely.

Khurt looked Saol in the eye, "If I even notice a questionable scratch on Khenzi, you will not have to worry about that wound closing up, Saol, because I will slice your hand off completely." He then looked at Salken and Saymon, "And your sons' hands as well." He grasped Khenzi by the shoulder and left the war room without waiting for a response.

CHAPTER 6
CONSCIOUSNESS

From **The Book of Orijin,** **Verse Two Hundred Ninety**
O Chosen Ones, We have chosen you to bear the Mark because you are the best of humanity.
You will make mistakes. You will have flaws.
But your Marks will signify you as examples for mankind.
Even at your lowest, remember your potential.

DESMOND OPENED HIS EYES again and turned on his side to lean over the bed. He vomited, hoping the bucket was where he expected it to be. He'd lost count how many times it had happened over the course of the night. He was sure it had been at least one hundred times in the week since he and Maximilian found themselves in Gangjeon. Most surprising was that he even had anything to throw up, as he'd only drank water for the past several hours.

Maximilian lay in the bed next to him, but the older man's wounds were more serious than Desmond's. Maximillian was recovering from several arrow wounds, and the nurses believed that there might be some internal issues as well, such as bruising or bleeding. They were keeping Maximillian sedated most of the time by forcing him to drink pepper tea every time he woke up. Usually, before the Maven could complain about the taste, he was already sleeping again. Desmond seriously hoped the nurses didn't decide he needed to be sedated as well. Pepper tea was extremely deceiving in its name. It was made by crushing pepper flies and boiling them in water, then steeping out any of the solids that remained. In order for it to be effective, it had to be ingested just like that, one could not mask the flavor with sugar or milk or lemon. When a person woke up after being sedated with pepper tea, the taste remained in the mouth for hours. Desmond wondered how long Maximillian would be tasting it once he was allowed to stay awake.

For Desmond himself, the injuries were far less visceral. Ever since releasing his manifestation at the House of Darian, when Maximillian had boosted his manifestation exponentially in order to keep the building standing, he'd longed to feel all of that power again. He hadn't even considered trying to levitate anything ever since. It started as a mild longing to hold it again, along with the exhaustion of using all that energy and then still being part of the battle. By the time he and Maximillian had been found in Gangjeon and taken to the infirmary, the headaches were intense and depriving him of sleep. The nurses were hesitant to give him any remedy for it, fearing he might become dependent on something else. For the last two or three days, he could not be completely sure since he wasn't really sleeping, Desmond's body would go into trembling fits every now and then. When he could manage to be still, the nausea was usually there, whether or not he ate anything. The worst part of it all was that Badalao had tried to talk to him a few times through their mental connection, but Desmond was incapable of holding a conversation. Even if he could, he knew he did not want to explain to Badalao what he was dealing with.

For days now, Desmond hadn't left the bed. Even the thought of sitting up made him more nauseous. His attendants spoon-fed him broths and even turned him over when he needed to urinate, so that he could use a bedpan. His life for the better part of a week was essentially to lie in pain, and every now and then someone would feed fluids into him, only for them to have to help him pee it out. As long as Badalao didn't enter his mind, these details would not be shared with his friends. He hadn't caught any of the attendants' names since he'd been there, but Desmond was aware that there were four of them tending to him and Maximillian. Two were men and two were women, and lately it seemed like only one of the men was looking after him, while the other three focused on Maximillian. Perhaps Maximillian needed more help than he did, but the man who cared for Desmond lately was never gentle or patient. It seemed as if each day, the man's patience for Desmond to get better grew shorter.

While he normally had trouble controlling his temper when healthy, being in this state shortened it even more. He lay on his side, facing Maximillian, who looked to be stirring as the effects of the pepper tea wore off from the previous night. He could see Maximillian's eyes flitting around, trying to make sense of their surroundings. Maximillian turned his head ever so slightly toward Desmond, likely the only movement he could manage while lying on his back. Desmond looked back at him and gave a nod. "You look the way I feel." Maximillian apparently had enough energy for sass, as he rolled his eyes at Desmond.

Just as Desmond started to entertain the thought that a good mood might be possible, his attendant returned with a bowl of broth. The tall, slender man put the bowl to Desmond's mouth without any warning, causing Desmond to cough up the hot liquid, spilling it all over himself and the bed. He summoned all of his strength, grabbed the man by the yellow apron, and pulled him down so that his head was tucked in Desmond's armpit, and the rest of the soup spilled on the floor. Desmond wrapped his left arm around the man's head and squeezed. He was somewhat taken aback. The man's hair smelled fragrant, of berries and perhaps other fruits. It only made it all the more pleasant for Desmond to maintain the headlock. The man flailed and struggled and convulsed until he managed to pull Desmond off the bed. The two of them crashed to the floor, with Desmond on top of the man. He barely noticed the soft touch on his shoulder but knew within moments that the hand belonged to Maximillian, as all of the energy he had drained and his body went limp. A moment later, his consciousness escaped him as well.

DESMOND WOKE UP TO Maximillian sitting at the side of his own bed, staring at him. His body was devoid of energy and he could barely move. He turned his head as much as he could toward Maximillian, and groaned, "Pepper tea?"

Maximillian chuckled, somewhat laboring. His voice was raspy and soft. "Not quite. Me. I've been stealing your energy for a few days now. You've been sleeping for a little over three days." Desmond blinked in disbelief. "You heard me correctly, three days. I needed the energy more than you did, and it kept you from attacking anyone. Not only have I been able to sit up, but the extra energy has helped with healing as well. Much of my swelling has gone down. It is likely that we will only need to continue this for two or three more days in order for me to be able to get up and around on my own."

"But..."

"No more talking. I cannot speak for very long." Maximillian leaned over and grasped Desmond's arm. At first Desmond thought the man was trying to comfort him, as he was too tired to process anything completely. By the time he realized what Maximillian was doing, his eyes were shutting and he was asleep again.

Desmond awoke several times over the next two days, but each time he was barely aware of his surroundings, beyond the fact that he was still in the same bed. On one or two of those occasions, he thought he'd heard Maximillian talking to someone in the next bed, and perhaps even sounds like moans or groans. Desmond barely trusted his senses, given the exhaustion and pain of the withdrawal he was feeling, but he had a strange premonition that what he heard was Maximillian with another man. Still, he knew better than to trust anything he saw, heard, or felt. He might be dreaming. Thinking about it all tired Desmond out enough that he fell back asleep for the rest of the night. He woke up the following morning to Maximillian once again grasping him, this time his shin. His leg jerked at the sight of Maximillian's hand, combined with the thought of Maximillian with another man.

Maximillian looked at him curiously. "Oh, I apologize. Do you not want the energy I am giving you? I thought that, now that I am much better from taking your energy, I could start giving it back to you, provided that you do not fight anyone."

"No, it's not that. Sorry, I'm still feelin' a bit nauseous. Haven't gotten myself back ta feelin' right just yet."

Maximillian placed his hand back on Desmond's shin. "I am almost done anyway. But you need to start eating, even if you are nauseous. It will help the nausea go away, having food in your belly. I know you have been sleeping or close enough to it for most the time that we have been in Gangjeon, but have you heard anything from Lao at all about the fate of the others? It is important to know if there are still others out there."

Desmond clasped his hands over his chest and stared at the ceiling. "I believe Lao has been tryin' ta contact me. I thought I heard him say 'Tower' when he was in my head."

Maximillian nodded, "That would make sense. Right now, the Tower of the Blind is the safest place for us to be, especially if we have numbers. Should I assume then, that you do not know who else managed to survive?"

"Yer assumption is correct. I haven't even responded ta Lao. Only thing I know is he's with Sindha. So there's at least four o' us."

"There are more. There must be. Savaiyon evacuated more of us, and he would only have put Descendants in safe places. Use this day to get yourself ready. We will rest in Gangjeon for one more night, and in the morning, we shall go to the Tower. Gangjeon is the closest city to it, so it will not take long. The travel will not tire us, and we can rest again once we get there. Have you ever been there?"

Desmond glanced at him, "No. We had a resident Blind Man in Vandenar. Never had a need ta go there. I'm not one ta really care about destiny. What happens will happen."

Maximillian nodded. "Very well. Regardless, the Augurs are quite hospitable. It is the one place in Ashur you can assure that you will not be judged, no matter your background. They do not take sides. And you are required to leave your weapons with them."

Desmond smiled. "So how do they manage our manifestations?"

Maximillian rolled his eyes, "Not all manifestations are weapons. But all are blessings from the Orijin. Besides, every servant there is trained by the Anonymi. Any one of them could kill us in our sleep without disturbing a fly. People do not go there to cause trouble. Did you not grow up in Mireya? How is it that you know so little about the Tower, even if you have never been there?"

"Not everyone is as privileged as ya Cerysians," Desmond eyed Maximillian sideways. "I spent most o' my life tendin' ta elephants, butcherin' elephants, or preparin' fer the elephants ta walk through the streets o' Vandenar. Never had ta worry about the Tower. An' I know about the servants an' the Anonymi trainin'. My cousin helps the Blind

Man who lives in Vandenar. When he's a bit older, I plan ta bring him ta Fangh-Haan fer trainin'. He'll be safe there, an' have a comfortable life."

"Orphan?"

Desmond nodded, "Farco's parents were killed on the Way o' Sunsets, ridin' down ta Khiry. Damn Vermillion thought they were hidin' Descendants. Only reason Farco wasn't with 'em was because I told 'em to let 'im stay with me so I could take 'im fishin'. Inadvertently saved the kid's life."

Maximillian shrugged his shoulders and then leaned forward. "Not all Cerysians support our king. We have no say in his doings. He certainly cares not for the counsel of others. When his own son and heir flees to the House of Darian for refuge, is there any other proof needed that he is a poor ruler?"

Desmond perked up at Maximillian's words. "What do ya mean? Garrison Brighton actually came ta us askin' fer asylum?"

"I thought that to be common knowledge in the House. Was it not?"

"No. Most o' us thought he was captured, or maybe chased out o' Cerysia. We had no idea he *chose* ta come ta the House. But he killed so many Descendants. Would Garrison be that daft ta think we would happily welcome him in an' act like his brothers?"

"So it seems. As soon as he appeared through the touch portal, he was begging for acceptance and mercy. Imagine that. How bad must things be in Alvadon, that the prince who once hunted and killed Descendants at his father's orders, thought his life would be better in the very home of the people he once terrorized?"

"Didn't he spend the whole time in the dungeons? Were there ever any plans ta release him? Give him a chance at redemption?"

"Marlowe did the merciful thing of keeping him in the cell. His uncle also made regular visits to the dungeon to make sure Garrison was safe. Can you imagine what would have happened to him if he was not protected by those bars? Why do you think only certain people were given dungeon duty? Baltaszar? That boy knew so little of Ashur that he likely did not even know a Prince Garrison *existed*."

"Yer right. I don't know if I woulda killed 'im, but I wouldn'ta stopped someone else from doin' it if I saw it happenin'."

Maximillian looked at him in the eye, "Good. Then you would not have a problem if it happened to his father, then?"

Desmond looked at him sideways. "What exactly do ya mean? You plannin' ta kill the king?"

Maximillian shrugged again, "Not me specifically. But it *is* going to happen, as soon as it *can* happen."

"Obviously ya need ta explain yerself."

"I assumed I would have to. Just know that if there was still a House of Darian full of Descendants I would not be so free with telling you. However, our survival is paramount, and the very fact that we were attacked means that Jahmash's return is not far off. Ashur needs to be defended and it needs as many resources as possible, as quickly as possible."

"Right, right, enough with the cautionary introduction. Just tell me already."

Maximillian smirked at him. "Once we regroup with the others, assuming Savaiyon and Vasher are alive and well, they will likely share this information anyway. Marlowe tasked the two of them with meeting with the Anonymi to arrange an alliance ahead of Jahmash's return. Marlowe wanted to affirm that we would have capable allies fighting alongside us, as he obviously would not rely on the Vermillion. However, the Anonymi did not trust Marlowe to hold up his side of an agreement, given how Marlowe was notorious for avoiding conflict and violence. The Anonymi told Vasher that the Descendants must kill King Edmund before they would agree to any alliance with us."

Desmond shot Maximillian a suspicious glance. "Why? An' how would ya know this? Yer an Anonymi in secret?"

"Vasher and Savaiyon were the ones who met with them. Savaiyon tends to confide in me a great deal."

"Fine, but why? Why kill the king?"

"The Anonymi are secretive and follow their own whims, so I could not tell you why they specifically want us to kill the king. Perhaps they want to see that we can stand up for ourselves against the man who has persecuted us so severely. What I *do* know, though, is that they are lethal. I would much rather fight alongside the Anonymi than the Vermillion. But imagine if we could somehow get the other Descendants to forgive Prince Garrison? We could kill the king and then have Garrison lead the Vermillion, making them loyal to us. Vermillion, Descendants, and Anonymi all working together against Jahmash and his armies. We would stand a chance."

"Ya talk like killin' the king will be easy. Like we can just walk inta the castle an' stab him an' leave, an' everyone will just applaud fer us once it's done."

Maximillian cut him off. "No, it will not be easy. But you underestimate how many people are loyal to Edmund simply because he is the king. As soon as that man is dead, Ashur will be a much different place. Our own lives as Descendants will be markedly easier."

"An' why do ya want this so bad? I don't like him at all, but it almost sounds like ya want ta kill him yerself."

Maximillian took a deep breath. "Imagine Ashur with an open-minded king, Desmond. Imagine what this world could be, could have been, under the rule of someone who appreciated Descendants. Imagine how different your own life would have been if you did not have to live your life in hiding. If we could come and go from the House of Darian whenever we pleased, without fearing for our lives.

"I was too young when I stood up to my father's abuse of my mother and sister. My manifestation grew out of protecting my family *from* my family. There should be no place in this world for bloodying up your wife and children. Yet, when I stopped my father from bludgeoning them, I was branded a criminal for developing a manifestation. My father kept his life and his freedom, while I was exiled and forced to abandon my family."

"Yer still talkin' about killin' the most powerful man in all o' Ashur. We don't even know how many o' us are left, an' ya think ya can rally Ashur ta kill," Desmond lowered his voice, "ta kill the king? People have been indoctrinated ta hate us fer decades now. That won't change overnight when Edmund dies."

Maximillian stood up, "But it *will* change eventually. Maybe not in a year, but maybe in a generation. It would give hope for our children."

Desmond paused for a moment at Maximillian's mention of children, then disregarded the notion that popped in his head. "I still have my reservations, but yer the expert, Maven. So the Anonymi, their offer is that simple? Kill the king an' they'll fight alongside o' us?"

Maximillian sat back down, looking somewhat defeated. He paused for a moment, then spoke. "I do not know. That is what Savaiyon shared with me. I believe the only condition is that Edmund's death must be by our hands."

Desmond took notice of Maximillian's hesitation, but knew he would get nothing else out of the man. It was clear that the golden-skinned Cerysian was holding some information back. Even with the House of Darian now destroyed, Maximillian was a Maven and Desmond could not make demands of him. He wondered what Maximillian wasn't telling him. Whatever it was, it was even bigger than having to kill Edmund, and Desmond felt uneasy at that prospect. Still, he couldn't help but push back, even a little bit. "I suppose I'll have ta take ya at yer word, then."

Maximillian eyed him curiously. "What is that supposed to mean?"

Desmond cracked his knuckles. *Too late ta shy away now.* "Yer obviously keepin' somethin' ta yerself. Ya hesitated so long just now that I coulda taken a nap in that time. Ya know more than yer lettin' on."

"You are free to believe what you would like to believe, Desmond."

Desmond raised his voice, "Don't ya dare talk down ta me. Ya may be a Maven an' I may be younger than ya, but I'm not stupid. I know there's more ta what yer sayin. I also know ya think too much o' yerself ta share it with me. Maybe ya need ta take a good look at yerself. Yer nobody in this world, just like me. Ya step foot in the wrong city, on the wrong road, an' they'll kill ya as easily an' quickly as they'd kill me. So don't ya think fer a second that yer better than me. Yer manifestation woulda meant nothing when the House was attacked if it wasn't fer me. We *both* kept the House up together, an' now I'm sufferin' because o' yer manifestation. Yer not better than me, Maximillian. Yer not above me. Yer not noble. Ya sneakily lay with other men while I'm sleepin' so ya think nobody notices."

Maximillian glared at him. "Is *that* what this is about? You are concerned about who I share my bed with?"

"I'm not *concerned*."

"No, it is my turn to lecture you now, boy. I am a grown man and I make my own decisions. Who I lay with and who I find comfort with are none of your business. You want to lecture me about not thinking that I am better, well then don't you dare judge me for my choices and lifestyle. I have been there for any and every Descendant in the House of Darian who has needed help or guidance. I have always been one of the few Mavens that could be confided in or relied on not to judge anyone. And you. You have known me for nearly two years and you had no issue with me in all that time. You want to know what everyone thought of you? You care so much about the man in my bed, yet when you and Badalao arrived at the House, you were so inseparable that most thought *you* two were sharing a bed regularly. For how many girls Lao laid with, it caused most people to believe even more strongly that you two were lovers and that he was covering it up."

Desmond reddened. "I..."

"Shut up, boy. Maybe you *do* fancy men and get angry because you have not come to terms with it. Maybe it is you that you are angry at, and not me." Desmond clenched his fist and lunged toward Maximillian and swung at the man. Maximillian dodged the punch easily, causing Desmond to land on the floor, face first, his choppy black hair covering his eyes. Maximillian stood up and placed his boot firmly on top of Desmond's neck. The man then crouched down and grasped Desmond's arm. Within moments, Desmond was devoid of any strength, and could barely move. Maximillian released his boot from Desmond's neck, but before Desmond could process any feeling of relief, that same boot crashed into his ribs. He blacked out again as Maximillian left the room.

FOR THE FIRST TIME SINCE coming to Gangjeon, Desmond left the infirmary room and tried to allow himself some levity. He walked gingerly to the inn across the street, the Valiant Rider, his ribs still aching. As he walked slowly, hand to his ribs, Desmond couldn't decide whether he was actually mad at Maximillian for their last argument. Luckily the inn was so close to the infirmary, he wouldn't have to think about Maximillian for very long. He would enjoy a nice glass of ale and perhaps a nice hot meal, something he could actually chew and taste.

Desmond crossed the street slowly. It was still somewhat early in the morning, and the streets weren't bustling, so he could take his time without being in someone's way. He'd awoken on the floor, in the same position he'd been in when he blacked out. The only difference was that a bowl of broth was set next to his head. *It was probably that stupid man who was always rude ta me.* He'd almost knocked it over in the process of waking up and getting to his feet.

He reached the entrance to the red building, but it took more strength than he expected to open the heavy doors. The large room seemed even more spacious, given how empty it was. Only a few patrons sat here and there. Desmond found a table close to the door and sat so he could still see most of the room. Even with the place so empty, he wanted to be able to see as much of the comings and goings as possible, especially if Maximillian happened to wander in. He didn't know what he would do if the man did come in, but Desmond told himself that he wanted to talk to Maximillian if the opportunity presented itself.

He'd gotten so distracted by the thought of Maximillian, that he didn't notice the barmaid walk up to him. "Mornin' handsome. Steak or stew? Ya look like ya could use some meat on yer bones. Both'll fill ya up right." The short woman was older, likely the wife of the inn owner, but still had her looks enough with her that she could effectively flirt with young men Desmond's age.

He grinned at her, "Ya got any eggs? If so, I'll take the steak."

"I can ask 'em ta cook ya some eggs, since it's still early. Ya want yer elephant steak or regular?"

Desmond raised an eyebrow, "How'd ya know I'm from Vandenar? Our accent's the same."

She nodded to his head. "Choppy hair like that? Ya got ta be from Vandenar."

"Fine then, elephant it is. Haven't had a good homestyle steak in a while. Let's see if ya make it as good as we do. An' some ale please. Might as well bring two mugs now. First one'll be done by the time ya walk away."

She winked and left. Desmond looked around. There were four other people, each sitting alone, scattered around the room. What caught his eye was a golden-haired girl sitting on the other side of the room. She sat facing him, but her head was down, focused on her plate, as she picked at whatever was left of her meal. Desmond glanced away before he got caught staring. He couldn't tell if it was a shadow, but he was almost certain there was a black line on her face. *There's no way she's Mireyan. Skin's too fair ta be Markosi. Maybe Galicean? An' she definitely wasn't at the House o' Darian. Wonder what her story is.* The barmaid returned with his mugs of ale and he fished out a few coins to hand to her. As soon as she turned to leave, he chugged down the first mug and set it back on the table. Desmond didn't want to set it too hard that the barmaid turned around to take it.

He moved the full mug to the side and concentrated on the empty one, while opening himself up to his manifestation. He hadn't used it since the battle at the House of Darian. Part of the reason was the lack of a need to, but deep down, Desmond knew it was fear more than anything else. He hadn't even let the melody flow through his veins, scared that he might like it too much and never let go. Even at this point, he was unsure if it was the best thing to do, but he knew the longer he put it off, the harder it would be to access his manifestation.

Back at the House, when they'd had the luxury of leisure time, Baltaszar had mentioned to him how he didn't fully know how to use his manifestation for a while. He'd told Desmond and some of the others how he and Horatio got caught riding on the Way of Sunsets and had to fight off some of the Vermillion soldiers. Baltaszar had made it completely clear that he froze from not knowing how to use his manifestation in the heat of the moment, as he had barely understood his powers and wasn't used to using them at will. As a result, an arrow had impaled his leg and Horatio had to fight off all of the soldiers on his own.

Desmond panicked at the thought of not being able to use his manifestation. He would not let himself forget the feeling of the melody in his veins, or of wielding his manifestation. There would be many more fights to fight and battles to win, and he could not afford to turn back into a regular man while his friends all sacrificed themselves. *Tasz. I wonder where he is. I hope he's alive. Marlowe. That stupid old man didn't even let him stay at the House long enough ta defend it. Imagine what we coulda done with fire.*

The barmaid set Desmond's food down on the table. She motioned to take the empty mug, but Desmond stopped her. "Leave that here fer a little while. I want ta try somethin' with it."

The woman eyed him quizzically. "Fine. But ya hurt anyone with it, an' we'll hurt ya back. Don't care if yer a Descendant."

Desmond nodded, "Don't worry, I don't need it fer anythin' like that."

"Workin' up yer courage fer *her* then?" The woman nodded to the other side of the room, "She's been watchin' ya on an' off since ya sat down." She left Desmond's table before he could ask for details.

Desmond looked over at the girl on the other side of the room. This time her head was up, and she was looking at something to her right, which put her Descendant's mark in plain view. The girl was beautiful, but Desmond found it difficult to put an age to her face. *She could just as easily be younger or older than me. Either way, old enough fer the House o' Darian. Wonder why she never made it there. Either way, Lao woulda got ta her first an' I'd never have a chance.* He looked back at his plate. *Then again, Lao isn't here now. There's nothin' in the way.* He dug into his steak and eggs, and every now and then, glanced at the girl to see if she was looking at him. Finally, as he was just about finishing up, she looked Desmond right in the eyes. He froze for a split second, then looked back at her and nodded his head for her to come over to his table. She half-smiled and looked down at her table, as if she was deciding whether or not to actually get up.

After a few moments, the girl stood and walked over. Desmond felt somewhat relieved that she waited, as it gave him time to finish chewing and drink more ale to get a little more courage. She sat down across from Desmond and looked at him sheepishly. "Hi."

"Hey. I'm Desmond. Ya don't have ta be shy. By the looks of ya, yer a far way from home?"

She clasped her hands on the table. "My name is...Schatza. It's nice to meet you, Desmond. I don't know too many Descendants, so I apologize for staring, if it made you uncomfortable. I don't really have a place to call 'home', and I was hoping to reach the House of Darian, but we both know that can't happen now. So I'm just trying to stay in places where people like us aren't being hunted and killed. Were you there? How did you manage to survive?"

Desmond was about to respond, when a voice popped into his head. *'Desmond, where are you? Are you safe? I've been trying to find you for days now. I know you're alive; otherwise I would not be able to do this, so please respond to me with something. Anything.'*

The surprise and discomfort must have traveled to Desmond's face, as Schatza responded to his expression. "I apologize, Desmond. I meant no offense. I hope that was not too forward."

Desmond recomposed himself. "No, it wasn't about ya. Somethin'...popped inta my head an' I wasn't expectin' it. Sorry. Mireya's the right place ta be if ya ain't got a home. Right side o' the world. That's why I'm here now. Those o' us who survived the attack on the House are all split up now. We had ta escape before we were all killed. One o' the Mavens, Savaiyon, he can create gateways outta thin air. He's the one who got us all out. I think he put us all in places where we'd be safe. I was recoverin' across the street fer the past week or so." Desmond realized then that he'd just exposed Savaiyon. It was frowned upon amongst Descendants to discuss the manifestations of others. He would have to be more careful.

Schatza's interest seemed to pique. She talked a little more excitedly, but still softly. "Oh wow, you were injured? It must have been such a battle. But I'm so glad that some of you were strong enough and brave enough to have survived. It's nice to not be the only Descendant around. Do you know where the other survivors are?"

Desmond cocked his head slightly. Something about her tone seemed...forced. "They could be anywhere. Only thing I'm sure o' is that they're all somewhere safe."

Schatza nodded, "Are you from here? Is that why you were sent to Gangjeon?"

"Nah, I'm from Vandenar. Same nation, different city. Lots o' similarities, though."

"Are you going back there once you leave Gangjeon?"

The thought of Maximillian popped into his head. "No, I am plannin' ta go ta the Tower o' the Blind. It's the safest place fer a Descendant right now. An' seein' as how there aren't much o' us left, we won't be much o' an imposition. Seems like that'd be the best place fer ya ta go, too. If ye want ta join me, it's fine. Probably safer ta not travel alone anyway."

Schatza bit her lip for a moment. "I'm not sure. I don't know if that is what's best for me. I've found that I'm much better off when I am on my own. More people means more opinions, more differences, and definitely more attention. I would rather follow my own choices and trust myself to survive."

Desmond shook his head in disagreement. "Yer a Descendant. There's no such thing as better off alone. No matter what yer manifestation is, if ya come across the Vermillion on yer own, eventually they can overpower ya. At least with more o' us by yer side, ya stand a chance."

She looked him dead in the eye, unapologetically. "Not so long ago, I was traveling with three other Descendants, one of them my little sister, Melina. We were hunted down by Prince Garrison Brighton's personal battalion, and I watched them behead my sister right in front of me, powerless to do anything, because not one single person in the crowd who surrounded us thought to put a stop to publicly murdering a little girl. You talk about safety in numbers, and I assure you, Desmond, that Ashur does not give a shit about us, whether we travel as an army or as one. At least by myself, I can hide. I can come and go with little suspicion."

Well, congrats Des. Ya made her hate ya an' there's no fixin' it now. He chugged down the rest of his ale. "Sorry. I'm sorry fer bein' so insensitive. Yer right, it *is* dangerous, no matter how we travel. But from here, we could lit'rally swim ta the Tower o' the Blind if we wanted ta. No armies ta get in our way. An' once yer there, there'll be no trouble. Anyone who wishes ta step foot inside the Tower must submit their weapons. An' if they try ta start trouble, all the servants in the Tower are trained by the Anonymi. There's no gettin' past that. Look, I'll be honest with ya, because I'd hate ta see ya get hurt or killed on yer own. The plan is fer survivors o' the House o' Darian ta regroup at the Tower. No idea what we do from there, but whether we leave or stay there fer a while, ye can decide what's best fer ya. Ye can stay at the Tower if ya want, an' be safe there. No matter what, it's the safest place fer ya ta go."

Schatza bit her lip again and looked down at her hands, still clasped atop the table. Desmond could easily see that this was a difficult decision for her. For whatever reason, she didn't trust too many others, not even Descendants. *Then again, if Garrison Brighton killed my sister right in front o' me, I'd have trouble trustin' Descendants, too. Damn that coward; what a traitor ta his own kind.* Schatza stood up across from him. "I'm going to go back to my table to think about it. As early as it is, I think I might think more clearly with some wine and time to be alone with my thoughts. Desmond, if you leave here before I do, come and talk to me. I'll give you an answer either way." She walked away and uttered a few words to the barmaid, likely asking for some wine.

Desmond watched her walk back to her table and took a deep breath. The barmaid looked at him and shrugged her shoulders. He looked back at his table and realized that the two mugs were still there. He opened himself to his manifestation and let the melody sing through his veins. It instantly reminded him of all the power he'd wielded while the House was under attack. Desmond pushed the memory out of his mind and focused only on the mugs in front of him. *One at a time. Don't overwhelm yourself.* He put his attention to the mug closest to him and concentrated, emptying his mind of everything else. He relaxed a little more and increased his focus, making the glass mug the only thing that mattered. After a few seconds, the mug lifted off the table an inch or so and hovered in place. Desmond smiled, allowing the small achievement to be a full achievement. He honed in again, lifting the mug higher in the air, nearly a foot above the table. Feeling a little more confident, Desmond allowed himself to focus on the second mug as well. He moved it next to the first one but started to feel slightly unsteady. The mugs both wobbled in the air as Desmond struggled to maintain his composure. He forced himself to focus on the mugs with all of his mind and felt a trickle flow from his nose.

Beads of sweat formed on his forehead, but Desmond refused to set the mugs down, partly out of stubbornness, and partly out of fear of breaking them. He knew at this point that others must be watching, even if the room was mostly empty. It added pressure to his focus, but he had to prove to himself and to others that he could handle this. Desmond steeled his resolve and moved the mugs higher into the air.

The barmaid commented from the kitchen door, "Remember what I said, ya break 'em, yer outta here." The comment was more promise than threat, but it was enough to throw off Desmond's focus. One mug fell straight down and shattered on the tabletop, sending a few glass shards into Desmond's face. In turning away from the pain, the other mug shot straight up and crashed against the ceiling, and its shattering caused a rainfall of glass in the room.

The barmaid yelled something into the kitchen and four men in aprons came running out. They pulled Desmond from his seat and two of them held his arms behind his back, while a third ripped his coin purse from his waist and handed it to the woman. Even if at full strength, Desmond knew he could not fight these men. The barmaid fished through it, took enough coin to satisfy herself, and then cocked her head for them to follow her. She walked out of the inn and into the dirt road, then tossed the coin purse into the middle of the road, uncaring of where it landed or whether it hit anyone. She nodded once more to the men holding Desmond and said to him, "I told ya. I told ya not ta be stupid. People're afraid enough of travelin' that we don't get many visitors here. We can't afford ta have ya breakin' our things. I took only what ya owed me. Don't come back. Ever." The four men lifted Desmond and tossed him toward his coin purse, then walked away as he landed with a thud next to his money.

Good thing the infirmary isn't far. He'd landed on his chest, elbows, and knees, and was sure that he'd gotten some scrapes upon landing. His chin felt a bit hot as well, and as he touched it, felt the tiny bits of rock mixed in with his blood and skin. Desmond pushed himself up to his hands and knees, sending streaks of pain into his ribs and making him think twice about standing up right away. He grabbed his coin purse and fastened it back to his waist. He'd assumed the street was so empty because it was early, but he hadn't even considered the notion that people didn't have much of a reason to be in Gangjeon, unless they were going to the Tower of the Blind.

Desmond put one foot on the ground and tried to push himself up to stand, but the strain on his ribs was too much. He breathed deeply for several moments, still unsure of whether he'd be able to do a simple thing like stand up. As he knelt there and contemplated his current predicament, he felt something loop through his right underarm and tug at him from above. He turned to look up and jumped at the sight of Schatza, with a condescending countenance. "You know, that was very rude of you."

Desmond rolled his eyes as she helped him to his feet. *She's stronger'n she looks.* "I know, I know. What kinda Descendant walks inta a friendly inn an' breaks their things. Ya don't really have ta rub it in, I'm embarrassed enough." They were both standing now, and he turned to face her. "Thanks."

Schatza lightly punched his shoulder, "I could care less about two stupid mugs. Though, your face says much differently. You are rude because you never checked back about whether I would go with you to the Tower, after I specifically asked you to."

Desmond shrugged, "I…"

"Is it safe to assume that that's the infirmary?" She nodded ahead and pulled him by the arm as she started walking. "Come, show me to your room and I can at least help you get cleaned up before I leave you."

Desmond furrowed his brow while his arm clung to his aching ribs. "Wait, so yer not goin' ta the Tower then? What's the point o' comin' out here ta help me then?"

As if purposely adding to Desmond's confusion, Badalao's voice popped into his head once more. *Des, where in all of Oblivion are you? I have been trying to talk to you for days now. If you do not answer me, I will completely take over your mind and look through your eyes. I know you are alive, fool!*

He didn't need Badalao to interfere then and there. "Shut up! Just go away!"

Schatza turned back and looked at him sternly, "Excuse me? I just had to come out and help you stand up, because you couldn't do that on your own. A little gratitude would be appreciated."

He could feel his face flush of color. "No! That wasn't meant fer ya. I've got…I've got some issues up in my head. I swear I wasn't talkin' ta ya! I'm thankful fer what yer doin', I promise. So confused, but thankful."

She eyed him curiously but turned and continued into the infirmary. "You lead the way now. What are you confused about? That I'm helping you but not coming with you? Why would I? Look at how weak you are, especially with your manifestation. Why would I want to travel around with such a liability? Despite what you might think, I am *quite* good at fending for myself and at not being noticed. You would be the worst companion for me to be with right now."

Desmond stopped for a moment, feeling more pain in her truth than in his ribs. He continued toward his infirmary room, "So what, yer just here ta pity me, then?"

Her voice perked up, "You could say that. I would feel bad leaving you in the state that you're in. The least I could do is help clean you up until a nurse comes in. Maybe I'll even give you a nice kiss before I leave you, that way it isn't a total loss for you."

As quickly as Desmond's face had gone pale, his cheeks were full of redness now. He did his best to not let on that Schatza had gotten to him and kept walking. "Oh, thanks." They reached his room and Schatza motioned for him to sit on the bed. As she inspected his face, he saw her eyes shift to something behind him.

"Hello," she smiled. "Your patient here got himself in some trouble outside. He's got some glass in his face and some scrapes here and there. Nothing too serious. I was going to clean him up, but I'm sure you would do a better job than me."

Desmond looked to his left as the same tall, slender, balding man he'd come to dislike walked toward him. He sighed at the sight of the man, unsure of whether it was the same man with whom Maximillian had been laying in bed, and even more uncomfortable about whether Maximillian had told the man anything about what Desmond had said. "Mornin'," Desmond said curtly.

The tall man rolled his eyes and said flatly, "I'm not sure he wants me ta help him. This feisty little boy doesn't care fer me too much."

Desmond took a deep breath, "It's fine. I trust ya. Ye can help me, if ye would be so kind."

The man nodded, "Very well." As he fished for something in his black apron pocket, Schatza moved back and sat on the other bed, which Maximillian had only recently been occupying. She smiled at Desmond and winked. The man held up a pair of tweezers, "Close yer eyes." He put one hand on top of Desmond's head and used his right hand to pull out the glass. After several minutes, a great deal of wincing, and even more blood and tears flowing down Desmond's face, the man was satisfied with what he'd pulled out. "That's the best I can do. Maybe ya know someone with a manifestation who'll fix ya completely. The rest o' yer injuries are superficial. It'd be a waste o' both our times fer me ta do anythin'. Ya look like ye've had a rough mornin' already. Take a nap if ya want, I'll tell the head nurse not ta charge ya fer stayin' today." The man nodded to him and then to Schatza, and headed to the door.

"Wait, what's yer name? If Max ever talks ta me again, it'll go a long way that I know yer name."

The tall man smiled, "Clyde. He'll talk ta ya again, Desmond. Ya know he will."

Desmond nodded, "Thanks Clyde, fer all yer help." Clyde nodded and left the room. Desmond turned back to Schatza, who sat only a few feet away at the edge of the other bed, now directly across from Desmond.

Schatza leaned forward slightly, "Good thing Clyde helped you. My hand isn't as steady as his; your face would've been carved up quite nicely."

Desmond smiled, "Good thing. I'm too young ta stop bein' handsome. In case you were wonderin', Clyde an' I didn't get along the whole time I was stayin' here, up 'til today. He an' Max...were quite close, though. Then Max an' I got inta a big argument before he left an' I owe him an' apology. He an' I were supposed ta go ta the Tower together, but I got him so mad that he left without me."

Schatza nodded, "Ah yes, the Tower. I guess then I should be going now, so you can take your nap and be off to the Tower."

Desmond looked down at the floor, then back at her. "Ya sure that's what ya want? I promise ya, once I'm back ta normal, I'm a great companion. Wouldn't just be me at the Tower anyway. Ye'd have lots o' travelin' companions ta choose from." He knew he was starting to sound desperate.

She shook her head in disagreement. "It doesn't matter. Like I said, I'm best at taking care of myself. And I'm not used to having others look out for me. Maybe we will cross paths again, though."

"Doesn't seem like I can do much ta change yer mind."

"No." She leaned forward even more. "But I did promise you a kiss before I left."

Desmond's eyes perked up as her face moved closer to his. She looked somewhat unsure of herself, which gave him some relief. *"Desmond Baek, I swear I am going to bloody beat you down when I see you again. Why is it so hard to just talk to me?"*

Desmond stood up just before Schatza's lips met his. "Lao? Light o' Orijin, why won't ya just leave me alone! I'll talk to ya when I'm ready! I've been through hell since I got ta Gangjeon!"

Schatza jerked backwards, "What are you talking about? Did you say *Lao*? As in Badalao? As in Badalao Majime? Descendant, your age, questionable hair? Was he in your head?"

"Desmond looked at her, dumbfounded. "How do ya know him? Lao is my best friend; we went ta the House together. He's been lookin' fer me an' tryin' ta talk ta me, but I didn't want ta respond until I was back ta normal. How exactly do ya know him?"

Schatza blushed, but it only enhanced her beauty. "I-I met him in the City of the Fallen. That is where I was before coming here. Is he...still planning to go to the Tower as well?"

"Yes, I told ya that all the survivors from the House will be meetin' there. Lao's the one who's coordinatin' with everyone ta make sure we all get there. Obviously ya know what he can do, so I don't have ta explain it ta ya." Desmond felt somewhat embarrassed now. *O' course she's met Lao already. But then why would she want ta kiss me?*

"Then perhaps I will join you after all."

"Ah, because o' *Lao*." *Damn ya, ya Markosi bastard.* "So, how about that kiss?"

Schatza half-smiled, "I've changed my mind." She stood and walked to the door, "Unfortunately for you, I'm staying at the Valiant Rider across the street. When you are ready, figure out a way for them to let you in, and come get me."

Desmond nodded as he laid back onto the bed. *Bloody Lao. Always has ta steal all the girls. Even when one is about ta kiss me, she stops at just hearin' his name. Some best friend, ruinin' my life.*

CHAPTER 7
GRAVE TRUTHS

From **The Book of Orijin,** **Verse Two Hundred Twenty-three**
Just as We have chosen you, We chose the Harbingers of the past. They too had flaws and fears.
Do not diminish the sacrifices of the Four on behalf of the selfishness of the Fifth.

SAVAIYON SIMALTI RECLINED in a heavily cushioned turquoise chair adorned with pillows and cushions of all patterns and colors. It was the type of luxury that most people in Ashur would never imagine, but he wouldn't allow himself to feel guilty about it. On most normal days, Savaiyon was coming and going at the whim and command of Zin Marlowe - a man he'd always respected but stopped liking years ago. *And now he is dead, and I feel like death. I cannot stop thinking, though. How did you die? You told the whole room that you would look like Drahkunov. Did Horatio sleep through it? Did he know he was killing you or did he really believe he was killing Drahkunov?*

Savaiyon had dwelt upon this since he'd had the energy to dwell upon things. He recognized the possibility that, during the attack on the House, Horatio might have been better off staying in the infirmary and resting, rather than leaving to fight. If anyone would have been responsible for ensuring Horatio stayed inside and rested, it would have been Savaiyon. He was the only one who saw what Horatio had experienced right before going to the infirmary. Their chase with Maqdhuum had taken everything out of them.

He could barely feel his body, as if it was one with the chair. As far as he could remember, he'd never even sat in this chair at any point in his past. It had been years since he'd been home, to the point where he didn't even know if any of the same furniture had been in the house the last time he was here. He looked around the spacious room, taking in every wall as well. The peculiar thing about the houses of the wealthy in Gansishoor was that they were built into the cliffs that overlooked the Sea of Fates. Decades ago, a wealthy family had hired some of the best Galicean builders to come and carve out the cliffs and build their home right into the rock. Other wealthy families caught on and followed suit. The builders were paid handsomely and even invited to stay. Some did and assimilated into the Gansishoori culture. Others went back home with their riches. Since then, these homes were reserved exclusively for the wealthiest families of Gansishoor.

"You look around this place like you don't know it. Although you sink into that chair like you're part of the room. When was the last time you were here?" Rhadames Slade smiled at Savaiyon from across the room, in a chair just as plush, except Slade sat upright.

Savaiyon didn't bother to look up or turn his head. "I left here when I saw roughly eleven or twelve summers. I traveled some before going to the House. That was almost thirty years ago. I've come back to Gansishoor a few times since then, but never back to this house. And now that I am here, I think I'm a fool for missing out on this."

"You can create doorways to anywhere, and you lament that you didn't take advantage of a chair?"

Savaiyon shrugged his eyebrows. "You are not sitting in it. Though I'm sure yours is just as comfortable. Rhadames, I have spent the last...however many years doing the bidding of Zin Marlowe. There was rarely time for comfort. Because of my manifestation, he expected a certain immediacy out of me. When I would finish with one mission, I would either be sent on another, or teaching young Descendants about the world. And in all this, all the missions, the travels, the experience, all the wisdom, nobody had a clue about Maqdhuum."

Slade perked up, "I was wondering when you would want to talk about that."

"It has been on my mind for as long as I've had consciousness since we parted ways with him. It baffles me that we knew nothing about this. We only saw Maqdhuum for the first time nearly a year ago, when he abducted Gunnar and Adria. As far as I know, he still has Adria and Gunnar with him, and now Garrison. Who knows who else is with him at this point?" Savaiyon threw a cushion across the room at the thought of Adria. He'd done so much to help her and encourage her since she'd arrived at the House, and despite all of it, he wasn't able to protect her. "I can only imagine what his mind must be like at this point. I've read books and books about the Five. Abram always sounded rather uncouth, but nothing like what I saw in Maqdhuum."

Kadoog'han entered the room holding a cushion. "A couple thousand years will do that to you. Was this cushion for me?" He tossed it back to Savaiyon.

Slade stood up. "You should know, Gunnar is dead. Jahmash only needed his eyes to find the House of Darian. Adria was more of a consolation prize. Maqdhuum likely thought it would earn him more favor with Jahmash by getting her too. That is an important detail to remember, though, my friend. Jahmash didn't trust me as much as Drahkunov and Maqdhuum, but I do know that he didn't know that Maqdhuum is really Abram."

Savaiyon leaned forward. "How would you know something like that?"

"Linas, Gibreel, and I were there when Jahmash ordered the attack on the Taurani. He trusted Maqdhuum enough to lead his armies. Up to that point, Jahmash only trusted Drahkunov with military responsibilities. It was clear that Jahmash had been inside Maqdhuum's head at some point, too. Somehow, Maqdhuum must have found a way to hide all evidence of him being Abram, because there's no chance Jahmash would have let him live if he knew.

"Either way, Maqdhuum and Jahmash are starting quite a formidable collection of Descendants. Adria and Garrison. They have another girl named Farrah—can kill you with a kiss. I don't understand how Descendants can be evil, but she's completely bought into what he wants. And Maqdhuum implied she was like that before Jahmash was controlling her mind. She came to him willingly. He kept one of the Taurani for himself, dull one named Aric. The boy is dense; he was easy for Jahmash to turn. That makes him dangerous: brainwashed, malleable, young Taurani fighter, and he can see in the dark. Farrah is the most dangerous; she *wants* to kill people, especially other Descendants. I think she has a grudge against Garrison. Maybe that's why Maqdhuum wanted him? Gain Farrah's loyalty by delivering the man she wants to kill."

Savaiyon patted his knee. "No, that does not coincide with the way he talked about Garrison. He said plainly that Garrison would be better off with him since the House left him to rot in a dungeon. You think he would bring Garrison straight to Jahmash?"

Kadoog'han chimed in, "That would make sense, wouldn't it? Heir to the throne of Ashur. He could blackmail Edmund for fealty with that."

Slade paced around the room. "No. Jahmash has his spies throughout Ashur. He doesn't care about Garrison. Besides, rumor is Garrison showed up at your doors *because* Edmund wanted to kill the boy himself. The only Descendent Jahmash cares about definitively is Baltaszar, which is why I'm in Ashur once again."

Savaiyon looked up at him. It wasn't until a few days after being in Gansishoor that Savaiyon realized he'd seen Slade before. Slade had been there with another man, conducting business with Marlowe, but it had been years before Savaiyon had become a Maven, and therefore, Slade's business there was none of Savaiyon's business. And if the timing of the memory was accurate, it was also around the time that Asarei departed. "You said that you lost your ear the last time, for being empty-handed. What will happen when you return again?"

Slade continued pacing and gently felt the scarred mess where his left ear had been. "I do not plan to return."

"What about the brother? You said Baltaszar has a twin brother, whom you delivered right to Jahmash. You can live with leaving him there? Surely you cannot expect Baltaszar to trust you once he knows that you served up his only kin to the Red Harbinger."

"Bo'az will be fine. Jahmash actually *likes* him, somehow. And he knows that keeping Bo'az alive makes it easier for Baltaszar to get to him sooner or later. I get the feeling that, in order for Jahmash to be stopped, either he will have to come here, or we will have to go to him. Having seen some war in my time, I don't like Ashur's chances if all of its forces have to take to the Sea of Fates to go fight Jahmash. Not only would it be too easy for us to be ambushed in the open sea, the whole continent would be left vulnerable. Let Jahmash come to Ashur. And let Baltaszar burn the seas away for him to get here."

"Something that big, it could kill him."

Slade nodded, "It could. I am confident that, by the time we get to that point, he will have considerable help." Savaiyon looked at him quizzically. "Do you remember where you sent him, when Marlowe banished him from the House?"

"The Never. Marlowe was specific about it. He wanted to be sure that Baltaszar would not die, but he wanted the boy to be hurt in the process of getting there. I created the bridge there high enough that he would fall through several tree branches before landing in the snow. At the worst, he'd break a few bones and would be knocked unconscious."

Slade snickered, "And you're worried that the boy will hate *me*?"

"Listen, I was given a command. I followed it. Marlowe also inspected the positioning of the doorway. The boy tried to burn down his own village, then set himself on fire. Whatever it was that set him off, that type of anger was still a significant danger to the House."

"I'll save my judgment until after I get his side of the story. I had one conversation with the boy and it was like talking to a younger version of his father. I knew Joakwin for a long time, and for all his faults, he was one of the best men I ever knew. Baltaszar has his heart in the right place. I have no doubt that he is unstable, scared, insecure, emotional, sheltered, and impulsive. But if Marlowe placed him in the Never after a year of being here, then he set Baltaszar on the proper path. By the time we see Baltaszar again, I guarantee you he will have matured considerably."

Savaiyon stood up. "Would you care to divulge exactly what you mean? You are being supremely vague right now, and details would help a great deal."

Slade glanced at Kadoog'han, then looked at Savaiyon suspiciously. "I'll tell you my secrets when you open up about yours."

Savaiyon stared at Slade for a moment. He dared not look at Kadoog'han; doing so would validate Slade's remark. Savaiyon wondered if Slade actually knew any of the secrets he was referring to, or if he was simply speculating. *He must know enough to know that I am on his side, or else he would not be here.* "I have no idea what you are talking about," he said flatly.

Slade simply nodded. "Very well. Let's get back to Maqdhuum, then. What do you want to do about him?"

Kadoog'han walked over and sat in the chair that Slade had recently been using. He shook his head, "Now I need to sit down. I don't know what the hell kind of secrets you two have, and I honestly don't care. But we do need to figure out what we do next."

Savaiyon put up a palm to try to halt Kadoog'han. "Be easy, Kad. Rhadames and I are not fighting. More like testing each other. I am sure we will be with our new companion for a while, so it's important to see where the parameters lie. Kad, I agree with you, but I am curious about what Rhadames just asked." He looked at Slade, "What do we *do* about him?" The man has existed for thousands of years and can disappear and reappear in the blink of an eye. He also rescues Descendants *and* kills them at his whim. Only a week ago, he chased me around all corners of Ashur like he was toying with me and hit me with so many knives; the Orijin himself might've mistaken me for a pincushion. And the only reason I survived it was because Horatio scared him away by striking him with lightning. Even Horatio did not walk away uninjured. Yet, you want to know what we should do about him. It seems to me, Rhadames, that Maqdhuum will do as he pleases. And if he wants to encounter us again, then hopefully he either stays in one place long enough to find out what he wants or long enough for us to kill him."

Slade continued his pacing. "Just because you have encountered the man, does not mean you understand him. Remember, he is working for the Red Harbinger. And nearly two thousand years ago, he *was* a Harbinger, and supposedly fought Jahmash to defend Darian. Everything we think we knew about that fight is likely wrong. What if Abram led Jahmash right to Darian and then went into hiding? Jahmash could have just told everyone he killed Abram."

Kadoog'han cut in, "Or, what if he *let* Jahmash think he killed him. Rhadames, you said yourself that Jahmash doesn't know now that he *used* to be Abram. You were originally under the impression that Jahmash and Abram were at odds. Perhaps that is still the case. Somehow and some way, Maqdhuum disguised his looks and managed to fool Jahmash. The only reason for him to do such a thing would be if he was plotting his own scheme against Jahmash. Otherwise, why not seek out Jahmash long before this day and age, and help him return to Ashur? If Abram had really wanted to help Jahmash fulfill his agenda, Abram could have done so centuries ago. All he would have to do is appear in front of Jahmash and bring him to Ashur. Neither of you bothered to ask me, but if you did, I would say Maqdhuum is rogue. He has his own endgame in mind and perhaps, just perhaps, it might even involve getting revenge on Jahmash. Jahmash has come to be known as the Red Harbinger. Do either of you know what label the books gave Abram?"

Savaiyon looked at Slade, who returned the glance. They both looked at Kadoog'han and answered simultaneously, "The Untamed Harbinger." Savaiyon looked down at the ground, processing everything Kadoog'han had just said.

Kadoog'han continued before either of them could add anything. "Untamed. Even before he was Maqdhuum, he was wild, whimsical, fastidious. Maybe now that he does not have to fix mankind, he feels the freedom to do as he wishes."

Slade looked at Savaiyon again. "You should have let Kadoog'han do the talking from the beginning. He makes so much more sense than either of us." He turned back to Kadoog'han. "What did you teach at the House of Darian?"

Kadoog'han laughed heartily, "Teach? I guarded the touch portal to the island. I stood at the base of a mountain and hid behind rocks. I argue with myself every day, and I never lose." All three men laughed.

Savaiyon was grateful for Kadoog'han's presence in the room, beyond his astuteness about Maqdhuum's possible intentions. The former porter to the House of Darian had also managed to ease the tension in the room and bring back some levity. With any luck, the other two men had forgotten about any secrets that might exist.

A head poked out from behind one of the doors and the middle-aged woman cleared her throat. Savaiyon looked over at his sister, Riha. "We'll be right there." She disappeared behind the door once again. "My sister has prepared lunch for us. Let us go sit in the other room.

Kadoog'han stood beside him and grasped his shoulder, "She still afraid of us?"

Savaiyon smirked. "Us? No. She is mostly afraid of Rhadames." He looked over at Slade, who rolled his eyes. "You have to understand, my sister lives a rather pampered and sheltered life. She grew up in a wealthy family and married a wealthy man. All she has had to do for the past twenty years is stay home and be leisurely. Her sons are old enough that they work most days with their father, and have tutors to fill the rest of their days. There are people hired to take care of most aspects of Riha's life, but our family has never believed in servitude, so she maintains the house and cooks more out of enjoyment than duty. The men with whom she interacts dress in gaudy outfits, adorn themselves in gold and jewels, and smell of berries and flowers. You may be the first vagabond she has had in her home."

As they walked to the table, Slade asked, "Should I leave, then?"

Savaiyon waved a hand dismissively, "She *is* used to overly-sensitive men, though." The questions reminded Savaiyon of his life here before leaving. Every male relative of his worked in the family's shipyard, either building ships or supervising the builders. As boys, they started with building the ships, then worked their way up. They were not given any handouts or perks; they earned everything they achieved. Savaiyon had worked as a shipbuilder for a few years, but his family gave him leniency because of the Descendant's Mark on his face. They'd expected he would want to go to the House of Darian to at least see what type of life was there. His parents hadn't forced him to stay or go, and Savaiyon had always appreciated the freedom he'd been given to choose his path. Every time he had come home, he was greeted with smiles and open arms, never with resentment.

Slade pulled him out of his reminiscence as they sat at a round, dark, wooden table. "Family of shipbuilders? How did you get a pass from that?" Savaiyon pointed to his left eye. "Ah, the Mark. Most wealthy families expect their offspring to follow in the footsteps of their parents, with no exceptions. Your parents must either be incredibly progressive, or you're terrible at building ships. Which is it?" Slade cocked his head and looked at Savaiyon diagonally.

Well, there it is. He's been holding that question for a while. Savaiyon sighed and looked down for a moment. *If I give him the honest answer now, there is a strong possibility that he will ease up on probing about other things.* He looked up at Slade, then at Kadoog'han, then back at Slade again. "These are not my true parents and sister." Just as he'd made the confession, Riha brought out a tray of several bowls and plates, with the scents of several herbs and spices wafting around them.

She looked only at Savaiyon as she set the tray down and walked away from the table, "You should not be speaking of this with them."

"It is my story to tell. I have faced death with these men; who better to share it with?" She shook her head and walked back to the kitchen. "She will be back. She has to bring bread for all of these curries. And do not worry. She is being protective. I have been part of this family for thirty-something years. They took me in when I was a boy, I believe somewhere between five and seven. I cannot be exactly sure, but I already bore the Mark by the time they adopted me."

As Riha walked back into the room, Kadoog'han stopped Savaiyon, "Savaiyon, you do not have to feel obligated to share this with us. Rhadames challenged you, and I understand you may feel the need to prove yourself, but what you are telling us—"

Savaiyon cut him off, "What I am telling you is what I choose to tell. The only person in the world who knows of this besides my family is Zin Marlowe. *Was* Zin Marlowe. I share this with you both because I trust you, and this gesture is an investment of trust going forward." Kadoog'han nodded. Riha set another few plates on the table with loaves of bread, plain flatbreads, and other flatbreads garnished with herbs, onions, and garlic. "Thank you, sister. If I were you, I would not be surprised if there is nothing left of this by the time we have had our fill."

Riha smiled widely at him and patted his head, "Then I will make more, Sava. You might still be growing, even at your age." She turned to the other two men, "I hope you enjoy it all, dear sirs. If anything is lacking or if there is anything you need, please come to the kitchen and let me know."

Savaiyon put a hand up, "You know as well as I do that this is the best meal these men will have ever had in their lives. Go rest, you outdid yourself for this and we will not be bothering you for anything."

"It is nice to have you back, even if only for a short while, Sava." She smiled even wider and then left the room.

"You two should start eating, while I tell you all this. It needs to be eaten hot." He took a large bowl of orange curry and ladled some into his own bowl, then passed it to Kadoog'han and accepted a flatbread from Slade.

As they ate and savored their food, Savaiyon explained to them the complete story of how he'd ended up with this family. His mother had been a Daughter of Tahlia and therefore, he had never met his father. He stayed with her and her partner, his second mother, Dorana. He didn't remember much of his mother, except that she was tall and her hair reached all the way to her calves when let down. Her name was Sivika, and Savaiyon remembered being happy with her. He had glimpses in his memory of playing with other children of Daughters and, while their lives were mostly simple, he remembered a lot of laughter. As he grew up, he deduced that Dorana had issues with him. At some point, she was no longer with him and his mother, but he never remembered his mother's explanation as to why. He'd just assumed she went on a trip somewhere and would perhaps return at some point. He'd seen many adults in Sundari do that.

After a few months of Dorana not being around, someone tried to attack the Daughters' home in the middle of the night. The sentries had difficulty fighting off the assailants, as it seemed they were familiar with the layout of the house. In the chaos, several Daughters were taken by the attackers and Savaiyon could not find his mother in the dark. He remembered clenching his fists and praying for someone to help him and the other children. He prayed to Orijin for them to be safe and for his mother to return. The one instant that had been clearer than anything else was the melody that flowed through him in the middle of all that confusion. He realized later on that it was the manifestation coursing through him for the first time, and a yellow-bordered rectangle appeared in the middle of the bedroom. He saw a road through the opening and tried to round up all of the other children to follow him through, but most of them were younger than he was and too scared to follow him through. From the other side of the rectangle, he saw attackers come kill the children and his sheer panic caused the rectangle to shrink and disappear.

Savaiyon swallowed, "I sat at the side of that road and cried for hours until the morning. It turns out that I was about halfway between Sundari and Gansishoor. I don't know why I picked the road; I suppose it was one of the only places I knew outside of Sundari. A merchant saw me and the Mark on my face and felt too guilty to leave me there. He was afraid someone else might come along and kill me. He was an older Gansishoori and figured I could blend in at the markets in Gansishoor. So he took me around through the markets. I'd already told him I was afraid to go back to Sundari, but I wanted to know if my mother was alive."

He noticed that Slade and Kadoog'han had both finished eating and, just as he'd predicted, every bowl and plate was devoid of food. "The man took me around the whole market, which, as you may have seen, takes up a great deal of this city. He asked anyone we passed if they could take me in for a short while to help me find my mother. After a while, a short, middle-aged woman grasped his arm and told us to follow her. She led us to the outskirts of the markets, where a man awaited her in a horse-drawn wagon. A young family out in the cliffside homes regularly hired her to buy fruits and vegetables at the markets. They had recently lost a baby in childbirth a few months before, and she thought that taking me in might help fill some of their void. I was skeptical, it was so much change in such a short amount of time, but I was also so scared of not having a home. I went with her to the family's house, and they sat me down, fed me, and talked to me about what I'd been through.

"As nice as they were, even their two children, who were younger than I, I still did not think I could stay with them. I was sure I would leave in the middle of the night. But then, the girl, she must have been only four or five years old at the time, she told me without even consulting with her parents, that they would bring me to Sundari as often as I wished to help find my mother. Her parents did not protest in the least. That little girl was Riha, and even though I am likely taller than her when I'm sitting down, she has never stopped being protective of me."

Savaiyon didn't want to stare or even look directly, but he thought he saw a tear trickle from the corner of Kadoog'han's eye, as the man stroked his short, chestnut-colored hair. He avoided eye contact and continued to tell them how, at first, the father would take him to Sundari once a week to find his mother. That went on for a few months, and as more time went on, Savaiyon felt less like going, tired of filling himself with hope on the way there and then crying from disappointment the whole way back. This family had made no hesitation to take him in, help him, and make him feel like he belonged. They even let him try to use his manifestation to get to Sundari a few times. After some time, he adopted their surname, as he hadn't even remembered his own, and accepted that he was part of their family. "So now you understand, Rhadames, why I was not expected to pursue a life in shipbuilding. Do not think the decision came easily to me. I never knew my birth father, but my adoptive father was a perfect example for me to understand how a man should act. He had to convince me over a period of months that I would not be letting him down if I chose a different path. He knew I had questions about the world and about my birth mother. They did not want me to always wonder or have regrets about not making my own choices. They allowed me to travel on my own, so that I might come and go as I pleased. They made sure I knew what places would be friendly to Descendants. So I traveled through Ashur for a while before going to the House of Darian, just to see what the world was like. I would also be lying if I said I did not spend a great deal of time in Sundari, trying to track down my mother."

Kadoog'han cleared his throat before asking, "Any luck?"

"No. Though I barely got anywhere with investigating. I was almost this tall when I left Gansishoor. Most people did not feel comfortable answering questions from a statuesque Descendant. I suppose many just do not see the gentle giant that I truly am."

Kadoog'han's solemn face spasmed as he broke into a laugh. "Oh Light of Orijin, thank you for that! It was too solemn at this table for my emotions."

Slade shook his head as he wiped his mouth and beard with his sleeve. "If we're done with the stories and emotions, we should figure out what our next step is."

Savaiyon said dryly, "I have already sorted that out. I have our next few steps set already."

"Perhaps you can speak for yourself and Kadoog'han, but I haven't agreed to anything yet."

Savaiyon glared at Slade. *Does he think he is our leader now?* "Look, Rhadames, I am a Descendant and a Maven of the...former House of Darian. My responsibilities are to the Descendants, especially the young ones who need some guidance. You may do as you please; you are not bound to us in any capacity. If you choose to stay with us, then you conform to our plans. Otherwise, I do not understand why you would stay with us. Surely we have different agendas."

Slade looked at him flatly. "It's pretty simple. I do not trust you. I know the House of Darian isn't your only allegiance, and I want to see exactly what you do going forward."

Going forward, I wouldn't mind punching you in the face. Or maybe pushing you into a river. "Do what you like. But my plans are my plans."

Slade looked across the table at Kadoog'han, "And you'll just go along with whatever he says?"

Kadoog'han nodded, "Trust him with my life. Bet ya anyone who survived the attack on the House says the same thing."

Savaiyon spoke up before Slade could get another word in. "First, we go back to the House of Darian. I want to retrieve Marlowe's body so I can properly bury him."

"You Ashurians and your need for burials. Why can't you just understand that the dead have no need for their bodies? You would put your life at risk just to honor a dead thing."

"Have you ever been to the Three Rings, Rhadames?" He didn't wait for an answer to the rhetorical question. "Exactly. But if there's a chance that Zin Marlowe's spirit can see us from whichever ring he ended up in, then I would like for him to see that someone cared about his death. I plan to bury him where the Harbingers and other Headmasters are buried." Slade perked up at the last part of what Savaiyon said. "Is that acceptable to you, Rhadames?"

"Actually, that sounds exciting. I've never had the privilege of going to the graves. Marlowe may have mentioned them once, I don't remember, but there was always business to handle and it never took me there. But I imagine you can get us there quickly. Dare I ask where the graves are located?"

Savaiyon was caught off-guard by Slade's eagerness. "I will tell you when we get there."

Kadoog'han stood up, "If you two are done seeing who can piss farther, then can we discuss when we're going and what the plan is when we get there? Chances are, Jahmash's soldiers are still there. I don't believe they would sail all this way to attack and then just leave. For all we know, some of our own could be prisoners. The longer we wait, the worse things could be."

Savaiyon nodded and stood. "Right. I apologize for forgetting myself, Kad. If you two are comfortable with it, we can go tonight. I would prefer the cover of night. I can even create a gateway small enough to ensure that we don't go where others might be. First, I want to get Marlowe's body. I can easily move him to where we'll bury him, then leave him there until we are ready. Then we can go inside the House and survey it for friends and enemies. Kad, your manifestation and mine will greatly help for what we are trying to do." He looked at Slade flatly. "And Rhadames, do your best to not get noticed. I don't mean that as a slight. You are roughly the same height as me; I know how difficult it can be to be inconspicuous."

Slade snickered, "Trust me, the last thing I need is for Jahmash's army to go back to him and tell him that I'm helping Descendants."

"Good. When we are inside, we do it the same way, track down any surviving friends and I will bring them away with a gateway, then come back and continue. Much of that will be touch and feel: we gauge it when we are there. If it is too dangerous to rescue our friends, then we go back another time with a better plan. It will not help them if we die fighting to free them. Once we can do no more, we bury Marlowe then regroup here. We can get a cirurgeon or leach here to help heal anyone discreetly. Until then, I suggest we all rest, eat again, and then go."

SAVAIYON PEEKED THROUGH the tiny, yellow-fringed rectangle, surveying for any signs of Jahmash's soldiers. "It is clear outside, as far as I can see. The ground is littered with bodies: I imagine they have no need to tend to any of the dead outside. Kad, when I make the gateway, you go through first. Obviously, your manifestation is best suited to going unnoticed."

Savaiyon was grateful that Kadoog'han, of all people, was with him. Not only was the man completely noble and trustworthy, but he could camouflage himself to blend into nearly any environment, which was why he was the porter to the House of Darian's touch portal. For many of the steps they would be taking going forward, it would be a great help to have a friend who could blend into the environment and remain unseen.

Slade spoke from behind his right shoulder, "Last time. You're sure that you want to do this? You're sure that this is necessary?"

"I have no doubt this is what must be done." Savaiyon didn't wait for a retort from Slade. He expanded the tiny gateway until it was big enough for the three of them to walk through in single file. Kadoog'han, clad in black like Savaiyon and Slade, walked through first and immediately blended into the night. Savaiyon only knew the man was there because he knew where to look.

Savaiyon had brought them to the northern shore of the island, where the battle had taken place. He remembered exactly where he saw Zin Marlowe fall from the lightning strike, looking like Drahkunov. Marlowe had stood looking like the Galicean general but then lay looking like the old man he'd revealed himself to be.

As soon as Slade was through the gateway, Savaiyon closed it and scanned the night sky. He looked around, first at the water, in which the shadows of hundreds of broken ships filled the horizon, then to his left to the shore where a handful of them had tried to fight off an army. He closed his eyes for a moment and saw Desmond and Maximillian, Horatio, Vasher, Badalao and Sindha, and Marshall and Reverron. As he opened his eyes, a small confidence surfaced in him that he might remember where he sent everyone if he concentrated hard enough. He would have to wait until they were done here, though.

They walked toward Marlowe's body and Savaiyon still surveyed the landscape. He knew what Marlowe's body had looked like, but he'd forgotten that cannonballs had shattered the front of the House of Darian. "Look at that," he whispered. "There is no front to it. The House was massive, and they destroyed it so easily. Desmond must have summoned so much power to be able to keep the wall from collapsing on us. I would be worried about him if he was not with Maximillian. To command that much power for so long, there would be a significant let down and withdrawal after letting it go."

They stopped walking as Savaiyon saw Marlowe's charred body on the ground. He put a hand down and knelt before the body. Even though it happened over a week ago, the smell of burnt flesh still caused him to turn away.

Slade stood behind him while Kadoog'han knelt beside him. "I understand that there's sentimental value in this for you two, but can you save that for later? Make the gateway and push him through. While our cover is good, I am sure you hear as well as I do the hum of people talking in the distance." Savaiyon looked up at Slade. The man stroked his thick beard and turned away from them. "There is no time for emotions or reminiscing now."

Savaiyon nodded. "Very well." He raised his hand while creating the small gateway on the ground, only big enough to just fit Marlowe's body, and then pushed the blackened mass through. He stood again and took a deep breath. "Did you know?"

Slade turned his head to Savaiyon, hand still running through his beard. "Know what?"

"Marlowe. That he was pretending to be young? From the time I met him, I thought his manifestation to be something along the lines of aging slowly. I knew he was not as young as he appeared but he never revealed to me that he could...mimic...other people. Did you know the truth about him?"

Slade shook his head. "No. Joakwin and I had no idea. We had no reason to think otherwise, and the nature of our meetings—we were always more focused on other things. I'm not sure if Asarei knew or not, though. Seems more likely that he would tell a fellow Descendant than us."

Savaiyon appreciated that Slade was entertaining this conversation. He started walking first, knowing they would follow him. "I would not use the term *fellow* when talking about those two. There was absolutely no fellowship between them." He remembered Asarei from long ago. Savaiyon was too young to know anything that went on between Asarei and Marlowe, aside from their stances on fighting and violence, but the tension between them was obvious. When Asarei left the House of Darian, everyone knew a hatred existed between the two men. "Perhaps you can explain that whole situation to me when we have more time."

"Situation?"

"You, Joakwin, Marlowe, and Asarei. He is our best resource now, as he was second to Marlowe at the House of Darian. As I understand it, he left because he wanted to be able to teach us to fight and Marlowe strongly opposed it." Savaiyon eyed Slade, hoping the man took the bait to divulge more information.

"Perhaps another time, then. Perhaps we should also discuss whether he is the best resource. But after we are done here." Slade stopped walking. "Are we really just walking right in?"

Savaiyon understood Slade's hesitance, as they were merely yards away from the front of the House. "No, Kadoog'han is walking right in. We will wait here until he lets us know it is safe. When he returns, we go in." He and Slade stood against one of the outside walls while Kadoog'han nodded at them and walked through the gaping hole that was once the front of the House of Darian. From the opening, faint wisps of light could be seen in the distance, but they were weak enough that the front of the building was still in darkness. Kadoog'han disappeared inside.

"How does that work with him?" Slade asked quietly. "The camouflaging, won't they still see his clothes anyway?"

"Actually, no. It took me a while to process how it works as well. Kadoog'han says that it affects what he touches, so he controls what he is wearing as well. You might have noticed that he wears his clothes rather fitted and close to his skin. He is not doing so to show off his manly physique; it is so that if he must hide at a moment's notice, he is always ready."

"Ha! He'd be a good fit for the Kraisos. They could use talents like those."

Savaiyon rolled his eyes and shook his head, "No. The Kraisos are a thieves guild. He would be a terrible fit for them. Kadoog'han is one of the smartest and noblest men I know. He always knows what he is talking about, otherwise he is not talking. He does what is right and thinks about the greater good before himself."

Slade turned his head to look at Savaiyon, "Sounds like you have some resentment toward them. Most of the Ancient Clan does, from what I understand."

Savaiyon was starting to get annoyed at Slade's constant mention of this. He turned his whole body to face Slade and did his best to maintain a whisper. "If you do not stop, I will leave you here. I'm sure Jahmash's soldiers would love to hear whatever story you have about why you have not been around. I am even more sure that Jahmash would love to hear it when they bring you back to him." Even in the darkness, Savaiyon could see Slade's countenance shift. "I doubt he would continue to trust you without being inside your head at that point."

"Fine, I will let it go. For now. But your secrets are going to catch up to you sooner or later."

Savaiyon dismissed the notion. He could worry about secrets another time. He peeked around the wall and could see Kadoog'han silhouette in the distance, drawing nearer. This part of the building must have been clear if he was allowing himself to be seen. "If I decide not to leave you here, then you will have plenty of time to get to know me. Until then, be quiet and do not mess this up for us."

Kadoog'han returned to them and didn't wait for their attention. "Most of the House is wreckage. The upper floors are gone, as is much of the ground floor. There are about two hundred soldiers inside, taking refuge in the western wing. Most of them are sleeping; they have a few lookouts. Seems like most of the bedrooms were destroyed, so they're out in the open. There may be more. It doesn't seem like they have much food left, so I doubt they'll be staying here long, unless they're expert fishermen. Even if our food pantry is intact, it will not last them very long. I wanted to check the infirmary, but it's blocked by fallen debris. There could be survivors down there, but you would have to get us down there, Sav. If it's blocked from up here, then an ambush down there is unlikely. Rhadames, how many soldiers did you sail here with?"

"Several hundred."

Kadoog'han nodded. "We didn't kill that many of them during the battle. And we would have known right away if hundreds of them were still here. The best bet is that most of them sailed back to Jahmash and left one or two squadrons here. I'm sure if we checked the shores closely, we'd find one or two of their ships anchored. I would imagine these ones who stayed behind are waiting for us. What's the next step, Savaiyon?"

"Infirmary. At least we know we'd be safe there. Although, if anyone was down there, I doubt they would still be alive. Marlowe got down there through a passage in the wall. Perhaps we can track that down and see what else we can access from there. I would like to avoid blindly using my bridges. The last thing we need is to cause something to collapse because of a foolishly placed bridge, and then draw attention to ourselves. Follow me." Savaiyon turned back toward the outside wall, summoned his manifestation, and created a yellow-outlined doorway. The melody flowing through his veins soothed him. If he didn't have to conserve his energy, Savaiyon would gladly hold onto his manifestation longer than he needed to. It was more than just a warmth flowing through his body. Summoning it brought peace, happiness, and confidence. There was a certain clarity to the feeling, but only when he took the time to pay attention to it, in which he felt almost as if he was connected to all of existence.

He led them through the opening into the infirmary and let it disappear once they were all through. All three men looked around in astonishment at the room. Dust particles floated around them like they were caught in the middle of a fog. The room was mostly free of bodies, but Savaiyon espied a lump on the ground next to some of the cots, a few paces away. He walked to it and knelt down, covering his mouth and nose the whole time. As soon as he turned the body over, he recognized it. *Jelahni.* Jelahni was also a Maven of the House, a Markosi renowned in the House for speaking out against King Edmund and Prince Garrison. Savaiyon had always noticed a pattern in which most Mavens were sent on missions, with Jelahni being the exception. The short Markosi man had never made a fuss about it, to Savaiyon's knowledge, but Savaiyon was sure that Marlowe didn't want Jelahni running around Ashur publicly defaming the King. *It is a shame you had to die so early, my friend. We could have used your passion and veracity with what we must do next. Ironic that now we must kill the king and you do not get to be a part of it.* Savaiyon summoned his manifestation and created a gateway next to Jelahni's body. He rolled the corpse through the opening, just as he'd done with Marlowe's. *How many times will I have to do this tonight? This is why I did not want Slade with us for this. He will not agree with the sentiment of all this.*

Savaiyon had learned long ago to not dwell on sentiment, but the way they'd all left the House was either by barely escaping or by dying, all during the middle of the night. Marlowe hadn't prepared any of them for anything of the sort. Most manifestations could be practical as well as used as a weapon. It made no sense to leave them all with no experience or guidance on how to use their manifestations in the event of an attack. Savaiyon knew that many Descendants took it upon themselves to practice using their manifestations for attacking or fighting. It only made sense that they would get curious; but it was dangerous to do that without supervision. Descendants could potentially harm themselves or others by doing so. *This is why we must go to Asarei. We need so much help in learning to fight and learning to defend ourselves.*

He rose to stand again and coughed as he tried to take in a breath.

"Let us continue on. Marlowe's secret passageway is still open along that wall. I have a feeling Jelahni got hurt and trapped down here in the process of getting others out."

At the other end of the room, the opening in the brick wall remained where Marlowe and Blastevahn had entered the infirmary. Savaiyon led the other two men toward it and walked into the darkness of the secret corridor, where the air was even thicker with dust and moisture. He followed the corridor, his boots crunching with most of his steps. It was likely that insects, dead and alive, covered the floor. Luckily, the path only led them in one direction, so there was no way to get lost or confused. There was no light, and no torch holders on the walls to even allow for it. *Marlowe must have memorized this passage.* The corridor continued on for several feet, with a few right and left turns here and there. All three men remained silent, save for the crunching of their boots and the occasional stifled cough. Savaiyon knew there was still a chance that Jahmash's soldiers could be down here, so they walked slowly as well.

Just as he'd turned his head to look behind him, Savaiyon tripped over a mound in front of him and fell hard to the floor. Kadoog'han and Slade followed right behind and fell on top of him. "What was that?"

Kadoog'han responded as he pushed himself up off of Savaiyon's back. "By the size of it, I'd say it's a person." Only after Kadoog'han responded and Savaiyon got back to his feet, did he hear the low groan coming from the floor.

He walked toward the sound, "I have an idea, but I need both of you to back away several paces. Both of you walk toward me and grasp my arm." Savaiyon held his left arm out for them to reach for. When both men had found him, he gave further instructions. "Now walk forward five paces. I am going to open a small gateway next to me, so that the opening will shed some light in here." Once he heard the others stop, he summoned his manifestation and opened a gateway beside him. If it was daytime outside, this plan would have been much easier, as he could have opened a gateway toward the sky. Instead, he opened it toward one of the walls in his home, that his sister always kept lit. As he expanded the gateway, the light poured in and he was able to see the mound in front of him, as well as Kadoog'han and Slade a few feet away. It was now clearly a large person crumpled on the ground. Savaiyon expanded the opening enough that all of them could fit through easily.

Kadoog'han stepped closer as Savaiyon nudged the body. It groaned again, and Kadoog'han helped Savaiyon try to unravel the person. Whoever it was, he or she wasn't strong enough to attack them. Once they made sense of head and feet, as well as wiped away the dirt and dead critters from the man's face, Savaiyon recognized him immediately.

"Blastevahn!" they sat the man up against the wall. His eyes were closed and his robe and clothes were in bloody tatters. Even through the dirt and dried blood covering his face, Savaiyon could see the dehydration on his lips and skin. "We have to bring him into my home to recover. You two carry him through. Kad, wake my sister and ask her to bring him water. Help her get him settled and comfortable; he will need to rest for a while. I have a feeling he has been trapped in here for the past week with no food or water. I am going to continue along this path to see where it goes, and I will check back in with you shortly."

Slade attempted to argue. "Keep the doorway open so we can come back and help you."

"No, we don't know if the soldiers have access to these corridors. The last thing we need is to let them walk into my house. It will take you some time to get Blastevahn settled in. I will not be long; my word is my bond." Kadoog'han tugged Slade towards Blastevahn so they could pull him up. The man was barely shorter than Slade and Savaiyon, but all muscle, even thicker than Slade. They pulled him through, into Savaiyon's home, and Savaiyon closed the gateway before Slade could say anything more.

Once he was alone, Savaiyon stopped and listened. There were distant echoes here and there, but Savaiyon didn't think they were coming from the passage. Most likely, they were from the floor above. He had to remind himself that he came from the infirmary, which was below ground. There had been no inclines or steps to indicate they'd come up to the main floor.

After walking on for a few moments, he came to a split, though he'd discovered it rather painfully by walking into a wall. He followed the wall in both directions and deduced that the passage continued on both right and left. Rather than overthink it, Savaiyon simply went right and decided he could always double back or get light from another gateway if he really needed to. The passage continued until finally Savaiyon tripped on a step while taking a step forward. He quickly realized what it was after putting his hand down to brace himself. After climbing about ten steps, he felt a ceiling right above his head. He probed around with both hands and finally found what felt like a latch. After fumbling with it for a moment, he managed to unlock it and pushed up ever so slightly.

Savaiyon tried to peek through the small opening between the door and the floor, but it was all darkness, with perhaps a hint of light in one or two places. He still heard nothing, which was reassuring. *Where could I be? Did this bring me back outside?* He summoned his manifestation and opened the door all the way. As he attempted to rise from the steps, something softly smacked his face and the front of his body. After the initial shock, Savaiyon laughed at himself. *A rug. A stupid rug.* As he took it off, he knew exactly where he was, and some regret kicked in again. He stood right behind Zin Marlowe's desk, where the man had sat and talked to him so many times before. Savaiyon quickly shut the hatch, locked it, and returned the rug to cover it. He looked around the dark room, but even without light, he could see that it had been destroyed. All the books were either gone or ripped apart on the floor. The desk had been left intact, as were most of the walls and fixtures. The room truly was a stronghold for headmasters.

Savaiyon walked the perimeter of the room and was immediately positive and thankful that Drahkunov had led this attack, rather than Maqdhuum. The soldiers took what they needed, followed their orders, and that was it. As a result, torches still hung on the wall and the oil and flints were still there as well. He lit a torch and placed it back on the wall, then looked around to get his bearings. The light did nothing to change the reality; the room had been raided for information and Savaiyon suspected they didn't even bother to look for secret passages. The books were enough wealth for them.

An anger rose in him, borne from the frustration, and sadness, and shame of having his safe haven destroyed and being powerless to stop it. He had never been a violent man, but seeing Marlowe's office ransacked was the final straw. If Drahkunov was still in the building, Savaiyon would kill him tonight. *It is time for Descendants to stop being victims. We have to stop allowing things to happen to us and start doing something in this world. That begins tonight. If we cannot find Asarei, then I will lead them and ensure they can fight. No one, not even the Red Harbinger himself, will push us around again.*

For a split second he considered opening a gateway to reunite with Kadoog'han and Slade but changed his mind as quickly as the thought entered it. *I will do this myself.* Savaiyon knew he would have some explaining to do later, but he would deal with that later. And if Slade was foolish enough to bring up secrets again, he might even consider punching the man in the face.

Marlowe's office had always been a rather bare and sterile room. There was no charm or personality to it. While Savaiyon would never have chosen that for himself, he respected Marlowe's tastes and the fact that it was a place of duty and responsibility. The room was to the point, just as its owner had been. And now it was the exact opposite. Chaos. Disorder.

Savaiyon opened the office door slowly and peeked out. There was no sign of anyone, so he left the room and continued to sneak around what was left of the House, looking for Jahmash's soldiers. Kadoog'han had found no survivors, and Savaiyon trusted his friend's ability to check everywhere without being seen, so focused only on the soldiers and what he would do to them once he found them.

There was something he'd wanted to try with his gateways for some time now but hadn't had the opportunity. *And better that Kad and Rhadames are not here to see it.* He walked to the western wing of the House, pressed against the walls where he could, or snuck along piles of wreckage and debris. He passed the front of the House, where they'd walked in, and continued to his destination. The anger still pushed him on, and while being smartly cautious, Savaiyon was all confidence. He came to the end of the final corridor before the western wing and crouched behind another pile of broken-down walls and floors. Two soldiers sat around the corner, talking softly to each other, but he did not recognize the language.

Savaiyon poked his head out and pulled it back in a heartbeat, just to gauge exactly where they sat. He needed to be able to attack without actually looking at them. He closed his eyes and pictured the exact location where they were sitting, then channeled his manifestation into a gateway. The only difference with this one was that it was parallel to the ground, like a fallen door, instead of upright. He placed it right behind them and then expanded it until the gateway was cutting through their torsos. Before they could even scream, their bodies from the chest up had already fallen through the gateway and Savaiyon closed it immediately.

He looked around the corner from behind the pile and saw the two headless, chestless bodies lying on the ground. He waited a moment for anyone to notice, then crept forward to the large opening of the western wing. He mentally patted himself on the back for choosing to come in the middle of the night. From what he could see, everyone else was sleeping. He scanned the room, inspecting every inch to ensure that he didn't miss any lookouts. The only curious thing he saw was someone tied to a column on the other end of the room. He was sure that, despite the boy's dirty face, there was a Descendant's Mark down his left eye. The boy was standing, but tightly secured to the column. Savaiyon wasted no time in creating a gateway to the other side, behind the column. The yellow-fringed doorway disappeared as soon as he was out, and he took a knife from his belt to cut the ropes, he created another gateway to the same island he'd sent Jelahni's and Marlowe's bodies. *Cannot afford to send him to Gansishoor now. Those two would start yelling at me and then it would all be over.*

Savaiyon cut the ropes and caught the boy from falling, then gently nudged him through the gateway and closed it immediately. *Malikai. Oh Orijin, that boy would be a blessing to us if he can recover. Focus, you fool.* He looked around at the floor once more and took a deep breath. *Breathe. You made one bigger than this when you hid the island from outsiders. One little room like this will be nothing.*

He sat down next to the column. It would be easier to get it right if he was lower to the ground. Once more he focused on the melody flowing through his veins, only this time Savaiyon kept his eyes open. Just as with the two guards, the gateway would connect to the Sea of Fates. Chunks and pieces of men would fall out of nowhere into the middle of the sea, providing a feast to the fish and sea creatures. The gateway would be a mere inch or two from the ground and, just like the previous one, would be flat instead of upright. He started the gateway in the very center of them all and in a flash, expanded it so that it covered the entire floor of the room. Within seconds, every soldier on the floor was cut in half in various ways. Savaiyon quickly crawled behind the column and turned away. If anyone ever discovered this room, they would likely vomit right away.

Aside from some of the dead bodies convulsing, there was no sound from the soldiers. No voices and no footsteps. As he created the gateway to the island where he'd brought Malikai, Jelahni, and Marlowe, Savaiyon smiled. He was satisfied with the retribution. He would tell Slade and Kadoog'han exactly what had happened. It would be easier that way. If his actions bothered either of them, at least they could make their decision now to go their separate ways. But he needed them to know that, going forward, violence would be completely necessary.

He opened a gateway to the other island and walked through. Malikai's health mattered more than trying to process what he'd just done. Malikai and the bodies of Jelahni and Marlowe had been left somewhat inland from the shore, where the trees began. The waves didn't reach this far inland, even at high tide. Savaiyon wondered if this island had looked the same when the Harbingers had first been buried here. It couldn't be much bigger than the island where the Tower of the Blind lay. He'd never buried anyone here himself, but he'd known that other significant Descendants had had the honor of being buried here. Marlowe certainly fit the criteria, and Jelahni would have to be the exception to whatever criteria had been set. *Dying in battle against Jahmash's army, defending the House of Darian should be the highest honor anyone could receive.*

Savaiyon hoisted up Malikai and hung the Markosi boy's arm around his shoulder. "Are you alive, boy?" He smacked Malikai's chest, which was exposed through a shredded black shirt, then shook his chin gently.

Malikai coughed up an answer in a raspy voice, "Alive. Tired. Thirsty. Starving."

Savaiyon already had the gateway open. He walked Malikai through, into the same room in his house where he'd been lying earlier that day. He eased Malikai onto the plush turquoise lounging chair.

Malikai was tall by most standards, but still a head shorter than Savaiyon. Still, the boy took up almost the whole chair. In terms of manifestations, Malikai was an important asset to have. He was able to adapt his skin to withstand elements and impacts, which meant that in battle, he could engage in combat with armed soldiers without getting hurt by swords or spears. Savaiyon wished he could say the same for Blastevahn, but in truth, he didn't know what the man's manifestation was. Blastevahn had spent almost all of his time with Marlowe, so it was likely that Marlowe had been the only one who knew Blastevahn's manifestation. Savaiyon wondered if it was because of Blastevahn's manifestation or size that Marlowe kept him close at all times. *Or perhaps they were just very good friends.*

Just as he was ready to turn to find his sister, Riha walked into the room with Slade in tow. She tilted her head to look at Malikai on the sofa behind him. Despite it being the middle of the night, Riha looked wide awake. "Is this the last one?"

"Yes. Unfortunately. It does not seem like many of us survived the attack. Why do you not look tired?"

Riha smirked, "I expected you to bring survivors here. Where else would you bring them?"

Slade cut in. "She was ready with water, bandages, and a bed the moment you closed the gateway. Blastevahn got water, some food, and now some much needed sleep. Kadoog'han is sitting in the room in case he needs anything. We had a lot of time to sit and wait, so now you can tell us what took you so long. You were supposed to come back and get us."

"Things changed. I did not need your help."

Slade rolled his eyes, "I need more than that. Enough with the secrets."

Kadoog'han must have heard the commotion, as he appeared from behind Slade. "This time, Savaiyon, I am curious about what happened. Not out of mistrust, but concern."

"You both can relax. I will tell you everything. But first, Riha, can you tend to this boy? Just like Blastevahn, Malikai is severely dehydrated and should be checked for wounds." He turned to Slade and Kadoog'han, "Let us go out to the balcony. Riha's husband and sons are sleeping. In the event that either of you gets...animated, I would rather us be outside so we do not disturb anyone." While he wasn't lying to them, the whole truth was that Savaiyon loved to be out on the balcony, watching the Sea of Fates. The view and sound of the waves calmed him. It would be much easier to tell them everything out there rather than anywhere else. Savaiyon also didn't want Riha to hear any of it. He wasn't sure whether she ever wondered if he'd killed anyone, but he didn't want her to hear it from him. *Better to not validate anything in front of her.* "Come," he waved for them to follow him outside to the balcony.

Once outside, Savaiyon leaned against the rail and looked out to the water. The sea was barely visible, even in the moonlight, but the waves crashing against the base of the cliffs was calming. Savaiyon listened for a few moments and let himself get lost in the splashes.

Slade broke the silence and brought him back to reality, "Are you going to say something? Why all this build up? Just tell us what happened." Kadoog'han stayed quiet, but Savaiyon could feel his eyes as well.

"I killed them all. Every soldier that was in there. Once I left you, I followed the passage to Marlowe's office. There was a hidden door built into the floor. They took everything from it. Every single book and document, either taken or destroyed. It just made me so angry that I swore I would kill every last one of them. I went to where you said they were, Kad. First I killed the two lookouts and then I killed the rest of them in one fell swoop. They were holding Malikai captive. I sent him away first, and then I used a gateway to slice all of their bodies in half while they slept. It was something I've wondered about for some time now, about whether it would work. I just never had the opportunity to try it until now." He took a deep breath, "Well, it works. It definitely works."

Slade walked up next to him at the stone rail and looked out at the sea. He turned to Savaiyon with a smile on his face. "Brilliant. Where did you send them?"

Savaiyon let his shoulders relax. Slade obviously was not going to chide him. "The sea. I thought I might as well put their remains to use and let the fish eat them."

Kadoog'han walked up to the other side of him and clasped Savaiyon's shoulder. "My friend, while I am surprised at this, do not misinterpret that as disapproval. The war against the Red Harbinger has begun, and you just killed hundreds of his soldiers in one move. I believe that we are past the point of wondering whether violence is necessary."

"I am relieved that you think so, Kad. My hesitance to share this is not out of shame for my actions, but out of uncertainty of whether you would see it the same way. Violence is the only way to stop Jahmash, and when we have such a blatant opportunity to strike against his armies with force, then we must take them. This is why we must go to Asarei. We are new to this, but he left us decades ago for this very reason. If there is anyone who can help Descendants prepare for a war, it is he."

Slade turned to walk back inside, "Then I guess Asarei it is. So what are we waiting for?"

"First we must bury Marlowe and Jelahni."

Slade rolled his eyes, "Yes, how could I forget."

SAVAIYON HAD RETRIEVED a few spades before creating the gateway to the island. It would take a while to dig graves for the two men, even with all three of them digging. He led Kadoog'han and Slade toward the interior of the island, past coconut trees and serpentfruit trees. The existing graves were situated in a massive clearing in the trees, too far inland to be seen from the shore. Savaiyon had already moved Marlowe's and Jelahni's bodies to where they needed to be, as there was no sense in tiring themselves out by carrying them.

"You should know, Jahmash will only come at us harder now," Slade pointed out as they walked on.

Kadoog'han quipped, "He's already sworn to kill us all. What is he going to do? Kill us even harder?"

Savaiyon chuckled. Of anyone, he was glad to have Kadoog'han with him. The man was intelligent, funny, and loyal, which would make for great company through all of this, especially since Slade insisted on staying with them.

"You underestimate him," Slade responded flatly. "Jahmash isn't aggressive for the sake of being aggressive. He is arrogant, yes, but also calculating and cruel." He pointed to his missing ear as a reminder. "He is also patient when it comes to making sure the time is right for his next move. Remember that he has waited two thousand years to get his revenge—on a man who died two thousand years ago."

They arrived at the clearing and Savaiyon led them to where they would bury the bodies. He started digging right away, and the other two followed suit. "If he attacks harder, then we defend harder. If his strategies are smart, then we make ours even smarter. He is doing all of this from an island far away from Ashur. He hasn't seen this kingdom firsthand in millennia, and his only knowledge of our people and culture come secondhand. Let me also point out that he is sending foreign soldiers to fight us. Historically, war favors the side that fights on its own soil. And unless you either do not know or are not telling us, their soldiers cannot wield manifestations. I am saying this as a matter of fact and not haughtily, but only an hour ago I killed two hundred of the Red Harbinger's soldiers in a few seconds, without any of them knowing what happened. I don't know how many of us are left, but imagine if even ten of us Descendants remain, how powerful we would be together? You said it yourself, Rhadames. Jahmash is arrogant. There is a good chance he will underestimate us or dismiss us as being inferior. And if any of us was fighting him one on one, then he would be right. Imagine the attacks we could put forth with Desmond moving anything with his mind, Horatio summoning lighting, Baltaszar wielding fire, my gateways."

Slade had removed his cloak as the sweat glistened on his forehead in the moonlight. "You had better hope so. Jahmash will send everything at Ashur. He is recruiting nations to fight for him. Even if the seven nations of Ashur all united to fight him, it is no secret that the only army belongs to the king in Cerysia. If Jahmash's forces arrived on the shores of Mireya, Galicea, or Markos, the whole nation would be destroyed before the Vermillion could save them. Even with your manifestation, you could travel to anywhere in Ashur within seconds, but what good is that if you don't know that we are being attacked?"

Savaiyon doubted that Slade could see him smirking, "Badalao."

"What's that?"

"Not what. Who. Badalao is a Markosi Descendant. His manifestation allows him to mentally bond with anyone. All he needs to do is touch you, and he can form that bond. He has already done so with his friends in the House. I believe, up to now, this talent was used more for mischief, but Badalao is how we secure Ashur."

"And you're sure that he's alive?"

"He did not die in the attack. I sent him away with Sindha, though I do not remember where. But I am nearly positive that, for anyone I sent away, I sent them someplace safe. And I do not think anyone was alone. Badalao is resourceful. And he knows how to talk to people to get the most out of them. I am certain that he and Sindha are well."

They'd cleared a hole a few feet deep and placed Marlowe's body inside. They immediately proceeded to refill the hole without taking a break. Slade responded, "This manifestation of his...you must keep it secret. It sounds eerily similar to how Jahmash uses his mind control. If Jahmash knew of it, I have no doubt he would launch a side mission just to go after Badalao."

"Then we shall keep it secret."

"Must you always speak so proper?"

"Actually, yes. I was raised by a wealthy family and given the best education they could buy. I was taught manners, etiquette, and speech, among other things. The way I speak has been ingrained in me for almost as long as I *could* speak." He looked up at Slade, who rolled his eyes and shook his head. They'd refilled Marlowe's grave quickly and were already digging Jelahni's.

Kadoog'han, shoveling from the other end, shook his head at both of them. "Two of you are like a married couple. Always bickering at each other."

Slade nodded at him, "Which is exactly why I never married. Who wants to spend their life bickering? What's your excuse, Savaiyon?"

"No time. I am too busy for any woman to be interested in me."

Kadoog'han chuckled, "With your money, I think there are some women out there who would be perfectly happy to live in a luxurious house on those rich cliffs in Gansishoor. It would likely be a perk that they wouldn't have to see you very often."

Savaiyon shook his head, "How would that benefit me?"

Kadoog'han shrugged, "Didn't say it would. I was just reassuring you, that there's still time and hope for you."

"Thank you for comforting me. If I survive the war against Jahmash, I will be sure to seek out a woman with aspirations of using my family's wealth to live a life of leisure, while interacting with me as minimally as possible." All three men laughed heartily at that for several moments. As the laughter died down, they used the silence to focus on finishing Jelahni's grave and then refilling the dirt once they placed his body.

Kadoog'han cleared his throat, which sounded more like he was trying to get their attention. He looked at Savaiyon and Slade sheepishly. "Since we're here, would either of you have a problem with me seeing the Harbinger's graves?"

Slade perked up, suddenly renewed with energy. "I think we *must* see them, given everything we now know."

Savaiyon looked at him sideways, "What does that mean?"

"Whose graves are here, Savaiyon?"

"Darian's, Linas's, and...and Abram's." Savaiyon understood. Slade wanted to see Abram's grave, perhaps even see what was in it. "I already know what you are thinking, Rhadames. And before any *bickering* can happen, I say we do it."

Kadoog'han smiled, "Really?"

"Look, these graves are sacred, but there is nothing sacred about Maqdhuum. And if he is out there somewhere, then we deserve to know the truth about who or what is actually buried there." Savaiyon turned and raced to the Harbingers' graves, which were only several yards away, surrounded by a tree on three sides. Savaiyon knew that if Kadoog'han and Slade had known where they were, they would have beaten him there. Darian's grave was on the left, with Lionel's in the middle and Abram's on the right. "Well, start digging."

All three men dug with renewed vigor, hungry to find out exactly what, if anything, had been buried in Abram's grave. They dug the plot for half of an hour in silence, each man's eyes filled with wonder and urgency. Savaiyon braced himself for the disappointment of an empty grave. He knew not to expect a body, but he expected *something* to be there. *Or else, why even make the grave? Whoever put it here knew there was no body to put in the dirt. Unless they believed Abram died and there were no remains to bury?*

Slade broke the silence, "Six feet? Is that the rule?"

Savaiyon shook his head. "During their time, yes. But that is a myth. Some idiot king long ago mandated that because he thought the corpses could pass diseases through the ground. He decided six feet would be enough to stop any transmission. But it is not true. If we see nothing by that point, then we…" A loud clang came from the end where Kadoog'han was digging.

The force of the impact must have rattled Kadoog'han mightily, as he dropped to a knee and held his head. After shaking his head for a moment, he looked back up at them. "Well, come over here and help me!" Savaiyon and Slade scampered over to him and looked into the hole that Kadoog'han had dug. Savaiyon saw something shiny reflecting from the dirt. "It is something metal. I see it faintly." He pointed, "Right there." All three picked up their spades and dug once more, but with extreme caution and precision. Shortly, they uncovered it enough to know what it was, but none of them dared reach down to pick it up or even touch it. They stared at it for several moments, in awe of what they were seeing. Savaiyon, even despite his disdain for Maqdhuum and everything Abram had become, marveled at the sight and caught himself getting lost in the wonder and profundity of it.

Kadoog'han broke the silence, "It's so beautiful. After all this time, look at it. Shiny, elegant, almost too pristine to have ever been used." He took a deep breath, "All right, so who is going to pick it up? Savaiyon, my vote is for you. You knew about this place and we are only here because it was your idea to bury Marlowe and Jelahni. The honor should be yours."

Savaiyon looked at Kadoog'han, surprised, then at Slade, who nodded in agreement. "Very well." He jumped down and knelt before the sword, taking it in completely before daring to pick it up. Kadoog'han was right; it was such an elegant sight, as if the dirt that buried it had never even touched it. Finally, he lifted the majestic weapon from the ground with two hands. It was remarkably light for such a big sword. The blade itself was wide and engraved in the ancient language of Imanol. The crossguard was shorter than modern day swords, but gold and simple. The hilt, however, was also golden with ornate markings and inscriptions from top to bottom, where the pommel was intricately shaped like the head of a snake, and small green emeralds for its eyes. After several moments, Savaiyon stood and passed the sword to Kadoog'han, who bent down to retrieve it, then climbed out of the grave.

Kadoog'han marveled at the sword for almost as long before passing it to Slade to do the same. Once he passed it along, he turned to Savaiyon with that familiar sheepish look. "So, since we've already started this process, we might as well…continue?"

Savaiyon stared at him for a moment, thinking he'd gotten Kadoog'han's meaning, but not entirely sure. "With what?"

"You know, 'inspecting' these graves for useful assets."

"You mean stealing weapons from the Harbingers' graves?"

"Whatever you want to call it. Either way, they would be more useful to us than to them," Kadoog'han nodded to the ground. "No offense, sacred Harbingers. But Savaiyon, imagine showing up to that battle against Jahmash, holding the swords of the very men the Red Harbinger betrayed."

Slade jumped in. "Keep in mind he also defeated all of them. I doubt the swords will automatically make any of you worthy of engaging him in a duel."

Kadoog'han nodded, "True. But still, there must be a good use for them. What if it came down to a swordfight with him? This sword is clearly superior to anything I've seen in Ashur. It might be the only sword that could match Jahmash's own, assuming he has one like this. You've both held it; it's lighter than any Ashurian sword. Try cutting something."

Slade walked to one of the serpentfruit trees. While they were relatively thin trunks, serpentfruit wood was known to be sturdy. Savaiyon watched, hoping that he would be surprised. Slade faced the tree but stood sideways so that his left shoulder pointed to it. He then raised the sword with both hands and held it sideways by his right shoulder. Savaiyon expected Slade to wait a few moments, but the man swung immediately, and so quickly that Savaiyon barely saw it. For a split second, Savaiyon thought that Slade had either missed the tree or that he'd barely touched it, as the strike was complete and the tree still stood. Savaiyon looked at Kadoog'han and then back at Slade. "What happened? Did you even get it?"

Slade glanced back at him over his shoulder with a wide grin, then walked up to the tree and half kicked, half shoved it with his foot. The tree fell over the opposite way, away from the graves and the three of them. Savaiyon blinked and stroked the top of his head. Despite the tree being completely down, he still could not completely believe what just happened. Slade walked back to them, still smiling. "That's all the convincing I need. Let's dig."

Kadoog'han was about to start refilling Abram's grave when Savaiyon stopped him. "Leave it. No one will be coming here for some time and Abram's body is not in there to be disrespected. We can always bring Desmond here at some point to fill it much more quickly. Save your energy for the next two.

As excited as they'd been to dig up Abram's grave, the three men shoveled with even greater vigor as they unearthed Linas's grave. "What should we be looking for?" Kadoog'han asked while tossing a spadeful of dirt. "Any idea how they buried the dead back then?"

Savaiyon paused for a second to consider, then resumed. "There would have been no one else with manifestations at the time, and everything we have been taught states that Lionel and Abram fought Jahmash so that Darian could get away. So Darian would not have been able to bury Lionel either."

Slade cut him off, "What you getting at?"

"I am trying to deduce at what specific point Lionel would have been buried. It is possible that this was not an island yet, if Lionel was buried right away. Darian supposedly led Jahmash on for days. My point is that, if Lionel was buried *before* the Drowning, then there is a chance he was adorned in some type of riches. However, if he was buried *after*, then someone would have had to sail out here with him, but there would be no way they would have ships big enough at the ready if Darian had just drowned the world. In that case, they would likely have wrapped Lionel's body in something simple."

Kadoog'han stopped shoveling and was staring at Savaiyon. "With all due respect, Sav, if you don't know, you can just say it."

Savaiyon rolled his eyes. The words were harder to say than he would have liked. "Very well. I do not know."

Slade chimed in, "And when we're all done with this, you can explain how Marlowe knew about this place to begin with.

Savaiyon continued to shovel at a fast pace, "Seems that I have much to do when we finish our business. Find a wife, tell you all of my *secrets*, as well as the complete history of Ashur and the House of Darian." Slade shrugged his eyebrows and continued to shovel without a word. They continued on for several minutes until Savaiyon's spade hit something hard. The other two heard the clink of the spade and moved closer to him to see what it was.

Slade rubbed his hand through his beard. "Don't think that's a sword."

Savaiyon shrugged, "Keep digging. We will find out soon enough." They cleared the dirt from where Savaiyon was digging and all of them were now hitting against something hard. "Wood. But rotted. I suppose that is expected after two thousand years. At this point, it will be easy to shovel out of the way. Keep shoveling. If the *wood* is rotted, we may not even find a skeleton, but this is still confirmation that Lionel was laid to rest here. Even if his skeleton is gone, the sword would still be here, since Abram's was."

They dug for a few more minutes, within where the wooden coffin would have been until they heard a familiar clink of metal against metal. "That's the sound I like," Kadoog'han stepped into the excavation and cupped away dirt with his hands. Once satisfied with how much he'd cleared, he picked up the sword from its hilt and inspected it. "It's honestly the most beautiful thing I have ever seen." Kadoog'han took the weapon in once more before passing it over to Savaiyon and then climbed out.

Savaiyon held the second blade as delicately as he would a baby. He respected this one even more than Abram's. He knew the swords were the same, but this one's owner was still pure in his eyes. He inspected it from top to bottom. It was almost identical to Abram's, except some of the inscription seemed different, and the golden pommel was in the shape of an eagle with black onyx eyes, rather than a snake. The three men looked at each other, then Savaiyon set the sword down on the ground next to the other, grabbed their spades, and refilled Lionel's grave within minutes. Immediately after, they ran over to Darian's grave, which was on the other side of Lionel's.

Savaiyon was caked in sweat, dirt, and grime, as were his companions. But they had one more grave to unearth, and this one was the most significant. They were about to start when Savaiyon paused. He eyed Kadoog'han, who looked just as nervous - as if he didn't want to be the one to start. Despite the two millennia that separated them, Savaiyon and Kadoog'han were both related to the man whose grave they were about to dig up. He tilted his head at Kadoog'han, signaling for the man to come over to him. Savaiyon knelt down on one knee and Kadoog'han walked over and knelt next to him. "Orijin, forgive us for what we are about to do. Only you know our hearts and intentions, and we intend no disrespect to our ancestor, Darian." He arose and Kadoog'han followed.

Slade must have sensed their unease and started digging first. He didn't bother to look to see whether they'd started, instead he continued to shovel. Savaiyon joined in first, then Kadoog'han. They dug for nearly an hour, until Savaiyon stopped and walked over to Abram's grave. He tried to gauge how deep they'd dug and then walked back to Darian's grave. Slade saw the confusion in his face, "What is it?"

"We have already dug deeper than Abram's. We did not even find a sword yet. It makes…"

Kadoog'han cut him off to finish the sentence differently than Savaiyon had intended, "Perfect sense. Darian led Jahmash quite far from here for their final battle. Remember, Jahmash is on an island somewhere north of Ashur. Just imagine how far that is from here. Darian would have had his sword with him. We also know that Darian died there, even if we don't know exactly how." Kadoog'han glanced down and then looked back at Slade and Savaiyon, "We got so excited to see these graves that we didn't stop to think logically. It makes more sense that Darian's grave is empty, rather than there being anything in it."

Savaiyon nodded his head. "You are right, Kad. We got too caught up in the moment and were blinded by excitement. Light of Orijin, we should have known. We wasted all this time when we could have been back in Gansishoor already. I apologize to both of you. All of us could have been sleeping by now."

Kadoog'han smiled and put a hand on his shoulder, "This is on all three of us, not just you. If any one of us had stopped to think about it for even a moment, it could've been avoided. This isn't your mistake. And to be honest, Sav, I likely would still be awake anyway, drooling over those two swords."

"Shit."

Savaiyon turned to Slade, "What is it?"

"It never seemed like anything significant until now. But I have seen Jahmash several times with a sword at each of his sides. He has them at his waist, but I never saw him take either of them out. I'd never paid them much attention aside from noticing that they were fancy, but both swords had golden hilts and golden pommels. He has it. Jahmash has Darian's sword. And if that's the case…"

Once again, Kadoog'han finished the sentence, "He likely has Darian's body as well."

Chapter 8
Shifting from the Norm

*From **The Book of Orijin**,* **Verse Three Hundred One**
Your manifestations will evolve, as will you.
Allow yourselves to grow. Adapt. Mature.
And your manifestations will as well.

"For the last time, Wassa, it is too late. He left already. You will get me and him in trouble if you keep pushing this. You said your goodbye, now be happy with that," Vasher's mother, Varana Jai, reprimanded her son in a hushed tone with enough of a rasp in her voice that Vasher knew he was being yelled at. "Must I really remind you that most young men in your position would kill—and I truly mean *kill*—to have what you have?"

Vasher sometimes wished that his sense of ethics wasn't so strong. He would have loved to use his manifestation to convince his mother that he should chase after his father for one final goodbye before the man left for his sea adventure. He knew there was no situation that could ever arise that would justify it, though. He gently kicked away the footstool and arose from his chair. "Listen woman, you can't talk to me that way. I have fought the armies of Jahmash. I have seen the inside of the Anonymi fortress. I have traveled all of Ashur." He lost his train of thought trying to keep a straight face. Vasher busted out laughing just about the same time as his mother, and he fell back into his chair holding his stomach.

Varana laughed so hard that her eyes teared. "I'm so sorry, big, strong, terrifying *Lord* Vasher. Tell me more of your brave adventures and conquests." They both laughed on for another couple of minutes. Vasher was sure that it lasted a little longer to offset any sadness either of them had about his father leaving on a journey with no set endpoint.

He leaned forward in the wooden rocking chair, "Mata, I've been here a week and it's taken me this long to be honest with you about him." Vasher paused and then looked up at his mother, who sat a few feet away on a sofa, facing him. She looked back at him curiously. "Don't get me wrong, I am happy for him. It was only a couple of weeks ago that I saw him, and I knew as soon as I saw him that he was bored. So I know he needs this. What upsets me, more than anything, is that I wish I could go with him. I wish the world wasn't falling apart and that I could just set the rest of my life aside and share the adventure with him."

Varana leaned forward now as well. "Then go."

"What?"

"Go. If that is what you want more than anything, go. Nobody on that ship will know who your mother is. You would not have to hide the fact that he is your father. You could make up for lost time and share a lifetime of memories and enjoyment." She looked at him so intensely that Vasher averted his eyes.

"You're mocking me, aren't you?"

"No. I know you are serious about this. Wassa, your happiness is paramount to me. You should know that. How many other children of the Daughters of Tahlia know who their fathers are? Talk to them. I have never found any issue with your choices, aside from the tambaku." She smirked while Vasher bit his lip. "Yes, of course I knew about that. Gossip in Sundari moves faster than a vrschiika's tail in the fighting pits. I wanted you to make your own decisions and I have seen far too many times that when a mother tells her child not to do something, the child only does it more often. Smoke your tambaku, just not around me. It is my hope that you will grow tired of it while you are still young."

"Uh, thanks."

"You distracted me. I was saying you should pursue whichever path will make you the happiest. Now, I know you well enough to know that you are a man of duty and honor. You are your father's son. A different type of soldier. But it doesn't matter what I say. All of Ashur, all of your Descendant friends could tell you to get on the ship, and you would not go. You feel a responsibility because of that black line on your face, and I believe you would feel more guilt being on that ship than *not* being on it." Vasher leaned back and looked up at the ceiling. "Wassa, I am not criticizing you, my son. It is admirable, the type of man you've become. You said Jahmash has foreign armies and I believe you. Much of Ashur will not, as they will refuse to accept the notion that there is life beyond Ashur, but most of Ashur is populated by fools. And that is why I have no issue with it if you prefer to go with your father. You would risk your life for a realm that hunts and kills the very people that are its only defense against complete annihilation."

Vasher put his hand through his hair, "I don't believe Ashur is that bad. Most of that is King Edmund's doing. If he were not in power, I think the mindset of Ashur would change drastically."

"You speak rather cavalierly about that. As if King Edmund is itching to renounce his throne. By the time Ashur gets a new king, I will either be dead or too old to care. Unless you're hoping that Jahmash does us the favor of killing him?"

Vasher leaned forward again and looked his mother in the eye. With his index finger, he beckoned her to do the same. He responded to her once she leaned in as well. "I am going to tell you something that only one other person outside the Anonymi fortress knows. If word of this gets out, I will know it's you who spoke. Then I will have no choice but to…"

"But to kill me?" She smiled with a wide grin.

Vasher chuckled. "Of course not, Mata. I was going to say lock you up in a cell somewhere. *Until* you die. But if you'd rather me just kill you, then I'm sure we can work something out."

Varana rolled her eyes, "Obviously I am terrible at keeping secrets; you'd better just kill me now."

"You might like this one. I don't think you'll have any trouble keeping it." Vasher took a breath, "Another Descendant and I met with the Anonymi. Our headmaster sent us to orchestrate an alliance with them, asking their help in defending Ashur against Jahmash. Their terms, though, were that King Edmund must die by our hands in order for an alliance to happen." The smile faded quickly from Varana's face, and she leaned back in her chair. Vasher looked at her curiously, "You don't look as happy as I thought you would."

"Wassa, I have no problem with the King being murdered. As horrible as that sounds when saying it aloud, I would sleep much more easily knowing that the man trying to hunt and kill Descendants is dead. My worry, though, is how Ashur reacts when that happens. Much of Ashur will not simply change their minds about you. And what of the Vermillion Army? Will they still do Edmund's bidding, or are they just blindly following his orders? Or will you have to kill them all as well?"

"Honestly, I don't know the answers to any of this. Like I said, I haven't told anyone. I'm planning to bring it up when we all meet at the Tower. Then everyone can weigh in and we can put a plan together. I'm not taking this lightly, Mata. I know there will be repercussions to deal with, but you didn't even ask *why* the Anonymi want us to kill *him*."

She rolled her eyes again and asked mockingly, "*Why* do they want you to kill *him*, Wassa?"

"The Anonymi said that he is the biggest threat to the well-being of Ashur." Vasher purposely left out the part about Marlowe. His mother didn't need to know about that, and Vasher still wasn't entirely sure whether Horatio had actually killed Marlowe. "If they believe that, and they only care for the well-being of Ashur, then they must be confident that things would be better with Edmund dying by our hands. I *do* know that most, if not all, of us who survived the attack on the House will be eager to go through with it."

"Then I will trust your judgment. Like I said, Wassa, I don't disagree that we would be better off without him. I just worry about any repercussions against you."

Vasher nodded his head as he stood up. "I will be fine. You know me, I can talk my way out of danger." He picked up the dark blue coat hanging on the back of his chair and put it on. "I should probably go get them now. We need to leave early while the good wagons are still available. And Horatio tends to always need extra time to get ready."

His mother stood as well and hugged him tightly. "Be safe, Wassa. Remember, I am always here if you need anything. I suppose I will not see you anytime soon?"

"I don't know. There is so much that is unknown now, and we don't have much of a safe haven. There's a great deal to discuss and decide upon as far as where we go next. We can't just stay at the Tower forever. I will try to come back or at least send word as soon as I can."

"Come back when you've killed Edmund. Then we'll celebrate together."

Vasher nodded. "Very well. Then you'll know for sure that it's done when you see me." He hugged her once more and walked to the front door of her quarters. He turned back to her and said, "I love you, Mata," and then left for Delilah's quarters on the other side of the square.

LINCAN SAT ON THE FLOOR of the leisure room, amongst a sea of small, bright pillows. Horatio walked by, inspecting his fingers, and entered one of the powder rooms. Lincan was sure that Vasher would be over soon, and Horatio showed no urgency in being ready. Lincan fell back into the pillows and closed his eyes. Vasher wouldn't care if they weren't ready yet, but Lincan hated being late, and Horatio was *always* running late.

He felt a shift in some of the pillows next to him but didn't bother to open his eyes or move. Unless Horatio was now using Delilah's perfume, Lincan knew right away that it was her. That sweet mixture of sunbursts and honey was specific to her. She hadn't had it at the House of Darian, at least not in the short time that Lincan had been sleeping with her. But now that they were staying in her sister's quarters, Lincan was grateful for the opportunity to smell her like this, as silly as it sounded. They had only been here a week, but the scent drove him crazy. He would be fine smelling it for the rest of his life.

Delilah's warm breath tickled the right side of his face and Lincan felt the whisper against his ear. "I think we need to stop our little...arrangement."

Lincan opened his eyes immediately. The color flushed from Lincan's face and the pillows instantly turned from pleasure to discomfort. He sat up and turned to face her. "Why do we need that?"

Delilah looked him straight in the eyes, "Don't give me that look. It has nothing to do with you. If this was happening with *any* man, the conversation would be the same. I am a Daughter of Tahlia, and I have not been true to the demands of that."

"You're also a Descendant and have other demands to consider," Lincan said coolly.

"Oh come, now, Linc. We've been sleeping together for what, a few weeks now? Where did you think this was going?"

Lincan scratched his head vigorously. He could feel his face heating up. "Going? With everything else that we've been through, the last thing I've wondered about is love. But what we've had has provided comfort and escape and stress relief. And you have to admit, it's been amazing."

Delilah smirked and nodded, "It *has* been rather amazing. You're welcome for that."

Lincan reluctantly let a smile escape. "*You're* welcome. But that's my point. Why would you want to stop so soon?"

Delilah sat up to be at the same level as him. "This is the most important time to stop. This is when it becomes addictive. We both wanted it, so it's not like anyone was being used, but the longer we sleep together, the more difficult it will be to stop. Being back here after so long, I'm reminded of the path I chose. Despite what many might think, we *choose* to be Daughters. We are not forced. We accept this lifestyle and all of the guidelines that come with it. Now, I am sure there are other Daughters who have regularly lain with men, or who have let their children know their fathers, but I no longer wish to stray. I have seen twenty-three summers, Lincan. It will likely be another few years by the time this war with Jahmash is over. By going to the House of Darian, I've already allowed myself to be older than most Daughters when they have children. There is no way I'm going to have a child until we've defeated Jahmash. So Linc, are you telling me that you're willing to wait until this is all over, just to lie with me again, for the sake of having a child, and then accepting that we can no longer speak?"

Lincan watched Delilah move her head and hands about as her long black hair cascaded on the pillows. He normally prided himself in always having a plan and thinking ahead, but this was beyond anything he could have been prepared for. There was no way he would even consider fathering a child at his age, no matter if he wasn't allowed to have fatherly responsibilities. He'd seen nineteen summers and planned to see many more before thinking about children. "I think I'm in over my head. There is clearly way too much here for me to bother arguing with you about this." He stood up, unsure of where he would even go, "But that doesn't mean that I accept it or that I'm happy about any of it. Remember, you came to *my* door. You initiated it and never for a second mentioned or showed any doubts about what we were doing. And to be honest, four of us are about to travel all the way to the Tower, which will take a few days. Why bring it up now? Do you really expect that everything will be the same for us? That we'll sit next to each other on a wagon and laugh at each other's jokes?"

Horatio reappeared on the other side of the room, his grin covering his whole face. "See! I'm all set! Ready to go and Vasher isn't even here yet!"

Lincan glanced down at Delilah disdainfully, then back at Horatio. "Great. Come outside with me, Raish. We'll wait for him out there. I'm going to try some of this mint tambaku he's been raving about." Lincan turned away from Delilah without looking at her again. He took two steps toward the dark wooden door when a knock came from the other side of it. *He's here already? Dammit, I'll have to process all this on the fly.*

"Come in!" Delilah's voice cracked as she said it. Lincan glanced at her out of the corner of his eye and saw her stand up and walk to her bedroom.

The door opened, "Everyone ready? I know it's early, but we have to get to the wagons early to get a good size. And one that will hide us once we cross over into Cerysia." Vasher walked into the leisure room and Lincan noticed his jovial countenance, as oblivious as Horatio to the conversation that had just happened. Vasher looked around as if expecting to see something, and looked at Lincan. "Sorry, I forgot that you and Raish don't have anything with you. Del and I both have the luxury of our families here, and I expected you two to have packs as well. My mother had some clothes of mine that still fit, so I brought some along just in case. It'll take us nearly a week to get to the Tower, *if* we make good time. If you fellows need to use anything of mine, just let me know."

Horatio stepped over a few pillows as he neared the door. He turned to Lincan and glanced at Delilah, then back at Lincan. "And don't worry, you two. I'll make sure to give you your privacy when you need it. The last thing I want to be is a burden on a trip like this." He looked back and forth at both of them once more, smiled, and walked outside. Lincan put his palm to his forehead for a moment and then scratched the back of his head again. *Light of Orijin, surviving this trip will be harder than fighting Jahmash.*

Delilah rolled her eyes at him, pursed her lips, then stood up and looked at Vasher. "I'll be out shortly. I have to say goodbye to Jennikah and grab my pack. I don't know when I'll see my sister again, so it may be a long goodbye."

Vasher nodded, "Understood. Try not to be too long, though. It would be a shame for us to die on a wagon a few days from now because we were too late to get a good one." Lincan surveyed Vasher before walking outside. He knew Vasher had likely spent the whole week making the most of every experience with his mother and appreciating every little thing, which was why it was easy for him to be on time now. He hadn't waited until the last minute to say what was on his mind or to be sentimental, while Delilah would likely take a while now to tell her sister how much she loved her and other things she could have said over the last few days. *Same way she chose today to end things with me.* Horatio was already standing outside when Lincan and Vasher left Jennikah's quarters.

Lincan looked back inside, then waved Horatio and Vasher to come closer. "She just ended things right before you arrived, Vasher. This journey is going to be awkward."

Horatio's eyes widened. "Really? This morning? Wow, I'm sorry, man. If I had known, I wouldn't have said all those things."

"It's fine, you had no way of knowing. I just wanted you two to know before we set out. That way you don't say anything that would make it awkward."

Vasher took out his tinderbox and lit his pipe, then chimed in. "We're going to end up being *more* awkward trying *not* to be awkward."

Lincan lit his own pipe, "Just act...natural."

"Does she know that you're telling us?" Horatio asked.

"Why does that matter?" Lincan said as he exhaled.

"Well, it would probably help with the awkwardness. You know, if she knows that we know, then maybe it's not as awkward. But then, if she doesn't know that we know, it gets more awkward because we have to be all secretive about not knowing. And then she might wonder why we're not saying anything about you two being together, and she starts getting awkward too."

Lincan's mouth hung open so far that the pipe almost fell out. He furrowed his brow. "Does that all actually make sense to you? Raish, do you understand any of what you just said? Or were you just talking to talk again?"

Vasher cut in before Horatio could respond. "Hey, I know exactly what he meant, Linc. He's not wrong. If all four of us know that the rest of us know, then it's a little easier because no one is stressed out trying to keep a secret." Lincan just shook his head. Vasher continued, "Listen, man, this is going to be a long ride to the Tower of the Blind. And honestly, we have a couple of days before we reach the Cerysian border, which means we can enjoy ourselves for a little bit. I don't want your nonsense to get in the way of that."

Lincan started to feel that his friends were pinning this on him. "Do you mean *my* nonsense or our nonsense?" He gestured inside to indicate Delilah.

"*Your* nonsense. You said she ended things. You two have been sleeping together for what, two or three *weeks*? Don't pretend like she broke your heart or something. She told you now because she figured you could handle it like a man and not be weird while we travel. The way I see it, Del's not going to be a problem. This trip only gets as uncomfortable as you make it."

Lincan knew he didn't have much of a case to argue back. Vasher was right and he hated to admit it. "I hate you two. You're supposed to be on my side. I told you two because you were supposed to be mad at her for this and maybe ignore her or give her an attitude. So what now, am I supposed to tell her that you two know?" Horatio and Vasher nodded simultaneously. "And how am I supposed to do that? What do I do, just literally tell her, 'Oh, hi Del. Vash and Raish both now know that you no longer want to sleep with me because you've reaffirmed your identity as a Daughter of Tahlia, and you don't have to worry about this trip being uncomfortable in any way.'"

"Oh good, Linc. I was worried that you would keep it all to yourself and just brood the whole trip." Lincan jumped at the sound or Delilah's voice as she walked out from inside her sister's quarters. He turned to Delilah while she walked up to them. Jennikah smiled from the doorway, as did everyone else when he glanced around.

He was glad his pipe wasn't in his mouth when Delilah responded, or it definitely would have fallen out. He took a puff and started walking without waiting for the rest of them. "Whatever. I hate all of you. Except you, Jennikah. Thank you for letting us stay."

Jennikah yelled back from the doorway. "My pleasure, Lincan! You are always welcome here! With or without Delilah!" Lincan heard laughter behind him and continued walking.

THEY HAD TRAVELED FOR almost three days and would reach Killington by the following morning, although they wouldn't dare go into the city. Lincan had grown up on the southern shore of Fangh-Haan, so he didn't have much experience with Cerysian cities, but Horatio had done a great deal of traveling before arriving at the House of Darian, and told the group that no Cerysian city should be trusted. Killington sat at a critical point. If they could get past it without being stopped by any of King Edmund's Vermillion soldiers, Horatio said they might easily pass between the Sanai River and the mountains.

They'd lucked out with the wagon Vasher found. The owner had a wooden compartment at the front of the wagon bed, just behind the seat, that was as big as a closet. It would be tight, but all four of them could fit in it uncomfortably. Lincan dreaded having to use it, as it would mean he'd be pushed up against Delilah. It was a ridiculous thing to be worried about, but it still made him uncomfortable. The mood had started of somewhat somber as they recounted the events of the attack on the House of Darian. But then it shifted to a certain lightness as they spent most of the time reminiscing about experiences and friends at the House.

Vasher was currently talking about some intrusive thing that Horatio had done. It reminded Lincan of a time shortly after Baltaszar became his roommate. "Raish, remember when you came into my room while Tasz was out? It couldn't have been more than a couple of weeks after you both got there for the first time. You saw his sketchbook and started drawing in it, even though I warned you not to. He was so mad at you for that!"

Horatio sat across from Lincan in the back of the wagon, next to Delilah. "He was? He didn't seem like he was that upset about it. I think he huffed and puffed a little bit and then that was it. I'm almost sure I apologized and that was it, and then I left."

"Yeah, after you left is when he let it all out. It was a little strange; I think he felt bad being mad in front of you, because he didn't want to hurt your feelings. Tasz is...odd...when it comes to certain things. Things like the sketchbook - he's quite protective about certain people and things, but I bet you if you had asked him to use a page of it or borrow it to draw something, he wouldn't have said no. He wouldn't have *wanted* to share it, but he would have anyway."

Horatio smiled, "Definitely odd. That doesn't make much sense."

Vasher, sitting next to Lincan, chimed in. "Think about it. Just about everything that he's had has been taken from him or has left him. He said his mother left when he was a baby. His father was killed in front of him. His brother refused to stay with him. The girl he loved is going to have his brother's child. And he has no one in his village that he can trust. I don't know, if that was me, I think I would be particular about certain sacred things as well. It might even be the same way with people, Raish. He didn't want to hurt your feelings because he didn't want to risk your friendship."

Lincan felt the mood starting to shift, so he tried to keep it light. "I miss Tasz, though. I hope we see him again soon."

Vasher responded, "Lao said he was in a dungeon in Alvadon. I wonder if Marlowe had Savaiyon send him directly to the dungeon, or if Tasz was sent to Alvadon and ended up in the dungeon."

"No, Lao said that Tasz told him he was sent to the Never. I remember wondering why there, of all places. Was Marlowe hoping Tasz would just get lost there? If Tasz was sent to Alvadon, he would likely have been killed on sight. Even now, why would he be in a dungeon? It makes no sense that King Edmund would imprison him when he's been hunting down Descendants for years. So either the King needs him for something, or..."

Horatio finished the thought, "Or the King doesn't know he's there! Lao said Tasz was in decent spirits. I've never been in a dungeon cell, but I can't imagine anyone being anything but tired and angry if they're truly a prisoner."

Lincan nodded. "I hope he manages to get to the Tower. Hopefully Maven Savaiyon also thinks to go there. He would be the best chance of rescuing Tasz."

Vasher perked up, "That's true. Speaking of Maven Savaiyon, there's something I've been wondering, Raish. It's about the battle at the House, when we were on the shores fighting. And don't get the wrong idea, I'm not accusing you of anything, but did you know that it was Marlowe, not really Drahkunov?"

Lincan held his breath. Deep down, this had been on his mind as well, but he wasn't sure of the best way to ask Horatio about it. There was some relief mixed in with the shock of hearing Vasher ask so directly. Horatio's reaction was quite the opposite, however. He slouched and deflated. Lincan suspected that Horatio had hoped to avoid that conversation, but it was too important a question to not be asked. Still, he felt a tinge of pity for Horatio, in that he thought Marlowe's death was an accident. He interjected before Horatio had to worry about a response. "Look, Raish, it's something that anyone who was there wants to know. But that doesn't mean that we think you're a murderer or anything like that. I *saw* the state that you were in when you and Savaiyon arrived at the infirmary. If I remember correctly, you slept through Marlowe's whole speech to us in there, which means you likely didn't even hear his plan. And to be completely honest, I don't know why any of us allowed you to leave it to go fight. You didn't have the physical or mental strength to be part of that battle. I'm dumbfounded that you were even able to summon lightning in the first place, with how out of it you were."

Horatio nodded and put his hand up for Lincan to let him speak. "The truth is, I don't know what I was thinking. That whole time out there on the shore, it's like a blur in my head. Linc, you're right. I don't remember anything about the infirmary, and definitely not anything Marlowe said. I didn't like some of the things he did, but I wouldn't kill him." Horatio breathed deeply and shrugged his shoulders, "I don't know whether you believe me, or whether anyone else will, but that's not me. I'm not a murderer. I know I talk too much and maybe I'm overbearing at times, but that's about as serious as my flaws get. I don't wish harm on anyone except those who want to hurt and kill *us*. For all of Marlowe's shortcomings, he still wasn't trying to hurt us. And even if I wanted to hurt or kill him, why would I do it in front of everyone where they could see me?"

"Like I said, I wasn't accusing you. I just wanted to know what your mindset was like when it was happening. We know you're not a murderer; you're not even a violent person under normal circumstances. But..." Vasher paused for a moment, "Oh...my..." He leaned forward and beckoned Lincan, Horatio, and Delilah to do the same, then lowered his voice. "What I'm about to tell you, I've only told Marlowe and Maven Savaiyon. So you're all sworn to secrecy until I'm ready to tell the others at the Tower. Understood?" They all nodded with confusion wrinkling their foreheads. "Good. When Savaiyon and I met with the Anonymi, they would only agree to help us if we fulfilled two criteria. Basically, since Marlowe would never let us fight, the Anonymi wanted us to prove that we could be violent for the sake of Ashur's best interest. So they said we had to kill the two men who were the biggest threat to Ashur if they were going to help us against Jahmash."

"What?" Delilah asked incredulously. "They want us to be assassins to prove we're worthy of their help? That's ridiculous!"

Vasher cut her response short, "Is it, though? Think about it. We're arguably the best equipped to defend Ashur, and up to now, we've done nothing to help it. We've been concerned solely with our own survival, but what have we really ever done to help others?"

Horatio answered him, "Didn't we just kill hundreds of Jahmash's soldiers? I'd say that's something."

Lincan spoke up, "Yes, but that's only because they showed up at our home in the middle of the night and attacked. We only did that to protect ourselves, or else we'd all be dead. It had nothing to do with Ashur. Vasher is right, and so are the Anonymi. Forget about what the King has done to us; we were chosen by The Orijin to wield these manifestations, and we've only used them for our own betterment. Vash, is it safe to say that one of the two men is King Edmund?"

Vasher nodded, "Yes. That didn't surprise me so much. It was the second name that confounded me." They all looked at him more intently. "The Anonymi also said that we had to kill Zin Marlowe." All three of them gasped, but Vasher continued before they could say anything. "Think about it. He was our leader. He could have easily trained us to be better with our manifestations and be a force of good in Ashur, especially against the King. Instead, he babied us and sheltered us. Look at what happened when we were attacked. We were totally unprepared and anyone who survived is just plain lucky. But my point in telling you all this now is that, regardless of Raish's intentions, he is the one who killed Marlowe. The Anonymi were quite clear that both men's deaths have to be by our hands. Everything else aside, Raish fulfilled their first demand. Now, I'm not saying I'm happy that Marlowe is dead, but if we want allies against Jahmash, then we're halfway towards getting some incredibly powerful reinforcements."

Lincan was starting to put pieces together. "So that's what we were really asking about when Marlowe wanted us to essentially question every Blind Man in Ashur. You said that you only told him and Maven Savaiyon, aside from your mother. Marlowe had you and Savaiyon lead a mission so he could find out how it would happen?"

Vasher nodded, "Precisely. We weren't allowed to tell you much. But then Tasz ran off and compromised the whole mission. I don't know if you were aware, but Marlowe was planning to send a group back out to see it through. Obviously, it's all inconsequential now."

Lincan cocked his head diagonally. "Actually, it's *not* inconsequential. If Tasz hadn't done what he did, then there's a strong possibility that Marlowe wouldn't have died by our hands." Vasher and Horatio looked at him quizzically. "Think about it. We were only at the House because Tasz ruined the mission. If he didn't do that, wed all have been spread out throughout Ashur, with likely no clue of the House being attacked. And if not for Desmond, it's pretty likely that the House would have come crashing down quite easily. At the risk of sounding arrogant, I'm certain that nobody would have survived that attack if we hadn't been there."

Delilah snickered, "Not arrogant at all."

Lincan rolled his eyes, "Look, Del, you can just sit there and be quiet since you have no idea what I'm talking about. Horatio and Maven Savaiyon managed to fend off Maqdhuum and keep him away from the House. Vasher, Desmond, Marshall, Kadoog'han, and Badalao all played a role in either keeping the House standing or fighting back on the shores. You and I were in the infirmary tending to the wounded, many of whom went right back out to fight." He shot her a glare, "So I'd say that my estimation is rather accurate. And back to the point I was making before you interrupted, if we weren't there, someone else would have killed Marlowe, and the Anonymi would have then left us on our own."

Delilah huffed, "Well thank you for saving our lives, Lincan." Lincan rolled his eyes. He realized then that Baltaszar's antics had also led to him and Delilah working more closely together, which is how they evolved into lovers in the first place. He hadn't meant to stare at her for as long as he did, but she must have picked up on what he was thinking. "And don't forget, that's how I ended up in your bed for so many nights. You should be extremely thankful to Tasz."

Vasher and Horatio both attempted to look away or down or at anything else but Lincan and Delilah. Lincan himself wished he could ignore it as well. "You two said it wouldn't be awkward if she knew that you knew. And now look, she's even more brazen about it *because* you know."

Delilah smiled, "I'm right here, you don't have to keep calling me 'she.'"

"The sooner I forget your name, the better," he quipped.

"Oh is that right?"

"If at first you don't succeed, destroy all evidence that you tried. I'll be perfectly fine forgetting about you. Believe me."

"Well how nice for you. I suppose I'd better watch out for you, then. Horatio might not be the only one killing fellow Descendants."

"Soldiers ahead! Looks like they're checking wagons! Get in the cabinet now!" The wagon driver yelled from up front. Vasher had made it a point to not exchange names with the man, for the sake of deniability if anyone was questioned. They scrambled into the hideout and set the wooden board back in place, but once they were secure, they couldn't dare move. Lincan had squished into one corner and, just as he'd imagined would happen, Delilah ended up right next to him. And as he'd feared, half of her backside was pushed up against him. Lincan was still mad enough at her that it was enough to prevent him from being aroused, but it doubled the sweat he'd already had from the four of them being stuffed in the compartment.

"Summon your manifestations," Vasher whispered from the other end. Lincan had already done so, but he could feel Delilah slightly shift, likely summoning hers at the reminder. Voices grew louder as the wagon rolled along until they stopped again. The voices were somewhat muffled, but it was clear that the checkpoint soldiers were questioning the driver. The wagon creaked as at least one of them climbed onto the back of the wagon, right where they had been sitting only minutes ago. Lincan heard the stomp of the boots as they would take a few steps, then stop, then do the same thing over and over again as they inspected every inch of the wagon bed. Lincan realized then that he'd been holding his breath the entire time, and refused to exhale until the soldiers left, lest they hear the faintest sound of him breathing. After another moment, the footsteps stopped and Lincan heard them grow more and more distant. In another minute or so, the wagon was moving again. It wasn't for a few more minutes that the driver yelled back that they could come out. Lincan and Vasher pushed the fake wooden wall out and the four of them spilled out of the compartment.

They pushed the wooden piece back into its place and then sat down in their original spots. Lincan breathed deeply a few more times to make up for the breaths he hadn't taken while hiding. He managed to calm down and the sweating stopped as well. The others seemed to calm down as well, but it was Delilah who spoke first. "Thank you, Lincan, for keeping us safe. Surely we all would have died without your efforts."

He was getting more annoyed with each of her comments. He was sure she was just doing it to get under his skin, especially since he hadn't handled it too well when she told him she wanted to end things, but Delilah was carrying it too far. "I'll let that one go. I'm sure you're just a little worked up and probably still a little excited from rubbing up against me while we were hiding." Once again, Vasher and Horatio did their best to pretend they had other things more worthy of paying attention to. To Lincan's surprise, though, Delilah simply smiled and nodded.

JUST AS VASHER had said, they'd traveled between the Sanai and the mountains for the past two days. There had been no incidents since passing Killington, but they would be coming upon Magnon on Sanai in the morning. Magnon and Killington were at each end of the mountain range, so the group decided to stop for a rest well before reaching the city. Everyone would sleep and one person would stay up as a lookout until he or she got tired. Lincan volunteered for the first shift. The others were all more tired than he was, as he'd drunk the last of the coffee earlier in the day. There had been rumors amongst the travelers that Vermillion soldiers were conducting searches in the night, so it was more important than usual for them to be prepared at a moment's notice.

Still, Lincan had gotten lost in his thoughts. His eyes were focused on a certain spot of the ground, yet his mind blocked him from seeing what was there. Instead, Lincan had fallen into a mental hole of wondering and worrying how his manifestation could be productive in battle.

Lincan, if nothing else, preferred to be honest with himself about who he was and what he was capable of. And the truth of it was that his manifestation didn't lend itself to be much of a weapon against enemies. He often joked with his friends that perhaps he could make his enemy too healthy in the heat of battle. At least Horatio could hurt or kill with lightning. Baltaszar had fire, Desmond could move enemies with his mind, and even Vasher could persuade an attacker against fighting him. But Lincan had nothing to use, and that was the main reason for his resentment toward Zin Marlowe. Marlowe knew full well that many in the House of Darian didn't have manifestations that could easily translate to battle, and he still refused to have them trained in any type of combat. Lincan had taken part in the secret sparring sessions that Gunnar had organized, but even those were minimal because of the secrecy needed.

He was excited to be able to reconnect with the other survivors. Lincan prided himself in always having a plan, and it would be nice for them all to let their guard down for once, talk about what needed to be done, and what steps needed to be taken. While Marlowe's death saddened him, Lincan was grateful that he would be able to put his life in his own hands and make decisions for himself.

Ever since the attack on the House, there had been so much uncertainty and tentativeness among the four of them, and Lincan had even sensed it in Badalao when in contact with him. He looked forward to some familiarity of seeing friends again. For the first time in a while, Lincan allowed himself to feel a sense of hope. If they could get past Magnon on Sanai without trouble, they could easily cross over into Galicea, a nation much friendlier to Descendants than Cerysia. Then they would be able to breathe easily, with much less of a chance of soldiers stopping them.

The footsteps were already too close for Lincan to wake the others discreetly. He'd snapped out of his reverie and knew the distinct sound of a soldier's boots crunching against the hard ground. He summoned his manifestation without hesitation or wonder of how he'd use it. They were all wearing black cloaks over their regular clothes, fashioned after the one Baltaszar had brought with him to the House of Darian, except these were thicker. Lincan hoped the hood would buy him a little extra time before the soldiers noticed the black line on his face.

To his surprise, only one soldier appeared at the back of the wagon, dressed in full armor, his helmet bearing the red crest of the Vermillion. The soldier held a torch in one hand, illuminating his golden Cerysian face. "Show your face, traveler. Off with the hood." Lincan didn't know whether the soldier had seen the others, but the man gave no indication of it, or perhaps he would handle them one at a time. Lincan thought it better not to wake them yet, as to avoid drawing too much attention. He kept his head down and slowly removed the hood. He wasn't entirely sure what he was going to do, but he knew he had to try his manifestation in some way. The soldier grabbed Lincan's jaw with his free hand and lifted Lincan's face. Lincan stared right at him and saw how the recognition of the black line changed the soldier's countenance.

Before the soldier could do anything, Lincan grabbed him by the wrist and held tightly. He focused on his manifestation, but with the intent to cause harm rather than heal. He focused solely on hurting the man as he stared directly into his eyes. At first, the soldier simply tried to escape, but after a few moments, his countenance changed to that of panic. Lincan was unsure of what he'd actually done, but he could feel the sweat building up on the soldier's arm, and his body temperature seemed to be getting hot. The soldier dropped the torch and his body went limp, causing Lincan to let go of his arm. The soldier fell to the ground. At first he lay still, and then his body went into violent convulsions and he vomited violently on the ground and on himself until he fell back to the ground on his back.

"What the...what did I do?" He whispered to himself. He heard movement behind him and slightly jumped where he was sitting. Lincan turned to see Vasher stand up and walk over to him. As Vasher reached Lincan, he must have seen the body on the ground outside the wagon as the soldier's armor reflected in the moonlight.

"What's going on?" Vasher was about to sit down but reversed course. "Is that a Vermillion soldier?" He scampered back to Horatio and Delilah and shook them awake. "Get up,

both of you. Up and awake, and clear your heads to summon your manifestations. I think we're about to have trouble." Both Horatio and Delilah looked at Vasher groggily, but neither argued. They both stood immediately, and Delilah opened her cloak to check the daggers in her belt. Each of them had at least one knife hidden in their cloak sleeves, but Lincan doubted the effectiveness of such a small blade against an armored opponent trained in combat. He only hoped he could continue to do what he'd done to the first soldier.

Just as Vasher had warned, trouble arrived in the form of three Vermillion soldiers inspecting the dead soldier on the ground. The notion gave Lincan pause. *Dead. I can't believe I killed someone with my manifestation.* The soldiers immediately looked up at the wagon, assuming they were the cause of death. Before the soldiers could utter a word, Vasher brushed Lincan aside and stood at the edge of the wagon. He spoke melodically to them, "My friends, you don't want to attack us. The people who killed that man are in a different wagon, and we pose absolutely no threat to you."

The three soldiers looked at each other and then back at Vasher. One of them, the tallest of the three, responded. "We have no quarrel with you, sir. We are looking for a different wagon."

As they started walking away, four more soldiers arrived, confused that these three were walking away. One of the new set eyed Lincan and immediately yelled to them all, "Why are you three walking away, there are Descendants hiding in there! They killed one of our men!"

"We spoke to them. We have no quarrel with them. We are looking for a different wagon." The other soldier looked at him and then at Lincan and Vasher, then shook his comrade and flung him into the other two who Vasher had spoken to. The jolt must have cleared their minds, as they no longer tried to walk away.

Lincan turned his head back to Horatio. "Raish, now might be a good time for lightning."

Horatio responded with his eyes closed, "I'm trying, Linc. It's not working. I don't know why I can't do it." He sighed deeply, "I think you three might have to do this without me. I don't know what's wrong with me."

Lincan turned around again to face the soldiers. "Del, come down with me, I think we'll have to do this ourselves." Lincan embraced a new confidence, and felt like if he could grasp each soldier in the right spot, he could inflict pain or illness on them, just as he'd done with the first. He hopped off of the wagon and heard Delilah follow. He held his arms up to imply that he had no weapon. Five of the soldiers had drawn their swords, but Lincan kept his arms high. "I have no weapons to fight you. I surrender. I'll kneel and you can bind my hands." He knelt and removed his cloak, then rolled up his shirtsleeves. He needed whoever bound him to touch his flesh. Sure enough, one soldier walked up to him as he thrust his arms out. Next to him, Delilah did the same. He heard Vasher and Horatio jump down from the wagon and walk up behind them as well.

The soldier who was binding Lincan used one hand to hold his wrists, which was all Lincan needed. He focused on pain and illness, just as before. The only difference was that now, Lincan knew what he was trying to do, so the results came faster. The soldier in front of him dropped immediately, just as the one binding Delilah did. He looked at her and she glanced back instantaneously. They jumped up and pounced on two other soldiers who'd brandished their swords. Lincan rushed ahead to grab the soldier's throat before he could raise his sword. The reaction was just as immediate as the last, and the soldier fell to the ground and writhed until he no longer moved.

Another soldier had attempted to advance upon them, but Vasher flung a dagger at his face. It missed, but distracted him long enough for Vasher to knock him down and draw another dagger, striking the soldier directly in the face. Delilah debilitated a fifth soldier using her manifestation to reach into his leg. She rematerialized her hand while inside of him, and pulled one of his shin bones right out of his flesh; he collapsed right away. The four of them didn't bother to admire their work, as two other soldiers remained.

Lincan found it curious that their weapons weren't drawn. In fact, he didn't think they'd pulled their swords at any point in the scuffle. "Why haven't you attacked? Are you cowards or are you just sensible enough to admit defeat?"

One of the two soldiers put his palms up in front of his chest. "We are part of a resistance within the Vermillion."

Lincan scratched his head and looked around at the other three. He noticed the wagon driver standing in the back of the wagon as well. They all looked as confused as he felt. "What the hell are you talking about? What resistance?"

The other soldier, the stockier of the two, removed his helmet and responded. "There are a growing number of us in the Vermillion who are loyal to Prince Donovan Brighton and Wendell Ravensdayle, our commanders, rather than to King Edmund. Simply put, we go to our posts and assignments, but we do not take part in killing Descendants."

Vasher spoke up while Lincan was trying to make sense of what they were saying. "Why? What started this?"

The helmetless soldier answered, "After Prince Garrison was named a traitor to Cerysia and before he was chased out of the nation, he ordered Prince Donovan and Commander Ravensdayle to train soldiers who would be loyal to them. Once many of us saw what King Edmund did to his own son, who we adored and respected, we began to shift our allegiance. Not everyone sees it the same way, which is why these men still attacked you." He nodded to the five men on the ground.

Lincan was skeptical. "So now what? Do we just say 'thank you' and go on our way?"

"If you go on your own now they will just stop you at Magnon on Sanai. It would be more of the same—some soldiers will attack you and some will not, but it may come down to luck as to whether you survive." He looked at his fellow soldier. "I can escort you. The four of you will hide in the back and I will sit up front with your driver. If they see me, they will know I have already inspected the wagon and will assume there is no threat. I can make up some excuse about knowing your driver, or that he asked me for help. Once there, I can talk to soldiers I trust, and you will have safe passage to wherever you are going."

Lincan turned back to the other three. He had some reservations about going through with this but wanted to hear what the others had to say. "What do you think?"

Vasher sighed, "Look, if these two wanted to attack us, they already would have."

Delilah quickly responded, "*Or* they know we would kill them, and this is just a way to stall in order to get reinforcements."

"Yeah, I was wondering about that, too." Lincan said reluctantly. He didn't want Delilah to know he agreed with her.

"Didn't Lao tell us that Tasz is in a dungeon in Alvadon, but in good spirits? What if that's because he's under the watch of people like these two," Horatio nodded toward the two soldiers. "What if it's Prince Donovan and…I forgot the other name. But wouldn't that make sense if they were telling the truth?"

Lincan saw Horatio's point. If they were being honest, it would make sense as to why Tasz was still alive. "That's a fair point. Realistically, we don't have much choice here anyway. And we need to act fast before more soldiers arrive. I say we do what he says. If at any point, we think he's lying, we kill him." The other three gave their affirmations. Lincan was surprised that Delilah agreed so easily, but now wasn't the time to question it. He turned back to the soldiers, "Very well. But we need to leave now, to avoid any more trouble."

The stocky soldier donned his helmet and walked to the front of the wagon. "Let us go then."

They turned to get back into the wagon as their driver walked to the front. Delilah walked over to the soldiers on the ground. "Just a moment." They all turned and watched as she walked to the soldier whose leg she'd broken. He still writhed on the ground, groaning. Delilah knelt down and passed her hand into his neck. She then looked at the soldier who offered to escort them and jerked her wrist. Without any expression or emotion, she walked back to the wagon and climbed into the back.

CHAPTER 9
SCHATZA

*From **The Book of Orijin**,* **Verse One Hundred Thirty-two**
State of mind will dictate everything in life.
A healthy mind creates a healthy body. A healthy life. And healthy relationships.
A tainted mind will kill you from the inside.

"THERE, AHEAD," BADALAO pointed at the clearing in the trees and turned his head to Sindha on his right. "Finally, the end of the forest." They'd ridden from City of the Fallen through the forest over the past few days, sleeping in shifts and doing their best to not inspect the corpses too closely.

"Holy haul, it's a miracle," Sindha said dryly. "At least it's early enough that we'll reach Gangjeon before sundown."

Badalao cocked his head towards her. "You say that rather often. Explain to me exactly what 'holy haul' means."

"Have you never met anyone else from Itarse?"

Badalao didn't turn to her but knew Sindha was rolling her eyes. "Actually, no. You're the first." He knew she was likely still rolling her eyes. "Oh come now, Sindha. I am a Markosi highborn and a Descendant. What reason would I ever have had to visit some small, tucked away village in the bowels of Shivaana?"

Sindha responded loudly, "Hmph. Wow." Badalao finally looked over at her again and regretted choosing to do so. She was angry. "You have made your highborn status painfully clear, Lao, and I don't mean that kindly. If you ever pulled your head with those three buns out of your ass, you would know just how large Itarse is. The city sprawls, and you would easily know that if you ever paid attention in Maven Savaiyon's classes. He showed us the city through a gateway, but perhaps you were too busy giggling and flirting with your pet, Desmond." She spurred her horse to trot a few paces ahead of him. "You loved to play swords with your friends so often back at the House, but I gather you never wondered where the steel came from. Most steel in Ashur comes from the mines at Itarse. Our people mine it, process it, forge it, and shape it. My father is a blacksmith in one of those forges. That sword at your hip would not be there if not for the *bowels* of Shivaana."

Ah, there it is; offended because of her father. "I apologize, I did not mean to disrespect your family. And *bowels* was harsh, I will give you that. But that still does not answer my question. Holy haul?"

"You got me worked up and I went off-topic. Jerk. Like I said, Itarse sprawls. It extends from the mountains all the way to the Sea of Fates. The city is likely double the size of the City of the Fallen, if not bigger. It's not just the steel that finances us; our fishing business thrives as well. Sundari and Vishadah have the benefit of being out on the open sea, while we are more settled into the bay and blocked by the islands off the coast. The thing is, there are no cities on those islands, which leaves our fishing boats a lot of area to cover. You'd be surprised at how many different kinds of fish are there. Even though my father is a blacksmith, we live close to the docks, so I've been out fishing with my uncles too many times to count. Sometimes, or I should say quite often, we bring back a haul big enough to feed the House of Darian, and that's just on one boat. That's what we call a 'holy haul.' We do a lot of business with buyers from Fangh-Haan and other Shivaani cities. Itarse isn't some dirt-ridden forgotten town, it's a flourishing city and well-governed."

Badalao was relieved to be done in the forest. They'd traveled through the entirety of it to avoid attention on the way to Gangjeon. It had been over a year since he'd been through this forest, but never had he seen it so full of corpses. Sindha was surprised as well, especially as most of the rotting bodies wore the armor of Vermillion soldiers. They'd been out of the forest for several minutes now, and Badalao scanned the field around him. There were more corpses sprinkled throughout the field. *More dead Vermillion soldiers. This makes no sense.* "Who were they fighting? This does not look like they won." Badalao hadn't realized some of his thoughts had manifested into words.

"What was that?" Sindha looked back at him.

"Sorry. I wasn't ignoring you. Just got distracted by all the bodies, and started thinking out loud. The corpses continue out here in the fields. I am having trouble understanding what happened here. There was clearly a battle, but with whom? Who could the Vermillion have been fighting that so many are dead? And I have yet to see a body of someone *not* in Vermillion armor."

Sindha slowed to let him catch up. "It's too bad Adria isn't here with us. She's perfect for solving these types of things. I'll see if I can think like her." She was quiet for a moment. "Perhaps they were fighting amongst themselves?"

Badalao shook his head. "To this extent? And this far away from Alvadon? That seems highly unlike…" He noticed a man's body, pinned under a dead horse, on the ground to his left. It had an arrow through the heavily tattooed skull, which proved quite serendipitous; otherwise he likely would not have given it much of a look. "Hold on, Sindha. Look at this one. Arrow through the head—a Taurani head." He looked around the rest of the landscape. "This is the only Taurani we have seen. Were they *that* skilled that it would take so many Vermillion lives to kill one Taurani?"

Sindha looked down at the corpses of the man and horse and stared for a few moments. "Taurani would not leave their village like this."

"Remember that their village was decimated a year ago. Judging by how rotted this one is, it might have been here for as long."

"So a survivor that managed to escape the initial attack. Still, where would he be going?" She ran her fingers through her hair a few times. "Wait. How long ago was it that Prince Garrison came to the House, begging for asylum?"

Badalao grew wide-eyed out of curiosity, "Probably about a year. Why?"

She looked at him sternly. "There were rumors that he'd gotten help from the Taurani in order to make it to the House, and that they'd sacrificed themselves for his survival. Chances are, we missed their corpses because we came from the City, not the mountain portal."

"And where did these rumors come from?"

Sindha smirked. "They? Them? You know the nature of rumors. It was supposedly a conversation that took place between Garrison, Marshall, and Tasz down in the dungeon."

Badalao's brow furrowed as they moved their horses on from the dead Taurani. "Ridiculous. Why would they even talk to him? We all hate him." He eyes Sindha curiously.

"Think about it. Of all the people who would have no reason to hate Garrison, one would be a Taurani who'd never left his village to know that Garrison had hunted and killed Descendants. Another would be a boy from *another* village hidden away in the Never, just as oblivious. Garrison's actions never affected them. They wouldn't even know to hate him. If anything, the three of them would get on swimmingly, as they'd all feel like outsiders in the House."

"You channeled your inner Adria quite well."

He noticed her cheeks redden a little as she smiled. "I'm a tiny bit proud of myself." Badalao noticed her smile fade almost into a frown. "I miss her. I hope she isn't hurt. Or worse."

He looked her in the eye, "You know as well as I do that she's the strongest and scrappiest of us. If anyone can handle themselves with Maqdhuum, it's Adria."

"Maqdhuum?"

"That's what Marshall said down in the infirmary before our final stand. He said that he and Maven Savaiyon were only a few feet away from her on one of the ships off the shore, and then Maqdhuum disappeared with her. Still, I think she could hold her own with him."

"Who even knows what his agenda is. First, he kills all the Taurani, then leads armies to kill all of us. Why take Adria captive then? Why not just kill her?"

Badalao shrugged. "There is a lot to figure out. Hopefully once we meet with everyone at the Tower, all of our minds collectively can piece things together."

They rode on for another hour or so in silence, through the field towards Gangjeon. Badalao looked forward to seeing Desmond again, but he'd seemed different when Badalao had tried to connect with him. Badalao knew something was off, but it was impossible to determine what without prying into Desmond's mind, and that wasn't something he felt comfortable doing.

After a while, Sindha turned to him, "Deep in thought, huh? You thinking about *her*?" She grinned widely, the slight gap between her two top teeth on full display.

Shit. "No. Who?" Badalao rolled his eyes and managed to stifle a smile. "I was thinking about Desmond. Why, you jealous?"

"Jealous of Desmond or Farrah?"

He could feel his cheeks redden at the mention of her name. "I guess it depends on which one of them you want to be." He eyed her peripherally. "I'm joking. Before you take that the wrong way, I am not insinuating anything."

Sindha pursed her lips together, "Oh please. Who haven't you flirted with or tried to seduce at the House? Don't pretend like *you* would be getting *my* hopes up, Lao. We had a very brief thing, and apparently I wasn't enough to satisfy you. And that's fine, but I wasn't going to just be some piece of food that you sample at the market, and maybe go back to get another piece while you try all the other options. I lost my interest in *you* and I don't regret any of it. We got a rise out of each other and enjoyed one night together, and then I learned that you are not the type of...man?...boy?...that I need to be with."

Badalao grew wide-eyed at her outburst. He knew she was right and he was not upset about it, but he hadn't expected that she would still have anything to say about what had happened between them a year or two ago. "I get it, I understand why you are upset. And I apologize for hurting you or leading you on, or misleading you, if any of those are applicable. My mindset with relationships is likely different than most other people's and that is not something I really understood until I spent considerable time at the House. As we've made quite clear, I am a Markosi highborn. It is expected that I marry another Markosi, and in our culture, it is...I doubt there is a way to say this without stoking your fire. But it is understood that young highborn men will have our dalliances before committing to our future bride." Sindha opened her mouth to respond, but he cut her off. "Before you admonish me again, you should understand that it is acceptable *because* we are expected to treat our wives exceptionally well during intimacy, and the only way to do that is through experience."

Sindha's eyes grew wide this time. "Oh. Well that's...interesting. And does this apply to only the highborn or are all Markosi men encouraged to be so...generous to their wives?"

Badalao smiled. "You know how most cultures are. Everyone emulates the highborn. This is no different. I would imagine that most common Markosi are better equipped than even the most reputable men in any other nation."

"All this carousing going on with you Markosi 'men.' I can only imagine how many of you have children before you can even grow a beard."

"One of the benefits of being Markosi is that silphica grows abundantly at the edges of the Never, all the way from Pyrrha to Constaniza. Both cities harvest it and sell it at the markets. It can be taken in tea or one can chew the leaves—it has a bitter taste but it is palatable. Within a few hours, it starts working, and just like that, it renders men sterile for a week or so."

"Seriously?"

"Yes. In fact, it is expected that young Markosi men take it regularly once our transition into manhood begins, up until the time we marry."

"Wow. I may have to pay a visit to Markos and find a nice common man to practice his techniques with me, and then I can marry him. And as for you, don't think that I forgot. Is Farrah another dalliance, then? You did say she's Markosi."

Badalao shrugged, "No clue. You might be putting more into this than me. My encounter with the girl lasted less than a day, and however good I might have thought it was, she left without a goodbye or an explanation. It really does not matter what I say or think—the truth is we may never even see her again. She ran off for a reason."

"While I'm truly sorry for all your confusion and stress, I can't help but think this is a nice dose of karum for you."

"Dose of what?"

"Karum. It's an old Shivaani word—balance, justice. Like perhaps you're getting what you deserve for all the times that you've done the same thing? And I'm not saying that to be bitter, I honestly believe in what the Book of Orijin says about balance and that eventually we all get what's coming to us."

"Oh, thanks. I'm glad you can justify this by telling me it's what the

Orijin wants."

Sindha didn't take his bait. "Any time. I'll always be glad to put you in your place."

Badalao pursed his lips and nodded. "How lucky of me to have such a great friend, whose highest priority is to keep me grounded."

"Well, your little boys group that you spend all your time with isn't doing anything to keep your ego in proportion, so it seems that someone has to. Come on, let's hurry up and get to Gangjeon so I can make Desmond jealous. Then I can leave you and go to Markos to find my future husband."

AS HUNGRY AS HE AND SINDHA were, Badalao wanted to see Desmond before doing anything else. A nurse directed them to Desmond's room as soon as they walked into the two-story building. Badalao knocked on the door several times until finally he heard someone grumbling and plodding toward the door. The latch clicked and the door opened to reveal a groggy Desmond.

"Hey," Desmond grunted and nodded, his eyes barely open. He turned and walked gingerly back to his bed without waiting for a response.

"What happened to you? You get roughed up or something?" Badalao scanned the room for any sign of a struggle. "And where's Maximillian? I thought he was worse off than you." Desmond grunted an inaudible response as he got back into the bed and covered himself with a wool blanket. "You can grunt all you want, but we want to know what's going on. Sindha and I have been traveling for days, and we're starving for a hot meal. But we're not leaving you here by yourself like this. So either we wait here until Maximillian returns or we wait here until you're ready to get up and do more than grunt at us." Badalao glanced at Sindha, who was standing next to him. She looked suspicious. Badalao also suspected that something was off. *He's hiding something. I've never seen him like this before.* He waited again for Desmond to respond but got nothing. "Fine. You want to be difficult. Sindha, you want to sleep next to him or do you want me to? We might as well get comfortable if Desmond is going back to sleep."

Sindha smirked, but he knew she was annoyed and hungry. She played along, "He's your friend; you two can snuggle and reminisce. I'll enjoy the other bed all by myself. If we're not going to eat, I might as well just get a good sleep."

"Dammit. I shouldn't have given you the option. I should just have gotten into that bed. Oh well, I guess he'll just have to deal with me sleeping next to him." Badalao set down his packs and jumped onto the bed, making sure he landed on Desmond.

Desmond's eyes shot wide open at the impact, as Badalao landed on his chest. "Bloody chuff! What the hell is wrong with ya! My ribs are cracked! Get off me!" Badalao felt a tinge of guilt and scrambled off of the bed.

"Oh, so you *can* talk! Thank you for actually using words! Now explain or I'll do that again. Your ribs were not cracked during the attack on the House. I know that for sure. So tell me how that happened. And where is Maximillian?" Desmond grimaced. He propped himself up and Badalao helped with adjusting his pillow behind his back so he could sit up. "Just tell us the truth. There's no judgment here."

"Max left fer the Tower a few days ago." Desmond held his side and winced, "He...said he wanted ta speak ta someone there before everyone else arrived." Badalao furrowed his brow out of curiosity. He saw Sindha do the same. Desmond must have noticed their expressions, "I guess he knows someone there that he wants ta catch up with before the rest o' us get there." He glanced at both of them and quickly pointed to his ribs and added, "This happened the day after he left. I got into a...misunderstandin' at the inn across the street an' they kicked me out. Pounded on me in the process. A Descendant girl helped me get back here. She was about ta kiss me an' then you decided ta jump inta my mind." Desmond paused for a moment, looking as if he was working something out. "She musta thought I was a bit off, because then she changed her mind about the kiss an' told me ta come get her when I'm leavin' fer the Tower."

Sindha sighed, "There's so much going on there. First, there is no way Maven Maximillian would just leave you on your own, especially in an infirmary."

Desmond cut her off, "He didn't just leave me. He knows the man who's tendin' ta us. A man named Clyde. Promised ta take care o' me an' it's not like I've been leavin' the infirmary anyway."

Badalao patted one of the loops of hair on the back of his head. "You just said you left the infirmary a couple of days ago and someone broke your ribs as a result. Where was Clyde then?"

To Badalao's surprise, Desmond glowered at them. "Look. If yer just goin' ta interrogate me an' think everythin' I'm sayin' is a lie, then both of ya can screw off. Just go ta the Tower now an' leave me. I'll leave in my own time an' go find Schatza, then maybe we'll go ta the Tower if we still feel like it."

"Schatza?"

Desmond rolled his eyes at him. "The girl I was just tellin' ya about. The Descendant girl. Her name's Schatza. If ya weren't so busy bein' suspicious o' me, ya would've been able ta keep up."

Badalao was about to say something snarky, but let it go. "Fine,

fine. Schatza. Sounds Galicean. I do not remember anyone by that name at the House. Sindha, that name familiar to you?"

Sindha was lying comfortably on the other bed, her legs dangling over the side. "Nope. Never heard that name before. Can we eat now?"

"Don't think she had any intention o' goin' ta the House. Said she's been on the run since she was younger. Now she's just roamin' Ashur like a vagabond."

Badalao sat back down at the foot of Desmond's bed. "This is all quite fascinating, Des, but more importantly, when will you be ready to leave Gangjeon? Whatever has been going on for you here, I cannot fathom why you have stayed this long when you could have easily ridden to the docks and taken a ferry to the Tower. The hospitality there must be vastly superior to what you would be getting in an infirmary."

Desmond sighed, "There are...reasons. That I don't care ta get inta right now."

Badalao shook his head, then stared up at the ceiling. "Very well. I am telling you now, Sindha and I are going to find a nice, hot, hearty meal, in shifts, because I do not trust you here by yourself. Something about you seems...*off*. We will sleep here tonight and then the three of us will find your new friend, then we'll all go to the Tower together. I do not care whether you agree with these plans or not, I am telling you that that is how it will go." He turned to Sindha, "Hey, you can go first. I know how hungry you are. When you return, I'll go eat."

Sindha shot up from the bed in a heartbeat. "No argument here. I am going to enjoy my dinner in peace and quiet." She walked briskly to the door to leave the room.

As soon as she was gone, Badalao walked to Desmond, who was still sitting up in the bed, reclining on some pillows. Without any warning or indication, Badalao slapped Desmond across the face. "Light of Orijin, I have no idea what the hell is going on with you, but you are not yourself and you'd better change that soon. Whatever it is that you are dealing with right now, either you can tell me about it and we can figure it out together, or you can keep it to yourself and you can figure it out on your own. Either way, get your shit right before we reach the Tower." He was rather surprised that there was no fight in Desmond. Normally, Desmond would've responded with a punch or worse. He still remembered how easily Desmond had neutralized Baltaszar's attempted attack, back when they were in Vandenar. This was just more evidence that something was wrong. Badalao slapped him again, just as hard. "I just wanted to see what you would do."

BADALAO FELT A GREAT DEAL of relief that they'd secured their packs to their horses and led them across the street. Considering how strangely Desmond had been acting since they'd woken him up, he thought there might be a chance that Desmond would make a run for it and desert them. At least with all of them ready to go, they could chase him down rather easily. They tied their horses up out front of the Valiant Rider.

"We couldn't just leave 'em across the road? Like anyone would steal 'em when we're standin' right here," Desmond chirped.

Badalao shook his head. "Yes, the horses would have been fine. But this was done to keep you in check. I still don't trust you to not run off. Maybe once we find this girl of yours, she will have you acting like yourself again. Speaking of which, will you go in and get her already? Or do I have to escort you?"

Desmond rolled his eyes. "I'm not allowed in there."

Badalao couldn't help but laugh. "Do explain, my friend."

"It was part o' that misunderstandin' I had the other day. Had ta do with the cracked rib," Desmond pursed his lips at the admission."

Badalao eyed Sindha, who was also chuckling. She joined in, "What you do Des, retch your catch all over their table or something?"

"Retch...what?"

Sindha shook her head. "You know, vomit all over the place?"

"No. It's a long story. I'll tell ya when I'm feelin' better, an' not bein' ridiculed by everyone." Desmond turned to Badalao. "Lao, go in by yerself. Just tell the innkeeper that Desmond is waitin' out front fer Schatza an' that I'm ready ta go. It's the least ya can do since ya cost me a kiss from her."

"Fine." Badalao raised his hands dismissively. He walked inside and was immediately greeted by a short, older woman behind the counter to the right.

"Mornin' darlin'. Set down where ya want, I'll be over in a minute ta' take care o' ya." She smiled at him affectionately and then turned back to whatever it was she'd been doing.

Badalao walked up to the counter to speak to her. "Actually, I am not here to eat. I have my horse and companions outside, and we are here to get Schatza. Would you mind telling her that Desmond is outside for her? She said to come and get her when I was leaving for the Tower."

The woman turned back to him and smiled again. "Shame. Ya see how empty it is in here. Ever since word got around that the House was attacked, people haven't been comin' around as much. But I understand ya Descendants have yer business ta get ta. I hope ya can all find a way ta stop Jahmash. Seems like yer our only hope. Doesn't look like Edmund cares much."

Badalao felt a tinge of guilt. "I apologize. Next time I am anywhere close to here, I will make it a point to come to the Valiant Rider for a meal."

"Thanks, dear. Oh, an' o' course I'll run up an' give Schatza the message. Didn't realize she had any other Descendant friends. She helped that one babo who broke our mugs tryin' ta impress everyone with his manifestation. We threw him out promptly. I hope ya don't know that fella. Doesn't seem very smart."

Badalao stifled a laugh, *so that was the 'misunderstanding'.* "Doesn't sound like anyone I know. And thank you. I will wait outside for her. She nodded and walked away. Badalao returned outside to a confused look on Desmond's face.

"Where is she? Was she not there?"

"Just hold onto your horse, loverboy. The nice lady had to go get her; I'm sure it will take several minutes for her to pack her things and come out."

A look of clarity appeared on Desmond's face. "Oh. Yeah, that makes sense."

"This girl really has some kind of hold on you."

"Shut up."

They waited there for several minutes, while Desmond resembled more a jittery jester than the person who single handedly kept the House of Darian standing against a barrage of cannonballs. Finally, as Badalao swore he might have to slap Desmond across the face again, a girl with golden hair walked out of the Valiant Rider and looked right at Badalao. At first, he hadn't recognized her and was momentarily mesmerized by her beauty. Then, in a flash, Badalao knew exactly who she was, and an ocean of questions flooded his mind. *Farrah?* "Gamokuso."

Desmond chimed in, "Huh?"

Schatza replied, "He said 'shit' in Markosi. Well, depending on the situation, it can mean worse. I suppose it's worse, given *this* situation."

Sindha cut in before any of them could get their wits together, "Oh. This is 'Schatza'? Wow, this is going to be a *fun* ride to the Tower. I can't wait to see how this all unfolds."

Desmond eyed them all suspiciously, "What am I missin'?"

Badalao didn't have the heart to leave his friend guessing, and he wasn't sure Farrah would speak up, considering she hadn't been exactly forthright with any of them. "Des, this is Farrah. We...encountered her back in the City of the Fallen. Got to know her pretty well, but then she deserted us in the middle of the night."

Farrah smirked, much to Badalao's surprise. He expected her to be more standoffish if he ever encountered her again, perhaps even defensive. She seemed nothing of the sort. The directness in her response surprised him even more. "Encounter, Badalao Majime? So you really *do* do that with plenty of girls then."

Desmond walked up next to Badalao, "So the two of ya…? Wow. An' it's Farrah? I shoulda known. Guess it's better I never got that kiss."

She smirked again, "Definitely better that you didn't." Badalao had been a bit suspicious of her back in the City of the Fallen, but let his guard down because she'd opened herself up to him. But once she left, and now, lying about her name in a different city, he was even more wary of what she might be up to and who she might really be. *But dammit, she is the most beautiful girl I've ever seen. And she's Markosi? Still, even if she IS a Descendent, there's something off about her.* She continued, "Desmond, aside from my name, I don't understand your confusion. You mentioned Badalao by name when we were in your room the other day. I told you that I knew him." She looked back at Badalao and Sindha, "If you two are wondering why I'm not surprised to see you, it's because I was there when you were in Desmond's head. I figured it was only a matter of time before you showed up here.

Well, that explains it. Even more information that Des is hiding. He looked at Desmond, "You kolos. You weren't going to tell us any of this?" He punched Desmond's shoulder. "Something is way off with you." He left it at that. Despite any disenchantment he felt, Badalao wasn't going to berate his friend in front of anyone else. "Farrah, do you have a horse with you?"

She nodded, glancing back and forth between the three of them. "Yes, she's right over there." She pointed to a mare tied up only a few feet from where their own were waiting.

Sindha twisted her mouth up, "So much for the fun. I guess you're the only one who's going to feel awkward about any of this, Des. Sorry." She walked with Badalao to help get Farrah's packs on her horse. They all then mounted up and rode toward the eastern gate of the city, where a ferry would take them to the Tower. Badalao knew this must be difficult for Desmond to swallow, so he let the two girls ride in front and stayed back with him. No words were spoken, but this tension was preferable to riding up front next to Farrah and making Desmond ride behind them and watch it all.

CHAPTER 10
THE GHOSTS OF ASHUR

From ***The Book of Orijin,*** **Verse Three Hundred Four**
A manifestation by itself can change one's situation.
Many manifestations working together, for a common purpose, can change the entire course of humanity.

DESMOND AND HIS THREE COMPANIONS stepped off the ferry and onto the dock. They'd all had to leave their horses back in Gangjeon, but Desmond and the others figured they'd have no use for them at the Tower of the Blind anyway. *Orijin, please let all o' the others be here already. The last thing I need is ta have ta be around Lao and Sch...Farrah the whole time.* By the time they'd stepped off the dock, a dozen men and women in white robes had flocked to them and greeted them. A tall, slender Shivaani woman, likely ten years or so older than them, spoke. "Welcome, Descendants. We are servants to the Augurs, and have been expecting you. Several others are already here and informed us that more Descendants would be on their way. Come," she beckoned them to follow with her hand, "we will take your packs." Half of the white-robed servants walked ahead and led the way toward the Tower, while the other half walked behind them.

Farrah was walking beside him and leaned over and whispered, "What is an *Augur*?"

Desmond wasn't sure if he was more surprised that she was asking *him*, or that she didn't know. He tried to sound as nonchalant as he could and whispered back, "Blind Man or Woman. That's the formal name fer 'em." She looked at him and smiled, then turned her attention to the sky. Desmond looked up, curious about what she was looking at. The Tower of the Blind stretched so far up into the sky that he could barely see the top of it. "Wow." Despite growing up in Vandenar, which was relatively close to the Tower, he'd never actually been here. He instantly regretted not having found a way to come here sooner. "It's so majestic." The others all responded in agreement.

The servants ahead of them stopped them once they arrived at the Tower's tall doors. The same Shivaani woman addressed them, "We ask now that you surrender any weapons in your possession. You will not need them inside, and everything will be returned to you once you are ready to leave."

Desmond looked around at the others, confused. Badalao looked over at him, as if he'd known what Desmond was thinking. Desmond suddenly felt something pop into his mind. *"Relax, Des. It's safe inside. The Anonymi trains every single one of these servants. Anyone stupid enough to attack this place would die before they made it inside."* Desmond appreciated the discretion of Badalao's explanation, rather than saying it aloud. He simply nodded at his friend. He had no weapons on him anyway, but Badalao, Sindha, and Farrah all produced several daggers from their cloaks. He was surprised that Farrah gave her weapons up without question or hesitation but figured that Badalao very well could have warned her about this while they were talking on the ferry.

Once everything was collected, the servants made way and opened the humongous doors for them. Desmond found even the doors to be marvelous. Tall, reddish-wooden doors carved with a face - Desmond realized it could be a man's or woman's, as there was no hair to discern that. The face bore no expression, but what made it memorable was the three eyes. Two closed eyes were placed where a person's eyes would normally be, but a third eye sat centered above them, at the bottom of the forehead, and it was open. Desmond didn't realize everyone was moving again until Badalao nudged him to walk. As they walked inside, it opened to a huge room, filled with white benches and servants coming and going in every direction, many wearing large square hats upon their heads. Desmond and the others were directed to sit at the nearest benches. He and Farrah happened to sit on the same bench, while Sindha and Badalao sat at one right next to them. A Cerysian servant approached them. "Welcome. Your belongings are being brought up to the floor where you will all be residing. The Tower is big enough to accommodate all of you. There are already ten of your acquaintances upstairs, and we were informed that others may still arrive as well. We have arranged for you all to be on the same floor, but we would strongly advise that you share rooms as pairs, so that everyone can be properly accommodated." They all nodded in understanding.

Desmond subtly glanced over at Badalao, who was already looking at him. Badalao smiled and nodded, *"Don't worry Lao, I wouldn't ditch you for a girl. This will be just like at the House."* Desmond smirked, attempting to stifle an ear-to-ear grin. He wanted to be mad at Badalao, but their friendship transcended petty things and he knew he would be stupid to play games. Still, there were other things he wasn't ready to talk to Badalao about. That could wait.

The servant continued. "Good. I am glad that everyone is in agreement. Now, before I lead you to your quarters, can I get you anything to eat or drink?"

Badalao spoke up for all of them, "No, thank you. We are coming from Gangjeon, so our trip was short. We're eager to see our friends and to get comfortable."

"Very well, then follow me. I should warn you, the floor that we've provided for you is rather high up. We understand that you may be here for some time and that you may have much to discuss. That being said, we do not want your stay to interfere with the Augurs or any of our other guests, nor for them to interfere with you."

They started up a ramp and continued to walk up in the same fashion for what seemed like an hour. Badalao walked in stride with Desmond and hooked his arm through Desmond's. Desmond hadn't wanted to say anything, but he was putting all of his energy into keeping up with the others. Sweat had coated his forehead for some time. Badalao asked the servant who led them, "I am curious, who is it that provided you with all the information about who and what to expect?" Desmond had wanted to ask the same question for a while but had been too focused on keeping up.

"Quite a few informed us that there would be others coming, but it was...I believe their names were Lincan and Vasher...who were able to provide us with more precise information."

Desmond's eyes lit up. *Linc an' Vash are here? Light of Orijin, thank ya!* He and Badalao looked at each other simultaneously with toothy grins. Desmond had almost forgotten what it felt like to smile like that. This might've been the happiest he'd felt since before the House had been attacked.

After a few more minutes, the servant finally directed them through a door that might as well have been invisible, as Desmond would never have known that it was there. He was thankful to finally be on a level floor, rather than a ramp. They walked through to another large circular room; the perimeter was littered with wooden doors, to what Desmond figured were the private chambers they'd all be pairing up in. The room was open and vast, and filled with couches, tables, and cushioned chairs. On the other side of the room, a small group stopped what they were doing and stared at the four of them. Desmond didn't recognize them right away, more because he almost believed he wouldn't see them again than anything else. A petite girl appeared and stood in front of the group. She tentatively walked forward, then finally spoke. "Des? Lao? Sindha? And..."

Adria? While Desmond thought it, Badalao exclaimed, "Mouse? You're alive! And in one piece! No bloody way!" Desmond's smile was even bigger than before when they were still walking up.

Adria ran toward them at a sprint. Desmond watched her face the whole time and couldn't understand why she wasn't smiling back. He and Badalao walked forward to her, and Desmond expected her to jump and embrace one of them, he just wasn't sure whom she would choose to hug first. As Adria approached, Desmond grew even more confused as she wasn't slowing down.

She drew nearer, and if anything, ran even faster, her countenance sterner. She ran right between them. Desmond turned quickly to see what she was doing just in time to see her pounce on Farrah and start pummeling her face and body. Her fists pounded Farrah non-stop while everyone else stood in awe.

"You bitch! How dare you show up here! I'm going to kill you for what you did!" Farrah flailed her arms in an attempt to defend herself, but Adria was too fast and too precise for it to matter. Sindha attempted to intervene. "No Sindha! I'm going to beat the bitch out of her!"

Finally, Badalao came to his senses and wrapped his arms around Adria, pulling her away. "Adria! Light of Orijin, what are you *doing*? Do you know her? We just got here; what the hell could she have done already to set you off?" Desmond looked at Farrah. Her face was a bloody, lumpy mess. Sindha had already knelt down to help her sit up.

Adria took several breaths to calm herself. It was only then that Desmond noticed she was crying. "Sindha, don't help her. Leave her there to suffer and rot."

Badalao yelled at her this time, "Mouse! Stop for a moment and tell us exactly what's going on!" By this time, all the others had come over, not only to see them, but also to find out what had driven Adria mad.

Adria, still struggling in Badalao's grasp, was mostly composed now. "This is Farrah. She bloody works for Jahmash!" Everyone's eyes lit up. "I'm not kidding." She looked at Badalao and then Desmond, as well as Marshall, who stood with Lincan, Horatio, Delilah, Vasher, and Reverron. "Lao. You, Des, and Marshall were there when Gunnar and I were taken away by Maqdhuum in the Taurani village. He took us to Jahmash. We were forced to do his bidding, got in our heads and controlled us. We were on the ships that attacked the House. They needed us to show the armies where it was. Well guess who else was on those ships." She nodded at Farrah, who was looking down and gingerly touching her face. "I was there when she killed Gunnar. She kissed him and...somehow poisoned him or drained his life, I don't know. But she kissed him and then he died. I saw it happen right in front of me."

Desmond froze and the color drained from his face. He looked at Badalao, who was just as pale as he felt. *What the...she killed Gunnar with a kiss? Why did she change her mind with me, then? Does that make me lucky? Why isn't Lao dead?* He imagined similar questions were bombarding Badalao's mind as well.

The servant who'd escorted them up interjected, looking directly at Adria. "We cannot tolerate violence or quarrels within the Tower. You have calmed down and appear to have regained your composure. Will there be any further altercations? If so, then I will need to have you removed from the Tower at once."

Adria took a deep breath, still wrapped in Badalao's hold. "No. I apologize, and I promise this will not happen again. Lao, you can let me go."

"Very well." The servant nodded in their general direction and left through a door on the other side of the room, that Desmond hadn't known was there until it was opened.

Adria continued as she looked around at everyone. "That busted up face will be nothing compared to the explanation that you owe us all, right here and now."

Farrah finally looked up as Sindha helped her to her feet, then immediately stepped away and put herself between Farrah and the door through which the servant had just departed. Sindha nodded to her. "Go ahead. Talk. Did you kill Gunnar?"

FARRAH TOOK A FEW BREATHS. She'd known that the only way coming here would turn sour was if Adria or Maqdhuum were here. *Well, at least this happened early. I can get the pretense out of the way.* She looked around; about a dozen Descendants surrounded her. She wasn't planning on running—couldn't have anyway. She made eye contact with each person in the room. "Look, I have no intention of fleeing. I had an idea of what I was getting myself into by coming here, and I knew it was only a matter of time before someone recognized me. I'll tell you everything, but can we please sit? My face and body are killing me, and…"

Adria cut her off, "No, stand and talk, you…"

Surprisingly, Sindha came to Farrah's defense. "Adria, I understand your resentment, trust me I do. But she's here, and she's willing to talk. We can't change what evil she's already done, but if sitting helps her give us the truth and better understanding, then it's a small compromise to make. Like it or not, she has a Mark on her face, so the Orijin *must* see something in her. Or at least she'd better hope so." Sindha nodded for Farrah to walk to the couches. The whole group traversed the vast room to the couches on the other side. They let Farrah sit first, then positioned themselves so they were surrounding her once more. *Great. Now they don't trust me and they're comfortable while they're doing it.* Sindha continued, "There, now you can talk."

Farrah nodded, then took a deep breath. "My name is Farrah…Shokan, though I rarely use my surname anymore. My father was Markosi, and my mother Galicean. They died of sickness in Galicea when I was young, and my little sister, Melina, was only a few years old." She paused to swallow away the lump in her throat. "We didn't have any family to go to, so we roamed Cerysia, Shivaana, and Fangh-Haan, staying where we could as long as it was safe. But that was never for very long, as Prince Garrison and his battalion seemed to always be nearby. We managed to find other Descendants in Fangh-Haan who were willing to help us, but, as many of you likely know, Fangh-Haan is not so friendly to—well I won't say 'Us' as I'm sure none of you accept me as one of you—so not friendly to Descendants. We hid in basements, sheds, closets, whatever we could find at the moment. Sometimes we would have to stay hidden for hours. You can't imagine how difficult that is with a little sister to look after." Once again, Farrah paused to maintain her composure.

"I got this manifestation warding off perverted grown men looking to take advantage of two helpless girls, shortly after my parents passed. Some drunken slob forced himself on me while I shielded Melina, and, well you all know how it works. You pray hard enough and I guess are *lucky* enough for something to happen. He dropped dead within a few seconds. I didn't stick around to inspect him, we fled Veidena right away and didn't return to Galicea ever again."

Adria cut in, "We appreciate all the backstory, but get to the part where you thought it was your duty to turn on us."

Farrah knew she would get nowhere arguing with Adria, especially in front of such a one-sided crowd. She rubbed her side, which led to a sharp pain. She winced, *damn, her punches are as harsh as her words.* "Very well. Melina eventually developed her own manifestation, which didn't make things any easier. A bunch of us found ourselves lying low in Rayan at some point, about two and a half years ago. It seemed like a smart choice, as someone's family was willing to take us in for a short while. Eventually, Garrison and his gang rode into town and we were discovered. That bloody *kolos* didn't even have the courage to do it himself. They lined us up in front of everyone, and Garrison had one of his soldiers..." She closed her eyes, but there was no stopping the tears. She was just relieved that it was only tears. Farrah didn't want any of them having the pleasure of seeing her break down. "They beheaded Melina right in front of me and the whole city. The soldiers whooped and laughed and celebrated. I believe I kissed one of them and one boy, Hansi, who could create illusions, secured our escape. We rode through the mountains into Shivaana without really stopping. We didn't even bother to seek refuge in a city. I swore then that I would find some way to get revenge on Prince Garrison for killing my sister."

To her surprise, Badalao asked her a question, "So you hate us all because of Garrison's actions?"

Farrah took another deep breath, then leaned forward and rested her elbows on her thighs. "Well, it's not that simple." She felt guilty for whatever she must be making him feel. "My hatred was directed at only him for a while. I separated from the other Descendants after Melina was killed and crossed into Cerysia. I really wanted to kill Garrison, but I wasn't brave enough to actually go to Alvadon to kill him. So, over the next several months, I bounced back and forth between Shipsbane, Linchester, and Roaldon, hiding out and hoping that Garrison might coincidentally be in the same city. Then, maybe a year ago or so, I remember being in Shipsbane and overhearing two maids talking about Garrison, that he'd fled Cerysia and been branded a criminal by his father. I was overjoyed, but then one girl shared the news that I suppose sealed my fate. She said that Garrison had fled to the House of Darian, and that you all had accepted him as one of your own." She'd spit out the last few words scornfully. "Once I'd heard that, that's when I hated *all* of you. That man has killed so many Descendants for no reason except that his father told him to, all the while, bearing the very Mark of the Descendant himself, and you all welcomed him into your home with open arms."

She looked around at them. Some seemed angry with her while others looked completely confused. A short Cerysian man, older than all of the others, spoke up. "They do not all know that Garrison was there. You blame the House of Darian for something that most of its residents were completely unaware of."

"That didn't cross my mind or matter to me at the time. I already felt alone in the world by that point, but once I heard that, I didn't think there were too many places I could turn. It was pure chance that Maqdhuum was in Shipsbane at that time. He actually wanted to kill me at first, but I told him that I wasn't like other Descendants. I told him I wouldn't mind killing other Descendants if they were just going to befriend the man who was killing them. He took advantage of my vulnerability and said he knew of someone who could help me. So, a few days later, we were on a boat to see Jahmash. I didn't really know what I was getting myself into. The only thing I did know was that I was angry and lonely, and that I wanted people to pay for making me feel that way."

The same Cerysian man responded to her. "My name is Maximillian. I was a Maven in the House of Darian, meaning that I was privy to more information than anyone else in this room." He looked around at the others, "This will be new to most of you, but most of the Mavens wanted Garrison killed the moment he stepped into the House of Darian. Farrah, we felt the same way as you. However, it is no secret that Zin Marlowe was a pacifist and would not grant those wishes. Especially once Roland Edevane, Garrison's uncle, arrived at the House and spoke with Marlowe privately. It was decided then that Garrison would rot in the dungeon until Zin Marlowe changed his mind, for better or worse. We can discuss Garrison further at another time." Maximilian's eyes darted around furtively. "What I am mostly curious about is, why did you not come to the House of Darian once you developed your manifestation?"

Farrah looked down at the ground, still processing what Maximillian had said about Garrison. "There were rumors that the House of Darian did not provide asylum to family members of Descendants. There was no way I would have left Melina with someone else. Also, I was afraid of my manifestation for a long time, and I was nervous about what others might say about me there."

Adria cut in again, sitting on the couch right across from her, "Seems a bit of a stretch. While I'm sorry for the loss of your sister, I'm having trouble understanding how you jumped from one end of the spectrum to the other. First, you were an innocent little girl, just trying to survive, then like most Descendants, you wanted to kill Garrison. And because he came to us for asylum, you essentially turned into the very thing that he'd formerly been? Sounds like there are some details missing here." Adria glowered at her.

Light of Orijin, she really is a bitch. "Garrison was raised to hate us. His father influenced his mind when Garrison was young, impressionable, and vulnerable. It wasn't much different with me. Maqdhuum found me at my most vulnerable and my judgment was clouded by anger and desperation. Jahmash used that against me, except that he was able to literally infiltrate my mind and directly take control of it. There have been so many times that I didn't know whether I was actually making a choice or if he was making it for me. Look, Adria, and the rest of you for that matter," she looked around at all of them, "I don't expect sympathy or forgiveness from any of you. My past is my past, and however good or bad my choices were, I made them. But my mind is free of the Red Harbinger now. Badalao can attest to that, as he's the one who removed Jahmash from my mind."

A collective gasp filled the room as everyone's eyes fell upon Badalao. He raised his hands in protest, "Hold on a moment, everyone. I'm just as surprised as you are. I knew that I'd kicked *someone* out of her head, but I didn't know it was bloody Jahmash!"

Farrah nodded and defended him. "That is true. He had no way of knowing that it was Jahmash. But Badalao, if you were able to do that for me, you would be able to do that for anyone else under his control. For you to remove *him*, you must be at least as powerful as him with your abilities. Imagine how many followers you could turn if you had access to them. Since you helped me, I haven't been the same person." She looked around again, "Surely if you could take in Garrison, willingly or not, you can give me a chance to prove myself?"

The rest of them all looked around at each other, as if they were looking for someone to make a decision about her. Maximillian spoke up, "We will give you the opportunity to prove you belong with us, but you will be on a short leash. Extremely short."

Adria added on, "If anything seems off in the Tower while you're here, I'll kill you. That would be the least I could do for Gunnar."

Maximillian held a hand up to stop Adria, "Easy. Let us stem the threats and start the process of coming together. Why don't the four of you get yourselves settled. All the time you've been here, you have yet to go to your quarters. I assume the servants explained to you that we are all paired up in our rooms?" Farrah nodded, along with the other three she'd arrived with. Maximillian continued, "Good. Seeing as how we've all paired up already, the four of you might as well do the same. Sindha, will you be able to handle bunking with Farrah?"

"Nothing to it. I'll set up a force field for myself while I'm sleeping, just in case."

So that's what she can do. Force fields. Interesting.

As they stood to walk to their rooms, Adria addressed her once more. "Oh, Farrah?" Farrah turned to her. "It seems like you have a great deal unresolved with Garrison and Maqdhuum." Farrah bit her lip. *What is she getting at?* "That's great news for you, because the two of them are sharing a room. We've instructed them to stay out of sight until everyone is here and properly prepared to handle their presence. But I can't wait for you to have a nice long chat with both of them so you can keep the past in the past and be that new person now."

As soon as I get the chance, I'm going to slap her so hard that the other cheek will feel it. As Adria walked away, Farrah heard her quietly tell Badalao, "Hey, I need you to get him out of my head, too." Farrah smirked. *Hypocrite. She knows exactly what it's like to have him in her head, and still pretends like I had full control of everything. I hope to Orijin that Jahmash made her bleed out of her ears and nose, like he did to me.*

"So ve are supposed to let zem both stay here? No trial, no punishment? Nothing?" Savaiyon was surprised at how pointed Blastevahn's voice was, considering the statuesque man's lethargic nature the day before.

"I sense that you woke up this angry, Blast. Under the circumstances, I find that encouraging, given that you had no energy to do anything but lounge and rest for the past several days." They sat on their respective beds, facing one another.

Blastevahn looked up at Savaiyon without moving his head, "Murderers and traitors have a vay of cooking my blood. I vould think you vould be just as angry."

He wouldn't dare let on to the others, but Savaiyon was exhausted. He'd been so busy overseeing the health of Blastevahn and Malikai, as well as delegating Kadoog'han and Slade on how to handle the Harbingers' swords, while instructing them not to practice with them inside his sister's home, that he'd barely slept. He wasn't ready to deal with the presence of Maqdhuum and Garrison in their company. "Blast, they are here of their own accord, and they arrived with Adria. If *she* saw fit to travel with them here, then she did so for good reason. I know you trust me, and I trust her. Besides, we should consider ourselves lucky that Garrison is back under our watch. Regardless, Blast, this is the Tower of the Blind. Maqdhuum knows violence is not allowed here, and Garrison is in no condition to start a fight."

Blastevahn shook his head, "Even ze safest place is von punch avay from being unsafe."

"Very well. I will take your protest under consideration."

"And you are our leader now?"

"Judging by everyone's attitudes yesterday, it seems that that is the silent consensus. I suppose I can handle the responsibility for now, at least until we can find Asarei. Then we can sort it all out. Unless you would like it?" He smiled at Blastevahn and stood up.

Blastevahn arose as well. "There is no vay I vant zat. Zhey all hate each ozer here. I vill let you sort it all out." He waved his hand for Savaiyon to walk first into the common area.

Several servants whisked around the vast room, taking trays of food from their broad square hats and placing them on the tables next to the couches. Savaiyon looked around the room, specifically at the walls and floor. There was a certain sterility to it, all white with no decor save for several sconces on the walls all around the room. *Not much need for decor if they cannot see anything. I suppose the servants have no need for it either.* As the servants cleared, Savaiyon noticed a group of people sitting at the couches and walked over with Blastevahn in tow. As he walked closer, he was able to identify them. "Desmond, Badalao, Lincoln, Horatio, Vasher, and Marshall." He sat down on one of the couches next to them. "Before the others stir, I am going to need your help." Blastevahn sat down next to him. "You all likely know better than I do that tensions are high right now. All of you, well with the exception of you sometimes, Desmond, are relatively calm and can talk others down from a tense situation. I need everyone here to let go of whatever quarrels they have with anyone else."

Horatio responded, "Does that include you and Maqdhuum? He was pretty intent on killing you the last time you saw him. I wouldn't mind getting some revenge."

"No. However difficult it might be, we need him. Everyone who is here, this is essentially who is left to fight Jahmash. We don't have the luxury of revenge right now. And there is more to Maqdhuum than you understand."

Horatio continued, "I think quite a few people here will disagree with you. Farrah is here. I'm sure Lao and Adria still want to put her in her place. Garrison—well everyone here wants a crack at him. Maqdhuum—well, it doesn't seem like Farrah likes him either. Linc here and Delilah—that's still awkward. I'm probably missing some, but everyone is rested now and likely back to their normal selves."

"Horatio, this is one of those times when you should stop saying everything that is going through your head. I was not asking you; I was telling you. I will take the lead on any plans we can put together, but I need your help with keeping everyone calm and peaceful."

Lincan cut in, "Essentially?"

"Excuse me, Lincan?"

"You said we are *essentially* all that's left. You didn't say we *are* all that's left. There's a difference."

Savaiyon smirked. *These boys are smart. There is no playing with words here. They deserve the whole truth anyway. If we are the only survivors, then they all deserve full disclosure.* "Very well. There is a chance that there may be other Descendants with whom we can align. The only issue is that…"

A loud voice cut him off, "They are difficult to locate." The crowd at the couches all turned to the source of the voice, and Savaiyon immediately summoned his manifestation and stood with clenched fists. Maqdhuum put up his hands, though one was wrapped in a bandage, "Easy, Savaiyon. I am here in peace. Just ask Adria." Maqdhuum looked over his shoulder as Adria, Garrison, and Delilah arrived at the couches with him.

Savaiyon nodded and sat back down. *If I'm going to expect the rest of them to trust him, I have to be the example.* "Just because you are here, does not mean that we are friends. That goes for you as well, Garrison. Sit with us. We have things to discuss. Adria, can you summon Farrah and Sindha, please? Marshall, same for Reverron, Malikai, Slade, Kadoog'han, and Maximilian." He glanced at the group present already. Since yesterday, Desmond had seemed aloof, but Savaiyon hadn't had the chance to talk to him directly the day before. "Desmond, are you well? You seem like something is…consuming you or distracting you."

Desmond glanced at him and then looked away, "I'm fine, Maven Savaiyon. Just worn out. I'll be back ta normal in no time."

Savaiyon nodded, "Very well." *Something is not right with him. I will have to look into it.* The others who'd been summoned were walking over now from various doors on the perimeter. Savaiyon stood and waved for those around him to follow. "Move the couches in a circle so that we can all face each other." The circle was formed as everyone arrived at the couches, and nineteen of them sat around like a council. Savaiyon knew he would have to be the one to lead them for the time being, but as he looked around at all of them, he knew that leading would not be the issue. Horatio and Slade glared at Maqdhuum, while Adria glowered at Farrah, and Farrah directed her scowl toward Garrison. In fact, most of them directed stern looks toward Garrison. Savaiyon walked to the middle of the circle. Everyone's attention shifted to him as he looked around at them. "The first thing that needs to be clear to all of you is that anyone who is here is on the same side. I want to see an end to the glares and scowls. Whatever grudges you are holding, you are letting go of them right now. I understand that there are certain individuals in this room whose transgressions seem unforgivable, but that is for the Orijin to decide, not us. Garrison and Farrah both bear the Mark of the Descendant, which means that the Orijin saw into their hearts and saw the goodness in them." He turned to Garrison. "You. This is your chance to explain yourself and what value you bring to us. Keep in mind that, if we were not in the Tower, many of these people would have tried, perhaps successfully, to kill you." Savaiyon sat back down.

Garrison shifted to the edge of the couch and leaned forward. He paused for a moment before speaking. "What many of you may not know about me is that it has been over two years since a Descendant has died by my hands or by my orders. I understand the magnitude of my crimes, and that is why I stopped. At a certain point, I took it upon myself to become educated about the truth of the Orijin and Descendants, rather than continue listening to my father. As soon as I knew for sure that he was lying to me, I stopped. Once that happened, my missions were purposefully fruitless, and I would simply tell my father that we'd killed Descendants, even though we hadn't." Garrison stood and looked directly at Farrah. "Farrah, I know who you are. I remember you vividly."

Savaiyon glanced at Farrah, whose face looked like stone.

Garrison continued, "I apologize deeply for everything I put you through. By the time we'd started that mission, I knew I didn't want to kill anyone anymore. My second in command, Willard, had a penchant for being overzealous and his excitement for killing you and your friends infected the other soldiers. I was too weak then to stop it, afraid of showing my true feelings in public. I fought back tears when Willard killed your friend, the little girl."

Farrah bolted up from the couch, "That was my sister, you *skahta!* My sister!"

Savaiyon put himself between Farrah and Garrison, though Farrah made no effort to advance at Garrison. Garrison fell back on the couch with glossy eyes. He choked out an apology, "From the bottom of my heart, I am truly sorry." He paused for a moment, "If it provides you any consolation, I killed Willard two weeks later.

Farrah continued, "Consolation? How in the Three Rings is that supposed to bring my sister back? You should have killed yourself, too, you bloody *kolos!*"

Garrison nodded curtly and offered a quiet response. "Believe me, I thought about it. But like Savaiyon said, the Orijin chose us for a reason. Farrah, you and I both have committed insidious crimes against our own people, but the Orijin saw into our hearts and chose to bless us with manifestations. Even if we have done evil, it does not mean we are stuck on that path for our whole lives."

Vasher spoke up for the first time, "What if you're just saying that now? Then you eventually become king and it's just more of the same as your father."

In that moment, Savaiyon instantly remembered about the Anonymi decree for them to kill Edmund. He hoped he'd managed to keep his reaction to a mere twitch. He darted his eyes around without moving his head to see the others' faces. They were all glued to Garrison. He took a deep breath. *Phew.*

Garrison answered Vasher, "That is not possible. My father renounced my princeship. My brother Donovan, is the heir to the throne. He knows my feelings about my father, and how I have changed my course on the treatment of Descendants. In fact, once I was banished from Cerysia, I ordered Donovan and Wendell Ravensdayle, the Commander of the Vermillion Army, to find any soldiers loyal to me and start a new army in secret. Factions had already been formed before I reached the House of Darian. In fact, they came to my rescue when the Vermillion were hunting me down in the forest at the southeast border of Mireya."

Badalao cut in, "So you did travel through there. Were there Taurani with you?"

Garrison nodded. "Three. All three sacrificed their lives to get me to the House of Darian, even though it was not their way." Savaiyon noticed Garrison eye Marshall and look back at Badalao, "One of them was Marshall's own mother, another his uncle. They all believed Marshall to be dead and fought ardently to ensure my safety and survival. They believed in me, despite my father's mistreatment of their people. And I am telling the rest of you, I can help you. And if you will allow me to, I can also get at least half of the Vermillion Army on our side."

Badalao responded, "Do we have your word that your brother and friend would be willing to help us?"

Garrison sat up straight, "My word is my bond."

Badalao nodded. "So if we were to go and get them right now, they would drop everything in a heartbeat and do what we needed."

Savaiyon was curious, "What are you getting at, Lao?"

Badalao directed his attention to Savaiyon. "Tasz is in a dungeon in Alvadon. I haven't had much of a chance to connect with him in days, but he told me that he's being treated well. For any Descendant to be treated well in a Cerysian dungeon, there *have* to be sympathizers there. Garrison, is there any chance you have friends in that dungeon?"

Garrison looked a little relieved, and his face softened. "By now, it is possible, even likely, that Donovan's and Wendell's influence have impacted various establishments throughout Alvadon, maybe even all throughout Cerysia."

Lincan chimed in, "We saw it first-hand." Lincan circled his finger around to include Vasher and Horatio, who sat with him. "Delilah, too. The four of us traveled here from Sundari, along the Sanai on the Cerysian side. The only reason we made it here is because of soldiers loyal to him." He nodded at Garrison. "They might've mentioned the name Wendell. Either way, it's real. Things are changing in Cerysia."

Garrison smiled for the first time. "I knew they would come through. How do you suggest we get Tasz? I met him briefly when I was in the dungeon at the House of Darian. Ironic that he now sits in one in Alvadon. Despite Wendell's and Donovan's work, I highly doubt that you can simply sail across the Eye and stroll into Alvadon."

Savaiyon took the opportunity to take the lead once more. "That will not be necessary. My manifestation allows me to create doorways from one place to another. If Badalao bonded us both, perhaps there might be a way for him to see your memory of the dungeon, and exactly where we can find Tasz, or at least your friends. We could simply get him and return in a matter of minutes." Savaiyon noticed some of the boys' faces lighting up with excitement at the newest developments of the conversation. He put a hand up to calm them, "Do not get ahead of yourselves. None of you will be going. This mission will only include me, Badalao, Garrison..." He looked around at all of them, "and Adria. The rest of you, stay and rest, and find ways to get along with each other. You three, join me in my quarters."

GARRISON STOOD IN A CIRCLE in the middle of the room, with Savaiyon, Badalao, and Adria. The height discrepancy was almost comical, as Savaiyon towered over Adria, but he didn't want to push his luck by laughing or pointing it out. In truth, he was grateful that nobody had attacked him the way Adria had beaten Farrah. He supposed that Adria had vouched for him with the others, and it helped that they were the first ones there, so she'd been able to ease the others into the news of his and Maqdhuum's presence.

Badalao, standing across from Savaiyon, had already bonded the tall man. All he'd done was put his hand to Savaiyon's head—after Savaiyon squatted a bit—then summoned his manifestation and closed his eyes. Once Badalao was done, Savaiyon seemed the same, so Garrison assumed this wasn't some ploy to torture him or kill him. Badalao looked at him and nodded. "You next."

Garrison nodded in affirmation and bowed his head for Badalao. The Markosi put his hand on Garrison's head, just as he'd done to Savaiyon, and then Garrison could feel a warm pulse of energy spread through his head, as if his mind was being comforted by a blanket. In another moment, Badalao took his hand away and stepped back. Garrison looked up at him, "Huh, for some reason I thought there would be more...discomfort."

Badalao responded, "Not unless I want there to be. From what others have told me, you'll know when I am in your head. You will feel it if you're paying attention. Regardless, I can only do this during the day, and I would never intrude, and never stick around in there without asking you first."

Garrison cocked his head, "What do you mean, only during the day? Manifestations can work that way?"

Badalao seemed uneasy. "I do not know how to explain it; it just does not work at night."

Garrison's interest was piqued; he was curious about how Badalao's manifestation could just stop. "Very well. I am simply curious, though, does it just...stop...once the sun sets?"

"Basically. Can we please not talk about this any further?"

Garrison nodded, but he noticed that Savaiyon also eyed Badalao peculiarly, as if something was off. "I apologize. Once you are finished with Adria, we can begin the process of contacting Tasz."

Badalao turned to Adria and began the process of bonding her. Once he finished, Adria turned to Savaiyon. "Before we start on any of this, Maven, you know what I'm going to ask."

Savaiyon smirked. "Why you?"

"Yeah. I wasn't sure if it was because you wanted to separate me and Farrah, or something else."

Savaiyon glanced at Garrison and then back at her. "That was part of it. But you and Garrison have both been with Maqdhuum long enough to know whether we can trust him. If he wanted to hurt any of us, he clearly would have already, so I know that is not his agenda. However, the man is clever and shrewd, and I find it difficult to believe that he doesn't have something stirring in that wasp's nest of a mind. And I trust he's told you who he really is?"

Garrison was about to speak up, but he knew that Savaiyon was asking Adria because he trusted her judgment above his. Adria nodded and responded, "Yes. Actually, he needs us. Just between the four of us in this room, Maqdhuum is afraid of Jahmash. He mentioned that Jahmash is a better swordsman, and extremely well protected by guards. And aside from all that, Maqdhuum is afraid of failing again. He failed as Abram, and the whole reason he's started this path is to put an end to everything. Now, if you want my honest opinion, the man is wild, uncouth, unpredictable, and morally confused. But I truly believe that he wants to stop Jahmash." She nodded at Garrison, "Maqdhuum could have easily killed either or both of us at any time and made our bodies disappear, but he's confided in us a great deal. As a matter of fact, before we arrived here, we were at the Stones of Gideon. Maqdhuum broke down in tears, apologizing to Gideon at his statue. As annoying as Maqdhuum can be, I believe that deep inside, it is Abram's heart, the one the Orijin saw, in there."

Badalao looked at them quizzically. "Wait. Am I missing something? Maqdhuum and Abram…you're saying that they are the same person? The man who led the attack on the House of Darian, is one of the Five?"

Adria nodded once more, "Yes. But Lao, don't run and tell the others yet. It's not something that we can just yell out to the crowd."

Badalao took a deep breath. "Fine. But…damn."

Garrison smirked, "Yeah."

Savaiyon looked at Garrison once more. "It would seem then, that our stay here is going to be an unforgettable lesson in forgiveness and patience. Right Garrison?"

Garrison nodded curtly. "Yes, sir. I certainly hope so."

"Good. Then let us finalize our plan for Baltaszar. I want us there and back as quickly as possible. Lao, reach out to Baltaszar. See if he can give you anything on where he is being held." Badalao sat on a chair between the two beds while the others watched him. On the surface, it was like watching nothing happen. Garrison and the other two stared at Badalao as he closed his eyes and concentrated, and they continued to do so for a few moments until Badalao opened his eyes once more.

"He is still in the dungeon, but nobody really knows he's there aside from…Wendell and Donovan?" Badalao glanced at Garrison for affirmation.

Garrison confirmed, "If he is under their watch, then he is safe. Does he have any idea where he is?"

Badalao continued, "He said he hasn't seen them in a while, but he's being taken care of. He does not know exactly where, except that there do not seem to be any other prisoners near him. He said that the only thing he remembers is that he was taken down two long flights of stairs to get to his cell."

Garrison's eyes opened wide, "That is where we used to keep traitors to the throne when my father wanted to question them or torture them. The upper level is usually full, and the lower level is simply more space for that same purpose. Baltaszar is down there because the level above has prisoners. It is likely that they covered his head to conceal his Mark from other prisoners."

Savaiyon cut in. "So you know exactly where he is, then?"

"I know exactly which floor, but not which cell. But if he is alone it will not matter much. That level has thirty cells on each side and is only one corridor. If we were to travel directly to that corridor, it would be easy to find him."

"Can you do it, Maven? Create a doorway there using Garrison's mind?" Adria asked.

"That is up to how vividly Garrison can remember the place in his mind. I need to be able to see the destination in my mind to get there." He turned to Garrison expectantly.

"Oh, do not worry about that. I have been down there so frequently that I could navigate it in the dark. But how exactly will this work?"

Badalao stood up again. "I will have to connect with both of you simultaneously. Garrison, you will imagine that corridor in your mind as vividly as you can, so that I can access it. I will then try to place that same image into Savaiyon's mind. Basically, Garrison, all you have to do is think of that place and keep the image of it in your mind for as long as you can."

"That sounds easy enough." Garrison was relieved. He had some reservations about returning to Alvadon and seeing familiar faces, but this would be a quick extraction and they wouldn't have to interact with anyone.

Savaiyon gestured for Badalao to come and stand between him and Garrison. "Let us begin, Lao. Adria, once the doorway is made and we're through, you must be the scout. Listen for any signs of others approaching. That is the other reason why I needed you with us." Adria nodded vigorously and Garrison closed his eyes to imagine the dungeon corridor. He could feel Badalao's presence like a gentle grip on the boundaries of his mind. He focused on just picturing the corridor and nothing else. Garrison concentrated so deeply for several moments that he didn't even realize right away when Badalao was nudging his shoulder, until finally he heard Badalao in his mind. *Garrison, wake up! It worked, the doorway is open!* Garrison opened his eyes in a hurry and realized they were all waiting for him to open his eyes so they could walk through. Savaiyon instructed him, "Garrison, you are new to this. Do not touch the edge of the doorway. It is large enough that that should not be an issue, but just be mindful." Garrison nodded as Savaiyon walked through first. Badalao motioned for him to go ahead, then Badalao and Adria followed him. Traveling this way was much easier than when he'd reached the touch portal to the House of Darian. He remembered how sick that had made him feel. Once they were all through, Savaiyon closed the doorway.

Garrison grew curious, "Why close it if we are going right back?"

"Precaution, just in case anyone tries to follow us or any trouble arises." Garrison was just about to assure him there would be no trouble when he heard a familiar voice behind them.

"All of you, stop where you are!" He turned around to see figures at the end of the corridor walking toward them.

"So much for scouting," Adria said dryly.

Luckily, they stood in the middle of the corridor and another voice cried out from the opposite direction. "I'm down here! It's Tasz, I'm down here at the end! Help!"

Savaiyon barked out orders as he ran towards Baltaszar, "Hurry! Follow me! Once we get to Baltaszar's cell, I will create another doorway to get inside it, that way we cannot be followed or attacked." Garrison immediately obeyed and ran behind Savaiyon. *Wow, that was some quick thinking. No wonder he is the one in charge.* He heard footsteps behind them as whomever else was down here was now giving chase. From the sound of it, they were quickly getting close.

"I said stop! By order of King Edmund, ruler of Ashur, I command you all to stop immediately!" Garrison knew it was his father's voice, but he also knew his father would not run after anyone. He didn't dare slow down to turn around and look. Savaiyon had reached Baltaszar's cell and was creating the yellow-fringed doorway right in front of the cell door. Garrison reached it just as Savaiyon leapt through and followed. Badalao and Adria were right behind him and made it into Baltaszar's cell—but before Savaiyon could close the door, two of their pursuers jumped through as well. Garrison turned, ready to attack, then realized who they were—and that one of them was hurt. The doorway was completely gone now, and as Baltaszar arose from the back corner of the stone-walled cell, Wendell Ravensdayle also got to his feet after his tumble through Savaiyon's closing doorway. Next to Wendell, Garrison's brother, Donovan, was on his knees, his head on the ground, clutching his right arm. As Donovan stood, Garrison immediately saw his blood-soaked arm, part of the sleeve seemingly sliced off. King Edmund finally reached the cell. "You are trespassing and are wanted criminals for those black lines on your faces. Wendell, Donovan, I shall summon guards to free you from there. The rest of you, do not even think about an attack, or trying something sneaky. I will have each of you executed at even the slightest provocation."

Garrison walked over to Donovan to check on him. He grabbed his brother's arm and inspected it. The cut ran almost the whole length of his arm and was deep. They would need to stop the bleeding quickly. Garrison turned to his father, "Would you not execute us all anyway?"

His father glared at him, "No, only you for now, Garrison."

Garrison turned to Savaiyon, "What do we do? My brother needs help; we cannot just leave him here to bleed out!"

Savaiyon seemed to contemplate for a moment, looking back and forth repeatedly between Donovan and King Edmund. He created another doorway from inside the cell. "Everyone, go through. We will take these two as insurance. Baltaszar, are you well enough to go through by yourself?"

Baltaszar hobbled over to Savaiyon's doorway, "I would be well enough to leave this place on one leg."

As Garrison guided Donovan through the doorway, he heard Savaiyon speak to his father. "Your majesty, we shall borrow your men to treat their wounds with our *dark magic*. We shall return them shortly."

A moment later they were all again in Savaiyon's chambers, now too crowded with three additional people.

Garrison set his brother down on one of the beds. He looked around at the others, "Can anything be done for him, or is it up to the servants of the Tower?" Badalao and Adria rushed out of the room at once. "Where are they going?"

Savaiyon responded, "To get Lincan. He will be able to heal your brother rather easily." He turned to Wendell, who stood next to Garrison beside the bed. "I imagine that you are Wendell, then?"

Wendell nodded, "I do not understand what happened to him. There was no attack."

"The doorway that you both jumped through to follow us— Donovan must have gotten too close to the edge. This cut is what happens when someone tries to go through and touches the boundaries of the doorway."

Lincan arrived at the room and Garrison and Wendell made way for him to inspect Donovan. "Don't worry, this will be easy." He grasped Donovan's arm with both hands and inspected the wound. Sure enough, Garrison watched Donovan's arm heal right in front of him, in a matter of moments. *And this is what father is so opposed to.* Lincan looked up at them, "See, nothing to it. He should get some rest before doing anything else, though. His arm will be sore for a short while. I can ask the servants to bring him some food."

Savaiyon responded, "Please do so, Lincan. Donovan, you can remain in that bed. Wendell, you can stay in this room with him. Blastevahn and I will find another room to occupy if we need to. Garrison, Baltaszar, let us go as well. They can join us in the common room when Donovan has rested up."

BALTASZAR HOBBLED OUT INTO the common room with Garrison and Lincan, and Lincan turned around and grasped Baltaszar's shoulder. "Wow, it's good to have you back. We didn't get to see what happened to you after the trial, but Maven Savaiyon told us. I'm sorry, man. Why don't you also take a rest? You look like shit, and I'm sure I could heal you rather quickly."

Baltaszar wasn't sure what to address first; he was just glad to be back with his friends. "You know, it's only been about two weeks since I was banished, but it feels like months and I've missed so much. And I feel like shit, too, but can you just heal me out here? Donovan and Wendell were beyond nice to me, but from the looks of it, there are a lot of people here that I remember and want to catch up with. Can we go sit with them?"

Lincan nodded, "Garrison, help me brace him and we'll walk him over to the couches." In a matter of seconds, Garrison and Lincan were on both sides of him and had his arms around their shoulders as they walked him over to the other Descendants at the couches. From the looks of it, they were in the middle of enjoying a lavish lunch. Baltaszar consciously kept himself from drooling at the sight of all the food, and the smell of it as well. Garrison and Lincan set him down on a couch, then Lincan instructed, "Stay here. I'll grab you some food. I just have to ask the servants to tend to Donovan." Baltaszar nodded as Lincan walked away.

Horatio immediately walked up to him with an ear-to-ear grin, "Is it great to have you back or what, Tasz? It's a shame that we couldn't be back at the House like how things used to be, but we should be grateful that those of us here survived and are well."

Baltaszar stifled a frown at the thought of the House of Darian and focused on his friend in front of him. "Raish, you mean like how you were in my room basically every waking hour, unless we needed to be somewhere else?"

Horatio chuckled, "That's exactly what I'm talking about."

"Yeah, I've missed that, too."

"So, I'll just go ahead and ask. How in the Three Rings did you get the scar on your face? Were you trying to give yourself a Descendant's Mark on the other eye? Light of Orijin, that thing looks painful!"

Baltaszar nodded, "It feels worse than it looks—feels like my face is cut wide open. Hurts to eat, too. But it's a long story and... complicated. Besides, once Linc heals it, it won't even matter anymore." Marshall, Badalao, Desmond, Vasher, Sindha, and Malikai all stood around him as well, and Garrison sat next to him on the couch. Baltaszar took a deep breath. He was overjoyed to see all of them again, especially all in one place, but also overwhelmed at the attention. "I'm sorry everyone, I don't have much of a great story for you. I wandered through the Never for a few days, wound up at a wall outside Alvadon, then got shot by an arrow and roughed up. Luckily Donovan and Wendell looked after me, or I probably wouldn't be here." He looked at Garrison and nodded with a half-smile.

Lincan pushed his way through the others and handed Garrison a tray of food. "Hold this for him, while I heal him." He then looked at Baltaszar, "Where exactly are you injured? I'm assuming too many places to count?"

Baltaszar smiled, "It hurts everywhere—I don't even remember the specific places. Let's see; obviously my face, then there's this shoulder, my ribs, my heart, and my leg. I think if you could get those, I'd be able to manage."

"Understood." Lincan put his hand on the left side of Baltaszar's face, closed his eyes, and concentrated for several moments. He began to look annoyed. Baltaszar noticed that his face wasn't feeling any better. "Tasz, what exactly is this injury? I can't seem to heal it, and it's producing a lot of heat. I've never seen anything like it."

Baltaszar wasn't sure if the horror in his mind matched that of his face, but he was consumed with panic as Lincan backed away. He touched his face, feeling the warmth of the wound emanating from it. Many of the others backed away to give him space. He closed his eyes and took several deep breaths. After a few moments, Baltaszar managed to calm himself. "I encountered...something in the Never. I'm not ready to talk about it all at length, but basically I have this wound, and one at my heart, as punishment for my outburst in Haedon. The one that got me banished from the House of Darian."

Adria spoke up from the couch next to his. "You said some*thing* did that to you?" He hadn't met her before this day but had heard a great deal about her. She looked younger than he'd imagined, and prettier.

"Some*things*. Actually, a lot of somethings. And believe it or not, they were on my side. But seriously, can I please save this conversation for later or another day? I know you have questions, but, Linc, I'm fairly certain that the rest of my wounds can be healed, aside from my face and heart. Can we please talk about something else while Lincan heals me?"

As Baltaszar made his request, Savaiyon appeared behind the throng around him, just as tall as Baltaszar remembered. The Maven announced, "Let us all resume our circle, like this morning. There is still much to discuss. And it would provide Baltaszar with the break he deserves." Savaiyon paused for a moment while everyone found seats on the numerous couches. "Baltaszar, while the focus is still somewhat on you, you should know that I am deeply sorry for the way I had to remove you from the House of Darian. I questioned Zin Marlowe on his order, but he insisted that that was what needed to happen. In speaking with Rhadames Slade, it seems that there is truth to this." Savaiyon glanced over at another couch and Baltaszar followed his eyes, blinking repeatedly at the sight of the bearded man who'd set him on his journey out of Haedon so long ago.

Slade? Seriously? Baltaszar smiled to himself while Lincan continued to work on his wounds, now sitting next to him instead of Garrison. "I know enough by now to realize that everything you do is in our best interest, Maven Savaiyon. Though, I have trouble believing the same about Zin Marlowe."

Savaiyon's nostrils briefly flared, "Baltaszar, I understand that you may have certain frustrations and resentments but let us not speak ill of the dead. Whatever shortcomings Zin Marlowe may have had, let them have died with him. We may have not agreed with all of his decisions, but the man made all of his decisions based on what he thought was best for Descendants."

Baltaszar considered biting his tongue, but Lincan's healing must have revitalized his brazenness. "Fine, but just one thing, Maven Savaiyon." Baltaszar leaned forward, as Lincan finished. "Sitting in a dungeon for...however many days gave me ample time to think. We throw around this word 'Descendants' as if it belongs to only us. But throughout Ashur there are hundreds, if not thousands of people who are likely descendants of Darian. So why do we call ourselves that like it makes us special? We are not gifted simply because we are descendants of Darian; we are special because of these lines on our faces, because of these manifestations that we have. But not every descendant of Darian bears this mark. Not every descendant is hunted or forced into hiding. It is only those of us who have been chosen."

"Baltaszar, I appreciate your explanation and clarity of this subject, but what is it that you are getting at? Do you wish for us to stop calling ourselves 'Descendants'?"

"It is not simply a wish. I think it is unfair to us to be grouped together with so many other people who have not had to live in fear the way we have, simply because we were asked to face an impossible situation as children and prayed hard enough for a way out. I am not saying we are better than anyone who does not bear this Mark, but I *am* saying that calling ourselves 'Descendants' is not entirely accurate for what we truly are." Baltaszar glanced around the room. He hadn't intended for this topic to sound as combative as it had.

Savaiyon didn't look as annoyed as Baltaszar believed him to be. "And what would you have us call ourselves, then?" All eyes in the room were now directed at Baltaszar, except he noticed Horatio two couches away, staring at the floor and concentrating.

Horatio blurted out, "Tasz, what was it I said the innkeeper in Khiry called us? I remember us talking about it, that it made us sound dangerous."

Baltaszar stood up, excitedly, "Ghosts! You said he called us 'The Ghosts of Ashur'!"

Savaiyon stared at Baltaszar with a smirk on his face. "You two would like for us to refer to ourselves as 'The Ghosts of Ashur' instead of 'Descendants'? Am I understanding this correctly?

Baltaszar wasn't sure what happened to his previous fearlessness, as he answered Savaiyon sheepishly, "Yes…?"

Horatio seconded the notion more emphatically, "Yes!"

Savaiyon simply nodded for a moment, as if in contemplation, then looked around at the rest of the group. "And the rest of you. Do you agree with our two brutally honest companions here?" Savaiyon barely finished asking the question when the room filled with a score of 'Yeses' and 'Ayes.' Baltaszar felt almost embarrassed that this had become an official order of business, but Savaiyon was the one who entertained it when he could have simply brushed it aside and moved on. Savaiyon continued, "Very well, then, *Ghosts of Ashur*. The name is appropriate, as you will need to exist like ghosts when I tell you what we must do in order to properly defend Ashur against Jahmash."

CHAPTER 11
SALVATION AS ONE

From ***The Book of Orijin,*** **Verse Four Hundred**
O Chosen Ones, your downfall can only come through dissention. Know that your common purpose is greater than any one of you, and remain loyal to one another.

GARRISON SHIFTED IN HIS SEAT. He was nervous about what Savaiyon might say, and as nice as it was to be included as a "Ghost of Ashur," he wondered how much he was actually *accepted* by these people. He knew that Adria and Maqdhuum had no quarrels, nor did Savaiyon. But were the others all completely trusting of him and willing to stand beside him in a fight? Would they turn on him or blame him the moment something went wrong? Would he have to worry about Farrah killing him in his sleep? He would proceed with caution for the time being and choose his words and actions wisely.

Savaiyon looked around the room, as if hesitant to continue. But he was the one who had spoken cryptically about what needed to be done to defend Ashur. Garrison was not keen on building things up this way, especially ever since he'd been blessed with the truth about people who bore the Mark and understood who he was.

Savaiyon finally spoke up after a deep breath, "Not long before the House of Darian was destroyed, Zin Marlowe sent Vasher and I on a secret mission to meet with the elders of Fangh-Haan to request their support in a war against Jahmash. Vasher managed to secure that on his own, which was a huge victory, though I may have not let him think so at first." Savaiyon glanced at a Shivaani a few couches away, that Garrison assumed was Vasher. "However, the other part of that mission was to secure an alliance with the Anonymi." Garrison heard a few grumbles around the room, but Savaiyon raised an open hand to quiet them. "Anyone in this room who was trained in the House of Darian, knows that Zin Marlowe was against violence. His credo was that violence on our part could only do us harm, as it would show Ashur that we are dangerous. So he thought an alliance with the Anonymi might properly complement any weaknesses we hold in combat. As a result, Vasher and I were tasked with gaining the support of the Anonymi. We managed to procure a meeting with them, to offer our proposal."

Maqdhuum cut in, "How did you manage to *procure* this meeting?"

Savaiyon eyed Maqdhuum from the corner of his eye, without

actually turning his head. He held the gaze long enough for Garrison to notice some contempt. Savaiyon continued, "We talked to people who could lead us to them. As I was saying, as a result of this meeting, the Anonymi informed us that…"

This time, Vasher cut in, "Sorry, Maven Savaiyon, but they informed *me*. You were taken somewhere else, remember?"

Savaiyon nodded, "Very well." He took another deep breath, "They informed Vasher that the only way they would agree to an alliance was if the Descendants killed the two men who were the biggest threats to Ashur." A low din arose once more, but Savaiyon didn't bother to quiet them. "They explained to Vasher that alliances are not their way, just as violence is not ours. Thus, if we could prove to be violent toward the kingdom's biggest threats, they would form an alliance in order to ensure Ashur's survival."

Baltaszar posed the question that was likely on everyone's mind, "So who are the two men? Who do they want us to kill?"

Savaiyon's gaze fell to the couch next to Garrison, upon Horatio. *Why would we have to kill Horatio?* "Horatio, I have not had the opportunity to speak to you, to find out your intentions, so it seems that everyone will find out together now. Did you know that it was Zin Marlowe you were striking with lightning, or did you think you were attacking Drahkunov?"

All eyes now redirected to Horatio, whose face looked sallow. Horatio swallowed several times before putting a loose fist to his mouth and clearing his throat. "I…um. I never actually knew the plan. When I…when I left the infirmary, I knew I missed some discussion, but I assumed it was just something inspirational from Marlowe. I didn't know. I didn't know he could look like other people. I was already exhausted, and didn't have great command of the lightning anyway, but I saw Drahkunov far off on the shore, and I just focused on trying to hit him." His voice cracked at the last part, and Garrison noticed his eyes were a bit glossy. "I'm sorry everyone, I promise you, I'm not a murderer. I'm not a traitor. I didn't know I was doing something wrong." Marshall, who was sitting next to Horatio, put a hand on his shoulder to comfort him.

Savaiyon spoke up again. "Be easy on yourself, Horatio. As terrible as it will sound to say this, you may have done us a favor in the grand scheme of things. Zin Marlowe was one of the two men we were tasked to kill." Once again, the room filled with responses and gasps of all sorts. Savaiyon nodded. "Believe me, Vasher and I were just as shocked, and it would have been near impossible for anyone in this room to kill Zin Marlowe willingly. Horatio, in your confusion, you completed half of our mission. As much as I looked up to him, I am certain Zin Marlowe would consider his life a small sacrifice for the protection of Ashur. Horatio, do not focus on why or how you did it. Instead, focus on the future and that, because of you, we are one step closer to an alliance with the Anonymi and being able to properly defend Ashur against the Red Harbinger."

"I guess I'll be the one to ask, since I'm not caught up grieving for Marlowe," Farrah interjected matter-of-factly. "Who is the second man? Is it Garrison or his father?"

This time, everyone turned to Garrison, who hadn't been ready for so much attention. Savaiyon answered Farrah before anyone could posit any theories, "The other man *is* King Edmund. I doubt *that* comes as a shock for anyone, nonetheless, I am sorry for this, Garrison. If this is too difficult for you, I understand if you would choose not to stay. We would allow you, your brother, and your friend to stay until you are all well again."

Garrison had no idea how to respond. He had the smallest inkling that Savaiyon would say his father's name, but it had no effect on the shock he felt. He looked down to grasp the situation and, surprisingly, did not feel sadness. He'd held a great deal of anger toward his father in the past few years, but he'd never really been sure if that anger was strong enough to want his father dead. Now that the time had come, he felt no remorse about the notion. *He was ready to have me killed right in front of him. Why should I feel sad about this? The Anonymi are right, he is the greatest threat to Ashur and to our ability to fight Jahmash.* Garrison looked up at Savaiyon and glanced around at the others. He was surprised that no one in the room had made any comments or jabs about him. This seemed like the perfect opportunity for the rest of them to show their true colors about how they felt about him. "This will not be easy…"

Savaiyon misunderstood his response, "I understand that. We hold no grudges if you cannot see this through."

"No, I mean it literally will not be easy. He is a coward and surrounds himself with guards. I know not how many soldiers Donovan and Wendell have recruited to their side, but my father will still have scores of well-compensated guards to protect him. I highly doubt that we will be able to…wait." Garrison suddenly realized that Savaiyon had had an opportunity to kill his father already. He stood up and looked Savaiyon in the eyes, "You." He pointed directly at Savaiyon. "You knew of this directive when we were rescuing Baltaszar. My father was alone outside the cell, unprotected. No guards were around. All you had to do was make one of your doorways back into the corridor and fight him and kill him. You *saw* him, he is not physically threatening—he is all mouth! Why did you not simply do it then? It would have been so easy to do *and* get away with. Why?"

Savaiyon grew wide-eyed, "I...well..."

Before he could put together a response, Maqdhuum cut him off and, with a wide grin, shouted, "Because he's not sure if it would have counted, if it was by his hands!"

Garrison cocked his head, confused. "What do you mean?"

Maqdhuum continued, "Ask Savaiyon. Right, *Maven*? I imagine it's quite difficult to decide if you are one of us or one of them?"

Vasher asked, "Is it true, Maven? Is that why you weren't in the room with me when they met with me?'

Savaiyon sat down, right where he'd stood, in the middle of the floor with the couches surrounding him. Garrison had lost count of the amount of deep breaths the man had taken, but Savaiyon took one more, then finally spoke. "Maqdhuum is correct, as are Rhadames's suspicions. I am Anonymi." He looked around and made eye contact with them, rather than looking down. "It was a secret that only Zin Marlowe knew, at least as far as I am aware. However, you should all know that this was kept secret, not because of Zin Marlowe or the House of Darian, but at the command of the Anonymi. It is not their way to have their acolytes out in the world. Acolytes of the Anonymi either stay in the temple for constant training and meditation, or are about in Ashur on various missions, hidden in plain sight. I am only divulging this information because of *where* we are, in a tower of Augurs who never leave, and servants trained by the Anonymi. Each of you here will swear this information to secrecy here and now."

"And if we do not?" quipped Farrah.

"Then you and I both face the wrath of the Anonymi. And trust me, they would not give you some swift and merciful death. It is likely that they know all about your sins and your past, Farrah. They would be quite interested in you." Garrison glanced at her in time to see her face turn pale. Savaiyon continued. "I understand if anyone here is offended or feels somewhat betrayed by my deception, but *you* should all understand that there are bigger things going on in Ashur than Descen...than the Ghosts of Ashur. And that is all part of what we must do next. So before I continue, I ask you all to swear this information to secrecy, and to keep it between the people in this room. All of you, your word is your bond."

Maximillian spoke up. Garrison hadn't really met him aside from a brief introduction. "With all due respect, Savaiyon, I do not think the phrase *my word is my bond* really holds much value anymore. The House of Darian crumbled and many of its secrets have been thrust into the air with all of the dust and ash. I am not judging you, but the fact of the matter is that you have lied to us, as did Zin Marlowe. As a Maven myself, I am losing track of how much information was kept from me.

Many of these young men and women only recently discovered that the prince was being held captive in our dungeons. It is fair to conclude that the House itself sat on a thick foundation of lies. Our word is not our bond, because our word has been worthless this whole time."

Savaiyon nodded at Maximillian. "You are right. Subterfuge was weaved into our daily lives in the House of Darian. So we will no longer pretend that we have been being honest with one another. 'My word is my bond' has lost its value and credibility. I suppose it is fitting, as we are no longer calling ourselves 'Descendants' either. Thank you for bringing that to light, Maximillian. And to the point I had been making, Garrison, you were in the middle of telling us that it would not be easy to kill King Edmund. We are going to need help. For every step we take now toward preparing Ashur for a war against the Red Harbinger, we will not succeed with just the twenty of us sitting here. We will need more and more help the closer we get to that war."

Marshall asked, "Are you going to lead us in this war, Savaiyon?"

Savaiyon stood up once again and smoothed his green breeches, "I am not sure that I am the most fit *to* lead you. As I was saying, we are going to need help. Our first order of business is to seek out Asarei. He is a former member of the House of Darian who was ostracized by Zin Marlowe, for being too caught up with combat. It is fitting that you asked, Marshall, because Asarei is a Taurani who left the village after disagreeing with some of their methods. He is an intelligent man and an excellent fighter."

"Except that he cannot or does not want to be found," Maqdhuum interrupted.

Savaiyon smirked, "Does that mean you were in Shipsbane? They are rather protective of him there. He watches over them. But if one knows what to look for, then one can find him."

Maqdhuum continued, "So you are one who knows what to look for?"

Savaiyon nodded, "Indeed, I know how to get to him. But before we even get to that part, I need to know that everyone here is on board with what comes next. There is another piece of information that has been held from you, and you all should know before anything else is decided." Savaiyon looked around the room at each of them, and his glance lingered on Maqdhuum a little longer.

Garrison smiled to himself. *He's going to tell everyone, isn't he.*

Finally, Savaiyon spoke again. "The man who has been most critical of me since we all arrived here, has been also lying to everyone the whole time." He looked directly at Maqdhuum now. "I am sure you all have been wondering how Maqdhuum could possibly be able to disappear and reappear, though he doesn't bear the Mark. Well, the truth is that this man is actually..."

"Abram." Maqdhuum stood up and walked into the middle of the circle as the rest of the group gasped at yet another revelation. "My name was once Abram. On of the Five, chosen by the Orijin to save humanity from itself. The Untamed Harbinger. Before any of you bother, I am not going to answer your questions about my life in the past two thousand years." The room grew deathly silent in an instant. "All you need to know is that I escaped when fighting Jahmash after he turned on us. I thought it better to live and fight back another time. All that matters is that I am here to help you defeat him. And I don't care if you don't trust me. Obviously Adria and Garrison stuck with me and allowed me to come here."

Garrison glanced at Adria, who was already looking at him. He raised his eyebrows and shrugged, not knowing what to say. Marshall stood up from the other side of Horatio, with fists and jaw clenched. He stared directly at Maqdhuum for a few moments, then stalked off to his room and slammed the door.

Horatio leaned forward with his fist in his palm, "That's it? You're a Harbinger who was literally alive *with* Jahmash and befriended him, and all you have to tell us is that you cowardly ran off while fighting him and now, two thousand years later, have summoned the courage to fight back? But we can't ask questions?"

Garrison had wondered what the reaction would be once others found out Maqdhuum's true identity, but he was surprised at Horatio's anger. He was so worked up that blood trickled from his nose.

Maqdhuum responded as Horatio wiped the blood away with the back of his hand. "Yes. That's it. Over time, I'll share more with you, as I learn to trust you. Look, I know my flaws and shortcomings. I'm not here telling you that you need me or that I'm better than any of you. Some of you, probably, but not all of you. However, I *can* help you." He looked around the room and his eyes settled upon Savaiyon lastly.

Savaiyon glanced at Adria, "Adria, you've spent the most time with him. What do you say?"

She shrugged. "He's an asshole, but we *could* use his help."

"Then it's settled. Maqdhuum is one of us. Remember, he is Maqdhuum, not Abram. Now, about Asarei. Once we go to Asarei, there is no turning back. We will do things *his* way, which is starkly different than what you are used to. If you want no part of this, then I ask you to return to your quarters now. There will be no judgment passed upon you from the rest of us."

Garrison looked around at the others. No one moved or even flinched. He was impressed at their sense of duty.

Savaiyon continued, "Good. We will need all of your help.

Everyone here has value. That being said, there are many others who will need to fight alongside us in order for Ashur to have a chance. We have already established that Asarei and his followers are the first step. And once we kill King Edmund, we will have the Anonymi with us as well. Some of you from the northwestern nations have likely heard of the Kraisos. They are a thieves guild as old as the Anonymi. While their numbers are small, there is much they could possibly teach us about tactics in diversion and getting the best of our opponents. We will need as much strategy as possible. I get the feeling that no matter what, we will be greatly outnumbered. Which is why, as improbable as it sounds, we will need the Vermillion on our side *after* we kill the king. Garrison, is that even remotely realistic? Perhaps you could summon Wendell, and he could apprise us of where the Vermillion currently stands?

SAVAIYON CLOSED HIS EYES while Garrison retrieved Wendell. *Thank you, Orijin, for letting all of that go smoothly.* He knew that at some point, he would have to reveal himself as an Anonymi acolyte, but he'd hoped it would be on his own terms. Maqdhuum clearly liked pushing his buttons, which only made revealing Maqdhuum's secret even sweeter. Savaiyon was still coming to terms that only weeks ago, Maqdhuum was chasing him through almost every city in Ashur, trying to kill him. And now he would have to force himself to get along with the man just to set an example for the others. *Maybe I can strangle him when no one is looking. Or maybe I can bring him back to the fortress and my masters can kill him.* At some point in the near future, he would have to return to the Anonymi fortress to notify the Masters that he'd been discovered. Savaiyon didn't know how that would turn out, as he'd never seen or heard of it happening to anyone. *Perhaps they will be lenient, considering the circumstances, and who it was that exposed me.* He heard footsteps nearing and opened his eyes.

Wendell and Garrison returned to the circle of couches, and Savaiyon gestured for them to join him in the middle as he sat on the floor once more. Both sat opposite him on the floor. "Wendell, I do not know if Garrison apprised you of anything we discussed out here. Regardless, the basic details are that we have been tasked by the Anonymi with assassinating King Edmund. It is the only way to ensure an alliance with them in defending Ashur against Jahmash. To do this, we will need your help. *And*, if we are successful, we will surely need the Vermillion Army's help once it comes time to defend Ashur. Can this be done?"

Wendell's eyes were already wide as he looked back and forth between Garrison and Savaiyon. "You have to *kill* King Edmund?" Savaiyon nodded in affirmation, and Wendell continued, "And *you* have agreed to this?" He looked at Garrison, surprised.

Garrison flinched, "He tried to have me killed. Twice. I told you and my brother that his day would come. I have no issue with this."

Wendell flipped away a few strands of his long golden hair and put a hand on Garrison's shoulder, "You misunderstood, friend. I was not judging you. I only wanted to assure your approval of it. This is not something I would proceed with if you felt uncomfortable."

Garrison reassured him, "I will be a part of this mission. I do not think I can be the one who actually does it, but I want him to know that I am there before it happens."

Wendell turned back to Savaiyon, "It has been several months since we started this insurrection, and we have just under half of the Vermillion loyal to me and Donovan, rather than to King Edmund. We will need to work on more of them before you carry out your mission, if you would like for them to be loyal to you. To kill the King while they are still loyal to him will only make him a martyr and prove him right to those soldiers still loyal to him. Donovan and I are getting results but it takes time to wear these soldiers down. There are years of blind loyalty to break through for some of them, especially those who were not present when Garrison's father decreed him a criminal and ordered the Royal Guard to kill him."

Savaiyon understood that it would take time, he only hoped it would be sooner rather than later. "How much time do you think you will need? Another several months?"

Wendell took a deep breath and looked down for a moment. "Given our progress so far, I would say six months, at most. By then, it will be summer—that draws King Edmund out more often, which means the palace itself is not as heavily guarded. More soldiers will be outside the palace."

Vasher cut in. "Perhaps I could return to Alvadon with them, Savaiyon. With my manifestation, I might be able to help quicken the process of convincing these soldiers." Savaiyon looked over, surprised to see Vasher sitting on the floor a few feet away from him. Most of the others had done the same, likely wanting to better hear the conversation. Vasher explained to Wendell, "I can persuade people with my manifestation. Change their minds. At least for a while, anyway."

Wendell shook his head in disagreement. "No. It is no offense to you, but their choice must be natural. I understand that you mean to help, but these soldiers need to maintain loyalty to us after your siege is over. I do not want them to come to the realization that they have been tricked or lied to. That will only lead to more trouble. Donovan and I are only telling them the truth and letting them see the side of the King that they had not seen before. I know it is a slower process, but it is the right course of action to take."

Savaiyon agreed. "Wendell is right, Vasher. There can be no tricks in what they are doing. But thank you for offering." He looked around at the rest of the group, "Six months will work well with what we must do. It gives us plenty of time to go to Asarei and train for combat. Along with hand-to-hand combat, I am hoping that he can guide us with how to use our manifestations in combat as well." He looked back at Wendell, "Wendell, once Donovan has regained his faculties, we will return the two of you to Alvadon. Will King Edmund simply accept the two of you back? Do you think he believed that we took you as hostages?"

"Yes. He has no reason to believe that we are plotting anything. And you were rather convincing back in the cell; there is no reason for him to believe otherwise. If anything, it confirms what he thinks of all of you anyway."

Savaiyon noticed a brief scowl on Garrison's face, but it disappeared by the time he blinked. He looked around at the others once more. "Once I have brought these two back, the rest of us will prepare to leave for Shipsbane. I will go first to secure a place to stay, and then I will bring the rest of you there."

This time it was Adria who spoke up, a few feet away from Wendell. "With all due respect, Maven Savaiyon…"

Savaiyon cut her off. "I should make this clear. If we are ridding ourselves of the customs of the House of Darian, then you must stop calling me 'Maven.' That title does not exist anymore. Continue, Adria."

"With all due respect, *Savaiyon*, we are about to embark on a long, new endeavor. I am fully committed to what must be done, but the truth in all this is that any of us could die during this siege. And even if we all manage to survive, who knows if Jahmash will have already begun his war by then?" She looked at him intensely, "I implore you to let me return to Fera to see my parents. It may very well be the last time I see them *and* the last time I return home. Even if it is only for a few days before we go to Shipsbane."

Before Savaiyon could respond, Marshall added something from behind Garrison, "I second that request, if that is fair. Not to go to Fera, but I would kindly ask to return to the Taurani Village to give my family the proper death ceremony. The last time I was there was a year ago, and we had to flee because…" he paused and glared at Maqdhuum, "Adria and Gunnar were captured, and we had to flee." Others began to nod and verbally agree.

Savaiyon understood their concern. It *would* be helpful for them all to return to loved ones and see the very ones they were fighting for. None of them had the luxury of being able to travel to any place in Ashur at a whim. It might also provide him the opportunity to return to the

Anonymi fortress and stand before the Masters for his judgment. *Better to do it now than not know when I would have time. At least if they banish me now, I can kill Edmund if no one else can see it through.*

"I am not opposed to this request. I think we could all benefit from taking some time for ourselves before embarking on this new path. Let us take a week to tend to our personal needs. However, there is *some* business that will need to be done during this time. Does anyone wish to go with Adria to Markos?"

Badalao, Malikai, and surprisingly, Farrah and Maqdhuum all spoke up. Savaiyon singled her out. "If I may ask, Farrah, what do you wish to accomplish there?"

Farrah took her hand away from holding her face up, "My father was from Sapphria. I would just like to go back one last time to see it. I have not been there since I was very young." She looked around at everyone else, as they all looked at her, "I promise, I have no ill intentions. The rest of them can accompany if they'd like."

Savaiyon nodded, "I will let you all sort that out. Maqdhuum, what about you?"

Maqdhuum smiled widely at Savaiyon and waved a few stringy locks out of his face. "The Kraisos are in Taiju. Might as well have a chat. They like me a lot more than you do. I'm sure that's not saying much. Either way, like you said, we'll need them."

Savaiyon nodded curtly. "Should it be any secret that I dislike you? Only two weeks ago you were hiding in my quarters, then chasing me throughout Ashur, trying to kill me. I had as many daggers stuck in me as there are people in this room. If not for my Anonymi training, you likely would have killed me. So yes, I will tolerate you. If I expect everyone else here to put aside their differences, then I must do the same. You have gained Adria's trust, so you have mine. But I still dislike you." He looked down at the floor for a moment, then continued, "More importantly, the five of you will return to Markos for a week. That should be plenty of time for you all to tend to your needs as well as meet with the Kraisos."

Malikai added, "Do not worry, Mav...Savaiyon. My family is from Taiju. I plan to return there, and then I can accompany Maqdhuum to the Kraisos. I also have an idea of where to find them."

Savaiyon smirked, Good. Then you can keep an eye on him. Maqdhuum, given your talents, you will not need me to bring you to Markos. I trust you can handle that?"

Maqdhuum nodded vigorously, "You have my word, my lord. Would you like a hug from me? I think you might feel much better about me if we just had a good, strong hug."

Savaiyon rolled his eyes and disregarded Maqdhuum. "Marshall, you asked to return to your village. Will anyone be accompanying you?" Marshall shrugged, but Maximillian and Reverron acknowledged that they would join him.

Marshall looked at Reverron, "Really?"

Reverron looked at Marshall and then down at the floor. "I figure we are friends now, since we traveled here together. Also, I am not on the best of terms with my family." He pointed to his Mark.

"No, it's fine. I'm just surprised that anyone would want to join me for this. Thank you. And you as well, Maximillian." Maximillian smiled at Marshall, then quickly glanced at Desmond and back at Marshall.

I still need to talk to Maximillian about Desmond. Especially now if we are all going to go our separate ways for a short while. He clearly wants to be away from Desmond. "Very well, that makes two factions. Anyone else?"

This time, Sindha came forward, "I would like to return to Itarse, please, Savaiyon. I have not seen my family in some time and would love the chance."

Delilah joined in, "If you don't mind, Sindha, could I join you? I have never seen Itarse and would love the opportunity, as long as it would not be a burden?"

Sindha smiled, "Of course! I would love to show you the city!"

Savaiyon chuckled softly, "Good. That will not be an issue. Anyone else?"

Lincan stood up from the back of the group, "I would like to return home as well. I haven't seen my family in so long, and I'd like to take advantage of the opportunity while there's still time. If you could bring me there, it would also reduce the risk of being seen."

Savaiyon nodded, "I can accommodate that. I actually plan to return to the Anonymi fortress, so I will bring you right before I go there." Lincan bowed his head in thanks and sat back down.

Vasher excitedly spoke up as Lincan sat, "I would like to join you, Savaiyon." Savaiyon looked at him quizzically. "It isn't what you think. I am not trying to pry into your affairs. Last time we were there, they walked us through several chambers and there was no time to stop and take any of it in. I would just like to go back and see those chambers again for myself. There were so many artifacts and tapestries that caught my eye."

Savaiyon rolled his eyes, but he wasn't upset at Vasher's request. He loved the chambers as well, and all the legends of the original nine Anonymi. "I suppose I would not mind the company. But that is all you will be allowed to do. Once your window of time has elapsed in the chambers, I will bring you to Shipsbane to await the rest of us." Vasher nodded excitedly. "Good. Speaking of Shipsbane, would anyone prefer to simply go directly there? Or does everyone have things to attend to?"

One by one, Garrison, Horatio, Blastevahn, and Kadoog'han all expressed interest in going to Shipsbane. Blastevahn commented, "I'm still tired. I could use a veek to rest before ve start zhis next step." Kadoog'han and Garrison nodded in agreement.

Horatio added, "I just want to stay out of trouble. Best for me to just go to Shipsbane and wait."

Savaiyon looked at Horatio guiltily, "Horatio, no one here blames you for what happened. There was no way you could have known that that was Marlowe. But perhaps Shipsbane will provide your mind with some needed rest."

Baltaszar stood up from behind Vasher and looked at Savaiyon sheepishly, "It's not family, but there is someone I need to see in Vandenar. I know...it's a bold request and probably something I don't deserve, but if this is our last chance to see to our personal affairs, then I humbly ask to go to Vandenar."

Slade also stood up, right behind Baltaszar, "I will join him, Savaiyon, and ensure his good behavior. There are things that I must discuss with Baltaszar anyway."

Savaiyon nodded, but before he could respond, he heard a quiet voice from the other side of the group. Desmond spoke, as if reluctant, "I would also ask to join them in going to Vandenar. I would like to see my family there."

Savaiyon stood up. "I believe that is everyone, then? Correct?" He paused for a moment to be sure. "Then it is settled. Everyone knows where they are going, and everyone has a week to carry out their wishes before I bring you all back to Shipsbane. However, before anyone leaves, Lao must bond you. And before anyone complains or protests, this is not a punishment. This is for safety and protection, and in case anyone needs immediate help from us. Aside from King Edmund showing up, Lao's manifestation worked extremely well with mine in terms of creating a gateway using an image from his mind. We must all work together now. Although we are briefly going our separate ways, we are all one. Everything we do now must be for the best of the group. Everything we do must protect the group and the greater good. Adria, you mentioned that some of us may not survive the coming conflicts that we will face. The only way to ensure the best outcome is for us to work together and care as much for one another as we do for ourselves. Yes, even Maqdhuum." The others laughed, breaking the tension that was starting to build.

Maximillian stood up next to Savaiyon and looked around at the others, who were all sitting. "Salvation as one. That must be our mindset from now on. Remember it. Repeat it. Salvation as one." And sure enough, everyone in the room, Savaiyon included, repeated the phrase over and over again, embracing and celebrating the notion.

CHAPTER 12
MUTINY OF THE BLACK COATS

From **The Book of Orijin,** **Verse Four Hundred Seventy-eight**
When faced with an insurmountable enemy, life is the greatest priority. Live for another day. Do not make foolish and unnecessary sacrifices.

BO'AZ LEANED AGAINST THE taffrail at the stern of the ship and looked out at the open sea as the sun began its descent. Deep down, he had known that this journey was inevitable, and yet, he still couldn't believe that he was on a ship, setting sail for a nation whose existence he only recently became aware of. Since the beginning of his stay with Jahmash, he'd tried to be open to new experiences as much as possible and maintain an open mind about as many things as he could. For some of it, he knew Jahmash had control of his decisions and, even when Jahmash was not controlling his mind, Bo'az knew the wrong choice could get him hurt or killed. Still, Bo'az didn't dread this journey because of the actual journey part. It was more about what he was missing by going on the journey. The only thing he really looked forward to anymore was to see his brother again.

In the past year away from Ashur, he'd somewhat managed to come to terms with Yasaman's death. There was some satisfaction in the thought that he'd killed Gibreel, her killer, but he still missed her. Or at least the idea of her. He'd been honest with himself about the way their last conversation had played out; she'd only slept with him because she knew she would die sooner rather than later, and she still loved Baltaszar. Part of Bo'az being honest with himself was recognizing that he resented Yasaman for using him that way. His feelings for her had been genuine, and he'd been ashamed of those feelings for so long, only to have her exploit and pervert them for her personal gain.

In the past few months Bo'az had come to understand he would have to tell Baltaszar what happened. He knew that it would strain their relationship; if he kept it secret, his brother would never know. But part of becoming braver and stronger was doing what was right, even when he could get away with doing the wrong thing. Baltaszar would never have a way of finding out about Bo'az and Yasaman, but it was right to tell him.

Despite the fact that they'd parted ways because of an argument and a refusal to see things the same way, Bo'az knew the first thing he would do upon seeing Baltaszar would be to give him a huge hug. If they could be reunited, Bo'az would do everything in his power to stop being a coward and trust his brother's judgment more.

"You are either seeing something out there that no one else can see, or you are incredibly lost in thought." Hansi's voice scared Bo'az so much that he jumped, which then scared him a second time. Hansi chuckled, "Ah, lost in thought, then. I didn't mean to intrude or scare you, I just wanted to see how you're doing. Also…" Hansi looked at him, then out at the sea, then to his boots, "have…you felt Jahmash since we left?"

Bo'az looked again out at the open water. "Now that I think of it, I haven't. I am so used to him being there, that I just assume that he's always there. But, he *did* say he would let us be for most of our time at sea. Are you upset? I'm sure if you think long enough about the wrong thing, he'll be right back in there to get you *thinking properly* again."

Hansi chuckled once more and shivered. "Trust me, the last thing I am is upset that I have my mind to myself for a little while. This is only our second day out here, and it's the freest I've felt in a couple years."

Bo'az glanced at him from the corner of his right eye. He wanted to believe that Hansi was being genuine, but it could be some ruse by Jahmash to test his loyalty. They were, after all, on a mission for the Red Harbinger, and the last thing he wanted was to be killed out here on the open sea, thrown overboard in the middle of winter. "Didn't you come to Jahmash willingly, though? I know we never got much time to converse back at the fortress, but I always assumed that you and Farrah *wanted* to work for Jahmash."

Hansi's smile grew tighter. "Eh. I followed Farrah once we escaped Rayan. She was in bad shape physically, emotionally, *and* mentally. I knew she had some bad intentions; I just didn't realize *how* bad. I'm decent enough with my manifestation to fool some people, especially in a quick bind. So, I can keep myself hidden pretty well with my illusions. It was easy to tail her without being noticed, but I just really got myself stuck in a bad situation when I saw her talking to that mehkiyep, Maqdhuum. I knew she was making a deal with him, but I just thought she was trying to negotiate some sort of protection. I walked right into her agreeing to leave Ashur with him, and me telling them I was going as well. Oh boy, even if Farrah had wanted to tell me 'no,' Maqdhuum was leading us to a boat within seconds, telling us both how brave we were and he just wouldn't stop talking." Hansi paused for a moment and looked out at the Sea of Fates, just like Bo'az. "He was bringing us as gifts to Jahmash, but it seems like he's fallen out of favor now. Any idea what that's about?"

Bo'az shook his head, "No clue. Jahmash is too smart and careful to trust us. He has other spies out there anyway, and I'm sure he has some on this ship to keep an eye on us. Hey, you said you can create illusions.

Why didn't he send you on that last mission to destroy the House of Darian? I'm sure something like that could be useful. And it looks like Farrah managed to..." Bo'az paused, contemplating whether to finish the thought, knowing Jahmash could pop in at any time, "managed to escape Jahmash."

Hansi continued to stare out, "Nah, I'm decent with my manifestation, but not good enough with it to be able to maintain it for long. Definitely not trustworthy in combat. Most of the time, I was only using it to hide or get away." He pointed to his face, "This line on my face doesn't mean that I'm automatically great with what I can do; it just means I can do something. Sure, I was able to trick some soldiers and villagers to escape, and I'll be able to impress some people in a faraway land who know nothing of this magic, but in an actual battle, I would be useless. It's hard to train yourself when you're always on the run. Especially when people could walk in any moment and freak out about what you're doing. Farrah's manifestation is different, not as obvious. Also, she *had* to use hers more often to keep men from raping her. Easy to perfect a manifestation like that when every lodeit in Ashur is trying to grope you."

Bo'az looked at him, "That's tough. And you couldn't get to the House of Darian?"

"The thing about Fangh-Haan is, unless you live in the south, near the coast, it's difficult to just leave the nation, especially as a Descendant. I grew up in Zebulon, right in the middle of Fangh-Haan, and the only access to leave would have been sailing along the Serpent, where guards would be waiting, then checking at the wall that divides us from Galicea. Basically the same as suicide."

"Yeah. What are those words you're using? I'm sure they're insults, but my exposure to anything beyond my little town in the forest was nonexistent. I couldn't even name all the nations in Ashur if you asked me. The only reason I even know Fangh-Haan is because I met you."

Hansi chuckled, "Those are the bad words in Haan. I actually don't really speak much of the old Haan language, but any Haan knows the bad words. Let's see, 'mehkiyep' is bad—it's basically someone who is so base that they would even lay with their own mother. That's my favorite one to say, oh and 'lodeit' is just an asshole. What about you? You're from where again?"

Bo'az sighed. He was tired of explaining it to the others, "Haedon. It's a village in the Never. From what I've deduced in conversations with all of you, it's far enough in there that people in Ashur don't even know it's there. I guess it's some kind of hidden city or something, right there deep in the forest and mountains."

"That's pretty neat," Hansi nodded, and his hood flopped as his head moved up and down, "makes you mysterious. Girls would love that."

Bo'az paused and turned to look at Hansi, confused. "What girls? There are no girls on this ship. Where we're going, no girls are going to give a damn about my stupid little town hidden in the forest. Matter of fact, we're trying to find people who want to destroy Ashur, so which girls are you talking about?"

Hansi backed away a step, "Sorry, Bo. I didn't mean to strike a nerve. I was just making conversation. I never met anyone from Haedon before. I figure if I'm intrigued by it, everyone else would be."

Bo'az waited before speaking again. He wasn't mad at Hansi, but the notion of even being interested in any girl or any girl having an interest in him was something he wasn't ready to consider. The Yasaman situation still stung, even after so much time, specifically because she'd died before Bo'az could finish processing her rejection of him. There was no way Hansi could have known any of that, especially since Bo'az hadn't shared it with anyone since it happened. He thought about just blowing it off and dismissing Hansi, but then thought about the person he was trying to become.

"Wait, no. It's not your fault. You did strike a nerve, but there's no way you could have known. You know I have a twin brother, which is why I'm here in the first place. But there was a girl at the beginning of my journey to Jahmash. She and my brother were...something, but I fancied her as well and never told anyone. I pretended to be him to see if something could happen between me and her, and then Slade, Gibreel, and Linas arrived, and I had to keep the lie going. We slept together while I was pretending to be my brother, and then she revealed that she knew I was Bo'az. The following day, Gibreel pushed her off the side of a mountain because she became a burden to our journey, and then I did the same to Gibreel." He eyed Hansi's fur-lined black coat, which was identical to his own, and was thankful that they were both warm enough to be out on the deck without any discomfort. "I never shared that with anyone. I've been a coward for most of my life and I was hoping to avoid judgment for it."

Hansi stared at him for a moment, as if taking it all in. "I have magical powers, and the first time I had the courage to leave my nation was to follow a girl I barely knew in order to try and protect her from herself, and in the process, I found myself working for Jahmash." He smirked, "Matter of fact, four of us on this ship are working for the Red Harbinger, the very messenger of Orijin that killed his own friends and plans to do the same thing to all of Ashur. *And* we're on our way to recruit more armies for him. Trust me, there is no one here that is in any position to pass judgment on you for your decisions, Bo."

Bo'az eyed Deacon a few feet behind Hansi, also nestled in his thigh-length black coat. "How long have you been standing there?"

Deacon smiled and walked up to the rail, "Long enough to vish I had come earlier. Hansi is correct, Bo'az. No one on zis ship is qualified to pass judgment. Ve vork for ze most evil man in ze vorld, and even if he controls our minds some of ze time, ve all made a choice to go to him. Alzough, from vat you told Hansi, you did not choose to be here. If anyzing, you are at least a better person zan ze rest of us."

Bo'az snickered, "Thanks, Deacon. I guess that's worth something. Still, I feel like we have to *do* something. Right? We're Jahmash's messengers, for Orijin's sake. I know we've all done some shitty and cowardly things in our lives, but I don't think I can just shrug this one off as a bad decision. We've made it this far because he knows he can control us. And the way I see it, right now he needs us to get him armies, so he won't kill us just yet. That means our window is this voyage to the nations of Bisitsad. Once we get there, we're under his control again, and he could kill us one by one in front of the leaders of Castiel, Yahaira, and Brogan, and it would likely still convince them to follow him."

Hansi eyed him cautiously, "Bo, you are not wrong, but to think that four of us nobodies could rise up against Jahmash—that's crazy."

Fittingly, Aric arrived at the rail and leaned against it, next to Hansi. "Why exactly are we crazy nobodies?"

Light of Orijin, why him. Orijin, why must he be here? Bo'az glared at the Taurani from the corner of his eye. "Nothing, Aric." Hansi and Deacon shifted, seemingly tense as well. "We were just looking out at the Sea of Fates. Nothing interesting."

Aric stared out, straight-faced, wearing his fur-lined black coat as well. His coat seemed more fitted, though, as he was easily the most muscular of the four of them. "Very well. I have no problem doing that as well."

Bo'az rolled his eyes. "Aric, have you felt Jahmash in your mind over the past two days?"

Aric continued to stare straight ahead, "I haven't, to be honest. It is rather peculiar."

"Why are you so...the way you are? So rigid? I get that Jahmash has been controlling the four of us for most of the past year, but Deacon, Hansi, and I have all at least offered *some* part of our personalities. But you have offered nothing, like you're completely dry of emotions. Even when Jahmash has allowed us to be ourselves, you've still acted exactly the same way. Why?"

Deacon, standing between Bo'az and Aric, looked like he was straining to look out at the water. He focused his eyes downward and maintained his gaze. Aric turned to Bo'az. "Why do you believe that you can speak to me that way? I have been trained to kill since I saw six summers. Do you know how easily I could kill you, Bo'az? And what would happen to all that *personality* of yours then?"

Bo'az shrugged, "Here we go again. I challenge your personality and you immediately threaten to kill me. How can you manage to be so wound up all the time? Isn't it exhausting? Also, to be clear, if you kill me, I'm almost certain Jahmash would do unspeakable things to you. I'm his special pawn for luring my brother. But go ahead, kill me like you are six, with all your training and everything."

Aric spit out into the water. "You have no idea the hardships I have faced before coming here. My village was destroyed along with my entire race, and I watched them all die, including Esha, the girl I intended to marry. Her brother, Marshall, and I engaged Maqdhuum in a duel, along with one other Taurani. I had to watch Maqdhuum cut down Marshall and Myron and the only reason why he spared me was because I was the last one breathing. Maqdhuum thought I would make a nice trophy for Jahmash, so after he defeated me, he bound me and tortured me the entire way to Jahmash's island."

Bo'az felt a hint of guilt at the thought of Aric's experience, but the truth was that every one of them was a captive of Jahmash. Even beyond the four of them, Adria, Gunnar, and Farrah had all suffered before and during their time with Jahmash. "I understand that you've been through a great deal and I'm sorry you had to go through all of that. But the rest of us have all been through things as well. We have all lost people, watched people die, feared for our lives, experienced suffering or torture in some shape or form. That doesn't mean that you can't loosen up from time to time. I can't speak for the three of you, but when Jahmash isn't in my head, I take as much advantage of trying to be my normal self as I can. At this point, I think it's the only thing that's given me some semblance of sanity."

Hansi and Deacon both nodded, and Hansi spoke up. "Aric, Bo is right. For all we know, the whole crew of this ship willingly follows Jahmash, which means it's only the four of us. We need to be able to trust each other and rely on one another. Who really knows what Jahmash is sending us to? Castiel, Brogan, Yahaira, they are all just names. We know nothing of the people there. Even with three of us having manifestations, it would be easy for us to be outnumbered and killed."

Bo'az chimed in again, "Aric, all we're saying is that you can be yourself around us. It would be easier to trust you and talk to you that way."

Aric sighed and nodded his head. "Very well. The truth is, I'm deathly afraid of Jahmash killing me. As far as I know, I am the last

Taurani, and I don't know how I could face the Orijin if I died allowing my race to end. But you're all correct; all we have is each other. I'll do better to remember that."

Deacon turned to Bo'az, "Now zat ve know he's von of us, vat's ze plan, Bo'az?"

"The plan?"

"You said our window ends ven ve reach Bisitsad. So vat do ve do to strike back at Jahmash?"

"I don't know." He looked around at all of them. "One wrong move and Jahmash is right back in our heads all the time. We cannot just act rashly to try to change things. We have to be smart and also not alert the ship's crew that anything is going on. We have to assume that someone is always watching. Even with our thoughts we have to be careful. I highly doubt he's just going to completely leave us alone this whole time, and who knows whether he can be in our heads without us knowing."

"So then killing the whole crew is out, huh?" Hansi asked dryly.

Bo'az nodded, "Definitely a bad decision. Besides, even if we managed to kill the entire crew, how would we row all the way to Bisitsad? Didn't Jahmash say it would take us between two and three months, even with full rowing crews?" They all looked at Aric.

He smiled, something Bo'az wasn't sure he'd ever seen. Aric responded, "Why are you all looking at me? Is this about my personality again?"

Hansi chuckled, "No you lodeit, it's because you have all the muscles."

Deacon stepped away from the rail and faced all of them. "I don't agree viz zis. I say ve strike hard vhile ve can. We can only do so much, so let's make it count. I say ve kill ze full crew except for ze oarsmen. Zree of us have manifestations; ze oarsmen would easily fear us and do vat ve tell them."

Bo'az had turned around when Deacon stepped away. He shook his head vigorously. "No. Not a chance. We do that and Jahmash will surely make us suffer for it."

"Vat can he do zat he isn't already doing?"

Bo'az responded "Deacon, look at the freedom we have right now. It has been two days since we've felt his presence like a glove on our minds. I can't remember the last time I've gotten to go this long without him intruding on my thoughts and memories. If we do something stupid and get him angry at us or let him see he can't trust us, we'll lose that freedom before we can even form a thought. Are you willing to risk that?"

Deacon shrugged, "Do you really zink zat will last, Bo'az? Sooner or later, he vill be back in our heads anyvay. Zis *freedom* you speak of, it is fleeting. You are losing sight of ze big picture and getting comfortable. Ve should always be on our guard."

Bo'az sighed. He almost wanted to acquiesce to Deacon's argument. He knew Deacon had already made up his mind and there would be little chance to change his perspective. Bo'az had been through this with Baltaszar more times than he could count. When his brother had his mind made up, there was nothing that could be said to change things. The old Bo'az would simply take the defeat and resign himself to the stronger will. One positive from his time away from Haedon was that Bo'az recognized how detrimental his passive ways had been to his well-being. Giving in to everyone else's will meant that his wants and needs were never prioritized. It was one thing to be a nice guy, it was another thing to let people walk all over him. He looked back at Deacon, "Deacon, I don't mean any disrespect, but why are you here? We know the rest of us were either captured or tricked into being here, but what about you? You've never told us how you got from Galicea to Jahmash. You were with Jahmash before any of the rest of us. We haven't gotten your story."

Deacon stared at Bo'az, then fixed his eyes upon Aric, and finally Hansi. "You're not ze only von who left from Shipsbane, Hansi. Ze only difference is zat I vent zere villingly and I left zere villingly." He glanced around at all of them. "You all know I am Galicean. My full name is Deacon Drahkunov."

Hansi gasped, "He's your father?"

Deacon shook his head vehemently, "No. No, 'Drahkunov', as you all call him, is my uncle. He has no children of his own. My fazher is his younger brozher. His given name is actually Jesper, zough I don't know vhy he doesn't use it anymore. But I digress. You see, my parents are especially devout and zey live a very pious lifestyle. Everyzing zey get, zey give zanks to ze Orijin. And growing up, I could never understand vhy my fazher would be zis way, vhile my uncle vould be so opposite. I have so many qvestions for ze Orijin, especially about Jahmash. Vhy allow zis man to do zese zings to ze vorld and not punish him? Now he is revarded viz a long life and so many followers, ven ze Orijin could easily end his life."

Bo'az interjected, not seeing what Deacon's story had to do with anything. "What exactly is the point of any of this?"

Deacon nodded, "I found my uncle in Shipsbane, knowing he often vent zere ven returning to Ashur. I asked him to bring me to Jahmash." A collective gasp came from Bo'az, Hansi, and Aric. "I understand your shock. It is not somezing I am exactly proud of. However, ze Orijin has chosen some of us to bear zis mark and has blessed us viz manifestations, correct? I vanted to see for myself vhezzer or not ze Orijin vould allow me to actually help Jahmash. I vanted to see if ze Orijin would actually stop me from going to Jahmash of my own free will."

This time, Hansi cut in, "Because if the Orijin didn't stop you, it would mean that either the Orijin was wrong about you, wrong about Jahmash, or doesn't care about any of this at all."

"Yes. Zis is my zinking."

Hansi waved the hair out of his face and stepped forward to face Bo'az and Deacon. Aric placed himself opposite Hansi so now they spoke in a circle. Hansi continued, "Deacon, have you read the Book of Orijin?" The Galicean shook his head to indicate he hadn't. "If I'm not mistaken, that was written by a Galicean Descendant, who could hear the Orijin speak to him in his mind. If we return to Ashur, you should take the time to read it. Anyway, in it, the Orijin explains that we are responsible for our own decisions and actions. Before we die, we will have multiple opportunities to atone for our sins, wrongdoings, and shortcomings. Which means that, even if we take the wrong path or lose sight of things, we still have the ability to atone before we die. So even you, even by choosing to be here, that doesn't mean that the Orijin has sealed your fate or deemed you evil. Maybe you are here for a purpose, or maybe by being here, you'll end up doing something that ends up hurting Jahmash in the long run. Maybe the Orijin has foreseen that you'll change your mind and do the opposite of why you came here in the first place."

Bo'az nodded along to Hansi's words. He knew he couldn't relate to the other three about bearing the Mark or having a manifestation, but they *were* all here doing Jahmash's bidding, and so they were all alike in that sense. He also hoped to have the opportunity to read the Book of Orijin one day. He knew it could help him to be a better person overall. "This whole thing," he waved his hand around to imply the conversation, "has been pretty heavy, so perhaps we should leave it at this for today. I think all four of us are starting to see things the same way, so perhaps we should have some dinner and then get some rest tonight. Tomorrow, we can take our time to plan something in-depth and strategic." He looked around at the others, who all nodded. Deacon still seemed troubled but nodded just the same.

BO'AZ SAT AT THE EDGE of his bed, his eyes still adjusting to being awake. He knew it was early, as he'd grown accustomed to waking up early daily, at the request of Jahmash. Sometimes, while still on the island, he was awakened by one of Jahmash's soldiers, and other times Jahmash simply popped into his head and stirred him. The surprise in that method was just as jarring on the hundredth time as on the first. Bo'az hoped things wouldn't resort to that while they were sailing.

Hopefully if he trusts us enough to carry out this mission, then he can trust us enough to wake up on our own. Regardless, Bo'az fell asleep looking forward to today and felt just as eager upon waking up. He changed his shirt and breeches and sat back on the bed, looking around the room. His quarters were meager, but still better than any of the ship's crew.

Planning some type of rebellion, no matter how minute, would require hours, even days of strategy and specific detail. They would have to ensure that every little thing went according to plan, and then have auxiliary plans in case anything went wrong. Being honest with himself, Bo'az didn't even know what they could realistically do to rebel against Jahmash, but just the thought of the four of them working together to plan something got him excited. *Speaking of excited, there is definitely a lot of bustle and excitement happening up on the deck. I wonder what's got them so worked up.* Bo'az exited his quarters, figuring the crew must have had a great haul of fish at dawn, when they usually cast out for the first time each day. He glanced at the others' doors, all of which were still shut, including Linas Nasreddine's, which was guarded by one of the crew. None of them had anything valuable enough to be stolen, so they tended to leave their doors open during waking hours. *Guess I'm more excited about this than they are.*

He walked up to the main deck to see the chaos of dozens of oarsmen running, standing, kneeling, and screaming over the entire length of the deck. As he looked around, Bo'az saw that deck was stained red with the blood of scores of dead crewmen. Bo'az didn't know where to start, with the disarray surrounding him. He walked to the helm, hoping to see the captain, who was thankfully there, but sitting in front of the wheel. Bo'az ran to the captain and helped him to his feet. "What happened? What is all this?"

The stocky man stroked his black beard and responded in a language that Bo'az didn't comprehend. Judging by the man's gestures and expression, he didn't seem to know how or why it happened. A thought struck the back of Bo'az's mind like he'd actually been hit in the head. He left the captain in a flourish and dashed back down to the subdeck, passing his quarters and pounding on Deacon's door so loudly that Hansi and Aric responded as well. All three of them opened their doors within seconds of each other. Bo'az looked directly at Deacon and grabbed him by the front of his shirt.

"What did you do?! Last night we said NO killing! We said NOT to kill the whole crew!"

Deacon answered nonchalantly, which angered Bo'az even more. "Bo'az, do not vorry. I did zis *because* it hurts Jahmash. I did it *because* you all said I could be redeemed. By doing zis, I have hurt his plans and set him back. Just like Hansi said I might be capable of doing."

"No, you fool. Don't you understand? You killed thirty or forty sailors who mean nothing to Jahmash. If they die, he can just find others with simple minds to manipulate. *They* are not the threat! Do you have any idea what Jahmash will—"

Before Bo'az could finish the thought, something squeezed his mind more tightly than ever before, like it was trying to choke it. In agony, he saw the other three wince and drop to their knees simultaneously with Bo'az. All four clutched their heads, tears streaming from their eyes. The pain was too unbearable for Bo'az to form a thought, but the voice in his head was clearer than anything he'd ever heard before.

The four of you belong to me. You are my property and you do as I say. If you think you are too valuable that I will not kill you, then you are gravely mistaken. But I am not going to allow you to die until I see you again. Deacon, I am not going to kill you now. But you will feel this same pain every day for the rest of your journey, and some days it will be even worse. When you return to me, that is when I will kill you after weeks of torturing you even more. Bo'az, Hansi, Aric, do not even think of helping Deacon die before he returns, or the same will happen to you. Remember, I control you. I can stop anything you do. I can stop any decision you make from happening. And now I will be with you every day until you return.

The grip tightened so much that Bo'az could feel blood flowing from his nose and ears, and he saw the same in the other three through tear-soaked eyes.

CHAPTER 13
A PIECE OF OMNEITRIA

From ***The Book of Orijin,*** **Verse Four Hundred Twenty**
O Mankind, Love in its purest form shall transcend any and all planes of existence.

BALTASZAR NEARLY JUMPED through the gateway that Savaiyon had created for him, Desmond, and Slade. It had only been a few weeks since he'd last been in Vandenar, but it felt like years. The gateway opened to the street right in front of the Happy Elephant, and Baltaszar debated sprinting inside without waiting for Desmond and Slade. He knew Desmond wouldn't care, but Slade seemed overly eager to catch up on things with him. Slade had been the catalyst for starting Baltaszar's journey, and he didn't want to seem ungrateful by ignoring the man.

Regardless, they would only be in Vandenar for a day or two, and that put his time with Anahi at a premium. He could still talk to Slade even after they returned to the group in Shipsbane. But Anahi—this would be the first time he'd be seeing her without the weight of Yasaman on his back. He clenched his fists at the thought of Yasaman and what she'd done, but there was no burden that came along with that anger. That was for her and Bo'az to sort out. For the first time in as long as he could remember, Baltaszar was virtually free of physical and emotional pain. The only thing that still hurt was his face, where the Jinn had scarred his right eye. Even his chest and heart were back to normal. And while thinking of his father still made him sad, Baltaszar understood more and more that that was a sacrifice his father had willingly made. *The only reason to be upset is if I fail in our fight against Jahmash.*

He looked back at Desmond and Slade and saw the gateway close behind them. Desmond walked up to him and grasped his shoulder, "I'm goin' ta see my family. Good luck in there...an' don't mess it all up again."

Baltaszar smirked, "Thanks. I won't. She's the only thing that matters now." Desmond nodded, then turned and walked across the bustling street, weaving through merchants setting up their wares for the day.

Slade nodded, "So that's what this is all about. A girl."

Baltaszar shook his head, "No. It's not just a girl. It's *the* girl. The one I plan to marry and have kids with, and spend every day with, growing old in peace. And this might be my last chance at having her give me the time of day."

"How did you mess this up before?" Slade chuckled.

"Eh, I still had some loose ends to tie up with a girl back in Haedon. That turned to shit in a major way, and I let my anger get the best of me. Set myself on fire, and some of Haedon, in the process." He glanced at the ground and then looked back at Slade, "Not my best moment."

Slade squinted at him curiously, "We'll address the burning down Haedon part another time, but when you say 'a girl back in Haedon', are you talking about Yasaman?"

Baltaszar cocked an eyebrow, "Yes? Weren't you there when your friend pushed her off the mountain?" The words had come out more sardonically than he'd intended. "I didn't mean that as harshly as it sounded. Either way, I trust you, Rhadames. You protected Bo'az and I know you would have told me by now if he was in danger. Right?"

Slade nodded curtly, "That's a safe estimation. Go inside to your girl. I can keep myself entertained in the common room. I'll wait a few minutes and then I'll go inside."

Baltaszar hesitated. He wanted to know more, but he knew being this close to Anahi was blinding him from making anything else a priority. "Fine. Before we leave Vandenar, you and I will talk at length. Clear the air about everything. But if I don't go inside now, I'm certain I'll go mad. Thanks." He turned and walked inside the Happy Elephant.

The room was exactly as he remembered it, though not as busy as the last time. The bar counter stood right before him, and dining tables littered the sprawling common room to his left. A few patrons sat around here and there, and Baltaszar scanned the room for anyone wearing a brownish-grey frock, especially someone short with straight, black hair. He studied every person carefully, nervous that he might overlook her.

"Baltaszar? Lord Baltaszar? Ya look different, boy, but not *that* different." Baltaszar jerked at the voice, but he knew it wasn't Anahi's. He looked back at the bar and saw Cyrus smiling widely at him.

He regained his bearings and smiled back. "Cyrus! It's so good to see you again! It feels like it's been ages!" Out of the corner of his eye, Baltaszar espied a figure entering the room from the kitchen door behind Cyrus. At first, he couldn't get a good look because Cyrus was in the way, but then the person drew nearer and Baltaszar knew for sure. His mind was going through all the criteria while all he could do was stand there and stare. *Brownish-grey frock. Black hair. Grey almond eyes. The most beautiful face I've ever seen.*

She stared back, as if caught in the same paralysis, her face bewildered. "Is...is it…"

Her words released Baltaszar of whatever restraints his mind had put upon his body. He shook his head as he snapped out of the daze and glided to her from across the room. Anahi looked like she was still trying to process the sight of him and cocked her head sideways. Baltaszar didn't wait for her to start talking. He cupped her jaw in his palms and kissed her deeply. Everything around him seemed to stop, as if the whole room stopped to see what was happening. She kissed him back, reciprocating his passion and longing, and wrapped her arms around his back. Baltaszar lost all concept of time. They could have been there for seconds or hours, and it would have felt the same to him.

Cyrus broke them out of their reverie, "Anahi, fer the love o' Orijin, leave! Two o' ya have some serious catchin' up ta do. Go ta yer quarters an' the rest o' us'll take care o' things." Baltaszar looked at him and nodded his thanks.

Anahi blushed and smiled at Cyrus and said "Thank ya." She looked Baltaszar in the eyes and smiled, then took him by the hand up the stairs at the back of the room. He intertwined his fingers in hers and walked beside her. They exchanged glances and smiles the entire walk to her chambers, never saying a word. They finally reached her room and as Anahi locked the door behind her, she melted into his arms. "A part o' me thought I'd never see ya again," she spoke into his chest and Baltaszar could feel the tears soak into his cloak. "After ya didn't come back from Haedon, an' then the House o' Darian got attacked, I was sure either ya would go back ta Yasaman or be too busy ta see me again."

He gently pulled her away from his chest and looked her in the eyes, "I didn't come back because I physically couldn't. It wasn't because of you." Baltaszar kissed her again, as if addicted to her lips. "Yasaman slept with my brother and she's having his baby. I was so mad," he paused for a moment. He hated having to explain what happened. "I was so mad that I basically tried to set myself and Haedon on fire. I got lucky. The others followed me there and found me while I was in flames. They had to bring me back to the House of Darian and Lincan healed me. Then Marlowe banished me to the Never, so I wasn't even there when the House was attacked." He held her closer to him, "Anahi, I'm not telling you this as an excuse about not returning. I'm telling you because I know how stupid and immature I was, and that I'll never let it happen again." He took a few steps to her bed and sat at the side, still holding her hand.

She wiped her eyes, "Look at this. I never cry, ya silly boy. Nothin' makes me cry. An' so what happens fer us now? I know yer not here ta stay an' I wouldn't dare ask ya ta' choose me over savin' Ashur from Jahmash. So yer goin' ta leave soon an' what does that mean fer us? Ya get ta travel the world an' meet girls everywhere ya go, so what would ya have me do, Tasz?" She sat down next to him. "I'm sorry ya had ta deal with Yasaman doin' all that, an' I know it must've broke yer heart, but at least it's in the past. I'm more concerned fer yer future."

"What can I say? You're right. I have responsibilities because of this Mark. But I have *two* allies now that can get me back to you in an instant whenever time allows for it. The moment I leave you, I'll be thinking about you nonstop. *You* are my reason for needing to stop Jahmash. The moment we kill him, I'm coming back here to you, and I'm going to marry you. Then we'll spend the rest of our lives building a family and a life together. We can grow old right here in the Happy Elephant and never leave Vandenar." Before he could lean in, Anahi pushed him back on the bed and laid on top of him. She put a hand behind his head and kissed him deeply.

"Should I let ya leave now, before ya end up fallin' in love with me?" She mumbled in between kisses.

"Too late for that. I fell for you a long time ago; I was just too stupid to realize it." He rolled her off of him so they were both on their sides, facing each other. "The next time I fall in love will be the next time I see you. And then every time again after that. Just like I did again today." He put his hand on her waist and she inched closer. She kissed him again, but Baltaszar stopped her so he could take off his cloak, then quickly removed his shirt and boots before laying back down. He pulled her close. "I would have burned all the seas and run through the Three Rings just to get back here to you." She moved his hand under her frock and he pulled it over her head, and she took it upon herself to remove her undergarments.

Baltaszar must have stared too long without much expression, because Anahi snapped him out of his daze, "So...am I too beautiful or too ugly, since yer starin' like that?"

He smiled and kissed her again, "Way too beautiful. I was just wondering whether this is what Omneitria might be like. I'd like to think I've lived a good life so far, but no matter where I end up in the Three Rings, this is Omneitria for me. A piece of my soul will always remain in this moment, right here with you."

Anahi smiled and kissed him again, then started to pull his pants off. Her hands and whole body were surprisingly warm. "That's enough talkin', silly boy. We can talk later." Baltaszar smiled and let his hands explore her whole body. Just as he'd told her, this was his reason for the fight against Jahmash. And also his reason to survive and come back to her.

BALTASZAR STIRRED AFTER ANOTHER dream with those red eyes following him from a distance. The only difference now was that he knew those eyes belonged to the Jinn, which didn't relieve much of the fear. He put a hand to his right eye, unsure of why he would have expected the scar to be gone.

"How did ya get that, anyway? It's big an' ugly. Makes ya look mean an' dangerous. An' clearly yer neither o' those things." Anahi's voice was raspy, and he realized he must've woken her up.

You are not permitted to tell her of our existence.

Baltaszar hesitated. He'd somehow forgotten that the Jinn had access to his mind. "It's...let's just say that the Never isn't the safest place to be alone, especially after you've fallen through some trees and broken some bones, while having no idea which way to go. There are creatures there that I've never seen or heard of before. I'm lucky for this manifestation." He rolled onto his side to face her.

"How did ya manage ta get out?"

"I just started walking in a direction and ended up at a wall. Turned out to be Alvadon, and they shot me in the shoulder with an arrow. I spent some time in the dungeon there, but then my friends who survived the attack on the House rescued me and brought me to the Tower of the Blind. We have some business to take care of, so everyone has a few days to sort their affairs, and then we regroup."

"I suppose ya can't share what's next, can ya."

He smiled at her. "No. But it's big. We have our work cut out for us, especially since our numbers are so small now, and it will take some time. It's important that what we're doing remains secret. I don't even really know where we're going."

"An' what's the risk o' ya not survivin'?" Her tone was flat, as if she was ready for any answer.

"Well, if we plan properly and all work together, I think we can all walk out of it with no casualties. Nothing ever goes completely according to plan, but if we prepare ourselves for anything, we should still be fine - especially with our manifestations."

Anahi touched his hand, "So it's possible that ya don't come back ta me then."

Baltaszar smiled to reassure her, "Slightly possible, but unlikely. I told you, you are my motivation. We are finally able to be together. This is our beginning, and we have everything in front of us. I see things differently now that we have each other. I know I have to be careful and smart. And I'm not going to put myself or you in a dangerous position if I can control it." He paused, "*However*, this line on my face means that I have a responsibility to protect you *and* the rest of Ashur from Jahmash. But trust me, I will make sure that he never reaches Vandenar, or even thinks about it, even if I have to surround the city with forty-foot flames to protect you. Is that fair?"

She looked somewhat relieved. "Fair. Are ya hungry? We should get dressed an' go downstairs." She nodded to the window, "It's still daytime. As much fun as it is, I don't want ta just spend the whole day in bed with ya." They both put their clothes back on and Anahi sat at the side of the bed and smiled at him. "I also want ya ta know it means the world ta me that ya came here, of all places, with yer free time. Ya could've gone anywhere an' ya came ta see me. I can't wait ta tell Fae, an' have ya meet her."

"Who?" Baltaszar fell over while trying to put on a boot. He winced, but Anahi chuckled at his clumsiness and her laughter infected him. He laughed while getting the other boot on, "Of course I would come here. You're all I've really thought about since the last time I was here. I've felt so guilty. And who's Fae?"

Anahi walked to the door, kissed his cheek, then pulled him by the sleeve. "Ye'll see. She's heard lots about ya. Good *an'* bad o' course. But let's eat first. Then ya can meet Fae an' I'll get back ta work until tonight. Let ya regroup with yer friends if ya need ta."

"So intuitive, huh? I came with Desmond and someone else. Desmond went to see his family, but I do have things to discuss with Slade, especially about my brother. I know it sounds messed up, but I needed to see you before anything else. Anything bad Slade might have to say about Bo'az, well, I doubt there's much I can do from here, or else Slade would have told me already. And that's what the idiot gets for not coming with me when we left Haedon."

Anahi looked at him and blinked a few times as they walked back to the common room. "Really? Wow!"

Baltaszar smiled, "No, not really. Of course I don't want anything bad to have happened to him. Even with everything between him and Yasaman, I could never wish ill upon him. He's the only family I've got left." She smiled at him sheepishly. Baltaszar looked at her, confused. "What?"

"Nothin'. Just that ya better handle yer Jahmash business quickly, that way ya can get back here an' get started on makin' more family fer yerself."

It was Baltaszar's turn to look at her incredulously, "To quote you, 'Really? Wow!'"

"I know, I know. It's forward o' me ta say. Maybe I'm just caught up in this idea o' spendin' the rest o' our lives together. It's excitin' an' I can't wait 'til ya can come back here fer good."

He held her hand as they walked down the stairs, "No, I completely understand, and I agree. That's what I want most, to come back here and live a life with you." Anahi put up two fingers for Cyrus to see as they passed him and sat at an open table. Baltaszar asked, "What's that about?"

"Two plates o' food fer us. Aren't ya hungry? I'm starvin'!"

"I've never looked forward to an elephant steak more in my life!" They sat and talked for a while, through their meal, making more plans for the future, from travel plans to the ideal house. Another maid came to the table and collected their plates, bearing a silly grin and eying Baltaszar. He understood at once, "Fae, then?"

She smiled wider, "Oh, she talks about me? That's so sweet, Anahi!" Fae looked back and forth between them and settled on Baltaszar once more. "Yer handsomer than she made ya out ta be, Baltaszar. Even with that big scratch on yer face."

Anahi's tone was defensive, "I never said he wasn't handsome. I said it wouldn't matter if he wasn't." She looked at Baltaszar, "Tasz, o' course I think yer handsome. Don't listen ta her, she's full o' wickedness. She's the one who was tryin' ta convince me ta move on an' find someone new."

Baltaszar started to feel like this situation had less and less to do with him. "Oh. If you say so, then."

"Ya see, Fae. Yer startin' trouble. Bring these ta the kitchen an' then ya can come back an' have a proper conversation with us." Fae snickered and walked away with their plates as Anahi yelled to her, "An' bring us some more ale!"

Fae did return with two full glasses and sat next to Anahi, across from Baltaszar. He decided to catch her off guard before she could get any upper hand, "So who did you have in mind for Anahi to settle down with? Can I meet him?"

As expected, Fae's eyes grew wide, but then she smiled, "Baltaszar, I don't need ta have someone. There isn't an unwed man in Vandenar that wouldn't marry her. Look at her. If ya mess this up again, I'll be sure ta line 'em up an' question each one o' them, ta see which one is deservin' o' her. The moment ya leave this town, men will be back on the prowl. Ya' better be careful, Baltaszar."

Baltaszar smiled back, "Maybe I should take her with me then, and you can have all the men for yourself."

Fae rolled her eyes, "As if any Vandenari man can handle me."

Baltaszar nodded, "As if. Although, I do know of some in my company that could match all that...vigor...that you have." He was surprised to see her face perk up, and then Baltaszar realized Fae was putting so much energy into this because she wanted the same thing for herself. "Maybe next time I come to Vandenar, I'll bring my friends, Fae. Then you can have *your* pick of them."

Anahi nudged Fae to get up and then pushed her out of her seat to stand up. "Tasz, don't put crazy ideas in her head. She's already crazy. Come, we have work ta' do now." Anahi looked at him as she stood, "I'll give ya yer time with yer companions, an' then ya can meet me in my room when yer all done. Oh…" She paused for a moment, and continued in a hushed tone, "I'm sorry. I assumed ya would be stayin' in my room. I should have asked first."

Baltaszar chuckled, "There is no way in the Three Rings that I would spend the night anywhere else or with anyone else besides you. Remember, I came here to see you." She smiled and blushed as Fae pulled for her to follow.

Baltaszar took a gulp of his ale and as he set the mug back down, he was startled by a man swooping in to sit across from him. Luckily, Slade's stature and beard could hardly be confused with anyone else, so Baltaszar let his guard down after a moment. Slade noticed the mug of barely drunk ale that Anahi had left, took a swig ,and wiped his beard with a sleeve. "We should talk."

Baltaszar looked at him flatly. "Bo'az. Explain how he ended up with you. And where he is now. I'm going to assume he's safe, or you would have told me otherwise already."

Slade nodded, "He's safe. But you won't really like the rest of it." He paused, as if to collect his thoughts, "He did it all to himself. We showed up at your house looking for you. He pretended he was you, with some stupid excuse about the Descendant's Mark disappearing. It threw me off, because your dad never mentioned Bo'az, most likely to protect him. But if Gibreel and Linas knew from the start that Bo'az wasn't you, they would have tortured him. I kept the lie going to keep him safe, but still, there was no way to abandon the mission without getting me and Bo'az both killed. And then he went and demanded that the girl come along, and it just made a mess of everything."

Baltaszar perked up, "The girl? Yasaman? He insisted for you to bring her with you? And where exactly were you going?"

"He refused to come with us unless she came too. Don't get me wrong, I completely regret that she had to die, but we made it clear to Bo'az that she was expendable, that the mission was about him and that there would be problems if she made things complicated for us. She got hurt, was going to hold us back, and that's when Gibreel pushed her off the mountain. I apologize, Baltaszar." Slade took another gulp of ale. "I know that she had more of a relationship with you than with Bo'az, but it had to be done. Probably better for her to die then than at the hands of…" he paused again, "of Jahmash—that is where we took your brother."

Baltaszar nearly shot out of his seat but didn't want to cause a scene in front of everyone. He also had to stop himself from raising his voice, and instead kept himself hushed. "We need to unpack everything you just said." He took a deep breath and then gulped his own ale. "First, Jahmash. Are you bloody insane? Light of Orijin, why in all of the Three

Rings would you be taking Bo—no, *me* to Jahmash? I thought you were *friends* with my father! Why shouldn't I leave right now and tell the others that you're a traitor?"

Slade put up a hand, and then pointed to his left ear. "You see this? You see how there's nothing left there? Jahmash had his soldier cut it off my head for not bringing *you*. And the only reason he didn't kill me was because I convinced him that Bo'az could be used to lure you to him. He wants you to burn the seas away for him, so that he can come to Ashur without having to deal with the seas. You are his way of returning and starting his war. I am back in Ashur to get you to go save your brother. But Jahmash doesn't control my mind the way he does with so many others. I am a soldier from Semaajj. Our minds are too strong for even Jahmash to penetrate. Which means that I have no intention of returning to him. The moment he has you, the war begins."

"Which means my brother dies?" Baltaszar was confused. He thought about Munn Keeramm's prophecy that he would be the one to kill Bo'az, and he struggled to put it all together.

"Like I said, Bo'az will be fine, at least for quite a while. Jahmash finds him likeable, for whatever reason, and Bo'az also does what Jahmash asks. He doesn't try to resist any of the control. He also has Bo'az going on a recruiting mission to other nations beyond Ashur. With all the time it'll take just to travel, Bo'az is safe for at least a year. Believe me. I basically grew up with your father. There is no way I would be cavalier with the lives of his sons. Your brother may be a coward sometimes, but he knows how to survive. Sometimes the wisest choice is to not be bold."

Baltaszar took a few breaths. *At least a year. I have to find a way to save him. But then, what if saving him only leads me to kill him? No. It doesn't matter; I have to save him.* "Fine. You started me on this path to get out of Haedon, so at least you did *something* to try to save me. But this means that we have to find a way to save him. You said he has about a year, which means we—and I mean *we*—have time to think of a plan to get him without getting me captured by Jahmash." The last part stifled him. Baltaszar suddenly grasped the notion that of all people in the whole world, Jahmash was after *him*. He shook the idea away. *If he wants me, he'd better be ready to burn.* He took a sip of ale. "Also, Yasaman isn't dead."

"What? We all saw her fall! How?"

"I don't know. She said she fell, was in terrible pain, and then was carried by *something* back to Haedon. I saw her myself. She was bedridden...and pregnant."

Slade nodded, as if to say, "Oh." He looked around the room for a moment, then back at Baltaszar. "They saved her life, then."

"Who?"

Slade grinned tightly. "You know who. The voices in your head. The ones you saw in the Never after Marlowe banished you."

"How could you even know any of this? You mentioned the voice when we first met but didn't give me an explanation. I understand that there was no time then. But there is now. Tell me about the Jinn. Tell me about my father and my mother. I know you know about it all. You are basically the only connection I have to my parents now, with both of them dead, and Marlowe as well."

Slade gulped down the rest of his drink and nodded for Baltaszar to do the same, "Not in here. We can go for a walk. Too many secrets that should stay between the two of us." He stood up, which drew the attention of Cyrus.

Baltaszar stood as well and patted his coin purse for Cyrus to see. Cyrus shook his head, then yelled over, "Yer coin's no good here, boy. Ya know that! Leave the glasses, we'll get 'em!" Baltaszar nodded in acquiescence, and still left a coin on the table to tip the barmaid. Cyrus saw and yelled, "Thanks!" The coin purse itself was a strange feeling for Baltaszar. He'd never carried one before, nor had to, but Savaiyon had provided each of the Ghosts of Ashur with coin for their travels. They stepped outside of the inn, and Baltaszar started walking away from the building. He waited for the statuesque man to meet his stride and they walked side by side through the side streets of Vandenar. "Now no one can hear your secrets."

Slade looked around them, likely gauging whether anyone was paying them any mind. "Might as well start from the very beginning. I'd say it was somewhere between twenty and twenty-five years ago. Your father and I were Semaajji soldiers; we started when we were younger than you are now. Semaajj is a nation on another island, Fah'Zavan, which we share with another nation, Domna Orjann. There is harmony on Fah'Zavan, but there are other nations out there that seek out conquest. So Semaajj acts as a protector for all of Fah'Zavan. We both rose through the ranks rather quickly and were highly respected by our commanders and leaders. But our statesmen believed that our army was still not strong enough in the event that multiple nations formed alliances to conquer us. Are you following so far?" Baltaszar nodded. "Good. Well, in Domna Orjann, there are Oracles, similar to the Augurs in Ashur. They informed our Master General of people in Ashur that were capable of wielding magic, who could strengthen our army one hundredfold. Obviously, that was an opportunity that our nation could not pass up, so your father and I were sent here to recruit Descendants.

"Some of our statesmen knew a man here who had a secret reputation for helping outcasts and expatriates from our nations and other nations foreign to Ashur. His name was Vitticus Khou, whom I believe you know well as Oran Von."

Baltaszar finally reacted, "He knew you and my father that long ago?"

"Yes. He was our first contact in Ashur. We sailed directly to the Port of Granis in Galicea, then rode to see him in Penzaedon. The convenient part is that our light brown skin is similar enough to Shivaani people that nobody paid us much mind. But Khou knew right away, from the way we dressed and carried ourselves. We told him what we were doing there and he took us in for a few days, then sent us off to the House of Darian to meet with Zin Marlowe. You want to take a guess about which Descendant escorted us to the House?"

Baltaszar furrowed his brow, "Asarei?"

Slade chuckled, "You can't be that dense, can you? No, not Asarei. It was a beautiful Galicean girl named Raya Hammersland."

"What? My mother? Seriously?"

"Seriously. She's the one who brought us to the House. The romance between your parents began on that journey."

Baltaszar felt goosebumps raise on his arms, back, and neck. Throughout his life, he'd remembered his mother in glimpses here and there, but this was the first time he'd tried to picture the two of them young and meeting for the first time. He felt his eyes get slightly glossy and even smiled to himself. He hadn't even realized that a small fireball hovered over his right palm as they continued to walk. "Damn. I only barely remember images of her. No conversations or interactions, nothing like that. Khou told me that she could travel to the Three Rings. Would you happen to know how she would even develop a manifestation like that?"

Slade shook his head, "Sorry, Baltaszar. You know those stories tend to be sacred, and there's no way I would've dared to ask about that. Khou made that clear to us right away, do not ask Descendants how they got their manifestations."

"I understand. I was just hoping."

"I know. I'm sure it's frustrating not being able to ask your parents about the details of their own lives. You want me to continue?"

"Of course."

"Well, the plan that your father and I came up with was rather simple. Meet with Zin Marlowe and simply ask for an alliance in which he would allow some Descendants to come back with us in exchange for our protection. Joakwin and I were both clear with each other that we didn't want to go through Ashur kidnapping Descendants, so this was the most sensible option. Marlowe took us in and heard our offer. He wasn't enthralled with the idea, mostly because he was skeptical that a nation so far away could offer any real protection or alliance. And I understand his skepticism. Still, he didn't reject us outright. He offered to let us stay at the House of Darian for at least six months, to see how we could coexist with Descendants. Obviously, your father was excited, because it meant he could see your mother every day. That's also how we learned of Jahmash and the history of all the Harbingers. Semaajj really only focuses on the Orijin, as most nations outside of Ashur do, I believe.

"During that time, we actually got along well with quite a few Descendants, and there were about five or so who were receptive to the notion of coming with us, especially one who was around our age, named Asarei Taurean. He'd renounced his Taurani culture and was eager to experience the rest of the world. Then, King Edmund happened. I'd say it was a few weeks before we planned to leave the House and return home, Edmund inherited the throne for himself and announced his decree against Descendants. Within a week of being king, he'd already started hunting and killing your kind. We thought this might only make Marlowe more eager to send Descendants with us."

Baltaszar nodded, "Yeah, exactly, to protect them. That's common sense."

"You would think so, but not common enough for Marlowe. He reversed his decision."

"Why?"

"He didn't want Descendants to be seen as weapons or as soldiers, even in another nation. He thought it would only reinforce Edmund's point. Marlowe told us that he would not permit any Descendants to leave with us, and that we must leave the House of Darian at once."

"So what did you do?"

"What choice did we have? We left. We returned to Penzaedon empty-handed. However, Asarei, being his defiant self, had it out with Marlowe, then used his manifestation to sneak out with Raya in the middle of the night, and return to Khou as well. None of the others who were originally willing to leave Ashur were willing to defy Marlowe, so it was only the two of them. Joakwin and I thought it best to maintain a respectful relationship with Marlowe, so we didn't bother arguing. We left it at that, figuring that if he ever changed his mind, at least we hadn't insulted him. We stayed with Khou for a short while—he was in the process of leaving society for good. He informed us that, to the public, Vitticus Khou was dead, and that he was now Oran Von. He was leaving Galicea to govern a community in the forest. I suppose he trusted us with the information because he knew we weren't staying in Ashur.

"Joakwin and I toyed with the idea of staying a while longer, to see if we could travel around Ashur and recruit Descendants. The only problem with that was that they…"

Baltaszar finished the sentence, "Were being hunted and killed by Edmund. As we still are today."

"Exactly. And that's when Asarei and Raya showed up. Raya insisted that we go with her back to the Port of Granis and we could stay with her brother, Hugo. Your uncle, I suppose. Their parents had already passed by that point, but I don't remember how." Baltaszar nodded. Marlowe had mentioned his uncle but didn't know where the man was. Slade continued, "We obliged. Joakwin and I needed to get ready to sail back to Semaajj, anyway. The only problem was that when the time came to leave, Joakwin couldn't do it. We'd been there a few months prepping, storing up enough food for the journey. Raya didn't want him to go either. So it didn't happen.

"Instead, we celebrated Hugo's first daughter being born, then Joakwin's and Raya's marriage, and helped them to build a house right next to Hugo's. At that point, I decided to travel Ashur in secret, looking for willing Descendants to go back to Semaajj. I honestly thought they might be eager to get away, but that just wasn't the case. The more I traveled, the more I heard about Jahmash and how afraid people were of his return, so I moved around from city to city, getting what information I could, probably for a few years. I also stayed in the City of the Fallen for some time, and wrote your father a letter to tell him about the things I'd learned. He wrote back and informed me of you, but there was no mention of Bo'az. I suspect that, by that time, your parents may have met with an Augur and learned of something that posed a threat to one or both of you. It seems the only logical explanation was to hide Bo'az."

"Why didn't you actually go back to see them? You were practically his best friend."

"Believe me, I ask myself about that often. At the time, I think I felt some guilt about not returning to Semaajj, and I knew that if I saw Joakwin, he'd feel the same way. I didn't want him to feel guilty for the life he'd chosen. He was happy. So I moved around some more, kept correspondence with Marlowe as well, in case he'd changed his mind. And then upon returning to the City of the Fallen, I found a letter from your father informing me about what happened to Raya. He told me that Asarei was on the hunt, looking anywhere and everywhere for her, and so was Hugo, to a degree. Except that Hugo also had two young daughters of his own, and he dared not leave them for too long. I left the City right away, to do my own investigating, but there was nothing."

Baltaszar had a thought, something he hadn't considered before. "What if...what if she went to the Three Rings and never returned? What if she's just been there the whole time?"

Slade nodded and even put a hand on Baltaszar's shoulder, "I contemplated that myself, but there is one issue with that. The Three

Rings is not a place for physical bodies. When your mother went there with her manifestations, her spirit, her soul, was leaving her body to do that. So if it was the case that she went and never returned…"

Baltaszar, feeling defeated, finished Slade's thought, "Her body would eventually have been found somewhere."

"I'm sorry. Asarei and I both spent years trying to find her. After a while, I decided to try to fight the big fight right at the source. I found a faction of Drahkunov followers in Galicea and sailed with them to Jahmash's island. It took a while to gain his trust, especially since he couldn't control my mind, and I had to do some immoral things in the process, but it also led me to being able to find you before Linas and Gibreel."

Baltaszar was grateful for everything Slade had shared, but it only frustrated him more. *I don't even know whom to be angry at. Marlowe? Edmund? Jahmash?* "I appreciate everything you've told me. It only makes me wish I had *more* time with them. We're going to be with Asarei in the near future. You think he'll be willing to share anything about my parents as well?"

Slade laughed. "Asarei is many things, temperamental, intense, brash, and above all else, a good man. Even when Joakwin and I decided against returning home he was supportive and understanding. I believe it gave him a new sense of purpose, to stay here and help Descendants who were like him—willing to fight back. So to answer your question, yes. Baltaszar, you look just like Joakwin. He'll know you right away." Slade paused for a moment, "Speaking of which, is that thing on your face there permanently?"

"Who knows. The Jinn cut into my face pretty deeply, and Lincan wasn't able to heal it, so maybe. Only makes me more noticeable at a time when I need to be as ordinary as possible. I guess it serves me right, though. I was stupid enough to think the Descendant's Mark was a scar, and now I'll have a real scar on the other eye. Not to mention, I tried to burn down part of Haedon."

"Well, have you learned or grown at all from it?"

Baltaszar hesitated, "The easy answer is yes. But I won't know for sure until I'm that emotionally charged again, will I? I'd like to tell you I've learned. I don't *want* to do that again. But I suppose my guess is as good as yours."

"I seriously doubt that the Orijin would bless you with a manifestation just for you to go around killing good, innocent people."

Baltaszar shrugged. "Look at Prince Garrison. I mean, he seems nice *now*, but he still hunted and killed a lot of people."

"Yeah, fair enough."

By the time Baltaszar stopped to look around at where he was, he realized they were just outside Munn Keeramm's home. "I didn't even think about where we were walking, but it makes sense. This is the only place I really know, aside from the inn."

Slade stopped and faced him, "Me too. I've been to this city, but not long enough to really remember any one place except for Keeramm's."

"You know him, too?"

"I've come to see him, but we're not very well acquainted. It was while I was searching for your mother. Hoping for any clues about anything."

Baltaszar was getting tired of hearing about the impossible search for his mother now. "And nothing useful, I presume?"

Slade nodded, "Nothing." They reached the steps in front of Keeramm's home, where Baltaszar recognized Farco sitting at the bottom, holding a girl's hand. Surprisingly, she had a Descendant's Mark down her left eye.

"Farco, hey! I didn't see you that long ago, did you get taller?"

Farco slowly peeled his gaze away from the girl to look at Baltaszar and smiled. "Hey Baltaszar. Probably. My dad was really tall, so I might have more growin' ta do."

Baltaszar was about to comment on the boy's deeper voice as well, but he didn't want to embarrass Farco in front of the girl. "Wow, you'll be a giant in no time. Who's your friend?"

The girl spoke up before Farco could. "Hi Baltaszar. I'm Avenira. Farco's been talk 'bout ya a bit lately. I think he's jealous o' yer adventures."

Baltaszar huffed out a laugh. "Adventures, huh. I almost killed myself setting myself on fire, then got banished from the House of Darian a day before it was attacked, and got my face ripped open while lost in the Never. I'll pick sitting on Munn Keeramm's front steps over that any day."

"Maybe yer just not makin' the right choices." She turned to Farco, "I could set ya on fire if ya want me ta. Then again, I'd have ta hear ya complain about it fer months after, so never mind."

Baltaszar grimaced at Farco. "We're going to go inside. Good luck working your way out of this one, pal."

Farco shifted over to let the two of them pass, then got up to follow them in. "Master Keeramm might need my help ta find a prophecy fer ya. I'll come in with ya just in case."

Baltaszar chuckled as he walked inside, "Suit yourself. You're only putting off your trouble until later." Baltaszar scanned the room; it was mostly as he remembered, only tidier than the last time. The tables weren't covered with stacks of books and the whole room seemed better organized. Baltaszar eyed Keeramm sitting in the back, holding a steaming mug, likely filled with tea.

The old man lifted his head, "I know that voice. How've ya been, lad? Yer laughin', which is a good sign. Last time all o' ya came ta see me, it felt much, much more serious. Ya had official business ta sort out." He braced himself to stand and Farco rushed over to help him. Farco took the Augur's arm and draped it around his shoulder, then took the mug from him. He wrapped his other arm around Keeramm and led him toward Baltaszar and Slade. "Ya see? He treats me like an old man. I coulda done it myself. Might've taken a bit longer, but these young ones have no patience."

Baltaszar smiled. He loved the old man's banter, and Farco took it all in stride. "You didn't have to get up for us, Master Keeramm. We didn't come for any real reason. We were on a walk and just...ended up here."

Keeramm nodded, "That means ya were meant ta be here. So what will it be then? A prophecy fer ya, Baltaszar? Ya said we...who's yer companion?"

Slade walked up to Keeramm and grasped his hand. "I came to see you a long time ago, friend. My name is Rhadames Slade. It has been so long I doubt you remember me."

The Blind Man smiled. "O' course I remember ya. Ye were lookin' fer someone. Fer a friend o' yers. An' I couldn't give ya what ya were lookin' fer. I do apologize fer that."

Slade patted him on the shoulder and helped Farco guide him into the desk chair. "Not your fault, Master Keeramm. You can only provide what you have access to. It was actually Baltaszar's mother I was searching for. Ironic how it's all connected, but at least I'm still around to guide him."

Keeramm nodded, "Indeed. Rather fortunate, then." He clasped his hands on the desk, "So ya said neither o' ya is interested in a prophecy. If I'd've known that I never woulda gotten out o' my chair back there! I woulda just told ya ta come back an' have some tea with me. So now I'm sittin' here. Might as well give ya somethin'."

Baltaszar looked at Slade, who looked back at him. He felt guilty but knew that Keeramm wasn't actually mad. "Maybe something that's not about me then. Is that possible? Can you share prophecies with us about others?"

Slade cut in, "Maybe something about the Anonymi and Descendants? We are currently working on an alliance between the two. So if you could share something related to that, it might help us to know if our plans will succeed."

Keeramm nodded and pounded his fist on the desk, "O' course we can find somethin'. Far, fetch as many volumes as ya can related ta

Descendants an' Anonymi." Farco went to the shelves behind Keeramm and scanned for the right books. "Ya notice how much cleaner the place is? I've been puttin' the boy ta work. I think he feels guilty fer spendin' so much time with the girl, so he cleans a lot more now. He's goin' ta be leavin' me by the summer fer his Anonymi trainin'; might as well get the most out o' him while I can."

Farco brought two books over and placed one in front of Keeramm. "Here is the first. I brought two for now, but there are definitely a few more."

Keeramm shooed him away, waving his hand, "Then go get 'em, boy. Let me get started." Keeramm got to work on the first giant book. He used his fingers to scan the pages, reading with his fingertips and eyes closed. After several minutes of going through every page, he closed the book and moved on to the next one. "Nothin' o' that sort in that one. On ta the next." Once again, his fingers raced across the pages as he flipped through the second book, and then the third. About halfway through the fourth, Baltaszar was about to tell the man he could stop, but then Keeramm did stop and looked up with unseeing eyes. "I've got somethin'. At the time o' the vision, I wasn't sure if I was embodyin' someone or just a separate observer, but this is what I saw. Remember, I don't know what the world looks like, so this could be anywhere. Two armies on an enormous field. One side is all the same—men in armor an' it looks like their arms an' faces have strange patterns on 'em painted in black. The other side is led by a woman? Girl? Could be either, but she leads an army of men an' women. I know it's Anonymi 'cause o' the type o' armor they have. Ya have ta keep in mind, my grasp o' colors isn't quite like yers, but their armor looks like every color I've ever seen in these visions, an' yet, no color at the same time. I can't explain it any better than that, but others have told me that's what the Anonymi wear. However, there are also Descendants mixed in the ranks, as I can see the line down their faces an' their armor is black, not like the Anonymi. An' the Descendants salute the woman or girl an' call her the "Maiden." Not sure o' the significance o' any of it, or when it happens, but it's clear that the two are workin' together."

Slade responded before Baltaszar could. "The Vithelegion."

Keeramm turned his head to Slade. "What's that?"

"The other army. It's the Vithelegion. You mentioned that they had patterns of black painted on themselves. That's who the army is. They are from the nation of Vitheligia, in the realm of Orol Taghdras. I had always assumed they did not form alliances, so I'm confused as to why they would come here to attack us on Jahmash's behalf." Slade turned back to Baltaszar. We should go. I need some time to process this so I can explain it to Savaiyon and the others." Baltaszar wouldn't have argued anyway, but Slade's normally stoic countenance showed obvious signs of worry.

He nodded in agreement, then turned to Keeramm. "We apologize for the short visit, but it seems as if what you've shared with us is an urgent matter, and we must go."

Keeramm nodded his head and put his hand up. "I understand. Not the prophecy ya were expectin', I imagine. But now duty calls. Go an' save the world. The rest o' us will never be offended because o' yer responsibilities. We understand. It is always my pleasure ta have ya here, an' I hope ya get the chance ta return soon. Far, see our guests out, will ya?"

Baltaszar reached out and clasped Keeramm's hand. "Thank you, Master Keeramm. One of these days, we will return the favor. I promise."

"Nonsense. Protect Ashur. That's the favor. Ya don't owe anything ta any o' us, Baltaszar Kontez. Those lines on yer faces mean yer supposed ta save Ashur, an' that's already unfair. Throw in the King tryin' ta kill ya, an' we should feel lucky that ya still want ta save the world."

Baltaszar gripped his hand more tightly and thanked him again. Farco walked over to lead them out. As the three of them left Keeramm's home, Baltaszar nudged Farco. "Hey. I know you won't be here much longer but spoil him while you can. He's going to miss you." Farco nodded. "And while you can, look out for Anahi, make sure she's safe. I don't know if I'll be able to make it back here before you leave, so if not, then good luck with everything. I'm not sure how this romance of yours is going to work out, but I'm sure you know the details of it better than I do."

Farco smiled at him as they walked down the steps outside, "She's comin' with me."

"Of course she is." Baltaszar nodded and smiled back. "I'm glad you've got it all figured out. Be careful out there, then. Especially with Avenira. That line on her face is a target and there's no hiding it. Travel wisely and trust minimally." Farco grew serious again and nodded. He stopped at the bottom of the stairs while Baltaszar and Slade walked on.

They returned to the inn after a quiet and direct walk. Anahi was sweeping in the common room in her grey working frock, but Baltaszar pulled her aside, by the staircase. "Hey, something has come up and Slade wants us to return to the others right away."

Anahi furrowed her brow, confused. "That's serious then. Are ya goin' ta be all right, Tasz?"

He nodded. "It's not about me. Something about another nation beyond Ashur and a battle on our soil. Slade doesn't give much away with his countenance, but he seemed nervous, and maybe even scared. We walked the whole way back in silence." He held her hand. "Listen, I'll be back to see you as soon as I can." Baltaszar kissed her deeply and then wrapped his arms around her. Anahi nestled her head into his chest. "As soon as we have the opportunity to take a breath the first thing I'll do is come back to you. It may be a few months, though."

She looked up at him, "I'm not goin' anywhere. I'll be here, listenin' ta Fay's lectures about how I shouldn't wait fer ya." She smiled.

"Then we should find someone for Fay, too." He smiled and kissed her again. "Let me go grab my things upstairs, and then I'll come and say goodbye." She nodded and Baltaszar ran up the stairs, skipping every other step. He grabbed his pack from her quarters and returned to the common room in a few moments.

"Wow, that was fast. Ya in such a rush ta leave me?"

He chuckled. "Of course. I can't wait to leave you for a bunch of people who up until two days ago, all likely wanted to kill each other. Seriously, though, you are my highest priority. Everything I do from this point is to ensure that I can return to you and we can enjoy the rest of our lives together." Slade appeared at the bottom of the staircase and Baltaszar nodded at him. He remembered that they had to get Desmond. Then one of them would have to mentally tell Badalao to get into Savaiyon's mind, so that Savaiyon would know to create a doorway.

Anahi smiled. "An' Fay, because no man will likely be good enough fer her."

"Fine, and Fay, too." He kissed her deeply once more. "I love you."

"Ye'd better. Yer askin' a lot."

He took her hand and kissed it before walking out with Slade.

CHAPTER 14
THE KRAISOS

From **The Book of Orijin,** **Verse Three Hundred Fifty**
Those who bear the Mark shall not be humanity's only hope against the Betrayer.
Allies shall arise in the fight for righteousness.

BADALAO RECLINED IN A CUSHIONED wooden chair facing the Markosi River, which started at the Sea of Fates and reached Constaniza, where it turned into a waterfall. He shooed away the two servants who attempted to offer him shade. "It is the middle of winter. What shade do I need?" He nodded toward his sister, who lounged in the chair to his right. "Tend to Kiryako. She only has two of you fawning over her. Clearly she needs more."

So far, the winter hadn't been particularly cold, and winters were never harsh in Markos, but that still didn't warrant the need for artificial shade. Surprisingly, one of the things Badalao missed the least about his home was the excess with which his parents surrounded themselves. He turned to his sister, who lay back on the chair with her eyes closed, long brown hair tucked into the few blankets she'd bundled herself into, "I see they have not changed at all."

Kiryako was two years younger than he, and had the pleasure of a normal Markosi highborn life, with no Mark on her face. She turned her head as minimally as possible, "You act as if you are above all this. Remember, these very servants were dressing you and wiping your magnanimous little ass for how many years?"

He glared at her from the corners of his eyes. Kiryako was the traditional Markosi highborn daughter: beautiful, well-educated, quick-witted, confident, strong enough to put any man in his place, yet gentle and coy enough to keep any Markosi suitor interested, rather than scared. In truth, Badalao wasn't sure if he'd ever be able to return to his home to become the head of the Majime household, if and when the time came. Regardless, he knew that Kiryako would be able to assume that role comfortably if need be. It was one of the reasons why he didn't feel much guilt leaving home in the first place. Despite their constant bickering, he and his sister got along quite well. She lived a pampered life, like the rest of the family, but the difference with her and Badalao, compared to the rest of their family was that they enjoyed those luxuries, rather than *depended* on them.

He waved at one of the servants facing him, "Gasho, please allow my sister and I some privacy. I must speak with her alone."

The elder, silver-haired servant nodded, "Very well, Master Badalao. Would you like for us to return at a later time?"

"That will not be necessary, my friend. Go and relax."

"Thank you, my lord." Gasho turned to leave, and the other servants fell in line to follow him back inside.

Kiryako turned her head more definitively this time, "What is *this* all about?"

Badalao had been dreading this conversation since Maqdhuum had brought him home the night before. He took a deep breath, "I know your first thought will be to tease me or brush it off as ridiculous, but please listen to everything I have to say."

She rolled her eyes. "No guarantees."

"Skáse." It was the Markosi word for 'shut up', and had been one of Badalao's favorite words to use at the House, because most others didn't know what it meant. "Listen, Kiri. After the attack on the House of Darian, I ended up in the City of the Fallen. I met another Descendant girl there whose mind was being controlled by Jahmash himself." His sister's countenance changed, and he knew she was taking him seriously now. "I did not know it at the time, and I actually rid her mind of him. I have not told anyone else this, but ever since, I have not been able to shake this feeling that he knows who I am, and that he wants revenge."

"Revenge, as in, you think he is going to attack Constaniza, or even all of Markos?"

"Precisely. It would be the only way to know he got to me, by attacking my family and my people."

"You know if you bring this up to mother and father…"

He cut her off. "Yes. I know. Which is why I am telling you, instead." He didn't need to be in her head to know what Kiryako would say. Their parents never worried about threats or anything of the sort unless given cause to by their Augurs. They had three Augurs who lived in their palace, and firmly believed that visions of those three revolved around their lives. No matter how much Badalao tried to convince them otherwise, they refused to listen. "They listen to you more. If we both speak to them, then perhaps there is a chance they will listen."

Kiryako shook her head, "You know anything we say will not matter unless it has been foreseen by the Augurs. The Blind are their prophets, and mother and father hang on their every word. It is a good thing they do not rule Ashur; they would have been toppled off of their thrones long ago."

Badalao sat up and faced her. "If they refuse to listen, then it must be *you* who takes action."

She reciprocated by sitting at the side of her chair, still wrapped in her blankets. "And what would you have me do, Lao? I am a daughter of the Majime family, and have barely seen eighteen summers. Who do you think would listen to me?"

He looked down at his feet, took a breath, and then looked back at her. "Every person in this city who is able to fight will listen to you if you tell them the directive came from me. Whether you see it or not, you are strong, intelligent, and firm. I am not asking you to form an army and ride into battle. But every single person in Constaniza must be prepared. Weapons in their homes, escape routes, a plan for the old, sick, and weak, as well as how best to engage an incoming army from any part of the city. There are plenty of people in this city who can help you with these strategies.

"I only have one day here, and then I have my own mission that I must see through. And that in itself will likely take months to complete. All I have time for is to try and talk sense into our parents, but I am fairly certain that it is futile, which is why I am putting my faith in you. We have several cousins, and friends close enough to be cousins. Seek their help first. You do not even have to tell them everything I told you. Simply tell them that I have given you word that Jahmash is coming sometime soon, and that they must be prepared. You can tell them I said that. It will be enough."

Kiryako closed her eyes. Her face, normally olive-toned, was flushed. "And what if I am not brave enough to bear that responsibility?"

"You will be. Unless, by some miracle of the Orijin, mother and father heed my advice, it will be up to you. And when the time comes, I know you will rise to the challenge. If nobody acts, then Jahmash's army will barrel right through our city, our home, and destroy everything in its path, and then move on to the next. And most likely, they will do it without Jahmash even being present. If I could stay to oversee this preparation, I would. But my mission is even bigger than what I ask of you."

She stared out at the waterfall, as if refusing to look at him. "And you are certain that we are a target?"

Badalao continued to look at her as he bunched up his hair behind his head and then let it fall. When not put up in the traditional Markosi fashion, his hair was as long as his sister's. "I am almost positive it will happen. And soon. And if I am wrong, then it is not all for nothing. Sooner or later, likely sooner, Jahmash will make his move against Ashur. When that happens it will be wise to be prepared for an attack anyway."

Kiryako turned back to face him, her olive complexion back to normal. "Very well, brother. If bravery is what you request of me, then I will oblige you, and I will not disappoint." He was about to offer gratitude, but she continued on. "However, if you must implore me to be brave and firm, then I must do the same to you." She smiled, almost wickedly.

He cocked his head, "Please, do explain."

"Tell me. Do you still refuse to use your manifestation at night?"

Shit. "What do you mean? Refuse? I was never *able* to."

She looked at him flatly. "No—not with me, Lao. Do not try to lie with me. I have always been honest with you about everything, even when upset or insecure." Kiryako stood up and shifted the blankets to wear as a shawl, then waved for him to follow. She walked to the rail at the edge of the landing. Once Badalao met her there, she continued. "You seem to forget that I was old enough to understand everything when you obtained your manifestation. I remember that you had trouble controlling it at first and would end up in people's minds at any time of day or night."

He'd normally prided himself on his ability to think quickly, but he knew Kiryako had the upper hand. There would be no way to wriggle out of her snare, and he could not keep up the lie, even if he wanted to. "Fine. You win. No, I have not used it at night ever since I…"

She continued to look straight ahead at the landscape, "Ever since your friend Kato snuck into our palace in the middle of the night and tried to steal from us?"

Badalao looked straight ahead as well and made himself picture the memory. He'd blocked it out for so long, that he was surprised how vividly he remembered it. When he was eight, one night he'd snuck out of his bed to steal some pastries from the kitchens. His parents had only allowed him one, and he thought that if he ate them in the middle of the night, no one could accuse him. The palace had been dark; crime was rather uncommon in Constaniza, and there was a smattering of guards outside, but no one patrolling inside. As he crept his way to the kitchens, he bumped into someone else in the dark, and fell on top of the other person. In his panic, Badalao entered the mind of the other person, and the shock of realizing it was his friend Kato was so strong that he must have gripped the boy's mind too tightly, injuring the part of Kato's mind that controlled his legs. Kato never walked again. Both boys screamed in terror, though everyone else believed that Kato's injury stemmed from an awkward fall. The only person Badalao ever told the truth to was Kiryako, who was maybe six at the time. He'd forgotten that detail until now. From that point on, he swore to never use his manifestation at night, for fear that he might seriously injure someone without intending to. The others at the House of Darian never really questioned it when he told them that he could not use his manifestation at night. "That is one way to look at it. But regardless of the context, the fact of the matter is that I crippled him. That is far too great a punishment for attempting to steal."

Kiryako nodded, "Indeed, *if* the punishment was intentional. You told me yourself that you acted out of fear and shock. The fundamental point of this whole situation is that if Kato was not wrongfully in our home in the first place, then he never would have been in a position to be hurt."

Badalao lightly pounded his fist on the top of the railing. He didn't want to have this conversation. "Either way, what is your point in bringing all this up?"

"If I am to do as you ask, for the betterment of Constaniza, Markos, and Ashur, then I ask the same of you."

He squinted. "What do you mean?"

She looked at him and, at first he thought she was about to smile, but her face remained stoic. "I will do as you ask, if you stop being a coward about your manifestation." She held up her hand and raised her index finger, as if knowing he was about to argue. "No, listen. That Mark on your face tells all of Ashur that you are dangerous. Not evil, but dangerous. That is no secret, and Kato knew that just as well as anyone else. Anyone who would wrong you after seeing your Mark, would do so with a willingness to bear the effects of whatever your manifestation can do to them. By limiting yourself you are also not giving all of yourself in your fight against Jahmash. If you stand by your word that you must protect Ashur, then do so completely. Stop hiding behind the guilt of an accident that was by no means any fault of your own." She had caught Badalao off guard with her request, and he hated it. But she was right, and there was no defense or counter to the deal Kiryako had just proposed. "And to make sure that you keep your word, you will begin tonight."

"What? How?"

"With me. Later today, after I've had my nap, we will present your concerns and plans to mother and father. Then they will laugh at you, reject you, consult their Augurs just to be sure, and then your request will officially fall upon me to carry out. After dinner, once the sun has set, you will meet me back out here and you will enter my mind. You will do so in front of me so that you cannot offer some silly excuse as to why you could not. If you fail to comply, you will have to find someone else to do your bidding."

He hit the railing harder. "Fine." He almost wished at this point that his parents would agree with him. It would be far easier than what his sister was proposing.

"And if, by some miracle of the Orijin, mother and father entertain your concerns, I will tell Mother the truth of it all so she can demand the same of you."

Badalao shook his head, "Light of Orijin, I'm beginning to wonder if it is you or me who has the manifestation."

MAQDHUUM EYED BADALAO as he sat before him. "You look tired, boy. Burdened. I would have thought a visit with your family would have produced opposite results." He flexed his hand, still surprised that Savaiyon allowed Lincan to heal it for him. It was a great relief to finally be able to use it fully without any discomfort.

Badalao looked back at him and shrugged, "I never intended for it to simply be a joyous reunion. I had some things I needed to ask of them. It turned out that they had some requests as well."

Maqdhuum lay back on his bed, "What an odd, yet fascinating family. Well, Lao, I do hope that you all managed to fulfill each other's requests."

"It certainly looks that way. I believe now that Constaniza, and all of Markos, will be prepared and in good hands if Jahmash's armies happen to land on our shores."

Maqdhuum leaned on his elbows to be able to look at Badalao. "Wow. Ever the soldier. Then again, that's the type of thing a military *officer* does when he returns home. We may have to see how you handle some military responsibility." Badalao nodded dismissively. Maqdhuum had Traveled to Constaniza earlier in the morning to retrieve the boy, and ever since, Badalao had had an air of self-satisfaction. Not necessarily cockiness, but certainly confidence. The two occupied the room with Farrah and Malikai, all four making it a point to spread themselves out. Maqdhuum was sharing the room with Malikai in an inn called The Pale Moon, while Farrah had her own room adjacent to theirs.

Aside from the tension in the room, mostly because Badalao and Malikai now knew of Farrah's transgressions, Maqdhuum knew that sooner or later he and Farrah would have to have their own conversation to clear the air. He was the one who had brought her to Jahmash in the first place. The way he saw it, he didn't owe anything to her, especially not an apology. She had made her decision and had violence and revenge in her heart. He simply used it as another way to gain Jahmash's trust. This wasn't the same as his first gift to his old companion. He knowingly used that Galicean woman for his own interests, then betrayed her trust by handing her right over to Jahmash once he didn't need her. As the years passed since then, he felt more and more guilty about it. He knew he would have to find a way to make it right for her sons sooner or later, but there were higher priorities at the moment.

Malikai broke him out of his self-reflecting, "Are you still thinking of the plan there, Maqdhuum? Seems as if we lost you."

He smiled, "No. Just sorting some things out. Why don't we all sit at the table and at least pretend that we're willing to tolerate being in the same room." He stood and walked over to the table, which he'd gotten by Traveling to the inn's common room and then leaving again in the blink of an eye with it. He had gone back for a few chairs as well and hadn't taken the time to worry about whether anyone saw him. He figured they wouldn't know where he was going anyway, so there would be no chance of following him, and he planned to return everything once they were done meeting with the Kraisos. He sat in one of the chairs, shifting around to determine the best position for comfort. "If they see us as separated, fractured, or anything of the sort, they will think an alliance is not worthwhile. Why work with us if we cannot even work with ourselves? I know there are issues. Sort them out another time. Not here. Put it aside for now. That is the very reason that I'm bringing Adria to Marshall and Max in the Taurani village, once she's done with her parents. I don't need her roughing you up any further, Farrah. I'm going to go to their lair and sweet talk them into meeting with us. It shouldn't take long. They know me. When I return, I'd better not see the three of you arguing, fighting, or destroying the room out of anger. Got it?"

They all nodded as they neared the table. Badalao and Malikai still elected to maintain some distance from Farrah. Maqdhuum expected as much from Badalao, given that there had apparently been something going on between the two. He assumed that either Malikai did the same out of loyalty, or because he felt discomfort with her past and didn't know if he could trust her.

At times he wondered whether it had been a wise move to give up his immortality for a mortal body, but he knew that if he hadn't, it would be too easy to be a coward. It would be too easy to avoid Jahmash and this fight and live as far away from it all as possible. Dealing with these squabbles was part of what he agreed to when making his request from the Orijin for a new body. Maqdhuum found comfort in the notion that it would all be over soon, one way or another. Either they would succeed in killing Jahmash, or he would die trying. Either outcome would allow him to finally move beyond a physical existence.

He glanced back at the three of them and Traveled to the Kraisos' lair. Since their inception, Maqdhuum had maintained the utmost respect for their guild. They worked in the shadows and did their best to maintain order in Taiju's infrastructure. Most people in the city had no clue they existed, and the ones that did, likely had never seen them. The only entrance to their lair that Maqdhuum currently knew of was in the back of a tavern, through a series of secret entrances. It was possible that the tavern owner didn't even know they were there.

He appeared in one of their common rooms. It had been years since his last visit here, but there was still a strong chance that he would encounter someone who knew him, even in his current body. In the room, several people were stretched out on cots or lounging chairs, all seemingly asleep. A voice whispered in his ear, "I was thinking about you not too long ago. It's been a while since you...popped in."

Maqdhuum convulsed slightly from the unexpected voice. He turned to see a young Shivaani woman, somewhat chubby and of a height with him. His fear drained quickly as he recognized her face, especially the smile that spanned both cheeks. He whispered back, careful not to disturb anyone. "Freesia? You've barely aged at all in the last...what, ten years or so? The last time I saw you, you were only *starting* to become a woman. No offense, of course, but look at you. Beautiful as ever."

She held out a hand, directing him to sit in an empty chair, while she did the same. Freesia belonged to the Vizard faction of the Kraisos. They were the moles of the Kraisos, who blended into society to gather information about everyday things and were masters of disguise and gossip. Vizards thrived off barely being noticed or remembered, while also being exceptional at conversation. They were all named after flowers, while other factions used different categories. The Slayers, the militant arm, were named after animals, and the Coinbearers, who handled everything related to finances, were named after spices. There was also the Footpad faction, who were the thieves and scouts, and were named after the natural world.

His words produced a wide smile from her. "Good thing I remember you, else I'd think you were flirting with me, or trying to butter me up for something. Either way, I'm sure you're not here just to check in on me. What's your business?"

He nodded; glad she wasn't trying to coerce him into small talk. "I need some help. Along the lines of an alliance. It's not a small job, though. Something kind of big. Almost grandiose. You have anyone with some pull that might be willing to entertain me? Sit and talk in my quarters for maybe an hour? Less if need be."

She twirled her curly black hair while mulling over his request. "You remember my brother from the last time you saw us?"

"Stream? Of course. Nice kid. Straight to the point, just like me."

"Yeah, he's the Master's Apprentice of the Footpads. Basically second-in-command. He would be willing to talk with you. Not sure what kind of alliance you need, but if it's militant at all, then eventually the decision would be left to the Slayers. But Stream is a good starting point. He gets along with everyone. I'll send your message along. You looking to meet with him today?"

Maqdhuum nodded, "The earlier the better."

"Done."

"Don't you need to know where I'll be?" She laughed at him as if it was the most ridiculous question ever. Maqdhuum smirked, "Ah. Right. If he doesn't already know where I am, then he'll find me."

She stood, "Exactly. It was good to see you. I know you can see yourself out." She kissed his hand, then walked away. He wouldn't have minded talking to Freesia a little more, but Maqdhuum didn't dare interfere with the lives and schedules of the Kraisos. Taiju was a secret gem at the northeastern-most tip of Markos and Ashur, devoid of crime and corruption, and free of political squabbles. Despite the Throne's inflated taxes, especially on nations and cities suspected of being friendly to Descendants, Taiju thrived financially. Maqdhuum marveled at the fact that the Kraisos essentially ran the city from beneath it, while those aboveground lived completely oblivious to that reality.

He Traveled back to his room at the Pale Moon, where the others sat in silence. Badalao perked up at his return, "That was quick. Is that good or bad?"

"Don't worry, everything went well. One of them will be meeting us here today to hear us out. Before he arrives, I must warn you about their system of names. This information stays between us. They are a clandestine society. I am only telling you this so you don't jeopardize our request. The Kraisos are made up of factions, and each faction has a different method of assigning names. The man who will be entertaining us shortly, his name is 'Stream.' Whatever his birth name might have been was shed when he was accepted into the Kraiso community. You will not laugh, smirk, giggle, or anything else at any mention of his name, or the names of any other Kraisos. Is that clear?"

Farrah and Malikai nodded, while Badalao shrugged. "That will not be a problem. I am sure my name sounds strange in most other nations. We are not as immature as you would like to believe, Maqdhuum. Yes, there is tension, but we know how to carry ourselves, especially around guests. Just because *we* are not two thousand years old, doesn't mean we can't act like adults."

Maqdhuum rolled his eyes. "Good. See that that doesn't change." He was wondering how long it would take for the Abram references to begin.

Farrah spoke up for the first time all morning, "Exactly how big is this, this...organization? They all live underground?"

"Their underground city is almost the size of Taiju. They don't have the luxury of building *up*, like we do above ground. So everything gets sprawled out. And of course, they're not all down there at the same time. Most of them are above ground quite often. I don't know what their numbers are like. Could be possible that they've expanded beyond Taiju. You're probably thinking they're all Markosi, and that's not the case. Two of the factions definitely send scouts to other cities to recruit, survey, and do reconnaissance. Can't *only* rely on generational expansion if they want to keep themselves going. It's just like the Anonymi. Have to be willing to accept new blood where you can get it." A knock came from outside the door. Maqdhuum eyed it suspiciously, as did the others. He wasn't entirely sure how he expected Stream to arrive, but simply knocking on the door was at the bottom of the list. He looked at the others, who still nervously stared at the door, and then walked to open it.

He opened the door slowly and peeked out while it was still ajar. However, there was no one standing there. Maqdhuum leaned out into the hallway and checked to see if anyone was standing anywhere down the hall. Still, no one. He shook his head then backed into the room and shut the door. As he turned around, a voice asked, "Are these seats saved for us?" Maqdhuum jumped, as Stream's presence scared him far more than Freesia's had earlier. He saw Malikai, Farrah, and Badalao all jump from their chairs as well. All three had been looking at Maqdhuum and had no inkling of the two men standing on the other side of the table. Both wore tan shirts and green breeches. Stream continued, "Did all of you really think that we would just knock on the door?"

Maqdhuum huffed. "No. That's why we were so confused. We didn't expect a knock on the door. How...you know what, never mind. It doesn't make sense to ask, as I'm sure you won't tell us how you got in anyway. But, yes. Sit. Both of you. I was only expecting you, Stream. But both of you are welcome." Stream was a tall, stocky Shivaani, with long curly hair, similar to his sister's.

"That's accurate. I wouldn't tell you." Stream pointed to the other Kraiso, who sat to his left. "This is Wind. He's an apprentice in my faction, so I'm letting him tag along. He hasn't been above the surface in a few days. Figured this would be good for him. He's quiet, though."

Wind nodded and smiled, "Hi."

Stream continued, "Right. Enough with the pleasantries. I apologize to you all if I come across as curt, but that's exactly what I am. And I do have to get back to my responsibilities."

Maqdhuum smiled, "Yes, your sister said you're important now. Very well. Here it is. The four of us here are part of our own faction, comprised mostly of survivors from the attack on the House of Darian. We now go by 'The Ghosts of Ashur.'"

Stream cut in, "Oooh. That's rather fancy. Sorry, continue."

"Right. Our numbers are small, but we are on the verge of an alliance with the Anonymi. I'd say by the time summer arrives, that alliance will be intact. The Ghosts are working to prepare Ashur for the coming of Jahmash. We know it's only a matter of time, at this point. We need all of Ashur to be prepared when that happens."

"So what does that have to do with us?"

"I know for a fact that the Slayers and Padfoots regularly go to other cities, even beyond Markos. I need the Kraisos to use your strengths to get every city ready for Jahmash."

Stream shook his head, "That's a lot to ask of us."

"If you knew what was coming, you would think it's not enough. Jahmash is recruiting *nations*, not cities or secret organizations. There are seven nations in Ashur, and no offense to anyone, but the Wolf's Paw is barely anything. Of those seven nations, there is only *one* real army. The Royal Vermillion, who is loyal to a king intent on exterminating the very people who can save Ashur for him. Sure, Fangh-Haan and the Galiceans both have soldiers here and there, but they won't hold up against an attack."

Stream smirked, "We have heard that the tide is changing. The Vermillion's loyalty to King Edmund wavers."

Maqdhuum shrugged. "Still, it is one army. What good will they do when Ashur is invaded by armies from at least five nations? What happens when armies show up on the shores of Markos, Shivaana, Wolf's Paw, Galicea, Fangh Haan, or Mireya? Or all six at the same time? By the time the Vermillion decide who they should save, all of those nations will have been lost. I am telling you now, Stream, there is still enough time to prepare these nations and cities to fight for themselves. I know it won't happen in a day or a week, but if Jahmash's armies invade, even the Kraisos would not be able to avoid them or go unnoticed forever. So I ask you to stand with us in this fight. You don't have to be on the front lines. You don't even have to actually fight. Just start preparing cities by infiltrating their systems."

Badalao cut in, "Sorry, Maqdhuum, but I should share this, as it is pertinent to this conversation. Stream, if you think we are asking too much, you should know that I just asked my sister to do this very thing for Constaniza yesterday. Shortly, she will be setting in motion plans to prepare the people of Constaniza to defend our city, should an invasion arrive on Markosi soil. We are practicing the very thing we are asking of you."

Stream looked at Wind and then back at the rest of them. "I don't know. Doing something like this forces us to lessen our focus on Taiju. It weakens the city and everything we've worked for."

Maqdhuum leaned forward, "And what good is any of that once Taiju has been destroyed?"

Stream was about to respond when Wind spoke up. "I'm sorry, I know I'm interjecting at an inappropriate time, Stream, but something just occurred to me, and I have to ask. Three of you have these marks on your left eyes, and I know I have seen that before. I've been trying to recall where and when, and only now have I placed it. I used to know a boy in my life before becoming a Kraiso. His name was Baltaszar. Except he told everyone that the thing on his face was a scar. However, you all have the same exact marking, which means either you have all been scarred in the exact same fashion, or there is a meaningful connection that you all share."

They all looked at Wind incredulously. Stream responded first, "That's probably the most I've heard you say in the past month. Seriously?"

Before Wind could respond, Maqdhuum added, "You haven't educated him about the Descendants? How could he not know about them?"

Stream rolled his eyes. "Why does he need to? None of you have affected his life at all until today."

Badalao stood up. "Back to the important part of all this. Wind, we *do* know Baltaszar. He has been a friend of ours for a while now. In fact, I can reach out to him right now, and let him see you through my eyes. And just to prove I am not lying, in case you are skeptical, I will ask him to share something he remembers about you that we would have no way of knowing."

Wind nodded uncertainly. "Sure."

Maqdhuum eyed Badalao as the Markosi sat back down and fixed his eyes upon the table. He then looked at Wind and stared at the young man's face. "You knew each other in Haedon. There was a game that you and other boys would play. You would see who could go into the Never and stay there the longest. He said you were the best of the lot. He also said that you disappeared with no warning or indication, and everyone was worried. He also told me your...former name? I am unsure if it would be insulting to repeat it."

Wind glanced at Stream, who simply shrugged. He then looked back at Badalao. "Go ahead. Say it."

"Your former name was Vikram Bhoodoo."

Wind's eyes lit up and his smile grew wider than Maqdhuum remembered Freesia's smile ever being. "Tasz! It's really him talking to you! Tell him he exaggerates about the forest games. He was always the best. And tell him that my parents knew about me leaving but were afraid of being excommunicated for allowing me to leave Haedon."

Badalao smiled, "He heard you."

Maqdhuum attempted to refocus them. "Lao, can you put your...mind away. I wholeheartedly appreciate the reunion, but we can't let it drag on. We have to be mindful of their time."

Wind spoke up again, to Maqdhuum's surprise. "Stream, up until this point, I might've seen your stance on not getting involved. But there is something here. Baltaszar was one of the best people I knew. If he is with them, then we can trust them. I can even be an ambassador to the Ghosts of Ashur on our behalf, to ensure that they are what they say. Perhaps a deal can be made, or conditions can be set in order to come to an agreement. Regardless, I don't think this meeting was just some coincidence."

Stream arose from his chair. "And you're willing to present this same argument to Bull?"

Wind nodded, "Just allow me the opportunity."

"Very well." He turned to Maqdhuum, "Your request depends upon Wind's ability to present his argument, and whether the Master Slayer agrees. How much longer will you be in this city?"

Maqdhuum took a deep breath, though he wasn't sure if it was out of relief or to ease the tension in his shoulders. "We plan to depart later in the day, after I've retrieved another one of our companions. But, as you know, I can return at any time."

Stream started walking toward the door and waved for Wind to follow. "Return to our lair at this hour in three days' time. We will have an answer for you by then." He didn't wait for an answer and walked out of the very door from which they heard the knock earlier. Wind followed but turned and smiled before exiting and closing the door behind him.

Malikai pointed to the door. "They just walked out the door? I was expecting them to crawl out of the windows or something."

Maqdhuum ran to the door and opened it, only two or three seconds after they left, and saw an empty hallway with no sign of anyone, nor the sound of any footsteps. He shook his head and closed the door.

CHAPTER 15
MODERN HARBINGERS

From **The Book of Orijin,** **Verse One Hundred Fifty-one**
It is only through knowing oneself that you may understand how others will properly fit into your lives.
If you do not know who you are, you can never truly know anyone else.

MARSHALL STARED OUT AT THE river at the outskirts of the remnants of his village. He was glad he'd taken the time to bury his father and sisters at their family's Lineage Tree first. Each family in the Taurani society was assigned a tree somewhere beyond the village, and when a Taurani died, they were buried at their family's Lineage Tree. This custom had been practiced for generations, and it was said that Lineage Trees grew stronger, based on how honorable of a life the deceased lived. Marshall remembered being a young boy, helping his father bury his grandfather. He'd always expected that he would have a son of his own to help him by the time his own father died.

Maximillian and Reverron had encouraged him to focus on finding his reflection before tending to his family, as he might be too emotional to embrace his manifestation if he tried to do so afterwards, but Marshall knew that he would be more at ease if he saw to his family first. Adria walked up next to him and gently put a hand on his shoulder. Maqdhuum had brought her about an hour before. "Just try to do the same as when you summoned your shadow." She must have thought he was nervous about retrieving his reflection, when in truth he was more confused about whether it would work.

If only her enhanced hearing could hear my thoughts. Still, he was surprised at her empathy and encouragement. The last time she had accompanied him to his former home she hadn't been nearly as friendly. He knew that was more his fault than anything else, but it still surprised him how much had changed since then. He glanced at her, "Thanks. I've got a lot on my mind; that's all. I just need to focus. Also, it's strange to try this at a river."

Adria chuckled at his attempted levity. "Unless you want to search your whole village for a mirror? Speaking of which, where would your people ever have gotten mirrors from?"

"We had one in the house, but they definitely were not common amongst my people. The rumors were that some of our envoys retrieved things every now and then from the Tower of the Blind. Mirrors were among those luxuries. Which only makes it even more confusing that my reflection would be part of my manifestation. But who am I to question the methods or intentions of the Orijin, right?"

Adria shrugged, "Can't argue with that."

He nodded and then walked to the river until the brisk winter water reached halfway up his boots. He turned to Adria, then to Maximillian and Reverron, who stood a few feet behind. "I guess I'm lucky it's a sunny day, or else I might not even know if it returns." He took a deep breath and stared down at the water, where his reflection should have been, then opened himself to his manifestation. The melody of it coursed through his body, and it felt like ages since that sensation had passed through him. Marshall closed his eyes and focused on the idea of his reflection, imagining it appearing at his feet in the river. He held that thought for several moments until a strange sensation attached to his mind. He wouldn't have been able to describe it to anyone else, but it was almost as if he was now aware of someone else in the world and able to share his thoughts and intentions with that entity, without even trying. The presence was as familiar as talking to himself inside his head, and it grew stronger with each passing second. Marshall opened his eyes and looked directly into the water, where he expected the reflection to be. "What? There's nothing there. I *felt* something. I really thought it would work."

He turned to Adria and the others, still allowing his manifestation to run through him, and put his palms up in confusion. Adria walked up to him in the water and tugged at his sleeve, "Look. It *is* there! It did work!"

Marshall looked back down into the water to confirm for himself. Sure enough, he saw his own reflection for the first time in over a year. "Wow, it worked!" He continued to stare at his reflection in the water, "Can you give me a moment alone, Adria?"

"Of course." She stepped back and joined the other two.

Marshall tried to think of what to do first, and decided to just speak to the reflection aloud, but quietly. He tried not to think of the others, knowing they were most likely staring at him. "So how does this work? Why were...you...not there for so long?" He wasn't sure if he expected an audible response, but he hoped that wouldn't be the case. Going forward, he didn't want to draw attention and strange looks from others who would wonder who he was talking to. To his relief, the response came mentally, and it was so subtle that it seemed as if the answer had already been there, without any indication of a conscious thought.

In a split second, Marshall was aware that he'd lost his reflection once he arrived at the House of Darian, which is also why it took some time to appear before him once he summoned it, as it had just traveled all the way from there. *Why did I not attempt this with my shadow?* And just as instantaneously, he remembered that moment after he had regained his shadow, Maqdhuum had appeared and abducted Gunnar and Adria.

He was aware now that both his shadow and reflection were components of his ability to control the light. His shadow had separated from him long ago when he and Aric had tried to flee from Maqdhuum's army. The information continued to become accessible in his mind. He suddenly knew that he could not die without both being connected to him, which is why he must have unwittingly detached it. Marshall knew that he would need to take the time to discover exactly what he could do with both, and what his limitations were, and as he knelt in the water to get a closer look at his reflection, he heard Adria gasp behind him.

He arose and turned quickly, and saw Maqdhuum standing, clad in his usual all-black attire, in front of Adria, Maximillian, and Reverron. Marshall stalked toward the man and grabbed Maqdhuum by his long, stringy hair, "The last time you were here, you stole her and Gunnar away. The time before that, you killed everyone here. I'm assuming you popped in for something else this time?"

Maqdhuum disappeared and reappeared behind the others in the time it took Marshall to blink. "It was nothing personal those times. And I could offer an explanation, but I'm sure you wouldn't care about anything I have to say."

Marshall nodded, "And you would be right." He remembered Savaiyon's words and swallowed his anger. "Save it. Why *are* you here?"

"Something's come up. Savaiyon and Slade want everyone in Shipsbane now. So Savaiyon and I are retrieving everyone."

Maximillian spoke up. "Are we in danger?"

Maqdhuum shrugged, "Don't know the details. I just know it's Slade who's worked up. Come on now, everyone grab ahold of me." Maqdhuum smiled and put his arms out for everyone to hold on to. In another blink, a blur of almost infinite colors flashed before Marshall's eyes, and they were all in a tight alley next to an inn, which Marshall presumed was in Shipsbane. Maqdhuum walked ahead, toward the clearing and waved for them to follow. "The inn's this building on our right. The others are inside."

They followed him into the grey and white stone building, and as soon as they entered, a tall, chubby Cerysian man sneered at them. "More? For the love of Orijin, how many are you bringing in here?"

Maqdhuum looked around at the room, which was mostly empty, save for their company. "From the looks of it, I'd say we're helping more than hurting you. We won't be here long, Cedric. Besides, people find out a bunch of black-liners were at the Tall Tale Inn, sooner or later soldiers'll come knocking. Sounds like more coin in your pocket. I'll make sure everyone here drinks. Might even pay for them!" He cracked Cedric a smile and then walked to the crowd in the back corner, who sat at various tables in proximity to each other.

Marshall realized they were the last group to arrive; Savaiyon and Slade were waiting for them. Neither had yet addressed the group, which numbered twenty now. As soon as Slade eyed them, he wasted no time in standing up and quieting everyone down.

"I'm sorry that we had to cut everyone's affairs short, but it's for good reason. Baltaszar can attest to this, though he would have no way of understanding the severity of it. We were in Vandenar, visiting the Augur Munn Keeramm, and he offered a prophecy. We asked for something on the subject of an alliance between us and the Anonymi, and what he shared is what has caused me great alarm.

"Keeramm envisioned some of us on a battlefield alongside Anonymi, but our enemy wasn't Jahmash. It was the Vithelegion army, from the nation of Vitheligia. They hail from the island realm of Orol Taghdras, which comprises five other nations. Up to this point, I never believed that the Vithelegion would be the type to align with Jahmash, but if they are coming here to fight against Ashurians, then I can't think of any other explanation. It would take around six months to sail from their shores to ours, but we have no idea if they departed six months ago, or if this battle will happen six years from now."

Marshall tried his best to not sound arrogant, "How serious of a threat are they? Could one nation, or one army, come to Ashur and wipe us all out?"

Slade nodded and stroked his beard, "Serious enough. Especially if they are working with others. I see two possibilities. Either they arrive before Jahmash's other forces and weaken Ashur enough for his big push, or they arrive with all the other armies and...well, then we likely don't have a chance. To put it in perspective, Vitheligia is one of the smaller nations beyond Ashur, yet no other nation has ever been able to conquer it or defeat it in battle. Even in my days in Semaajj, it was understood that you don't attack Vitheligia."

Savaiyon stood up next to Slade, rubbing his closely shaved head. "This means we need to go to Asarei at once. This prophecy means we will be successful in this next mission, but we don't know at what cost. And we don't know how long after we complete our mission the Vithelegion will arrive. So the more time we give ourselves now, the better prepared we will be for that fight, when it comes."

Badalao spoke from the table next to Marshall's. "Are we ready to go, then?"

Savaiyon cocked his head, "Nearly. There are some things I should warn you about before we leave here. Asarei was ornery and aggressive twenty years ago, so I have no idea what time, age, and seclusion might have done to him. Remember, we are going to him unannounced and uninvited. Rhadames is the only one here who has had a friendly relationship with him, so we follow his lead. Any questions?"

Marshall asked, "You said he left the Taurani society because he disagreed with our ways. How will he feel about my presence?"

Slade responded, "It might be different with you, Marshall. For one thing, you're *with* us, which is a similar path to his. Also, you no longer have your tattoos, so he might not even realize you're Taurani. Just stay quiet at first."

Reverron spoke up to ask a question, which surprised Marshall. "So, are any of the rumors true? I've heard Asarei was banished from the House because he hurt Marlowe in a fight."

Malikai joined in, "Heard that one, too. I've also heard that he has a pet nashorn. One of those massive leathery things with all the horns on its head."

"And that he went mad after trying to summon his manifestation for too long," Lincan chimed in.

Slade put his hands up to stop them. "Honestly, Asarei has a...colorful personality. He's intense, but also charismatic, as well as many other things. Any rumors you've heard about him likely have some truth, with varying degrees depending on which rumor. I can tell you he never harmed Marlowe, though. They didn't get along, but Asarei wouldn't do that."

Badalao stood up, "Well let's go, then. How do we get there, Savaiyon?"

Marshall was surprised at Badalao's eagerness. He was curious about Asarei and the next steps they would be taking, but beneath everything else, there was a sense of unease as well. They were about to commit to killing the King of Ashur, and there were bound to be casualties in any combat. He hated to think that some of the people in this same room would not survive the mission. He glanced at Adria, who stared ahead stoically. He knew she would not need *protecting*, but he wouldn't be able to forgive himself if something happened to her.

Savaiyon responded, lowering his voice. "There is a touch portal at the shore, just outside the city. I have never used it, but I imagine the process is the same as the one to the House of Darian. It connects to the large island out beyond those two off the shore. Rhadames, Maqdhuum, you two will wait for me to create a bridge for you to use. The touch portal only works for us. Assuming everyone has whatever little belongings they own, we can go there now. I recommend we walk in smaller packs, so no one gets curious about following us. This inn is near the edge of the city, which is why we're at the Tall Tale to begin with. Unless there is any other business, we can proceed. It will likely be even colder at the water; I hope everyone's coats and cloaks are warm enough." He nodded his head in the direction of the door as he walked toward it with Slade, nudging Vasher to walk with them, and reminded them to leave in smaller groups.

Baltaszar spoke, just short of shouting, "I can help if anyone's having trouble with staying warm."

Maqdhuum stood and looked at Marshall and Adria. "Come on." Before getting to the door, he walked over to Cedric and placed a pouch in the man's palm. "No time for a round of beer, but this would've covered it. Thanks." He then walked out of the Tall Tale without waiting for a response. Marshall and Adria followed quickly.

"That was nice of you. Having a good day?" Adria asked sarcastically.

He responded without turning around, "I tend to be nice to people who are nice and patient with me."

Her tone changed to anger, "Yeah, I'm sure Gunnar would agree."

Marshall nodded, "And the entire Taurani population." He nudged Adria, "Hang back, we can walk by ourselves. Savaiyon is tall enough for us to follow anyway." She nodded in agreement. They slowed for Maqdhuum to walk several feet ahead, then moved to the other side of the road, and matched pace. The street was fairly busy, as this side of Shipsbane hosted dozens of fish merchants. It was late enough in the morning that most were back from their early ventures and setting up their wares. Marshall had never been part of the groups that fished at the river by the Taurani village, but he'd never eaten a fish that he didn't like. He wouldn't have minded returning to Shipsbane every now and then to eat a freshly caught fish. "Hey, how do you feel about all this?"

Adria looked up at him, "What do you mean?"

"What we're about to do. Lao seems extremely eager, as do some of the others. It's as if they have no concerns. And as a Taurani, I'm not afraid of dying in battle, but this mission we are about to begin, some of us may not survive it. There are only twenty of us, and even with some of the Vermillion Army on our side, how many battles do you know of in which either side had no casualties."

"Of course I'm nervous as well, but this is what comes along with the line on my face. On your face. Once we get to Asarei, we plan, we strategize, then create auxiliary plans and backup plans for those. We prepare for everything, and even then, I agree, Marshall. Any of us could die and some of us will. But I guarantee you that each of the twenty of us has concerns. Lao never shows it. Neither does Linc. I'm not sure what's going on with Desmond, because he looks like he's not behind those eyes, but normally he shows no fear either."

"You noticed it, too. I think it might be from the attack. Someone mentioned the Asarei rumor about going mad from too much power. I feel guilty about it now, but I'm the one who suggested Max transfer energy into Desmond so he could keep the House up. And now it's destroying him."

"We just need to be vigilant with him. If everyone watches out for him and keeps him from doing anything stupid, he'll be better with time. His body has to wean itself from wanting all that power."

"You sound like an expert. Have you seen this happen before?"

She smiled, "No, but I read as much as I can. There have been documented instances of this and numerous cases of people successfully recovering from it, with the proper help."

"Got it." He hesitated for a second, but then continued with what he had wanted to say. "Also, thank you."

She looked at him with a confused countenance, "For what?"

"We wouldn't be having this conversation if you never saved me in the first place. I was rather hard-headed when we first met, and I don't remember if I ever showed any gratitude. There was so much to process when I first awoke at the House, and I'm sure I could've handled things better. And then *that* shiteater," he nodded at Maqdhuum, who was still several paces ahead, "took you and Gunnar. So I never got the chance to really be nice to you. I figure I should thank you now, before I lose the opportunity again. It would have been easy for you to continue to be angry with me and many others back at the Tower." He thought he saw a hint of red in her cheeks.

Adria looked at the ground for a moment and then straight ahead as they walked on. "Everything I went through after Maqdhuum took me—it allowed for a lot of empathy on my part. I never looked down on you, and there wasn't any real grudge. You were just being so stubborn and, well, I think I've had to fight to get my way my whole life. Even my parents still treat me like I'm some small child who has never left Fera. I know I *look* like a child, but light of Orijin, I survived being Jahmash's prisoner." Marshall felt her glance at him quickly. "But I'm digressing. I was glad to help you and save you. Now that we know each other better, it's nice to talk to you. And you never talk down to me or feel the need to unnecessarily help me or *rescue* me from things. It's a relief to have someone around who just sees me as another person, and not a little girl. So many boys at the House of Darian used to do that."

They'd followed the others while talking for so long that Marshall didn't even realize that they'd left the city and were looking out at the Sea of Fates. Savaiyon stood in the distance, waiting with Slade and Vasher. Marshall turned to look behind him and realized exactly how far away from the city they were. The good thing was that, unless anyone was following them, no one would have much reason to trail them to the beach. The docks were way off in the distance, so they wouldn't be seen by fishermen either.

As everyone reached Savaiyon, the tall Shivaani spoke. "Well, this is it. None of us really know what to expect. Who knows if he'll even be there right now. But the touch portal is that big craggy rock that juts out of the water." He turned and pointed to a slick black rock that stuck out of the water about twenty feet out. *At least the sea is calm*, Marshall thought. If and when they managed to settle in and be comfortable, he would make it a point to ask who created the touch portals. *Were they some magic by the Orijin, or perhaps created by a Descendant? Are there others throughout Ashur that we don't know about?*

Savaiyon continued, "I will go first and create a bridge for Rhadames and Maqdhuum right away. After me, the rest of you can go whenever you are ready." He didn't wait for any of them to respond or ask questions. He turned and walked into the water; the bottom of his thick cloak dragged as he went farther in. As he reached the giant rock, the water was barely to his calves. Savaiyon put his hand on the giant rock without turning around and disappeared right away.

Marshall looked at Adria and tugged her forearm. "Come on. If there's any trouble on the other side, he will likely need help right away." All the others must have had a similar sentiment, as everyone in the group, save Maqdhuum and Slade, rushed toward the rock in the water, uncaring of the wetness or cold. Most of them reached it around the same time and blinked out of sight.

Just as with the touch portal to the House of Darian, Marshall found himself surrounded by utter darkness. Even the surface beneath him could not be seen, though he knew he was moving along on something. By the time he thought about speaking to see if the others could hear him, Marshall was already out of the blackness and standing firmly on gravelly ground. All the others appeared around him, and just as Savaiyon had told them, Maqdhuum and Slade walked through a yellow-fringed doorway a few feet away from Marshall. It closed as soon as both were through, and just as Marshall looked around at everyone, a large figure approached them from a small, thick grove of trees.

Marshall knew that the man had to see the Descendant's Mark on all their faces, just like the one on his, but his solemn countenance didn't waver. He was nearly as tall as Savaiyon and Slade, and thicker than both of them. Marshall noticed that he wore no cloak, though his shirt bore long sleeves, and his brown complexion resembled that of Savaiyon, Vasher, and Sindha. The sword that was holstered on his back was the biggest that Marshall had ever seen.

When he finally finished his slow walk to Slade, who stood in front, he spoke in grunts. "Who are you? And why are you here? You are not welcome."

Slade responded, undiscouraged. "My name is Rhadames Slade. I am an old friend of Asarei's, back when he was still at the House of Darian. My friends here and I seek his help with a mission that we must complete soon. We are in dire straits else we would not be here."

The other man seemed unaffected. "There is no one here by that name. Please go now. And do not return." He turned and started to walk away, when Vasher navigated through the group and stood next to Slade.

"Wait, friend. My name is Vasher Jai, from Sundari." Vasher's voice seemed different than Marshall had ever heard it, but it was soothing to listen to. "We are not here to cause you any trouble or discomfort. We need to speak with Asarei about a matter that could affect all of Ashur, including any of you residing on this island. All of life as we know it could hang in the balance. All of us here are your friends, your new friends. You should take us to see Asarei at once, as he would be thrilled to see Rhadames again, after so long."

Marshall realized after, that Vasher was using his manifestation on the other man, and that he had become caught up in the hypnosis or Vasher's persuasion. He assumed that since it wasn't directed at him, the effects didn't stick. He whispered to Adria, "Clever. How long will that last?"

She leaned her head towards him, "I'm not sure. I don't think I've actually seen Vasher use his manifestation before."

The large man looked at Vasher curiously for a moment, then finally responded. His voice was much softer and more amicable. "You know, I think Asarei would enjoy meeting all of you. I should take you all to him. Please follow me and do your best to leave the trees unbothered. By the way, my name is Manjobam. But just call me Bam." Once again, Manjobam turned and walked back towards the grove. Vasher turned to all of them with a wide grin on his face and nodded his head.

They followed Manjobam through the trees for a short while, and eventually came to a point where he pulled back a large flap in the ground and signaled for them to walk down the short flight of stairs that opened up beneath. "Please friends, enter and wait for me at the bottom. I must ensure that this is placed back properly. Do not worry, though. It is well-lit down there with several torches along the walls."

They followed his request and descended the stairs. Once Manjobam rejoined them, he led them once more. They walked through several corridors, all well-lit just as Manjobam had promised. After another few minutes and a few more descending staircases, they arrived at a doorless entryway, which opened to a large room with nothing in it except for the torches along the walls. At the other end of it, a bald man knelt, facing away from them. Without any indication of movement, the man spoke. "I heard the echoes of all your footsteps for so long, I was wondering whether you got lost down here. Bam, who else is with you?" His voice bounced off the stone walls all around.

Manjobam responded excitedly. "I have brought you several new friends, and one old one." Before Manjobam could continue, the other man sprang to his feet and turned to face them. He was shirtless and his head, neck, and body were covered in tattoos. He glided toward them, barefoot, with a scowl on his face.

"You fool. One of them tricked you with a manifestation. How dare you allow anyone down here that you do not know!" He reached Manjobam and smacked the larger, younger man across the face with the back of his hand. "I thought you were bringing the others down here to speak with me or meditate, and instead you bring these," he paused to look at all of them up and down, "these beggars here?"

To Marshall's surprise, the man, whom he assumed was Asarei, eyed Slade closely and gave no indication of recognizing him. Slade spoke up, "Asarei, can we slow down for a moment. It's me, Rhadames Slade. One of my companions *did* use a manifestation to persuade Manjobam to let us see you. That is our fault, not his."

Asarei quickly pivoted from Manjobam to Slade and brandished a dagger from behind his back. "It is *his* fault for being fooled so easily." He then placed the dagger at Slade's throat. He was several inches shorter than Slade, of a height with Marshall, but his demeanor was imposing, and he didn't seem to care that he was outnumbered. "Rhadames Slade. You dare abandon me, what...more than twenty years ago? And then have the balls to show up here asking favors?"

Slade put his hands up to show he had no intention of fighting back. "Asarei, I don't know how you saw it as abandoning you. I thought you wanted to stay in Galicea after our search for Raya proved fruitless. I apologize, but I didn't know." Marshall darted his eyes around at all the others as he opened to his manifestation.

Asarei looked up at Slade, then around at Marshall and all the others standing behind Slade. He pulled the dagger away and his mouth opened to an enormous grin, followed by a hearty roar of a laugh. "Rhadames! Of course I'm not angry with you! I can't believe you thought I would actually attack you! How have you been, old friend? It's been so long! And you look so old! Look at this beard! It's terrible!"

Marshall took a deep breath and relaxed. *Wow, they weren't kidding. That was a little too intense.* Slade must have also been rendered speechless, as it took him a moment to respond. "I should've known you were joking. I've been keeping myself busy. Traveling the world, getting myself into trouble, and now trying to prepare for that final battle that's in the back of everyone's mind."

Asarei nodded and scratched his dark brown beard, which was full, but kept somewhat short. He smiled and then looked at everyone behind Slade, "You should all know that you are in the presence of a legend. If any of you knew exactly what this man has been through, accomplished, and been willing to do for his friends, you would cry at the realization that you are not worthy of his friendship." Asarei's eyes fixated on someone in the crowd. "Speaking of friendship, you must be one of Joakwin Kontez's sons." Marshall and the rest of them turned to look at Baltaszar, whose jaw tightened. It was obvious he was caught off guard and managed a nod. Asarei was direct, but Marshall realized he was also astute. The man put his hand on Slade's shoulder, "Shit, I'm sorry. How long ago did it happen?"

Slade didn't allow any time for Baltaszar to respond. "Somewhere around a year ago. Joakwin went to Haedon with Khou after we stopped searching for Raya. Ended up sacrificing himself to spare Baltaszar from the others. You know how non-Ashurians feel about magic, and Haedon is full of them. Poor kid never really got much of a chance to face it all. Left Haedon the same night and got caught up with all the shit that comes with that black line. His brother is with Jahmash," There was a collective gasp from everyone except Slade and Baltaszar. Slade raised his voice for everyone to hear. "He's safe for now. As I've told Baltaszar, I can guarantee he'll be safe for about a year. And as long as Baltaszar is alive, then Bo'az will be as well. It's Baltaszar that the Red Harbinger wants, not Bo'az."

Marshall found himself not satisfied with Slade's explanation. "Why? Why would he want Tasz?"

Before Slade could answer, Asarei interjected. "All of you. Sit. Clearly there's much to discuss and it seems like we might be here a while. Get comfortable. Except you, Bam. You go to the wall and stand until I tell you otherwise."

They all sat on the ground tentatively and watched as Manjobam followed Asarei's orders. As they all settled, Slade answered. "I honestly don't know how he found out about Baltaszar specifically, but he believes that Baltaszar can burn away the entire sea, which would allow him to travel here without having to deal with the sea."

Marshall looked over at Baltaszar, expecting him to react. But this time, Lincan had a question. "Wouldn't it make sense for him to use Savaiyon? Or Abram, I mean Maqdhuum, who actually worked for him."

Maqdhuum spoke over Slade, "He didn't know who I was or what I could do. The whole point of me working for him was to gain his trust and then infiltrate, so I would know how to strike at his weaknesses."

Asarei stood up. "Wow. You all speak about this so casually, but is it true? You are Abram in the flesh?"

Maqdhuum pursed his lips and rolled his eyes as he put his head back against the wall. "Not in the flesh. Long story, but I explained my intentions to the Orijin a while back. Got a new body out of it: can still Travel anywhere. Only difference is I get older in this body. There's more urgency when time actually matters."

Asarei nodded and smiled. "I'll save this conversation for another time. I have too many questions. Sorry, Rhadames. You were saying?"

"Right. Honestly, Lincan, I don't know. He may not even know about Savaiyon, for all I know. But just like Maqdhuum, I worked for him for years, and it was always about Baltaszar."

Asarei shook his head. "Filthy bink, have all of you here worked for Jahmash at some point? Hey! Bam! Come sit; these people who tricked you into bringing here, turns out it might not be your fault." Marshall eyed Manjobam as the massive Shivaani sat next to Asarei. "Look, all this is well and good, but the truth of it is that there are twenty of you in here, many carrying weapons, and I really only know two of you. And Baltaszar, I'm only counting you because of how close I was with your father. So what I need to know is, what in all the Three Shitty Rings are all of you doing on my island?"

Marshall nodded. He was starting to wonder when Asarei would confront them on that, as well as when they would have to share their plan with him. Slade and Savaiyon, who sat beside each other in front of Asarei, looked at one another. Slade nodded to Savaiyon. "You know most of the details. When you finish, I can add on the new facts."

Savaiyon nodded in agreement. "Very well." He turned back to Asarei. "You may or may not remember me, Asarei. I was young while you were still at the House of Darian, perhaps not as tall, though. My name is Savaiyon Simalti."

"You look familiar, but that was a long time ago, and there were other things capturing my attention at the time. Go on."

"The people you see in this room are all that are left of the House of Darian. I am not sure how much you focus on the affairs of Ashur, but…"

"The House was attacked and destroyed, most likely by Jahmash's army. Yeah, I'm on an island, but I'm not stupid. Anyone in Ashur who doesn't know by now, likely doesn't even know who Jahmash is."

"The first reason why we are here is because we need help. *Your* help. All of us have spent years under Marlowe, and never had much of an opportunity to learn how to fight. We need the proper tutelage in mastering physical combat, as well as learning how to weaponize our manifestations. I am sure some of us have dabbled in using our manifestations in various ways, but we are each limited to the boundaries of our singular imaginations.

"It was no secret among anyone in the House of Darian that you and Marlowe differed in your philosophies, specifically on the topic of violence and combat. Our home has been destroyed and we do not have many options for seeking refuge. We could use your help with anything you would be willing to teach us, and in turn we would earn our keep."

Asarei closed his eyes for a moment and smiled. "How exactly do you plan to earn your keep? You don't even know what we do here."

"We could learn. We are in need of your help and would willingly do what you ask in order to stay here. Whatever that might be."

"You truly must be desperate, Savaiyon, to all come here and throw yourselves at me, saying you'll do whatever I ask if you can stay. I must say, though, I'm not convinced. You said there are two reasons why you're here. Give me the second."

Marshall continued to watch Savaiyon's every move, as only Maqdhuum sat between the two of them. The former Maven took a deep breath and continued. "This is the crazy part. Well, here goes. Shortly before the attack on the House, we met with the Anonymi to request an alliance in fighting against Jahmash." Maqdhuum was about to say something, but Marshall quickly punched him hard just under the shoulder blade. Maqdhuum turned quickly, and Marshall responded by simply shaking his head and then putting his index finger to his mouth. Marshall was expecting a response, but the former Harbinger just turned back around and kept quiet.

Adria leaned to his ear and whispered, "Wow. You just punched a Harbinger and rendered him speechless. Maybe you should just lead us." Marshall couldn't be sure if his heart was racing from the Maqdhuum interaction, from Adria's compliment, or from the idea that she was comfortable enough to be whispering things to him. He kept his emotions internal as he broke a wide smile and kept it at that.

Savaiyon had continued on with explaining the Anonymi's request for them to kill King Edmund, which shocked even Asarei. He'd left out the part about Marlowe, though. Marshall assumed that that was information that could be explained at another time. Asarei's reactions seemed to be more intense with every new piece of information he was provided. "You're shittin' me, right? You're serious that you met with the Anonymi, and they told you they would agree to an alliance if one of you kills the king? This is a real story that you're telling me and expect me to believe?"

Savaiyon nodded. "I was present when they made the decree, as was

Vasher." He pointed behind him. "In fact, Vasher is the one who spoke with the Anonymi in their private chambers. We are not here to lie to you or trick you, Asarei. The Anonymi looked down on the passive ways of the House of Darian under Marlowe's watch. That is why they set these terms. We must be the ones to kill King Edmund, as they see him to be Ashur's greatest threat, and then they will take us seriously. If you are concerned that we will ask you to do it for us, that is not the case. We need your guidance in terms of strategy, preparation, and planning. But we know full well that one of us must be the one to kill the king."

Asarei looked at Slade, who confirmed Savaiyon's story. "He's not lying to you. I agreed that seeking you out was the right move. Jahmash is slowly taking out his biggest threats in Ashur. First the Taurani, then the House of Darian. I'm sure the Anonymi are in the back of his mind as well. If Edmund wasn't trying to kill anyone with a black line, I fully believe that Jahmash would be targeting him and the Vermillion next. My friend, I know you came here to get away from everything that Marlowe touched, but the people in this room are *not* his followers. They are not Descendants any longer. We have renamed ourselves the Ghosts of Ashur. Jahmash likely believes we are dead, and we must now do everything in secrecy. Once we are fully prepared to strike against Edmund, then we will leave you. I promise."

Asarei stood up and clenched his fist. "If people weren't so damned idiotic, all of you wouldn't even be here. This is why I left the Taurani in the first place! All these tattoos do is cover up the black lines so they don't have to admit the truth. And if they hadn't been lying to themselves, they wouldn't have been wiped out." Marshall noticed Slade glance at him to gauge his demeanor, but Marshall surprisingly wasn't mad about what Asarei was saying. A year ago, he would have been in Asarei's face, ready for a fight. But he'd come to see that Asarei's view was right. A good fighter doesn't deny himself his best weapon. That's exactly what his people had done for generations.

Asarei continued his rant. "Same goes for the House of Darian! Marlowe was so worried about coexisting that he literally wiped his people out of existence. Light of Orijin, what a damn fool. If he had done his job, then the House would still be standing and none of you would be here. Some would be hurt, perhaps a few dead, but even armies of Jahmash should be no trouble for a hundred weaponized Descendants. Dammit, Slade, this makes me so angry. I haven't wasted my time thinking about that man in years, and now he's not even alive and he's still pissing me off!"

Marshall and the rest of the Ghosts of Ashur sat there speechless. He wasn't sure if Asarei was mad at just Marlowe, or at all of them, but none of them wanted to say anything to set the man off even more. To everyone's surprise, Blastevahn stood up from the back of the group. Since he was nearly as tall as Savaiyon, everyone seemed to notice right away. Oddly enough, he didn't say anything at first. He closed his eyes and seemed to concentrate for a few moments. Marshall suspected that Blastevahn was opening himself to his manifestation, which was even more curious, in that he was almost certain that no one in the room had ever seen Blastevahn use it before. At the House of Darian, Blastevahn had always been attached to Marlowe, so they rarely saw him.

Finally, Blastevahn opened his mouth to speak, but what came out surprised everyone even more, though no one said a word. Blastevahn started singing,

"In days of peril, times of sin,
Came Harbingers of Orijin.
Good Lionel, fair Gideon,
Fierce Abram; brave Darian.

And then Jahmash betrayed his friends,
Now banished to an island.
He vows his anger will not end,
Til his revenge on Descendants.

And now our king, he hunts us til
We all are silenced, all are killed.
We'll save their lives and even still,
King Edmund vows his dreams fulfilled.

We are the Ghosts of fair Ashur,
We'll save you when Jahmash returns.
Rise our lives as the Drowned Realm burns.
We are the modern Harbingers."

As the song finished, Marshall blinked his eyes several times to snap himself out of what felt like a trance. As his mind grew less cloudy, he looked around and noticed everyone else doing the same thing. Eventually they all looked back at Blastevahn and stared him, waiting for some sort of explanation.

Sindha spoke from the other side of the group, "Blastevahn, that was beautiful. I never knew you could do that. Your song, it put me in a trance; it's like your voice was mesmerizing and I couldn't do anything except listen. And it almost seemed as if...you'd lost your Galicean accent?" All the others in the room nodded and shared verbal agreements.

Blastevahn smiled and nodded. "Zank you, Sindha." He looked

around at the whole group. "I am fairly certain zat none of you have ever seen or heard my manifestation. Zat song has been in my head for some time now, and I didn't know vy, or ven to share it. However, sitting here, it seemed like ze right time, vith Asarei, and all of you. If it isn't clear, ve are ze Harbingers now, no offense Maqdhuum. Ze burden is upon our shoulders to save mankind. I vonce heard an Augur say zat Ashur vould burn like vild fire once Jahmash returns. I don't know if zat is Baltaszar's doing or not, but it does not sound good eizer vay. Ze time to vork togezer is now. Ve must start preparing now, and zat means zat anyvon viz zis line on our faces must be on ze same side." He looked Asarei directly in the eyes, "If you choose not to help us, zen it means you vould razzer see Ashur burn. Ze choice is yours."

Most of them in the room were now wide-eyed and looking at Asarei, awaiting his reaction. Marshall felt Adria nudge him with her elbow, but out of the corner of his eye, he saw that she still looked straight at Asarei. He didn't dare look away from the man, as he didn't want to miss anything.

Asarei stared back at Blastevahn. He looked somewhat confused, as he must have been caught up in the trance that came with Blastevahn's song. Whatever the trance was supposed to do, Marshall wasn't entirely sure, but it had definitely softened Asarei's intensity. He finally responded to Blastevahn's words. "Blastevahn. You're not wrong. But I lived my life a certain way up until about an hour ago, and now twenty of you are here expecting all of that to change." He looked at Manjobam, "Bam. I must go consult General Grunt about these matters. Take them to the dining room, summon the others, and see to their needs. When I return, I'll have an answer for you. Either way, it's my duty to be a good host. Eat and drink until you're full. Rest until you're refreshed. I'll return shortly." With that, Asarei left the room from where they'd entered.

Slade stood up and looked at Manjobam, "Did...he say General Grunt? Do you actually have an army on this island?"

Manjobam briefly smirked, but then it was gone in an instant. He stood and gestured for all of them to do the same. "We...are not allowed to discuss General Grunt. It is a sensitive subject for Asarei." He then started towards the entryway, "Come. Follow me." They all arose and followed.

Marshall looked at Adria and raised his eyebrows, "Mysterious!"

"Right? Why would he be touchy about a military officer? What a strange man. Even stranger for Blastevahn of all people to put him in his place."

Horatio, who was right behind them, chimed in, "But wasn't that the most beautiful song you've ever heard?"

Marshall chuckled, "It really was."

Horatio continued, "If he could sing to us every night before we went to sleep, I wouldn't spend hours staring at the ceiling."

Adria responded dryly, "Perhaps you should offer him something in return for his services, and he might oblige."

Horatio took her seriously. "I might just have to do that." They walked on, but only went one flight up and then followed new corridors. Shortly, they walked into another large chamber, though smaller than Asarei's meditation room. This one had plenty of couches and cushioned seats, as well as a large wooden dining table at the center.

Once they all found a seat, Manjobam addressed them. "I hope this room is to your liking, my friends." He smiled at Vasher, "See, now I can call you that without your tricks." Marshall laughed to himself, *I guess the effects don't last forever.* Manjobam then addressed the whole room again, "I am going to retrieve the others who inhabit this island, as well as request some food and drink be served. Take this time for yourselves. I won't be very long."

As soon as Manjobam left, Marshall looked over to Slade, who was lying down on a long sofa. "Rhadames, you said he was intense. You never mentioned that he's full on crazy!"

Slade responded without even looking up, "He's got a lot of anger and he's too noble to take that out by hurting the wrong person."

"If you say so. But it's probably best if he doesn't know I'm Taurani. He might kill me in my sleep."

Badalao had sat on the adjacent couch to Marshall, Adria, and Horatio. He directed another question toward Slade. "And who is this General Grunt? If he's confiding with a general on an island far offshore, then where is he hiding the actual army? Perhaps this underground labyrinth is much larger than we think?"

Once again, Slade didn't move. "I know nothing of this general. You all need to keep in mind that I haven't seen Asarei in about twenty years, give or take. I'm not accountable for the man he is now. But I can tell you that he is still noble, honest, and honorable."

Kadoog'han yelled from a chair on the other side of the room. "Can everyone just be quiet about Asarei for a while? My friend Blastevahn just sang the most beautiful song I've ever heard, and *that's* what we should be focusing on!"

They erupted into shouts and cheers in agreement. They focused on Blastevahn for a while, which transitioned into various banter, until Manjobam returned with some others in tow. He shouted to regain their attention, "Friends! I have returned with most of the others!" They all stopped their conversations to focus on the new faces in the room, who looked as bewildered at what they were seeing as Marshall felt.

Manjobam continued, "Let me give you a proper introduction." They all lined up next to him and he introduced them in order. "Next to me is Krissette Luuk, then Neraiya Neikos, then Trevor Nightsmythe, and Ahvedool Bain, who most of us just call 'Dool.' After Dool is Asarei's wife, Candra, and daughter Dafne."

"What?" Marshall was glad his reaction was soft, as nobody heard him, but he instantly felt overwhelmed by his thoughts and emotions. Asarei having a daughter meant that she was half Taurani, and also the strongest candidate for repopulating the Taurani. Marshall glanced at Dafne again. She was thick like her father, looked of a similar age with Marshall, and not what he would consider pretty. *But should that matter when duty is at hand? Dammit.* He had made such strides in getting closer to Adria, and Dafne's mere existence threw it all into chaos. He tried to shake away all of the confusion and focus on Manjobam, who was introducing the two girls at the end of the line, who seemed closer in age to him than Dafne was.

"Lastly, these two young ladies are the Sisters Hammersland. Vilariyal and Faryal."

"Light of Orijin, are you bloody joking?!" Marshall turned to the source of the shout, which came from Baltaszar, a few couches away. In fact, everyone in the room looked at him as he jumped out of his chair and ran to the two girls who'd just been introduced. Marshall thought Baltaszar's eyes seemed glossy, but he couldn't be sure with how fast he'd moved. "My name is Baltaszar Kontez. My mother was Raya Hammersland, which means *we* are related." Baltaszar dropped to a knee and spoke more softly, "Which means I still have family in this world."

CHAPTER 16
HOLDING BACK

From **The Book of Orijin,** **Verse Three Hundred Two**
You must learn to hone your manifestations through focus and concentration.
If you would do so with your minds and your blades, the same must be done with your abilities.

DESMOND LEANED BACK AGAINST the tree trunk and focused on the blue-green winter apple in his hand. He had been so enamored with it for the past several minutes, that he'd almost forgotten why he picked it in the first place. He'd never seen apples of this color back in Vandenar, or anywhere else, for that matter. He held it farther away from him so he could concentrate more on levitating it.

He tried to let his manifestation take its course, rather than fighting it like he'd done in the past few weeks since they'd all gotten to the island. He stared at the apple and concentrated as hard as he could. After a moment, the apple jostled in his hand and then barely levitated from his palm. Desmond tried with all of his will to keep it there and lift it higher, but the small fruit defied his wishes and fell, bouncing off his hand to the ground.

"That apple would help you more in your belly than floating above your hand, *or* on the ground."

Desmond turned sharply towards the source of the voice. "Yer spyin' on me now?" Asarei stood behind him, to the right of the tree. To his surprise, the man didn't look angry.

"Hardly. I let you know I was here, right? If anyone's being deceitful, it's you. How many times since you've been here have you come out to the orchard to be by yourself? That's shitty if you ask me. Bam and Krissette are doing their damndest to train you all in combat and doing a hell of a job with all the others. You, you halfass everything, look like you're too tired to lift a sword, and then go off to hide and sulk once training is done."

Desmond didn't bother to move or stand. Instead, he looked straight ahead. "I've got some things ta sort out. Won't help if I'm around the others. Ain't like they're worried about it, anyway."

Asarei sat at the tree next to him and grabbed the apple that had fallen. "I get the feeling you've probably pissed some of them off with your attitude. Don't blame them because you'd rather feel sorry for yourself. Everyone's got their shit to deal with. You start telling yourself that your life is so much harder than everyone else's, well that's a hole that you'll just keep digging deeper."

"I can't even control my manifestation anymore. Seems like this hole's already deep."

"Do you know what my manifestation is, boy?"

Desmond shook his head, which tended to bring on more discomfort these days. "Nah. I don't think ya showed any o' us yet."

"There's not much to show. It's one of the reasons why I've put so much emphasis on being able to fight with my hands and with weapons, and others being able to as well. My manifestation is in my senses. They're heightened. Stronger. Even in the darkness of my meditation room, I could see how pale your skin is compared to the others. And I know you're Mireyan, so don't tell me your skin is supposed to look like that. I bet that if I tried to listen to your heart right now, it would be slower than it's supposed to be."

Desmond was starting to grow annoyed at him, "An' what's yer point? Ya sayin' I'm sick?"

"I'm saying you haven't nourished yourself properly since you got here, and at this point, it seems almost intentional. You've been here for weeks and you are exactly the same as when you got here. If this is your path, then why did you even come? You know as well as I do that you are not an asset to your friends' mission. You're a liability. You will only hurt their chances of succeeding if you insist on continuing this way. What will you do, help by staying out of the way? That's what Dafne used to do when she was too little to help. Is that what you've become? Will that be your legacy in the grand scheme of things?"

He clenched his jaw, unsure of whether he was angrier at Asarei or at himself for letting the man anger him. "I stopped the House o' Darian from crumblin' on us all when Jahmash's army attacked! Me! Every single one o' my companions is here right now because o' what I did. That's my legacy!"

"And you're content to stop there? The world hasn't stopped needing to be saved."

Desmond stood, then looked down at Asarei, "An' yet you chose ta hide here fer the last twenty years. Yer legacy up ta this point has been ta desert yer brothers an' sisters at the House o' Darian when ya could've helped in secrecy." His anger had reached its boiling point, and Desmond knew hitting Asarei would be imprudent, so he made a fist and punched the tree. He immediately crumpled to the ground and regretted the decision.

As he writhed in pain, choking on a scream that wouldn't or couldn't come out, Asarei knelt down next to him. "I wish you would've waited another half a second to do that, I would've told you not to. Though it's unlikely you would have listened to me. On the bright side, it looks like you do have some strength in you. The bad news is that you probably just broke your hand. And you know what, you're going to just deal with it, as a constant reminder to stop acting like a shithead. You think your friends don't care about you? Do you know how many of them have expressed their concern about you, but were convinced that talking to you about it would be futile? That's why I'm here. They figured you would listen to me."

Desmond continued to hold his hand, which felt so mangled that he dared not try to move it. He shut his eyes tightly as tears formed at the corners. In between holding his breath, he managed to respond, "Please...shut up. No lectures."

"I apologize for being so insensitive. Should I carry you back?" Desmond didn't respond to him. He stayed as he was, knees, feet, and forehead all against the ground while he kept his hand close to his body. He was sure that Asarei's presence had magnified the pain. The man continued his attempt at a conversation. "It should start to numb in a little while. Then perhaps you'll be more receptive. Anyway, let me help you up. You don't have to talk to me, but it'll be in your best interest to listen." He put a hand under Desmond's right armpit and pulled him to his feet. Desmond couldn't be sure whether Asarei pulled from that side because it was easier or because the other arm was hurt. As Desmond stood, Asarei looked at his face, "You know what, stay here for a minute. I'll get something that will help you." Asarei ran off while Desmond stood there, thinking about what the man could be doing. A few minutes later, he returned with a few long vines in his hands and, without asking or warning Desmond, used them to create a sling by wrapping them behind Desmond's neck and under his arm several times. He fastened it tightly enough to keep it close to Desmond's body, but without causing too much additional discomfort.

Desmond looked at him and uttered a "thank ya," through gritted teeth, which was more from the pain than a reluctance to show gratitude.

Asarei simply nodded, "Don't mention it. I figure the tree wasn't going to try to help you, so it might as well be me. Come on, let's walk. You mentioned that you saved a good number of lives during the attack on the House. I fully believe your courage and sacrifice saved the lives of many of your brethren, but I don't believe that you did it on your own. Maximillian already told me what happened, especially because he's seen the worst of your withdrawal. And that's what I want to talk to you about more than anything. I am likely the only one on this island who can honestly tell you that I know what you're going through. I know what it's like to try to manifest too much power and cling to a manifestation for too long."

He noticed Asarei picking a few more apples. They walked through the orchard and, for the slightest moment, Desmond forgot about his hand and gave Asarei his full attention, "Ya do? How?" He still needed to grit his teeth when talking.

"It was a long time ago. I'd say somewhere around twenty-five years ago? A friend of mine—his wife was taken from him right out of their house, and there was no trace of her. He couldn't go searching for her because of his young boys, actually you know Baltaszar. It was Baltaszar and his twin brother, Bo'az. Their father wouldn't dare leave them, and so Rhadames and I searched as much of Ashur as we could, with no luck. We both searched for over a year, and at one point, I got so fed up that I tapped into my manifestation as hard as I could, thinking that if I tried hard enough, maybe I could see her or hear her. I think I pressed on for over an hour until my body just gave out on me and I collapsed. Luckily, I was right outside the Colored Road Inn, in the City of the Fallen. Lots of friendly faces there. Some good people dragged me in, and I was bed-ridden for a while. No energy, no appetite, no will to do anything but lie there and try to get a taste of my manifestation again. And of course, without any energy or nourishment, the manifestation wasn't going to happen, which caused me to lose more hope."

To Desmond's surprise, Asarei had piqued his interest. He still talked in huffs, as the pain refused to subside. "How did ya get out o' it then?"

"There were a few others there who had seen it happen before. They gave me a lot of advice and pounded it into my head to do two things. First, eat, eat, and keep eating. That's the best remedy for fighting withdrawal, but it takes your body a while to get back to normal. It takes even longer to fix your mind. First few times you eat a good meal, there's a strong chance you'll throw some of it up. Second thing is to keep things small, meaning focus on each step and not the endpoint. One minute at a time, one bite at a time, one movement at a time. Appreciate those small victories and eventually they all add up."

Desmond had noticed that they'd left the apple orchard, as the trees were no longer dotted with those blue-green apples. He also realized that they hadn't gone down into the underground fortress. They'd passed the entrance a few minutes before and just kept walking. He wondered where Asarei was planning to go. His hand was still in terrible pain and he knew his body was growing weaker the farther they walked. "I know yer tryin' ta help, but where are we goin'? An' can we walk a bit faster ta get there?"

Asarei chuckled, "Oh I didn't think you could go faster than this. I guess a bloody broken hand will do that, huh. Yeah let's walk faster.

Don't worry, if you get too weak, I can always carry you." He flexed his arm as a show of his strength.

Desmond tried to slow his breathing, hoping that it might help with the pain, and maybe the anger as well. "The advice those people gave ya. Did it work?"

"Yes," Asarei responded adamantly. "But it didn't end quickly, which was the whole point of what they were saying. Focus on the small steps, rather than days or weeks at a time. If you can start doing that today, then I guarantee you that you'll feel like a new man by the time you're all ready to leave here."

Desmond nodded as his hand throbbed some more, "Are ya really not goin' ta help me get my hand healed? Can't I lose it if it's not tended ta in enough time?"

"You should've thought of that before you tried to hurt my tree. Maybe if you can keep yourself conscious until we get where we're going, I'll get someone to look at it."

"An' ya still haven't told me where we're goin'."

"We have a lot in common, believe it or not. More than I do with the others who stay here with me. Don't get me wrong, I get along well with all of them and would do anything for them, but none of them are really like me. Bam is the size of two trees, but also about as smart as one. Sweet as a lamb, though. He's not angry like me. Not holding anything in. Same goes for Trevor and Doolie. Nice boys but not aggressive. You on the other hand, you keep that anger inside of you, almost like a second manifestation. It can be good, but right now it's not going to help you, so we're going to go get rid of some of it. And after today, we'll do the same thing until it's all gone. Come on, you're slowing down again, let's pick up the pace again. We're almost there."

Desmond knew he couldn't go much longer than Asarei was suggesting. It was taking all of his focus to continue on when they finally reached the beach. The shapes started to get blurry, to the point where he couldn't tell if he was looking at trees or people in the distance. He heard Asarei point out that General Grunt was standing in plain sight not too far off, but by that time, Desmond was sure his eyes were playing tricks with him. "Wait, is that…?" Before he could finish his thought, he fell to the soft sand, still clutching his hand.

Before he completely blacked out, he heard Asarei complain, "Ah, shit on me, Orijin. I really thought he would stick it out. Dammit."

ADRIA WATCHED ON AS LINCAN and Delilah worked together to fix Desmond's hand. They seemed somewhat tentative in communicating with each other, though Adria had no idea why. *How much did I miss in my time away?* It was breathtaking to watch, though. Lincan had

Desmond's hand rested on his own, while Delilah used her manifestation to insert her fingers into his hand and reset the broken bones. Desmond remained awake and without any medicine at Asarei's orders. She caught a glance from Asarei and wasn't sure if he knew exactly what she was thinking, as he spoke to everyone in the room. "If anyone feels bad for him, don't. The pain he's going through right now is exactly what he wanted to inflict upon my apple tree."

She saw Desmond send a sharp look Asarei's way, but that was all he could muster, given the agony he was enduring. Adria wasn't sure if public healings had been a regular thing for Lincan or Delilah while she was away from the House, but it seemed everyone wanted to watch them fix Desmond's hand. All of the Ghosts of Ashur were present, as well as Asarei's people, and everyone stood in silence as they marveled at Lincan's and Delilah's work.

Once Asarei had agreed to let them stay on the island, the difficult part was determining where everyone would sleep. Of the twenty of Adria's company, sixteen were men, and there were no large quarters designated for guests, since no one even knew Asarei was on the island. They quickly turned the dining room into the men's sleeping room, as it had plenty of space on the couches and floor for them. Adria, Sindha, Farrah, and Delilah were the only females in the group, and they were able to turn the small study room on the other side of the fortress into quarters for the four of them. It had definitely been awkward being near Farrah, especially in such close quarters, but she tried to remember Savaiyon's advice every time she felt like punching the girl, which was quite often.

They had all been training with hand-to-hand combat and with weapons for the past few weeks, and every time Adria had to imagine a target, Farrah's face came to mind. Krissette, who was teaching them along with Manjobam, had even complimented Adria on her focus. *If she only knew who I was focusing on.* Krissette often chose Adria as a sparring partner, especially since they were of a similar height. They'd gotten along well in the past few weeks since training had begun, and Adria was glad for it. Despite Krissette being a few years younger, she was really the first girl that Adria had started a friendship with.

She supposed a big part of it was that Krissette loved to make fun of all the boys, and there were so many that there was always something to make fun of. Adria knew that most of them were good people and meant well, but nearly all of them tried a little too hard during training sessions. And Krissette's manifestation was the ability to mimic anyone's voice, which she used for mischief quite often. But that's what formed the connection in the first place. The first time Krissette had used it in front of them, she mimicked Badalao missing badly with a bow and arrow.

Once they all realized that the voice came from Krissette, Adria must have laughed nonstop for at least a few minutes. They instantly bonded after that.

She had gotten so lost in thought that she forgot about what was going on in front of her. A loud groan from Desmond reminded her. "Light o' Orijin, how bad is my hand?"

Delilah looked up at him, "How hard did you punch the tree? It seems like you broke every bone in your hand. And there are so many bones that I have to make sure each one is set in the right place for Lincan to heal. That's just the bones. Lincan will have to sort the rest of it out on his own." She looked at Asarei then back at Desmond, "Asarei was right to release everyone of their sympathies. Your idiocy is costing Lincan and me time and energy. Next time, don't be so stupid." Her words seemed to surprisingly humble Desmond, as he had no response except to purse his lips.

Adria blinked a few times at that. *Wow. That must've been some talk that Asarei gave him. A normal Desmond would have argued right back.* Asarei broke the tension for everyone, "How much more time do you two think you will need? Not that I'm rushing you."

Lincan looked up and wiped his brow, "Once we're done with the bones, Del can leave. It will take, I'd say less than an hour to mend the rest of his hand."

Asarei nodded. "Good. The rest of us will leave and let you finish in peace. I believe Neraiya has caught us a feast of fish for dinner. We will eat in two hours and then we will have a meeting afterwards. Every single person in this room is expected to attend. You have been here a month now, and I believe it is time to start setting in motion a specific plan for how to actually kill the King. At least we know for sure that Maqdhuum secured the alliance with the Kraisos, but that's not our focus right now. Everyone please leave the room and be prompt for dinner in the meditation room. Lincan, Delilah, I will be in the next room. Please inform me when you are finished, as I would like to speak with Desmond privately."

Adria looked at Asarei and then at Lincan and Delilah, who nodded in agreement. She was glad that Asarei was willing and able to help Desmond. He'd looked so sickly and unlike his normal self since they'd all arrived at the Tower of the Blind.

A voice spoke softly behind her, "Want to go have some private time?" At first she thought it might be Marshall being incredibly forward, but then the voice sounded strangely like Maqdhuum's, which freaked her out. Adria turned around cautiously and saw Krissette grinning widely. "Sorry, I couldn't help myself."

Adria let her guard down and laughed heartily. She grabbed

Krissette by the arm and filed in with the others as everyone left the room. "Actually, some private time with you wouldn't be so bad. Maybe some sword fighting before it gets dark?"

"How could I say no to that?" They walked on through the corridors, which Adria could now navigate much more easily than a month ago. Within a few minutes, they reached the training grounds, which were near where the touch portal had originally brought them. They both selected their two-handed swords from the armory wall and walked out to the open space in the middle of the training grounds. Krissette assumed her ready stance and eyed Adria. "Ready?"

She nodded, "Whenever you are."

Krissette stalked toward her as the last word left her mouth, eyes set on Adria's eyes the entire time. As she concentrated on Adria, the smile faded from her face. Adria focused on Krissette's movements as well. She wasn't sure if her friend would attack first, as her moves were more predictable during the group training. Adria continued to circle and take calculated steps. She was hesitant to make the first move, but also knew that in a real fight, she might have to. She kept her focus on Krissette's eyes and thrust her sword towards the girl's torso. Krissette sidestepped the strike with ease and countered with an overhand strike. Adria got her sword up in time to defend it, but it was clear that the strike wasn't full force. If it had been, Adria knew the fight likely would have been over already. She shoved Krissette's sword off of her own and reset. "Damn, I'm still too slow at this." She nodded at Krissette, "Come on."

They sparred for another half of an hour or so, but nothing changed for Adria. She struggled to defend Krissette's attacks, despite Krissette clearly holding back. "I know you will be upset, Adria, but I think we should stop."

"But I need to get faster. The only way to do that is to keep sparring."

Krissette cocked her head toward the armory, and Adria followed her reluctantly. They put their swords away, but as Adria was about to turn and walk back to the underground fortress, she saw Krissette sit on one of the stools. "Sit. There's no rush; we
still have much time until dinner." Adria listened and sat on a stool facing Krissette. *This is...unexpected.* Krissette looked her in the eyes again, just as when they were sparring. "It is only because we have become friends that I feel I can be so direct with you. You are older, so I don't want this to come across as disrespectful."

Adria was even more intrigued now. "Say what's on your mind. You won't offend me."

Krissette smirked, "That's what most people say before they take offense. But fine, friendship means honesty, so here goes. You have clearly made strides since we've begun training, both with and without weapons."

Here comes the 'but'.

"But, you are not slow because your body is holding you back."

"What do you mean?"

Krissette tapped a finger against the side of her head. "Whatever is limiting you is up here. There's something on your mind, and I don't blame you. Everyone has so much to think about these days, that it would be surprising if anyone was *not* stressed. But I've noticed that your focus lately has been off. That is normally your biggest strength."

Adria stared at the ground for a few moments. She knew *what* had been bothering her, she was just annoyed that someone else was able to notice it. Even worse, she was angry that it was affecting her ability to better herself. She decided that she might as well get it out of her system now, rather than let it continue to affect her. She looked back up at Krissette, "Can I confide in you?"

"Of course."

"Something *has* been nagging me, and it's silly, which is why I didn't really want to tell anyone else about it. It's new to me and I haven't been sure if it's a normal thing to be bothered by, or if it just means that I'm overreacting."

Krissette rolled her eyes, "Oh just get on with it. What is the matter?"

She took a deep breath. "Well, there is...something...happening between me and Marshall. I think? It seemed like when we were at the Tower of the Blind and then even in Shipsbane on our way here, there was something...blossoming. And I know I can't be imagining it because up to this point, I haven't thought of anyone that way, *especially* the boys from the House of Darian. But Marshall and I had just been connecting very well for a short time." She looked at Krissette tentatively, unsure of whether her friend would judge her.

"And obviously something changed along the way?"

"Shortly after we got here, I'd say after the first day or two, it's almost as if we haven't been able to get to that same level again. But it's more that he's been aloof and not as willing to engage. I've tried to have the same conversations and it's not the same anymore. And it's so frustrating because I don't know what I did that made him not want that anymore."

"I'm guessing that you haven't brought any of this up to him."

"That's another part that's frustrating me. Normally, I would have no problem being direct with someone and getting straight to the point. But I'm nervous; I'm hesitant to find out what it is about me that changed Marshall's mind."

"You're being too hard on yourself. What if it's something about him and not you? So many things changed the moment you all stepped onto this island. Maybe *he's* seeing something in a new perspective. Or perhaps he's stressed about something the way you are, and is so preoccupied with it that he does not realize he's acting differently."

Adria furrowed her brow, "Whose side are you on? You're supposed to be *my* friend."

Krissette smiled at her, "I apologize, I don't know what I was thinking. Forget everything I said. It's all his fault."

They both laughed for a few moments, "Thanks. I needed that."

"My pleasure. You should still just talk to him, though. That's always the most sensible thing to do." She got up, "Come. Let's go sit out there and look up at the sky. Now that it's dark, we can just look at the stars and not think about anything else." She took Adria's hand and they brought their stools out of the armory to look at the sky.

They stayed there for a while longer and then went inside to get ready for dinner. Even throughout the meal, Adria stuck with Krissette and kept quiet most of the time. She contemplated her friend's advice and knew that she was right about talking to Marshall, but that didn't make it any easier to actually do. By the time she finished her meal, Adria decided that she would wait to see what happened at the night's meeting, and then she would decide when to confront Marshall.

Once everyone had finished, Savaiyon created a few gateways into various rooms so that everything could be cleaned up and put away, save the tables and chairs. Once everything was sorted, Savaiyon closed the gateways and Asarei stood at the head of the largest table. "Twelve can sit at this table, and the rest can stand and gather close by. There are thirty of us in total, and no one is to be excluded. Come, gather around or sit."

Adria, Krissette, Neraiya, and Dafne were encouraged to sit, as they were the shortest. None of them took it as a slight. Dafne sat at the head of the table and Asarei stood behind her. Savaiyon asked, "Where should we begin?"

"First, I should make one thing clear." Asarei looked around at all of them. "For all of the guests to this island, we will gladly train you, prepare you, equip you with anything you need, but we will not be coming with you. And before anyone argues one way or another, let me explain." He rested his arms on the back of Dafne's chair. "You said the Anonymi's decree was that Edmund must be killed by someone who followed Zin Marlowe. They didn't say any Descendant could do it. If any of us from this island comes with you, then it enables the possibility that Edmund is not killed by the right person. If you want to ensure that this alliance happens, then that is my request. And I think it's fair."

Savaiyon walked over to stand next to Asarei. "He is right. We came here only to be trained for our mission, not to recruit more people." He turned to the rest of them, "And I should also make something understood. It is likely that I will not be able to help the rest of you either, nor will Rhadames or Maqdhuum."

Asarei looked at Savaiyon confusedly, "What do you mean?"

"Another secret to add to the collection. I also belong to the Anonymi. Marlowe was the only other person who knew. That is why Vasher had to make the request to them." Adria was stunned, but quiet. She hadn't considered that Savaiyon might not be part of the mission. It almost felt like being in an army without a general to lead them.

Asarei nodded, "Wow. For once, I'm speechless. That's almost as big as this one being Abram." He pointed across the table at Maqdhuum. "I would ask what else you're all hiding, but I guess we could probably spend a whole week just getting all the secrets out of you. Fine, that makes things more difficult for you, but definitely not impossible. Well first things first. Prince...I apologize. I'm aware that you're no longer a prince to that shitty king. Garrison, how big is your father's palace and what is the most sensible way to attack it?"

Garrison was standing at the side of the table, behind Desmond. "It would help if I could actually show you. Can someone grab...plates or mugs or something that I can use to create some kind of map on the table?"

Within a second, Savaiyon had already created a gateway and walked through it. In a few moments, he walked back out with plates, bowls, and mugs stacked and balanced in his arms. Garrison quickly took some from him and put them on the table, and Savaiyon set the rest down. "That should be enough." He then closed the gateway.

"Thanks." Garrison arranged the various items into a pattern on the table, then rearranged here and there until he was satisfied. "Well, it will have to do. That cup and plate there are the entrance and throne room. That is how most people enter, and where my father sees people publicly. In truth, he avoids that room as much as he can. I'm assuming we will infiltrate at nighttime, which means he will be in his chambers. Right there." He pointed to a small bowl that sat on a plate, surrounded by a few mugs. "It is difficult to explain, but his and my mother's chambers are below the castle. That big plate is the grand ballroom. Along the northeastern wall...I think...is a secret entryway to the underground corridors that lead to his chambers. I've never actually used it myself, as Donovan and I never have any reason to go down there.

"Without Savaiyon or Maqdhuum, we have no way to sneak in. That means that we'll be noticed at some point, and we'll have to fight guards inside the palace. Once that happens, my father will almost definitely be in his underground chambers, protected by more guards." Garrison looked up from the table and glanced at everyone around the table. "I hate to say it, but in order to do this, we're likely going to have to kill and hurt a lot of people."

To Adria's surprise, and annoyance, Farrah responded. "Interesting how killing people bothers you now, Garrison."

Adria was glad that Farrah was on the other side of the table so she couldn't hit her. "Farrah, shut up. The rest of us are putting our differences aside and have been for the past month. If you don't grow up, I'll kick you so hard that you wouldn't need the touch portal to land back in Shipsbane." Adria didn't wait for a response, though Farrah's glare hinted that there likely wouldn't be one. She turned to Garrison. "Garrison, if we wait long enough for your brother to turn them, perhaps their numbers will be low enough that we can just capture any guards there who actually fight back."

Garrison shrugged, "I do not know." He looked around at everyone again. "Realistically, what is our timeline to actually do this? If we are willing to wait, then it will help Donovan's and Wendell's cause. But what they are doing is not something that simply happens overnight."

Baltaszar stepped forward between Lincan and Horatio. "Do you know if they freed Virgil from the dungeons, or is he still a prisoner in there?"

Garrison's eyes grew wide, "Virgil is a *prisoner*?"

"Yeah, we spoke while I was there in the dungeon, before your brother and Wendell moved me. He was rather open with me about his allegiances and deeply regretted taking your father's side over yours, Garrison. He mentioned he was one of the King's Royal Guards; surely that holds more weight than a regular soldier. My point is, perhaps he can be used to help sway some of the other soldiers, and even Royal Guards, who need more convincing."

Garrison nodded. "That could actually help. The next time we connect with my brother, I will have Lao suggest it. Still, though, we have to prepare for a fight in which we are vastly outnumbered. Any suggestions?"

Asarei responded, "That depends on your manifestations. I know they are a private thing and by no means am I forcing anyone to share, but your manifestations will dictate how this siege goes, far more than anything else. Not only that, but along with regular combat training, it would be prudent to start learning to use your manifestations more...violently. I know at the House of Darian, that is not something you focused on, but for the sake of this mission, *and* to be able to fight Jahmash and his armies, you will need your manifestations to be your most powerful weapons."

Baltaszar spoke again, "Once we have a better idea of what's what in the palace, we can find a place for me to start a fire. That's bound to get the soldiers inside on the move."

Garrison replied, "It could work. You start a fire on one side, then perhaps Reverron can...carry you back to us?"

Reverron nodded, "He is not too big where that would be a problem. No offense, Tasz."

Baltaszar smiled, "You just said I'm not too fat to carry. None taken."

"Aside from Tasz's fire, are there other manifestations that could be used to attack?"

To Adria's surprise, Desmond, who also sat at the table, responded first. "I can levitate things. Or I'll be able ta by the time we're ready fer this mission. Used it ta hurl all the broken pieces o' the House at all the ships that were attackin' us."

Horatio added, "I can summon the lightning. As long as I'm not exhausted, I'm decent at hitting my targets."

Malikai stepped up to the back of Krissette's chair, "My skin can harden to the point where it's basically a weapon. I've punched some holes in walls before. I figure it'll work on people."

Manjobam looked at Malikai, "We should have a contest one day about who hits the hardest." Shortly after they'd arrived on the island, it was revealed that Manjobam was incredibly strong, more so than several people combined. Asarei explained in great detail that Manjobam had basically created the underground fortress all by himself, just hitting away at the dirt and rock underground. It had taken several months to create the basic structure and outline, but he did it all. Asarei told them it was why he started calling him 'Bam' as a nickname, because he loved to hit things as hard as he could.

Malikai smiled at Manjobam, "As long as it's not each other, I'm always ready."

Lincan raised his hand and spoke up, "I don't know if this counts, but on our way to the Tower of the Blind, I learned that I can use my manifestation to make people sick as well. I don't just heal people. It has to be through physical contact, but it can still be helpful."

Savaiyon shook his head, "Lincan, I appreciate your intentions, but your ability to heal is far more important than being able to attack, at least for a mission like this. The Ghosts will assuredly take on injuries, and we will need you ready to heal. If anything were to happen to you, it would be a huge blow to us." Lincan nodded and darted his eyes around the room. Adria looked away to avoid eye contact. She knew for sure that he wanted to be able to fight.

Asarei responded, "Agreed. Anyone else?" The room was quiet for a few moments. "Very well, then. Four attackers, which means four fronts. Each of you will lead a group, composed of the rest of you, who will train tirelessly to fight with your hand and with weapons. I will still gauge your manifestations and see what can be done to weaponize any of them, or at the very least, make them even more useful for a mission like this. Blastevahn, this is not meant as a slight, but even something as innocuous as singing could be turned into an asset. So, if any of you are insecure about your manifestations, don't be."

Garrison added, "I can also get to work on weapons and armor that might complement your manifestations."

Asarei nodded, "Good."

Sindha chimed in, standing on the other side of the table from Adria, "My father is a blacksmith down in Itarse, and is quite well-respected at the armory there. Before we leave for Alvadon, with your permission, Savaiyon, I could go there and ask for any weapons and armor that he can spare. I could do it discreetly, so no one connects it with what we're setting out to do."

Savaiyon nodded, "That would help, Sindha. I agree; within the next few days, you will go there and see your family, and then see what your father can do. Likely he will have to measure us for armor, if he's willing to supply us with that. Anything he can give us will be of great value. Preferably swords, shields, and armor."

"Now comes the hardest part." Asarei patted his daughter's head. "Which of you is going to actually kill King Edmund?"

Adria looked around the room and took a deep breath. All the others looked around at each other as well, dozens of eyes shifting around without actually looking at anyone in the face. In this moment, Adria realized a truth about them, though she wasn't sure how to take it. This whole time, they'd been planning for a siege, as well as engaging in discussions about an eventual showdown against Jahmash. Up until now, those had all been words and plans for some day far into the future. She could see it in all their faces, and knew the same expression was on her own. They were not killers or assassins. Some, if not most of them, had killed before, for survival or self-defense, but this mission was different. They were initiating an attack on the most powerful man in Ashur, with the intent to kill.

She understood now why the Anonymi set these terms. King Edmund aside, if they wanted to have a real chance of defeating Jahmash and his armies, it would not just be a fight for survival. They would have to go on the offensive and strategize how to kill hundreds of enemies. The tension in the room signified that none of them were close to being ready for that.

"I'll do it." Malikai sheepishly raised his hand and looked around the room. "I figure I have the best odds of making it that far, right? As long as I maintain my manifestation, I can make it that far, and I can do it."

Malikai's courage spread to Horatio, "I'll join him. Between the two of us, we can definitely get it done. Besides, I should probably redeem myself after what happened with Marlowe." Adria whipped her head around to look at Savaiyon, and just as she expected, his stoic countenance distorted into a grimace. There was never any formal discussion about Marlowe's death, and whether or not to talk about it in front of Asarei. But they had all, or all except Horatio, understood that if Savaiyon hadn't shared it with Asarei when he had the chance, then nobody else should do so.

Asarei cocked an eyebrow, "What happened with Marlowe?"

Horatio glanced back and forth between Asarei and Savaiyon until finally Savaiyon turned to Asarei. "Another secret that we get to share with you." To his credit, Asarei didn't look surprised, upset, or offended. Adria assumed he was used to this by now. Savaiyon continued, "The Anonymi's terms actually consisted of two parts. They told Vasher that those of us at the House of Darian were responsible for killing the *two* biggest threats to the well-being of Ashur. The first threat was actually Zin Marlowe, while Edmund is the second."

"Holy shit. They told you to kill Marlowe and you just did it? That easily? Horatio, you underestimated me."

Savaiyon put a hand up to stop Asarei, "It is not that simple. Vasher, Marlowe, and I were the only ones who knew about these terms. This secret was kept until we all reconvened at the Tower of the Blind. So Horatio didn't even know what he had done. Furthermore, Horatio didn't mean to target Marlowe in the first place." Adria looked over at Horatio, whose excitement seemed to turn to embarrassment. "During the attack on the House, basically everyone you see here regrouped in the infirmary. Marlowe revealed to us that his manifestation was the ability to change his appearance to resemble anyone. The plan was that he would go outside and make himself look like Drahkunov and tell the enemy to retreat back to the ships. While this was all happening, Horatio was in and out of consciousness on one of the cots, oblivious to what the plan was.

"So, when we all went up to make a final stand, Horatio eventually followed. Out on the shores, he thought he was striking Drahkunov down, when in actuality it was Marlowe. When he says he wants to redeem himself, he means that he wants to kill Edmund on purpose, as I told him it was a lucky mistake that Marlowe died by his hands."

"Why didn't you just tell me that back when you told me about Edmund?"

Savaiyon sighed. "More than anything, I was trying to protect Horatio. We had only revealed everything a few days before that. Also, there was so much to discuss, that I didn't think that needed to be shared right away. I wasn't sure how you would react to it, and it wasn't a pressing detail at the time. Asarei, you *heard* that the House of Darian was destroyed less than two months ago. We *lived* through that destruction. And if not for Lincan's ability to heal, or me, Kadoog'han, and Rhadames going back there, a few more people would not be standing in this room." He waved his finger at everyone around the table. "Most, if not all, of them have not even seen their twentieth summer yet. They are not seasoned warriors like you or Rhadames. They will *become* warriors by the time you are done with them, but you must understand what they are coming from in order to prepare them for where they are going."

Asarei gave Savaiyon a toothy grin. "That was so poetic. If you survive Jahmash, you can be a bard when it's all done. But I see your point. Based on what you're saying, Garrison, your brother will need time to convince more soldiers to switch sides anyway. So we don't need you all to be ready in a week or anything. Which is good, because it's going to take some time to work with all of you and see what you can do. We start tomorrow morning. Desmond, Raish, Tasz, Kai, you will work directly with me. The four of you will be the front lines of the attack, which means you all need to be perfect at what you do.

"Bam, Krissette, you will continue to train them. Trevor, Doolie, Neraiya, the three of you will also instruct them on how to fight." He looked at the Ghosts around the table, "Those of you who call yourselves Ghosts, these five are not your enemies. You listen to them; you do things exactly as they say. I will sort out all the other arrangements in the morning. Everyone, go to your quarters and get a good night's sleep. Starting tomorrow, you will likely be sore and bruised every night."

CHAPTER 17
FAMILY SECRETS

From **The Book of Orijin,** **Verse Eleven**
Life without truth is not a full life.
Always seek to share truth and learn it.

YASAMAN TOOK ONE OF THE SAILOR'S hands as she eased herself over the side of the boat and onto the small dock, and secured Zane against her chest with the other hand. "Thank you," she said softly. Zane was still sleeping and she didn't want to ruin that. The last few days had been rough for him, as she never felt comfortable staying in one place for very long. Even when she slept, she found herself waking up every few hours. She wasn't sure if there were real threats in the Never, or if all of the stories just put it in her mind, but she wasn't going to take any chances with Zane, who was barely over three months old. "So how do I get to Vandenar from here?" She was glad that Oran Von had reminded her of the city's name before she left, or else she would have easily forgotten it.

The sailor, whose name she definitely forgot, replied, "My dear, that's where we're headed with our fish. No way we'll have ya get there all by yerself, especially with a baby. These are changin' times an' it's not safe ta be travelin' by yerself anymore. Even worse if ya got a black line down yer face. Come. We have a wagon waitin' fer us a little ways ahead, where the road begins."

She was grateful for their offer, as she wasn't looking forward to more walking. Yasaman also just wanted to get somewhere where she could change her clothes and lie down on a bed for a while. Walking alone would only prolong that. She'd waited on the other side of the river for nearly an hour until she saw this boat, just as Von had advised her to do, and managed to track it down. The other sailor hefted a barrel over the side and onto the dock, then hopped over to join them. *Ugh they stink. Hopefully it doesn't wake Zane.* She tried to stay pleasant, especially since both men had been extremely nice and accommodating to her.

The wagon ride to Vandenar lasted a few hours, and Zane slept for most of that time. She knew he was making up for the past few days, and Yasaman hoped to do the same once she could get a bed. Oran Von had given her a coin bag to hold her over for a while. He'd gotten to see firsthand how her mother treated her, and Yasaman could see the sympathy in his face when she told him she was ready to leave Haedon. *If only I'd known that there was more than just Haedon, I would have left sooner, before everything got so crazy.*

By mid-morning, they finally rode into the city and stopped shortly after. The driver hopped out and came around to help her down. "Our stand is right up there. We'll just carry the barrels over an' set up. Ya know where yer headed?"

"Not exactly. I would like to start with a nice bed and something to eat."

The wiry man nodded, "Easy enough. Happy Elephant is right there, on the other side o' the road. Cyrus is the innkeeper; he'll take good care o' ya."

Yasaman smiled, "Thank you."

The other man walked up holding her pack. "Need me ta carry this over fer ya?"

"No, that's not necessary. It's not too heavy, but thank you. And thank you for all of your help and hospitality. Good luck."

Both men waved as she walked away, and the wiry one replied, "Same, dear. Good luck with yer search."

Yasaman nodded and walked toward the inn that they'd pointed out. She was somewhat nervous, as she'd never actually been in an inn before. She didn't like the idea of being around too many people, so she hoped that it wasn't too busy inside. Zane was awake now and strapped securely to her front, inside her coat. Luckily he was still quiet and just looking up at her. She stopped at the doors, took a deep breath, and walked in. She was relieved to see that the place was not bustling. *Maybe it's busier at night?*

A chubby, bald man stood behind the counter to the right and smiled at her as soon as she looked at him. "Welcome, welcome, dear! This is the Happy Elephant, an' I'm Cyrus. Here, let me take yer pack! No need fer ya ta be carryin' that around. Ya plannin' ta spend the night?"

"Yes, well…"

"Great! If yer ready ta go up, I can have 'em bring it up fer ya. Or if yer hungry, ya can stay down here an' have a bite first."

Nice man, but way too excited. "Maybe I can stay and eat, and have my pack brought up? If that's no trouble?"

"O' course that's no trouble. You go sit, I'll take care o' it. An' I'll send Fae over ta tend ta ya."

"Thank you, that's very nice of you. I'll sit right there." She pointed to a small table along the wall, away from other patrons. Cyrus smiled and nodded, then returned behind the counter.

Yasaman sat at the table and looked down at Zane, who was trying to pull at her shirt. She adjusted his knit hat, which was halfway off. "Hi baby, you're happy this morning, aren't you? Finally got some good sleep?" Zane giggled back at her, as he normally did when her voice got soft and melodic. She played with his hands and made faces until a maid walked over to the table.

"What a cute baby! What's yer name, little one?"

Yasaman smiled and looked up at the girl, whom she speculated was around the same age as her. "Thank you. His name is Zane."

"Aw. pleasure ta meet ya, Zane. An' ye too, dear. My name's Fae." She eyed the empty seat across the table, "Anyone else comin'?"

Yasaman pushed aside her annoyance at the assumption. She knew she wouldn't get far in a new world if she treated idiots like idiots. She would have to be nice and smile at people, even when they asked stupid and annoying questions. She would also have to draw sympathy from strangers. *And sweet, innocent Fae is probably a good start.* She smiled back at Fae, "Thank you. I'm Yasaman, or just Yas. Just me and Zane, thanks. I'm actually setting off to search for Zane's father. He's one of those...what do you call them? With the black lines?"

Fae's eyes perked, "A Descendant? Oh wow. Too bad ya didn't come a while back; we haven't had any in town in a few months. Ever since the House o' Darian was destroyed, seems they've all gone inta hidin'."

Yasaman realized there was a lot she didn't understand about Ashur, or about Baltaszar's life beyond Haedon. She tried to follow along, "How many of them are there?"

Fae shrugged, "I honestly couldn't tell ya. Most o' my days are spent here, an' these days we don't get many outsiders, so there's not much gossip. But if the House o' Darian was destroyed, then I imagine there can't be many left. Oh, I'm bein' rude. Are ya hungry?"

Yasaman was waiting for her to ask; she was starving. "Oh yes, I'm famished. A nice big breakfast would be amazing. Also, do you think there's anyone in Vandenar who might be able to help me locate Baltaszar Kontez? Even point me where to go beyond Vandenar?" She noticed Fae's expression changed from happy to confused for a moment, but then changed back to a smile.

"Did ya say...Baltaszar?"

"Yes! Baltaszar is Zane's father and he left Haedon while I was still pregnant. I need to find him so our family can be reunited."

Fae's eyes shifted up for a moment, then alternated back between Yasaman and whatever was on the ceiling. *Has she met him before or something?* "Ya know what. I think I know someone who might be able ta help ya. I'll send her over when yer food's ready. Now ya said yer hungry, right? Eggs an' elephant steak then? That's our specialty, better than anywhere else in Vandenar."

Yasaman cringed, "Elephant? Like in the stories? No, the eggs will do fine. If you have potatoes or any other vegetables, I'll have that with the eggs."

"If ya say so, but the steak is pretty darn good. I'll bring it out in a bit, an' I'll bring Anahi with me. Ya can tell her about yer search fer Baltaszar." Fae turned to walk away and her smile was bigger than before.

Yasaman nodded and looked back at Zane, who was starting to fuss. "I agree, little man. She is a strange girl. I hope the rest of the people in this town aren't as annoying as she is." She looked around the room to gauge the crowd, but it was mostly empty. She wriggled her shirt down to feed Zane, and he suckled for a minute or two and pulled his mouth away. Yasaman adjusted herself and then put Zane to her shoulder to burp him. She patted him for another minute or two until he made that sound that made her smile every time.

As she was about to secure Zane back into the sling that hung from her neck, Fae returned with a plate of food and another girl. "Came up pretty quick, since ya didn't want the steak. I tried ta get them ta give ya extra vegetables, just ta help with yer nourishment. I'm sure feedin' that little cutie takes somethin' extra out o' ya. Got ya some cider, too." Fae placed the plate and mug on the table in front of Yasaman. "Oh, my apologies. This is Anahi; she also works here. She's met Baltaszar before, an' if ya just tell her everything ya just told me, I'm sure she can help ya in some way." Fae slowly turned and walked away.

Anahi sat at the table across from Yasaman and looked at her so deeply that Yasaman thought she was trying to look through her. She would never tell the girl, but her grey eyes were beautiful, and like nothing she'd ever seen. After a second, Anahi spoke. "It's nice ta meet ya...what was yer name again?"

"Yasaman. It's nice to meet you as well. Fae told me that you might be able to help me? I'm searching for someone." She awkwardly shifted Zane, who was drifting off, to grab her fork and take a bite of her eggs.

Anahi smiled, "Here. Why don't ya let me hold him while ya eat. It'll be easier fer ya."

Yasaman eyed her curiously, "Are you sure? That would be extremely helpful." Yasaman couldn't remember the last time someone had offered to give her a reprieve. Most of the times at home, she resorted to eating while Zane napped, but she couldn't remember her mother ever offering to take Zane off her hands.

"O' course I'm sure. We don't get many babies at the inn, it'll be nice ta hold one." Yasaman nodded and slowly lifted Zane as Anahi stood and came around to take him. She cradled him in her arms and sat back down. She looked down at Zane and then up at Yasaman with a smile. "So how can I help ya?"

"Oh. Right." She finished chewing and told Anahi about Baltaszar and how she knew he was out in Ashur somewhere. She also told the girl how Baltaszar was Zane's father and how he'd left Haedon before Zane was born, and that she just wanted to find him so that all three could be together again. She was surprised at how interested Anahi was; it was almost as if the girl hung on every word she said. "You seem really interested; I didn't think it was that exciting of a story."

"Well," Anahi paused for a moment, "We don't get much excitement up here. An' the Descendants are as interesting as they come, so anytime someone has stories about them, we eat it all up." She smiled at Yasaman. "We've met Baltaszar here before. Stayed at this inn a couple o' times. He never mentioned a wife an' baby, though."

Yasaman talked through chewing a seasoned potato. "We never got married, he had to leave Haedon before we had the opportunity, and before Zane was born, so Tasz never actually met him. Maybe he was too worried to want to talk about it. He didn't want to leave, but I told him that he had to. But now that Zane is here, I feel like we could be there to support him, help ease his tension." She noticed that Anahi's countenance grew intense.

"Ya know, Tasz *did* mention that he has a brother. Bo'az?" Yasaman's face tightened at the mention of Bo'az. Anahi continued to stare at her, "Why didn't he want ta come with ya an' find his brother? Would be a lot easier fer ya ta travel through Ashur with someone, rather than by yerself."

Yasaman paused for a moment. The thought of Bo'az had caught her off-guard. "Bo'az...is not in Haedon anymore. He left a long time ago and I don't know where he went. You're right; it would have been nice to have someone to keep me company and help with Zane, but I don't have that luxury. Besides, I'm a strong young woman, likely just like you." She noticed a half-grin appear on Anahi's face as she took her last bite.

"Oh are ya all done? I'll have Fae come over ta grab yer plate." As Yasaman chewed, Anahi called for Fae to come to the table. She swallowed it down and took a gulp of the cider, which was surprisingly good. Fae arrived at the table, but she wasn't smiling as she had before. She looked back and forth between Anahi and Yasaman. *What the hell is going on? She gets stranger by the minute.* Yasaman was about to offer to take Zane back when Anahi stood up from the table and turned to Fae. "Fae, would ya be a dear an' hold this sweet baby fer a moment. An' then ya can take her plate away."

Fae nodded and put her arms out to hold Zane. "O' course." Anahi gave her the baby and stepped up to the table, right in front of Yasaman, who still sat.

The confusion was engulfing Yasaman's mind at this point. "What is going…"

Before she could finish the question, Anahi struck her across the face with the back of her hand so hard that Yasaman felt bits of food fly out of her mouth. Yasaman held her cheek and turned back to Anahi. "No, don't move. Don't stand up. Yer goin' ta sit there an' ye'll listen, because all ye've done since ya got here is lied ta me an' Fae. Yer a huge pile o' elephant crap, thinkin' ya can fool us!"

Yasaman tried to play the fool, calling Anahi's bluff. "I don't know what you're talking about."

"Ya talked enough. Now's yer turn ta shut up. Ya know exactly what I'm talkin' about. I know the truth, because Baltaszar has told me the truth. That baby isn't his, it's his brother's! An' he doesn't want ta be with ya. He's had enough o' ya an' he's moved on. All o' us in the 'Elephant', we've met him and talked to him, an' know him well. I'm goin' ta give ya one chance ta leave here peacefully with yer baby an' yer things. If ya don't, ya should know I can hit harder than that first slap." Anahi eyed her up and down, gauging her next step.

Yasaman stood and glared at Anahi. She knew she would not fight the girl, but wouldn't dare let either of them see her looking weak. "Give me back my child." Fae handed Zane to her and they walked with her to the entrance.

Cyrus was still at the front counter. He stopped talking to another man and looked on curiously. "What happened? What's the matter with our new guest?"

"They are kicking me…" Yasaman tried to get a word in, but Anahi cut her off.

"Cyrus, ya remember our boy, Baltaszar?"

"O' course! He was just here, what, a month or two ago? Love that boy."

"Well, Yasaman here is tryin' ta find him, an' is spreadin' lies about him in the process. Ya see, her cute little boy here is actually the son of Baltaszar's twin brother, but she's spreadin' lies that it's Baltaszar's child."

Cyrus scratched his head, "Why would she do that?" Once again, Yasaman tried to defend herself, but Anahi denied her the opportunity.

"Because she's a bottom feeder, like the catfish at the bottom o' the river. Yasaman, ya see, we cherish the Descendants here, like they deserve ta be. An' when rubbish like yerself comes here an' tries ta spread lies about them, that makes ya no longer welcome."

Cyrus nodded his head, "She's right." He turned to walk the other way. "I'll be right back." He hesitated, as if he was about to say more, but then kept walking.

Dammit. What the hell do I do now? I have to find another inn. "Fine, but can you at least tell me where I can find another inn? If not for my sake, at least for my son?"

Anahi looked at her flatly, as if seeing through her attempt for sympathy. "The Vandenar Pub is not far up the road. Ya can get a room there." Cyrus returned shortly with her pack and handed it to Yasaman, and she slung it around her back while adjusting Zane and went on her way. She was hoping to think of something sharp to say to them as she walked out, but nothing witty enough came to mind.

BALTASZAR SAT ON THE other side of the armory from the training grounds, waiting for Lincan to finish his sword training. They'd started their more focused training over a month ago and Baltaszar could see the strides he was making. Asarei had taken the time to see what he, Horatio, Malikai, and Desmond were capable of. He had focused on each of them individually, sometimes for whole training sessions, just to try new things. Baltaszar had told him about the fire drops that he'd created in Haedon, and they worked on perfecting that for days. Asarei had gotten Baltaszar to concentrate hard enough that he could even control the exact area he wanted the fire drops to cover. The only issue was that doing so took a tremendous amount of energy out of Baltaszar, so it wasn't something he could do on a regular basis.

They found that out the hard way after a day in which Baltaszar worked on it for a few hours without stopping. Baltaszar collapsed in the middle of the training grounds and blood flowed from his nose and ears. Asarei was likely the best person who could have been there, as he'd seen it happen many times before, and had even experienced it. He had brought Baltaszar in immediately and laid him down on a couch, then forced him to drink what felt like a river. After a few days of just resting and eating, Baltaszar had finally been able to resume training.

As a result, he could control multiple fireballs at a time, and Asarei had instructed him to practice that on his own. He kept pushing himself to control more and more and, now, Baltaszar could create nine fireballs at one time, while being able to control each one simultaneously. Asarei had wanted him to be able to get to at least ten. Baltaszar figured that might take another month or so, as it took all of his concentration to focus on nine.

Vilariyal and Faryal, his cousins, came and sat on the ground a few yards away from him, which altered his focus just enough for him to lose control of the fireballs. Luckily he'd learned to just let them dissipate quickly when that happened. He'd been spending as much time as he could with them, which hadn't amounted to much, as they were busy tending to the needs of everyone, such as cooking, cleaning, gardening, and traveling back to Shipsbane for goods.

They were also of a similar age as Baltaszar, as Vilariyal was a year older than him, and Faryal two years his younger. He looked at them and smiled, "It's been a few days, huh? Asarei is really keeping you busy."

Vilariyal shrugged, "We're just filling in for some of the others who are training all of you now. It's not as bad as you think, it's just we're quite used to a life of leisure here. Not that we don't help with things, just usually not to this extent." She nodded at her sister, "Also, this one is in bed after dinner every night now."

Baltaszar laughed. He'd wondered why he hadn't really seen Faryal at night anymore. "Well, while I have you here, would you mind if I asked a few things? Before you have to run off and tend to something else?"

"Ask away. We might have answers," Faryal said. "I know we've mentioned this before, but we're also excited to know we have family as well. All this time, we thought we were the only ones left."

"It's so strange, right?" Baltaszar mused, "It's like, we should have known each other our whole lives, and even though we only met a few months ago, there's a familiarity."

Vilariyal nodded, "I know exactly what you mean. So what do you want to know about?"

"I'll ask what I think is the easier question first." Baltaszar hesitated a moment. He wasn't necessarily nervous, but he hoped the question didn't offend them. "I know my mother's family was Galicean. And so I'm assuming you two grew up there. Why don't you have Galicean accents?"

The two girls looked at each other and laughed heartily for a few moments until Faryal finally regained her composure enough to respond. "Asarei made us lose them."

He cocked his head sideways, "Lose them? What do you mean?"

Faryal's expression became serious, "Well, it wasn't all funny. It all stemmed from sadness actually. Our father, your uncle, died about five years ago. Asarei kept in touch with him frequently, and even came to see us usually about twice a year while our dad was still alive. He got sick, and our mother had already died a few years before that, so we wrote Asarei to tell him what happened. He came immediately to look after us for a short while. We knew we couldn't stay there; the farm was just too big for the two of us to maintain, and we didn't have much interest anyway. Asarei eventually sold our parents' home and farm for a good amount of coin and then let us decide what we wanted to do. We could take the money and look after ourselves, or he offered to let us come with him here, and told us that we would never have to use a single coin for as long as we stayed here, and we could leave whenever we want to.

"The only condition was that we had to lose the accents, because he couldn't stand them. Honestly, we had no idea what he wanted us to do, but he told us to just be patient. And so, once we got here, every day he would spend time with us to change our way of speaking."

Baltaszar was baffled by the explanation. He wasn't sure what the answer would be, but he wasn't expecting that. "Wow. So how long did that take?"

Faryal continued, "Not as long as you might think. I guess because we worked at it every day, maybe it happened faster. I would say less than two months? And of course, everyone you've seen here was here before us, so we had people to talk to all the time. It was easy to practice because we were interacting with them regularly."

Baltaszar shook his head, "That's crazy. He's got so many little...quirks, that it's hard to keep track of. Speaking of which, do you two know anything about General Grunt? He keeps mentioning that he has to meet with this man, or consult with him, and I don't know why the rest of us haven't gotten to meet him. Why have a secret person on the island? It doesn't make any sense to me."

Vilariyal stuck out her bottom lip and shrugged, "We're not at liberty to speak about General Grunt. Sorry."

"Of course. I should've known. Fine then," he paused and stared at the ground for a moment. He'd only asked the question as a stalling tactic for what he really wanted to ask. It had been one of the things he'd wanted to know for so long, especially once he'd found out that his mother had been abducted, rather than killed. His two cousins were the only ones who might possibly have information about what happened the night his mother disappeared.

Vilariyal softened her voice, "What's wrong, Tasz? You look upset."

He took a deep breath and then looked at both of them. "There's something I've wanted to ask you both since the moment we met, and either I've been too nervous or there wasn't enough time. So while there *is* time right now, can you tell me anything you might know or remember about the night my mother was taken?"

Vilariyal nodded and clasped her hands on her lap, "I don't remember much. I think I had seen about three summers by that time. What I know about that day is a mix of glimpses of memories and what my father told me. Fary was just a baby, so both of us were in the house with our mother. I'm not sure if you know, but our house was a stone's throw away from yours. Whenever your mother brought pies over, they were still hot when they got to our house." She fiddled with her fingers,

"Anyway, I think it happened in the morning, because my father was already out on the farm, tending to the animals. I think either you or your brother was being fussy, which caused your father to still be inside helping your mother, or else he would've been out already as well.

"At first I believe there were shouts, and then the fire started. It wasn't long before we saw it, and I know it didn't take my father very long to run to your house. From what my father told us, a man was in your house, and he grabbed her and left. Your father swore they were gone so fast, that by the time he even tried to give chase, the fire broke out. He was there when the line on your face appeared. Your father said that he thought he saw the man return and attempt to get at him, but the fire was so thick and strong that he couldn't reach your father and he left. My father was able to help get you and your brother out without anyone getting hurt.

"The one thing I remember most was that Bo'az didn't say a word, and the only thing you kept repeating was 'They disappeared,' over and over again. Of course, you were younger than I was, so you might've been babbling. But I feel like it was all you said for days. After that, you three stayed at our home until your father decided it was time to leave."

Baltaszar didn't realize until she was done speaking that his eyes were closed. He was trying to picture everything Vilariyal was describing to him, but it was difficult. He couldn't blame her; if he had no memory of the event, her recollection wouldn't be much better. "Thank you for telling me everything. I had a feeling you wouldn't be able to tell me exactly what happened, but what you did share was helpful. I just wish my father could have told me the truth about everything before he died. It's like I've been left to piece my own life together, and all of the pieces have been some huge secret from the world and from me."

Faryal offered some encouragement, "I can't imagine how difficult it all is for you, but you should know that the two of us are here for you every step going forward. Things will be different now."

He nodded a thank you. "The same goes for both of you. We're all that's left of our family, which means we have to keep intact the memories we *do* have."

They talked about lighter topics for a while longer, which helped to lift Baltaszar's spirits, and then the girls had to leave to prepare for dinner. Baltaszar went back in with them and headed to the men's quarters. He'd pushed himself hard throughout the day, and wanted to lie down for a short while. Dinner wouldn't be served for another couple of hours, so he had some time to decompress and clear his head. The room was empty, except for Lincan, who sat on a cushioned chair with his legs folded in front of him, reading a book. He was somewhat caught off guard, not realizing that Lincan had left the training grounds before he had.

Baltaszar would have been disgruntled by the presence of anyone else, but Lincan always provided good company, and they hadn't had much time to catch up since Baltaszar had been banished from the House of Darian. "Hey man, what are you reading?"

Lincan looked up from the book, "Hey. It's *The Making of the Fangh/Galicean Wall*. It's about everything that happened that led to the wall being built. I just started it, so I haven't gotten into too much of the specifics just yet. You look tired."

"Sounds interesting. Yeah, I've just been pushing myself with these fireballs. Asarei wants me up to ten at a time before we set off to Alvadon." Baltaszar sat down in the chair next to him.

Lincan stood and put the book down on the chair. "Sounds like the training has really been helping. I know my manifestation is important for everyone's health, but I wish I could have a chance to be fighting. Or at least even how to weaponize my manifestation. Back when we were on our way to the Tower, I actually managed to fight off some Vermillion by sickening them. I don't know what changed, but it was so exciting to be able to actually fight back with my manifestation."

Baltaszar noticed a curious look on Lincan's face. "What?" Lincan raised his eyebrows and nodded. "Am I missing something? I don't...wait. No. There's no way."

Lincan smiled. "Come on. I'll go easy, and then heal whatever I do. Anything I do to you can be undone."

"I understand that, but that still requires you to either hurt me or make me sick." Baltaszar shook his head vigorously."

"Just let me try once. I'll just work on your foot, then. I'll keep it simple."

"What do you mean 'just my foot!' I need my foot; I need both of them!"

Lincan's eyes got wider and his voice more desperate, "Please! You know I won't do anything too serious! I promise, I'll start small, with something simple, and I'll heal it right away." He stopped for a moment, then continued as if realizing something, "Besides, you owe me. I'm the one who basically brought you back to life after you set yourself on fire. *And* I made you impervious to your own fire! Just let me try one time. After this once, if it's too much, I won't ask again." He paused, "I'll probably try to find someone else. But just let me try."

Baltaszar knew he owed his friend for saving his life, and Lincan never asked anything of him. Even now, Lincan wasn't asking to be selfish; he was trying to better himself for the greater good. Finally, he nodded. "Fine. But like you said, if you go too far, I'm not doing this again." He rolled his pant leg up and removed his boot and sock. "Are you really planning to touch my foot? That's not awkward to you?"

Lincan nodded in agreement, "Fair enough. Your shin, then." Lincan kneeled down next to Baltaszar's outstretched leg.

"So I have to sit here and just let you hurt me?"

"I don't know. Concentrate on something else then. Talk to me about something."

"That won't distract you?"

"I'll tell you when to be quiet."

Baltaszar shrugged and sat back in the chair, then looked up at the ceiling. "Makes sense." He'd had Bo'az on his mind as of late, and perhaps Lincan might be able to give some helpful advice on the matter or ease his mind at the least. Lincan grasped his shin, just above the ankle. "I've been concerned about my brother for a while now."

"Shh. No talking." Lincan glanced at him, "Just kidding; go ahead. Concerned about what?"

"You're an ass. Anyway, Slade said he knew Bo would be safe for another year or so. He's on a mission for Jahmash, which means Jahmash needs him until it's done. But when that's over…" He winced as Lincan started the process.

"When that's over, there are no guarantees. You said a year? By then, we'll have been done with this king mission for months. When we finish this, we can turn our attention to rescuing your brother. Maybe Maqdhuum can do a quick snatch type of mission, where he goes back, figures out where Bo'az is, then returns to get him when no one is around."

Baltaszar nodded as the pain started to increase, though it was still tolerable. "What exactly are you doing?"

"Removing the skin first. Like I said, I'll start small, like a simple bruise or scrape. Then I'll heal it back up."

"Fine. You can keep going. It's not that bad yet. Anyway, I'm not necessarily worried about the extraction part with Bo, or Jahmash killing him." Lincan looked at him curiously. Baltaszar paused for a moment, "That sounds bad. Let me explain." He looked around to ensure that no one else was in the room, then continued. "You can't share this with anyone else, got it?"

Lincan nodded, "Sure."

Baltaszar was so caught up in focusing on Bo'az, that he didn't even know whether Lincan was trying to hurt him anymore. "I got a prophecy from Munn Keeramm a while back, and it's pretty bad."

"You don't have to share if you don't want to."

"I know, but I *need* to. It's been eating at me for a while now, and I think I need someone else's perspective on this. Keeramm told me that

I'm going to kill my brother." Lincan stopped what he was doing and looked at Baltaszar intently. "See, that's what's got me so knotted up. Bo'az will be fine with Jahmash, because Jahmash isn't the one who's going to kill him. I'm going to."

Lincan backed away from Baltaszar's leg, "Hold on, let's start at the beginning. What exactly was the prophecy? If you don't mind retelling it?"

Baltaszar nodded and explained what Munn Keeramm had told him over a year ago. "Keeramm said he saw everything through my brother's eyes, and that I told him I would never forgive him for his sins. I called him 'brother.' Then I stabbed him several times until he died."

Lincan scratched his head for a moment and stared at the ground. "I wonder."

"What?"

"Did Keeramm actually say 'Bo'az'? Like his actual name?"

"Not that I can remember, why?"

"Well, did he give any indication that it was definitely Bo'az? Like a description? Or did he specifically say 'twin brother?' Anything like that?"

"Well...no. What are you getting at?"

Lincan went back to working on his shin, "One thing I've learned with these prophecies is, they are not all exactly as they seem. You have to keep in mind that the Augurs are interpreting a vision that they see. And those interpretations are given to us as described by men and women who cannot see the physical world. Sometimes, things get misconstrued in the process of translating them from the mind of the Augurs to the pages of their books."

Baltaszar exhaled deeply, "So you're saying that I'm *not* going to kill Bo'az?"

Lincan shrugged, "I'm saying that Bo'az might be one of several possibilities. Think about it. When you got to the House of Darian, we made it clear that we all referred to one another as brothers and sisters. Keeramm might only have said 'brother' because you said it in the vision."

"That makes sense."

"I have a tendency to do that."

"Yeah, yeah. But then, who the hell am I going to kill?"

CHAPTER 18
GENERAL GRUNT

From **The Book of Orijin,** **Verse Thirty**
We have filled the worlds with a wondrous variety of life.
Every thing, every mind, can benefit existence in some way.
It is your duty to seek out those benefits.

"I'M NOT STRONG ENOUGH. I think I still need more nourishment. I need ta get bigger again." Desmond released his manifestation and wiped the sweat from his forehead. His hair, which was normally shorter and choppy, had grown out to an awkward length and he had to tie it up to keep it from constantly falling in his face. The few logs he was trying to levitate fell to the ground.

Asarei shook his head and pointed to the others on the training grounds. "Even smaller than your normal self, you're bigger than Baltaszar. Yet he is working up to being able to command ten fireballs at a time, while focusing on each one separately. Malikai and Horatio are bigger than you, but not by much, and their command of their manifestations far exceeds yours. The issue isn't your size or physical strength. It's your will power. You've been here, what, about four months? And you still give up too easily. I commend you on making strides with everything that you've been going through, but I get the feeling that your mind still craves all that power. Your body might be back to normal, but your mind isn't."

Desmond shrugged, "An' how am I supposed ta fix myself, then?"

"Train yourself to focus again. It just takes practice and will power. Force yourself to concentrate on something for a few moments. Then keep doing the same thing for longer periods of time. While you're doing it, focus on nothing and push all the thoughts and emotions aside. Just like when you're controlling your manifestation. For me, I close my eyes and picture a small triangle in the distance and everything else is black. I just focus on that triangle and push everything else away."

He looked at the others on the training grounds, "There's no quick fix fer this, is there? This is goin' ta take a while?"

"Depends on you, really. The more work you put into it and the harder you push yourself, the faster your mind gets stronger."

Desmond was about to respond, but hesitated. He knew that turning his thought into words would solidify the notion, and that he wouldn't be able to take it back. He also knew the answer to what he was about to ask, and once Asarei responded, he would have to commit to those next steps. But as he looked around, he understood that Malikai, Horatio, and Baltaszar would all do what was best for the whole group if put in the same situation. *Ta hell with it. Can't call myself a Ghost if I'm not goin' ta do what's best fer the other Ghosts. Salvation as One.* "Would ya say it's in my best interest, then, ta take a break from the manifestation trainin'?"

"Would *you* say it's in your best interest?"

"I already know that it is," Desmond nodded. "Maybe I need a break. I can use the time ta work on my thoughts an' makin' my mind stronger. I'll be no help ta the rest o' the group if I can't even help myself."

Asarei smiled, "Look at you, starting to think responsibly. For a while now I thought I might have to keep wiping your ass for a long time. Remember what we talked about when you tried to hurt my apple tree? I told you it would take longer to fix your mind than your body. And to be honest, until you learn how to focus properly, you won't make much progress with your manifestation."

Desmond grasped his right hand with his left, "It sounds familiar. It's hard ta take in a lecture when every bone in yer hand is broken."

"Understandable. Why don't you start now? Take a walk by yourself and clear your head. I'm not trying to rush you on this, but you don't have *that* much time to fix yourself. What did Donovan and Wendell say? Another two months or so and they'll be ready."

He nodded and left the training grounds. *Shit, that's right.* Desmond had forgotten that the whole group would be ready that soon. Maqdhuum had retrieved Donovan and Wendell about two weeks before, in the middle of the night. They were having some success with increasing their followers in the Vermillion, but several soldiers chose to remain firm in their allegiance to the king. *They said there's enough ta cause us a problem.* According to the pair's updates, Edmund had increased his personal guard ever since Garrison left, and those guards were with him all the time. Not only did he keep some knights by his side, no matter where he went, but more guards stood at every doorway of whatever room he was in. Wendell had told them that, deep down, Edmund knew it was only a matter of time before Descendants made an attempt to attack him, once Garrison was no longer hunting them down.

Desmond agreed with that sentiment, but throughout Ashur there were barely any reports of Descendants causing trouble, much less being seen. He had been inclined to believe that most Descendants were reticent toward being seen once the House of Darian had been destroyed. It was one thing to have to hide from the Vermillion, but to be full-on attacked by the armies of the Red Harbinger, in a supposed safe haven for Descendants, that would terrify anyone with a black line on their face.

He walked back to the orchards where he'd gone the first time he wanted to be alone. He'd returned to the same tree several times and every time, before sitting at its base; he patted its trunk and apologized for punching it. Desmond felt the urgency that Asarei had suggested and wasted no time in closing his eyes. *Clear everything out an' focus on...nothin'. Great, push all the thoughts out. Definitely don't think about Farrah an' Lao. Or how they're not even talkin'...dammit. This is the opposite o' what I should be doin'.* He sat there with his eyes closed until he was able to push everything out of his mind and just focus on a small circle. He preferred that to the triangle that Asarei had suggested. He sat there for a few minutes until the thoughts started to creep back in, but surprisingly, he wasn't angry when they did. *He said it'd be tough an' that I have ta keep practicin'. So here we go again.*

Over the next couple of weeks, Desmond continued to strengthen his mind in solitude. He found that it helped to put his mind at ease and made it easier to sort out everything that was going on. It also made him more observant. While he'd abstained from training on the training grounds, he still went there to see what the others were doing, check on their progress, and offer encouragement.

Asarei had started working with more of them on their manifestations. Baltaszar and Horatio were both incredibly dangerous with their fire and lightning. In fact, Horatio was no longer limited to summoning it from the sky. He could generate it from his own body and use it at close range. Desmond knew that that would be deadly if used properly in their siege.

He was also surprised at Reverron, whose manifestation allowed him to dash forward several feet. The word was that Reverron was an adequate swordsman, but likely wouldn't overpower anyone, which Desmond thought was a shame. Wielding a sword well would have superbly complemented Reverron's manifestation. Regardless, the Cerysian *was* now able to scale short walls and even briefly run along walls while dashing ahead. It would still help when fighting in tight corridors.

Sindha had better and more precise control of her force fields. Desmond remembered that before, her force fields stayed the same once she created them. Now, she could manipulate their shapes and sizes while wielding them.

Even Garrison had shown off his abilities, but in the form of what he was creating. The nature of his manifestation was more about what he could create or invent while harnessing his manifestation. He'd requested several items and ingredients from the mainland of Ashur, and Asarei and Savaiyon had entertained those requests. As a result, Garrison had produced dozens of pouches in a variety of colors. He'd explained to the rest of them that the pouches contained certain combinations of ingredients that reacted differently when exposed to another element, such as water, soil, fire, wood, blood, or even spit. He'd used pouches just like them when on the run from the Vermillion after Edmund had banished him from Cerysia. Desmond was beyond excited to see what they could do, but Garrison warned them that the contents of the pouches were too valuable to waste on trial runs. He already knew what combinations to use, and how they'd react, so it would be foolish to waste any of them.

Watching his peers allowed Desmond to fully realize what each of them was newly capable of doing as he witnessed firsthand how hard they were all working, day in and day out. Even those who couldn't necessarily use their manifestations to attack were learning to use their abilities in new and creative ways, as well as pushing themselves in combat training. The older men, including Maqdhuum, Savaiyon, Slade, Kadoog'han, and Blastevahn were training alongside the younger folk. They were all pushing themselves to their limits in numerous ways, even those who seemed to be struggling. Adria made no secret of spending almost all of her free time with Krissette in sparring sessions. Desmond was proud to see her excelling in combat, especially because there were so many at the House who would have scoffed at the notion of her as a fighter.

Marshall had also been doing his best to elevate his fighting skills. Like Desmond, Marshall also seemed to be a project for Asarei. He suspected it had to do with both being Taurani, but harnessing the full potential of Marshall's manifestation seemed to stump Asarei. If Marshall wasn't sparring with Asarei on the training grounds, then he was challenging Manjobam, Trevor, and Ahvedool to swordfights. Sometimes it would be one on one, or other times Marshall would challenge two or all three to spar simultaneously. It seemed as if Marshall improved every time, and Desmond and the others tended to watch their sessions, either to learn new strategies or just to see who would win. They would also switch up their sparring, sometimes using two-handed swords and sometimes using shields and one-handed swords. After a while, they'd even started to place bets on who would yield first.

Some nights, they'd sit around and talk in the men's sleeping quarters. The same group that Desmond had bonded with at the House of Darian tended to make up the gatherings. At the House, they normally consisted of him, Badalao, Lincan, Horatio, Baltaszar, Vasher, and Marshall. However, Malikai, Garrison, and Reverron tended to join them these days. One thing that surprised Desmond the most was that the feuds and gripes between most of them had withered away, at least for the ones in the room. Adria still consistently snapped at Farrah, and most of them were leery of Maqdhuum, which he expected would likely last for the duration of their alliance.

Marshall admitted to the rest of them that he was adamant about being the best fighter possible, because of what happened to his people. He was embarrassed at how easily the Taurani had been defeated in their own village, and at how unprepared they had been. Desmond remembered seeing the destruction of the village, and how completely demolished everything had been. So many rumors had swirled through Ashur about the Taurani before that attack.

Horatio called his name from a chair to his right, "Desmond, it's been weeks now and I've been holding my tongue about asking, because I'm sure I know the answer. But I can't help it anymore. I know you've been going off to talk to this 'General Grunt' that Asarei is so secretive about. What's going on? Who is it? Does Asarei actually have some military man hiding out somewhere on the island?"

Desmond smiled. *I should've known that if anyone would ask, it'd be him.* "I can't tell ya. I'm sworn ta secrecy as well. All I can say is that regularly talkin' ta General Grunt is a big help ta me. Gets a ton off my mind."

Vasher chimed in, "He's not a real person is he? Asarei just carved a face on a tree or a rock, and pretends it's a real person. Right?"

Desmond, along with all the others, laughed. "He's very real an' very alive. If ya want ta know more, ya have ta convince Asarei ta tell ya." They ribbed him for a while longer and eventually everyone went to sleep.

The following morning, everyone assembled at the training grounds for combat training. Asarei stood before them and was about to assign them to different tasks, when Horatio interrupted him. "With all due respect, Asarei, I have a question. Last night a bunch of us attempted to get the truth out of Desmond concerning General Grunt. However, he refused to oblige us. In fact, he told us that we had to convince you to share. What I want to know is, why is this General such a big secret? Why do only you and Desmond get the benefit of meeting with this general? What if the rest of us could be helped by meeting with him? Is General Grunt even a real person? Vasher said that perhaps you carved a face into a tree or a rock, and you have delusions of talking to a real person." Desmond glanced over at Vasher and could see the annoyance in his eyes. Horatio continued, "I think it's time we knew the truth."

By this time, all eyes were on Asarei. Desmond was sure that Asarei was about to attack Horatio, and he was sure that all the others were thinking the same thing. *Why must he always just say everything that's on his mind?*

Asarei rubbed his beard while staring at Horatio. "Raish, either your balls are made of steel, or you have no clue about anything. Either way, you just say whatever the hell is on your mind, don't ya?"

"Sorry?" Horatio replied sheepishly.

"Too late to apologize now." Asarei looked around at the rest of them. "I'm going to assume most of you have been talking about this. And that speaks to those of you with whom I've entrusted this secret. That being said, Raish is right. There's no real reason for General Grunt to be a secret anymore." He nodded to Vasher, "He is completely real. Why don't we all take a walk? Those of you who know the truth already, you can stay here." He started walking into the forest, "The rest of you, come with me. I'll share the truth with you now. Perhaps *everyone* can benefit from meeting General Grunt."

The whole group, except for Asarei's people, followed him north into the forest. They walked on for a while on the very path that Desmond had used so many times. He was thankful that they'd all stayed quiet while walking. He was somewhat nervous and embarrassed for everyone to know about General Grunt. He wasn't sure whether they'd all laugh at him or if they would embrace the unorthodox nature of it all.

They finally reached the clearing that gave way to the northeastern shore of the island, but Asarei stopped them. "As soon as you see General Grunt, your first instinct will likely be that I am crazy, or something of the sort. I ask you to suspend your judgment and be open-minded. Embrace the unorthodox, just as Desmond has. Also, when you see him, approach General Grunt with love and calmness, as he will know if anyone has ill intentions."

Desmond took a deep breath. *I can't believe we're doin' this. At least I don't have ta keep any secrets anymore.* Asarei proceeded and they all followed. They walked out of the forest and onto the long beach.

Horatio dared to speak again, "So where is he?"

Asarei nodded ahead, at the large grey and black mass on the beach.

"Is he lying behind that big black rock?"

"No idiot. He *is* the big black rock."

"So I was right then?" Vasher responded.

Desmond shook his head, "It's not actually a rock."

Kadoog'han passed them all and stood in front of Asarei. "Is that what I think it is? There were rumors that you had one, but I thought they were just rumors! They don't even have those at the Sundari fighting pits!"

Vasher perked up at the mention of Sundari. "What is it?"

As if knowing they were talking about it, the grey and black mass shifted and rolled until it was standing on four legs, each one thicker than a tree trunk. It untucked its head and looked directly at them all with eyes bright like emeralds. Now that it was standing, its horns were also on full display, one over each eye, another massive horn on its nose, and two more horns that started on top of its head and curved around its short ears and jutted just in front of the corners of its mouth. "A scaled nashorn," Kadoog'han responded.

They all walked closer to it, cautiously, but Desmond maintained his pace and walked up to the beast first. He decided to embrace the situation and be proud of his connection with the beast. Its scales were not really noticeable until up close, and the others marveled at them. Desmond put a hand on General Grunt and patted his nose. The nashorn responded with a friendly grunt, which is how he'd earned his name. He then gently nudged Desmond with the side of his face. "Asarei is right. If he knows your intentions are pure, he's like a cat that just wants to lay around and play."

Asarei added, "But if he sees you as a threat, he can kill you in a heartbeat. He's faster than he looks."

Kadoog'han continued to marvel at General Grunt. He walked up to the beast and stroked his scaly body. "Where did you find him? Couldn't have been on this island."

"Found him at the edge of the Never, just north of Roaldon. He was injured and by himself. Mother probably figured he wouldn't survive. Got him on a wagon, bribed someone in town to stitch him up, and brought him back to Shipsbane."

Kadoog'han looked at him incredulously, "You got him through the touch portal?"

Asarei chuckled. "No, that likely would've killed him. Put him in a boat with me and we sailed out here together. He's got plenty of space to do as he wishes, though he seems to like the beach. Generally stays around here."

By this time, most of them were standing around General Grunt and petting him. Desmond knew right away that General Grunt would be getting a lot more visits than he had before.

Kadoog'han continued to marvel. "Is he full grown?"

"The hell if I know. Can't imagine him bigger than this, though."

Slade answered as well, "No, he'll get bigger."

Asarei's eyes widened, "You're sure?"

Slade nodded. "Positive. I've seen them in the Never before. Definitely saw bigger."

"Hear that, boy? You're still growing!" Asarei nodded at General Grunt, who fittingly grunted back at him."

Marshall spoke up from the other side of the beast, "You know, if you were able to tame him and bond with him, then it might be possible with others of his kind."

Asarei laughed, "What, you mean just appear somewhere in the Never and start cuddling with nashorn? Sorry, don't think so."

Slade countered, "Marshall might be onto something. Suppose you appeared with General Grunt, riding on top of him or something. Perhaps he might be able to communicate with others of his kind. Imagine having a squadron of nashorn riders in the battle against Jahmash?"

Before Asarei could speak, Desmond responded, "Sure it sounds crazy, but only as crazy as tamin' one nashorn, then bringin' it ta yer secret island, an' tellin' it about all yer problems."

Asarei nodded, "Fine. I get it. But let's focus on one thing at a time. First, kill the king, then build an army of nashorn. And before I forget, now that you're all here and," he looked at all of them petting General Grunt, "familiar with him, feel free to come talk to him. He likes it. He likes it even better if you bring him food, especially the winter apples."

MARSHALL LOWERED THE WOODEN SWORD and finally noticed how sweaty his hand was, as the hilt stuck to his palm. He took a few deep breaths and looked back at Asarei, "I think I've had enough for tonight."

"Good. As much as I love to spar, I'm not fond of a middle of the night session like this one. I know fighting in the dark is a legitimate concern, but your opponents will not be able to see either." Asarei walked closer to him. They'd lit two of the perimeter torches, which provided only enough light to see each other when movements were made.

Actually, Aric can, if he's still alive. They walked over to the armory to put their swords away. Marshall had consistently insisted on using the wooden swords for sparring, as they were heavier than most swords, especially the Itarse steel swords that Sindha had promised to equip them with. "Actually, there is something I was hoping to discuss with you. Something that has been on my mind since we arrived, and I'd rather not talk about it in front of the others."

"I know, I know. Your manifestation." Asarei took a deep breath. "Look, I'm sorry, Marshall. I can't seem to grasp the nature of it. You might have to work it out on your own and tinker with things. I think it's beyond my help."

Marshall shook his head, "No, that's not it. I understand that I might just be on my own with it."

Asarei patted him on the shoulder, "Well, if you're smitten with me, I'm flattered, but as you can see, I have a wonderful wife and daughter."

Marshall laughed and was thankful for the levity. "Actually, that's not far off from what I wanted to talk about." He sat on a stool, "Obviously, I'm *not* smitten with you. But you *are* Taurani, as am I, and

I think there are matters to be discussed."

Asarei sat on another stool. "Concerning?"

"Well, rebuilding our people, of course. Isn't it our duty to revive the Taurani people?"

Asarei wiped the sweat from his forehead and eyed Marshall curiously. "We haven't talked about very much besides combat, but I've assumed you're not dense like most Taurani, Marshall. First of all, Taurani never left the village, aside from scouting and trading. And those types of things didn't happen that frequently. They always stayed in the village or returned to it if they did conduct business elsewhere. What I'm getting at is that aside from the two of us, there *are* no more Taurani. Which brings me to my second of all. You may have noticed that both of us are men. And I'm not sure if anyone ever explained to you how it works, but it's impossible for two men to rebuild a population." He cocked his head sideways, "You *do* know that, right?"

Marshall closed his eyes and took a deep breath, "Yes. Of course I know how it all works; I'm not stupid."

"So then how do you think it could even work?" Marshall's eyes darted back and forth between Asarei and the ground. Asarei's eyes and mouth opened wide in shock. He leaned forward and punched Marshall hard in the chest. Marshall was solid enough to take the punch, but it still hurt a bit. Asarei then pointed a finger in his face, "You get those thoughts out of your head right now. Now I know why you didn't want anyone else around, you little shit. You even look at my daughter again while you're here, I'll bloody kill you. Got it? That's what you've been up to this whole time? Hoping that I'd agree to let you lay with my young daughter? Dafne's barely seen sixteen summers."

Marshall put his hands up to try and settle Asarei down, "That's *not* what I was trying to convince you to do. But ever since our people were obliterated, I haven't been able to shake the notion that it's my duty to start the Taurani over. I promise, this isn't about your daughter; it's about me and this calling in the back of my head that just feels like something I must do."

"Why? So you can all walk around the Never with your heads up your asses and then fall apart the moment you're challenged by an enemy?"

Marshall swallowed his anger at Asarei's harsh words. He knew the man was right. "It wouldn't be the same. They could be taught the truth and how to avoid the mistakes of the past. It could be a new community better equipped for the world."

"Communities that feel the need to hide in the middle of a forest do more to hurt the world than heal it."

Marshall was starting to get annoyed at the pushback. "Oh, but doing so on an island is brave, right?"

Asarei smiled tightly. "This only *looks* like a community. *I* live here with my wife, my daughter, and my pet. All of the others know full well that they are free to leave the island whenever they want. They have not been commanded or bound to stay here by any decree or cultural rule. Although I suspect Bam would never consider moving back to the mainland. But I'm not forcing any of them to stay and they all know that."

"Fine. You're not a coward. You're extremely brave for living here."

Asarei shook his head, "Your words are not going to get to me, boy. I know exactly who I am, what I've been through, and how my decisions impact the well-being of me and my family. Let's backtrack for a moment, seeing as how this isn't all about Dafne. She is the only female that either of us knows of, who carries Taurani blood. *But*, she's not pure Taurani anyway. Even if you were to start a family with my daughter, it would be a lie."

Marshall nodded, "I know. But she's the closest to a pure Taurani that there is anymore." He paused for a moment, "Look, this was all a suggestion anyway. It's not like I was coveting your daughter the moment I saw her. In fact, there's someone else who's captured my affections for some time now. And I sort of cooled things between us because I thought this Taurani situation was a higher priority."

Asarei nodded, "Look, Marshall. It's noble to think that this responsibility should fall on your shoulders. And if the Taurani hadn't been so misguided, I would agree with you. In fact, I would never have left in the first place and we likely wouldn't be even having this conversation. But the Ghosts are your family now, your people now. And even twenty of you are stronger than that whole damned village. You know why?" Asarei didn't wait for him to respond. "It's because you all *want* to be here. You all believe in a common thing, and you're willing to die for that. The Taurani sent their children into life-threatening situations as early as five or six, knowing that some of them wouldn't survive. Some of them even knew that their children would develop manifestations and went along with the custom, even though they would hide those manifestations with all the damn tattoos for the rest of their lives. That notion sickens me. Stick to the people you're with now. They respect who you are and accept you for all of your differences and original thoughts." He stood up and started walking out of the armory, "Especially Adria. And now you can go back and fix whatever it was you had with her."

Marshall jerked his head as he stood up to follow. "You knew?"

"I only just put it all together. I mean, it's obvious you both fancy each other, with the number of glances each of you takes when the other isn't looking. I just figured the romance hadn't started yet. But you should go make your amends before it's too late. Strong women like her don't wait around very long for fools like you. You're just lucky she's stuck on an island without any new prospects."

They walked away from the training grounds and toward the fortress steps. "Trust me, I know how lucky I am. I'll talk to her first thing tomorrow. But back to this manifestation thing of mine. Instead of working on it at the training grounds, I'd like to have that time to go off by myself to work on it. I think I need to start without any distractions, and then once I have a better handle of it, then I can work on it with people around."

"Fair enough. On your manifestation training days, go wherever you think is best. Oh, and about that stupid rebuilding idea of yours. You do realize that if you tried that, it would mean having children with my daughter? And then your children would have to have children with each other?"

Marshall didn't bother to respond. He looked at Asarei flatly and with defeat in his eyes, and walked on. They walked back to the underground fortress and parted ways. Marshall went directly to the men's quarters and rinsed off at a basin before going to sleep.

The following morning, Marshall approached Adria at the start of breakfast. Krissette was sitting next to her, as usual. "Krissette, would you mind if I spoke to Adria for a bit?"

She looked at Adria and raised an eyebrow, "Of course not. I'll come back when I see you leave. Then she can tell me everything."

Marshall rolled his eyes as she walked away. He sat across from her at the small table. "I should start with the apology. I know I've been distant for a while now, and you've given me that space, whether you wanted to or not. I'm sorry for that. The truth is that it wasn't about you at all, so please don't think that there was anything you did." He looked down at the table and then back at her face. Her eyes were fixed on his, waiting for his explanation. "Ever since my people were decimated, one of the things that's been on my mind *all* the time is how I might be able to restart the Taurani civilization. And I guess when I found out that Asarei was also Taurani, and that he has a daughter, that it might somehow be my duty or responsibility to wed her in order to start that whole process."

She squinted at him. "Wait, you're saying that you stopped talking to me because you thought you might have to have children with Dafne? That's really what you thought?"

Marshall shrugged, "When you say it like that, it doesn't sound as noble."

"So what was your plan? Were you going to butter up Asarei and ask him for permission to marry Dafne?" He looked down at the ground. "Light of Orijin, you already did! Are you only here then because he rejected you?"

He was having trouble gauging her response. It was hard to tell if she was genuinely amused or being facetious about the situation. Marshall was definitely not even sure whether she was mad or not. "No, I never intended to ask to marry her. But I did ask him for guidance on the situation. I wanted to know if the idea itself was worthwhile or futile. Obviously he told me that there was no sense in doing so. He also punched me in the chest for even bringing up Dafne in that regard. But he showed me that what I have with the Ghosts is better than any Taurani community, past or future."

Adria ripped a piece of bread from the chunk in her plate. "Marshall, I know how dumb you boys tend to be, so I should point out that I'm not mad about Dafne. I know your people were important to you, of course they would be. But I am upset that you wouldn't just tell me what you were going through. That's not really a good way to start off...whatever it was that we had."

He nodded, "You're right, but I had no idea how to have that conversation. How do you tell someone, 'I fancy you, but I think I may have to start a family with a stranger so that I can repopulate my people'? In my head, I think it was easier to make you angry, in the event that I really did have to do that."

She closed her eyes and shook her head. "I think I may have given you too much credit when this whole thing between us started. You're an idiot." Her smile put him at ease.

"I am. In all fairness, I don't think I ever said I *wasn't* an idiot. But can we start over? I promise, if I ever see another girl who might be Taurani, I won't ignore you and try to marry her."

"Well how could I say no to that? As long as you promise to not be an idiot anymore. So many of the other boys here—your friends—are idiots anyway. We don't need any more."

He smiled and stood up to leave. "Thanks for giving me another chance. I won't disappoint you. I'm going to go eat so that Krissette can come back and hear the whole stupid story."

"Oh, she will definitely get the whole *stupid* story." She smiled back at him as he turned and walked away. Marshall took a deep breath. He'd only slept the night before because he was exhausted. As soon as he woke up, his shoulders and back were tight in anticipation of this conversation. Asarei had been right about not waiting too long. For her to forgive him so easily, Marshall knew that he couldn't be so foolish again.

He let the happiness and confidence carry him through the day, especially once it came time to focus on his manifestation. He walked into the forest, in the direction of General Grunt. He remembered that there was a small clearing along the way, in which the sun broke through enough to cast a strong shadow. Asarei had agreed to send Vilariyal and Faryal to Shipsbane, in order to procure a few mirrors for Marshall. Until that happened, he would have to focus only on his shadow.

Marshall stood at the center of the clearing and cleared his mind. He let the manifestation flow through him as he looked down at his shadow. The more he focused on it, the more he seemed to understand it, as if sharing a thought with someone, without having to consciously acknowledge it. He knew what the shadow knew, and it knew what he knew. As he concentrated more and more on the shadow, he focused specifically on sending it away. He was wary of sending it too far and then losing control of it. As he thought about what was around him, Marshall decided to send it to General Grunt. He closed his eyes and pictured the destination, and opened them again, hoping he might be able to command his shadow to go. Sure enough, it detached from him and moved, almost like a slithering blob, in the direction of General Grunt.

As the shadow moved farther away from him, Marshall could instinctively tell where it was and how far away, and he could picture its whereabouts in his mind. After a few minutes, he could feel that his shadow had reached the nashorn on the beach. As he thought about what to do next, he realized his shadow was quickly returning to him. As it drew close, he heard and felt thumps on the ground in the distance. After another moment, Marshall realized that General Grunt was chasing his shadow all the way back to him.

The nashorn stopped once Marshall's shadow reattached itself to him. Marshall walked over to the beast and petted its face. General Grunt responded with a nudge. "Come on, I'll walk you back to the shore. I'm glad Asarei rescued you. I've heard bad things about the animals at the fighting pits in Sundari. They say many of the beasts are kept in cages so that no one gets hurt." Marshall ambled through the forest, toward the shore, and General Grunt walked by his side. "Cages. Almost like prisoners in a dungeon." He remembered the dungeon at the House of Darian, and how Garrison had been treated as a prisoner. It made him shudder to think of someone doing that to an animal as well, and he imagined what General Grunt might look and like if deprived of food the way Garrison had been.

Suddenly, a thought came to his mind. "Oh no." He turned to General Grunt, "Garrison wasn't one of 'us' at the House. He wasn't a disciple of Marlowe. What happens if his involvement in all this ends up violating the Anonymi's terms?" He patted General Grunt. "After I bring you back, I have to bring this up to the others."

CHAPTER 19
CATALYSTS

From ***The Book of Orijin***, **Verse Two Hundred Nine**
There will come a time when you must stand and act.
When others will need a leader to follow in their darkest hours.
When your heart will know that you must be the voice to rally others.
And when that time calls upon you, Rise.

Khurt watched from the middle of the stairs that led up to the deck, as Khenzi sparred with one of the crew members. In the past few months, Khenzi had markedly improved with his swordsmanship, and was dueling with the crew on a daily basis. The softness about him faded a little each day, and while Khenzi wasn't thick or stout, Khurt could see that the boy was all muscle now. He was still too small to defeat either of Saol's sons in a duel, but he would be able to defend himself and perhaps even inflict some damage.

To Khurt's surprise, neither Saol nor his sons had boarded his ship to harass him or Khenzi since Khurt had been demoted to Eighth General. Khurt had been sure that there would be some form of torture or intimidation, but that hadn't been the case. Still, he kept his guard up each day and night, with the expectation that that each day would be the day they boarded his ship. He knew that the moment he relaxed, that would be the moment that Saol would appear on his deck, with his sons right behind him.

What made Khurt proud, more than anything else, was that Khenzi had insisted on practicing and sparring every day. The boy had taken it into his own hands and even seemed to have a schedule every day. Khurt hadn't had to force him or even suggest anything. He knew that it had all spawned from the confrontation in Saol's meeting room, but that was as good a motivation as anything. Khenzi had even taken to applying his own paint to his skin, rather than waiting for Khurt to do it.

He turned his head slightly toward Davala, who was now Fifth General, after Khurt's demotion. "You see him? After all the ridicule and disrespect, Khenzi might end up a better general than I."

Davala nodded, "That's the point of it all, isn't it? Live our whole lives as an example to them, in the hopes that our examples are good enough to make them better than we could ever be. Khenzi has your stubbornness and drive, and your wife's intelligence. If the Orijin blesses him with a safe return to the motherland when this is all over, I think he very well could be the best of us all. I only hope that Darvel can turn out the same way."

"I wouldn't worry about that. Darvel has the compassion and empathy to balance out his size. He has great potential to become First General someday."

"Thank you for your kind words, Khurt. But why am I here on your ship? I can't imagine you asked me aboard to talk about our sons." Even in quiet conversation, Davala's deep voice boomed.

Khurt turned and sat on the step, then gestured for Davala to do the same. He took a breath, "This whole conflict with Saol has been eating at me. I know a soldier follows orders, and I know that a good general does as well. But this whole approach of his seems wrong."

"What is it that bothers you so much?" Davala reached into the breast pocket of his dark blue general's coat and retrieved a pipe.

"I think it's the unknown of it all. We're headed toward a continent for which we've done minimal scouting, and whose population is likely exponentially larger than ours. Yet, Saol believes that we can easily walk through each city and destroy everything. This is not the way of the Vithelegion. We don't conquer. I firmly believe that infidels must pay the price, especially those who choose to follow Darian instead of Abram. But I draw the line at killing children. That is not our way, and Saol's father would never have made a command like that."

Davala nodded as a puff of smoke left his lips. "His father was a good man. The only problem is, Saol is our commander, not his father. Nothing we can do to change that. Khurt, I don't disagree with you. But my personal views are not more important than the well-being of the entire Vithelegion. Going against Saol will only lead to dissension, and it will fracture our army. If that were to happen, I strongly believe that all of our wives back home would soon become widows."

Khurt hesitated and lightly punched his palm. *The worst that happens is he says 'no,' and then I'm right back to where I began.* "What if we could get others on our side? What if we could meet with the other generals, but without Saol being there?"

"And do what? Secretly plan to overthrow Saol?"

"Well it sounds stupid when you say it like that. But I don't mean a full on mutiny. I just wonder if we can devise some sort of plan or system to save people without Saol knowing."

Davala stood, "Khurt. I have always respected and admired you. But I must do my duty as a higher ranking general and demand that you comply with Saol's orders."

Khurt stood in a last attempt to convince him. "Wait, just entertain one request. Organize a meeting with the two of us, Bragha, and Ezera. The four of us are the lesser ranked generals. I will tell the two of them what I have in mind, and if they disagree, then I promise, I will comply."

Davala's eyes grew thin as he puffed at his pipe. Khurt took the opportunity to be more persuasive. "All I'm asking is for the three of you to be in the same room with me and listen. It doesn't even have to be on my boat. I'll let the three of you decide that. Again, if you're all against it, then I'll never bring it up again."

Davala waved for him to ascend the stairs. Once they were both on the deck, Davala pointed at a ship out in the distance. "That's my ship. Tomorrow morning, right after breakfast. I will entertain you there. Bragha and Ezera will be there as well."

Khurt nodded vigorously, "Thank you, Davala." They grasped forearms and then Davala briskly walked away to return to his own ship. Khurt sat back down on the steps that descended from the deck. *Tomorrow morning? That's less than a day from now. That leaves barely any time to rehearse or practice any powerful speech that might move them. My men will know something is off if I spend the rest of the afternoon and evening in my quarters. I will have to speak with urgency from the heart and hope that it's enough.* Khenzi came and sat next to Khurt as he punched his palm a few times. "Hey boy, good job out there. You're getting better with every day and every sparring session."

"Thanks, Dad. I saw Fifth General leave, and thought it might be a good time to stop. Is anything wrong?"

"It's nothing dire. I'm still a bit cross about Saol's plan to take no prisoners. I'm trying to see if the other generals are willing to...follow a different path." He could feel his son staring at him.

"Wouldn't you get in trouble for something like that?"

He looked at Khenzi, "Only if I push too hard against something that doesn't want to be pushed."

"Or someone."

Khurt smiled, "Or someone. Don't worry; I am being gentle and cautious in what I'm trying to do. If it can't be, then I'll let it go. Why don't you go and clean up? It's nearly time to eat."

Khenzi stood at the suggestion, and put a hand on Khurt's shoulder. "I just don't want anything to happen to you."

Khurt nodded, "I understand, my son. Nothing will happen to me. I'm too smart and I love you too much to allow myself to get into any trouble. Especially before the war even begins. Now go and clean up." As Khenzi entered their quarters, Khurt stood and ascended the stairs back onto the deck. He surveyed the ship, taking in all the hard work of his men. Most of those who were up top were resting after their rowing shift had ended. Khurt felt as tired as they looked, but envied that they were only tired from rowing, rather than the moral crisis he was currently wrestling with. He quietly walked the perimeter of the deck, too lost in his thoughts to interact with anyone.

He didn't know what the possibilities would be if Ezera and Bragha saw his point of view, but he was sure he would have to convince them with conviction and confidence. To be fair, Khurt was not short on either of those qualities, but still worried whether it would be enough. The relationships between the eight generals were not necessarily cold, but they were formal. None of the three he would meet with tomorrow would side with him just because they got along well with him or favored him for a particular reason. That type of informal camaraderie occurred between a general and his own squadrons. They were the ones who spent the most time together, and knew of each other's quirks, tastes, faults, and all of the other little things that a man might be constructed of.

As the sun began its descent, Khurt regained his bearings and realized that most of his crewmen were walking to the lower deck, likely heading to supper. He'd heard them celebrating throughout the day due to a great haul of fish from both the nets and the rods. Khurt set foot in the same direction, eager to see what the cooks were serving with the day's bounty.

He went back to his quarters first, where one of his crewmen was already waiting with a bowl. "Thank you, Navren, but I could have gotten it myself."

"Ah, nonsense, General. It's clear as the sea's horizon that you've got something big on your mind. We all noticed it up top. Take the bowl and go clear your head. We'll be fine."

Khurt patted him on the shoulder, then took the bowl. "Thank you, my friend. I'll do as you say." Navren nodded with a smile, then walked back to the others. As soon as Khurt shut his door and sat down, he slurped down the fish soup. He was somewhat glad that Khenzi had already left the room to eat with others. Within minutes Khurt finished, a combination of him being famished and the soup being one of the tastiest meals he'd had since sailing off.

He lay back in his bed, boots still on, and fell asleep envisioning how the morning's meeting would play out. He woke up early the next morning with a crick in his neck and his feet sore from the boots, and still, Khurt's thoughts went straight to the meeting and refused to let anything else steal his focus. The only thing he took the time to do before leaving his quarters was to paint the darker skin patches on his face, using a tiny mirror that he kept on the chair. Even Khenzi seemed to understand his preoccupation as soon as Khurt saw him, and the boy gave Khurt a hug and ran off to find a sparring partner.

The bell for breakfast rang, but Khurt's thoughts filled his gut too much for him to fit in any food. He instructed some of his crewmen to prepare a messenger boat for descent and stared out at Davala's ship until his boat was ready. As much thinking and planning as he'd done the day before, Khurt's mind couldn't focus on a specific thought at the moment. He closed his eyes and took a deep breath, then walked to the ladder that would bring him down to his boat.

He dismissed the oarsman who awaited him and told him to return to the deck. "I have to sort out my thoughts. The rowing will help me focus." As the man climbed back to the deck, Khurt embarked toward Davala's ship. By the time he boarded Davala's ship, Khurt had barely a semblance of what he needed to say and how he needed to say it. He knew the fear of opposition tightened his mind's ability to prepare, but he held out faith that he might be able to embrace the moment once in the room with the other three. One of Davala's crewmen led him to the others, who all awaited in a small cabin at the lower deck. When Khurt entered, Ezera, Bragha, and Davala looked at him flatly, with barely any expression on their faces. *So that's how this is going to go.* "Good morning Generals. Thank you for entertaining my request." They each nodded curtly, but their expressions were less harsh, even with their darker patches of skin painted black. So much of Bragha's face was painted black that it resembled a mask. "I'm sure that Davala informed you of my intentions, but let me explain myself. I would like to propose an idea, and I assure you that if you disagree, I harbor no hard feelings."

Ezera nodded, "Understood. But get to the point, Khurt. Either we agree or disagree. No need to dance around the subject."

"Very well. I think that if enough of the Generals can come to an agreement, there might be a way to counteract Saol's decision to take no prisoners in Ashur."

Bragha stood upright after leaning against the wall. "Enough of the Generals? You're proposing a split in the Vithelegion."

Davala added his own question, "And what would you even propose to make that happen, anyway? How could we secretly keep prisoners without our Commander knowing?"

Khurt shrugged, "Honestly, I don't know. The first and hardest step was to get all of you on board with me, then we can work on a plan once I know you all agree."

Bragha stepped closer to Khurt. "Back to my point, though. You would risk the Vithelegion just to pursue your own agenda? Khurt, how did you ascend to First General in the first place, if you would willingly betray the entire nation?"

A voice came from the doorway, which was now open. "Precisely. Which is exactly why he was demoted, and why the Eighth Squadron will now pair with my own forces, so that I can keep watch on him myself, and order any traitor to the Vithelegion killed." Saol Suldas stood in the doorway, filling all the space in the opening. "Everitas, you're lucky that I am not having you stripped of your rank outright. But we are too close to our destination to be able to train a new general and go through all the proceedings and ceremonies. That's also why I'm not considering having you executed or making you walk the plank. Until our mission is completed, there will be eyes on you the entire time. And on your men, too."

Khurt lowered his eyes, then looked back at the other three generals. The weight of Saol's decree burdened his shoulders just as heavily as the betrayal of Bragha, Ezera, and Davala. He knew they owed no allegiance to him, but he wholeheartedly thought they shared the same philosophy about prisoners. He looked back at Saol and walked toward the door. "I understand, Commander. I will not be a burden to the mission going forward."

Saol moved aside for Khurt to exit the room, then followed him out. He walked with Khurt back up to the deck and softened his tone, "Stop for a moment, Everitas, and talk to me." Saol stopped at one of the rails and looked out at the sea. "I know you second-guessed my motivation for embarking on this mission in the first place. You think this is an unnecessary war." Saol instinctively put his hand up, stopping Khurt from speaking. He continued, "As clever as you think you are, some things I just *know*. Regardless, my father prepared me on every single meticulous detail about being a general and commander, especially on the subject of war. I know what we are up against as clearly as we can see the sea before us." He looked at Khurt and then back out at the water.

Khurt could see his ship in the distance and wondered if his men had any idea about what was currently happening. "As I said, Commander, I will follow your lead from here on, and do what is best for our mission. For the Vithelegion."

"I know you will," Saol nodded. "I'll tell you what, follow my orders for the first few cities we attack. Just do as I say and you'll understand why I insist on taking no prisoners. After two cities, only two, if you think that I'm wrong and my strategy is flawed, then I'll consider doing things as you suggest. I'll even allow you to formulate a strategy on how best to take prisoners."

Khurt eyed him curiously, "Seriously?" This conversation with Saol had confused him on more than one level. He had never heard Saol speak so casually and at first, wasn't sure whether to take the man at his word. But for Saol to first insist on seeing his way through, Khurt finally saw a glimpse at why Saol might be a good Commander.

"Seriously. What I said in there, in front of the others, just let it go. Take some time to think about things, and I promise you, my methods will all make sense." Saol extended his forearm and Khurt grasped it for their traditional embrace.

In the moment, Khurt also saw and felt Saol's bandaged hand, and felt a hint of guilt for stabbing the man in front of his whole crew. He decided it was best not to bring it up. Khurt was so thrown off by the man's kindness that he even formed a half smile. "Thank you Commander. I'll do as you say and take some time to think."

"Good. Good. Now let me help you with some extra time to think about it all." Saol tightened his grip around Khurt's forearm, and then he grabbed Khurt's shoulder with his other hand. Before Khurt understood what the man was doing, Saol pivoted and heaved Khurt over the railing. As he plummeted toward the water, he could only imagine the sinister smile on Saol's face as he neared what he expected to be certain death.

ADRIA FOLLOWED KRISSETTE through the dim corridor toward the meditation room. This late at night, all of the dinner furniture would be gone and the room would likely be bare. She was honest enough with herself that she knew she couldn't be in any kind of trouble, but to be summoned by Asarei and Savaiyon at this hour was beyond curious. More surprising was that Krissette had been instructed to escort her all the way to the large room. Krissette stopped at the entrance and turned to Adria, her long braid swinging around her shoulders in the process. "Like I said, Adria, I doubt it's anything bad. Most likely, the only reason they would want me to escort you the whole way is to make sure nothing happens to you. Not that anything would, but I guess they are being overly cautious."

Adria nodded, "I suppose I'm about to find out." As she was about to walk in, Adria grasped Krissette's forearm, "You don't have to wait here for me. It's late and you should get to sleep. Besides, whatever is about to happen in this room is likely something that will be on my mind for a while. I'll probably prefer to be alone with my thoughts by the time I'm done."

Krissette hugged her tightly, "Good luck." She smiled at Adria as Adria turned and walked into Asarei's meditation room.

Inside the room, Asarei, Savaiyon, and Slade sat by the far wall, facing each other. The only torch in the room was on the wall just above where they sat. In fact, she could barely identify their faces. She only knew that Asarei would be here, and even sitting, Savaiyon and Slade were taller than anyone else on the island, save Blastevahn. Adria walked toward them, trying hard not to walk too fast, but also not wanting to make it look like she was holding herself back. She was naturally light on her feet, which made her wonder whether she should do something more to make her presence known.

As if reading her mind, Savaiyon called out to her once she was about halfway across the room. "Thank you for coming, Mouse. Please have a seat with us. There is some business that must be discussed."

Once she drew close, the three men shifted around to make room for her on the ground. She sat on the ground to join their circle and looked around at their silhouettes. "Well, it's late, so let's discuss this business."

Asarei, who sat to her left, nodded. "Good. I like the attitude. And that's why you're here in the first place. We need you to be a leader."

She looked at him curiously while gripping her knees tightly, "A leader of what? Or whom?"

He smiled back at her, but his countenance seemed more sinister in the dim light. "*The* leader. Of this mission." *What?* "The three of us here have come to a decision that you are the best choice to lead this mission. Over the last few months, you have shown incredible dedication and poise, and you may not realize it, but the other Ghosts have followed your example."

Savaiyon added to Asarei's point, "Don't for a second think that we've chosen you because no one else is fit to lead. There were definitely other options, but all three of us trust you more when it comes down to it. Add your manifestation to it all, and you are the easy choice."

She looked around at all three of them, hoping for any of them to reveal that they were joking with her the whole time. "This is...a lot. What does my manifestation have to do with anything?"

Asarei answered, "The siege will happen in the dark, which means you will not be able to rely on sight. With you in charge, you can use your manifestation to make decisions based on what you hear. You have shown incredible strides in your ability to pinpoint certain sounds and predict what might happen as a result."

Savaiyon spoke up again. "Badalao and Kadoog'han will be your seconds-in-command. You will make the decisions and then relay them to Lao, that way he can relay them to everyone else."

"Wouldn't it make more sense for him to just be in charge, then? I don't know if I even want this. What if I mess something up?"

Asarei leaned in and grasped her hand, which still rested on her knee. "Adria, the greatest leaders have never been the ones who sought to lead. They have been the ones who rose to the occasion when the situation called upon them. When their people needed them. And that is what we're telling you now. We need you. Ashur needs you. You do not need to be anything more or different than who you already are. Trust in yourself and you will succeed."

She took a deep breath. "Am I here because you are asking me, or telling me?"

"We cannot *force* you to do anything, but we hope that you will answer the call. If you recall, the Book of Orijin states that our leaders will stand tall during our darkest hours. This is one of those hours." Savaiyon's voice was soft, but insistent. "Believe me, I would gladly lead, but I am almost certain that the Anonymi will not allow me to go with you. The universe calls upon you now."

She cracked a smile, hoping the humor would ease the tension in her shoulders. "The Orijin has a strange sense of humor, then, doesn't He. Asking the shortest person here to stand tall." The three men all broke out in laughter; even Slade's stoic countenance broke.

After the laughter subsided, Savaiyon finally looked at her and asked, "Is that a 'yes,' then?"

"Can it be a 'probably, and let me sleep on it'?"

Savaiyon nodded, "Very well. Go sleep. You can give us your answer at breakfast."

Adria stood and walked away. As she neared the other side of the room, she could hear their voices again, and resisted the temptation to use her manifestation to eavesdrop. *That's not what a leader would do, is it?.* She left the meditation room and slumped against a wall after only a few steps. She wasn't upset, nor scared, but the weight of what they were asking suddenly blanketed her entire body and Adria felt as if she couldn't move. She didn't bother trying to walk any farther, and instead, knelt on the ground and took a few deep breaths. Even that was a struggle. After a few minutes of just breathing and not even trying to form a thought, she pressed her forehead against the cold brick wall. The chill brought instant relief to some of the weight dragging her down, but only for a few moments. *Get it together. They chose you because they know you can handle it. Stop acting like the girl your parents think you are, and act like the one you know you are.* She pushed herself off of the wall and stood up. *Marshall. I should talk to Marshall. He'll tell me I'm capable enough to do this.*

She forced herself to start walking, and proceeded towards the men's quarters. She had only visited the room infrequently, but the thought of how the men slept brought a flash of amusement. She remembered seeing them just strewn about, like a room full of house cats all napping wherever they could find the space. The men slept in all types of strange and awkward positions, while the women had sorted out an arrangement for sleeping. Of course, there were far more men on the island, so Adria and the other ladies had the luxury of more space. *I hope he's still awake; I don't want to have to wake him up just to have to listen to my problems.*

After walking slowly for several minutes, she arrived at the entryway to their quarters, and was surprised to see Badalao sitting on the ground, against the wall, looking exactly as she felt. "Hey. What are you doing?" She kept her voice low, not wanting to wake anyone up and also because she was certain Badalao didn't want anyone else to know he was here.

He looked up at her, "Eh, just trying to stop my head from exploding."

She sat down next to him and realized that his hair was down, rather than up in his traditional ancient Markosi style. "Didn't realize your hair was that long. Things must be rough if you're willing to look like that with other people around." He cracked a small smile. "But, you actually look the way I feel. Want to share?" She'd remembered some of the elders in Fera would often say something about miserable people loving company, or something of the sort. *Maybe it'll be easier to sort it all out with Lao, instead of waking Marshall.*

"Maybe. You first?"

Adria nodded, "Fine." *I'd rather get this all out of my head as soon as possible, anyway.* "I just met with Asarei, Savaiyon, and Rhadames. They want me to lead the siege." She stared at the floor to avoid any emotion surfacing. "As in, I make the decisions, relay them to you, and then you relay them to the rest of the Ghosts."

Surprisingly, Badalao scoffed. "Dammit."

"What?" She glanced at him.

"I'll tell you when it's my turn."

Adria shrugged in acceptance, then continued. "I *know* what they see in me, and I know that those qualities are real, but I think it's that this siege...it didn't become..."

Badalao continued her thought for her, "It didn't become real until tonight."

"Yeah. Exactly. Even with being captured by Maqdhuum and Jahmash, I never had to make the calls. Those things *happened* to me, but I was never in control. Then Maqdhuum rescued me and again, I had no control over the situation. I've always told myself that I was strong and that I could lead, but I think those things are easy to say when you aren't put into any difficult situations."

She could feel Badalao's gaze upon her as he started to speak. "You know, most of us in the House of Darian were somewhat afraid of you, right?" She looked at him quizzically. "Yeah, sounds crazy, doesn't it? But it's true. I think many of us saw your potential, and knew that if you were pushed hard enough, you could easily put any of us in our places. That wasn't fear out of dislike or mistrust, it was fear out of knowing just how powerful you are. It was reverence. I speak for every man in that chamber right now when saying that we would follow your lead on any mission."

Adria stared at the ground again, even more intently, to focus on holding the tears back. She had been oblivious to any of these sentiments while at the House of Darian, but she knew that Badalao was telling her the truth and not just trying to make her feel better. She clenched her jaw to steel her resolve, then responded, "Th-thanks. That means everything to me."

"I know. And just in case you think I'm just being nice, you can ask any of them tomorrow. They'll tell you the exact same thing. You were made for this moment. And as long as you stay true to yourself and trust your instincts, I have no doubt that we'll be successful under your watch."

"I get it. Stop saying all these nice things now. If I cry in front of you, I won't be able to hang this hair thing over your head."

Badalao finally chuckled. "Honestly, you can have the hair thing. Go ahead and cry. I would never use that against you. There's been so much tension building inside of each of us, that I think everyone on this island has cried multiple times over the past several months." As soon as he said that, Adria knew it would be impossible to stop the rush of tears, and allowed them to fall. They gushed down her face as she smiled at Badalao. She looked at him, unable to get a word out, and surprisingly, he smiled back with tears of his own streaking down his cheeks. "See, told you."

They sat there for a few moments in silence, just letting all of the tension and emotions escape, and Adria finally summed up the ability to speak again. "Whew, that was...cathartic. Now it's your turn." As she turned to him, she saw that Badalao now stared at the ground.

"You sure you don't want to keep talking about you?"

"Positive. The only thing uglier than me crying with all kinds of fluid coming out of my eyes and nose is me crying with nothing coming out. I'm all out of tears now. Maybe by the time you're finished, I'll have more." She wiped her face with her sleeve, then patted his forearm. "Whenever you're ready."

Badalao nodded, "Fine." He paused for a moment, then continued. "I'm assuming that if you're relaying your orders through me, that I'm your second-in-command?"

"That's what they said."

"Well, then it might be me who ruins the mission."

"What do you mean?"

"All this time, I've been a phony. I've been lying to everyone." She was about to ask him to clarify, but he continued. "I think from the time I arrived at the House, I told everyone that my manifestation didn't work at night, and that is actually not true." He took a breath. "The truth is that I went through something traumatic when I was younger, where I didn't handle my manifestation properly in the middle of the night, and hurt someone severely as a result. After that, I never used my manifestation in the darkness again, for fear that I might hurt someone in a panic."

Adria took it all in and searched for a solution to offer. "I understand. But that was one situation a long time ago. You've got it under much better control now; I'm sure Asarei could easily help you master it before we're ready to go."

"That's the thing; my sister is the only one who knows that I've been lying about it, and she makes me enter her mind every night, to help me get past this block. And I do, and it works. Obviously I haven't hurt or killed her, but she thinks I'm expanding to other people, and I cannot bring myself to do that."

"You haven't hurt or killed her *because* she's your sister and you're likely extra cautious. Come on. Try it on me."

"What? Not a chance."

She jabbed her finger into his chest. "Lao. You removed Jahmash from Farrah's head with no problem, and mine as well. Do you really think that you're going to hurt me just because the sun has set? You're being ridiculous. Now invade my mind or I'll have Savaiyon send me to Constaniza just so I can tell your sister the truth." She paused for a moment, "Not only that, I'll tell all the ladies about this horrible tunic that you apparently wear to sleep."

She managed to evoke a smile from Badalao once again, "See, now you've got my attention. This...thing...belongs to Trevor. I believe it's a Cerysian fashion, so perhaps this is how Cerysian men get the women to notice them."

"Stop stalling."

He grunted, "Fine. Sit back against the wall and relax." Adria did as he said as he closed his eyes. "This should be no different than any time before but let me know if there is any discomfort."

"Understood, second-in-command." She briefly considered pretending that he was hurting her, but decided against it. The last thing she wanted was for Badalao to take it the wrong way and swear off trying to get past his mental block. After several moments, she felt a slight tightening inside her head, but not to the point of being uncomfortable.

Am I being too rough?

No, this is fine. You're doing great. Stay as long as you need to. But don't get too nosy.

I'm just here, I'm not digging into anything. It's like my eyes are closed.

While you're in here in my head, you might as well talk to me.
About what?

She rolled her eyes. *About anything, fool. I'm just helping you get comfortable with doing this. Why don't you pick something to talk about?*

He was silent for a moment, but Adria still felt his presence. Finally he spoke again. *I am curious about something. Your father is Markosi, but your mother is not, correct?*

Yes, that's right. Why?

It's just that 'Adria' isn't very Markosi. Is it Galicean then?

Adria sighed audibly. *Dammit. I made it through the destruction of the House of Darian without any of you ever asking about my name, and now I'm in the middle of trying to help you, and this is how it's going to come out.*

Did I strike a nerve? We can talk about something else if you'd like.

She pursed her lips, *No, it's fine. You might as well know, since we've already shared so much. My full name is Adrianza Mariako Varela, and that's about as Markosi as it gets. I don't know how or why my mother allowed that to happen.* She could feel Badalao's emotion and tone change, even within her head.

Light of Orijin, that's almost as outdated as my hairstyle! In a split-second, the grip on her mind was gone and Badalao leaned forward, unable to contain his laughter. He kept his hands over his mouth to stifle his cackles, not wanting to wake anyone up. It proved infectious, though, as Adria started to laugh and couldn't bring herself to stop. They sat and laughed like fools for what felt like hours until sleep overtook them both.

CHAPTER 20
RETURN TO THE ANONYMI CHAMBERS

From *The Book of Orijin*, **Verse Twenty-five**
What is worthwhile shall rarely be obtained easily.
Success, happiness, and appreciation shall be hollow without sacrifice.

"ARE WE JUST NOT GOING to talk about it?" Vasher eyed Savaiyon as the taller man stepped through the yellow-fringed gateway and abruptly made it vanish. Savaiyon had been relatively quiet throughout the morning, at least toward Vasher. If anything, the dry, desolate landscape in front of them matched Savaiyon's attitude at the moment.

"Talk about what?" The former Maven was unsuccessfully trying to sound coy, and Vasher wasn't going to let him get away with it.

"You know what. Adria and Lao both sleeping in the hallway outside the men's quarters. Did that have anything to do with this morning's announcement that Adria would lead the siege?" A gust of wind blew past their faces, and Vasher was glad for the lined cloak. Despite the early spring, on some days, the remnants of winter overpowered the new season. To be fair, most Shivaani got cold easily, though Vasher couldn't be sure why that was the case for his people.

As Vasher matched strides with Savaiyon, the taller man exhaled deeply. "I suspect the spectacle that we saw this morning was a result of Adria being given the news late last night. If you must know, she did not readily accept the leadership responsibility, and asked for the night to think it over. My guess is that she sought out some counsel after meeting with me, Asarei, and Rhadames, and ended up working it all out with Badalao. Despite what they looked like early this morning, their talk must have worked, as Adria was fully on board with what we asked of her by the time breakfast began."

"That's interesting." As Vasher finished the thought, Savaiyon extended his right arm straight into the air and clenched his fist, then brought it back down. "We're getting close, huh. They didn't want to send us one of those masked babysitters this time?"

Savaiyon glanced at him and smirked. "Funny you would say that. He was only sent because they weren't sure they could trust you. If you had done a single thing out of line in the process of entering the fortress, he would have killed you. Why are you so curious about Adria? Do you disagree with this selection?"

Vasher shook his head, "No, of course not. But she's so reserved;

she's the last person I would've expected to see asleep in the corridor. And what happens if I step out of line this time? Would *you* have to kill me?"

"Why don't we try it and see?" Savaiyon's smile grew larger.

"You wouldn't kill me," Vasher rolled his eyes. "You like me too much. Either way, I'm glad the other guy isn't here this time. That armor and cloak, something about them made me so uneasy. I was honestly getting nauseous just looking at him."

Savaiyon nodded, "That is part of the function. The armor helps to camouflage as well as somewhat disarm opponents. We spend days upon days staring at it until it no longer affects us. It does take a while to get used to." A ramp opened from the ground in the near distance, and Vasher looked around for anyone who might have seen Savaiyon's fist signal, or who might've signaled for the ramp to open, but there were no signs of life besides the two of them. As they descended, Savaiyon spoke again in a hushed tone. "You came along because you wanted to spend more time in the Ancient Chambers. You have until I have finished explaining to them that my secret has been revealed."

Vasher nodded as they reached the bottom of the ramp, and kept his voice low like Savaiyon's. "So they might actually kill you then, huh?"

Savaiyon shrugged, "It is a possibility, but excommunication is more likely. And if that is the case, they would still watch me for the rest of my life to make sure I don't reveal any secrets."

"No way," Vasher waved his hand. "Once they know that it was Abram of all people who saw who you were, they'll come around." The bottom of the ramp gave way to a large, poorly lit chamber. Vasher remembered the last time he'd been here and looked forward to revisiting the ninth chamber. There had been something about the nine warriors that had drawn his curiosity, and he couldn't wait to return to it and take it all in, especially knowing he might have the time to learn something, since Savaiyon was the one with business to tend to. The entry room was not as bright as he'd remembered it the last time, but the light was sufficient to see his surroundings. Vasher waited for Savaiyon to make a move. The last thing he wanted to do was misstep and end up in some Anonymi dungeon.

"Come. They'll be waiting at the Ninth Chamber." Savaiyon waved for him to follow and then walked on.

Vasher followed excitedly, "Is that the one that I asked to stay at for a while?"

"Yes. There will be two novices there ready to instruct you on anything you want to know about the Okike—the Nine who originally led the Anonymi." Savaiyon paused, almost as if dramatically, "Within reason."

Vasher nodded, "Understood." He made his best attempt to not let his tone reveal his excitement. They walked on through the chambers and Vasher saw two masked figures standing in the distance. Each chamber somewhat flowed into the next one, as there were no doors, but large doorways instead. As they drew closer, he realized the Ninth Chamber was illuminated more than the previous eight that they'd walked through. The light also made their robes more noticeable, the same robes that nauseated Vasher simply by looking at them. He couldn't comprehend their color; it was as if they were every color and no color at the same time. He chose to focus on their masks instead, which were black as pitch, instead of the silver one that he had seen others wear the last time. He deduced that perhaps mask colors indicated a hierarchy among the Anonymi, and different colors signified different ranks or levels. *Novices wear black. I wonder what rank the one who escorted us last time was. Do they attain silver after novice? I'll have to ask Savaiyon.* He wished he'd been able to better see his surroundings the last time when he was in the room with all of the small enclaves, as he was now certain there were more colors besides black and silver.

Savaiyon stopped once they entered the Ninth Chamber, "These two are here to answer your questions. They will not speak unless addressed. They also will not answer questions that are not about the Original Nine. So before you even finish the thought, you do not ask if you can join, and you do not ask their names."

Vasher nodded. He wanted to be snarky, but that would diminish his appreciation for Savaiyon's efforts. "Got it."

"And no asking about me, either," the taller man added.

"Of course." Vasher smirked and then turned to the two novices as Savaiyon walked away. He eyed them both up and down, and almost lost his confidence to ask questions. He turned his attention to the tapestries that had mesmerized him the last time, and regained his bearings. "First, when did they start the Anonymi, and what were their names?"

SAVAIYON CONTINUED THROUGH the underground fortress. After departing from the entry chambers, the corridors were all unlit. It was expected that Anonymi could navigate their way to wherever they needed to go based solely on memory. He walked slowly through the dark halls, nervous more about what the Komytii might tell him in the Crucible, the room where all decisions were made, than about finding his way around in the dark. Although it had been a while since he had to get around on his own, Anonymi training was intense enough that he neither would nor could ever forget the intricate layout of the underground fortress.

After several minutes, Savaiyon arrived at the Crucible and

hesitated before opening the large, heavy door. He knew that the entire Komytii was there, awaiting him. Since arranging this meeting, he expected only bad news, and as realistic as he'd been about the limitations of the siege, he knew that this meeting would solidify all of those rules and boundaries. He took a deep breath. *Might as well get it over with.*

He entered the dark room. It tended to seem bigger when he didn't want to be there. The torch at the center of the room was lit, jutting a foot or so from its holder in the ground. He walked to the torch and retrieved the metallic red mask that lay next to it on the ground. The process could not begin until he was masked. As he placed it on his face and pulled up his hood, Savaiyon felt himself calm significantly. *Remember, we are here to act in Ashur's best interest. Any decision made is for the best of Ashur.* Savaiyon then took his place along the perimeter of the large inner circle, where dozens of other silver and red-masked acolytes stood, silently waiting. He thought about the last time he came here with Vasher, imagining what Vasher must have thought about this room. It was no wonder that Vasher had almost missed the opportunity to speak with them.

The entire Komytii circled the perimeter nine times, until the torch's flame blew out. Then, every acolyte filtered into their enclaves, each of them separated from all the others. In the enclaves, they were free to remove their masks if they chose, but required to wear them when speaking. The masks themselves were forged in Domna Orjann, far across the sea, using a dense metal native to the floating islands there. While wearing them, one's voice grew deeper and louder, which allowed them to mask any markers of their identities. Ironically, though, Anonymi rarely spoke outside of the Crucible, except during training. They mostly relied on visual cues and communication, using signs and gestures. Some acolytes who struggled with that aspect tended to request to be sent to the Tower of the Blind as servants. Savaiyon had considered that option a long time ago, but changed his mind once he was granted special permission to join the House of Darian.

A voice boomed through the room. "Speak, Acolyte. State your business."

He knew that that was meant for him. "I seek counsel about the siege on King Edmund."

The voice boomed again, though there was no way of telling whether it was the same one or a different one. "What counsel may we provide?"

"I need to know the extent of the help we are allowed. You stated that only followers of Zin Marlowe can be involved in killing King Edmund. Does that mean that no help is allowed from others?"

"Ashur must know that Zin Marlowe's followers acted independently of anyone else. You have named yourselves 'The Ghosts of Ashur'. Only a Ghost of Ashur may be involved in your mission, with the exception of you, Garrison Brighton, Rhadames Slade, Adl Maqdhuum, and Farrah Shokan." Savaiyon had forgotten whether their knowledge of all of those names had come from him, but even if they hadn't, he wasn't surprised at the depth of their knowledge. He would have no way of knowing whether another acolyte was tracking him. The voice continued, "The remainder of your 'Ghosts' are permitted. But remember, we will know if our requirements have been met. Acolyte, you have had a foot in both of these worlds for some time. That time must come to an end. We require you to stay and complete your ascendance. We have made an exception for far too long."

What? Savaiyon almost removed his mask to think more clearly. "Are you saying that I am no longer allowed to be out in the world?"

"An exception was made on your behalf because of your potential influence on the new Harbingers. They no longer require your guidance, as they have others who can fill that role. You will stay here and accept a new assignment." The voice boomed louder inside Savaiyon's head than it did in the enclave.

Dammit. He tried to take deep breaths to stay calm and keep his head clear. "Very well. My business in the Crucible has ended," he said reluctantly. He stood from the chair in the enclave, then stepped out of it simultaneously with all the others, and they all filed out of the Crucible. Once into the corridors, the group knew to match pace, no matter the destination. Savaiyon slowed to the appropriate speed and set course to return to Vasher. He now regretted returning, and knew Vasher would have questions he didn't want to answer.

VASHER SAT AGAINST THE WALL while everyone trickled into the meditation room. He still wore his heavy cloak, lined with fur. Most rooms in Asarei's domain had a chill, despite all of the torches. He had returned a short while ago, and immediately summoned everyone to Asarei's meditation room, which was used more as a dining hall or meeting room since they'd all arrived. He wanted desperately to just be able talk to Lincan and Baltaszar about the Okike he'd learned about at the Anonymi fortress. Unfortunately, with Savaiyon having to stay there, the burden now lay upon him to share the Anonymi's decisions.

As more people entered, the group started to walk across the room and sat near Vasher. Asarei and Rhadames sat next to him, which surprised him, but brought comfort.

"I have just returned from the Anonymi fortress. Without getting into any details, Savaiyon is needed there and must remain there for the time being. I have no answers about it, so please save your questions." Vasher looked around and knew the group was uneasy. *Stick to the business.* "I'll be blunt, so here is what we have to work with. No one who was not a follower of Zin Marlowe at the House of Darian may be a part of the siege." A few voices chattered, but he raised a hand to silence them, "What that means is, only the following people will go to Alvadon: Adria, Badalao, Desmond, Baltaszar, Horatio, Kadoog'han, Maximilian, Marshall, Reverron, Malikai, Sindha, Delilah, Blastevahn, and me. That is fourteen of us. Originally we said four squadrons. Does that still work?"

"Three will be better." Garrison stood up and then walked to Vasher. He turned and faced the group without sitting, "There are three entry points from different parts of the castle. If it is only fourteen, your best chance is to divide the guards. This decree from the Anonymi means that Donovan and Wendell cannot help either, which means even the Vermillion who are loyal to them will not be able to interfere."

"That means that we'll also want Tasz, Raish, and Desmond separated," Badalao added. "Their manifestations are the most weaponized out of all of us. No offense to the rest of you, of course. But you three should be the ones at the front of each group."

Vasher was impressed with Garrison and Badalao, especially as he glanced at Adria. "Savaiyon asked me to speak on behalf of him. Adria, as the one leading this mission, what do you think?"

She looked at him blankly, then blinked. "Hold on a moment." She shifted her gaze to the ceiling as if pondering, then stood and joined Vasher and Garrison at the front. "Three squadrons. The first will include me, Tasz, Marshall, Blastevahn, and Vasher. The second will be Lao, Desmond, Rev, Sindha, and Delilah, and the third will be Kadoog'han, Raish, Malikai, and Maximilian. I think that evens out our abilities best, and allows certain manifestations to complement each other. That also means that I would like for each squadron to train separately before we depart. I want us to have a certain level of synchronicity when the time comes, so we know how and how *much* to depend on each other. Speaking of which, when *do* we depart?"

Vasher looked at Asarei, then at Sindha. "Sindha, do you think your father would have had enough time to finish everything by now?"

Savaiyon, Asarei, and Slade had sent Sindha back home to Itarse months ago, to request that her father make armor for them. Measurements had been taken for all of them, and her father warned that it would take months to make everything while also forging what he was already required to. Savaiyon had offered him a generous payment for the services, but her father refused, saying it was his honor and duty to do so. The other men who agreed to help the Ghosts all shared the same sentiment.

"Depends on whose armor he's finished. Remember, we originally asked for armor and weapons for everyone. I…"

Vasher missed Savaiyon in this moment. "Maqdhuum, Savaiyon would've been able to just make a gateway. Any chance you can take a few people to check and just find out for sure? The easiest way would be to ask him."

The stringy-haired man nodded, "Of course. Who's coming? You'll have to actually touch me to travel with me. Don't be shy."

"Take Marshall, Garrison, and Malikai for now. Obviously Sindha, too." Sindha nodded at him with a smile and blinked out of sight with Maqdhuum and the others.. He looked at all the others, and then at Adria. "If everything is ready now, then we have a week to prepare. The longer we wait, the more things will get in the way. We're not even allowed help with traveling, so we'll have to get there like…regular people. And we will need to be cautious with that as well. Maybe we leave in separate squadrons, and then find a common meeting ground. Though, without Garrison with us, we might have difficulty finding a safe place."

Adria shook her head at him. "The Stones of Gideon. It is far enough outside of the city to keep us from being noticed, and no one goes there."

Vasher nodded as he eyed Asarei and Slade, wondering if he was overstepping any authority or boundaries. He would have loved to have known what was said between Adria and Badalao during that hallway conversation that resulted in them both falling asleep on the floor. Whatever was said, Adria was now confident and in command. "Will all three squadrons know how to get there?"

Maximilian responded, "I am familiar with it. I can direct my team there."

"As can I," Reverron added. Vasher noticed a tinge of nervousness in his voice. He was about to ask Reverron about it when the others returned with Maqdhuum and a hefty haul of weapons and armor.

"We're going to need more help!" Malikai beamed as he carried a black breastplate in each arm. The other three each carried the same thing. Vasher wondered how they managed to do that and still maintain contact with Maqdhuum. As they neared the group, they delivered the breastplates to the person each was made for.

Asarei nodded to the group, "You heard him. Go help to retrieve the rest." Over the next several minutes, weapons and armor started to fill the room, including breastplates and vambraces, helmets, swords and daggers, shields, lances, gauntlets, axes, and hammers. By the time they finished, the whole group stood in silence and marveled at what lay before them.

Once they were done, Vasher sighed, knowing what had to be discussed next. He was starting to hate being Savaiyon's stand-in. "Everyone, please sit once more. Again, please remember that I speak on behalf of Savaiyon, who relayed all this direction to me before sending me back here." He paused for a moment. "Adria, you placed Horatio and Malikai together. Are you two still willing to go through with killing Edmund?" Both nodded confidently and solemnly. "How will this work, logistically, then?"

Adria smiled. "I've been thinking about this as well. While you and Savaiyon were gone, Garrison and I discussed that three groups would be ideal. The reason being is that my squadron and Lao's would enter from the more heavily guarded areas. Our groups would draw the bulk of the soldiers, which would allow for Kai to lead the third group against a lighter opposition. That should help to clear the way for Raish and Kai to get to Edmund without much pushback. As a contingency, if my squadron or Lao's happens to get to Edmund first, then one of us will have to do the deed."

Vasher lost his train of thought. He'd never thought poorly of Adria, but he now saw exactly why Savaiyon thought so highly of her. As he fumbled with a response, the only thing he managed to say was, "Unstoppable."

Adria looked at him curiously, "I'm sorry?"

He chuckled at the sound of what he said, and didn't bother to backtrack. "It's clear that we'll all be unstoppable under your leadership." He looked around the room. "Seriously. If we follow her lead and trust her decisions, I think we'll undoubtedly succeed. Savaiyon would be really proud of you." She blushed and Vasher shifted the focus by providing the group with Savaiyon's final direction. He'd discussed this with Asarei and Slade just to make sure they were on the same page as well, and both agreed. "As I said before, we'll depart one week from today. For the next five days, our training will consist of two parts. As Adria stated, we'll train with our teams to become a cohesive unit. We'll do this after breakfast until midday. We'll then break for lunch and a short relaxation. Then, the second part will be constant sparring with various opponents after lunch until dinnertime. After dinner, we'll all return to our chambers and sleep. On the sixth and seventh days, we'll use the time for resting, bonding, and revelry. Even on the seventh day, which is the day we will depart, we're expected to enjoy ourselves from the time we wake up until it is time to leave. Is this understood?" As he looked around, the rest of them nodded confidently. "Good. Salvation as one. Now let's play with our new toys." He tilted his head towards all the new armor and weapons. They repeated the motto and joined Vasher in going through all the new things.

CHAPTER 21
INVASION

From ***The Book of Orijin,*** **Verse Two Hundred Eight**
Intention and emotion can only take you so far, for they only exist within you.
Conviction without action is an unsheathed sword.

KHURT LAY IN HIS DISHEVELED BED, which felt smaller and smaller every day. His feet ached and burned, but he found solace in that he was finally able to fully move his toes since his fall from Davala's ship a few days before. He'd had the wherewithal to tighten his body and point his feet downwards, but the impact of such a long drop still took its toll. Under any other circumstance, Khurt knew that he might've felt the pain right away, but too many men had fallen in the sea and not returned for him to want to find the source.

He remembered vividly how numb his feet and legs had been, and still somehow he managed to swim to the surface and find his boat. It had taken some time for him to regain his composure as well as his breath. By the time he'd rowed back to his own ship, his arms and shoulders burned as well, and it took a few of his men to get him up the ladder and back onto the deck. He'd been bedridden ever since, despite his protests that he didn't need Khenzi and his crewmen tending to him as if he'd been crippled.

The door creaked open slowly as Khenzi's head poked through. "Still think you're invincible?"

Khurt propped up on an elbow and cracked a welcome smile. "Well, I'm alive and I will be ready for battle when we arrive in a few days. So perhaps *almost* invincible."

"Well, you're staying in here until we tell you that you can leave. Everyone knows that you would try to do everything if we let you. Show me your feet. I bet they're still all kinds of strange colors." Khenzi pulled the blanket away from Khurt's legs and exposed his discolored feet and shins. "You see. You wouldn't even have to paint the light skin patches on your legs, they're almost black anyway."

"You sound just like your mother, you know." Khurt grimaced while rubbing his shins and calves.

"Thanks!" Khenzi smiled, the sarcasm lost on the boy.

Khurt shook his head, "No, I meant that as…never mind." He didn't have the energy or patience this morning to reason with a boy who was acting his age. "Look, boy. We are days away from the western shores of Ashur. I am still the Eighth General of the Vithelegion, even if that barely means anything to the other ships. That means it is still my responsibility to lead the men on the ships of the Eighth Battalion and inspire them. With or without your help, I will be up on the deck to speak to my men. So you can either go now and gather them up, including the oarsmen, so that everyone is present by the time I get up there, or you can be stubborn."

Khenzi eyed him with a wicked smirk, "What happens if I'm stubborn?"

"You stay on this ship for the duration of our stay in Ashur. I would literally tie you up and leave you in this cabin." He thought for a moment, "How about this; if you do as I say, I'll arrange for you to spar with Demetri later today." Khenzi's eyes widened and he shot out of the room without a word.

Khurt knew it would take a while for him to even get out of his bed, but he needed to show his men that he could stand before them, ready for the upcoming war. He let both of his legs hang over the side of the bed, then gingerly set his feet on the ground. They still ached with even minimal weight upon them, but the pain was tolerable. He leaned over to grab the breeches on the floor, and awkwardly put them on, maneuvering in various positions to find the least painful. Finally he stood slowly, and the pain increased in his feet from the weight of his full body. He took small steps around the tight quarters, and the pain became more tolerable with each step. Khurt knew that putting on his boots would only increase the pain. The only benefit of taking so long was that it would provide enough time for all of his men to reach the deck and await his arrival.

After several minutes, he walked off the initial soreness of his feet conforming to his boots, and settled on a way of walking that wouldn't look too awkward or show how much pain he was in. He walked carefully up the stairs, glad that nobody remained below deck. As he reached the top, rows and rows of his men stood shoulder to shoulder, waiting for him. At the front of them all stood Khenzi, his solemn countenance every bit the look of a soldier awaiting his general.

Khurt walked slowly until he was about ten yards away, hoping that his pace seemed more dramatic than weak. He looked around at his battalion; they all looked eager and proud, which Khurt appreciated more than he could ever tell them. They were loyal soldiers, and loyal to him more than the Vithelegion itself. Not one of them even hinted at leaving him once he'd been demoted, which they were allowed to do. That was the one detail that Khurt kept close to his heart. It was the one piece of evidence of him being a good leader, despite what the other generals thought.

He spoke calmly, yet loudly. "In a few days, our war begins. We have never faced an enemy this large before, but we do have the advantage of surprise. I look at all of you and I have no doubt in my mind that we are the best battalion!" That roused the men to cheer and yell. He nodded, then raised his palm to quiet them. "You have learned techniques that no other battalion in the Vithelegion knows. You have trained every day of this voyage and are prepared for everything. We will attack in the middle of the night, and let these Darian-worshippers transition easily from a normal sleep into an eternal sleep! We will not be stopped. We will not be defeated. We will feast on Ashurian flesh and bathe in Ashurian blood. We will fight as we have been told, and will take no prisoners. The risk is too great. We will fight as one cohesive army. Then we will burn Ashur to the ground and return to our wives with scars and stories to make them proud. We will make the Greatmother proud! We are Vithelegion!"

The shouts and roars of his men made Khurt forget about his pain for a short while. As he looked around at them, he knew that nothing could strip their dignity and pride, not even stripping their general of his title as First General. Khurt knew for sure that he would not defy Saol, but regardless, his battalion would be the one that determined the success of the entire Vithelegion.

KHURT LOOKED OUT OVER THE RAIL at the blackness of night. The water was calm enough that if one relaxed his eyes, it would look as if the ship was floating in a world of black, with no way of distinguishing the sea from the sky. The black paint on his pale patches of skin brought confidence, as did the two swords at each side of his waist. He wore the traditional Vithelegion armor, which consisted of a black steel breastplate, helmet, and vambraces. Most soldiers opted for the vambraces over gauntlets, as the vambraces allowed for more flexibility when using a sword.

He put his hand on Khenzi's shoulder, who stood next to him also staring out into the darkness. In the night, even Khenzi looked formidable and fearsome with the black patches of paint on his face. "Son, within the hour we will be marching on the shores of an unfamiliar realm. I trust in you and your abilities, especially because I trained you myself. However, I expect that you will stay by my side and fight along with me." He saw Khenzi rubbing the ridge of hair down the middle of his otherwise shaved head, and knew the boy was about to protest. Before Khenzi could speak, Khurt continued. "I know you are going to think I am coddling you or treating you as a baby but remember that I am your father and it is my duty to ensure your well-being. You have barely seen seven years, and I would be a terrible father if I allowed your first battle to be your last. So please trust me. I will not stand in the way of you fighting, but I will watch out for you, as will the other men of this battalion. Otherwise, I expect you to trust in your instincts and remember your training. If we get separated, trust no one outside of the Eighth Battalion. Do you understand?"

Khenzi looked up at him and nodded, "Yes, father. I guess staying with you also means I have to keep you safe."

Khurt laughed heartily, "Well of course! That's the most important part!" They stood and watched some of the men preparing the small messenger boats at the side of the ship. In a short while, all of the ships would anchor far enough off the coast to remain undetected, and they would all row to shore in the small messenger boats to maintain their cover in the event that anyone was scouting the coast. Khurt looked out across the black void ahead of him. He wondered what the people would be like across the expanse between his ship and Ashur. He wondered if they would see him and the Vithelegion as infidels, just as he saw them. He wondered how well they would be able to fight back, and whether they would be as merciless as Saol Suldas wanted the Vithelegion to be.

He knew these kinds of thoughts were dangerous, and if he lingered on them for too long, they would affect his ability to be effective in combat. He tried to focus on the notion that they supported a Harbinger that was almost as bad as Jahmash. A man chosen by the Orijin, who killed countless innocent people in the process of drowning the world, instead of just killing Jahmash. A man who allowed his friends Abram and Lionel to sacrifice their own lives, just so he could run away. Darian was a coward, and anyone who celebrated him was not only incorrigible, but destined to rot in Opprobrium. And Khurt would be happy to send them there.

The messenger boats were finally ready for boarding. Throughout the voyage, they were primarily used to send couriers between ships. Now, though, they would deliver the Vithelegion's message to Ashur, that the price for celebrating Darian was blood and death. "General, your boat awaits." Demetri, his First Captain, stood a few feet away, ready to usher him and Khenzi to the ladder at the side of the ship. Khurt nodded and followed with Khenzi in tow. He descended the rope ladder first, so that he could assist Khenzi once they reached the bottom. As steady as the crewmen kept the messenger boats when boarding, they always rocked a bit because of the water.

Once they were both in, an oarsman boarded their messenger boat and positioned them ahead of the rest of the battalion. Khurt stood and faced his battalion behind him, who were all filing into their boats. He removed his dagger from his thigh holster and clanged it against his breastplate, indicating for them to mobilize. The Eighth Battalion responded by repeating the same sound with their own daggers, and Khurt sat as his oarsman started rowing once more.

They reached the sandy shore after several minutes, and the half of the Eighth Battalion that would be part of the night's attack filed into two lines behind Khurt as he and Khenzi walked farther inland. Every battalion was instructed to leave its current oarsmen behind, as they'd need time to rest, and the Vithelegion wouldn't need the entire army to overtake one city. In the moonlight, he could see the shadows of a city in the distance. It would be an easy target, as there was no wall or gate or even towers to protect it from an attack. *Arrogance. That will be their downfall.* Khurt couldn't fathom how a city could be so open and unprotected, but he wouldn't complain about his job being easier.

The air smelled only of the salty ocean and wet sand. The lack of ash or smoke in the air meant that most people were in their homes, likely sleeping, instead of outside using fire to stay warm. In the distance, he saw the other generals leading their battalions, with Saol's personal squadron not far ahead. Their black armor and black-painted skin camouflaged them well in the darkness of night, especially with barely any light coming from the city ahead.

Khurt saw the glint of Saol's silver dagger just before Saol clanged it against his own breastplate. It was a single, minimal command for them to proceed. *The war begins.* He whispered to Khenzi, "Remember, stay close. Trust your instincts." Khurt led his battalion ahead of the other seven, as Saol had commanded him to pair with Saol's own forces. As he neared Saol, the Commander acknowledged him with a curt smile and a nod. Khurt knew there would be no wasted words on the eve of battle, and he knew that for Saol, the only thing that mattered was what was happening at the moment. Not a week before or a day before.

The other generals arrived and formed a circle with Khurt and Saol. Saol wasted no time in relaying orders. "Hector, Raiza, Bragha. Your battalions will march toward the southern side of the city to enter from another point. Rafa. You, Thiel, and Ezera will do the same from the north. No point in all of us pouring in from here and allowing them to flush out from the other end. March on and once your battalions are out of sight, Davala, Khurt, and I will storm the city from here." The generals returned to their own battalions and Khurt watched as six of them marched on to other sides of the city.

As the last of the soldiers disappeared from view, Saol hit his chest plate once more with his dagger, and the three battalions marched into the city. The streets were bare, save for one or two merchants pulling carts. Saol raised his right arm high, then thrust it down. In a matter of seconds, soldiers had run down anyone remaining in the street and quickly killed them. The battalions then broke ranks and stormed every building and home in sight.

Khurt led Khenzi and a small group of soldiers into a two-story building. They broke through the front door with ease, and Khurt pulled Khenzi aside as his soldiers continued on. "I want you to stay here at the front. If anyone besides one of us tries to leave this building, you are going to kill them."

"But, father…"

"Khenzi, this is not a request from your father. It is an order from your General. Do you understand?"

The boy pursed his lips in frustration and rolled his eyes. Khurt wondered where he'd gotten that from; it certainly wasn't him. "Yes, fa…General."

"Good." With that, Khurt turned and stealthily navigated the building. He didn't expect much in the way of a fight. They were massacring these people in the darkness of night, while they slept, which was the biggest reason why he needed to keep Khenzi away from what they were doing. Khurt crept up a staircase and found a closed door. His men had already covered most of the building. Another soldier reached the top of the staircase and Khurt signaled for him to follow. Khurt slowly and quietly opened the door and entered the dark bedroom. In it, a couple slept, facing away from one another. Both snored loudly, which only made Khurt's job easier. He and the other soldier stood at opposite sides of the bed and unsheathed their daggers at the same time. *In the name of Abram.* They slit the sleeping couple's throats, and Khurt turned and left the room as the man opened his eyes in shock and clutched his neck. There was no time for sentimentality. If anything, they were killing them as mercifully as possible, since slitting their throats would allow for a quick death.

He left the room and searched the rest of the floor for anything unchecked. All of the other doors had been opened. They returned downstairs, where Khurt saw Khenzi waiting, his hand clutching the sword hilt at his waist. Khurt walked to him and smiled, "Well done. Let's go." As they stalked on to the next target, Khurt noticed a blaze on the other side of town. "Dammit. That is going to bring attention." *That has to be Ezera's battalion that started it. Way too early.* He turned to the group of soldiers in his company, "Hurry! To the next house!"

Khenzi ran alongside him, "Can I help this time? Can I do my duty as a soldier?"

"I need you to look out again."

"But I can help!"

Khurt looked at him as they reached the door of the next target. "Do you really want your first kill to be someone sleeping with no means of defense? No, of course you don't. You saw that fire outside; that means it is only a matter of time before an army arrives. Then you will have your chance. For now, I need you to be our lookout." He patted Khenzi's shoulder as the boy nodded, defeated. Khurt walked past him, further into the house. He found a door near the back of the ground floor and entered quietly. From the moonlight that crept through the window, he saw the silhouette of a child sitting up in the bed.

"Are ya here ta kill me?" The boy whimpered, his young voice cracking in the process. As Khurt walked up to the bed, he could see the tears streaming down the boy's face, and smelled the sour odor, indicating that the boy must have wet himself. Khurt maintained a stoic face, but couldn't bring himself to speak, so he nodded in affirmation. The boy looked down and then back at him. Despite his trembling, he managed another question, "Will it hurt?"

Khurt crinkled his nose and shook his head. In truth, he had no way of knowing whether the boy would feel much pain. He just knew that the process wouldn't last very long.

The boy asked one final question, saving the hardest one for last. "Why must ya do it?"

Khurt took a deep breath, glad that he had steeled himself enough to hold back any tears. He looked down for a moment, and finally at the boy once more, "You worship Darian, a Harbinger whose crimes are unforgivable. And for that, you must die."

"Who's Darian an' what's a Harbinger?"

Khurt knew the longer the conversation lasted, the more likely it would be that the boy lived. He looked at his dagger and took a step back towards the door, then remembered that Khenzi awaited him. If he didn't do his duty and follow Saol's orders, it would be Khenzi who suffered. He sat on the edge of the bed, then put a hand on the boy's sweat-soaked head and clutched the dagger. "I'm sorry, boy," his voice cracked. "I must choose between you and my own son." *In the name...of Abram.* Khurt quickly covered the boy's eyes and swiped the dagger across his tender neck. He pulled the boy to him and held him there as the life drained from his body, until the convulsions stopped.

He laid the boy's body back down in the bed and closed his own eyes for a moment. *Is this really what Abram would want? For his followers to kill children in the middle of the night?* He shook off the emotion, remembering that if he took too long, his soldiers would wonder what was going on. As he left this room, he didn't bother to check the rest of the house. He walked back to Khenzi, who dutifully awaited outside the front door. Khenzi's eyes grew wide at the sight of him, surprised at the sight of blood.

"Did they start fighting back?" Khenzi looked at him with wide-eyed wonder.

Khurt shook his head and paused for a moment, "Not quite, but they wanted to."

"Must have been someone big with all that blood! Glad I didn't have to fight him!"

"Me too." He looked toward the other end of the city. The fire was growing and engulfing several buildings, likely visible to others beyond the city. Khurt turned to his company, "All of you, go on to the next available target. Khenzi and I are going to stay outside to monitor the fire. I have a feeling we'll be seeing combat shortly." He walked farther up with Khenzi by his side. He looked off into the distance, struggling to see the fire past the image of the boy in his head. Khurt kept telling himself that if it wasn't that boy, it would be Khenzi. Even though the notion was true, he had a hard time believing it as he told himself that over and over. He saw Saol through a crowd in the distance, leading his own company toward the fire. *Thank the Orijin.*

Khurt's company silently returned from another house and gathered around Khurt and Khenzi. They looked out at the blaze, just as Khurt and Khenzi did. One of the soldiers asked, "How much time do you think we have, General?"

Khurt shook away the thought of the boy. "There's no telling. I doubt there are soldiers right outside the city, else they would be here already. That means that an army could arrive at any time. We will have to stay alert outside. Inside the houses is the easy part." *At least for them. I'd rather be killing people who fight back.* "We'll have to stay vigilant out here, keep enough men outside on watch to be prepared. We don't know how much time we have, or how big an army would come."

"We'll be ready." One soldier said, and then the rest in the company agreed with and repeated the sentiment.

Khurt found himself not wanting to enter another house. Despite the folly of setting the fire so soon, it would allow him an easy excuse to not have to kill any more children or sleeping victims. "Come. We'll place ourselves near the blaze and rally others to be ready for anyone or anything that enters the city." They walked on toward the blaze as other companies ran in and out of homes and buildings. As they continued on, more and more soldiers of the Eighth Battalion rejoined their ranks and followed. Khurt also recognized members of Saol's personal battalion walking alongside them.

They reached the location of the fire, which had spread to several buildings, and Khurt approached Saol. "Wall?"

Saol nodded. "Wall."

Khurt stood in front of his battalion and raised his right arm. He outstretched his fingers and spread them apart, then waved his arm from side to side twice. As his soldiers saw, they repeated the command down the line for those farther in the back to see. The lines quickly broke and fanned out wide instead of deep until they spanned almost the entire width of the wide street. They faced the edge of the city, where it would be easy to see any oncoming soldiers. Khurt stood a few paces in front of his battalion with Khenzi and turned his head to the soldiers behind him. "Once they arrive, I need you to also be extra eyes for me. Look out for my son. He can hold his own with a sword, but it will be easy to lose sight of him once the melee begins."

His soldiers nodded and one responded, "Don't worry, General. Khenzi will be standing by our sides at the end of it, covered in the blood of those infidels. And once we have killed them all, we will celebrate your son as a war hero. He will have the first selection at every meal starting tonight."

Khurt nodded and smiled with pride. He knew that trying to keep track of Khenzi during combat would compromise his ability to fight effectively. Knowing that his men would share in the responsibility eased his mind and allowed him to focus better on the battle that would eventually come.

They stood in place, each soldier quietly waiting for and expecting an enemy at any moment. After several minutes, Khurt turned around, curious about the silence behind him. The soldiers no longer ran in and out of buildings. The speed in which they'd eradicated the residents impressed even Khurt, who thought the process might still need more time to complete. Most of the Vithelegion stood behind them, though Saol had signaled for the First and Second Battalions to stand by at the northern and southern entrances to the city, respectively. Once any army or cavalry committed to attacking the mass that stood inside the city, the other two battalions would march around to stop the enemy from being able to retreat.

Most of them heard the rumble at the same time. Khurt and many others looked around at each other and muttered the same word. "Horses."

The sounds of hooves grew louder. As Khurt and the rest of the army assumed a ready stance, Saol shouted out a command, "Ready yourselves! They approach on horseback! Do your best to save the horses! We will be much better off with them at our disposal once we destroy these men!" As planned, the archers took up the rear. They would be the first to attack upon Saol's command, especially if the enemy soldiers were charging on horseback. Saol continued, "Archers! Be ready!"

Khurt planted his right foot and drew his sword, assuming the *pillar of wind* stance. He made sure to keep his right leg from tensing up. He looked down at Khenzi, who'd drawn his own sword and copied Khurt's stance. Khurt subtly glanced around at the other soldiers and noticed that most of his own battalion assumed *pillar of wind*, while all of the other battalions assumed the classic stance that Saol had instilled in the whole army, their legs apart, holding their swords in front of them. The stampede of hooves grew louder. Khurt could feel the rumble now, as well as shouts in the distance.

It wasn't until now that he realized how bad his feet hurt. In the midst of all the chaos, he'd forgotten about the pain; standing and waiting had allowed him to focus on himself. He almost hoped that the enemy would arrive soon to take his mind off it.

After another moment of waiting, armored soldiers adorned in red-plumed helmets appeared in the distance. They rode right into the city on horseback and charged directly at the Vithelegion without hesitation. Saol shouted, "Archers!" and held his left arm up, with his index and middle fingers extended for the archers in the back to see, then bent them down and put them back up. In an instant, arrows flew overhead and rained down ahead, most falling upon the riders. Some clanked off of the enemy's armor, some hit the horses, and others successfully impaled riders. Saol repeated the command and another throng of arrows glided towards the riders. More riders fell, and more horses rollicked and panicked, flinging riders in several directions. The enemy's charge grew chaotic as frantic horses disrupted their progress. Khurt and the Vithelegion maintained their position, knowing better than to advance. Khurt knew Saol's tactics too well by this point. More than likely, they would disperse to the sides of the street to allow the riders to breach the middle with little to no casualties.

Sure enough, as the Ashurian army regrouped and maintained their advance, Saol yelled out, "Break to the sides! Disperse!" The riders were upon them now, but too close to change course. As they stumbled forward, the Vithelegion cleared the center of the road and attacked from the sides. The Ashurians in the middle of the charge proved impotent in the fight, as they couldn't reach anyone at the sides. Khurt kept Khenzi behind him, knowing that the boy might protest, but there was no way Khenzi would be able to reach the horsemen to spar with them. Khurt quickly switched in *steelmaiden* and then attacked the nearest rider. The soldier swung his sword one handed at Khurt, who struck the sword out of the soldier's hand. The rider's momentum took him past Khurt, where one of Khurt's soldiers waited and struck the rider underneath his arm, through the torso. The rider slumped and shortly fell off his horse.

Khurt continued to fight horsemen with the same strategy as they rode past, focusing on disarming them and letting the next Vithelegion soldier attack. The strategy worked for several minutes, mostly because any rider who stopped would be trampled from behind. Khurt noticed riders in the distance turning away before reaching them. *Are they retreating or regrouping for a new strategy?* From his vantage point, it was impossible to know the difference. Either way, he could only control those who were in front of him. He continued to fend off the oncoming soldiers. Fighting this way was easier than sparring on equal footing.

The riders started to wise up and halted their advance. Even those in front of him changed course and turned back to create more distance. The wide street was littered with men, mostly those with red-plumed helmets. Nearby, Saol shouted, "Vithelegion!" and then raised a fist in the air for them to reassemble as a wall in the middle of the street. Within moments, the Vithelegion stood shoulder to shoulder, just as they had when the enemy arrived. Only now, the enemy's numbers were significantly smaller.

One of the Ashurian riders at the front dismounted and sheathed his sword, then slowly approached. He kept his hands up and spread away from his chest to show he was not coming to attack. Khurt noticed that his golden skin tone was the same as all of the soldiers. "Strangers! I am General Easton Grey of the Royal Vermillion Army! Who are you and why are you laying siege to innocent people in their sleep? What nation are you from and what is your quarrel?"

Saol stepped forth and sheathed his sword. "I am Saol Suldas, Commander of the Vithelegion, Descendant of the Greatmother Ashota. We hail from the nation of Vitheligia, across the sea, in the realm of Orol Taghdras. We have arrived on your shores to bring you to justice for your infidelity!"

Easton Grey looked back at his soldiers, then cocked his head slightly. He was somewhat tall compared to his own soldiers, but still a head shorter than Saol. "What infidelity do you dare charge us with?" Khurt wondered why they would charge first, then retreat, and then think to talk. *Poor leadership.*

Saol responded, loud enough for all to hear, "We are loyal followers of the Harbinger Abram, who was killed by Jahmash and betrayed by Darian. We are here to rid the world of Darian's followers and bloodline, both of which thrive in Ashur."

Grey seemed to smirk, but it was gone before Khurt knew whether it was there in the first place. "Commander Suldas, I must inform you then, that you are mistaken. We Ashurians follow Orijin before anything, and we do not put any single Harbinger before the others. If you were to ride south, you would see that in the City of the Fallen. There are statues of all Harbingers except Jahmash, towering over the city. The only Ashurians who specifically celebrate Darian are the Descendants, who wield dark magic and seek to terrorize our lands."

Saol turned back to the Vithelegion, "Generals, come!" Khurt looked around and then walked to Saol. The other seven joined Saol as he turned to them. "This man, General Easton Grey of the Royal Vermillion Army, claims that Ashurians do *not*, in fact, worship Darian. What do we make of this?"

Khurt said flatly, "They are stalling for more time. Likely trying to find a way to surround us or find a weakness." The other generals responded in agreement.

Grey shook his head, "No, you have my word, it is no scheme."

Khurt responded, "Then why would you charge against us, and then want to talk afterwards?"

"You have decimated the entire city of Yongradae and set it ablaze! Why would we not attack?"

Saol cut in, "And suppose we take you at your word, General Easton Grey? What would you propose we do from here?"

Grey looked around at Saol and the other Vithelegion generals. After a moment, he looked at Saol with a certain realization in his eyes. "You say that you have traveled here to rid the world of Darian's followers, correct?"

Saol nodded. "Indeed."

Grey smiled, "Then perhaps we have a mutual enemy." Khurt squinted at him in confusion. Saol must have given a similar look, as Grey offered an explanation. "For years now, at the order of King Edmund, the Royal Vermillion has done our best to hunt down and kill these Darian sympathizers. However, because of their magic, they tend to be too strong for us. Their stronghold was destroyed several months ago by…an army. Now what remains of them is in hiding.

"This very city is one that sympathizes with them, as well as every other city in this nation. If you agree to do the same to all of the other cities in this nation of Mireya, then the Royal Vermillion Army can conveniently stay out of the way. In doing so, you will rid Ashur of thousands of Darian's sympathizers as well as those who would harbor his Descendants. Once you finish, we will join forces with you to hunt down the rest of them throughout Ashur."

Saol looked around at Khurt and the other generals once more, slightly nodding his head. "If we do you the favor of decimating these cities, then we hold dominion over any city that we lay siege to. Including any assets that we find within them."

Grey took a deep breath. "I will have to ask my king about the terms, but I believe that as long as you agree to be peaceful with anyone who is not a follower of Darian, then you may do as you please."

Saol nodded, "If I even suspect that you are going against your word, I will rip you apart starting with your fingers and toes, then hands and feet, then arms and legs. I will cauterize each wound immediately to prevent you from bleeding out until you are just a stump of head and torso. Then I will cut out your eyes and shove them down your throat until you choke to death. I will do all of this in front of your own soldiers and king, so they see what it means to betray me and the Vithelegion." Khurt swore that Saol glanced at him for a split second, but he was too busy looking at the sweat on Grey's cheeks to know for sure. "Do you understand me, General Easton Grey of the Royal Vermillion Army?"

Grey nodded quickly, "You have my word, Commander Suldas. I will also leave a small company of my own soldiers with you, to help you navigate. My only request is that you set no more fires. The clandestine nature of this alliance requires that we bring as little attention as possible to what you are doing. The Royal Vermillion can only stay away if we do not know what is happening here."

"Very well. Send your company. We will extinguish the blaze and then ride to the next city at sunrise." Saol turned to the generals. "Generals, send your envoys back to the ships. Gather the rest of our army and instruct all to be ready for invasion tomorrow morning."

By the following morning, those Vithelegion that had stayed back on the ships had joined the others in Yongradae, ready to advance to the next target. Most of them walked through the tall grass and sparse trees, but Khurt, Khenzi, and the other generals and their sons, along with a select few others rode on horses taken from fallen Vermillion soldiers. Easton Grey had left about twenty of the Royal Vermillion with them as guides. They had informed Saol and the Eight Generals that the closest city to Yongradae was one named Khiry, about a day's walk to the east. Once they lay siege to Khiry, they could choose the next target from there, as the other cities were mostly equidistant from Khiry.

ADRIA TRIED HER BEST TO NOT SLUMP in her chair. She wasn't tired at all, but the news and the implications drained her to the point that she felt impotent in her ability to do anything about it. Not having Savaiyon around only drained her more. Seven of them sat around the table that had been hastily moved into the meal room, along with any chairs they could find. "I'm sorry, I can't seem to process this, Donovan. One more time, please?"

Donovan Brighton spoke, rubbing his short black hair and looking almost as frayed as Adria. "It's fine. We just found out ourselves, and both of us tried to call out to Badalao once our messengers brought word. A foreign army decimated Yongradae and all its people, as well as the Vermillion who tried to stop them. They were supposedly going to Khiry next, and after that, it could be any of the remaining cities in Mireya."

"Vithelegion. It has to be," Slade cut in.

Asarei pounded his fist from the head of the table. "Dammit. From Khiry, they have options. Vandenar, Bakh Ratan, even the City of the Fallen. If their forces are big enough, they could even attack two cities at once."

Wendell Ravensdayle nodded; his lion's mane hair tied up atop his head. "The messengers said that it could not have taken them much time to destroy Yongradae. Rhadames, what was it you called them?"

Slade answered. "Vithelegion. It must be them. Jahmash doesn't have the armies yet to dare attack Ashur. Savaiyon vanquished the only army that he *did* have. But the Vithelegion, they are good enough and smart enough to not need numbers. Especially in Ashur, where the majority of the army is in the north. They are from Vitheligia, a nation in the realm of Orol Taghdras. I have never personally experienced them, and that's only because most nations beyond Ashur know better than to quarrel with them. The strange thing is why they're here in the first place. It's not their way to conquer or seek a fight. They *end* fights. Did your messengers happen to find their motive?"

Wendell and Donovan both shook their heads, but Asarei responded. "Motive doesn't mean shit at this point. No offense, Rhadames. They are a fire that we need to put out." He looked back at Donovan and Wendell, "Are your own armies prepared to fight at a moment's notice? Once we know where they are headed, perhaps Maqdhuum can transport your armies to intercept them. I can accompany you with the few people I have here. It's not many, but they are great fighters, even without their manifestations."

Donovan responded, looking at Wendell and then back at Asarei, "I'm afraid our forces will be small as well." He paused for a moment and took a deep breath, "We relayed the news to my father first, and he instructed us that the majority of our forces must stay in Cerysia. He told us flatly that he must ensure the safety of himself and all of his kingdom, and he wants to know more about them and their tactics and tendencies before sending a large contingent."

This time Adria pounded the table. "Coward."

Wendell nodded and raised his hands, palm up, indicating he'd known that truth for a long time. "He is willing to mobilize five hundred men to Mireya to combat the Vithelegion. I don't know their numbers, but for them to have sacked Yongradae so quickly and quietly, it had to have been a much larger army than five hundred."

Adria did her best to process the whole situation. A foreign threat had arrived days ago and already laid waste to one city, most likely two. Yet, the King thought it wise to sit and wait to see what they do. While she couldn't believe that a king could be so cavalier about his own people's lives, she also didn't know why she should be surprised. *This is why we're planning to kill him, after all.* She was about to bring up the siege on his castle, but knew that they needed to sort this out first. To her surprise, Maqdhuum, who sat next to her, joined in the conversation.

"I might be able to discreetly pop in on the remaining Mireyan cities to see whether the Vithelegion has attacked yet. Should I start in Khiry, or should we assume that it's already fallen?"

Asarei stood up, unable to contain his anger while sitting. "No wonder even the Anonymi want him dead. Honestly, Maqdhuum, if these two only got this news now, we have to assume that Khiry has been defeated. Wendell and Donovan need to leave quickly and must waste no time. I say we send them back to Alvadon to ready their battalion. In the meantime, you check Bakh Ratan first. As soon as you know whether they've been there or not, return and tell us. Without Savaiyon here, Maqdhuum, we're limited in our ability to mobilize them quickly. How long would it take you to transport five hundred men?"

"Not sure. If they're all prepared, hopefully less than an hour. It will be tiring to do it, but as long as I'm bringing them all to the same place, then that makes it easier.

Asarei nodded, "We might as well get started then. Check Bakh Ratan first."

Maqdhuum rose from his chair, adorned in his usual all black shirt and breeches. He pushed in his chair and then walked around to Donovan and Wendell, grasped their shoulders, and all three disappeared instantly. Within a minute, Maqdhuum had returned, coughing heavily. He had his hands on his knees, but then waved toward them, shaking his head. He stopped coughing long enough to croak out, "Bakh Ratan...destroyed! I told the other two already. Told them," he paused to cough again, "they have an hour to get ready." He sat down once more to have a drink of water.

Slade turned to Maqdhuum, "What happened there? What did you see? Did they destroy the whole city?"

Maqdhuum shook his head, "No. That's the strange thing. The city is intact. Just corpses everywhere. I dared to arrive in the middle of the city, to get the best evaluation. Nothing torn down, barely anything broken. Just death everywhere. Whatever it is they want, they're efficient." He looked at Asarei, "I hate to tell you this, but five hundred soldiers and the five of you who live here aren't going to be enough to stop them."

Asarei pounded his fist once more, "Dammit. Maqdhuum, you're to bring them all to Vandenar. My gut tells me that's their next target. Thinking as a soldier, it would be harder for anyone to reach them there."

As Asarei spoke, Adria heard a commotion from the doorway on the other side of the room. She looked over and saw the rest of their companions walking in, looking confused. She already knew the cause without looking at Badalao but smirked at him anyway.

On cue, Badalao explained to the others around the table, "I told them all to come. They need to know about all of this. Even though this is a different concern, it is nonetheless a concern that affects all of us." Those around the table nodded in agreement.

Adria glanced around at those who'd just arrived. Asarei and Slade explained all of the new developments to them, including Donovan and Wendell bringing troops to fight, and Asarei offering to join. Most of them still looked confused, just as Adria had, trying to come to grips with all of it.

Desmond, who looked more his old self than he had in a while, asked the first question. "If this new threat is wipin' out Mireya, then shouldn't that be our biggest priority? We should *all* be goin' there ta fight!" Baltaszar and a few others voiced their agreements.

Marshall echoed the sentiment. "Agreed. With all of us there, we could beat them handily and then still have plenty of time to prepare for the attack on the castle."

Asarei stopped them from continuing, "No. Maqdhuum will have it under control. He will already be working with Wendell and Donovan to take on the Vithelegion. I will go with Manjobam and Trevor. Not only are they good fighters, but their manifestations will protect them well."

Desmond responded. Adria knew he was doing his best to maintain his composure. Vandenar was his home and that mattered more than anything. "All due respect, Asarei, ya said yerselves that ye'd have trouble containin' them. How can ya stand there an' tell me I can't defend my own home? Stop my own family from bein' killed?"

Baltaszar asked, "Do they have Descendants on their side?"

Asarei looked at Slade, who answered after a moment, "As far as we know, there *are* none beyond Ashur."

"Then how can we lose? Send us there and we can end this early. Stop them before they kill another Ashurian." Adria knew that Baltaszar had fallen for a girl in Vandenar, but she didn't realize how much it all mattered to him until now.

Slade tried to calm him down, "Tasz, I understand why you want to be there. Believe me, I do. But we have to stick to the plan."

Baltaszar raised his voice, "Plans bloody change, Slade! It was easy to plan the siege on Edmund when we didn't know we were about to be invaded! How are we any better than Edmund if we stay here and let innocent people die? Imagine how much faster we can stop them if we all go instead of three people!"

Adria knew that the argument might never end if someone didn't intervene. She stood from her chair. "Listen. All of you have valid points, but I have something to say. So please just let me say my piece.

"It is foolish to enter any battle with the mindset that anything will be easy. Especially if you know nothing about your opponent. Desmond, Tasz, the people of Vandenar will not be exposed. Within the hour, Maqdhuum will meet with Wendell and Donovan to mobilize their forces. Maqdhuum and Lao will continue to monitor the process to find out exactly where the Vithelegion goes next. As soon as they know for sure, the entire battalion will arrive to fight them, including Asarei, Bam, and Trevor.

"Remember that we're doing this without Savaiyon. Maqdhuum can only transport so many people at a time. You have to trust that our allies will do their jobs as they've trained to do. What happens if all of us go there to fight and any of us are injured or killed? Our own mission will be compromised. The repercussions of this siege of Edmund are bigger than our ability to stop the Vithelegion right now. I know how bad that sounds, but if we lose this potential alliance with the Anonymi, then that cripples our abilities against Jahmash, which is the biggest threat."

Baltaszar glared at her. He didn't know her familiarly like the others did, so she understood why his trust was thin. "The biggest threat is always the one that's happening now."

Desmond chimed in before Adria could respond. "Mouse, I love ya, but would ya be so unwillin' ta fight if the Vithelegion were headed ta Fera, where yer parents are?" Desmond didn't wait for her to answer. He and Baltaszar turned and walked away, leaving the room. Adria pressed her fists into the table and bit her lip. She knew why they were mad and defiant. She even knew that Desmond had made a good point about whether she would trust others to defend her own city without being there. She *didn't* know her answer to that, though. More than anything, it made her wonder whether the issue was her own leadership, or just the supreme stubbornness of Desmond and Baltaszar.

CHAPTER 22
NEAR AND FAR

From *The Book of Orijin*, Verse One Hundred Twelve
The world of flesh is but one phase of life.
Life does not end with the destruction of flesh.
Only in the Three Rings will you truly understand existence.

YASAMAN EYED THE TALL TALE Inn to her right, a dark brick building with the name painted in yellow lettering on a plank that hung from a pole above the door. Curiously, the "l" in Tale extended down farther than the other letters, and now that she'd noticed, Yasaman realized that the Happy Elephant in Vandenar had the same writing style. She wondered if the owners knew one another and she shuddered at the thought of Anahi and Fae bullying her. She grasped Zane more tightly. He was wrapped against her chest and wide awake, taking in his surroundings as well. For everything that they'd been through since leaving Haedon, Yasaman knew that her son was a good baby. He barely fussed and only cried when he was hungry. He didn't fight sleep or wake up too often. The past months could have been much worse if Zane was more troublesome.

She entered the inn, which was mostly empty save for a few people here and there. Yasaman looked around for a table positioned where she would be able to see everyone. The people in Gangjeon had told her that the last news of Descendants, apparently that's what Baltaszar and others with black lines were called, was that some had been seen in Shipsbane. They'd also said that this inn would be the best place in Shipsbane to find a Descendant. She sat at a table along the wall, where she didn't have to worry about anyone behind her, and then shifted Zane to her breast to feed.

One of the maids made eye contact with her from across the room as Yasaman adjusted her shirt to position Zane properly. The woman nodded and mouthed that she would give Yasaman a moment before coming over. Yasaman knew already that she would like this place better than the stupid Elephant Inn in Vandenar. The golden-skinned maid walked over with a big smile. "I hope your appetite is as big as his is this morning, dear!"

Since leaving Vandenar, she'd tried to stretch the coins that Oran Von had given her as far as she could. Sometimes, innkeepers or strangers would sympathize with her situation and would give her food free. Sometimes they would accept a partial payment or provide something small to take with her. The rhetoric was always that she needed to keep her health and energy for the baby. Before Zane had been born, Yasaman knew that pride would have gotten in the way of accepting so many handouts and preying upon people's sympathies. But she was set on finding Baltaszar, and the only way to make it to him was to rely on others. Once she convinced him that he needed to be Zane's father, then she wouldn't need to worry about help from anyone else.

She smiled back at the maid, "I'm starving." She pulled out the coin purse from her waist, "I've been traveling from Vandenar and this is all I have left. If I can't afford any food, might you have any…coffee? I think that's what it's called. I had some in Bakh Ratan and it was delightful. They mixed it with milk and sugar and I swear it was what Omneitria might taste like if it had a flavor."

The maid raised her eyebrows at the few coins Yasaman had left. "You've traveled from Mireya with a baby on this little coin purse? Where exactly did you come from?"

She sighed deeply, more so than she normally might, "I am from a town called Haedon. It is in the Never, north of Vandenar."

The maid's eyebrows got even higher. "Seriously?"

"Yes," Yasaman nodded. "There is a town hidden in the Never. I escaped with my baby. My mother was practically throwing me out with nothing anyway. It was either stay there with her judgment and abuse, or leave and find my own way."

The maid sat down across from her, "What about the baby's father? Did you need to leave him behind as well?"

Yasaman shook her head and looked down at Zane for a moment, then looked back up at the maid, whom she realized couldn't be much older than her. "Zane's father is a Descendant. He left Haedon before Zane was even born so he could find others like him." She saw the other girl's eyes soften. "That's why I'm all the way out here. Back in Gangjeon, they told me that my best chance of finding him would be here at the Tall Tale Inn in Shipsbane. As you can see, I don't have much. And I don't want to be in your way or become a burden. If my remaining coins might be enough for some coffee and a small bite, then I would only ask that perhaps I could sit here for a while to see if any Descendants wander in. Of course, only until you need the table for someone else. And then I could just stay outside and keep watch for any Descendants who might enter."

She gauged the girl's reaction. She was getting better and better at evoking pity from others, although she wasn't necessarily proud of it. Zane had finished suckling and she moved him to her shoulder to burp him. As she patted his back, she thought of the scars on her forearm and more specifically about the fact that she hadn't cut herself since leaving

Haedon. If she could be proud of something, it was that she hadn't felt the need to release any emotional pain in a while. For everything that her parents had put her through, she deserved for someone to take pity on her and maybe even feel sorry for her.

The maid looked at her incredulously once more. "You cannot really believe that we would push you out while you're trying to nourish a baby *and* trying to find your husband." *Husband does have a nice ring to it.* "My name is Violet. You should know that we are nice people here. Not only do we secretly help Descendants, but we would obviously take care of their families as well. Stay here." She reached out and grasped Yasaman's hand. "I'll bring you some coffee and hot cakes; you'll love them. Claim this table for as long as you need. I'll also have a room set up for you in case you need to rest. That way, if any Descendants do come in, we can inform you. What's today, Dariday? You might be in luck. Manjobam usually stops in for a meal every Dariday. He usually comes into town to shop at the markets once a week and then goes back to wherever he goes."

What the hell is Dariday? "You don't know *where* he goes?"

"It is not polite to intrude upon the lives of Descendants. They have certain secrets that they must keep in order to protect themselves."

Yasaman nodded, "I understand. And thank you for such generous hospitality. Normally I might refuse out of decency, but I am in dire straits and I know that if I could just find Baltaszar, then I wouldn't need anything else anymore. I promise I will be out of your hair as soon as I can find a Descendant who will help me. My name is Anahi." She almost cringed at the sound of using Anahi's name, but she had to be smart. The last time she saw Baltaszar, he left her in a rage and almost burned down Haedon. Yasaman knew for sure that if word got out that someone named Anahi was looking for him, Baltaszar would be much more open and welcoming than if he knew it was her.

Violet left and returned after a short while with a mug of steaming coffee and a plate of hot cakes slathered in butter. Yasaman's stomach grumbled at the sight and smell of her breakfast and barely stopped herself from drooling right onto Zane's sleeping face. She'd wrapped him back up against her body while Violet left so her hands could be free.

She was about to devour the food, as had become habit while traveling with Zane, but then stopped herself after realizing she didn't have to rush off somewhere else. Zane had just eaten and would sleep for a while, and she could savor the meal and hot coffee that she'd been looking forward to. Yasaman took her time to eat and enjoy every bite and sip. She sat for a while, just to observe the room for herself. Barely anyone came in over the next hour. When Violet returned to take

Yasaman's dishes, she explained that Dariday was a big day for the markets. The inns tended to be slower as most of the townsfolk were either selling their wares on the long, narrow main road, or shopping. One way or another, almost the whole town was at the markets. Some might come in for a meal, but most were more interested in going right back home to cook their fresh fish.

Violet encouraged her to go up to the room that had been set aside for her and Zane, and that she would come up to get Yasaman once Manjobam arrived. There was little reason to argue, and a soft bed had been few and far between since leaving Haedon. She stood and grabbed her pack, then followed Violet up to her room. As soon as Violet left and shut the door, Yasaman set Zane down in the middle of the bed, tugged off her boots, and lay next to him. She placed a pillow on the other side of the baby to prevent him from rolling, and then closed her eyes.

She barely even knew that she'd been sleeping when she heard the loud knock on her door. After realizing the implications of the knock, Yasaman jumped up and mustered a raspy, "Coming!" in response. Zane was stirring as well, which made things easier. She opened the door to let Violet in, shoved her feet into her boots, then scooped Zane from the bed and secured him to her front. "I'm sorry to keep you waiting. I didn't realize how tired I was, I guess."

"You're a mother, Anahi. You don't need to apologize!" Violet led her back down to the main dining room.

"Is he here? The one you said would come?"

Violet glanced back and smiled. "Never fails. Yes, Manjobam arrived not too long ago. I told him that you need his help, so he is at a table expecting your company." As they entered the room, Violet pointed at Manjobam, who sat at the table next to where Yasaman sat earlier. Yasaman could not avert her gaze as she walked to the table. The man was massive. Even while sitting, she could easily tell how tall he was. His brown skin reminded her of Baltaszar's, except that Manjobam's was notably darker. She eyed his long black hair and almost felt jealous of how much healthier his hair looked than hers.

As he noticed her, she smiled and approached the table. "Anahi, is it? Please, sit. My name is Bam."

Yasaman sat and watched Manjobam as he worked at a plate with twice as many hot cakes as she'd had. "Those were my breakfast earlier, too. I could eat them every day."

He nodded, "This is the best part of my day right here. Without fail, I have them once a week. I guess they're the best part of my week, actually. Violet said you need some help. You're looking for someone?"

"Oh, yes. I'm looking for Baltaszar Kontez. I need him and so does his son. He left us because of his duties as a Descendant, and I thought I could handle all of this on my own, but...but I can't." She tried to give him the same expression that she'd mastered, evoking pity from him.

Manjobam seemed surprised more than anything else. "Wow, all this time he never mentioned that he had a child. That's so strange."

Yasaman knew that this part might be the most challenging. She interjected before Manjobam could start down some path of wild theories. "I...I don't think he was very excited about the baby, if I must be honest. And that is why I need to see him. I need for us to be together. I need a father for my son, and I need Baltaszar to be there for us."

She saw Manjobam biting his lip, though she couldn't be sure if it was from emotion or habit. Finally he responded. "I cannot simply take you to him, Anahi. First, I will have to mentally reach out to Lao, who will then likely need to confirm with Asarei, Maqdhuum, and Tasz, and then if they all approve, Maqdhuum will come to get you. I can also not explain to you *where* exactly he is."

Yasaman looked at him confusedly, but nodded to move the process along. "Sure, but just one thing. Please do not mention anything about the baby. In your...mental discussion? Please just say that Anahi desperately needs to see him. Can you do that?" She eyed him curiously, wary of how a Descendant's magical powers actually worked. Manjobam nodded in affirmation and then stared at the table for several moments. She felt too awkward to look directly at him, so she looked around the room and glanced back at him from time to time. She dared not interrupt him, but the longer it took, the more Yasaman wondered if her plan would even work. *This was stupid. They all have to know. If they can talk to each other in their minds, then they surely know that it's not Anahi looking for Tasz. This will be so embarrassing if he rejects me. What do I do then? Just go back upstairs? Violet will kick me out just like Anahi did.*

Finally, after several minutes, he looked up at her. "Tasz has agreed to see you. Some of the others are excited as well. Maqdhuum will appear here shortly. He will bring you there instantly. You should understand, though, that they are in the middle of worrying about an invasion, so your time may be cut short, depending on how things go." She put her hand down on the table to stop it from shaking. Manjobam half-smiled, "Nervous about seeing him after so long, huh? I hope it goes well. You seem very nice."

Yasaman forced herself to smile, and a man appeared right behind her as she was about to stand. He startled her so much that she shrieked as she sat back down. He grabbed her, then saw Zane and put his other hand on Zane's head. Yasaman saw a flash of more colors than she'd ever known existed. They were blurry and streaked toward her until all of a sudden, she found herself in a large stone room with two men sitting at a table in front of her. Maqdhuum, who'd just brought her there, sat down at the table next to the other two.

Once again, she found herself alone in an unfamiliar place. She walked to the table and took in the three men who sat there. All three stared at her, but it was the one who sat directly across from where she stood who finally spoke. Yasaman found herself constantly glancing back at him, unable to determine why he seemed so familiar. "Well, for starters, *Yasaman*, I supposed I should tell you that I'm glad you aren't dead. I never actually wanted you to die, and I was rather angry with Gibreel for pushing you off the side of a mountain." One of the other men, whose entire body and head were seemingly covered in tattoos, was about to stand, but the one who had spoken to Yasaman stopped him.

Her eyes were wide open. *No. It can't be.* "S…Slade?"

"In the flesh, just like you." He nodded at Zane, who thankfully stayed quiet. "Is that the product of your night with Bo'az?"

She continued to stand. Sitting seemed like it would only invite more ridicule. "You have no idea what I've been through. You people killed my father."

Slade stood and shook his head. "No. That's on you. You and Bo'az were never supposed to come with us. We were looking for Baltaszar. And then Bo'az had to go and lie, and the only way to make it work was for me to also pretend that he was Tasz, in order to fool Gibreel and Linas. Anything that happened to you on that journey is on you for insisting on coming in the first place. If we didn't currently have more pressing manners, I would entertain this conversation more. But there are more important things to worry about, so you can walk to the door over there and wait for Tasz. I don't know what you've told yourself about how this will all work out, but he is going to be pissed when he sees you there instead of Anahi. You'll be lucky if he even speaks to you."

BALTASZAR RACED THROUGH the corridors toward the meal hall. He couldn't fathom how Anahi could have gotten all the way here from Vandenar, but he could barely keep himself from tripping over his own feet with how fast he wanted to run. *I can't believe she's here! She came all this way to see me!* The doors were in sight and she was either already in the next room or would be there shortly. He'd been so angry about Adria's decision the day before, especially because of the risk that it meant for Anahi. Her being here managed to stem his anger somewhat, though he still knew that Vandenar needed saving. There were countless others there that would die without any intervention from the Ghosts of Ashur, and Baltaszar knew it was their responsibility to do something.

He let the anger go for now. Today would be dedicated solely to catching up with Anahi and having time alone with her. He would think of nothing else. He reached the doors and flung them wide open. Baltaszar was so excited to see Anahi that he almost looked past the girl who stood before him as soon as he opened the doors. His eyes knew who he saw, but his mind couldn't accept who was standing there. "You...I don't...Did you tell them you're Anahi?" He froze. As much as he wanted to run back the other way, his feet grew heavy and kept him in place. He opened himself to his manifestation, almost wanting to burn her to ashes right there. If not for the baby on her chest, Baltaszar thought he actually might have done so.

Her mouth shrugged. "It was the only way you would see me. If I told Manjobam it was Yasaman who wanted to see you, I wouldn't have made it here."

"Go the hell back to wherever you were. I don't have time for you." He turned and walked back down the corridor.

She followed him and walked just behind him. "Please, Tasz. I need your help. There is no one in Haedon who will even give me a kind eye, not even my own mother. But even after leaving and trying to survive in Ashur, all I have to rely on are scraps and handouts from generous strangers. I can't do this on my own. I know you aren't Zane's father, but I need *someone* to be a father to him. And you're the closest thing in this world to that."

He stopped and clenched his fist. "He has a father. His father's name is Bo'az Kontez, who just happens to be my twin brother. Bo is currently doing Jahmash's bidding, mostly because he wanted to impress you and keep you alive, and if he's lucky, we may be able to save him before Jahmash kills him. That's what *you* do to people who love you. You use them and expect everything from them, with nothing in return. I *begged* for us to stay together and you refused. Do you remember? I was still in Haedon for a time after that, and you never once came to see me with any thoughts of getting back together." He walked on, moving so fast without any inkling of where he wanted to go.

Yasaman continued on behind him, rambling desperately to change his mind. "I told you. I thought I was going to die. All I wanted was one last night of comfort and Bo'az was the only one there to provide that."

Before he realized it, Baltaszar was outside the underground fortress and walking through the orchards. "That's exactly what I mean! You used him too! You knew how he felt about you, and you used those feelings against him just so *you* could feel better. You didn't care how he would feel afterwards! So you know what? You can have him! That's your family now! You and Bo and this damn baby that will forever remind me that you didn't want me anymore, but still laid with my brother. And you know what? It doesn't matter anymore, because I love someone else. When I'm done with my responsibilities, I'm going back to Vandenar to spend the rest of my life with Anahi." He paused for a moment, looked up at the sky, and then back at her even more angrily.

"What now, Tasz? You look like you want to kill me."

He shrugged, "It has crossed my mind. You know, I didn't realize when I first saw you behind those doors what it all meant. You used her name to fool all of us into getting here. Which means you met her. You've seen her and you knew that *I* would want to see her. How else would you know to tell Manjobam to tell us it was Anahi, not you?" The implications made Baltaszar slightly smile. "You met her in Vandenar. Probably mentioned my name, that you were looking for me." He looked directly into her eyes, "Did you tell her that the baby is my brother's, or did you try to tell her it's mine?"

Yasaman attempted a response, "I told her…"

"I already know. I know you would sink that low. She's too smart to believe you. And if I'm working out the timing of it all, you were probably there not long after I was there last. What I have with Anahi is stronger than what you and I had. What she and I have is built on trust. Honesty. Love."

PEOPLE STORMED INTO THE HAPPY ELEPHANT, desperation in their eyes. Anahi stood in awe at the bar counter with Cyrus, knowing that this was the moment but still refusing to believe it. Finally, someone shouted to them, "They're here! The enemy army has engaged the Royal Vermillion!" They had been notified by the royal army a day ago that a foreign army might be heading this way. It was a lot to explain and most of the people of Vandenar were still in disbelief, but Anahi knew that all of Vandenar was about to see the truth.

They had offered the Elephant as a refuge for people to hide, though Anahi wondered how much it would really help. If enemy soldiers stormed the inn, everyone inside would be like a herd of animals just waiting to be slaughtered. Anahi, Fae, and the other maids ushered people up the stairs to various rooms, where they would hide out, while Cyrus locked the doors to the inn. She had wanted desperately to run to Munn Keeramm's home to usher him to someplace safe, but Cyrus and Fae had stopped her. It was just too far away, and they hoped that Donovan Brighton and the Royal Vermillion Army would stop the enemy before they got too far into the city. She'd already asked The Orijin hundreds of times since the day before to keep them safe and alive.

Once they got everyone to safety, they went back downstairs and hid in a supply closet. Many of the maids had stayed upstairs, too scared to come back down. Even from the closet, they could hear the shouts and screams of battle. Men were killing and dying throughout Vandenar, and she could not be sure which side was doing which.

"But I love you too, Tasz. I always have. It's just, I was so naive then, thinking that my parents might give me some leniency if I showed them I could be a good, obedient daughter."

Baltaszar shook his head. He still clenched his fists, tempted to create a fireball. "Do you simply tell the lies, or do you actually believe everything that you lie about?"

Tears started to form at the edges of her eyes. "I'm not lying. I love you. I was young and stupid and I have made…too many horrible decisions so far in my life. As a result, my father is dead. I am dead to my mother. Bo'az is gone. Baltaszar, I gave birth to two sons, and had to bury one of them. Zane's twin brother, Zaid was born first and never took a breath. In the same breath that my mother was encouraging me to push out the babies, she was calling me a murderer of my own son."

Baltaszar sighed and looked down at the ground. He felt bad for what she'd been through, but he knew he didn't have an obligation to love her just because her life had been difficult. "I'm sorry you had to go through all of that. I really am. I know your parents were tough and you had a hard time with them. But that doesn't justify how you've treated people. You forget that less than two years ago, I watched my father get publicly hanged. And I stood there helplessly as the rest of Haedon cheered. Then, not long after that, I found out that the fires were all caused by me, which means that my father took the blame for something I was doing and was willing to die with that secret."

She stepped closer to him and touched his sleeve. "You see? Our lives are parallel. We have seen the same horrors and can help each other heal. Be with me, Tasz. Or let us stay with you. We can be there for each other."

He looked at her. Her face and tears and beaten down posture asked for pity, and he had no room in his life to provide that for anyone. "The only similarity that we have is that we are both severely damaged people. The difference, though, is that I am trying to fix that damage and move on. You are trying to manipulate someone into filling those voids that haunt you."

Every few seconds, the whole building seemed to shake, and the ground never stopped rumbling. Anahi, Fae, and another maid, Sadie, held each other tightly toward the back of the closet while Cyrus stood by the door with a butcher knife. He was a brave man and willing to sacrifice himself, but Anahi wondered how much of a fight he could provide against a soldier. Out of nowhere, Cyrus whispered, "Oh no!" Anahi looked at him curiously. "I locked the door! If they try ta come in, they'll know we're here if the door's locked! If I unlock it, then they can walk in an' see that it's empty. An' then maybe they'll just leave."

"Cyrus, don't it's foolish at this point. Too dangerous ta walk out o' this room. Just stay put."

Cyrus shook his head. "No. I can't. It could be the difference between everyone in the Elephant livin' an' dyin'." He lifted his arm to show he was ready to use the knife, and the blade glinted from the few rays of sunlight that crept through the spaces between the wooden wall boards. He quickly left the closet and shut the door completely. Anahi and the other two hugged each other even tighter. Fae was crying, likely sure she'd seen Cyrus for the last time. They stayed as quiet as possible, hoping to be able to hear Cyrus's every move. Even Fae kept her sobs muffled. Anahi heard the jingling of keys in the distance and knew Cyrus had reached the door. In the next few moments, the patter of footsteps grew louder until the closet door opened again.

Despite her expecting it to be Cyrus, Anahi still felt a sense of dread when he opened the door and exposed them to anyone that might be outside. She whispered, "Did ya do it?" He nodded. "Did ya hear anythin' while ya were out there?"

"No," he whispered back, still clenching the butcher's knife. "Still so many shouts an' screams. They sound farther away now, though."

Anahi let go of Fae and Sadie and sat on the ground against the wall. The cool stone helped to calm her a bit, but all she could think of was that she wished Baltaszar was here. And Desmond, and the other Descendants in their group. The Royal Vermillion was all well and good, but the battle would go much differently if they had magic on their side. She wondered if Baltaszar and the others even knew about what was happening and prayed to the Orijin to send him to help.

SHE TRIED TO GRASP HIS HAND, but Baltaszar pulled it away. "I am not being manipulative. Aside from this beautiful little boy, everything in my life is horrible. Fine, I admit that what happened with your brother was a terrible thing to do, and you know what? If I was dead right now then it wouldn't even matter anyway, because I wouldn't be here in front of you, and neither would Zane. And Bo would *still* be off wherever he is. You would have gone back to Haedon to find me, and my mother would have told you either that I ran off and didn't return, or that I was probably dead somewhere. And then what? Would you be happy then? That the girl who broke your heart was dead? Would that have been easier for you?"

Probably. Baltaszar took a step back and looked her up and down. Her baby was awake and looking around, taking everything in. *Poor kid. She's going to ruin his life just by being around him.* "I don't wish death upon anyone. Knowing the truth about everything you've done, though, has definitely made my life more difficult. If you don't understand that, then I doubt there is much hope for you to find happiness."

"Baltaszar, I need *you*. You understand me. We have a connection. This is your nephew. I can be a better person. I'm a good mother to Zane and I could be a good wife to you."

"Stop! If you want to be a better person, then it has to start with you understanding that there is nothing here! Your son has a father who is alive. If you don't want to wait around for him, then go out into Ashur and find a new husband for yourself! Maybe if you go back to being the Yasaman I knew a long time ago, you'll have a better chance at it!"

She looked at him with saddened eyes, "But not a better chance at you?"

"Dammit, girl. I've already told you; I've promised myself to Anahi."

THE FOUR OF THEM WAITED IN the storage closet for what felt like hours, but Anahi knew it had only been a matter of minutes. They dared not speak or even move. All of them sat on the floor, bracing against something. Fae sat next to Anahi and the two of them held hands. Most of the rumbling around the inn had died down and the fact that no one had entered gave Anahi some optimism that perhaps the Vermillion were winning the battle.

She continued to think of Baltaszar and knew that if he was in Vandenar, this would be the first place he would come. She sighed. *He probably has no way of knowin' what's goin' on here. Maybe we'll be all right without him. Maybe the Vermillion are actually holdin' off the enemy. If we survive this, though, I'm goin' ta tell him he owes me forever fer not comin' ta save me.*

Just as she managed a small giggle to herself, they heard the door to the inn violently forced open and several sets of footsteps rush in. Anahi and the others looked up at each other. Even in the darkness, she could see the terror on the faces of the others. The soldiers seemed confused at the empty inn, but then someone barked out an order. "Check upstairs! If anyone is in here, then they're all hiding! All of you, go up!"

No. No no no no! Everyone is goin' ta die up there! We let them all in an' promised ta keep them safe! They're all goin' ta die because o' us! She heard more footsteps storming about the common room, seemingly searching high and low for any survivors. Anahi could feel her heart pounding through her chest. She hugged Fae tightly and Fae reciprocated. Sadie scooted closer to them and joined. *Baltaszar, please. Orijin, please.*

"What makes her so special?"

Baltaszar glared at her. "She appreciates me. Puts her faith in me. Accepts me for who I am and believes in my potential. Not once has she ever made me feel bad about myself or judged me for my shortcomings. For everything I didn't know, she never used it against me. She educated me instead, and has made me a better person. I don't mean this as a slight to you, Yas, but I've never felt this about anyone else. Anahi and I together are a greater magic than any manifestation. We are made for each other. By each other. Of each other."

Khurt surveyed the inn's common room as members of the Commander's Battalion and the Eighth Battalion exterminated any remaining townsfolk that might be hiding. Once again, slowing the pace brought the ache back into his feet. Slowly, soldiers filed back down the stairs with confirmations that the upstairs had been dealt with. Most of them bore splotches of blood on their armor and faces. It was an honor amongst the Vithelegion to wear the blood of the enemy. The red added another layer beyond the black paint that covered their pale skin patches. Once this battle ended, all of these soldiers would celebrate with great pride at the ease with which they decimated the city and the enemy army.

"Go back out and help the others finish off the opposition. It seems as if we have cleared out this place. A few of us will stay behind to make sure the rest of it is clear." The soldiers nodded in agreement as over a hundred of them exited the inn. Khurt shouted across the room, "Demetri! The rest of us will handle anyone who remains." He turned to Khenzi, "Check the kitchen behind that counter." Khenzi nodded with a smile and ran off. Khurt knew that anyone remaining would pose little threat, and so far Khenzi had done well to hold his own and follow orders. He rewarded the boy with more trust.

Khurt joined in on inspecting the ground floor. Most of the common room was spread out to the left of the staircase. Directly next to it, on the right were a couple of doors. *Most likely closets*. And off to the right side was the kitchen that Khenzi was currently inspecting. Demetri and the others seemed to have most of the other side covered. Khurt assumed the *greatmother* stance as he prowled toward the closets. He held the dagger upside down in his left hand, in front of his torso, while holding his sword in his right hand, diagonally away from his body. He stalked on quietly, in case any fools actually hid in there. He slowly turned the handle and swung the door open quickly. *Empty. Good.* He breathed a sigh of relief. In truth, he preferred to be outside in regular combat, but Saol insisted that Khurt handle this task.

"If she's so special, then why aren't you two together now?"

Why aren't you in Vandenar with her? Why am I the one here and she's so far away?" Yasaman eyed him with an air of smugness.

Baltaszar realized as the words left Yasaman's mouth that she'd distracted him from everything else that was currently happening. He was supposed to be inside, waiting to hear whether the Vithelegion was attacking Vandenar or the City of the Fallen. He brushed Yasaman out of the way and sprinted back underground.

AS HE TOOK ANOTHER DEEP BREATH, the other closet door swung open and a round, older man sprung out toward Khurt. He actually managed to knock Khurt onto his back with the charge, and as the man held both hands over his head in an attempt to bury a butcher's knife in Khurt's head, Khurt struck the man through the heart with a dagger. The heavy corpse slumped onto Khurt's torso and he pushed it off. As he got to his feet, he saw three girls trying to sneak behind the counter, just as Khenzi was walking back in. Smartly, Khenzi aimed the tip of his blade toward them and nodded for them to turn back.

"I'd do what he says, girls. You see the blood on him? He's killed more dangerous people than you today." The three girls stood straight and walked toward Khurt, just in front of the staircase. "Stop there. On your knees."

One of them, who knelt in the middle, spoke up. "Look. If yer goin' ta kill us, then just kill us. No need fer torture."

The girl to the right of her looked at her incredulously. "Anahi, be quiet. I don't want ta die!"

"Fae, have ya seen what's happenin'? They've killed everyone already!"

"Enough. Be quiet." Khurt looked at them, wondering if there was any hope against Saol's plan. Perhaps he could just send them upstairs to pretend they were dead.

Khenzi walked closer and removed his helmet, then sheathed his sword. "This thing is so heavy." The long stripe of hair down the middle of his head had been matted down from all the sweat. "Do we have to kill them?"

Khurt took a deep breath and whispered, "I don't know, boy. I don't really want to. It's one thing to fight soldiers in combat, but this…this is different. Look at them. They're not dangerous."

Behind him, the door to the inn swung open and Saol Suldas stormed in with his sons and a few other soldiers. "You're not done yet, Everitas? I need you back out there! The other half of the enemy army is pushing back! Kill them already and let's go." As Khurt turned to Saol, he heard one of the girls jump up. Before Khurt could react, the girl who'd been called 'Fae' by her friend ran to Khenzi and unsheathed his sword. She stood behind him with the black to his exposed neck. *Fool boy, I should have stopped you from removing your helmet.*

"Let all o' us go or I'll kill him."

"Everitas. End this stupid scene now," Saol said flatly.

Khurt knew that she didn't have it in her to kill, much less kill a little boy. He shook his head and in two quick movements, glided toward the maid who had been kneeling on the left and slit her throat with his dagger. He looked back at Fae, who still held the blade to Khenzi's throat, but looked on the verge of tears. "Is that not enough to let him go?" He grew tired of waiting for her.

The one maid who remained looked up at him, straight-faced, tears streaking down her face. She croaked, "He's going ta find ya'. I'm betrothed to a man who can wield fire. He an' his friends are comin' fer ya. An' they're goin' ta kill ya all." Khurt rolled his eyes at the threat and slit her throat as well. Before her body hit the floor, he turned to Fae, lifted his helmet, and rubbed the blade against his face to cover it in the blood of the two maids. He had been so focused on scaring the girl that he barely noticed Khenzi's horrified face. Khurt was about to speak when a throng of soldiers barreled through the inn's front doors.

They were led by a man with long blonde hair flowing from under his helmet, which matched the ridge atop his helmet. The man looked directly at Khurt and charged at him while several other soldiers engaged with Saol and the other Vithelegion inside. His golden-skinned face made Khurt think of the soldiers in the Royal Vermillion Army. Khurt wondered if there was a connection between the two armies.

His opponent was of a similar height, but not quite as thick. Khurt knew that slimmer didn't always mean faster with a sword, but in this case, it did. The blonde-haired man proved to be aggressive. He swung at Khurt relentlessly and quickly, which forced Khurt back. Khurt placed himself in front of the wide staircase so that at least he could maintain a higher ground, but even that proved difficult as he had to navigate up the steps. He was tempted to unsheathe his second sword at his left hip, but he didn't want to risk losing focus while defending himself. *My damn feet. Saol didn't kill me by pushing me overboard, but it might lead to my death now. Stop. Focus.*

The younger man continued to attack up the stairs. By the time Khurt reached the top, he realized moving backwards would be even more difficult. Bodies were strewn all throughout the hall. As the other man reached the same level, Khurt knew he couldn't continue to give ground. He parried an advance and hacked back as quickly as he could. While he regained some control, he drew his other sword and assumed the *apple tree* stance, holding both of his elbows out with both swords in front of his chest. Khurt could see the surprise in his opponent's face at his ability to fight back. Khurt knew his chances would be better if he wasn't also trying not to cringe with every step.

He proceeded to the *whirlwind* attack from his stance, in which he repeatedly attacked the other man with overhand strikes using both swords. The only problem was that the other man was as strong as he was fast, and he could parry both attacks from Khurt. Khurt couldn't keep the intensity up for a lot longer. He would slow down eventually, which would be a death sentence. He continued an overhand strike, which was blocked, but then spun into a backhand strike using his left hand. In mid-spin, the other man kicked him in the ribs hard enough to knock Khurt down the stairs. He bounced down a few times and hit his head hard enough against the ground that his vision was growing spotty. He saw some of his own soldiers run up the stairs after the man, but then everything went black.

FARCO CREPT INTO THE KITCHEN DOOR behind Avenira. The beauty of it was that it barely looked like a door from the outside, so he hoped that no soldiers had known to come in through this way. Anahi and Fae had shown him a long time ago, when he'd just started working for Munn Keeramm, just in case he needed to grab something quickly for the Blind Man. Farco hesitated a moment at the thought of Keeramm.

The old man had sacrificed himself so that he and Avenira could hide in his home. Avenira had protested, arguing that her manifestation of unbreakable bones could protect them, but Keeramm told them that unbreakable bones meant nothing if she was stabbed in the body and bled out. He'd had a point, and Farco knew there was no arguing with the man, even about little things. Something big like life and death wouldn't be an argument they would win.

They hid in an underground library of Keeramm's, beneath the main floor. Keeramm had had books down there that the Tower of the Blind wanted to be kept safe, and only Keeramm and Farco had known about it. Now Avenira knew as well. He hadn't cried when he heard it happen, though he knew at some point that would come. For now, he needed to see if his friends had survived. They'd snuck through Vandenar to get to the Elephant, with Avenira leading the way. It was an easy decision to let her go first, given that she could better defend herself.

As they tiptoed into the kitchen, they maintained their silence. He heard a commotion coming from the butcher block. Avenira had heard it, too; she set course toward the noise. As they turned the corner around a counter, he saw Fae keeping a boy in place with a sword pointed a few inches from his nose. "Fae." He was about to shout but remembered they might not be alone in the building. "What is this? Are there any others left?"

Fae pursed her lips together as she kept her gaze on the boy. "N...no. They killed Cyrus an' Anahi an' Sadie right in front o' me. Everyone inside is dead. This one's a general's son. Figure he might be a bargainin' token ta keep me alive. He keeps insistin' he doesn't want ta go back with his own people, but I figure that's exactly the kinda lie that a little boy would tell."

Farco nodded and walked up to the boy, who sat with his back to the counter, then crouched down. He eyed a dagger strapped to the side of the boy's leg and pulled it out. "How did ya manage ta get free from the others, Fae?"

"Ya remember the two generals who came ta warn everyone yesterday about the invasion?" Farco nodded. "Well, right after this one's father killed Anahi, one o' those generals, I think his name was Wendell somethin' or another, he stormed in with a bunch o' soldiers an' they all started fightin'. That's when I took this one an' slipped inta the kitchen. It's been quiet fer a few minutes, so I dunno if they all killed each other."

He pointed the dagger at the boy, still coming to terms that Anahi and Cyrus were dead. "What's yer name?"

The boy looked at him and answered through a raspy throat, "Khenzi."

"Khenzi, where are ya from an' why are ye an' yer people here, killin' everyone?"

"You talk strange. We're from Vitheligia, on the island of Orol Taghdras, across the sea. We've come to rid Ashur and the world of people who worship Darian."

Farco looked around at Fae and Avenira, confused. "Who told ya that we worship Darian?"

Khenzi looked at him with less conviction now. "My father, Khurt Everitas, General of the Eighth Battalion of the Vithelegion. As well as our Commander, Saol Suldas. We follow the Harbinger Abram and celebrate him."

Farco shook his head. "This is all so stupid. Khenzi, we don't worship any single Harbinger here. At least no one I know does. We celebrate all o' them, except Jahmash. But I've never met anyone who's singled out Darian ta worship an' said that Abram was lesser."

Khenzi simply shrugged. "You should talk to my dad then. And Saol Suldas and the other generals."

Farco almost chuckled at the notion. "That's not likely. But why were ya tellin' Fae that ya don't want ta go back ta yer people?"

Khenzi worked his mouth over for a few moments. He was starting to look more like a little boy now. "I don't think I can keep doing this. I trained and fought and everything to make my father proud and to continue the tradition, but I don't want to fight in battle like this anymore. At least not like this. They went into people's houses and killed them while they slept. I don't want to do that, and the Vithelegion will keep doing that to every city in Ashur."

Farco waved Fae off, then stood and pulled Khenzi up to stand. "If we can bring ya ta safety an' hide ya from yer people, will ya agree ta not try anythin' stupid? Khenzi nodded vigorously. "Good. Because ya see Avenira, here? This is my girlfriend an' she has unbreakable bones. Which means that she could keep punchin' ya over an' over again in the face without ever breakin' her knuckles. Got it?"

Khenzi looked up at him, and then at Avenira, terrified. "Y-yes I think so. But what about my father? Can we save him, too?"

They ushered Khenzi towards the side door. "If he's there in the other room, then Avenira an' I will come back fer him. An' then we can bring him back ta ya."

They snuck back out of the Elephant and through broken down and abandoned homes to get back to Munn Keeramm's home. After what felt like an hour, they finally snuck through a window in the back of the house. Farco went first, then helped Fae and Khenzi through, and Avenira entered last. They removed the proper floorboards and showed Fae to the hideout beneath the floor. Each removable board had a handle attached to the bottom so that they could be pushed out. Some even had posts extending down, to help support the weight from up top.

They helped Fae and Khenzi down and Farco stayed up to talk to Avenira. "What do ya think? Wait it out an' still go ta the Tower?"

Avenira sat next to him and criss-crossed her legs in front of her. Her soft and silky black hair still looked beautiful, despite everything they'd been through. "Wouldn't that be the safest place fer now?"

"I dunno. If this army isn't from Ashur, then they won't care if the Tower is sacred. They may attack it anyway. Even if the Tower is filled with servants trained by the Anonymi, would they really be able ta fight a whole army like this?"

Avenira met his eyes, as if she understood exactly what he was getting at. "So then, straight ta the Anonymi fortress fer trainin'?"

He shrugged and smirked, "Right?"

"Right. But what about Fae?"

"Let's just get out o' Vandenar first, then we can worry about what she wants ta do next. If we can sneak out from the north end, then we can get ta a fishin' boat at the river an' take that ta the Tower. We could drop Fae off there, an' they could even tell us where we need ta go. It's not like we'd know how ta find the Anonymi on our own anyway."

She eyed him curiously and whispered, "Ya weren't serious about goin' back fer the boy's bloody father, were ya?"

Farco's eyes widened, "Fer the love o' Orijin, no. I hope he's layin' in the Elephant, dyin' a slow death an' wonderin' where the hell his son is."

She smiled at him and leaned in to kiss his cheek. "I can't wait til we know fer sure that we're safe. Then we can train an' turn ourselves inta proper weapons, gather an army, an' wipe out these bloody bastards."

He grabbed her hand, "We'll fight side by side in every battle an' take down our enemies side by side. We'll become legends in Ashur an' we'll call ourselves 'Near an' Far'."

Her cheeks looked almost like they'd reddened, "Near an' Far?"

"Well yer Avenira - so it's like 'Near'. An' I'm Farco, so 'Far'. But it also sounds like the words near an' far."

Avenira's cheeks were definitely bright at this point. "How long have ya been thinkin' about that?"

It was his turn to blush. "Since the first time I met ya. Is that strange?"

"Absolutely it is. But also amazin'. An' I love the sound o' it. Near an' Far."

CHAPTER 23
CRACKS IN THE GLASS

From *The Book of Orijin*, Verse Four Hundred Ninety
The time will come when you shall look upon your horizons and think that the end has come.
Listen to the voices around you and know that if you are righteous, even the end should bring you no fear.

MAQDHUUM APPEARED IN THE basement of a battered house, where Garrison's brother, Donovan Brighton, awaited him. The prince looked worn down. His hair and clothes were matted with blood, and his armor stained with it as well. Most likely it was a mixture of his own blood and his opponents'. Maqdhuum vaguely remembered his days of hand-to-hand combat, except that he'd never really had to worry about his opponents hitting back. The first fight he'd ever lost was the one against Jahmash.

"Destinations?"

Donovan removed his gauntlets and put his hands to his hips. He was still breathing heavily. "Soldiers back to Alvadon. Training grounds. Those of us who are healthy can bring the injured to the infirmary. Bring survivors to the Tower of the Blind. The Augurs will not object, but let them know it is just temporary until we know what to do with the survivors."

"Fair enough." Maqdhuum nodded. "I guess that means I have to go house to house?"

Donovan looked down, and then met his eyes. "We lost a lot of soldiers in this battle. Which is why we're retreating in the first place. I'd say we're lucky if we still have one hundred men. Find whom you can. Be thorough if you can. If you happen to find any of our soldiers protecting surviving townsfolk, bring them all to the Tower. We can always sort it out when everyone is safe."

"Guess I'd better get started then. You first?"

Donovan looked guilty at the question being asked. "I suppose. It'll be easier to direct them when they see me. What about you? Will you be able to do all this? Bringing us here was one location to another. Now you have to get through the whole city while the Vithelegion are still attacking."

He smiled, partly to ease his own mind, but also to help Donovan worry less. "I'm already exhausted, but trying not to die will help me get through."

"It would have been much easier if Savaiyon was here to help as well. Sorry that the burden is on you."

"We each have a part to play." He stepped to Donovan and grasped his shoulder. "Let's move before it's too late." In an instant, they were at the training fields of Alvadon, where Maqdhuum had met them to transport them in the first place. "I'll be bringing them as soon as I find them, so be ready. Keep this area clear. This is where I'll show up. Don't want us appearing in the middle of someone else's body. That gets ugly."

Donovan nodded. "Thanks."

Over the next hour, Maqdhuum scoured the homes and buildings of Vandenar, searching for surviving soldiers and townsfolk. The constant transporting of people from Vandenar to the Tower of the Blind and Alvadon wore him down. He was growing sluggish in his ability to appear and disappear quickly. Throughout the process, Badalao checked into his mind to make sure he was safe. There had been a few offers to help, and Maqdhuum knew that those offers were more Badalao's attempts to quiet Desmond and Baltaszar than anything else. The two of them had grown unbearable with their incessant demands to come to Vandenar to fight. Maqdhuum was almost glad that he had this opportunity to be away from them. At least the people he was finding were grateful, despite their surprise and hesitance to go with them. He understood their reluctance. They knew Descendants because they were easily recognizable with the black lines down their faces, but he was something completely different. To explain to them who he really was would have been complicated, time consuming, and most likely futile.

Some places were empty of life, but the scenes were gruesome. Bodies hacked apart in every manner imaginable. Maqdhuum had seen this before many times since Jahmash had betrayed them. Usually it was one nation seeking to instill its dominance over another, or an argument over borders. To Maqdhuum, it was always something stupid. Even during his days as a Harbinger, the quarrels were always the same. He often wondered what the point was of Orijin sending forth messengers to fix things. Mankind would always be violent and jealous and angry. It was just in the nature of man to be that way. Sending a message to one generation would just give the next generation something different to fight about.

He was surprised that the Vithelegion had traveled so far to attack Ashur. He'd been somewhat familiar with their nation and had even fought alongside Ashota, the founder of Vitheligia, when she decided to attack her persecutors for their abuse of her. Over the centuries, Vitheligia had been renowned for its warriors, and most nations knew better than to seek a fight with them. Similarly, Vitheligia didn't look for fights with other nations. They tended to keep to themselves unless provoked.

Maqdhuum dwelled on what Ashur could have possibly done to become the target of the Vithelegion's wrath. The Vithelegion wasn't nearly large enough to wipe out all of Ashur. As efficient as they were, Ashur was simply too large for one army to travel from city to city, expecting extinction. There was also no way that they were working for Jahmash. Jahmash had made it clear more than once that the Vithelegion had refused his offers.

He kept his routine of bringing survivors to the Tower of the Blind. Most people were injured, but every so often he came across a few people who hadn't been hurt, and they usually had with them a child who bore the black line. Maqdhuum wondered if this Vithelegion invasion might spark an outbreak of new children with manifestations.

As he appeared in the next house, he walked into three Vithelegion soldiers. He blinked away to the Alvadon training grounds, but was almost positive that one of them turned and saw him.

Donovan stood almost exactly where he expected him to be, directing soldiers to and fro. He saw Maqdhuum and nodded, "You look like you need a break. Why not stop for a few minutes and catch your breath? We may be able to get you some food and drink as well."

Maqdhuum hadn't realized how heavily he was breathing until he actually stopped. He felt soreness and exhaustion in every fiber of his body, but he knew he couldn't rest yet. He squatted down to catch his breath. "I'm almost done, Donovan. The Vithelegion is still there. If I don't get the people out now, they might not survive."

Donovan looked at him flatly, knowing he wouldn't win the argument. "Then be careful. If you don't survive, then you can't save anyone."

Maqdhuum nodded, "Point taken. I'll be careful." He took a few more breaths and stood up. As he traveled back to Vandenar, he was more conscious than before of just how slow he was. Even the process of traveling seemed to take longer. He appeared in a room, staring at a bare wall. Something about it looked familiar, and then he heard the voices behind him. As he turned around, he saw the same three Vithelegion soldiers that he'd just seen. *Shit. Same house. How did that happen?* Instantly, one of the soldiers hefted a spear at him, piercing him through the left shoulder. The hit dropped Maqdhuum immediately. He knew he needed to get away before they could attack again, or he might not have the energy to travel.

He thought he heard one of them say "Again," and he closed his eyes. Just as something pierced his side, Maqdhuum disappeared from the room.

EVERYONE STOOD, SURROUNDING Badalao. The long table sat only a few feet away, but no one dared sit. Or speak. They watched Badalao intensely, waiting for something, anything, after he told them he'd lost his connection with Maqdhuum.

After several more moments of anticipation, Baltaszar couldn't stay quiet any longer. "Nothing? That's it? Is he hurt? Alive, even?"

Badalao looked up from the ground, and at the whole group. "There's enough there that I know he's alive. But I don't think he's even conscious right now. Which means I don't know where he is. It's similar, Tasz, to when I was trying to reach you while you were in the dungeon at Alvadon. I knew you were alive, but not the extent of your injuries, and I had no way of telling where you were. At least with you, I was fairly certain that you were in Ashur. With Maqdhuum, he could be anywhere here or beyond."

Baltaszar wasn't mad at Badalao, more at the situation. Perhaps mad at Asarei and Maqdhuum as well. Adria and Slade could also be thrown into that category. They were the ones who prevented him and Desmond from going to help. Others would have come along to fight as well, if it had been allowed. He stepped forward and looked at the group, singling out Adria and Asarei specifically by pointing to each of them. "This is *your* fault. We told you we needed to be there. Desmond and I were ready. We could have helped. We could have saved more lives. Now Maqdhuum is hurt, too. And with Savaiyon gone, we have no one who can travel quickly if something happens."

Asarei stepped to him. "Watch your tone, Baltaszar."

Baltaszar wouldn't back down. "No. *You* listen. We've trained for over six months to better our manifestations and to perfect our combat abilities. And as soon as a situation arises in which we can help and put all of it to use, *all* of you in charge tell us that we're not ready. That the risk is too great. So what in Opprobrium did we just bloody train for? Why are only *you and your people* good enough to fight? Wouldn't this have been a good opportunity to see if we're ready for the siege on Edmund? And if anyone was hurt, Linc and Delilah could have treated us with plenty of time to be ready for the siege."

"And what would Linc and Delilah have done if you died? How could they have helped then?" Adria sounded defensive.

Baltaszar was about to respond, but Desmond came to his side. "All due respect, Mouse, isn't that the risk we all accepted? That death is part o' the whole thing? We're supposed ta be protectin' Ashur."

Baltaszar nodded. "So what is the plan for the Vithelegion? We're just going to allow them to march through Ashur and overtake every city?"

Adria looked flustered, "No. But if an alliance with the Anonymi is on the line, then we have to make sure we focus on that first. Jahmash is bigger than the Vithelegion. We also need to put things in place to be able to fight Jahmash when the time comes."

"An' what is the Anonymi doin' right now ta stop the Vithelegion? They're supposed ta protect the balance in Ashur. Look out fer Ashur's best interest. All they're doin' right now, Savaiyon included, is hidin' in their fortress an' lettin' Ashur crumble."

"I don't know the answer to that." Adria shrugged.

Baltaszar was growing frustrated. It was almost as if the siege was the only thing that mattered, and they'd accepted that innocent lives would be lost.

Asarei spoke up, "That's it, I'm getting tired of the two of you insulting everyone. You don't think Savaiyon would be here helping if he could? Clearly there is something important that is keeping him with the Anonymi. Maybe they *are* planning how to fight the Vithelegion. Maybe that's why they need him there, because he can't help with the siege anyway. Do not judge anyone unless you know exactly what they're going through."

Baltaszar couldn't hold himself back. "Well, Desmond has a point. If they are planning something, they're taking a really long time to do it. They've just let the Vithelegion destroy four cities. Within a week all of Mireya will be lost. Might as well call it New Vitheligia now. Adria, Desmond asked you last time what you would do if they arrived on the shores of your city. Would you just sit here and let Asarei go fight with a few other people? And just hope that everything worked out? Would you be so cavalier about losing innocent lives? Would your parents be worthy sacrifices to the greater cause? Just because Jahmash is coming? When you eventually see them in the Three Rings, would that be your rationale? That you let them die for the greater good, without lifting a damn finger to help them?" Baltaszar saw her expression become crestfallen, but it didn't make him feel bad for her. "Oh good, you're upset now. That look on your face is only the slightest particle of what Desmond and I feel about Vandenar."

Asarei interjected again. "Stop. You're being disrespectful and hurtful now."

Baltaszar looked him in the eye. He wasn't done with his attack. "What do you know about any of this? You abandoned your people and don't give a damn about anyone outside of this island. The Taurani were slaughtered and you did nothing. The House of Darian was destroyed while you sat here, oblivious. Now, Mireya is being dismantled, and you bring *two* people with you to help!" He summoned his manifestation, unsure of why. He hadn't created any fire just yet, but he was ready to.

Asarei somehow seemed to sense this, "Calm down, Baltaszar. You're getting too angry for your own good. Let go of your manifestation."

"No. You don't care about Ashur! All you care about is staying safe! You have everyone you love here. Protected and unknown to the rest of the world! Nothing will ever happen to your wife and daughter, because all you've done with your life is hide!"

Asarei walked up to Baltaszar and grabbed him by the neck. Baltaszar was too taken by surprise to even think about fighting back. Asarei pushed him back as he tightened his grip around Baltaszar's neck. He wasn't actually choking Baltaszar, but it still hurt. Baltaszar backpedaled all the way to the wall. The hard rock was cold against the back of his head. Asarei whispered to him. "Let's take a walk. Do as I say and it'll just look like I calmed you down. Continue to be an asshole and I'll choke you so hard that you'll shit your pants. Got it?" Baltaszar wanted to take a deep breath, but couldn't. He wiggled his head as much as he could to show that he accepted the terms. "Good. Let's go." Asarei released him and turned to the others, all of whom were staring at the confrontation that just happened, "We're going to take a little walk. Lao, continue to monitor anything from Maqdhuum."

Baltaszar followed Asarei out of the room. He expected that Asarei would start putting him in his place immediately, but they walked on in silence until Asarei led him outside. As they stepped into the open air, Baltaszar remembered that he'd left Yasaman out there and had no idea what had become of her after. "What happened to…"

"Don't worry about her. She's not your problem now. My *protected* wife and daughter are going to take care of her for a little while, and then we'll send her back to Shipsbane."

Baltaszar nodded. "Thanks."

They walked on, away from the orchards and past the training grounds. "I understand that you're angry. Believe me, I do. I know what it's like to lose a loved one. I know what it's like to fear for someone else's life. You're scared. There are people in Vandenar that you love and you don't know if they survived or not. Once we hear from Maqdhuum, we can sort that all out."

The walk had started to calm Baltaszar down. He felt somewhat guilty for insulting Asarei and Adria, but he was still angry. "I'm sorry for insulting you before, but it doesn't change the fact that Anahi might be dead. Desmond's family might be dead. And the plan is to just wait and see."

"How do you plan to get to Vandenar?"

Baltaszar worked his mouth for a response. "Now, there's no way. That was my whole point in the first place. Send some of us there to help fight, and preserve lives. Now, there's no hope."

"I'll entertain your point. What if we had brought you there to fight? What would you have done?"

Baltaszar looked at him flatly, "I would have burned them all."

Asarei looked straight ahead as they walked on. "Simple as that, huh? Just would've stood there in the middle of the street and set everyone on fire? You do realize that in battle there's no such thing as an easy target. Even if you can control fire. There are people running around everywhere. People on either side. Looking to do two things. Kill the enemy and stay alive. And there's a fine line in that. You're trying to act so quickly and make sure that you're protected at all times, that you also have to make sure you don't hurt your own people. So even if you're standing in the middle of the street, burning everyone, chances are you're killing your own men. Chances are, you're also not paying attention to everything around you. So while you're focusing on setting fires, anyone could run up behind you and kill you in a number of ways. Most likely they'd stab you through the neck, though."

"Fine. Then I could have done it from a rooftop."

Asarei snickered at him. "Right. Stood at the edge of a roof, in plain sight, setting people on fire. Easy target for an archer. Or would you have a soldier escort you while you're up there? Have them cover you while you set your fires? Then they would die not long before you would. What else?"

Baltaszar clenched his teeth. "Look, I don't know because I wasn't there. But I bet you I would've had a decent strategy either way."

"You saw Trevor return with me and Bam, correct?"

"Yeah."

"He looked like he was in decent shape? No injuries?"

Baltaszar shook his head, "No. Nothing noticeable, anyway."

"You want to know why?" Asarei didn't wait for an answer. "It's because his manifestation is that he can heal quickly. He was able to take a beating in Vandenar because the wounds would heal. Now, that doesn't mean they don't hurt, but Trevor tends to be a little aggressive, knowing that he'll be fine sooner or later. Bam, on the other hand, well you've seen and been told what he can do. I'll admit, Manjobam is one of the gentlest souls I've ever met, on a *normal* day. But he takes his fighting seriously. And boy, he was scary as hell in Vandenar. And as for me, my senses are much, much better than a normal person. I can feel and smell and hear an attacker coming. It's also why you were so surprised that I knew you had opened to your manifestation."

"Oh. Yeah."

"The point I'm making, Tasz, is that the three of us went because our manifestations allowed us to be the lowest risks out of anyone else here. We were the most likely to return in one piece. And even still, we lost. The Vithelegion is that good that they could still defeat us. But now we know what we're up against and we can use that to bring a better fight next time. You're right. This does suck. People are dying and we don't have Savaiyon around to help, which is a huge blow. But this is war, and as much as you hate to believe it, people are going to die in war. Even the siege that you're all about to undertake, there's a huge possibility that things won't go according to plan. You have to accept the possibility that some of you will not survive. Including you. It's not training anymore. As soon as you step into that castle, there will be people trying to kill you, and if you let your guard down for even a moment, you could die."

They walked on through the trees and stayed quiet for a short while. Baltaszar did his best to process everything Asarei was telling him and not argue back. There was sense in what the man said, whether Baltaszar liked it or not. He hadn't really considered the option of failure. He had just assumed the whole time that, since the Ghosts had their manifestations, they could win any fight. Asarei's advice made him think of the attack on the House of Darian, and how so many Descendants were killed by an army with no manifestations.

It wasn't until they reached the clearing that Baltaszar realized they had been walking toward the beach the whole time. He looked out and just as he saw General Grunt, Asarei verbalized the confirmation, "There he is. Here are a couple of apples. Go talk to him and clear your mind. If you get angry enough and can't contain yourself, his scales are impervious to fire. Only his scales though. Take your time and come back when you've let it all out."

Baltaszar nodded and walked toward the nashorn, unaware that Asarei stayed within the forest to watch him. He clutched the apples in his hands and walked up to General Grunt. He patted the beast and put an apple in front of his snout. General Grunt sniffed it and then grabbed it from Baltaszar's hand with his teeth. After chomping it down, he gently licked Baltaszar's hand with his coarse tongue until Baltaszar offered him another apple. General Grunt ate it quickly and then licked Baltaszar's face, much to his surprise.

"Thanks, pal. I kind of needed that." He kept one hand on the animal's snout and put the other on its neck. "Does it ever bother you that you're here and not with your family? Seems like you're happy every time we see you, but it's got to be tough to not be with others like you. Maybe after this siege is done, we can work on bringing you back to the Never." The beast continued to nuzzle against his hand. "I don't know, General Grunt. It all seems like too much is going on. Sometimes I wish my life could be simple like yours. Like it was back in Haedon, but *before* all that shit with my father started. It was all so simple. Just farming all day, spending time with the animals, going to the markets every now and then. Arguing with Bo about stupid things. The worst thing about that life was the looks people gave me about this black line on my face. But at least *they* weren't trying to kill me."

"You know who I really hate? The man who took my mother away. If that had never happened, my parents would still be together, enjoying a quiet life, and they'd both be alive. Even better, the four of us would still be together and I wouldn't have this blasted line on my face. Or this damn scar on the other side of my face." He touched the scar, as if checking to see if it was still there, hoping that it might be gone. "If I ever find out who took her, Grunt, I swear I will rip him apart." He looked out at the sea, staring at the horizon as if change might start out there somewhere. "You know what I feel like? I feel like a piece of glass, and all of these things are like rocks that keep putting cracks in me, but not hard enough to break me apart. Soon, though, it's going to be too much. I mean, how many cracks will it take before I shatter into a thousand little pieces?" He could feel a tear form in the corner of his eye, and he let it follow its path. "Especially if Anahi didn't survive the attack on Vandenar...I...I think I would set the whole world on fire."

Baltaszar let go of General Grunt and stepped away. He walked a few steps past the beast and continued to stare out at the sea. The tears had overtaken both of his eyes. They blurred his vision just as his emotions had blurred the realization that his manifestation flowed through him. Baltaszar continued to stare off at the horizon until he created a fireball so large far out over the sea that even he was scared at the size of it. Instead of just allowing it to dissipate, he released it and let it fall into the sea. Even from the beach, he could see the steam rising from the water.

He remembered what he'd done the last time he was this emotional, and considered it a small victory that at least he'd only killed fish this time, instead of putting people's lives in danger.

"Not bad. Maybe once the siege is done, you can drop one of those on the Vithelegion before they get to another city." The voice behind him startled him, especially once he realized it was Asarei, whom he assumed had left him alone. He was even more surprised to see Adria standing next to Asarei.

ADRIA STOOD WITH HER HANDS on her hips, hoping to exude confidence and so that Baltaszar would back down from arguing. She expected that he might be angry and perceive this as being spied on by her and Asarei, but he surprised her.

He wiped his reddened eyes and cheeks, though the teary gloss remained. "Adria, I'm sorry for my outburst before. It wasn't about you at all and I know that what I said was incredibly out of line."

She shook her head and waved off the apology. She didn't need it. "I've been thinking the whole way here about what you and Desmond asked me. About if I would just sit here and accept not being able to help if the Vithelegion had invaded Markos instead. And the truth is, Tasz, if Fera was the next city they were going to, I don't know what I would do. I would like to say that I'd trust those with more wisdom and experience than me, but I can't say for sure. I know that's not definitive, and I apologize, but it's an answer.

"What I *can* say definitively, though, is that we have a job to do. Fourteen of us do. And while we focus on that, Asarei and the others can look to the Vithelegion and make their own decisions. If you're angry about all of this, then hold on to it and use it against the idiot who sits on the throne in Alvadon, who wouldn't even send his whole army to stop the invaders. We *need* to succeed with this, and we have to get to Edmund before the Vithelegion do. If they've traveled east since Vandenar, then that means they're already closer to Alvadon than we are."

Baltaszar walked up to her and Asarei, patting General Grunt on the way. "So what exactly are you saying? Adria, I don't dislike you, so please don't get the wrong idea. All of the guys who I've become friends with are the same ones who have raved about you for months. I've never doubted them for a moment. But I'm not really looking for a pep talk right now, so if that's why you've come out here -"

Adria rolled her eyes. *They're all stupid. Every boy. Every single one of them. Dimwits.* "No, you idiot. I'm here to tell you to get your ass back to the fortress and get your things together. Armor, weapons, clothes, and any supplies you'll need. We're leaving for Alvadon today. The fourteen of us will go to Shipsbane first to stock up on food and buy horses, and then we'll travel separately in three different factions. The meeting point is the Stones of Gideon, just like we all discussed. Once we get there, we rest, go over the plan of action, and then we go kill a king."

For the first time, saying it was the same as believing they would actually do it. For so long, Adria had seen the siege as something far off that would happen in the distant future. But now she felt it deep inside, as much in her core as when her manifestation ran through her body, that the Ghosts could and would kill the king. She turned and walked back to the fortress, not worrying about whether the other two were following her. She was the leader now and they would follow.

CHAPTER 24
THE EDGE OF THE PRECIPICE

From ***The Book of Orijin,*** **Verse Two Hundred Ninety-one**
To doubt yourselves or your purpose is to doubt Us.
Believe in your ability to be a vessel for Good, and have faith that Omneitria awaits you.

HORATIO TOOK A DEEP BREATH as the other two factions came into view. Kadoog'han had led him, Malikai, and Maximilian to the Stones of Gideon and Horatio was relieved to finally be around the others again. The journey from Shipsbane hadn't been overly bothersome; they'd been harassed once or twice, but neither time had things escalated into violence. Just as he'd seen when traveling to the Tower months ago with Lincan, Vasher, and Delilah, some of the Vermillion soldiers were sympathetic to them and reminded the others that the real threat was the Vithelegion that was attacking Mireya.

There were times when he'd held onto his manifestation just in case, but he hadn't actually summoned any lightning since training on Asarei's island. For the few days that they'd been traveling, Horatio had been mostly preoccupied with the notion that he and Malikai were the ones expected to kill King Edmund. When the question had originally been asked, he volunteered because it seemed that no one else would step forward. But as the siege drew closer, and grew more real, Horatio knew more and more that he would have great difficulty going through with it. He refused to tell the others, knowing that it was too late to change the strategy at this point. He clung to the hope that either he would be able to summon the will once the time came, or that Malikai would reach the king first and he wouldn't even be needed.

This is what happens when you try to be brave. The stress of it had given him terrible headaches throughout the journey. Oftentimes he'd try to think back to simpler times, like when he was traveling through Ashur on his own. Thinking about the past tended to make the headaches worse, though, especially when he tried to find comfort in thinking about his brother Leonard and their mother. It had been years since he'd seen them. He'd wanted to travel Ashur and take in all of the cultures and sights and cuisines, so his mother gave him her blessing to leave home and travel, with the understanding that Horatio would then go to the House of Darian. That was the last time he'd been back in the Wolf's Paw. Sometimes he desperately wanted to go back and see them, while other times he felt like he was forgetting who they were. He shook his head as they rode toward the rows and rows of stone warriors frozen in place.

The other factions had arrived earlier in the day, and most of them sat about or relaxed on the ground. Horatio dismounted along with his own company, and they led their horses farther in. They walked to the others, who took their horses and tied them to stone soldiers. Horatio walked over to Malikai, who was being greeted by a few of the others. They were laughing about something, which put Horatio somewhat at ease. *At least they're not feeling the stress of all this.* He nudged Malikai's shoulder, and as Malikai turned to him, Horatio asked, "Hey, can I talk to you off to the side for a moment, Kai?"

Malikai nodded, "Of course." The look in the short-haired Markosi's eyes softened, as if he knew what Horatio needed.

They walked a few paces away from the others, and Horatio spoke softly, "Are you sure you can do this? Sure you can go through with it, I mean?"

A half-smile grew on Malikai's face. "I think so. Of course there's some hesitation now, but the group needs me and this is a pretty important task. You having doubts, Raish?" Horatio shrugged. "Listen, by the time we get to the king, you'll have killed dozens of soldiers. Killing him will be easier than anyone we fight before him. If our faction gets to his chamber first, I'll do it with you. Or if you're still unsure at that point, I'll take it upon myself to do it."

Horatio took a deep breath, "Thanks, Kai. That means a lot. I think maybe it'll all be fine."

Malikai chuckled, "Good thing you didn't kill me with your lightning back on the island, huh?" Horatio laughed nervously. He was glad that Malikai could joke around about it, but Horatio still hated thinking about the incident that had occurred during training. While they practiced their manifestations on each other, Malikai had been trying new things with his ability to harden his own skin. They had tried various weapons and attacks to hurt Malikai. After Baltaszar had been unsuccessful with fire, someone had suggested Horatio try lightning next. Horatio had had serious reservations about doing it, especially because of what had happened with Marlowe. Lincan had assured him that he could heal Malikai right after if it didn't work.

Horatio had walked tentatively to Malikai in the middle of the sparring circle and directed a single bolt of lightning at Malikai. Malikai instantly flew several feet and stayed unconscious for a few moments. Lincan immediately ran to him and healed him, but not before Horatio considered never using his manifestation ever again. He was surprised to see his manifestation work on Malikai's toughened skin, and even more terrified to see his friend hurt.

Malikai had been fully healed for a while and bore no hard feelings toward Horatio. Horatio was grateful for the forgiveness but still found difficulty in forgiving himself. "I'm glad, too." Malikai patted him on the shoulder and walked back to the others. Horatio wished he'd had the conversation with Malikai while they were still traveling to the Stones, but with Maximilian and Kadoog'han with them, it was difficult to find a long enough period of time when the other two weren't around. He turned and saw the figure of Gideon in the distance and walked over to it. Some of the others were around, but none were too close. He'd wanted to come to the Stones of Gideon for some time, but the proximity to Alvadon and the king scared Horatio.

He stood before the young Harbinger, who stood with his legs apart and arms stretched out, looking up to the sky in agony. Horatio closed his eyes and pictured the battlefield, imagining the sacrifice that it must have required to stop so many soldiers from fighting. He imagined the agony that Gideon must have felt to the point that Horatio felt like he was there with the Harbinger thousands of years ago. It wasn't until he opened his eyes to look at the stone figure that he realized tears flowed down his cheeks. What surprised him even more was the sob that came out as he stared at Gideon. He thought the noise had been quiet enough to cover up with a cough, but Adria and Marshall came over to check on him.

"Everything alright, Raish? Why are you crying?" Adria grasped his arm.

He nodded and looked at her, wiping his face and fighting the headache. "I'm fine, thanks. I just got caught up thinking about Gideon and the sacrifice he made, just to show mankind the error of its ways. I think in a way, the same burden has been passed to us, right? We're the ones who have to fix this world, and some of us are probably going to die in the process."

She nodded as she continued to clench his forearm. "You're right. It *is* our burden now, but if we do this properly, maybe we can infiltrate the castle and complete our mission *without* any casualties. Come on, I need to talk to everyone anyway." He followed her to where the majority of the group congregated.

ADRIA WALKED TO THE CROWD WITH HORATIO and Marshall in tow. She'd let go of Marshall's hand before addressing the group. "Ghosts, can I say something to you all?" The others nodded and stopped their conversations and drew in around her. One thing that brought Adria relief was that it wasn't hard to lead this group. They all respected her and believed in her, and ever since Baltaszar and Desmond came around, no one questioned her decisions. "Horatio just reminded me of something. We stand here before Gideon, who made the ultimate sacrifice thousands of years ago, to save humanity. He was younger than any of us standing here, but he knew what he had to do. The same is true for the fourteen of us here. We are the new Harbingers, just as Blastevahn sang. We are the ones who must now save the world, and Edmund is the first step toward doing that. In order for that to happen, we all must be willing to make the same sacrifice. I know that's asking so much, but this fight is bigger than any one of us."

Badalao shouted out, "Salvation as one!"

Adria smiled curtly, "Salvation as one. We fight for each other and for the cause. If for any reason, Horatio and Malikai are unable to kill Edmund, then any of the rest of us must be up to the task. Even though Garrison gave us an idea of the castle's layout, we are still going in blind. Not everything will go according to plan. Keep your heads clear to hear Lao's orders and messages, as they will come from me. If you need to warn the rest of us about anything, relay it to Lao, and he'll tell the rest of us. We only succeed tonight if we act as one. I know we'll be in three separate factions, but we'll be three arms of the same beast.

"We've done well to get past all of our personal grudges against each other, and tonight will be the ultimate test for each of us. In everything you do tonight, remember *why* you're doing it. Remember that Ashur is being torn down in the west. Remember everything that we did to survive the attack on the House. Remember our fallen brothers and sisters, like Gunnar, Jelahni, and Marlowe. Remember all the others who aren't here that need us to be victorious tonight. Remember our friends who have gone through the same struggles and can't be by our side, like Lincan and Savaiyon. If we remember everything and everyone we're doing this for, then maybe we can all make it back home."

Adria almost got choked up at the thought of any of them not surviving but pushed it down and looked around at the rows and rows of stone soldiers. She looked back at the group, "Let's spend the rest of the day until nightfall enjoying each other's company, resting, sleeping, and doing as little as possible." The others nodded and smiled and shouted in agreement.

Before they all dispersed, Badalao walked up to Adria and hugged her tightly, then whispered, "Thank you," before walking away. To her surprise, the others followed Badalao's lead and did the same. By the time Kadoog'han, the last of the group, hugged her too tightly, Adria had been crying for a while.

Marshall took her hand and led her away from the others. They walked far down a row of stone soldiers and Marshall finally stopped and sat down against one of the stone figures. He beckoned for Adria to sit with him, so she sat between his legs and leaned back against his chest. If they had been close enough for the others to see, Adria knew she would avoid looking so vulnerable, but she knew she needed some time to be comforted and held before they left the Stones of Gideon. *When night comes, I'll have to be the strong one, more than any of the others. I can have this moment.* She closed her eyes and rested her head against Marshall's shoulder. She asked him quietly, as if nervous that the stone soldiers might hear, "Are you still upset? About your manifestation?"

He whispered back, "Only with myself, but I've bettered myself in combat. There's nothing to worry about. We don't have to talk. We can just sit here and…be."

She smiled at the suggestion. She didn't really want to talk. She preferred to just sit and enjoy the semblance of privacy. The only thing that mattered was that she and Marshall were both at peace. Throughout their time training, Marshall and Asarei worked and worked at Marshall's manifestation and ways to use it. They tried focusing on the daylight first, especially because Marshall had made the whole world go dark less than a couple of years ago. When that proved futile, they tried to work on manipulating Marshall's shadow and reflection, but nothing worked and Asarei ran out of suggestions for Marshall.

Adria suspected that the frustration might have mounted enough for Marshall that his emotions prevented him from being able to focus properly, but she wouldn't dare say that to him. She wasn't afraid to, but she knew it wasn't what he needed to hear. Once the siege was over, she planned to give him some suggestions about different things to focus on. She was tired of thinking though, and even more tired of thinking about how to solve problems. She cleared her mind and focused on the darkness. In only a few moments, she drifted off into a deep sleep.

When Adria finally opened her eyes again, Marshall was nudging her shoulder and kissing her cheek. She felt her cheeks redden, but only until she realized that the sky was dark. Adria jumped to her feet, feeling both refreshed and anxious. Marshall arose next to her and as they walked back to the others, Adria noticed a ball of light at the end of the row. *Tasz must be providing light for everyone to get ready.* She smiled at the thought and, as they walked out into the clearing, Adria saw fireballs hovering all around, helping the others see to put their black armor on. "Everyone ready to do this?" The response was a resounding yes from all of them.

The others broke into their factions and helped each other suit up and find the desired weapons. Adria walked to the other groups to check on them. She first stopped at Horatio and Malikai, who were both donning breastplates, along with Kadoog'han and Maximilian. Kadoog'han nodded at her, "Captain."

She smiled. "Kad. Ready?"

"Aye. Always."

"Good. Raish? Kai? What about you? Ready to kill a king?"

They both replied. "Ready," though Horatio's smile seemed tentative. She didn't blame him, though. It was hard enough to kill an enemy in battle. They were being asked to kill the King of Ashur.

She walked to Badalao's group, where Sindha and Delilah were examining daggers and comparing the weights. "Armor looks good on you two ladies. Weapons, too. I'm sorry you two had to be with these disgusting boys, but I need you to keep them in line." She smirked.

Sindha cackled, "Oh don't worry, they're in good hands. At least Rev here is sensible, too. But don't worry, my queen, we won't fail you."

Adria's eyebrows shot up, "Queen?"

Delilah grasped her hand, "You're leading us to go kill a king. That means you will be our Queen."

Adria blushed, and then whispered so that only the girls would hear, "Does that make Marshall the king?"

Delilah snickered, "Light of Orijin, no. Marshall is your throne."

She was glad it was night, as she knew her face must have been several shades darker. She wasn't sure of Delilah's connotation, but she assumed it was meant to be suggestive. Adria didn't mind, though. It was nice to talk to girls for a change. She sorely missed Krissette, who was back on the island with Asarei and the others, likely preparing to fight the Vithelegion. "Del, you're too much. I'm sorry I haven't spent more time with the two of you. I think when this is all done, we need more time to bond."

Sindha nodded vigorously, "And to share all of the secrets about these boys."

"Absolutely. It's a deal then."

As she walked away, Delilah said loud enough for only Adria to hear, "Bye, my Queen." Adria blushed again but composed herself before reaching her own faction.

"Everyone here ready?" Marshall, Baltaszar, Blastevahn, and Vasher were all adorned in full armor, and were sheathing their swords and daggers.

Vasher nodded, "Ready as we'll ever be. Just give the order and we'll be ready to move out. The horses have been fed and prepped; I think everything is ready."

Marshall helped her with her armor, putting the breastplate on and securing it in place. "I know we haven't really faced combat like this but listen for my orders. If you find yourself in a bind, trust your instincts. Trust your gut."

Baltaszar cut in, "The last time I trusted my gut, I shit myself."

Adria cocked her head and looked at him with squinted eyes. Vasher must have been equally as confused and responded. "What? Are you serious? What the hell does that even mean?"

Baltaszar laughed, "Actually I don't know. Seemed like the right thing to say. Sorry, just trying to lighten the mood a little. I know this is serious, but this may be the last time we get to smile and laugh for a while, depending on how tonight goes."

Adria understood Baltaszar's point. "That's fair. I understand. I know you get my point, Tasz. I'm not worried about you. And please don't shit yourself tonight."

Baltaszar winked at her and smiled, "I'll do my best."

The other factions joined them once they were all dressed and armed. Adria sheathed her two swords behind her back, as well as her shield. She looked around at all the others. She knew they weren't expecting another speech; in fact, most of them weren't even looking at her. But Adria felt it would be bad leadership to just embark without saying anything. Once she had all of her weapons properly equipped, she decided to address them. She didn't bother to stand in front of the group or try a dramatic opening. Adria just took a deep breath and started talking. "Look, I know we all have our fears and doubts. I know we haven't done anything like this before. And I would be lying if I told you that I wasn't nervous, too. But tonight, focus on the mission. If you let fear make your decisions, I guarantee that this will not end well for us. Remember that we all have each other's back. Remember that some of us have manifestations that can help in a bind. And most importantly, remember that we are one unit. Salvation as one."

The rest of the group chanted 'Salvation as one' as they followed Adria's lead in finding their horses and mounting.

"Rev, Kai, you'll lead us to the castle?"

Reverron nodded, "My pleasure, captain. This way, Ghosts." Reverron rode past Gideon and away from the Stones, southwest towards Alvadon. "It won't take very long, so I advise everyone to stay quiet and put out any fires."

Adria nodded, "Good." She turned around to look at the others, and noticed that Baltaszar's fireballs had already vanished. The light of the summer moon and the stars would be their only guide in the dark. As they left the Stones of Gideon, Adria reminded them once more that her faction would enter the castle from the south, while Badalao's would enter from the north, and Kadoog'han's would wait for the other two to draw the majority of the guards before entering from the west. "The target is to get to the grand ballroom, and then find the royal chambers beneath it. Garrison said the staircase is hidden behind a wall, so whoever gets there first, you'll have to do some searching. As soon as we get there, Tasz will set a fire on the eastern side once everyone is in place, to draw more guards away. As soon as I hear a reaction to the fire, we enter. Remember, Garrison said his father keeps the guards inside, to allow a false sense of security for attackers. It's unlikely that guards will be outside, but we have no idea what the inside of the castle will be like."

CHAPTER 25
KINGSBANE

From *The Book of Orijin*, Verse One Hundred Forty-eight
The greatest trials will break down your mind as well as your body.
But the stronger your mind, the more your body can withstand.
Your body will only fail if your mind allows it to.

Badalao looked all around and oddly felt confident because of his helmet. Sindha's father and the forgers had seemingly gotten all of the measurements perfect. The helmet fit perfectly and covered the top half of his face, while exposing anything beneath his nose. The locations of the eye slits were accurate and big enough to see peripherally as well as straight ahead. The tops of the black helmets were lined with spiked ridges, which helped him to feel the slightest bit more dangerous.

He led his faction through the northwestern corridor. Baltaszar had started the fire as planned, and Adria confirmed that soldiers rushed to the scene to analyze the threat. Badalao and his group entered the castle first, hoping to draw some of the soldiers who were near the fire. Sindha led the way for them, her force field large enough to shield them all from any arrows. They carried shields with them, but the unfamiliar hallways meant that they would have to keep their shields up all the time. They walked carefully yet quickly in the hopes that they'd be seen sooner, rather than later. *Quiet on this side so far*, he relayed to Adria and Kadoog'han. They neared an intersection in which the corridor branched into two paths. To the left, he saw a group of soldiers down the hall, through Sindha's force field. *Rev, can you hold Sindha while dashing like you practiced?* He shared the thought with Sindha and Reverron, to make sure they were both on the same page. *Des, Del, and I can charge right behind you to attack after you two knock them all down.*

Reverron responded excitedly, *I definitely can. Just watch my back in case we miss any.* As soon as he finished the thought, Reverron walked past Badalao to Sindha. He put his arms around her waist as she nodded to him, and Reverron dashed down the hallway with her, going faster each time he dashed. Badalao waved his arm forward for Desmond and Delilah to follow, and the three of them ran after. As soon as Reverron and Sindha reached the surprised soldiers, Sindha's force field knocked them down, pushed them out of the way, or flung them backwards.

Badalao didn't hesitate to engage the enemy, nor did Desmond or

Delilah. Their swords were in hand as they hacked away at the lame Vermillion soldiers, who still struggled to get their bearings and understand what had happened to them. *Adria, Kad, we've engaged the enemy. We'll continue to do so until you tell us to stop, Captain.*

Adria responded, *Good work, Lao. Tasz just rejoined us and we're entering from the south.*

As they fought through the downed soldiers, more got back to their feet and shook off their dazes. Desmond, standing next to Badalao, sheathed his sword and stared deeply into the enemy soldiers before them. As Badalao watched, several of the soldiers were raised off their feet into the air, and hung there for a few seconds before Desmond flung them into the soldiers that stood behind them. A moment later, Reverron dashed back toward them, holding Sindha. Her force field knocked even more soldiers out of the way. Once all five of them were back together, they advanced on the enemy once again. Sindha's force field vanished so that they could use their swords. Most of the few dozen soldiers lay on the ground, piled on top of each other. Badalao thought about every single Descendant who'd lost a life or who'd been hunted down because of these men. He looked for vulnerable spots and openings in their armor and helmets and struck them repeatedly. Without saying anything, he connected to the minds of the rest of his faction and felt the same anger in all of them.

He knew that the idea of 'Salvation as One' was more than just a saying. Anyone who'd feared for their lives because of the black line on their faces would know this anger. Would give anything for the chance to get this kind of revenge. The five of them advanced through their enemies and killed them all. Desmond even levitated every single body to check for life. Every Vermillion soldier was dead, but it only took a few moments for Badalao and his group to hear voices in the distance, getting closer. *Behind us. Turn around,* he told the other four.

Desmond responded quickly, "Hurry, get past these soldiers an' I can use their bodies against the next wave!" They did as he said and in no time, the dead Vermillion soldiers were all floating through the air, almost like a wall blocking the corridor. They could barely see through the mass, but as soon as the voices of the enemy soldiers revealed themselves to be around the corner and close enough to attack, Desmond hurtled the mass of dead bodies through the air at the second wave of soldiers. As soon as Badalao heard the crunch of metal falling on metal, he saw Desmond drop to one knee.

"What's wrong, Des?"

"Nothin'. Don't worry about me. I'm fine. Need ta take a break from my manifestation is all." Desmond remained on one knee and took several deep breaths before standing again.

Badalao connected to Delilah, Reverron, and Sindha, *Desmond is still dealing with some of the withdrawal. The rest of us need to step it up.* He adjusted his black spiked helmet and stalked toward the new set of soldiers. The others followed, with Desmond in the rear, regaining his bearings. As the soldiers began to climb and clamor out of the mass of dead bodies, Badalao sped toward them. The Vermillion advanced in deep rows, four men wide. As Badalao got close, Reverron dashed past him with a mace in hand. He swung the round, spiked head of the weapon like a wheel as he burst through the crowd, and used his shield to push others back. Badalao was about to mentally relay to him to be careful, but he didn't want to create any distractions that would throw Reverron off. Several soldiers fell either from the mace's blows or from the force of Reverron's speed.

He'd gone far enough to be out of Badalao's sight, but in a matter of seconds, as Badalao neared the enemy, he saw Reverron coming back and repeating his mace attack. Just as Reverron was near the front of the enemy force, one of them must have managed to trip him up. Reverron sprawled forward and his mace went flying. His other arm was bent awkwardly. While many of the Vermillion soldiers were brought down in the commotion, others had escaped and avoided Reverron's attack. They ran toward him as he lay on the ground, face up with a Vermillion soldier on top of him. As Reverron struggled to get the body off of his chest, no more than ten feet away from Badalao, a Vermillion soldier struck his sword right through the opening in Reverron's helmet.

"Nooooooo!" Badalao didn't hear himself scream, or feel himself advancing upon the enemy, but in a split second, he was hacking down the remaining soldiers with Desmond and Delilah by his side, both equally as aggressive. While they attacked with swords, Sindha used her force fields to keep other attackers at bay, shielding them from being able to advance. Once they'd taken care of the remaining soldiers, Badalao finally reached out to Adria. *Adria. They killed Rev. He's heard the Song of Orijin.* He waited a moment, but there was no answer. *Adria, did you hear me? Reverron is dead. Adria? Come on, where are you?*

After another few seconds, Adria responded. *I heard you, Lao. We're in the middle of our own fight here; I'm sorry.* She paused and then continued. *I don't even know what to say about Rev, I want to cry but I can't right now. We have to stay focused.*

Badalao responded, *Agreed. Should I tell the others?*

Yes. Adria's response surprised him. *They need to know that it can happen to any of us. That way they don't suffer the same fate. How are the rest of you?*

We're doing our best. Badalao hesitated, unsure of whether to tell her about Desmond. *We'll have to keep an eye on Des. He might be trying too hard with his manifestation. I'm concerned he might wear himself out.*

Got it. As Adria responded, he saw from the corner of his eye, Sindha created another force field the size of the entire corridor.

Go fight. We have more company. As he turned toward Sindha, Badalao saw another contingent draw near. "Sind, can you leave it in place there for us to leave, or do you have to be near it?"

"I can leave it up. As soon as I lose enough focus, like by fighting or using my manifestation on something else, it will probably come down, though."

Badalao took a few deep breaths. "We'll have to come back for Rev's body later. We have to go and find a better location where we'll be less vulnerable." He walked down the corridor, away from the force field, with Desmond, Sindha, and Delilah right behind him.

BALTASZAR STOOD SIDE BY SIDE with Vasher. He had eight fireballs floating in front of him as he flung two toward oncoming soldiers. Both hit his targets in the faces, right in the openings of their helmets. Before they completely fell to the ground, Baltaszar had already flung three more at the soldiers behind them. The Vermillion had engaged them only a few minutes before, and Baltaszar and his faction were holding their own so far. Baltaszar had yet to draw his sword but knew that he would eventually need a break from using his manifestation.

He felt a bit guilty, as his attackers never made it within an arm's reach, while Vasher was constantly engaged with his sword and shield. Whenever he had a moment to check on Vasher, Baltaszar hurled fireballs at Vasher's attackers. He wanted to simply set the whole corridor on fire and have the group escape to another room, but Adria had strongly advised him against it. She didn't want the fire to spread too quickly and then hurt their ability to get to the king. Baltaszar knew she had a point. He could dissipate the fireballs that hovered in the air, but for some reason, once the fire came into contact with something, he no longer had control. It would be too big a risk.

Not far down the corridor behind them, Adria, Marshall, and Blastevahn engaged another group of Vermillion soldiers. From the looks of it, they were handling the other threat easily, especially since both Marshall's and Blastevahn's statures took up a considerable amount of room, so no one could get past them.

Just as another set of Vermillion soldiers climbed over their fallen brethren to engage Baltaszar and Vasher, Baltaszar heard Vasher talking to them. Even stranger, Vasher's voice was calm and almost amiable. Baltaszar listened to him as he summoned more fireballs. "You don't want to attack us. We're your friends. The men behind you are your enemies. *They* are the ones you need to fight." To Baltaszar's surprise, the three men turned around with their swords drawn and started fighting the other soldiers behind them.

Baltaszar guffawed at the sight and looked at Vasher, "Wow. That worked!"

Vasher couldn't hold back his smile, "I was getting tired of using this sword so much, Tasz. See! My manifestation comes in handy for combat, too! You're not the only one here who's weaponized."

Just as Vasher finished his comment, Badalao's voice popped into Baltaszar's head. The same must have happened to Vasher, as his focus changed and he stared upward as if to concentrate. *It's Lao. Listen, we just lost Reverron. The Vermillion killed him. The rest of us killed the Vermillion who were here, and we've advanced but all of you need to be careful. Do not take this enemy for granted. And don't get overconfident. Just because all of us have manifestations doesn't mean that we can't be hurt or killed. Be safe. Salvation as One.*

"Dammit!" Baltaszar shook his head, "How?" The question received no response, and Baltaszar wouldn't bother Badalao for an answer. Despite the brief levity with Vasher only a moment ago, Baltaszar knew that that was a luxury they could no longer afford. The three soldiers that Vasher had convinced to turn on their own were still sparring with other Vermillion soldiers. Baltaszar sent fireball after fireball past the three until only they remained standing.

They turned back to Vasher and eyed him suspiciously. Baltaszar assumed they were out of their trance and were trying to determine whether Vasher was friend or foe. Before they could think of attacking, Baltaszar concentrated and sent fireballs directly at each man's face. He knew their metal armor and boots would never catch, so he continued to hit each man with a fireball to the face and neck until each fell.

Vasher took a deep breath, "Thanks, Tasz. Damn, I can't believe we lost Rev. Especially so soon. I really believed we could all make it out of this." He nodded his head toward the others and they quickly joined Adria, Marshall, and Blastevahn.

Baltaszar realized that they had barely advanced since entering the castle. Garrison had told them that from the southern entrance they could go straight to the grand ballroom, though it was down a level. However, they had yet to move on from the corridor where they'd originally entered. There had been no guards outside, they were currently fighting the third wave of soldiers, and from the looks of things, more soldiers were arriving behind them. "Light of Orijin, where the hell are they all coming from? It's like every soldier in the castle knows we're here!"

Adria shouted to him and Vasher, "Tasz! Vash! I hear more coming from behind us! Take up your previous positions. Use fire if you have to; there are too many!"

Baltaszar turned to run back to where he and Vasher had stood only a few minutes ago. He smiled tightly as more Vermillion soldiers appeared from around the corner. He held his sword in his left hand, letting them assume he would spar, but as soon as a few dozen were in sight, Baltaszar created a fire big enough to span the walls, ceiling, and floor, and thrust it down the corridor. The soldiers in front immediately tried to turn and retreat, their faces contorted with terror, but in stopping their charge, the whole battalion crashed into each other. The fire engulfed all of them and Baltaszar reveled in the screams as the Vermillion fell. His tight smile turned into a grimace as he sent another enormous fire down the corridor, just in case anyone was spared.

"Tasz! Vash! We need you!" Baltaszar turned around to see only Adria and Marshall fighting against the oncoming Vermillion. Blastevahn, unmistakable due to his gigantic stature, was slumped against the wall with the hilt of a dagger sticking out of his neck and blood smeared on the wall. A Vermillion soldier was entangled with him and looked to be dead as well. "Get out of the way!" He yelled at the other three with more rage and urgency than he'd ever felt. As soon as Adria and Marshall withdrew from their fight and Vasher was by his side, Baltaszar unleashed a torrent of fire toward the remaining Vermillion soldiers. Just as before, their screams confirmed their deaths. Baltaszar didn't stop until well after the final scream was heard, and finally he let go of his manifestation. He fell to a knee from all of the energy he'd just spent. Sweat soaked his brow and face, and he sucked in the air as if each breath was his last.

HORATIO'S HEAD FELT LIKE IT WAS going to split apart. He'd dealt with the headaches for most of his life, as far as he could remember, but he'd never felt so disabled from one as he did in this moment. His squadron was lucky in that the western entrance to the castle was quiet. They'd descended a flight of stairs to enter and walked a narrow corridor with no evidence of Vermillion soldiers. Horatio was rather surprised that, even with the diversions on the other ends of the castle, there were no soldiers around. In a way, it brought a sense of relief. Just before they entered the castle, Badalao had informed them of Reverron's death, and only a moment ago, he relayed another message about Blastevahn's death.

He'd known all along that the mission would be serious and dangerous, but he never imagined that any of his friends would die so quickly. He, Malikai, Kadoog'han, and Maximilian all walked the corridor tentatively, as if they were only safe as long as they stayed there.

Kadoog'han led them, while Malikai and Maximilian followed, and Horatio defended the rear. Kadoog'han insisted on staying in the middle of the corridor, rather than trying to camouflage himself against the stone wall. He told the rest of them that they would have trouble following him if he did that, and the last thing he wanted was for them to get lost or killed because of him.

They reached the end of the corridor and Kadoog'han advanced into the new hallway before the rest of them. In the span of a short breath, a throng of silver-armored soldiers overtook Kadoog'han. They wrestled him to the ground and stabbed and stabbed until they were satisfied. They must not have realized that Horatio and the other two were there, as they seemed surprised when they looked up and saw them.

As soon as Malikai saw that they'd been spotted, he rushed toward the enemy soldiers. Horatio saw his hands and face harden to resemble the rock on the walls. *Steel armor on top of rock skin. He might kill them all.* He heard the clang of steel and rock against steel, knowing that Malikai might defeat the whole group with his bare hands. Horatio peeked into the opening and saw frustrated Vermillion soldiers breaking their swords on Malikai's stone hands. Despite their inability to hurt Malikai, they still vastly outnumbered him.

Strike them down. All of them.

The voice caught him off guard. He wasn't sure if it was even his own. He knew that if he summoned the lightning, there was a chance of hurting Malikai, and he couldn't take that risk. Horatio shook off the notion, but his head throbbed even more than before. The pain was becoming so severe that it angered him; he needed to release it somehow. He stumbled forward into the corridor, holding his head in agony. Horatio turned to Maximilian, whom he'd pushed behind him. He gritted his teeth as he tried to speak. "Get back. Far back!" Maximilian listened and wasted no time in retreating to the end of the corridor. Horatio immediately turned his attention back to the soldiers Malikai was fighting. Lightning exploded from his every fiber and shot through the corridor from end to end. Horatio screamed a feral scream as the outburst provided catharsis and eased the agony in his skull. Before he even looked up at the havoc he'd just wreaked, Horatio felt a sense of happiness and peace at the calmness of his mind. The tension was gone, and he breathed deeply.

Not a single man stood anywhere in the corridor. Horatio shook off the daze of euphoria and realized that Malikai was also somewhere in the piles and heaps of men that littered the ground. "Kai! Kai! Malikai!" He ran to one down one end of the corridor, shoving and kicking silver-armored Vermillion soldiers out of the way. He heard Maximilian behind him doing the same thing down the other end of the corridor. Finally, after a few moments, he uncovered Malikai, who'd been trapped under a mountain of blackened bodies. Malikai groaned as his rock-like skin slowly turned back to normal. It was impossible to tell whether he'd been burned, but Horatio had never seen Malikai's skin turn to anything like this back on the island. "Light of Orijin, you're alive!"

Malikai grasped his hand and allowed Horatio to pull him up. He smiled once he was on his feet. "Last thing I expected was for you to attack me, but yeah, I'm alive!"

"Sorry, I know they weren't hurting you, but it seemed like sooner or later, that many soldiers would get the best of you."

Malikai nodded as they walked down the corridor toward Maximilian, and the ballroom that would lead to Edmund's chamber. They passed by Kadoog'han's body as they walked on, and Maximilian stopped and knelt on one knee next to the man. Horatio and Malikai joined him and stayed silent. He knew that Maximilian would hurt much more, having known Kadoog'han longer, as would Savaiyon and Asarei. Maximilian looked up at them, "I know we cannot stay here long, but I couldn't just go on without honoring him first. We probably won't have another chance to do so." Maximilian put a hand on Kadoog'han's arm, "Rest easy, friend. We'll see you again in the Three Rings."

As they stood and continued on, Horatio heard faint voices behind them, likely coming from around the corner at the other end of the corridor. The other two heard the same at almost the same time, as Malikai's and Maximilian's eyes both darted between the direction of the voices and back to one another. Without a word, they ran toward the north of the castle. As they gained speed Malikai asked, "Should we turn back and fight?"

Maximilian responded before Horatio could think of the right answer. "No. Remember, the mission is for you two to get to the grand ballroom and then find the entrance to Edmund's chambers from there. Garrison said it is near the wall at the northeastern corner, which means that you two need to be in there as quickly as you can, find the entrance, and complete the mission."

Horatio turned and glanced at Maximilian on his left, "And what will you do?"

"I'll draw them off. The ballroom is around the corner ahead. You two will make a sharp right turn when we get to that opening, and I'll keep running straight. With any luck, I can either hide or catch up with one of the other groups. Either way, you two are the priority!" Just as Maximilian got the last words out, arrows whizzed by them and hit their backs. Horatio thanked the Orijin under his breath, as arrows dinged against his armored back and the back of his helmet. Sindha's father had forged their armor with the best steel and Horatio knew that the worst the arrows could do from so far away was to make dents.

Maximilian slowed a little to let Horatio and Malikai get ahead of them. Horatio yelled at him, thinking he was about to sacrifice himself. "What are you doing?"

"Falling back a little to throw them off! The last thing they'll see is me going straight! If they see you two turn then they'll follow you! Run faster! As soon as we get to that clearing, you're going to make a hard right, almost as if you're turning completely around! Get through the ballroom doors before I catch up, and make sure they're closed behind you!"

Horatio didn't wait for more; he ran as fast as his legs could push him as Malikai matched pace. The only thing he yelled back to Maximilian was, "Salvation as One!" In another moment, he and Malikai reached the clearing where the corridor split, and they turned quickly to the ballroom doors. As they opened the doors and rushed in, Horatio put a finger to his mouth and looked at Malikai, "Shh," he whispered, "There may be soldiers in here. We can't alert them while the ones outside are running past here." Malikai nodded and they gently shut the doors. They stood vigilantly beside the doors in silence and listened to the stampede go by. *Orijin, please protect Max. Please let him find a way to escape the attackers.* Once the sounds of footsteps were far enough in the distance, Horatio stepped away from the wooden doors and faced the ballroom. He hadn't even realized that the room was pitch black until turning around, and he wasn't sure why it surprised him.

As he stepped farther into the room, he had the strange feeling that he and Malikai weren't the only ones here. Within seconds, Horatio's suspicions were confirmed, as the one torch that was lit, moved in the shadows and another torch was lit, followed by more and more. At first, the light was far enough away that Horatio didn't realize that someone was actually holding the torch. As the room gained more and more light, Horatio saw a few dozen soldiers waiting for them. They stood at varying distances in the room, but none rushed forward to attack, much to Horatio's surprise. One soldier stepped forward, in full steel armor, with the red-plumed helmet of the Vermillion. "Lay down your weapons, Vithelegion. This is to be your end in the realm of Ashur."

Horatio eyed him curiously, "Vithelegion? We are not Vithelegion."

"Now is not the time for your lies. You are severely outnumbered, and it is only a matter of time until you both meet your death."

Malikai responded, "We belong to the Ghosts of Ashur. We have no allegiance to the Vithelegion. In fact, we plan to annihilate them as soon as we have killed the king."

Horatio saw the tall Vermillion soldier smile in the light of the torch. The soldier responded, "Oh, you have? Well, good. All you have to do is get past those of us in this room, and King Edmund is all yours." He drew his sword and assumed a ready stance, as if about to pounce.

As Horatio let his manifestation run through his veins, the pain in his head returned. This time, he knew that if he succumbed to it, it could mean his life. He pushed back against it and focused only on the melody that ran through his veins. Horatio closed his eyes, opened them briefly to see where all of his attackers held their torches, then clenched his fists and summoned the lightning. Once again, he let it continue for so long that the bodies beneath the armor were charred black. The fallen torches flickered for a few moments against the tiled floor before going out, and Horatio picked up one to keep the light going. As he stood, he felt a warmness touch his mouth. He licked his lips to get rid of the sensation, and tasted blood. After another few seconds, it flowed down his neck and dripped from his chin.

THEY HAD BARELY FINISHED MOURNING Reverron's death, when another horde of Vermillion soldiers charged against Badalao and his faction. Despite their ability to use manifestations, it was simply tiring to continue fighting over such a long period of time. Badalao knew they would have to reach the ballroom soon, in order for the others to rest. While he was only tired from the hand-to-hand combat and wielding a sword, Desmond and Sindha had to be twice as exhausted for doing the same while also using their manifestations for so long and with so much force.

The current corridor opened into a square room that was separated by a wall in the middle and had a few wooden chairs against the far wall. The middle wall would be a helpful barrier as this new set of soldiers was more aggressive than the last. Sindha blocked off one side where the wall ended with a force field and kept it there, allowing them to dictate the fight. Badalao looked around the side of the wall and saw the battalion coming, not far down the corridor. He was tempted to tell Sindha to block off the other side of the wall so that the Vermillion couldn't reach them. They would have enough space to leave the room through the western door and would be almost to the ballroom. It would be a huge gamble, though, and not one that needed to be made. If the Vermillion knew of a way around the wall, they would eventually get to the ballroom anyway. Better to fight here and eliminate them earlier than let them continue to be a problem. Before the Vermillion even reached them, Badalao realized that Desmond stood next to him at the side of the dividing wall. Desmond stared ahead at the oncoming enemy, and in an instant they were all hurtling backwards against each other, back down the other end of the corridor. Desmond even sent the chairs flying after the soldiers and made sure that they crashed into them as well.

"Nice work, Des." Badalao assumed that his friend was done, but Desmond continued to fling them around in the distance, as if he needed to be personally sure that every single soldier was killed. After a few moments, Desmond flinched and looked at Badalao as if surprised to see him there; he exhaled and clumsily collapsed to the ground.

Badalao immediately knelt down to check on his friend. Desmond was still awake, much to Badalao's surprise. Desmond whispered, "I'm fine."

"Bloody seas, you're anything but fine," Badalao whispered back. Sindha and Delilah ran over and knelt next to Badalao.

Sindha grabbed Desmond's hand and asked, "What happened?"

Badalao saw Desmond try to respond but cut him off. "He got carried away with his manifestation, overexerted himself again. I've a feeling that his mind is less ready than his body to fully use his manifestation. I need you two to keep him safe." He tilted his head toward Desmond to have them help him pick him up. Desmond attempted a small protest in the form of grunts, but the three of them got him to his feet, where Badalao draped one arm around his shoulder and started walking in the direction that the Vermillion soldiers had come from. Sindha collected Desmond's other arm and hung it around her shoulder as well. Just beyond the square room, Badalao eyed a door on the right. Delilah opened it, revealing a small servant's pantry inside.

She turned to Badalao, "You want us to stay in *here*? What will you do?"

He looked at Sindha. "I'm going to the ballroom. I haven't gotten any confirmation from Adria or Kadoog'han about whether they've reached it yet. I haven't heard from either in a while. Hold on," he took a deep breath and tried once more to connect with Kadoog'han, but it was almost as if the man's mind had vanished. "Dammit, not again." Badalao looked down at the ground for a moment, while Delilah's eyes followed him.

"What happened?"

"I think Kadoog'han is dead. I can't connect with him. Enough of this shit. You two keep Desmond in here. Only come out after you haven't heard any fighting in a while. I can't be sure if anyone has gotten to the ballroom yet, so it could be filled with more Vermillion soldiers. Either way, someone has to get in there." He left the pantry and closed the door, then tried to connect with Maximilian as he crept towards the ballroom. *Max, what's your status? Are you safe? I can't connect with Kad. What happened?*

After a few moments, he finally got a response. *Lao, I'm safe for now. Hiding from Vermillion. I drew them off so that Raish and Malikai could get to the ballroom. Not sure what was waiting for them in there, but I know they made it. Kadoog'han has heard the Song of Orijin. He perished as soon as we engaged the enemy, as if they were waiting for us. I'm just staying safe until I can figure out how to reach Adria's group or yours.*

Badalao took a deep breath as he stood outside the ballroom doors. Losing Kadoog'han meant that they'd lost three of their own since the siege began. *Too many.* He responded to Maximilian, *Stay there. I'll let you know when it's safe. I'm about to enter the ballroom, but I'll check with Raish and Kai first. Salvation as One.*

Maximilian responded immediately. *Thanks. Salvation as One.*

Badalao leaned against the wall beside the ballroom doors. He tilted his head back against the wall and his helmet shifted slightly. Having Horatio and Malikai on the other side of those doors would help greatly, but he wondered what condition they might be in. He reached out to each of them in his mind, first Malikai, but felt the same void as when he'd tried to connect with Kadoog'han. He closed his eyes and gritted his teeth. He tried Horatio next and felt Horatio there, but something was pushing back against him. *Raish? Are you in the ballroom?* There was no response, but more emotions than Badalao could field at one time. He knew waiting around could cost lives and even the chance to kill Edmund, so he flung the door open, which was much lighter than he anticipated.

He stalked in, sword in hand and armor weighing his shoulders down more than ever before. The ballroom was vast, bigger than any room he'd seen in Constaniza. Ornate tapestries covered most of the walls, with golden torch holders at set intervals between the tapestries. Many of the torches were lit, but the shadows they'd cast made the room seem even larger. As he looked around at the ground, dozens of Vermillion soldiers littered the tiled floor. To Badalao's surprise, he didn't see much, if any blood. *There was no fight. They were struck down quickly.* "Raish?" The name came out sheepishly, as if afraid to disturb the ghosts of all these dead men. He walked around and scanned the floor more meticulously, looking for Horatio or Malikai. Finally, he found Horatio lying face up on the ground next to what he could only assume was Malikai's body, in the middle of all that death.

Badalao shifted his eyes back and forth repeatedly between Horatio and Malikai. He was almost afraid to look at Malikai's remains for too long, as all that was left was a blackened crust of a man, with what was likely blood oozing out here and there. Horatio lay there, blinking and staring up at the ceiling. "Raish, what happened?" It wasn't until Badalao spoke to him that he realized Horatio's helmet was off and that he was bleeding from his nose, mouth, and ears.

After what felt like ages, Horatio looked at him straight in the eyes and said, "Lao. Kill me. *Please*."

ADRIA THOUGHT SHE'D FELT BADALAO nudge her mind several minutes before, but hadn't had the time to acknowledge it or make herself available. As soon as they'd advanced on to the next room, outside of the ballroom, they had been bombarded with Vermillion soldiers. The only advantage they'd had was that the room was narrow, which allowed them to keep their attackers in front of them, but they still fought attackers in both directions. Adria fought beside Marshall, while Vasher and Baltaszar fought side by side, with their backs to Adria. It would only be so long until they were overrun.

Desperately, she called out to Baltaszar, "Tasz, you have enough in you to take them all out with fire?"

"I think so! It might take all I have left, but I don't care! Only other thing is, there are a lot of things around that will make the fire spread! We could risk it spreading throughout the castle!"

Adria considered the options, and knew the risk had to be made. "Do it! At least we have a fighting chance against the fire! We can't hold up much longer!"

As soon as she was done speaking, Adria heard the screams and shrieks of men being burned. She stabbed a soldier through the neck and briefly glanced behind her to see the whole corridor alight because of Baltaszar's manifestation. Baltaszar was now facing her direction, and yelled to her and Marshall, "Duck down! I'm going to light them up!"

She and Marshall squatted down and covered their heads with their shields as Baltaszar opened his palms to direct the forthcoming blaze. Adria peeked out as the fire was quickly formed and beams of fire shot past them, scorching the Vermillion that had only a moment ago been clamoring to reach them. More screams filled the air, which was starting to feel heavy. As Baltaszar finished off the soldiers, Adria nodded her head at Marshall and then at the ballroom doors. She stayed low and crept toward the doors with Marshall right behind her. "Tasz, you and Vasher follow us when you're done!" Baltaszar nodded to acknowledge the command. Adria stood to open the doors and pushed them open. She walked through tentatively, with Marshall now beside her.

They walked through a dim entryway with huge, cushioned couches the size of massive beds on each side. As they passed them, the entryway gave way to an enormous ballroom with armored bodies scattered on the floor throughout the room. Vasher and Baltaszar jogged up to them from behind. Baltaszar sucked in air and finally said softly, "I'm not sure how much I have left. If we have to fight again, I may accidentally light one of *you* on fire. I'm lucky I was able to control it as well as I did just now."

Adria nodded as they all inspected the room, "One last favor and then you can lay down and blend in with all of these soldiers. Light the rest of the torches around the perimeter. I just need to be able to see. I could have sworn Lao was trying to tell me that he was in here."

In an instant, the torches were lit and the room grew brighter. Still, there were so many bodies on the floor that Adria took a deep breath and let her manifestation run through her. She concentrated on the sound of a heartbeat, just as she'd done so long ago when she found Marshall barely breathing in his own village. She listened patiently for any sign of life in the room besides her three companions. Finally, she felt the faintest echo in the distance, coming from the middle of the ballroom. Adria sprinted toward the source, and the other three followed her. In the middle of all the dead Vermillion soldiers, Badalao lay on the ground with his helmet off, not moving. Adria choked up at the sight of him but steeled her resolve with the others around her. She couldn't stomach to look at his face again, as his eyes looked like they'd been burnt out. Where his eyes had once been, there was only blackness now. The rest of his face looked mostly unharmed, as did the rest of his body. Adria listened once more and knew that the heartbeat was his.

Next to Badalao's body lay another Ghost of Ashur. Adria couldn't recognize the face, as it had been completely blackened to the point that it matched the black helmet and armor that the corpse still wore.

Vasher finally spoke up, "What the hell happened here? Who would've been able to do that to Lao? Is he even alive?"

Adria nodded, "He's alive, but barely." She came to a new realization upon thinking about Badalao. "And to make matters worse, without him, we have no connection to the outside. There's no way to tell the others that we need help, or even other Ghosts in the castle to come find us here."

"Someone burned his eyes out. Do we know who that is that's next to him? Judging by the size, I would say Desmond, Horatio, or Malikai," Baltaszar conjectured.

"I don't know," Adria shrugged. "I imagine we'll only find out once we can gather everyone back together." Another realization arose, "Look, despite all this, we still have to find Edmund and kill him. If this *is* one of those three, Tasz, then most likely one of the Ghosts who was supposed to hunt down Edmund is dead." She took a deep breath, "I need you three to stay up here and protect Lao. We don't know if more Vermillion are coming, but I do know that we're all exhausted. I can find Edmund on my own once we find the entrance in this room. I think we've reached the point of this mission where we must act out of desperation. At least four or our group have been confirmed dead. For all we know, the four of us might be all that's left. Marsh, you and Tasz stay here with Lao. Vasher, come with me. I need you to bang on the walls on the northern side of the room. I'll listen for differences and echoes while you do it. I'm pretty sure I can sort out the difference between a solid wall and a hollow one." She turned and walked to the walls of the ballroom as Vasher followed. She'd asked Vasher with the hopes that Marshall wouldn't try to follow her. She knew he would want to, but she dared not risk his life while chasing after Edmund.

They started along the side and worked their way along the perimeter. Adria had Vasher hit the tapestries as well, since most of them hung all the way down to the floor. When they reached the northeastern corner, Adria finally heard what she thought was a louder echo behind one of the tapestries. She stopped Vasher and had him help her lift the bottom of it up, revealing a subtle rectangle in the wall behind it. The handle was so small that it didn't even make the tapestry jut out. Adria nodded at Vasher, "Thanks. Now go back to them. I've got this."

Vasher smiled at her and nodded curtly. "I know you do. I heard that the girls have been calling you 'Queen.' While they're not wrong, I kind of see you more as an unfit king's worst enemy. Like a king's bane."

Adria smiled in response. "King's bane. I like the sound of that. Now let me go and make myself worthy of that title. Thanks, Vasher." She pushed open the door and walked through quietly, then slowly shut it behind her. As soon as she was by herself, Adria sighed deeply, closed her eyes, and then dropped to one knee. *You can do this. You have to do this. There's no one else left and you're not 'Mouse' anymore. You're the captain of this mission. People are already dead, and if you fail now, everyone fails.* She whispered to herself, "Get up, Adria. Get up and be everything that everyone else already sees in you. Be everything that you've ever doubted you could be." She formed a fist and pounded it against her black chest plate.

She descended the few short flights of stairs with her sword ready in her right hand, and her dagger in her left. The bottom of the stairs led to a stone corridor with torches sparsely providing light from sconces along the walls. The dimness would be to her advantage, as she was still drawing upon her manifestation, listening for any sounds of life or movement ahead of her. She continued to follow the corridor along a few turns and straightaways. After several minutes, she could hear the banter of a few guards from around a corner. As she peeked around the corner, she let out a frustrated huff. *Dammit. Four of them. They're all facing this way. So much for the element of surprise.*

Adria tried to think of various strategies that might work, and she briefly wished it were Badalao or Marshall doing this instead of her. At least they were more creative with ways of attacking. She thought of removing her armor and trying to hide her sword, so that perhaps the guards might not see her as a threat. *No, that's stupid. Why else would you be down here, except as a threat?* She decided the only way to defeat them would be for her to take them on and hope that she could handle all four of them.

Sweat crept down her brow as Adria turned the corner. She walked slowly, unsure whether her tired legs or her nervous mind was more to blame. The four guards didn't notice her until she was about twenty feet away. Once they turned to face her, Adria stopped and gripped her sword and dagger. One of the silver-armored guards stepped forward and, with a smile, addressed her. "If you are down here, then you have accepted death. I must say, though, girl, as crazy as you are to come down here by yourself, I admire your bravery." The four guards drew their swords, ready to pounce on her. As they stalked closer, Adria tried to listen to their heartbeats, but to her dismay, all four soldiers seemed calm. A moment later, she felt one soldier's heart speed up, and when she looked at him, she realized that he was looking behind her.

If not for his faster heartbeat, Adria would have thought it a ploy on the soldier's part to distract her. She listened to the footsteps behind her and knew that her burden had become a little easier. Marshall walked up and stood by her right side, also ready to fight. Before any of the soldiers made a move, the whole corridor went pitch black. In the few moments of confusion, all Adria could hear was the groans of struggle and pain. She dared not move, but waved the tip of her sword around in front of her. No one was near her. *None of them advanced upon me.* "Marsh? Did you do that?"

After another moment, the darkness dissipated and Marshall came into view once more. He wore a wide smile. "It *was* me. I guess in the heat of things, I managed to use my manifestation successfully."

She half-smiled at him, "I could have taken all of them, you know." She hoped the sarcasm in her voice was evident.

He continued to smile, "I know, but I was helping you save your energy for the king." He tilted his head and started walking past the four dead guards.

They walked down the corridor, and after a short while, noticed more guards in the distance. Once again, the corridor went dark and she heard Marshall run towards the group. She couldn't be sure whether he was able to see what he was doing, but after another several moments, the darkness disappeared once more. Before her, Marshall stood over a throng of dead Vermillion soldiers, grasping his arm and breathing heavily. "In there. You hear anything inside? Any chance there are more guards in there?"

Adria paused and opened herself to her manifestation. She listened carefully for heartbeats. She focused beyond Marshall's racing heart and put her attention to the room behind the door. She hoped there would be no more guards, for Marshall's sake. As she focused more meticulously, all she only heard two heartbeats. "I'm almost positive it's just him and the Queen in there. I only hear two."

Marshall nodded and kicked the door open for her. They both knew immediately that this was the room they'd been looking for. It was the largest bedroom she'd ever seen, with plush couches around the perimeter and a sprawling bed centered at the back wall. At the foot of it sat two people, one in front of the other, both in their night robes. The woman, whom Adria assumed was the queen, was in front, being held from behind by a man who was likely King Edmund. He held a dagger to her neck.

As soon as Adria and Marshall had stepped into the room, he yelled out to Adria, "Take another step and the Queen is dead!"

Adria stopped, sword still in hand. "What kind of king, or man, are you, that you would kill your wife to save your own life?" She took off her helmet and held it beside her, "Either way, look at my face so you know who your killer is."

"Your judgment is beneath me, Descendant witch."

"Fair enough, but I came here to kill you, Edmund. It's going to happen whether or not the queen lives. Killing her won't keep you alive."

Edmund stood, his arm still wrapped around the queen's waist, the dagger still at her throat. He side-stepped until he was completely past the bed, then slowly backed up. *There's no way he's backing himself into a corner. Secret doorway back there?*

Marshall confirmed her suspicion with a whisper, "Pretty sure there's a hidden door behind him."

Adria watched the king back away a few steps more, even more tentative than before. She eyed the queen quickly. She looked so defeated that she didn't even attempt to struggle. *She might prefer death to escaping with him.* Adria took a step closer as Edmund neared the back wall. As soon as he saw her move, he pressed the blade of the dagger into the queen's neck and sliced it across. Adria and Marshall both ran toward them. She put her helmet on again as Edmund released the queen and pushed her toward Adria.

Queen Valencia stumbled forward, clasping her neck. In the brief moment that Adria looked at her, Edmund escaped through a door that had opened in the wall. Adria briefly thought about stopping to save the queen's life, but there was nothing she could do for the woman at this point anyway. And to stop now would ensure the king's escape.

Once more, Marshall was on the same page as her. "Go after him,

Adria! There's nothing we can do for her. I'll keep a lookout for more Vermillion and make sure they don't get to you. Go!"

Adria sheathed her sword behind her back and sprinted through the new doorway in the wall, then followed Edmund, who scampered ahead several feet away. He was surprisingly fast for an older man, but his frame was also rather slender. Adria estimated that he couldn't be much heavier than she was.

She followed him, trying desperately to make ground. The constant battles, extensive use of her manifestation, and emotion of losing friends all slowed her even more. She wanted to throw off her armor, but that would take too much time. After accepting that she would simply have to follow him, Adria retrieved a dagger from her thigh, held the tip of the blade between her thumb and index finger, and then threw it at her target.

As soon as she threw it, she knew that it was on target. Adria smiled as it hit Edmund just under the left shoulder blade. The strike was enough to send him hurtling to the ground; he stumbled and rolled several feet, until finally sprawling on his stomach. In the process of falling and rolling, his robes had come off, revealing only his smallclothes. Edmund pushed himself up onto hands and knees as Adria drew near. She eyed him, inspecting his body for more weapons. He looked up at her with fear and dread painted his wide eyes.

Adria stood over Edmund as he shifted and tried to sit face up. The agony of the dagger in his back was evident as he winced with every movement. "Please, wait." Edmund put up his right hand as he managed to sit on the ground. "Grant me mercy, I beg of you." Adria gripped another dagger at her waist and unsheathed it. She sliced Edmund's palm open as he held his hand out.

"You, who have reigned with no mercy to my kind, would dare ask me for it?" Adria took another step toward him as he tried to scoot backwards, away from her.

He held his bloody palm with his other hand, and then held up his good hand. "Please. I can change. I see the error of my ways now! I can become a good man!"

Adria sliced at his other hand, cutting open his left palm. The wound caused Edmund to lie on the ground, clutching his hands to his body. "On the precipice of death, you suddenly can change. Yet, only a moment ago, you killed your own wife to try to get away. Less than two years ago, you branded your own son an outlaw and had your soldiers hunt him down." As Edmund lay whimpering, Adria unsheathed her sword and sliced through his calf. He jerked again at the new wound and held his leg.

"Please! Don't!"

Adria shook her head at him as he writhed even more. "The wounds you'll bear today are nothing compared to the pain that you've caused so many Descendants in your lifetime." She sliced through the back of his left arm as he screamed even more. "Your son, Garrison, whom you cast away as an afterthought, helped us plan this siege. Think about that for a moment, you worm. You are so despicable that your own son helped to plan your death." Edmund continued to twist and turn on the ground, his sobs unending as Adria continued to slice him open at various points of his body.

She stood over his torso and pinned down his arms, then looked down into Edmund's tear-filled eyes. "If I were to die tomorrow, I would do so with a smile, knowing that I had this experience. Knowing that I was *blessed* with the opportunity to kill you. Knowing that when I would arrive in the Three Rings, scores of dead Descendants would be rejoicing in your death." She sliced open his cheek as she continued to pin down his arms. "I almost wish that the Orijin would create a fourth Ring just for you, so that Descendants could come to get their vengeance." Adria positioned her sword downwards and pressed the point against Edmund's chest. She applied the slightest pressure as his mouth contorted and his chest convulsed. "Feel each death that you caused. Die with the same agony that you wished upon all of my brethren." She pushed the blade slowly through his torso and watched Edmund's convulsions slow and stop.

BALTASZAR SAT NEXT TO BADALAO'S BODY, along with Vasher. They were sure that no more soldiers were coming, but that did nothing to ease their panic. The truth of the situation was that Badalao had been their only means of communication. Especially with some of the castle now on fire, their time was running short. As they sat in silence, tired and defeated from worrying so much, Baltaszar heard Marshall return from the hidden doorway behind the tapestry. Baltaszar nodded at him, expecting an update.

Marshall waited until he was just in front of them, and then spoke as he sat down. "All clear. There were a lot of guards, but she had the king handled. I stayed with her for a while to ensure her safety. Edmund killed his own queen to get away. Once Adria was alone with him, I figured I'd just keep lookout for more soldiers. Emptied the corridors down there before coming back up here. She's going to want to gather her thoughts and emotions after she kills him, before seeing any of us."

"King's bane!" Vasher exclaimed.

Baltaszar turned and looked at him, "Huh?"

"Before we parted ways at the door over there, I told her that she was a king's bane. If any of us could handle leading this whole group, then going off to kill the king, it's her."

Baltaszar nodded, "Yeah. I feel bad for making things hard for her back on the island. She definitely didn't need any of that." He briefly thought of Anahi and Vandenar, but it was too much to focus on with everything that was currently going on. He would worry about that once they survived their escape from the castle.

Marshall tried to reassure him, "You had your reasons. We all have things and people we care about outside of our group. I firmly believe in the idea of 'Salvation as One', but that doesn't mean that this group is the only thing any of us should care about."

Baltaszar's attention shifted from Marshall as he saw Horatio enter the ballroom from the far northwestern corner. Baltaszar stood up and watched as Horatio limped over to them. He rushed over and helped Horatio back to the group. He wondered what had happened to his friend, as Horatio's nose, mouth, and ears all had lines of dried blood streaking down from them. Baltaszar helped him sit on the ground next to Marshall. "Raish, what the hell happened to you?"

Horatio closed his eyes and took a few deep breaths. He looked over at the others, then down at Badalao's body, and flinched at the sight of him. He moved several feet away, lay flat on the ground, and looked straight up. "I just went around the castle to find any remaining soldiers. I killed them all with lightning and I'm drained." He took another deep breath, "I need you three to stay away from me. I think I'll need everyone to keep their distance. If I accidentally summon lightning, I don't want to hurt anyone."

Baltaszar nodded and looked at Vasher and Marshall, who looked back at him with concern. Baltaszar turned back toward Horatio, "Just rest, Raish. We'll let you be. Let us know if we can help with anything." Baltaszar tried to process what might be going on with him, and it seemed that Vasher and Marshall might've been as well, but they all just sat there and checked on Badalao's breathing from time to time.

Several minutes later, Baltaszar heard a few voices from behind him and turned. From the southeastern entrance, Sindha, Delilah, and Maximillian walked in, helping Desmond to walk. Desmond was alive and aware but looked almost as exhausted as Horatio. As the others reached them, they saw Badalao on the ground and a collection of gasps followed. They let down Desmond, who kneeled by Badalao's side. "What happened ta him?"

Vasher shrugged, sitting next to Desmond. "We don't know. We found him like this. And I guess if you and Raish are both here, that means that's Malikai lying next to Lao." The whole group glanced over at Malikai's blackened body.

None of them spoke for a while until finally Baltaszar broke the silence. "The one good thing is, Lao is still alive. Adria heard his heartbeat before going off to kill Edmund, and Vasher and I have been making sure he's still breathing. Linc can do wonders with his healing, but it looks like Lao's eyes are completely gone. I don't know if he can regrow eyes, but at least we still have him. We have to figure out how to get out of here now. Any of you see fire out in the corridors?"

Maximillian stepped forward. "The castle is definitely burning. The fire is spreading slowly, but we need to make haste in escaping. Is this everyone? What about Adria?"

"She is in the process of killing Edmund," Marshall responded.

"Actually, she already killed him!" They all turned to the northern side of the room to see Adria walking toward them from the wall. She wore a reluctant half smile and carried her helmet and chest plate in her hands. "He's dead. I made sure of it."

The whole group erupted in cheers. Baltaszar's eyes grew a bit misty. Despite everyone they'd lost throughout the night, the king's death lightened the blow just a bit. Marshall stood up to hug Adria tightly and lifted her in his arms as she dropped her armor and kissed him. Baltaszar eyed Horatio in the distance, hunched over on his knees, holding his head. *He must've used so much lightning to kill all of the guards.*

Vasher nudged his arm, "See, I told you! Adria Kingsbane!" Vasher shouted the name repeatedly and eventually Marshall heard him and repeated it himself. He let go of Adria and let her stand on her own to be celebrated. As Adria put her hands up to quiet everyone down, Baltaszar saw Horatio getting to his feet. Small sparks of lightning danced around in his hands, and trails of new blood came down from his nose and ears.

In only a few seconds, everyone else had noticed, and they all backed away from him. Baltaszar stood at the front of the group, who all made sure to keep Badalao's body behind them. "Raish, what's going on? Just let go of your manifestation! If you release it, then it can't harm anyone."

Horatio looked up at him, staring him in the eyes, but Baltaszar felt like there was someone else behind them. Horatio continued to stare, as if struggling to speak. Finally, he opened his mouth and blood escaped with the words. "I...can't control it. Please, Tasz. Anyone. Kill me, please. Before it's too late."

Just as Baltaszar thought about taking a step toward Horatio, Maqdhuum appeared with Donovan by his side, in the empty space between the group and Horatio. The two of them faced the group, with Horatio behind them. Somehow, Baltaszar was so focused on Horatio that he barely processed that the two of them had appeared, until Maqdhuum finally spoke. "Damn. None of you look like you're happy to see us. Guess you'd all rather..."

Before Maqdhuum could finish his sentence, Donovan convulsed right next to him. His body shook and contorted so fast; it almost looked like he was vibrating. Bluish-yellow lightning frantically danced around his body, as Donovan was powerless to defend himself in any way. As Donovan's body fell forward, toward Baltaszar and the group, Horatio's face became visible once more. His grin was bloody and full of terror, almost as if in pain, and even his eyes bled. He spread his arms once more, and as lightning was about to strike the rest of the group, a force field formed around all of them except Maqdhuum, who disappeared and reappeared behind Horatio. Baltaszar stood, frozen and unable to comprehend what was unfolding before him. By the time he thought to fight back, Maqdhuum did the unthinkable and disappeared with Horatio.

MAQDHUUM REAPPEARED WITH HORATIO in a place he'd swore he'd never return to, no matter how long he would live. He stood with Horatio in the middle of a clearing of serpentfruit trees, though strangely, one looked like it had been cut down. As he looked behind him, he also saw that the ground seemed to have been dug up in a few places. He couldn't focus on that at the moment, though. As soon as he let go of Horatio, the boy fell to his knees. Maqdhuum knew there was something else going on; Horatio wasn't acting on his own.

Just as the thought passed through his mind, Horatio perked up and lightning crackled from his eyes. Maqdhuum disappeared and reappeared behind Horatio as a small bolt of lightning flew past where he had just stood. He punched Horatio in the back of the head and knocked him over. "Look, I can disappear faster than you can throw lightning, and I know it's not just you living in that head of yours right now. So who wants to speak to me, Raish? You or the other thing in there?"

The voice that came from Horatio's mouth was not his own. "Funny that you would talk about more than one person being inside someone's mind, *Maqdhuum*. Since that's what you prefer to be called now. It seems like there were three of us in your head at one point, no?"

Maqdhuum almost choked. "Jahmash? How the hell is that possible?" He disappeared and reappeared in front of Horatio. "When would you two ever have met?"

Horatio looked up at him and continued to speak with Jahmash's voice. "Oh, Abram. I suppose it doesn't matter now that he's been found out. Horatio is my son. I've been in his head since I sent him off to Ashur. My hope was to put him in a position to gain a manifestation and infiltrate the House of Darian. It worked, with mediocre results. He fought me the whole time, though. Kept pushing back every time I tried to force his hand. I got tired of it all and pushed him harder than he liked."

Maqdhuum disappeared again and reappeared behind Horatio once more, and walked around him in circles. He took a few deep breaths, knowing that he might not like the answers to the questions he was about to ask. "Who…who is the mother, then? If this is your bloody son, who gave birth to him?"

Horatio looked at him once more and his mouth opened into a wide, bloody grin. "You know. Of course you know, Abram. How could you not? His mother is the very woman you brought to me as a gift. What, some sixteen years ago or so? I actually count the years now. And this beautiful son of mine would never have existed if not for *you*. You brought his mother to me. You told me that she could bring me to the Three Rings, and that I could face Darian and Gideon and Lionel again to get my closure. But you know what, Abram? I didn't want to. I have nothing to say to Darian. So instead I impregnated her. Let her believe she was happy the whole time."

Maqdhuum found himself panicking at Jahmash's words. "No, it can't be. You made her have your baby and then killed her?"

Horatio's grin grew even wider and the corners of his mouth looked torn. Jahmash continued to speak through him. "Always so quick to judge others, despite your own misdeeds. You stole her from her own family and brought her to me in the first place. Did you ever go back and tell them what became of her?"

Maqdhuum hung his head as he continued to walk around Horatio. "I couldn't. I felt too guilty for what I'd done. She had a husband and children. But people are strong. I've seen it over and over again. People overcome loss. It gives them strength."

Horatio laughed heartily, still with Jahmash's voice. "You are so bloody right, Abram. I lost my own wife to a man I thought of as a brother. And it made me so strong that I'm going to kill every last one of you."

In an instant, Horatio fell over and his grin was gone. He struggled to push himself off the ground and made it to his hands and knees. His voice was faint, but discernible. "Are…are you going to let me die now?"

Maqdhuum paused for a moment to try and shed some of the emotions that smothered him. "Raish. It would be a crime against the Orijin to let you die now. You're more important than you could know. Is *he* still in there right now?"

Horatio shook his head laboriously. "I don't feel him in there now. For the first time in a while. Can I ask you something?"

Maqdhuum sat down in front of him. "Ask anything. I owe you

answers."

"I've always known something was off with my family, and it's felt like I've grown up with two sets of memories. There was a woman down in Damaszur who raised me like her own. But I think I've always known that something was off. Who was my real mother? What was her name?"

Maqdhuum thought about fighting the tears that were ready to storm out of his eyes, but knew it would be too hard. As they rained down his cheeks and face, he looked Horatio directly in the eyes. "Her name was Raya Hammersland. I stole her from her family. Her husband's name was Joakwin Kontez. Her sons were Baltaszar and Bo'az Kontez."

EPILOGUE

From *The Book of Orijin*, Verse Four Hundred Ninety-five
The darkness harbors the unknown.
Just as the unknown may harbor Evil, so too may it harbor Good.
If the future is unknown, then force the good to come of it.

GARRISON ARRIVED IN HIS PARENTS' sleeping quarters with Maqdhuum and Adria. It had been a few days since the siege, and since the deaths of his parents and brother. He'd prepared himself for accepting his father's death. It was a necessary sacrifice in the best interest of Ashur. He was glad that he didn't have to be a part of the siege. As much hatred as he held for his father, he didn't want to be there when the man was killed.

Through all the hatred, however, melancholy had taken control of him since the others had relayed the news of his brother and mother. Emptiness had bloated his mind, the way gas might bloat one's stomach. He found that he had no capacity to process anything or feel emotion about anything else. But he needed to return to his parents' chambers for one thing, before anyone else had the opportunity to storm the castle and steal it.

The spacious room had been cleaned and any evidence of violence and death had been removed. He looked around, curious about what had transpired between Adria and his parents but unwilling to ask for the specific details. For as long as he lived, Garrison knew he would never want to know, especially after hearing that his father had murdered his mother in an attempt to save his own life.

"There." He pointed to the mantle in between two sconces on the wall. "That's why I came back." He walked over to it and reached for the sword that rested horizontally above the mantle, and then removed it from its holders. He inspected it, seeing it for the first time in what felt like ages. It was the lightest sword he'd ever lifted and the design on the hilt and pommel were so intricate, that Garrison wondered how it had been forged. Inscribed on it were words in Imanol that Garrison couldn't read, nor could his father. On the pommel was the face of a growling lion, with two yellow diamonds set for its eyes. He knew that most would kill for the diamonds more than the sword. Garrison turned back to Adria and Maqdhuum and held the sword up to show them. "This sword has been in my family since the beginning of our ancestry. It has been passed down from king to king for generations." He took a breath, thinking of Donovan. "It should have been Donovan's next. I still can't believe the truth of Horatio."

"I know. I'm sorry." Maqdhuum walked over to inspect the sword and touched the blade. "May I?"

"Sure." Garrison nodded and let the man take the sword from him. To his surprise, Maqdhuum only held it in front of him and stared at it. Garrison would have expected anyone unfamiliar with it to inspect the hilt and pommel, and even swing it. "What is it? What's the matter?"

Maqdhuum continued to stare at the blade. "This is Gideon's sword. I've wondered what happened to it. He threw it down before he even stepped onto that battlefield. He was sure he wouldn't use it or need it. The rest of us were so distraught and shocked at his sacrifice that we never really thought about it. But here it is. Savaiyon told me some time ago that he'd found Lionel's and mine, but I hadn't really put much thought into them until now."

Garrison nodded, "Then it is yours, not mine. It seems more like an ancient ancestor simply *found* this sword, rather than earned it."

"We can worry about who it belongs to another time. I'm just glad we found it."

Adria walked over to look at the sword for herself. "What's so special about it, aside from it being so shiny?"

Maqdhuum grinned. "The steel used to make our blades is only found in Domna Orjann, and forged on the floating islands in the middle of the nation. It is lighter and stronger than any metal I've seen anywhere else in the world. It can literally cut through other metals. Even our scabbards had to be specially constructed to accommodate these blades. If a master swordsman was to wield this in battle, he," he looked at Adria, "or *she* could likely take down a whole battalion."

Bo'az stepped onto the shore of Castiel, with Aric, Deacon, and Hansi. Linas Nasreddine followed, his wrists bound and led by Aric with a rope. They all wore their black coats, though the Casteyan air felt a bit warmer than the winds on the Sea of Fates. He didn't have to look at the others to understand their discomfort; he felt it as well ever since Deacon had betrayed Jahmash.

He turned to the rest of them, "So this is Castiel. Let's go build an army." Bo'az walked inland; the walls of a city could be faintly seen in the distance. For the first time in a while, he wondered whether he would ever have the ability to think freely and comfortably again, or even make his own decisions. Just as the notion offered him the tiniest bit of comfort, his mind felt like it was being squeezed again and he wiped a small stream of blood from his nose, hoping that it would only be his nose this time, and not his ears and mouth.

Farco sat in a dark alcove, a blindfold over his eyes. The last thing he remembered seeing was several silver-masked figures overtaking the wagon. Farco, Avenira, Khenzi, and Fae had left the Tower in haste with barely anything besides food and sailed to Galicea before procuring a wagon. The whole time, all Fae had concerned herself with was keeping Khenzi safe and swearing to get revenge for Anahi's death. Once the masked people had arrived, Farco and the others were hit when they tried to speak, so they all learned quickly to stay quiet. No words had been said, and there was not even a struggle between those in masks and the servants from the Tower of the Blind who'd escorted them on the journey.

Surprisingly, Fae, Avenira, and Khenzi offered little protest, which Farco hoped meant that they hadn't been kidnapped. However, he hadn't seen them since the wagon abduction. He assumed he was in the Anonymi fortress, though no one had confirmed that in the short time since he'd arrived. His notion of time was severely distorted, but he believed it had been less than an hour since he felt the heat of the outside world.

A voice boomed and echoed all around him. "Farco Baek. You sit in the Crucible of the Anonymi Fortress. You have requested an audience with us. State your business."

He'd wondered whether any of the others were somewhere else in the room, but if they were addressing him directly, then he was most likely by himself. "My city was destroyed by an invading army. I have nothing left except the three that I came here with. Before Vandenar was destroyed, I was apprentice to an Augur named Munn Keeramm. I had planned to come here to train, in order to be a servant in the Tower of the Blind." Farco paused to calm his nerves. He could feel his hands shaking and his thigh twitching.

The voice responded before he could continue. "Is your intention still to serve as a Servant of the Augurs?"

Farco breathed deeply for a moment, to stop the tears from coming. He didn't want the Anonymi to think his intentions were based only on emotion. He gritted his teeth and clenched his fists, and the swarm of emotions calmed. "No. My intention is to stay here to train as an Anonymi soldier. The legends have always stated that the Anonymi exist to maintain balance in Ashur. Well, Ashur is now out of balance and I want to be a part of what sets it right again."

He sat there for several moments as silence loomed all around. He was about to stand up and remove the blindfold to see if anyone was left in the room when the voice boomed again with a response. "Very well. You will train as an acolyte of the Anonymi. You will not leave this fortress until your training has ended. Your training begins today."

MAQDHUUM APPEARED ON THE ROOF of one of the houses that still stood on the western side of Yongradae. He'd returned Adria and Garrison to Asarei's island, and then stopped to check in on Horatio, mostly just to bring the boy some food. There was some obvious resentment from the Ghosts about Maqdhuum taking Horatio away after murdering Donovan, but he knew that Jahmash's son was more help to them alive than dead.

He currently had other things in mind, so he focused on the tents that were set up in the streets of Yongradae instead. The leader of the Vithelegion was a man named Saol Suldas, and if he'd studied their procedures correctly, Suldas was in the biggest tent, at the center of all the others. Maqdhuum stroked his long, stringy hair. He disappeared from the roof and reappeared on the ground, just outside the perimeter of tents. He took two steps before a pair of Vithelegion spotted him and advanced upon him.

The shorter of the two men acknowledged him. "Stop where you are. Who are you and why are you here?"

The taller soldier added, "Choose your words wisely, or they could be your last."

Maqdhuum rolled his eyes and disappeared again. He reappeared behind the taller man, unsheathed his dagger, and slit the man's throat. Before the shorter man finished turning around, Maqdhuum appeared again a few feet away. He squinted at Maqdhuum and almost spit the words out, "What *are* you?"

Maqdhuum grinned widely at the man. "I am someone who is looking to speak with Saol Suldas. I strongly suggest that you bring me to him, unless you want to end up like your friend here. You can walk me to him, and I promise I won't try to kill you."

The man shook his head and looked at the ground. "What choice do I have, then?" The man walked past him and waved him on to follow. Before Maqdhuum followed, he grasped the dead soldier and disappeared with him into a house, then reappeared behind his new escort. Every few paces, the man turned his head slightly to check on Maqdhuum. They walked past several other soldiers who all eyed Maqdhuum warily. The soldier who escorted him assured them all that Maqdhuum was with him and posed no threat. The eyes of the others still proved wary, despite the explanation, but no one attacked.

Once they reached the large tent, the soldier approached one of the sentries who guarded it. Maqdhuum's escort whispered to the sentry, and it seemed as if he was having no luck with convincing the sentry to allow them to enter. Maqdhuum walked up to the two of them, and as the sentry was unsheathing his sword, Maqdhuum patted his escort on the shoulder. "I've got it from here, my friend. Thank you." He disappeared and arrived in an instant inside the tent. As he gained his bearings, Maqdhuum looked up to see eight men standing around a table, with one giving directives to the other seven.

"Excuse me, friends, is there room for one more at the table?" He walked up to a chair and stood behind it, resting his hands on its back.

All eight men quickly turned to face him, their swords drawn instantly. The one who was speaking addressed him first. "Do you know who I am? I am Saol Suldas, Commander of the Vithelegion. Who are *you* and how did you get in here?"

He grinned widely once more. Before any of the men could get a word out, Maqdhuum repeatedly vanished and disappeared, stealing all of their swords in the process and dropping them behind the chair he'd leaned on. The process was complete in only a matter of seconds. Once he had taken their swords, Maqdhuum returned to the chair and sat in it. He leaned back, rested his foot on his other knee, and clasped his hands, maintaining the same grin. "I hear that the Vithelegion follow and worship the Harbinger Abram. Well here I am." He spread his arms wide. "Worship me."

GLOSSARY

Acolyte - an Anonymi apprentice
Adria Varela - A Marked Descendant and a Ghost of Ashur. Her parents are from Markos and Galicea. She grew up in Fera, Markos. Her manifestation is enhanced hearing.
Ahvedool Bain - A Marked Descendant, one of Asarei's followers. Lives on Asarei's island, originally from Maramarosa, Shivaana.
Anahi Yeon - a maid at the Happy Elephant in Vandenar
Anonymi - an ancient organization that resides in the underground of Fang-Haan and works secretly to maintain balance in Ashur.
Aric Taurean - A Marked Descendant and Taurani. Currently under Jahmash's control.
Arild Hammersland - A Marked Descendant from decades ago. He was able to receive messages from the Orijin, and used them to transcribe the Book of Orijin.
Asarei Taurean - A Marked Descendant and Taurani
Augur - Commonly referred to as a Blind Man or a Blind Woman. Capable of receiving prophecies.
Avenira Gwonahn - A Marked Descendant, resident of Vandenar. Her manifestation makes her bones unbreakable.

Badalao Majime - A Marked Descendant and a Ghost of Ashur. Highborn from Constaniza, Markos. His manifestation is the ability to mentally connect with anyone he touches.
Baltaszar Kontez - A Marked Descendant and a Ghost of Ashur. Grew up with father and twin brother in Haedon, in the Never.
Blastevahn Handschuh - A Marked Descendant and a Ghost of Ashur. From Eris, Galicea. His manifestation is the ability to mesmerize others by singing.
Book of Orijin - A sacred text transcribed by Arild Hammersland, using words direct from the Orijin. The text provides directions to normal humans and Marked Descendants about the proper way to live.
Bragha Drusus - Seventh General of the Vithelegion, native to Vitheligia.
Bo'az Kontez - Twin brother of Baltaszar, son of Joakwin. Originally from Haedon. Currently under Jahmash's control.

Candra - Wife of Asarei. Originally from Roaldon, Cerysia.
Cerys - One of the original three Harbingers, who predated the Five.
Clyde - Nurse at the infirmary in Gangjeon, and native to Gangjeon, Mireya.

Cyrus Baek - Owner of the Happy Elephant Inn in Vandenar. From Vandenar, Mireya. Uncle to Desmond and Farco.

Dafne - Daughter of Asarei and Candra, lives with her parents.
Darian - One of the Five Harbingers. Could control and manipulate water, had multiple wives. Darian led Jahmash away from civilization and summoned the seas to create an island in order to trap Jahmash, sacrificing himself in the process.
Darvel Valoran - Son of Davala. Native to Vitheligia.
Daughters of Tahlia - A group of women in Sundari, Shivaana, who follow Tahlia's example. A Daughter of Tahlia takes a woman for a life partner and forms agreements with men for the sole purpose of procreation. Once Daughters of Tahlia bear a child, they cease their connection with the father of the child.
Davala Valoran - Sixth General of the Vithelegion, native to Vitheligia and father of Darvel.
Deacon Drahkunov - A Marked Descendant, nephew of Jesper Drahkunov. His manifestation is the ability to not feel pain. From the Port of Granis, Galicea. Currently under Jahmash's control.
Delilah Fakhri - A Marked Descendant, a Ghost of Ashur, and a Daughter of Tahlia, from Sundari, Shivaana. Her manifestation is the ability to alter her cellular density in order to move through objects.
Descendant - 1) any person from the many lineages of Darian. Because of Darian's numerous wives, a descendant can have a vast array of physical features. 2) Marked Descendants are descendants of Darian who bear a black line down their left eyes, signifying that they have a manifestation and can wield magic given by the Orijin.
Desmond Baek - A Marked Descendant and Ghost of Ashur from Vandenar, Mireya. His manifestation is the ability to levitate objects and move them around.
Diya - The midwife for Yasaman, from Haedon.
Donovan Brighton - Prince of Cerysia and Ashur, and younger brother to Garrison Brighton. Donovan is currently the heir to the throne, due to Garrison renouncing his title as prince.
Dorana - One of Savaiyon's mothers and a Daughter of Tahlia, from Sundari, Shivaana.
Drahkunov (Jesper) - A former general from the Port of Granis, Galicea during the Galicean/Fang War. Currently a general of Jahmash's armies.
Easton Grey - An officer for the Royal Vermillion Army, from Alvadon, Cerysia.

Edmund Brighton - The King of Ashur
Ezera Albes - Eighth General of the Vithelegion, native to Vitheligia.

Fae Miyung - A maid at the Happy Elephant in Vandenar. From Vandenar, Mireya.
Farco Baek - Apprentice to Munn Keeramm, an Augur in Vandenar. From Vandenar, Mireya. Nephew to Cyrus Baek and cousin to Desmond Baek.
Farrah Shokan - A Marked Descendant and Ghost of Ashur whose parents are from Markos and Galicea. Her manifestation is the ability to release venom from her lips.
Faryal Hammersland - Daughter of Hugo Hammersland and younger sister of Vilariyal. From the Port of Granis, Galicea.

Garrison Brighton - A Marked Descendant, Ghost of Ashur, and former prince of Ashur. From Alvadon, Cerysia. Previously renounced title as heir to the throne. Brother of Donovan Brighton and son of Edmund and Valencia Brighton.
General Grunt - A resident of Asarei's island and source of stress relief for those on the island.
Ghosts of Ashur - A group of Marked Descendants, whose mission is to kill King Edmund.
Gibreel Casteghar - A former soldier of Jahmash, who perished during the journey to bring Bo'az and Yasaman to Jahmash. Native of Castiel, a nation beyond Ashur.
Gideon - One of the Five Harbingers, who sacrificed his life to end a war between nations. Gideon could turn things to stone.
Gunnar Richteven - A Marked Descendant from Wasseron, Galicea, who was captured by Maqdhuum for Jahmash. His manifestation was heightened vision. Gunnar was killed by Farrah on a ship, on the way to attack the House of Darian.

Hansi Huu - A Marked Descendant from Zebulon, Fangh-Haan, who can create illusions with his manifestation. Hansi is currently under Jahmash's control.
Hector Calidus - Third General of the Vithelegion, native to Vitheligia, father to Hector.
Hernan Calidus - Son of Hector, native to Vitheligia.
Horatio Mahd - A Marked Descendant and Ghost of Ashur from Damaszur, Wolf's Paw. He can summon and create lightning with his manifestation.
Hugo Hammersland - deceased father of Vilariyal and Faryal, and brother of Raya Hammersland. From Galicea.

Iman Qaja - The nation that existed before Darian drowned the world

and created Ashur.
Imanol - The language of Iman Qaja.
Ihsan Adin - Deceased father of Yasaman. From Haedon.

Jahmash - One of the Five Harbingers. Killed Lionel, fought Abram and Darian. Can control and manipulate others' minds after physical contact. Trapped on an island north of Ashur.
Jaya - Jahmash's former love interest, from the time of the Five Harbingers.
Jelahni - A Marked Descendant who was killed in the attack on the House of Darian, from Shivaana. His manifestation was the ability to communicate with animals.
Jennikah Fakhri - A Daughter of Tahlia and sister of Delilah. From Sundari, Shivaana.
Joakwin Kontez - Father of Baltaszar and Bo'az, originally from the nation of Semaajj. Raised sons in Haedon and was publicly hanged before Baltaszar left Haedon.

Kadoog'han Valatteir - A Marked Descendant and Ghost of Ashur from Kharza, on the Wolf's Paw. His manifestation allows him to camouflage his skin based on his surroundings.
Khenzi Everitas - Son of Khurt Everitas, native of Vitheligia.
Khurt Everitas - First General of the Vithelegion, father of Khenzi. Native of Vitheligia.
Kiryako Majime - Highborn girl from Constaniza, Markos. Sister of Badalao.
Kraisos - a thieves guild that operates in secrecy beneath Taiju, Markos.
Krissette Luuk - A Marked Descendant and follower of Asarei. Lives on Asarei's island, parents originally from Cerysia and Markos.

Leonard Mahd - Older brother of Horatio, from Damaszur, Wolf's Paw.
Linas Nasreddine - soldier of Jahmash who was tasked with finding Baltaszar and eventually brought Bo'az to Jahmash. Blinded by Jahmash for his mistake. Native of Castiel, a nation beyond Ashur.
Lionel - One of the Five Harbingers, had the ability to speak any language. He was killed while fighting Jahmash, in an attempt to help Darian flee.
Lincan Vo - A Marked Descendant and Ghost of Ashur, from Xuyen, Fangh-Haan. His manifestation is the ability to heal others.

Magnus - One of the original Three Harbingers, who predated the Five.
Malikai Aitos - A Marked Descendant and Ghost of Ashur from Taiju, Markos. His manifestation is the ability to change the texture of his skin,

depending on the threat.
Manifestation - an ability given to those chosen by the Orijin. Manifestations tend to be given when a person is between the ages of five and eight years old, and puts their utmost faith in the Orijin during a dire situation.
Manjobam Gidda - A Marked Descendant and follower of Asarei, originally from Agralun, Shivaana. His manifestation is enhanced strength.
Maqdhuum/Abram - One of the Five Harbingers as Abram, and disappeared while fighting Jahmash. During present times, has been granted a new body and changed his name to Maqdhuum. Currently allied with the Ghosts of Ashur, has the ability to teleport to anywhere.
Marika Taurean - A member of the Taurani civilization, which descends from Taurean, one of the original Three Harbingers. She was the mother of Marshall Taurean, and died while helping Garrison travel to the House of Darian.
Maximilian Eddington - A Marked Descendant and Ghost of Ashur from Benjam, Cerysia. His manifestation is the ability to absorb energy and redistribute it to other people or living things.
Melina Shokan - The younger sister of Farrah, who was killed at the hands of Garrison's soldiers while Garrison was still hunting down Marked Descendants.
Munn Keeramm - An Augur from Vandenar, Mireya.

Neraiya Neikos - A Marked Descendant and follower of Asarei, who resides on his island. She is originally from Darling Harbor, Markos and her manifestation is the ability to breathe underwater.

Oblivion - One of the Three Rings, reserved for those who chose inaction over good or evil.
Omneitria - One of the Three Rings, reserved for those who lived righteously.
Opprobrium - One of the Three Rings, reserved for those who lived evilly or unjustly.
Oran Von/Vitticus Khou - A Galicean man who is currently the Chancellor of Haedon. Originally from Penzaedon, Galicea.
Orijin - The god of this universe.

Raffa Canus - Second General of the Vithelegion, native to Vitheligia, father of Ravindra.
Raiza Malleolas - Fifth General of the Vithelegion, native to Vitheligia.
Ravindra Canus - Son of Raffa, native of Vitheligia
Raya Hammersland - A Marked Descendant from Galicea. Mother to

Baltaszar and Bo'az Kontez, and wife to Joakwin Kontez. Her manifestation was the ability to travel to the Three Rings. She disappeared when Baltaszar and Bo'az were very young.
Reverron Maidenfield - A Marked Descendant and Ghost of Ashur from Alvadon, Cerysia. His manifestation is the ability to move quickly via bursts of speed.
Rhadames Slade - A former soldier from the nation of Semaajj, and former friend of Joakwin Kontez. Pretended to be loyal to Jahmash, but is now working with the surviving Descendants.
Riha Simalti - Older sister of Savaiyon. Lives in Gansishoor, Shivaana.
Roland Edevane - Uncle to Garrison Brighton and a Marked Descendant from Cerysia, whose manifestation is the ability to create astral projection.

Sabouros Majime - Father of Badalao Majime, from Constaniza, Markos.
Sadie - A maid at the Happy Elephant Inn, in Vandenar, Mireya.
Salken Suldas - Older son of Saol Suldas, native of Vitheligia
Saol Suldas - Commander of the Vithelegion, native to Vitheligia
Savaiyon Simalti - A Marked Descendant and Ghost of Ashur from Shivaana. His manifestation is the ability to create yellow-bordered gateways to any location he has been before.
Saymon Suldas - Younger son of Saol Suldas, native of Vitheligia
Seylaan Jai - Older brother to Vasher, from Sundari, Shivaana
Sindha Taravari - A Marked Descendant and Ghost of Ashur from Itarse, Shivaana. Her manifestation is the ability to create force fields.
Sivika - A former Daughter of Tahlia, and Savaiyon's birth mother. From Sundari, Shivaana.
Sopira Majime - Mother of Badalao Majime, from Constaniza, Markos.
Stones of Gideon - A historical location on the outskirts of Alvadon. This is where the Harbinger Gideon turned a battlefield to stone, including himself and all of the soldiers, in order to teach humanity a lesson.

Taurean - One of the original three Harbingers, who predated the Five. The Taurani people were direct descendants of Taurean, as was the Harbinger Darian.
Thiel Aquilas - Fourth General of the Vithelegion, native to Vitheligia.
Three Rings - The domain of the Orijin, where souls are sorted after their departure from the world of flesh.
Trevor Nightsmythe - A Marked Descendant and follower of Asarei. Lives on Asarei's island, originally from Shipsbane, Cerysia.

Vanna Wynchester - A young woman from Alvadon, Cerysia, and

Garrison Brighton's former love interest.

Varana Jai - A Daughter of Tahlia, and Vasher Jai's birth mother. From Sundari, Shivaana.

Vasher Jai - A Marked Descendant and Ghost of Ashur from Sundari, Shivaana. His manifestation is the ability to persuade through speaking.

Vermillion - The Royal Army of King Edmund, named for the red-dyed crest of hair on their helmets

Vikram Bhoodoo - A young man from Haedon, in the Never, who was friends with, and of a similar age as Baltaszar Kontez. He disappeared from Haedon about two years before Baltaszar left Haedon.

Vilariyal Hammersland - Daughter of Hugo Hammersland and older sister of Faryal. From Galicea.

Vithelegion - The Army that hails from Vitheligia.

Wendell Ravensdayle – Commander of the Vermillion Army, best friend to Donovan and Garrison Brighton.

Yasaman Adin - A young woman from Haedon, in the Never. She was previously the love interest of Baltaszar Kontez, but is currently carrying the child of Bo'az Kontez, Baltaszar's twin brother.

Zin Marlowe - The former and final Headmaster of the House of Darian. Marlowe was originally from Maradon, Cerysia, and perished during the attack on the House of Darian. His manifestation was the ability to change his form to look like anyone.

ACKNOWLEDGEMENTS

Special thanks go out to my brother, Ahmed. Aside from being a fan and a support, he's been a huge help at all of the author events, and oftentimes the nudge I've needed to be more outspoken. It's no secret that I'm an introvert, and his outgoing nature has always inspired me to advocate for myself more than I normally would.

While it also goes without saying that my wife and daughters deserve a great deal of credit, I'm so grateful for their constant involvement. I love that my kids think the first book is called "Rose of the Red Hamburger", and I guess the only thing left to do is write a kids version of this story about an evil hamburger who tries to take over the world.

"Harbinger" had already been published by the time I started my current job a few years ago. And *somehow*, my department already knew that I was an author before I started. It was amazing to have people like Jamie, Sarah, and Matt all show immediate interest in reading "Harbinger" and offer feedback and insight after reading it. I'm so appreciative of that, especially because I didn't want to come across as arrogant for mentioning that I'm an author. I'm so grateful for Shawna, Amanda, Gabby, Greg, Nicky, Ellen, Alison, and Jeff - the Ivory Tower, who have continued to ask about my progress and have been proud of me every step of the way. I couldn't ask for a better department to have my back.

Having been an English teacher for fifteen years now, so many of my students and former students have been exposed to my progress throughout this whole endeavor of writing a fantasy series. One of the most amazing parts of this journey is seeing firsthand how these people have continued to track my journey, even after moving on from high school. It's surreal to be a teacher and then have those same students turn around and tell you that they're also proud of your accomplishments. People like Nicole Merced, Arbron Krivca, Vanessa Morales, Sanjay Singh, Conner Barrett, and James Ur, who have consistently been fans since this all started, are directly responsible for inspiring me to find the urgency to keep writing and not get lazy. I am indebted to them for believing in me.

For anyone who doesn't know, my background is Guyanese. And if you're Guyanese, that generally means that all other Guyanese people are family, literally and figuratively. For me, that family includes Sandy, Travis, Mala, Deo, and Rey, all of whom have been my biggest supporters since I started writing. Sandy and Travis even allowed me to miss their wedding so I could go to Chicago BookCon and promote

"Harbinger". I honestly cannot thank them enough for how much they've supported me and for being so genuine with their questions and feedback. I hope "Ghosts" has been worth the wait for all of them.

Lastly, I need to thank someone who has inspired me artistically throughout my entire life. From the time I was a snotty and bratty little kid, my Uncle Al was the best artist I knew. From Pictionary games to computer-based sketches, he was always the physical evidence that creativity was in the genes. And ever since "Harbinger" came out, he's been right there with real, constructive advice about the story and series, and has been an advocate for my work in his own circles. If there's anyone who I can say is responsible for inspiring me to be creative and artistic from an early age, it's Al. His example alone has allowed me to better myself in so many ways, and I'm incredibly grateful.

ABOUT THE AUTHOR

Khalid Uddin is a New Jersey based author and high school teacher. He enjoys partaking in local author events and appearances throughout New Jersey whenever he can, and loves to interact with readers to learn about their interests and tastes.

Khalid is also a husband to a wonderful wife, and father to two adorable girls who moonlight as demons. They've grown up knowing that their father is a writer and already try to emulate him with their own stories and "books".

Aside from his family, Khalid is heavily into pop culture, including Star Wars, most fantasy series, all kinds of music (you should see his writing playlists), and most comic book related things. His creative spark started from the pages of Spider-Man and X-Men, and those roots still hold strong.

There is rarely a time, if ever, that Khalid will pass up on donuts and coffee, especially those that are locally made. He has been known to drive great distances for good donuts, so feel free to mention your favorite spots and he'll be sure to try them. It is probably only a matter of time before an author signing/donut shop tour comes into existence.

Going forward, Khalid plans to start writing Book Three (this series is slated for four books) in the summer of 2022. There was a five-year gap between the first two books, and he hopes to shorten that for the next one. In the meantime, Khalid will be getting his podcast, "Mr. Write Now" up and running, which will focus on various aspects of writing, pop culture, branding, local & small businesses, and anything else that needs to be talked about. You can find him on most social media platforms: IG: @khalid.uddin.author; FB: Khalid Uddin - Author; Twitter: @kaluddin23, and his website is www.khaliduddin.com. He loves to hear from readers and fans, so feel free to reach out to him with your thoughts, reactions, questions, and predictions.

Made in the USA
Middletown, DE
11 September 2025